IN BED WITH A SWISS BANKER

Parker Belmont

WHITE
MOUNTAIN
BOOKS

White Mountain Books is an affiliate of
The Arcadian Group S.A., Case Postale 431,
1211 Geneva 12, Switzerland
Copyright © White Mountain Books 2018

Database right White Mountain Books (maker)

First published 2018

ISBN 9781941634301

Designed and typeset by *et al* design consultants,
London & Oxford
Printed in Great Britain by CPI UK
141–143 Shoreditch High Street
London E1 6JE
Typeset in Monotype Arcadian Bembo

DISCLAIMER

Although based on the author's experiences, it should be noted that this book is a work of fiction presented entirely for entertainment purposes. The author and publisher are not offering professional service advice. The stories and their characters and entities are fictional. Any likeness to actual persons, whether in terms of character profiles or names, either living or dead, is strictly coincidental.

DEDICATION

This book is dedicated to all my children and relatives who have not broken a leg in the Alps.

FOREWORD

In one way or another, each of the characters in this novel are inspired by certain observations I have made of people I have known personally. Having first visited Switzerland over forty years ago, and having now lived in the country for more than twenty years, I have experienced many different angles of Swiss society, and met many of its quirkiest characters. This is not to say that this is a *roman à clef*: everyone who appears between these pages is purely fictional. I merely wish to emphasise that I have drawn character traits from many people I have encountered, whether they are Swiss bankers or mountain farmers, aspirational immigrants or art dealers. Though my descriptions may be humorous, and though many characteristics have been exaggerated, I hope that it is obvious to the reader that they have their genesis in both my instinct to be truthful and the great affection I feel for the country I now call home.

The same must be said of the portrait of Switzerland that I've drawn. There are no sour grapes in this novel. I've been a banker for over twenty-five years, and shared many successful connections with the world of Swiss banking. I love skiing in the Swiss mountains. I've spent time in all the locations mentioned in the book: Zurich, St Gallen, Lucern, Neuchatel, Saas Fee… One could say that I've done my Swiss research. In some sections, this could almost be called a travel book! That said, above all it is a humorous novel.

I do firmly believe that Switzerland has changed less than one per cent in the past twenty years, which is even lower than the returns one gets on a portfolio in a Swiss private bank! But writing this book has made me love Switzerland at least ten per cent more. I found such joy in the act of drawing up a collection of all the most Swiss things I could think of. I wanted to present both outsiders' and insiders' perspective on the Alpine country, in order that the reader might fall in love with it as much as me.

If there is any criticism in the book, it is only the gentle ribbing of a close friend. Perhaps the Swiss might even see this book as a mirror, in which to see themselves and laugh at their traditions! In fact, whenever I mention this book to a Swiss person, they laugh at the observations and anecdotes that I recount; the title in particular elicits a giggle. I suspect this is a good sign.

Last but not least, I wish to thank my team at White Mountain Books, in particular Elodie Olson-Coons, Elena Feehan and Johnny Walker, for their input and consistent diligence in helping to bring this book to fruition.

Chapter One
Geneva, 1984

'*Chéri?*'

Gabriel de Puritigny rolled over in bed, switched on the bedside table lamp, put his glasses back on and reached for the *Financial Times*.

'Is that it?'

Gabriel slowly unfurled the pink newspaper, without looking at his wife. 'Yes,' he said firmly. 'That is it, as you say.'

Clarice de Puritigny sat up in bed, straightening her shoulders. 'I see,' she said slowly, with a little shrug. Her long, dark hair tumbled over her antique lace nightshirt.

'It is already six thirty,' Gabriel said, without looking up from his newspaper. 'I need to finish this article and eat, before my first meeting at the bank.'

Primly, Clarice reached for her grey silk kimono and tucked it around herself before emerging from bed. 'Very well. I will go lay the breakfast table, then.' She disappeared behind the bathroom door, and the noise of the shower faintly filled the air.

Gabriel continued to read. After a few minutes, he sighed, set down the paper, slipped back the white Egyptian cotton sheets and stepped onto the cold stone floor. Tiptoeing through the early morning darkness to the window, he pulled apart the velvet curtains and let morning light into the dark and stuffy room. Sunlight streamed down the narrow cobbled streets of Saint Antoine. He nodded, as if satisfied, and headed to his armoire. The bathroom door clicked open, and he could hear the quiet sounds of his wife dressing, across the room, but he did not turn to look. Instead, he inspected his array of shirts.

At last he chose: a white starched cotton shirt, blue suit jacket and trousers, light red silk tie. He smoothed his dark hair, pulling a stern face in the antique mirror, and adjusted the slim, expensive frames of his glasses. He pulled on each item of clothing carefully, making sure it was unadulterated by creases, straightening every edge of fabric. At the end of this performance, he nodded again, curtly, and closed the armoire door.

The de Puritigny family portraits stared down from their black backgrounds and gold frames, over the oak table in the dining room: a dour patriarch in burgundy velvet, his pointed beard as luxurious as his gold pin; a beautiful grandmother in an embroidered cap, a white ruff and pearls; a pale infant in a gauzy dress holding a small dog. Gabriel sat down at the head of the table, pulling the bread basket towards him.

'Some books arrived in the mail yesterday,' Clarice said disinterestedly, toying with the buttons of her white silk blouse.

He looked up. 'You came home late from your business dinner, so I'm not sure you saw them,' she continued. 'I believe they're from your father.'

Gabriel nodded, using a letter-opener on the brown paper package. 'I see. I requested some of the family manuscripts be sent here,' he explained. 'I wanted to have a look at some of our history.'

'Very well,' Clarice replied. 'Would you like some jam?'

'No thank you; no sugar this morning. I wanted to know more about the parquet, you see.'

'The parquet?' Clarice repeated blankly.

Gabriel pulled out two heavy, leather-bound stacks of paper from the envelope and, after brushing the tablecloth clear of invisible breadcrumbs, set them down on the table with satisfaction.

'Yes. You see, this house was first purchased by my great-great-great-great-great-grandfather when he emigrated from France along with other Huguenots, after the Edict of Nantes.'

'I am well aware,' Clarice replied with a faint smile.

Gabriel nodded, not listening. 'The de Puritignys left their home in Argenton, in Normandy, with only a horse and carriage, and followed the footsteps of Jean Calvin: to Besançon, then Metz, and finally Geneva, resting place of that original Protestant.'

'His teachings were catching on like wildfire, if I remember the history correctly.' Clarice was looking at her bread, inscrutable.

'Exactly,' her husband replied distractedly, pushing his glasses back on his nose. 'Couldn't have put it better myself. So around the start of the seventeenth century, my family settled here and had this house built, in the center of the Old Town. Everything, from the *cave* to the attic, is original. Now, I'm sure you've noticed, when cleaning, that some of the parquet has begun to warp beneath the weight of the books in the grand library. I'm a little worried about this. Beautiful old Swiss oak, you see. Tremendously expensive. I thought if I could find the original plans, I might be able to understand what has changed, and what we can do about it without resorting to external help.'

'Doesn't wood naturally change when it ages?' she asked, her voice neutral.

'I don't know, I'm not a carpenter,' Gabriel replied briskly. 'All I know is that you cannot put down *moquette* in a house like this, only carpets that can be taken out, washed and aired in the sun. The parquet needs to breathe. I have no wish to modify this house. The beauty of our domicile is that the window handles are the originals from the 1600s.'

'Yes,' Clarice smiled. 'Have some more coffee,' she said. 'Now, I wanted to talk to you about something.'

'Yes, thank you,' he said, his eyes still on the manuscripts in front of him. He picked up a piece of now-cold, dry bread and bit into it.

'When we go to church this weekend, some of the committee might approach you,' she continued.

'Not a single piece of wooden parquet in this house came later than the eighteenth century,' he continued, his voice settling into a drone. 'Not a single piece.'

Clarice nodded, spreading butter neatly on her *tartine*. 'Yes, I know, *chéri*. The committee will approach you, because I may have mentioned that we could be willing to offer them some funds.'

'Funds?' Gabriel looked up from the manuscripts. 'What kind of funds?'

'The church is fundraising for a new roof,' she said patiently. 'They're holding a fête in the countryside next Sunday. I thought it might be fun to attend; a little outing, supporting the community.'

'Fun,' Gabriel repeated drily. 'A fête! Well, I'll think about it. You know we have to be careful with the inheritance.'

'You inherited a whole bank from your father,' Clarice replied lightly. 'I would think you could spare a few thousand, for the works of Our Lord.'

Gabriel looked up from his bread, blinked, and sighed. 'I said I would think about it. Besides, how can I worry about the church roof when I have my own parquet to consider? My ancestors laid this floor four hundred years ago, paying for it with the bags of gold coins they carried all the way across old Europe.'

'Ten thousand gold coins,' Clarice said softly.

'Everything depreciates,' Gabriel said sternly, his eyes on the manuscripts. 'Furthermore, it is no longer my father's bank. Von Mipatobeau is my bank. Now, let me finish my *tartines*. I have to go to work.'

'Yes, so do I.' She paused. 'You'll wear out your eyes, reading all the time like that,' Clarice observed. 'You could at least look at me when you're speaking, Gabriel.'

He raised his eyes slowly, and reached his hand slowly towards his wife as if to caress her, before doing up the top button of her silk shirt. 'There you go,' he said. '*Veni, vidi, vici*. Now, time for work.'

The Swiss marble of the entry hall at Bank von Mipatobeau gleamed white, grey and green in the early morning light. Gabriel walked in, adjusting his lapels, barely noting the glory of the Empire style decoration: gilding, leather, mahogany. It was 7.30. The four *huissiers* stood in line, guarding the entrance in full morning dress: black tailcoat, white bow tie, white waistcoat and shirt. Three of these bodyguards were ancient and weathered, their *queue-de-pies* fitting them as if they were born into them, as if they had guarded this doorway for a hundred years.

Gabriel squinted at the fourth, a youngster. He didn't recognise the boy. A grin split across the lad's face and he rushed forward.

'Good morning, monsieur!' he cried. 'I am Astorg, the new guard. I am at your service, Monsieur de Puritigny.'

Gabriel looked at him, unblinking. 'The first thing you learn about Swiss banking,' he said coldly, 'is never to use names in public. Have you never heard of Swiss banking secrecy, boy? Never, ever mention names, account numbers, addresses, residences. You don't mention seeing them before. You don't recognise anyone. You don't greet anyone. You don't try to shake hands; have you never even thought about cultural correctness? You don't ask questions. Don't tell me your name, and certainly don't tell me mine.'

Astorg swallowed. 'Yes sir,' he croaked. 'I am... being trained.'

Gabriel nodded, his face softening imperceptibly. 'Good. Now, do you know how to operate the elevator?' Astorg shook his head, blushing crimson. 'Then learn that.'

Gabriel walked off towards the front desk, shaking his head, one of the older *huissiers* scuttling after him.

⸻

The gilded elevator scudded smoothly up its shaft towards the third floor. Gabriel adjusted his slick hair in the mirror before stepping out.

'*Bonjour*,' he said to the red-headed receptionist. She was wearing a rather flashy turquoise suit, he noted, with those large shoulders. He would have to speak to Caroline about that.

'*Bonjour*,' she replied brightly, blushing furiously.

'*Bonjour*, Caroline,' he said to his secretary, as he stepped into his office.

'*Bonjour*, monsieur. This is your schedule,' she said at once: 'eight appointments, the first one at 8.30 with Mr Schön.' Caroline was dressed impeccably in a pale grey tailored suit. Her face was powdered and her lips severely pencilled. Her lacquered blonde hair, turning white day by day, was pulled back in a tight bun.

He nodded. 'I need to finish some administration. Hold my calls, read through my mail. Make sure none of the meetings go over half an hour. I'll be taking an eleven thirty lunch, as usual.'

'Yes, monsieur.'

'And bring me a carafe of sparkling water,' he added. 'I'll be in the conference room.'

The conference room in question was large enough for twenty people. At its centre loomed a vast elliptical mahogany table, surrounded by leather-covered chairs in the Napoleonic style. The light filtering through the half-lowered blinds was turning from blue to white. Gabriel settled down at the beautiful table and checked his gold watch for the time.

Caroline appeared at his shoulder, quietly setting down a silver tray containing a stack of letters, an antique letter-opener, a linen napkin and a crystal carafe of water. She had switched her suit jacket for a cashmere cardigan, which softened her figure slightly.

'Thank you, Caroline,' Gabriel said, already opening the first letter. He caught a whiff of her expensive perfume, reminding him strangely of older women he had known.

'Don't you ever tire of the paperwork?' she asked gently, an almost motherly note creeping into her voice.

'Not really,' he replied, not looking up. 'It's part of the job. I've ten minutes left before Schön barges in,' he added, rather pointedly.

'I'll leave you to it,' she said quickly. She shut the door silently behind her.

Gabriel sighed and turned back to his letters. Just one moment of peace. That was all he needed.

'Well *something* is different today, my old friend,' a voice suddenly boomed. 'Your little redhead. How long were you going to keep her a secret from your favourite client?'

The door slammed behind Mr Schön, who was wearing checked trousers, a crimson shirt, and a green tie decorated with exotic painted flowers. He opened his arms magnanimously, as if aiming for a hug, but then swung them back down upon seeing Gabriel's face.

'*Bonjour*,' Gabriel said, without standing up. 'Yes, the receptionist on this floor is indeed new. She is in training.' He sighed, taking off his wire-framed glasses and polishing them on a piece of cloth. 'I hope she did not cause offence.'

'Oh, anything but! Samantha, she told me she was called. What a pretty little thing. I'll try for her phone number next time.'

'She should know better than to tell you her name,' Gabriel said half-heartedly, 'let alone her number.'

'Ah, but I pressed her so! I have certain powers, you know. I made her blush nearly the same colour as her beautiful curly hair. She's a perfect addition to your other set of beauties, with their kaleidoscope of blue-green-black eyes: the suave brunette at the entrance, the voluptuous blonde upstairs, and of course your mysterious exotic –'

'Mr Schön,' Gabriel cut in, 'would you like a coffee before we get down to business?'

'Oh yes,' he said. 'Make it a double ristretto. Your *petits cafés* are lovely here. Compliment whoever makes them.'

Gabriel picked up the phone and delivered the order, without adding the latter remark.

'Do you know,' Mr Schön continued thoughtfully, 'Samantha wasn't the only unusual thing that happened this morning. Your youngest bodyguard took me all the way up in the elevator! Is everyone new these days?'

Gabriel sighed. 'There've been a few changes because of our expansion. It's not what I would have wished, for Von Mipatobeau, but apparently it must be so.'

'Not to worry, not to worry. Ah, lovely,' he said to Caroline, who had presented him with his coffee. 'And how about some chocolate almonds?' He winked. Caroline repressed a smile.

'Schön,' Gabriel said sharply, 'we are not in a restaurant.'

'Oh, don't worry, monsieur,' Caroline replied hastily, 'I know they are his favourite. I always have some for him. I will bring them straight away.' She bustled away. Had she put on *lipstick* since she had first left the room?

'Sorry,' said Schön, with a grin. 'Although, say, come to think of it, this little misunderstanding gives me a great idea: shall we go out for lunch next time? We're always meeting in these drab and frosty conference rooms.'

'I prefer to eat alone,' Gabriel said calmly, smoothing down his collar. 'I cannot be seen with my clients, you see. Geneva is a small town. The families, they know each other.'

'Ah, jealous Swiss bankers, worse than wives. I understand.'

Gabriel's lip curled imperceptibly. 'Your own wife, she is well?'

Mr Schön's booming laugh filled the room. 'I have no idea,' he said. 'Haven't seen her for days. The bills and the deliveries keep coming, so I assume she is.'

'She has left Geneva?' Gabriel asked curiously.

'She hates the damn city,' Mr Schön replied expansively. 'Spends every weekend away she can, and weekdays too. Italy this time, Sardinia perhaps.'

'How curious. My own wife detests spending time away from Geneva and the Genevois, you see.'

'Such fidelity!' Mr Schön cried. 'But let me tell you a story I heard yesterday, about your beloved Genevois. A friend of mine, a Swiss man, was invited to dinner by old friends who live in a beautiful house in a cul-de-sac. He parked in their courtyard, and proceeded to have a lovely evening of dinner and a few drinks. Upon leaving, he decided it would be easier to manoeuvre out of the cul-de-sac by making a U-turn than to crawl out in reverse. That was against the law, as I'm sure you know.'

Gabriel, not seeing the point of this story, did not respond.

'So my friend drives back to his home, a short drive away, and when he comes home his wife is standing at the door in her nightie, stony-faced, telling him she's had a call from the police. Turns out he's been fined seventy francs for his U-turn. And do you know who sold him out? His own damn host! He called the police on his own friend, in his own driveway!'

Mr Schön slapped his thigh in throes of mirth.

'What an amusing story,' Gabriel replied. 'Now, shall we get down to business?'

His client wiped his eyes. 'Of course,' he said, with mock

politeness. 'Whatever *monseigneur le banquier* desires.'

At this moment, Caroline arrived with the chocolate almonds. 'You are sure you do not want anything, monsieur?' she muttered apologetically.

'Quite sure,' Gabriel replied. 'Now...'

At this moment, the phone rang. Gabriel de Puritigny exhaled heavily as he picked up. 'What now?' he exclaimed. 'Caroline, I told you to hold all calls.'

'Yes, monsieur,' she said, frowning sternly. 'I don't know what could have happened. It must be urgent. It must have come through the downstairs reception.'

'Very well. What is it?' Gabriel barked into the receiver. 'Samantha? I am well aware that you are being trained but – Diderot?' His tone changed sharply. 'Something has happened? Very well – yes, of course, fine, put the boy through.'

Mr Schön raised his eyebrows in incomprehension.

'Please forgive me,' Gabriel said smoothly, laying a hand over the receiver. 'There has been... what the French call *un contretemps*. Occupy yourself as you will with your chocolate almonds, or by going over your portfolio figures. I'll just be a moment. Yes?' he said after a pause, his tone transformed again. 'Yes, Jason? Hello.'

From the receiver came the distinct sounds of a child sobbing. Mr Schön raised his eyebrows further.

'Hello?' Gabriel continued. 'Jason, I need you to focus. Can you tell me what happened? Your father? Why do you think he is dead?'

Mr Schön's eyebrows threatened to disappear into his receding hairline.

'I see. He isn't breathing? Blue, you say? He did not wake up this morning. Right. Yes, of course I am your godfather, yes. Calm down.' Gabriel removed his glasses and ran a hand over his face. 'Look, Jason, just stay where you are. I'll come get you, and take you to school. Thank you for calling me. Good day.' He paused, considering for a moment, before explaining: 'Mr Diderot is my partner. Jason is his eight-year-old son. Please forgive my interruption.'

'The man is dead? *Dead*?' Mr Schön appeared to be in shock.

'So it would seem.' Gabriel picked the phone up again and dialled. 'Caroline? No, we don't need to fire Samantha. Turns out Diderot died in his sleep. Forty years old! Yes, I suppose that qualifies as an urgent matter, although I'd refrain from sharing that information with the receptionists. I don't want them to think they can ring up at any hour of day. No, I need you to do something else for me. Can you call the funeral parlour? Thank you. Afterwards, I need you to go to the man's house, pick up the child and take him to school. No, I'm sure you will not see the dead body. The school is in Contamines; you know the one. He cannot miss school. No. Goodbye Caroline.'

'He's eight?' Mr Schön repeated.

'I don't see what is strange about that,' Gabriel replied. 'We were all eight once. Now, where were we? I believe we were just about to look over your portfolio.'

Mr Schön swallowed. 'Yes,' he said hesitantly. He blinked for a while in silence, before grabbing a handful of chocolate almonds and stuffing his mouth with them, as if hoping to dull the shock. 'Alright,' he said at last. 'Let us get back to business.'

'Your accounts are doing well,' Gabriel began. 'You have accumulated a neat two per cent return on your investments.'

'Pah!' Mr Schön replied, spattering small crumbs of chocolate almond across the mahogany. 'Two per cent? Two measly per cent? I am supposed to be grateful for this to your smooth Swiss face?'

'Yes,' Gabriel replied, neatly sweeping the spittle and crumbs up with a linen napkin.

'Do you know what the interest rate on deposits alone is in France? At least eight per cent. America? Fund managers in America do twelve per cent and more. What on earth would make a client like me stay with yourselves?'

'Swiss banking fees are expensive,' Gabriel said, throwing the napkin into a silver bin on the floor, already half-full with other linen napkins. 'There's a reason people come to us and there's a reason people are willing to shell out for our services. You have to pay for this level of secrecy, the low taxes. Let me remind you that you have to pay extra fees to be in a private bank anywhere in the world. We have something special to offer: service and secrecy.'

At this moment, there was a bang on the door, and the sounds of sobbing were heard once more in the conference room. 'Diderot!' the man was crying, stumbling and clutching at his blonde curls. 'Oh, my little *liebling* Diderot! Whatever will we do without him!'

'Thomas,' Gabriel said with a profound sigh, 'what have I told you about interrupting my business meetings?'

Thomas was wearing crumpled beige linen trousers and a tie decorated with edelweiss. '*Ach,*' he exclaimed, sinking down into one of the Napoleonic leather chairs. 'What a world we live in!'

'I cannot believe this son was only eight,' Mr Schön added, impulsively grabbing Thomas's hand. This appeared to have been a mistake, as Thomas turned to him and buried his great head of curls in Schön's besuited shoulder, weeping loudly.

'Gentlemen,' Gabriel said sternly. 'We have business to attend to.'

'The poor son!' Thomas was sobbing. 'I will adopt him! We will move to the mountains. I will raise him, we will sleep in the barn together and go bicycling and –'

'THOMAS,' Gabriel said sharply. 'Get out of here. Get Caroline to make you a cup of warm milk. I will speak with you in no more than twenty minutes. If you are still crying, you are fired. And try and iron those trousers, will you?' He turned back to Mr Schön. 'Now, those portfolio figures...'

Mr Schön gave a dry little laugh. 'So you are saying I should be thankful for these measly returns just because I am in Switzerland? Mr de Puritigny, I am well aware that I am in Switzerland. I can see the damn Alps from my hotel room. What you are really telling me is that I must pay for your gigantic mahogany table, and your weeping German, and your four beautiful receptionists with their stupid hairdos? So you can keep your floor so clean you could eat off it?'

Gabriel sighed. 'Mr Schön, I do not understand why you choose this of all mornings to be so contrary. We have always done good business together. Why change that?'

'I am very Swiss, you know,' Thomas said suddenly.

'Yes, I can see by your tie,' Mr Schön replied with a wry smile.

'My parents were German, but I am Swiss. I have been Swiss for twenty years. Switzerland is my country, the mountains are my home, the edelweiss is my –'

'Thomas,' Gabriel said, not impatiently, 'I seem to remember requesting you leave the room some ten minutes back.'

'Come now, you've got to admire his tie,' Mr Schön said.

Thomas grinned. 'I found it at the flea market in Plainpalais, last Saturday.'

Gabriel steepled his fingers and leaned forward slowly. 'Thomas, what country are we in?' he asked quietly.

Thomas paused. 'Switzerland?' he replied hesitantly.

'And what sort of institution are you currently working for?'

'A bank!' he replied, more confidently.

'And what are Swiss banks famous for?' Gabriel continued.

'Gold?'

Gabriel sighed. 'Secrecy,' he said. 'Do you remember what banking secrecy is?'

Thomas blinked. 'Have you forgotten, Monsieur de Puritigny? Sometimes I am worried about you.'

Mr Schön gave a raucous burst of laughter. 'He is clever, your little German,' he said. 'I like him.'

'You are one of our favourite clients,' Thomas said with a conspiratorial grin.

Gabriel looked ready to bury his head in his hands. 'Thomas,' he said slowly, 'there is really no need to keep talking. You are here – well, to tell the truth I am not *entirely* sure why you are here, since I sent you off to be looked after by Caroline, but in the broader sense of the term, you are here to serve our client Mr Schön. We are managing his funds, you see. That is my job. That is your job.'

'*Ja, monsieur,*' Thomas replied brightly. 'That is right.'

'The commentary on his accounts will be right at the bottom of the papers: division of stocks, bonds, cash, all sitting there in a circle. You can read, Thomas. There's simply no need to tell us about your strange sartorial decisions.'

Thomas's friendly, red face transformed at once into an aggrieved mask. 'I will withdraw like an army sergeant, facing you both,' he said, his eyes wide. He stood up and began edging towards the door. Gabriel took a deep breath.

'Three per cent,' Mr Schön said. 'That's all I ask.'

Gabriel was silent.

'By the way,' Thomas said from the door, craning his neck as if trying to hail their attention from a great distance, 'do you want me to organise the funeral?'

'God, no,' Gabriel replied, 'and if you repeat this information to anyone, I will personally remove your edelweiss tie and have it buried in a garbage can, where it belongs.' Thomas, still walking backwards, ran into the door and disappeared. 'One cannot have word of this getting out,' Gabriel told his client by way of explanation. 'Partners dying at forty! People will gossip. They'll say it must be the pressure, tension, banking — bad for the heart.'

'I take it you will also burn my tie if I repeat this story?' Mr Schön replied, innocently.

Gabriel stared at him. 'It was a joke, Mr Schön.'

'Three per cent,' he repeated.

'And you are being humorous in return! What a delight. No, not today,' Gabriel said briskly, closing the file. 'If you wish to withdraw your funds, that is your business. I can ring Caroline at once, if you like.'

Mr Schön shook his head, half-disgusted, half-admiring. 'I won't stop trying, you know. Why don't you come to my boat next time? We can sail around good old Lac Léman, I'll pack a picnic, a little Moët, we can go right across to Vevey if it's sunny…'

'Don't be ridiculous,' Gabriel snapped. 'Do you think I can just waltz out of this bank carrying your accounts, where they could be stolen in the street, or fly out across the waters? What kind of banker would drink in the midst of important business negotiations?'

'Ah, so you *are* prepared to negotiate, then!' Mr Schön grinned in delight.

'My patience is wearing thin, monsieur,' Gabriel said, delicately massaging his temples. 'That will be all for today.' He picked up the phone. 'Caroline? Oh, damn, of course she's gone to Contamines with the child. In that case, never mind.' He slammed down the receiver and poured himself another glass of water.

To comfort himself, he let his mind drift back to that quiet, dark morning, when, half awake, he had received such a lovely surprise: the perfect package of manuscripts he had unwrapped, and their fascinating information about the house's parquet! What a joy it would be to read through the rest of them that very evening. But first, seven more meetings. The Swiss man sighed happily and opened up his files.

Chapter Two

'*Chéri?*'

Gabriel rolled over in bed, sighed deeply, and reached for his glasses.

'That's all?' Clarice's voice was not quite as soft as it had been the previous day.

Gabriel slowly unfurled the *Financial Times*, without looking at his wife. 'Yes,' he said. 'That was quite enough for this morning. I have to be at work soon.'

Clarice sighed. 'You truly cannot spare twelve minutes? It's only seven. You have at least half an hour before you go,' she added crisply. 'Come on, just a little? I'll keep my eye on the clock.'

'I should like to finish this article,' Gabriel continued, apparently unfazed, though his ears had gone the same colour as his newspaper. 'Then I will need to shower, of course. Do you expect me to turn up at work sweaty? I must eat my *tartines*, drink my *café au lait*, and go to meet with one of the bank's most influential clients.'

'Would you like coffee in bed?' she cajoled.

'You know the rules,' Gabriel replied calmly, shaking his head. 'No food outside the dining room. I don't know what's gotten into you, *chérie*. This is not the time of day for amorous pursuits.'

'And when, *chéri*, is the right time of day?' Clarice was calmly braiding her long dark hair, her face hardening. 'Your bank always seems to be receiving its most important clients. Do you only have two, then? I also have work, you see, but last night you were asleep before nine thirty, your precious manuscripts draped over you like a blanket. I had to tuck you in like a child.'

Gabriel made a coughing noise, like one disgusted. 'A child! A child would not have had eight meetings at the bank, in an extremely trying start to the week.' He shook out his newspaper in a petty little gesture. 'Perhaps I should have given you children, ten years ago. Then you might leave my manhood alone a little.'

'This is not about children,' Clarice retorted. 'This is about your duty as a husband.'

'Clarice,' Gabriel said calmly, 'I am a responsible and charitable man. Instead of donating babies to the world, I have donated considerable amounts of hard-earned banking profits to local institutions. Babies, you'll remember, cost more than a Mercedes.'

'Don't pull that Calvinist argument on me again,' she spat. 'Have you even donated to the church yet?'

'It's about time as well as money, my dear. Be reasonable. Instead of investing ourselves in infants, we advanced our respective careers: your gallery, my bank. We are successful and content. Now, let us cease this squabbling. I must get dressed, and someone must lay the breakfast table.'

'Well, I must get to the gallery, *chéri*.' Neatly, Clarice flung back the blankets, and swished across the room, not even pulling on her kimono.

Gabriel looked back at his newspaper, hastily.

———•◆•———

Clarice de Puritigny stared into the antique mirror, her face calm, though her hands were trembling on the edge of the sink. She pinned back her long dark braid into a tight bun – still only a few grey hairs, though they were progressing slowly. Her eyes looked tired, and her sharp cheekbones were pale. Quickly, sternly, she drew on lip pencil. She repressed the emotions rising up beneath her breastbone. There was work to be done. Oh, to be sitting behind her desk in the gallery!

Gabriel sat at the breakfast table, eating a single piece of dry bread.

'You couldn't lay out two plates?' she asked, coldly.

'I have other things on my mind than these trivialities,' he replied calmly, reading his manuscripts. 'You'll be pleased: I believe I may have found a solution to our parquet situation,' he added with a smile.

Clarice stared at her husband, unblinking. 'Please inform me when you have found a solution to our...*couple's* situation, then.'

Gabriel steepled his fingers. 'My dear, are we really to have this conversation again? We agreed we would not have children. It was a shared decision. Remember? I distinctly remember you saying it would be a waste of twelve years, since they would only run away at the end. Oh, oh, and have you forgotten how you used to feel about the idea of a parasite growing inside you?' By this point, his cheeks were uncharacteristically flushed, and a few tendrils of hair stuck to his forehead.

Against her will, Clarice winced. 'Gabriel, I am *not* talking about children,' she said. 'I am talking about... communication.'

But Gabriel was not listening. 'You hated the idea of your body changing, being taken over, being exposed nude to doctors, all of it. The emotion, the drama, the humanity. I specifically recall you suggesting you might be able to face raising children, if they were sent off to an expensive boarding school from the age of three, like the British aristocrats used to do.' He smiled grimly, recovering his poise. 'We were above all that, you and I. I am an important banker, and you wanted time for your gallery. We had schedules, priorities.'

Clarice stared stonily at the empty breakfast table. 'Yes, we do,' she said.

———◆———

Clarice strode down the cobbled streets of the Old Town of Geneva, her heels clicking against the ancient stone and echoing. The sky was grey, a fine rain had started to fall, and her face was set. Ignoring the friendly greeting from the baker at Le Jardin d'Eden, and the waft of warm, sweet aromas from inside, she quickened her pace towards the gallery. Work would clear her mind, she told herself. She wanted nothing more than to be enveloped by the utter, pregnant silence of the place, quiet and alone. It disturbed her, this rush of emotion. It was so unlike her; the contained, middle-aged Swiss woman that she was. Perhaps it was the *foehn* blowing in from the mountains, bringing with it wild thoughts.

There it was, dark and comforting, the narrow entrance on Rue

Calvin, hidden behind its nondescript glass front – nothing in the window for fear of sun damage, vandals, exposure; everything hidden away in a series of rooms, each deeper and darker than the last, as if endless. At last, in the depths, the wanderer would find storage space and old document archives, their tidy figures yellowing and alphabetised. In her strange mood, Clarice found herself imagining that the high ceilings yawned above her, welcoming her back to her domain. She took off her coat and shook out her hair to dry. There they were, the familiar paintings, hung in series from the ceiling on long wires.

Albert Anker was the first Swiss painter to form the heart of her collection. All around her, his plain, glowing, brooding paintings hung. Clarice looked with satisfaction at the simple subjects: a blonde child peeling potatoes; a still life of ham, rustic bread, a cup of wine; serious children sitting with beautiful babies, or sewing, reading, or at their parents' deathbeds; a busy schoolyard scene; a family meal; a village funeral. There were soft woodland watercolours, and dark chiaroscuros, the humanity of their subjects glowing forth in gold and ochre from the black backgrounds. Poverty and loneliness illuminated the subjects in such a strange way, Clarice found herself reflecting. Yes, it gave them gravitas, but what sadness to choose for art! All those struggling families. Surely the painter was almost glorifying misery? Calvin would have approved, she told herself firmly. It was important to know the world around oneself. She wondered if Gabriel had donated anything to the church tombola. The morning's conversation threatened to come rushing back into her mind, and firmly, she repressed the tide. There was nothing further to be thought on the topic. She had work to do.

Ferdinand Hodler's world was populated by graceful, symbolic figures of woodcutters, reapers, workers, farmers. *The self-same peasant backbone of Switzerland,* she thought to herself, *but transfigured through Impressionist watercolours.* These were more joyful visions of Swiss country life; all socialist propaganda, Clarice reflected with a smirk: how amusing that they should now hang in the Old Town, selling for millions to brokers, yacht owners and socialites. The highlights of Clarice's Hodler collection, in any case, were the landscapes. There was a beautiful view of a mountain lake, the perspective taking in the ripples on the rocky shore as well as the peaks in the distance, washed in purple and blue. Another painting of Lac Léman showed Château de Chillon perched above the waters in all its Romantic glory. She was particularly proud of another painting of the lake, however, all in bright yellows and turquoises, like a vision of the Côte d'Azur, with soft, puffy clouds around the top. It was fanciful, but something about it had charmed Clarice. It had a place of honour amongst the dark faces of labourers and the still lives of meagre dinners: the beautiful lake that she had loved so, as a child.

She sat down at her desk, facing out towards the rainy street, and pinned her hair back tidily. The simple, modern desk was the only vestige of the twentieth century to have made it into the gallery. She kept its surface immaculate, without a stray sheet of paper anywhere in sight. A bone cup containing two matching pens, and a plastic-covered gallery catalogue, were all that lay on the surface. She opened a drawer, pulled out a sheaf of letters and sighed in satisfaction.

———————

The glass door flew open with a clunk, letting wind and rain blow in. The wild wind had a way of blowing down from the mountains at the most unexpected moments, turning the weather bitterly cold. A blonde man in a gigantic hat was standing in front of her, his booted feet splayed far apart. 'Howdy,' the man said, in a thick Texan drawl, removing his hat and smoothing down his hair with a small comb. 'Nice place you've got here. Would you grant me shelter from the storm, my lady?'

'Good morning, monsieur,' Clarice said with a thin-lipped smile. 'I see you're unused to Swiss weather. What can I do for you?'

'Well,' he said, his chest swelling out, 'I saw your pretty little self sitting all alone and I thought you might need some company.'

'I'm sure there's no need for that,' Clarice said shortly, her English clipped but perfect. 'There is only one real reason to come in here, disturbing me at my work. The rain is no excuse. We do not harbour vagrants in our art galleries. Are you interested in Swiss art?'

'My, your English is fantastic!' he exclaimed. 'I am still slow with French, even though I've been coming to this strange little country for twenty-five years.'

'I prefer French,' she replied, 'but I understand that sometimes, when dealing with foreign clients, it is necessary to speak other tongues.' She straightened the collar of her white shirt.

'You guys sure have a great lake out there,' the Texan replied, not really listening. 'I thought it might be nice to have a look at some of these as souvenirs — for my kids, you know. They're into their motorboats, waterskiing and whatnot.'

'I see,' said Clarice. 'You would like a painting of the lake?'

'Hey, look at that one with the castle!' The man gave a long, slow whistle, hooking his thumbs into his belt loops. 'I just love me some of that. Texas only has recent history, you know. Cars, politics, a few buildings. The oldest damn thing around is a hundred years old. These look, like, five hundred years old.'

'Yes, they are indeed very old; the castle and the painting both.'

'Looks right out of one o' them poems,' he said thoughtfully.

'Well, Lord Byron, the famous English poet, spent part of a day there,' Clarice replied smoothly. 'Along with many other writers and poets. Switzerland has long been considered a source of inspiration to those that visit it.'

'Byron, eh? Well I'll be damned. Those English, they get everywhere. They took over our country, you know, from the Indians. Oh, them and the Spaniards that saved Texas from tea-drinking.'

Clarice stared at the man in steely silence for a minute. 'Would you like to purchase one of the paintings?' she asked at last, her voice still silky smooth.

'Yeah, that one,' he said, gesturing at the image of Château de Chillon. 'How much is it?'

'Would you like the price in dollars?' she replied coolly, sighing internally. The old adage along the lines of 'if you have to ask, you can't afford it' sprang to her mind.

'What do you think? I can't count in anything else.' He spread his hands with a grin.

'One and a half million dollars.'

'I'll be damned!' he exclaimed. 'That piece of... something! I have a cowboy picture at home that also has water and rocks like these, and I only paid two thousand for it!'

'Perhaps this is not the painting for you, then, sir. It sounds like you already own something quite similar,' she said, unsmiling.

'I only came in here for the view anyway,' he said, flashing a sharkish grin, 'and I don't mean the painted kind. My name's Wyatt.'

'Well, monsieur,' Clarice replied, looking back down at her paperwork, 'I am not particularly interested in your name. I have a lot of administration to finish.'

The man stared at her for a moment, then put his hat firmly back on. 'A man's gotta know when he's failed,' he said with a show of gallantry. 'I bid you good day, you cold –'

The slamming door cut off his last word. Clarice sighed with relief. The rain was now pouring down outside, which would hopefully deter anyone else from coming to disturb her. Most passers-by who stumbled into the gallery were nothing better than time-wasters. Those who truly intended to buy, tended to make an appointment through their secretary weeks in advance: mostly distinguished gentlemen, retired bankers, old Swiss ladies in furs. Of course, there was always the occasional opportunist...

As if on cue, the door flew open again, this time bringing a few wet leaves flying across the gallery floor.

'Good morning,' the man said loudly, brushing raindrops from his shoulders.

Sighing inwardly, Clarice put on a faint smile. 'Good morning,' she said. *Two foreigners in one morning!* she thought to herself. *How very unusual.* Perhaps this week was some Catholic holiday she had forgotten about.

'I am Pyros,' the man said rather imperiously. He had taken off his coat and was holding it over one arm, looking around as if expecting staff to come and remove the inconvenient item from him.

Clarice looked him up and down slowly. Greek, she surmised, both from the name and from his olive skin and dark, greased-back hair. Pyros was short, with large, bright, white teeth. He was wearing an expensive polo shirt, unbuttoned to show a flush of chest hair. Overall, the impression the man made on Clarice was not favourable. *Flashy,* she thought to herself; *new money.*

He craned down over the desk, so close that she could smell his strong eau de cologne. 'What's this?' he said. 'Do you art people have secrets, just like the bankers?'

Clarice pursed her lips and pulled the papers back sharply. 'It's really quite rude to look at people's private documents. What do you think you are, some kind of spy?'

Pyros gave a raucous laugh. 'I may be foreign, but I am not a spy. I'm a shipping magnate. I'm looking to buy a painting.'

At this, Clarice lowered her eyebrow, and her face softened imperceptibly. 'Well,' she said. 'In that case, perhaps we can talk. This is my inventory list,' she added by way of apology. 'It is a private document.'

'I own many ships,' Pyros continued, somewhat bombastically. 'I should like a watery painting of some sort, to put it in my ship.'

'In your ship?' Clarice's heart sank. 'Won't that be a rather damp environment for an oil painting?'

'I wouldn't know,' he replied airily. 'Who cares?'

'It might damage the paint. These are important artworks,' she said. 'The Swiss masters are highly prized the world over.'

'What Swiss masters?'

'Anker, for instance. That's one of his landscapes you're pointing at with such emphasis.'

Pyros narrowed his eyes, sensing her disapproval. 'Anchor?' he repeated. 'Perfect for a ship. Maybe I'll stop in the middle of the ocean and throw it overboard.' He threw back his head and laughed happily.

'In the middle of the ocean, on a ship, you want a painting of water? To remind you...?'

'In case I forget,' he said with a wink. 'Now, enough of this chit-chat. You want a lot of money for this piece of canvas?'

'That one?'

'Yeah, that...' At this moment, Pyros paused. 'Wait a minute, how about this?' He pointed at the turquoise-and-yellow Hodler.

'That's Lac Léman,' Clarice replied, her heart sinking further. 'A silly little painting, really.'

'I like it!' he exclaimed with gusto. 'Makes a nice change from the rest of these dreary children. They all look positively diseased. Come on, give us a price for the postcard.'

'You wouldn't like this view of Château Chillon? It's the same lake. Or how about this water scene? There's even a little sailboat in it.'

'I hate sailboats. I need big engines. Come on, what does the yellow one cost?'

'One and a half million dollars,' she replied at last, reluctantly. 'About four million Swiss francs.'

Pyros paused, considering. 'Isn't that a little expensive for this Anchor guy?' he asked. 'I'm pretty sure I've come across him in auctions.'

'No,' Clarice replied firmly, fully aware the man was bluffing. 'These are my prices.'

'I love it,' Pyros said suddenly, coming to a decision. 'I want it on my ship and I haven't got all day. I'll write you a cheque right away if you give it to me for three mil.'

'The price is four million,' Clarice replied, 'whether you pay by cheque, cash, or transfer to an account at a private Swiss bank. If you have the money, I'll sell it to you for four, but not a penny less.'

Pyros shook his head. 'You drive a hard bargain, lady. Three and a half million?'

'You're forgetting,' Clarice continued smoothly, 'the charges for VAT, which add on a few per cent. Of course, after that there is the question of handling, and I have my insurance for the year to cover.'

He stared at her for a moment. 'Did you just increase the price on me?' he asked, disbelieving.

'I'm not increasing anything,' she replied. 'I told you the price, and now I'm telling you the costs.'

'I've never heard anything like this in my life,' he said, outraged. 'How long have you been in this business?'

'I've been running this gallery more than ten years. If you don't want the painting, you can go,' she said quietly.

'I want the damn painting! But I want to negotiate! That's how it's done!' Pyros looked like he was a few seconds from stamping his foot on the ground.

'Not in Switzerland,' she said, 'or in my gallery. I have no need to lower my prices. Why would I?'

'Because you want to sell the painting.'

'Yes, but I wouldn't want to sell it under value, would I? That would be a waste of everyone's time. Besides, maybe I don't want to sell it. Maybe I like it right here.'

'Why would you have this gallery, then?' Pyros was becoming impatient.

'It amuses me.'

'Who pays the rent?' he sneered.

'Don't be impertinent,' she retorted sharply. 'It's none of your business. The only business that concerns me is whether you'll be buying this painting or not.'

'I don't understand why you're sitting here in this expensive place, wasting my time. Does your husband approve?'

'How dare you,' Clarice said, her temper threatening to flare. 'What kind of man would insult a woman in such a way? This is *my* gallery. I pay my own damn rent. Is that all you Greeks do, gossip about each other's lives, and the lives of strangers? My family life is absolutely none of your business, you weasel.'

Pyros laughed. 'So you're running away from your husband! You see, in my country we do tell each other everything. It makes us very good at reading your pale Swiss faces, repressing everything since birth. Yes, we talk about everything. Salaries, affairs, dinners, children.'

Clarice swallowed. 'What a strange culture,' she said bitterly. 'I shall make a note never to visit.'

'You're one to talk... sitting in a shop all day and not selling anything! Switzerland is awful. I think I'd commit suicide if I had to live here.'

'What a country you must come from, expecting to buy without paying.'

'You are bizarre,' he said, shaking his head, 'and distinctly unpleasant. On top of this, you know nothing about retail.'

'The price is five million now,' Clarice said quietly, with a satisfied smile.

'You're crazy!' he cried out. 'You crazy old Swiss woman! You've just increased the price by twenty-five per cent! This is the only place in the world where you start to negotiate, and the price goes up instead of down!'

'The Swiss are rarely crazy, and I am certainly not old. I just want you to get out of my shop. Now, if you'll excuse me, I have work to do.'

Pyros slammed the door so hard it bounced open again, swinging in the wind and rain. Clarice let a smile spread across her face, looked up contentedly at the bright turquoise and yellow painting, then stood up to close the door behind him - a good morning's work.

Chapter Three

The jagged peaks rose into the sky in rows of white snow and rock, fading into the fog of distance. Across the greening valleys and pine forests far below, rising up into the first snows of autumn, late bluebells were scattered. Gabriel breathed deep, looking around him at the brightness, his trekking poles held tight in his gloved hands. Even the clouds overhead were pure, crisp white. On the horizon, the stark tip of the Matterhorn shone in the morning light. In the valley, the sprawling town of Saas Fee was visible, its rooftops glowing gold as the sun rose.

It had to be one of the most breathtaking sites in the world, Gabriel reflected with satisfaction, even just before the start of the true skiing season. And it was all his, or at least that was how it felt. He almost preferred it in autumn and spring, even if the first and the last snows were of inferior quality: no-one was around. Everything so pure, so clean, so bright! He sank forward onto his cross-country skis and pushed himself with his poles along the curve of the mountainside. He had chosen this location for his luxury chalet, based on its excellent statistics: the best snow year-round, excellent cross-country skiing tracks, the fewest foreign tourists; all this as well as the impressive glaciers. These appeared in the distance, blue-grey rivers of ice inching their way down towards the valley.

Isolation: this is what he longed for. True, the scenery was wonderful, the skiing conditions were flawless, but above all, he was far from everything and everyone: no luxury shops, no tacky cowbell souvenirs, no chattering masses of children flailing their way downhill; none of the swarming excitement of Chamonix or Val d'Aosta or even Zermatt, which was just forty minutes away. Yes, here above Saas Fee, Gabriel de Puritigny had silent and solitary mountain bliss. He slid powerfully across the snow towards the glaciers.

Looking up at the sky, however, he noticed a few clouds gathering. A trail of bright powder was blowing from one of the nearest peaks like an aeroplane trail: the winds above were strong.

It would be November soon, and the rains that whipped through the streets of Geneva would grow colder by the day. He shivered at the memory. In any case, he should probably head back to his wife, Gabriel thought with a sigh. He did love the chalet, which he had constructed in as pure a design as he could, but he had left Clarice down there chattering away to Serge, the chalet's architect, and he wasn't sure he was in the mood for conversation - not the kind that ended in requests for thousands of pounds, and not after this wonderful morning walk. How tragic it seemed that even two thousand meters above sea level, one could not escape humankind! If only he could stay up here, in the harsh beauty of the autumn mountains, clambering across the rugged glacier or slipping down the little hills towards the bluebells!

Gabriel sighed and turned back towards the chalet. It was, he had to admit, getting a little cold.

Firelight flickered across the beautiful blonde parquet, shined to a golden sheen with pure beeswax.

'Five million francs?' Clarice nearly dropped her silver teaspoon in shock. 'Five million? Serge, do you have any idea how much my husband and I have already sunk into this damned chalet? This whole extension project is a ridiculous idea. Mark my words, most of the year it'll only house our ski jackets and bicycles.'

'Monsieur de Puritigny implied it would be for guests,' Serge said graciously, wiggling his toes in the forty-thousand-dollar hand-woven white carpet.

'There are no guests,' Clarice said firmly. 'Nobody comes, and do you know why?'

'No, madame?'

'Because we do not invite them,' she said.

Serge burst out laughing. 'I see,' he replied.

Serge and Clarice were sitting in the chalet's large, open-plan salon, lounging on the pure white sofas. The coffee pot and a small china plate of chocolate *carac* tartlets were laid out on a vast glass coffee table.

'I understand that this extension was a part of the original plan,' Clarice continued calmly. 'When we first designed the chalet. I mean, we obviously originally thought the place would one day need room for children, as well as visiting family and guests. Do you know how many people have visited so far? I could count them on the fingers of one hand, and that includes you and Thomas, Gabriel's idiotic German associate from the bank. He's a recluse by nature, my husband, whatever his charm might imply. I don't think he can even stand most of his employees. You met him through the bank, so you'll have been subjected to the full seductive client treatment.'

Serge laughed. 'I suspect I was quite an important client of Von Mipatobeau, so no, this doesn't surprise me. I first came in to deposit money; a matter of portfolio management. Monsieur de Puritigny was indeed very charming from the first day onwards.'

'It's all an act,' Clarice said, shaking her head; though whether in bemusement or affection, it was hard to tell. 'He knows how to sound polite, even sociable, because it's necessary to his career, but I believe he would truly be happiest if he could spend all day up there in the snow.' She sighed. 'Would you like some more coffee, Serge?'

'Yes please. It's lovely and strong: just what a man needs in the morning!'

Clarice was quiet. After pouring the coffee from a china pot, she sat down again, suddenly earnest. 'Tell me, Serge,' she asked, 'why do you think Gabriel is so attached to this idea of the expansion? I honestly don't understand it.'

Serge raised his eyebrows. 'You want my honest opinion? I believe he's doing it for art, as a decorative hobby. I also believe he considers this to be a solid investment – no, don't interrupt, I am giving you my personal thoughts on the matter. I'm sure you are aware that in purely financial terms, the bigger the chalet, the better. The third reason I would give you is that I suspect Monsieur de Puritigny has a sort of patriarchal instinct, whether or not he will have descendants:

he wants to feel like a prince in his own palace.'

Clarice nodded. 'I think you're right about that. But what kind of prince doesn't want to entertain, doesn't like sharing food, doesn't enjoy conversation? What kind of prince doesn't want a court full of courtiers? What is the point of a palace if there are only the two of us to wander its lonely halls? Let me tell you something: if there was nobody in paradise, nobody would ever want to go there. Hell would be more fun.'

'That's a great quote,' said Serge. 'I'll use that in the architectural promotion of my next catalogue.'

'Yes, go on and use it. Use my husband's money, too. You're blinded by your love for it.'

'Now, that's not fair. Remember, you hired me! I'm in love with your husband's vision, his taste, his artistic flair.'

'Flair?' Clarice nearly choked on her *carac*. 'Have you looked around you? You no longer question the necessity to remove your shoes at the door, as if you were entering some sort of sacred temple, but do you see what colour this entire room is?'

'I helped design it,' Serge said hesitantly. 'I am not blind.'

'It's like stumbling into a snow bank,' Clarice said shortly. 'The sofas, the bedding, the throw pillows. Not even off-white, not even cream. One morning, we'll come down here at dawn and go snow-blind.'

Serge laughed out loud. 'But Madame, it's fashionable! Besides, the curtains are red.'

'Do you know why? So that they match Gabriel's ties,' Clarice said crisply.

'It's incredibly stripped back and modern,' Serge continued. 'If your husband would allow it, I'd have your chalet on the cover of the decoration magazines. Not a single tasteless bear skin, antelope antler, or tiger claw on the walls. No thick furs in front of the fireplace. Not a single heavy oaken wood carving! It's radical. It's wonderful. *J'adore!*'

'Do you know where the heavy oak has all gone? Straight into that damn fireplace, in great hunks, so that the temperature is always just a little uncomfortably warm. Sometimes I suspect my husband is something of a lizard, always needing to be in hot and sunlit places.'

Serge shook his head. 'You've a wicked tongue, Madame de Puritigny. I don't remember you being this sharp in our previous meetings.'

'That's because my beloved husband is out on one of his interminable cross-country ski hikes,' she replied primly, adjusting herself on the white sofa. 'I become the châtelaine in his absence, you see. When he returns, I am the shrinking violet.'

'You must understand, Clarice, if I may call you that: your husband is one of my very favourite clients. I do not intend to flatter either of you, but I do love the radical nature of his artistic vision. Yes, of course, in a way I am in love with his fortune, but only because it allows me to live out my most ambitious visions as an architect and interior designer. But what do you think of the *carnotzet*, incidentally? Surely that cannot leave you cold?'

'You are mistaken,' she replied: 'it can. Why on earth would a Germanic wine cellar excite me? Gabriel barely even drinks. We've had it for, what, four months, and it's never seen any use.'

'Ah, but don't you admire the design? Monsieur de Puritigny only used the most marvellous wood. He had no fear of spending ten million on this room.'

'I am well aware of all that, but Gabriel is a Genevois born and bred,' she retorted. 'Why this German creation? If you want my honest opinion, I must confess I find it rather tacky. These silly panels on the wall, made out of flour paste, if I'm to believe my husband!'

'The history of your family, through your skiing trips,' Serge said hesitantly, before reeling off with growing confidence: 'Courchevel, Val Thorens, Tignes, St Gervais, Chamonix, La Clusaz, Meribel, Interlaken...'

'Stop! It's too many.'

'It's the biggest carnotzet in the region,' Serge replied with satisfaction, 'a glorious wooden-panelled room immortalising your best mountain memories. You'd be able to seat a hundred people without trouble. Oh, and the wines you can collect! Riesling,

Sylvaner, Pinot Gris, Gewurztraminer...'

Clarice stared in disbelief. 'Did you even hear what I said earlier? I believe we've had a total of four guests here, one of them a business associate. We haven't filled your perfect wooden wine racks with a single bottle.'

'Well, you need more people, then! More wine! What is the point of an empty carnotzet?'

Clarice sat back in grim satisfaction. 'My point exactly. More coffee?'

'No!' Serge slammed his fist down on the empty glass table, making both of them jump. 'Sorry,' he said hastily.

It was Clarice's turn to laugh. 'I like your enthusiasm,' she said. 'I'll tell you what: how about you organise us a fondue party for tomorrow night? I'll get Gabriel to rustle up a few of his mountain buddies. I say we never entertain, but I believe my husband has a scattering of acquaintances hidden up in these hills: ski instructors, farmers, and the like. You figure out the fondue, I'll set the room up, but Gabriel has to find people for you to invite. You'll be the guest of honour.'

A blast of cold air filled the room as Gabriel closed the door, shivering. 'Find people for what?' he asked coldly, unwrapping his scarf and hanging it up carefully. This transition from glorious mountain solitude to stifling interior with architect was harsher than he had expected. Even with the white furniture, it was so much warmer and darker than outdoors.

'Your fondue party!' Serge exclaimed. 'It will be the event of the opening of the ski season. I will invite everyone, but you must come up with the list.'

'That won't be necessary,' Gabriel replied, slowly unbuttoning his winter coat. His stomach sank further and further. 'Clarice, did you agree to this party idea? Couldn't you wait for me to get home?'

Clarice shrugged. 'You're home now. Have some coffee, *chéri*,' she said. 'I never know how long you'll be gone on these ski trips of yours. Serge was very convincing. Besides, frankly, I think it'd be nice for your wooden wine shack to go to some use.'

'This was meant to be a relaxing weekend!' he sighed.

'You've had your long solitary bout of gazing at snow,' she replied. 'Come now, prince: enjoy your palace.'

Gabriel looked at Serge quizzically, but the architect only shrugged.

'Doesn't he look nice in his ski gear?' Clarice asked innocently. 'He doesn't even match the curtains.'

———————•◆•———————

'*Santé!*'

The sound of clinking glasses filled the wooden room. On the walls, painted scenes in auburn, forest green and ochre opened for upon the guests: buzzards, mountain goats, and chamois, as well as edelweiss and bluebells. *Well, it was certainly Swiss,* Clarice thought to herself, adjusting her shoulder pads under her sheer white blouse. She was rather satisfied with the turnout. If only she could keep track of all the guests' names! Guillaume, Olivier and Pascal were local farmers. Edgar and... Adam? Arnaud?... no, Alain were various other neighbours. Charles was a British skiing instructor. For the last ten minutes, he had been eagerly grilling the architect on the decor, which he kept declaring 'absolutely spiffing' and 'marvellous.' Clarice repressed a smile. *If he likes it so much,* she thought to herself, *he can have the damn place.*

'The preservation of Swiss heritage is essential,' Serge was saying seriously, leaning across the table. 'Woodwork is an essential part of our culture. Consider the beaver: I once had one in my own pond, in my garden. In fact, it was the only time I ever had a fight with a neighbour,' he continued dreamily. 'He called it an oversized rat! Fancy that. In any case, the industrious little critter was a wonder to watch, sawing down gigantic old Swiss trees, cutting them up, building dams in his little pond for his little family!'

'You're quite fond of birds, too, aren't you?' Gabriel asked. 'Never seem to keep track of them myself. That's why I had him design the panels, you see. I'd probably have chosen three ducks and a peacock without Serge's ornithological guidance.'

'I did my research,' Serge said modestly. 'Most of my family library consists of plans and photographs of old chalets; various architectural miracles of Switzerland. The floral and ornithological life of the mountains inspires me.'

'So, you must tell me: how much would it cost me to immortalise every single one of my skiing trips?' Charles was asking, a twinkle in his eye. 'I mean, I've been on *many*.'

Serge shrugged. 'I designed the panels myself, for pleasure. I love nothing more than drawing wildlife. I've always been an avid birdwatcher, you see, so it is a hobby. After that, I bring the designs to a painter in Zurich, who is well-versed in the local techniques. He creates this sort of dough – can you see how the drawings are raised? – and paints it thickly to create the beautiful effect you can see all around you. As you can imagine, his services are rather expensive,' he added apologetically. 'I seem to recall he charges around three hundred Swiss francs an hour.'

Charles let out a low whistle. 'Not a project for this winter, then,' he said cheerily. 'Poor deprived wife of mine, with no carnotzet in our chalet!'

The men laughed. 'Chalets are expensive, we all know it,' Alain said earnestly. 'After all, most of us had to work pretty hard to earn our way up into these mountains!'

'You're forgetting Pascal,' Olivier chimed in. 'Not all of us are bankers. He's Saas Fee born and bred.'

Pascal nodded. 'Every time I step into one of your houses, my jaw drops to the floor.'

'Not all of us had the good luck to be born a peasant,' Olivier laughed, clapping his friend on the back.

'Or a beaver,' Serge added wistfully. The men laughed.

'Gabriel's place is something else, though,' Guillaume continued. 'I don't think I've ever seen such a steeply tilted roof! Like one of those great properties outside of Berne...'

'It's not every chalet that makes you take your shoes off as if you were entering a mosque!' Pascal added. 'I guess you have to be a managing director to get that...'

'Perhaps he likes looking at nude men's feet,' Charles suggested with a cheeky grin.

Gabriel glared at him. 'I cannot help it if my carpet is hand-woven and perfectly white,' he retorted seriously. 'If I could make you all wear slippers, trust me, I would. My wife has assured me, however, that this is impractical to provide for.'

'The sultan's palace, and all of us in embroidered white velvet slippers!' Serge exclaimed in delight. 'Please, remind me of this idea at our next meeting.'

'Relax,' Charles said, seeing Gabriel's face turn a darker shade of red. 'I think we all quite enjoy the novelty of it.'

'Besides,' Olivier added, 'imagine when a few lovely young ladies come to stay? It won't always be knobbly and hairy old banker's toes you'll have to stare at...' Suddenly recalling Clarice's presence, he stammered slightly: 'Except for our dear hostess, of course.'

Clarice smiled blankly. Her mind had been elsewhere. 'I'm glad you're all having a nice time,' she said. Everyone nodded, relieved.

'Shall we bring out the fondue?' Gabriel barked suddenly. It bothered him that his wife should appear so absent. If he was making an effort to host this awful event, shouldn't she be too? He had spent many a day in the hills of Saas Fee with these men, and had even sipped a glass of wine in one or two of their houses after hiking or skiing, but this was still far more social interaction than he was used to.

As Clarice stood up to fetch the cheese, Olivier followed her movement.

'Why don't I get us another chilled bottle?' he said smoothly. 'A little Gewurztraminer, perhaps?'

A murmur of assent went round the table, and glasses were refilled. Gabriel sipped at his now-warm glass of Pinot Gris.

'I've never quite understood drinking culture,' he said slowly, ' - not here, not in other countries. I usually let myself indulge in the pleasure of a fine bottle three times a year: Christmas, Easter, and my birthday. How do you all manage to want to get tipsy every single time you sit down at a table?'

'Ah, but it's essential to the fondue experience!' Pascal exclaimed, his farmer's cheeks flushed red. 'If you don't drink wine, the cheese will clot in your stomach, giving you terrible indigestion.'

Gabriel shook his head slowly. 'I highly doubt that,' he said.

'I'll make sure the man takes a medicinal digestif after the meal,' Serge assured his friend with a wink. 'Just in case a whole wheel of gruyère is trying to reconstitute itself inside him.'

At this moment, Clarice reappeared at the door of the carnotzet, holding aloft a gigantic red metal vat. The scent of hot, melted cheese, wine and garlic washed through the room. Spontaneously, one or two of the guests applauded, and Olivier leapt up gallantly with his lighter, to light the little flame under the pot.

'Beautiful!' Guillaume exclaimed.

'Mm, I'm starving,' Pascal added.

Baskets of fresh bread were passed around, as well as platters of local dried meats and pickles. The cubes of bread, cut tidily on Clarice's specific instructions, were threaded one by one onto the long forks. Then, after a chorus of *bon appétit,* the men began diving into the cheese. A satisfied silence followed.

'I didn't know your Clarice was such a fabulous chef!' Charles cooed.

Clarice smiled thinly. 'I ordered it from a restaurant in the village. It's nice, isn't it?'

'Come now,' Gabriel retorted, obviously cheered by the cheese, 'my wife happens to make a wonderful chicken salad.'

'Yes, let us drink to our hostess, the restaurant cooks, and to the chalet extensions!' Serge exclaimed.

'To ten million francs not spent in vain,' Clarice said, raising aloft her glass with a small smile.

Pascal choked on his pickle. 'Ten...' He did not finish his sentence, choosing instead to shake his head and reach for another hunk of bread.

'She doesn't mean the fondue, you know,' Olivier grinned.

'Ten million's nothing, for a luxury chalet,' Guillaume said gently.

'I don't know. Given that our dear friend Serge here already charged a million pounds for the initial structure...' Alain shook his head knowingly.

Pascal made a noise like a mouse being trodden on, and copiously refilled his glass of wine.

'Your chalet is your palace,' Serge said expansively, looping cheese around a particularly large piece of baguette. 'What the patriarch desires, he should have.'

Alain shrugged. 'If you can afford it, I suppose that is true! In this case, let us drink to Gabriel's health, and to his palace projects!'

'And his wife,' Olivier added. Clarice ignored him.

'And here I was thinking our own kitchen investments were out of hand,' Pascal said with a grin, wiping his mouth on the back of his sleeve. 'My wife has just bought a *pierrade,* you see.'

'A pirate?' The ski instructor looked at him questioningly.

Guillaume laughed. 'You know, it's a sort of heavy granite stone, from the word *pierre* meaning stone, heated from beneath. You can cook any kind of meat on top of it.'

'Very caveman-like.' Olivier nodded approvingly. 'I shall have to investigate.'

'You know this carnotzet has its own kitchen attached? A glorious thing, all stainless steel,' Serge said proudly.

'Just the thing for chicken salad preparation,' Olivier said with a wink.

'Come,' said Gabriel hastily, 'let's toast to one of the first real fondues of the season! The snow will soon be ready for alpine skiing... Who is excited?'

An enthusiastic chorus came back to him. He smiled.

'Every year,' Pascal said dreamily, 'I am so excited from the first day the leaves change, and the air grows cooler. It is as if you can smell the snow coming from the North.' He took a deep drink from his wine glass.

Alain slapped him on the back affectionately. 'I wish I could read the seasons like a real country man. I only know it's autumn when the shops start advertising Christmas.'

Guillaume laughed. 'You know, though, this year the leaves are falling early. I think we could have snow as soon as this month. Before November even starts.'

'Oh, I must ask you something!' Charles suddenly said, leaning forward. His cheeks were flushed with wine. 'Your talk of snow has reminded me of something. Almost every time I come to this valley, I see this strange man on a donkey. Who is he? What is his story?'

'Ah yes,' Pascal replied philosophically. 'The knight.'

Serge raised his eyebrows. 'The knight?' he asked.

Pascal grinned. 'We call him that around here: nobody knows who he is. A great hulking man riding a white donkey. What a sight! The real question is where on earth he got that animal. I've never seen the likes of it in Switzerland. Someone once suggested it might be from Cyprus.'

'Perhaps,' Gabriel said quietly, 'he is carrying the mail. That would explain why it never seems to arrive.' Everyone laughed. 'I have wondered the same thing myself,' he added. 'He often seems to appear on snowy days.'

'When did you build this chalet, then, Gabriel?' Guillaume asked with interest. 'I can tell, from the wood panelling, it was no casual undertaking.'

'Just over five years ago, I believe,' he replied, 'although of course the work is never done. Even the question of woodwork is seemingly never-ending, and so fascinating! We chose the best local pine wood, you understand, from the highest Swiss pine forests. Mountain wood for a mountain home. As you can see, it has very, very few knots. It's perfectly smooth.'

'Very nice,' Alain commented.

'The office, of course, contains the most expensive wood in the house: solid pear wood. Now, most undertakings in pear wood choose to use the beautiful substance only as a thin veneer. My dear wife, here, was adamant on having rosewood or lemonwood, something luminous and exotic, even just for the skirting – but I refused.'

'I did,' Clarice said, suppressing a smile. 'I do love the darkness of rosewood. He said it was a hippie's choice, far too adventurous.'

Gabriel nodded proudly. Clarice noted with pleasure that, as her husband's voice sank into its characteristic drone, his interlocutors eyes drifted slowly to their wine glasses. Pascal refilled his again, wine sloshing onto the tablecloth, and drained it neatly. 'I wanted something simple, classic, and very expensive. That's why I chose pear wood, smooth, salmon-coloured and easy to clean.'

'It cost him four million francs,' Serge added cheerfully. 'They had to wait for two years just for the cut wood to dry, then they had it exported and shipped to a special cabinet maker in Italy for him to fashion it into boards.'

'Then, of course,' Gabriel continued eagerly, 'we had to *import* the cabinet maker to Switzerland, along with the wood, to stay with us while he was panelling the walls. The whole thing was a dreadful bore. But those wooden walls are perfection itself. I shall have to show you gentlemen, after dinner.'

'Shall we have some more wine?' Olivier asked, rather more loudly than necessary. Pascal smiled beatifically.

'I don't know,' Serge replied. 'Don't you think it might be time for something a little stronger?'

'Oh yes! But first, a toast to the pear wood,' Pascal cried, in pink-faced confusion.

'Come to think of it, I've brought you a little something,' Charles said, standing up and tiptoeing gingerly across the carpet. From his bag, he extracted a bottle. 'A fine amber colour, and smooth. Perhaps not salmon, or easy to clean...'

The men laughed. 'Alright then,' Olivier replied, 'give us a sip.'

Charles unscrewed the bottle and Olivier leapt back in mock fright. 'Goodness!' he exclaimed. 'What kind of Scotch is this? Have you brought us a bottle of your wife's Chanel number 5?'

Charles roared with laughter. 'Never tried an American bourbon, I gather? Come now, why would you sip smoke when you can sip vanilla?'

Olivier screwed his face up, and dipped his lips in. He licked them like a cat, contemplating. 'Drinkable,' he said, 'but no elixir.'

Charles shook his head. 'Anyone?'

'Me!' said Pascal, unsteadily holding out his wineglass.

Gabriel stood up and walked to the sideboard. 'We also have eau-de-vie, Calvados, Armagnac, cognac, and Scotch and Irish whiskies.'

'There's a bottle of absinthe in there somewhere,' Serge added, 'for the real Swiss men.' He winked.

'To the real Swiss men,' Guillaume repeated, sloshing himself a generous measure of the absinthe.

'The real men!' Pascal replied, unsteadily.

Various drinks were poured and the glasses clinked again.

'I think you gentlemen will soon be toasting to toasting,' Clarice said, standing up elegantly. 'I bid you all a good night.'

'You won't stay for a little absinthe? A little brandy?' Serge asked. 'I promise I'll get Olivier to leave you alone.'

'*Bonne nuit, chérie*,' Gabriel said dismissively. 'Do close the door behind you. The draughts can be rather chilly. Now, for whom can I pour another glass of this fine perfume?'

Chapter Four

In the reflection of a marble column, Gabriel adjusted his red tie.

'Caroline,' he said, smoothing his hair, 'I need you to wipe all the data from this computer.'

'Of course, monsieur,' she replied, before hesitating. 'Must you really carry the whole thing with you, all the way out of Switzerland?'

He shrugged. 'I have carried heavier bags up the Alps,' he said, 'though none so precious.'

'Don't they have rules on these planes about how much you can take with you?'

'No,' he said.

'Forgive my impudence, but what are you even going to need the computer for, if it's empty?'

'I'll need to take notes,' he replied. 'I will be... typing. Otherwise, my attendance at this conference will be a total waste of time.'

Caroline looked him up and down. 'And where are your clothes?' she asked, pinching her lips sternly. 'Man cannot live on files alone,' she added.

Gabriel held up a tiny suitcase. Caroline raised an immaculately pencilled grey eyebrow.

'I'm only going for two days,' he said. 'One change of suit is all I will need. A change of underwear, a change of socks. Pyjamas, of course,' he added hastily, blushing a little. 'A toothbrush.'

'Toothpaste?' Caroline asked, her expression unreadable.

'I always use soap,' he replied. 'It's far more frugal.'

She received this information without comment. 'Let me wipe those files for you. Have you checked your phone, as well?'

'The phone is empty,' he replied.

'Excellent. Then your journey can commence.'

Gabriel sighed. 'I really have no desire to travel so far out of Switzerland,' he said. 'Why a banking conference should take place anywhere else than here, I cannot understand.'

———— ◆ ◆ ————

'*Bonjour, monsieur,*' the customs officer said, bowing and waving him through. He wore a smart white starched shirt, with a pointed collar under a black and navy blazer. *Swissair,* Gabriel thought with satisfaction. *What a respectable institution.* Spring sunshine blazed through the airport windows.

His computer briefcase was heavy, but his suitcase was light. He knew there was no trace of information on him, and that his hair was impeccably combed. Sometimes, he thought to himself, being a Swiss banker was rather satisfying. Everyone seemed to be smiling in acknowledgement of his status, Gabriel noted with pleasure, and everyone's clothes were perfectly finished.

The day seemed to be off to a good start.

'*Bon voyage!*' a neatly-dressed air hostess said. 'Rivella? Toblerone?'

———— ◆ ◆ ————

The flight passed without incident, sipping sparkling water and staring out over the clouds. At last, through the swirling grey, Gabriel saw a city: London. He adjusted his tie. Time to go meet some English bankers.

Unfortunately, upon flashing his passport and his most professional smile, he was merely waved on, by a man with terrible teeth, towards a red archway. CUSTOMS, this hurdle read. Gabriel sighed. Didn't they *know* he was a Swiss banker?

'Hello,' he greeted the two men standing by the side, obviously paired for their gross size disparity – the Laurel and Hardy of the UK Border Force, he thought grimly. He noted with distaste their cowboy posture and crumpled suits. One of them even appeared to be chewing gum!

'We'll need to see inside that briefcase, sir,' the shorter man told him abruptly.

'I'm sorry?' Gabriel was flabbergasted.

The tall man, still chewing gum, sighed. 'What is your business?' he asked. 'Where are you travelling to today?'

'I am a banker,' Gabriel replied crisply. 'I am headed to London.'

'And where in London are you staying?'

'I can't tell you that,' he replied.

The man blinked. 'Can I see your address book, sir?'

'Absolutely not!' Gabriel replied defensively, before smiling thinly as he remembered his preparations for the trip. 'I don't have one.'

The short man stared at him. 'Why ever not, sir?'

Gabriel ignored him. 'What is the purpose of your trip, sir?' the tall man asked suspiciously.

'I am a banker,' he repeated patiently. 'I'm attending a banking seminar.'

'I see,' the man replied, squinting in doubt. 'Could I see an invitation to this banking seminar?'

'I do not have one,' Gabriel replied, flustered. 'I do not need one.'

'Any proof that this story holds true?' the short man added abruptly.

'I am not carrying paperwork,' Gabriel said, as smoothly as he could.

'You came here without *any* documents?'

'Yes. My passport will serve as identification at the front desk of the hotel. I have memorised the address, as well as the name of the men I must meet.'

The short man frowned. 'Sounds 'ighly suspicious, if you ask me,' he told his companion. He turned back to Gabriel. 'Open up your briefcase,' he snapped. 'For all we know, it could be loaded with hundred dollar bills.'

'You fool,' the tall man hissed back. 'He's Swiss! They'd be gold ingots.'

Dollar signs practically sparkled in the short man's eyes. 'Go on then.' He reached out a hand for the case, and staggered when it was dropped into his hands. 'Cor!' he exclaimed. 'You wouldn't carry this thing with two fingers! I bet you walk tilted over at a thirty degree angle.'

'You'll end up with a slipped disc,' the other man observed.

'A slipped desk?' Gabriel asked, momentarily thrown. 'What desk? Where?'

'You'll pull the bones right off your shoulders!' he explained.

'Are you threatening me?'

'Never mind.' The man rolled his eyes.

Gabriel gave a thin smile. 'Whatever this desk business is about, if you weigh my case,' he said, 'it will become apparent that I am not carrying gold ingots. Neither am I carrying stacks of hundred-dollar bills. Furthermore, I believe you are miscalculating your suspicions. Truly, if anyone is smuggling laundered money across Europe, it will be West to East. Would a banker really be carrying gold *out* of Geneva? I'd suggest you interrogate me and crack open my briefcase upon my return. If I understand airport regulations correctly, you are not allowed to open my personal case without my permission. I highly doubt that will be necessary today.'

The two men exchanged a glance. 'Not sure this one is worth it,' the short man hissed. The tall man shrugged. 'OK,' he said to Gabriel, 'you can go through. I just hope you know we don't appreciate your sorts around here. We'll keep an eye out for you, on the way back.'

Gabriel gave them a deep bow, worthy of the most senior *huissier*, and walked off jauntily. *Grosvenor Hotel*, he thought to himself with satisfaction. *Graham Wilkie, Harold Walton.* The briefcase really was quite heavy, though.

The conference hall was full of chattering voices and the clinking of champagne flutes. Champagne, this early in the day! Gabriel shook his head. The English really were terrible booze-hounds. Drinks had already been spilled on the beautiful lacquered parquet – if they were not mopped up soon, they would leave awful stains. And why must everyone be so loud? What would English bankers have to laugh about? Certainly not the state of their currency, Gabriel thought with a grim smile. No-one seemed to be ashamed of their eccentric shoes, their yellowing teeth, not even the occasional tweed jacket. Did these people have no pride?

He sighed. How on earth was he going to recognise Wilkie and Walton? There must have been five hundred people in the room. He decided to circumambulate slowly, hoping he would recognise the more distinguished guests.

'My good man!' someone exclaimed, rushing up to him. Gabriel did his best impression of a smile, in case this was one of his new clients, despite his rude approach. 'How on earth do you not have a glass in hand? The stuff is free!' The man was red-faced and pot-bellied. Judging by his appearance, Gabriel guessed it was not his first drink of the day – or the week. Walton, perhaps? 'What are you,' he continued gaily, 'one of the organisers? In which case, excellent work.'

'No. I am Swiss,' Gabriel replied. 'And in answer to your first question, I am not particularly interested in early morning drinking.'

'Come now, it's nearly eleven! What kind of hospitality would it be to refuse us a glass or two?' The man paused, rocking back and forth slightly. 'Swiss, eh,' he said thoughtfully. 'So, have you come to rob us of all our money?'

Not Wilkie *or* Walton, then. 'Surely I'd be more interested in stealing your clients,' Gabriel said calmly.

The man eyed him nervously, then laughed. 'Ha ha,' he said. 'That famous Swiss sense of humour. Well, I must be off.'

It took Gabriel a good deal of self-restraint to keep from rolling his eyes. He walked slowly in the opposite direction, wondering how much longer he would have to wait before the actual seminar began. Perhaps some of their food would be edible? He meandered in the direction of the snacks, and sighed as he arrived. What *were* these things? He recognised eggs, although they appeared to be filled with some kind of yellow cream. How abhorrent! More mystifying was the line of large deep-fried balls, labelled *Scotch Egg*. More eggs, then.

'Excuse me,' came a voice from his side.

At last, he thought, *Wilkie*!

'I was wondering whether you were planning on taking that

piece of cheddar.'

'There are two pieces left,' Gabriel replied in bemusement.

'Yes, but if you take the one, there will only be one left, and I will not be able to take it.'

Gabriel looked at the man. 'I am Swiss,' he said. 'While I do occasionally enjoy eating cheese in the morning, I do not understand your strange etiquette. You may have the second-to-last piece.'

'Thank you kindly,' the man said graciously. Gabriel tried to edge away from the table, but it was too late. 'I'm Abe,' he said through a mouthful of cheese. Not Harold or Graham, Gabriel thought sadly. 'Short for Abraham.'

'I'm Gabriel,' Gabriel said unwillingly. *Short for 'leave me alone'*, he thought. He did not stick out his hand to be shaken. For one thing, he did not want cheese crumbs on his cuffs.

'Isn't that something!' Abraham exclaimed. 'A Biblical meeting. Are you here to tell me the good news?'

'I don't think I have any news for you,' Gabriel replied, confused and slightly offended.

'Are you here to meet anyone from the city?' Abe continued.

'Yes,' Gabriel said shortly.

'Who?'

'I can't tell you that!' he snapped.

'Oh yeah,' Abe said airily. 'That Swiss confidentiality nonsense. How are you going to look for them, then?'

'Secrecy,' Gabriel replied, ignoring the second question. 'You'll find it's known as Swiss secrecy. It happens to be the law in our country.'

'Well how do you manage to keep everything secret?'

'I can't tell you anything about our software.'

'Do you have conferences about secrecy?'

'And why would I tell you about that?' Gabriel was losing patience. 'How do you think secrecy works?' Seeing Abraham's stricken face, he softened his tone. 'I can tell you one thing, though: one bank officer does not even know the names of the other bank officers working in his bank. Everything is kept isolated.'

'I see.' Abe, apparently sulking, was not interested in this revelation.

Gabriel sighed. 'Look, I'm here to meet two potential clients. I should probably go look for them.'

'Try the reception,' Abe suggested. 'If you can reveal their *secret* names, they'll be able to find them on the books.' With that, he took the last piece of cheddar and flounced off.

At the reception, Gabriel discovered that neither of his potential clients had turned up yet. 'Perhaps they'll be here this afternoon,' he was told. Cursing himself for having failed to memorise their phone numbers, Gabriel stormed back into the conference hall. At least he remembered their home addresses.

As he walked back towards the snack table, fuming, he heard an unexpected sound. The sound was somehow familiar, yet out of place. What could it be? Yes, it was a German accent! he realised all at once. Better than that: a Swiss German one! The man was tall, handsome, with bright blue eyes and a wave of blonde hair, elegantly swept back. He was impeccably and conservatively dressed, and he was frowning. Gabriel's heart leapt in his chest. Perhaps he was not the only *Schweizer* here!

'Basel, Bern or Zurich?' he asked, pouncing on the man.

The handsome blonde man looked him up and down, lowering an enormous portable phone. 'From your lack of social graces, I'd guess you're not English,' he said with a smile. 'The answer to your question is Zurich.'

Gabriel blushed. 'I'm so sorry,' he said, 'I got a little carried away at the thought there might be other Swiss people here.'

'You look like a fish out of water,' the man said kindly. 'And you're not even drinking!'

Gabriel shook his head. 'I only really drink three times a year,' he explained.

'Goodness; do I gather from your accent that you're from the *Suisse Romande*?'

'*Oui!*' Gabriel grinned. 'Genevois born and bred. I'm Gabriel,' he said, extending a hand.

'Dieter,' the man replied, shaking it enthusiastically. 'So, Gabriel, are you a commercial banker like me?'

'Oh no,' he explained, 'I'm the managing director of a private bank. Von Mipatobeau. I doubt you'll have heard of it.'

'Ah, I see! I'm the managing director of CBS in Zurich. The Commercial Bank...'

'... of Switzerland, yes, I know!' Gabriel felt positively dizzy with enthusiasm. Is this why the Brits all drank so much?

'You never meet Swiss bankers at these events,' Dieter said thoughtfully, 'although that doesn't mean they're not here. They're just being... secretive.'

'We're both fish out of water, then,' Gabriel said chummily. 'We'll have to swim together for the next hour, before the speeches and study groups start.'

'Do you mind if we swing by the bar?' Dieter asked. 'I'd quite like a refill. Besides, I can recommend some of the stranger non-alcoholic drinks, here. What about a light shandy?'

'Even half a glass of beer is still beer,' Gabriel said sternly. 'And that ginger stuff makes me cough.'

'Have you ever heard of dandelion and burdock? It's a soda made out of plant roots, not unlike Rivella. It's surprisingly lovely. You should try it.'

'Very well.'

———◆◆◆———

Drinks in hand, the two Swiss men set themselves up in a corner of the room, ignoring everyone else. *Two handsome fish out of water in impeccable suits*, Gabriel thought dizzily.

'So what is your business generally, in the *Suisse Romande*?' Dieter asked.

'Portfolio management, mostly,' Gabriel replied. 'What about you?'

'Oh, commercial banking, trade finance, real estate loans,

industrial finance,' Dieter reeled off casually. 'There are a few French and German banks that try to rival us, but really we rule the roost.'

'Well, you're one of the biggest commercial banks in Europe! You're not so much a fish out of water here as a whale!' Pleased, Gabriel took a sip of dandelion and burdock.

'Exactly.' Dieter grinned. 'The rare and beautiful whales of Lac Léman. So tell me, Gabriel, what exactly brings you to this seminar? You seem distinctly unexcited at having been invited, if you don't mind me saying. If I may push the metaphor a little further, one might even compare you to a beached whale.'

Gabriel laughed. 'Netted, beached, caught - hook line and sinker... Yes, it is true! As for exactly why I'm here...' He hesitated. 'Well, I'm not meant to talk about it, but I suppose you're not exactly competition. I can trust you to respect the Swiss laws. These two Englishmen, Mr Wilkie and Mr Walton, they're interested in setting up a fund in Geneva. They're just starting to deal in trading options, you see, and they're looking to transfer their capital somewhere it will be well looked after.' He grinned sharkishly. 'All four million pounds sterling of it. Each.'

'So the seminar is an excuse to meet with them.' Dieter nodded in approval. 'Excellent work.'

'I don't travel often, as I find the whole operation rather unnecessarily stressful, but in this particular case, I decided the potential acquisition of these two new English clients seemed worth the journey beyond Swiss borders.' He sighed. 'Except that they're not here.'

'I'm sure they'll turn up,' Dieter said drily. 'Meanwhile, we'll be having this, no doubt, wonderful seminar talk, which will be of great relevance to both of our interests...'

'Dieter, do I detect a trace of sarcasm in your voice?'

'I couldn't possibly say,' Dieter grinned.

'Why are *you* here, then? I know my own failed reasoning, but what brings you to these inhospitable shores?'

'Schmoozing,' he said coolly, emptying his glass. 'Unfortunately,

I can tell I've already met the most interesting person here. I also happen to know from experience that the lunch buffet is the worst of any I've encountered. Have you eaten a lot of British food in your life? Are you familiar with the symptoms of food poisoning?'

Gabriel felt a smile creeping across his face. 'Dieter, are you suggesting we... get out of here?'

'Gabriel, I think I am.'

Speeding down the alleyways of London in a black cab, despite the threatening clouds above, Gabriel felt like a teenager who had been allowed to escape from an awful dinner party. Dieter seemed similarly enthused, although especially at the prospect of eating out.

'Shall we go for fondue at the Swiss Club?' Gabriel offered genially. 'I am spending the night there.'

Dieter laughed, as if Gabriel had made the most hilarious joke. 'Not in London, my dear friend. Their fondue is half cornstarch, and their wine is Italian. No, we must be more adventurous than that. Do you like Turkish food? Indian? What about Chinese? It seems to be taking over this city...'

Gabriel hesitated, not wishing to seem uncultured in front of his new friend. 'I'm not familiar with any of those cuisines,' he had to admit.

'Well, you have plenty to discover!'

His excitement abated further as they turned onto a dingy side street. Men hovered in doorways, by windows of broken glass. On the ground, empty wrappers and bin bags blew in the wind.

'This is Woodfield Road,' Dieter said conversationally.

'It looks filthy,' Gabriel replied, aghast.

'We've entered the backwaters of Tottenham Court Road. Most of this area has been burned to the ground twice in the last ten years, probably for insurance. However, it's famous for absolutely wonderful Indian food. Ten years ago, a few chefs rocked up and opened one-room restaurants: one plate with the food served up together, not even a napkin, and you had to eat with your hands. Nowadays, of course, it's a little more civilised.'

Gabriel swallowed. 'A hidden gem,' he managed to say between clenched teeth. A mangy street cat darted out of the taxi's way and ran into the dirt, hissing. 'Isn't it supposed to be Spring?'

Dieter shrugged. 'Have you never been to England before? It's grey and rainy for all but four days of the year: two days of dirty snow, two days of sunshine so everyone can burn their noses bright red.'

'In Geneva, it was so beautiful,' Gabriel said sadly.

'Can you smell the curry?' Dieter continued.

Gabriel shook his head, holding his breath. 'I have never tasted Indian food,' he gasped.

'Oh, my friend, you're in for a treat!' Dieter said, rubbing his hands together. 'Indian food, for a start, is so spicy your tongue feels like it might fall off. You have to eat yoghurt with cucumber, to recover.'

'Absolutely not,' Gabriel said flatly, beginning to wish he had stayed at the conference. 'I don't even like black pepper. I don't think that's for me.'

'Well,' Dieter said, 'you're missing out on one of the culinary staples of this whole country. There are many kinds of spiced and creamy curry sauce, roasted oven tandoori, little crunchy papadum with seeds. They make a wonderful thick flatbread called naan. You're telling me none of this can tempt you?'

'I am not interested in these things,' Gabriel replied dully, staring out the window.

'What about Turkish food? Thai? Ethiopian?'

'I don't know,' Gabriel said, beginning to feel embarrassed. 'Just please take me away from this street.'

'Enough tourism for the Swiss man! I know,' Dieter said decisively, smiling. 'Come with me: we're eating Chinese!'

Beneath the painted red beams and the hanging golden bells, and just behind a gigantic fish tank, Gabriel and Dieter were seated with their menus.

Prawns with ginger and cashews. Mushrooms in oyster sauce. Fried chicken in orange sauce. Grilled octopus salad. Black bean rolls. Crispy seaweed. Gabriel's eyes roamed over the page, as he began to panic slightly. What were these things? What on earth was he doing here?

Dieter laughed lightly, noting his expression. 'Don't worry about the Chinese characters,' he said. 'Just pick something that sounds nice.'

'There must be over two hundred dishes here,' Gabriel said, trying to keep his tone light. 'How can a man possibly choose?'

'I'm having the Peking duck,' Dieter said. 'Join me, if you like.'

'What is that?' Gabriel asked cautiously.

'The duck is marinated with spices, covered in syrup and roasted in a special fashion so that the skin is very crispy, and then sliced thinly. You serve it with spring onion, cucumber and a sweet plum sauce, wrapped in little pancakes.'

'Pancakes?' Gabriel could not believe his ears. 'Duck pancakes?'

Dieter laughed uproariously. At this moment, the waitress appeared.

'I should like the chicken soup,' he said carefully, his ears turning red.

'The Szechwan chicken soup? An excellent choice. Would you like corn in it?' she asked.

'Corn?' Gabriel turned to his companion in agonised confusion. 'What is corn?'

'Sweetcorn,' Dieter explained. 'Maize. I had forgotten the French are so wary of it.'

'If you mean *maïs*,' Gabriel said slowly, 'that is what we feed our pigs.'

'Well, the Germans and the English enjoy it in their salads,' Dieter said easily. 'It's a small, sweet vegetable. Delicious.'

'No thank you,' Gabriel said firmly, to both of them. 'I think that is quite enough adventure for me.'

Gabriel stirred his soup, picking the bony bits of chicken from the broth suspiciously. He sipped from his spoon, and made a face. 'It's a little... spicy,' he admitted. 'And sweet!'

Meanwhile, Dieter was deftly lining up little pieces of spring onion, cucumber and duck in a pancake – a pancake! Through the thick glass of the window, they could see clouds scudding across the greying sky.

'You're lucky we didn't go for Indian food,' Dieter teased. 'In curries, you have to make sure they're chicken bones and not cat bones! With a biryani, everything is so buried in rice and sauce that you can hardly tell...'

Gabriel's face turned grey, and he nearly spat out his piece of presumed chicken.

'Don't worry, my friend,' Dieter said, laughing. 'We're in safe hands here.'

Gabriel swallowed. 'So,' he said weakly, 'what is life like in Zurich these days?'

'Business is booming, of course,' Dieter said, crunching on a pancake. As a new thought crossed his mind, he paused mid-crunch. 'Gabriel,' he said, 'are you meaning to tell me you've never been to Zurich?'

'I rarely have a reason to venture outside my canton,' he replied. 'I have not had the pleasure.'

Dieter clapped his hands together in delight. 'Oh, my friend, my friend, what a treat you have in store! I'm a firm believer in the idea that the businessman must be a traveller, must come out of his shell, be open-minded and always ready to adapt. You must experience other cultures and traditions: you must learn! So much to see, so much to do!'

Gabriel shook his head. 'You're an interesting man,' he said. 'I am not sure I am as interesting as you.'

Outside, rain had begun to fall.

'Nonsense!' Dieter exclaimed. 'You're simply a neophyte. I know I'm a little younger than you, but I've simply had other priorities.

There's no shame there. In any case, I wasn't going to suggest whisking you away to Bombay. Only Zurich: would you like to come stay with me and my wife? Winifred would absolutely love to meet some Genevois. She's a classical music aficionado, you see, and often travels to the city to catch this or that opera. Perhaps you could bring your own wife?' He paused, frowning slightly. 'You are married, aren't you?'

Gabriel smiled grimly. 'Yes, I am. I'm sure Clarice would love to come along.'

Catching his expression, Dieter laughed. 'It's too early in the day to investigate whatever brings that look to your face: let's just say that it will be lovely for Clarice and Winifred to meet. Come for a weekend, save on hotels! How about in a few weeks' time?'

'Absolutely,' Gabriel replied, forgetting about his chicken soup. 'I would love to see Zurich,' he confessed, leaning forward eagerly. 'I have seen too little of my beloved country of late. When I was younger, I loved nothing more than to take the trains and zoom from one mountainside to another. I would go alone and hike for days, lost in the Alpine beauty.' A dreamy air crept into his eyes.

'Excellent, a mountain man like myself!' Dieter said enthusiastically.

'Oh, you are too?'

'Oh yes. I love nothing more than a brisk two-hour circuit followed by a nice *pression* beer. We must go walking together sometime.'

'I am usually a solitary man,' Gabriel said carefully, 'and I have never understood the alliance of outdoor sports with beer-drinking, but it would be a pleasure all the same. I have a chalet up near Saas Fee, you know, with ample room for guests. It's high up in the mountains, hidden away, a perfect refuge. We could have a weekend there, man-to-man. We have just finished a new expansion, you see. We have wonderful parquet, solid pear wood walls, and a beautiful carnotzet...' He beamed. 'I can't wait to show you,' he said.

'Yes,' Dieter said distractedly, spreading plum sauce on a pancake, 'that would be great. I'm sure Winifred would love to come along.

We would also enjoy a visit to Geneva, to be honest.'

'Of course!' replied Gabriel, his cheeks reddening.

'In the German parts of Switzerland,' Dieter continued, carefully aligning his sprigs of spring onion, 'we admire the Romande part of the country for its international peacemaking institutions, its countryside, the meeting point of the Alps and the Jura, Lac Léman and the Rhône; even the excellent French food. That is something we do not have much of in Zurich. We do, however, have the country's best fondues.'

'Oh, I beg to differ,' Gabriel said. 'There is only one way to resolve this challenge to the honour of Geneva: I will come visit you in a few weeks' time.' He sat back, eyeing his soup like a hunter looking over a slain lion. 'Well, Dieter,' he said, 'perhaps international cuisine is not so bad. All the same, I suspect I will prefer Zurichois to Szechwan.'

'I can guarantee even a cat-meat curry would be better fare than the lunch we were going to be served at the conference.' Dieter checked his watch. 'Speaking of which, they'll probably be wrapping up soon. We should get back and schmooze some more. What were your gentlemen called again?'

'Graham Wilkie and Harold Walton,' Gabriel repeated. 'My soon-to-be clients.'

'Well, my friend, I'm sure you'll find them. Meanwhile, I think it is time for a little digestif. Let us go see what the bankers of London have in store for us...'

Chapter Five

The priest's voice droned peacefully through the high stone arches, his soothing words drifting across the congregation. The simple, heavy wrought-iron chandeliers hung above them, casting luminous shadows across the pure-hearted and the sinners alike. No towering saints of stained glass here, no gilding, no elaborate and terrifying paintings of Hell: most of the church was plain stone, the pulpit a simple hunk of carved wood. '*Au nom du père et du fils,*' the priest intoned, '*et du Saint Esprit.*'

'Amen,' Clarice murmured, staring down at her hands.

It was odd not to have Gabriel by her side, frowning intently, as if he was the first man ever to hear the words of scripture for their true value. Often, he would attempt to debate some small point with her after the service, tugging distractedly at the collar of his black suit, as if trying to prove himself a natural ecclesiastical scholar. She usually ignored him, nodding demurely.

Today, instead, she had the strangely comforting presence of her parents, in their Sunday black. Sitting between them, she had the odd sentiment of being transported back to her childhood, tapping her foot impatiently through the service, waiting to be released back into the sunlight.

The last hymn began, and Clarice sneaked a look at each of her parents. Adam Louis Saint-André-Tobbal winced at every new chord from the organ. Eugénie clasped her delicate hands in her lap, wrinkled eyes closed as if beatifically transported. Neither of them sang, so Clarice kept quiet, although she knew every word.

Clarice laid out the three china plates of chicken salad. She watched her parents' hands pick up their heavy silverware and compose delicate bites: Eugénie's slender white hands, wrists clasped in a silk chemise and pearl bracelet; Adam Louis' wrinkled fingers deftly angling his knife and fork to carefully separate his chicken into minute bites. Their matching tailored black suit jackets sat on the back of their chairs.

'Did that husband of yours finally agree to make a contribution to the church tombola?' Adam Louis barked.

'Yes, father,' Clarice replied demurely. 'He was always going to, you know.'

'Yes, well, I don't trust a man like that, who spends all his money on wood polish... Too attached to earthly vanities, if you ask me.'

Clarice sighed. 'Not all earthly things are vanities,' she replied. 'Doesn't the church deserve a new roof?'

Adam Louis gave a short laugh. 'He probably only donated anything because you told him it was for a new wooden parquet.'

'Papa, that's not fair,' she replied. *It's also not untrue*, she thought with a sigh.

'Gabriel should understand that supporting the local church is an essential part of participating in the community. Does your good-for-nothing husband even pay taxes?'

'Of course he pays taxes,' she replied cuttingly, adding mentally, *I think*. 'He certainly has an accountant who helps him file his tax return every year.'

'Well, if I ever find out even a hint to the contrary, I will report him to the authorities. You tell your rich and handsome de Puritigny man that. And that he should do it on time, too.'

'Papa,' Clarice said sharply, 'I don't remember you having any objections to me marrying an extremely rich private Swiss banker ten years ago. In fact, I seem to recall you encouraging it. Now, I suggest you keep your thoughts on this private matter to yourself.'

'Now, now,' Eugénie said graciously, '*le déjeuner* is no time to be airing these grievances, *chéri*,' she berated her husband. 'Come, our daughter has made a beautiful lunch.'

Adam Louis poked it harshly with his fork. 'I'm not sure it counts as 'made' when you buy the chicken from Migros,' he said. 'Oh, I'm sure somebody slaved for hours over a hot stove, roasting it – but it wasn't my daughter.'

'It's not from Migros,' Clarice replied fiercely. 'What kind of woman do you take me for? It's from the *traiteur*.'

'Well, the vinaigrette is too strong. Mustard won't hide the fact that your dish has no taste, darling. And these greens are days old. Can't you see how shrivelled they are?'

Clarice swallowed, her eyes stinging. 'I am sorry it displeases you, Father,' she said.

'Adam Louis,' Eugénie rebuked her husband primly, 'do not be so unkind. We accepted the invitation, and are therefore our daughter's guests. Have you forgotten your manners?'

Adam Louis shrugged, tossing his thin hair back. 'If I had manners, I would serve my guests something more substantial than chicken salad.'

'It's springtime,' Clarice retorted.

'It's good for your blood pressure,' Eugénie added shortly, a twinkle in her eye.

Adam Louis pushed his plate back. 'Well, I'm going for a walk,' he announced, 'to help my blood pressure.'

'Fine,' Clarice replied. 'There isn't any dessert, anyway.' She stared at her plate, where a few chicken bones sat in the remaining dressing. 'Perhaps the vinaigrette *was* a little strong,' she said quietly.

'Nonsense,' Eugénie said crisply. 'Your father has been in a hideous mood since he found out the results of the latest horse race.'

Clarice stared. 'Since when has father been interested in gambling?'

Eugénie shrugged. 'He calls it "supporting the local community",' she explained with a delicate laugh. 'I couldn't care less, really, as long as he doesn't sink the family fortune into it. Luckily, he's too much of a Calvinist.'

Clarice shook her head. 'He's one to talk about Gabriel's financial oddities!'

Eugénie took her hand in hers. 'You mustn't take these things to heart, my darling. You know what your father's temperament is like.'

Clarice stood up suddenly. 'Don't you think it's a little dark in here?' she asked. She walked quickly to the window and stood there in silence for a minute. Below, the hustle and bustle of Saint Antoine on a Sunday was oddly comforting.

Carefully, Eugénie stood up from her chair and walked daintily across the floorboards, her sensible heels echoing on the parquet.

'I'm so glad it's spring. Winter in Geneva never gets any easier,' Clarice reflected aloud as she pulled the curtains wider.

'You shouldn't complain, my dear. It didn't even rain that much this year.'

'Don't you find it depressing, mother? The constant onslaught of darkness...'

'To be perfectly honest, at times I find it comforting. It's a good excuse to batten down the hatches, make a chocolate cake and eat it in front of the television.'

Clarice looked over, startled. 'Goodness, Mother. Is that really the sort of thing you do nowadays?'

Eugénie shrugged. 'Your father leaves me to my own devices most of the time. I'm having a second youth of sorts.'

'Aren't you worried about your figure?'

Eugénie laughed, surprising her daughter again. 'Why on earth would I worry about my figure? My days of seduction are long behind me. Childbearing marks a point of no return, my dear. You will have new elements in your life to wrap your pride around. Your tiny waist will no longer matter. Only the pitter-patter of tiny feet.' She gave a small sniffle, and extracted an enormous pocket handkerchief.

Clarice stared. 'Would you like some tea?' she finally asked.

'Yes please,' her mother replied.

Clarice walked back to the table and began to gather the plates.

'How are things with Gabriel, anyway?' Eugénie asked gently.

'Well, let's see: last month, in April, it was our tenth wedding anniversary.'

'How marvellous,' Eugénie said, clapping her hands together gently.

Clarice resisted the urge to shrug. 'The whole thing was something of a bore,' she admitted. 'Gabriel got it into his head that he wanted to invite all his uncles to a dinner – it was meant to be one at first, and then some sort of egalitarian spirit seized him, and our house became some sort of de Puritigny charity institution. Cousins everywhere.'

'What's wrong with a little company?' Eugénie asked gaily.

Clarice sighed. 'Well, you have to hide all the valuables. The crystal ashtrays, the silverware, the Hodler miniature, the antique manuscripts... I have these wonderful plastic covers, that you can tie on with ribbons, you see. I put them on everything worth more than ten francs. I wouldn't even leave my eyeglasses on a table around this crowd, I tell you. It's like inviting a bunch of robbers into your home.'

Eugénie shook her head. 'I've never understood this obsession of yours, my dear,' she said gently. 'Do you remember the time you didn't even let the party into your house, preferring to serve everyone tea in the maids' quarters, for fear of exposing your oh-so-precious things to... people?'

Clarice stared. 'I'll have you know, Mother, that it was you who instilled these values in me. Surely you'll agree that the family crystal is worth protecting?'

Eugénie shrugged. 'Of course,' she said, 'but not if it means spoiling a party. Come on, my darling, live a little!'

'I am almost entirely sure,' Clarice said vehemently, 'that Gabriel's uncle once stole from me a carafe made of crystal. Somebody once stole the ironing board, and many of my husband's socks.'

'Socks?' Eugénie raised an eyebrow. 'Why would anybody steal socks?'

'They are silk,' Clarice said shortly. 'I am certain there is a place for them on the black market.' She picked up the plates and marched to the kitchen. It was comfortingly dark and immaculate there, the old oak cabinets looming over the stainless steel countertops. As she arrived in the small and spotless room, the phone rang. *Gabriel, of course,* she thought. Clarice sighed and ran a manicured hand through her hair, then walked into the salon and picked up.

'*Oui, chéri*? How is London? Oh, so you found the clients? If they didn't turn up to the conference, how on earth did you... Threadneedle Street? Oh, I see, their home address. Isn't that near where Jack the Ripper committed all his murders? No, never mind. Yes, things here are going well. My parents are here. Mother is... never mind. Chicken salad, of course.' There was a pause. 'Cat bones? Dieter? Who is Dieter? What on earth are you talking about? You've been invited to Zurich? Oh, I see. Yes, well, we can discuss that when you come home. Yes, dear. Of course. Enjoy the rest of the conference. Yes, I will. Have a safe trip home.'

She sighed and set down the receiver, then walked slowly back into the kitchen. 'What has got into everyone today?' she muttered to the chicken bones. 'Maybe it's springtime.' She glanced out of the small window overlooking the courtyard and garden patch, and was startled to see her father sitting outside, staring at the grass. She shook her head and opened the door.

'Papa?' she asked cautiously, standing in the doorway.

His pale face was angled downwards, his white hair catching the sunlight. In this position he looked ancient, vulnerable. Clarice almost felt sorry for him.

'Clarice, I am of the opinion that your grass is much too short,' Adam Louis said, still looking at the grass. 'It will be summer soon, and everything will scorch. There will be nothing left.'

'I thought you'd approve of the tidiness,' she replied bitterly, without leaving the doorway.

'You have just twenty square metres of grass,' he continued. 'How hard can it be to take proper care of it? Your salads are too wet and your grass is too dry. Have you no respect for the natural order of things?'

'Well, I hope all this worrying helps you digest your chicken salad,' Clarice said shortly, closing the door a little too firmly behind her.

She squared her shoulders and walked back into the dining room, forgetting the tea. Seeing her mother, she stood for a moment as if at a loss, smoothing down the creases of her skirt with a blank expression.

'Oh dear,' Eugénie said. 'Did you run into your father?'

Clarice gave a curt nod. 'I don't understand how such a boring person can be so consistently disagreeable,' she muttered.

Eugénie shook her head. 'You mustn't let your father get to you. How do you think I've survived forty years of being married to him?'

'Heaven knows,' Clarice replied.

'Ignore him. He's never talked very much, never looks at anything, never interacts. He tends to turn away when you speak to him – have you noticed that? Ignore Adam Louis for long enough and eventually he'll get a headache and go to bed.' She shrugged. 'It's not been a difficult life since I figured that out.'

Clarice let a small laugh escape. 'Does he still go to bed at nine thirty every night?'

'Oh yes,' Eugénie replied gleefully. 'Like the old, bland man that he is. On the bright side, he'll agree with almost everything you say, out of an unwillingness to make the effort to maintain conversation.'

'That doesn't seem to extend to me,' Clarice said ruefully.

'As I said, he's in a hideous mood today. Perhaps we should play some jazz music to cheer him up?'

Clarice laughed, genuinely this time. 'These pop musicians will be the downfall of civilisation!' she said, miming her father's stern expression. 'All this dancing! This loudness! These scantily clad singers should be banned.'

'Sometimes I used to wonder what Adam Louis's story really is,' Eugénie mused, sitting down on the couch. 'Is he a bitter man? Did he survive some traumatic incident at a young age? Is he is... a psycho? Where does this hatred of music come from?'

'Come now,' Clarice teased, 'I seem to remember him enjoying a little Strauss.'

'Quiet waltzes only,' Eugénie replied. 'And the Wedding March.'

'What about "Happy Birthday"?'

'Yes, he'll sing along to that,' her mother said wistfully. 'Though it's been a long time since we've been to a party together.' She sighed. 'Clarice, can I ask you something?' She patted the sofa by her side.

Clarice nodded and sat down next to her mother, smoothing her skirt around her.

'I raised you alone,' Eugénie said thoughtfully. 'I watched you grow from a pretty young girl into a beautiful woman. I saw your body change, and the way your eyes began to sparkle in the company of certain young men. I saw you fall in love with that haughty banker. I must ask you one question: do you still make love with Gabriel?'

'Mother!' Clarice exclaimed, genuinely shocked. 'How could you ask me such a thing? This is not a very Christian question!'

'Nor is it very Swiss,' Eugénie replied with a hint of a smile. 'But who are we to be limited by these features? Listen, my darling, we are alone. I am your mother.'

'I do not speak of these things with anyone,' Clarice said hesitantly, beginning to blush. 'It is no-one's business what goes on within a marriage.'

'I was supposed to have taught you things,' Eugénie said, her voice turning melancholy. 'I never told you anything before your wedding night. I never asked you about your first kiss. I don't even know what you two did, ten years ago. What is Gabriel like as a husband, as a lover? Tell me, darling, are you still making love?'

Clarice, mortified, felt the blush deepening across her cheeks. She squared her shoulders. 'Mother, do you want me to give you statistics, describe for you our positions, his technique?'

'You're offended,' Eugénie replied. 'I apologise. You must understand...'

'He's awful,' Clarice burst out suddenly. 'What do you want me to tell you? That it lasts twelve minutes? That he reads the *Financial Times* afterwards? That he is utterly without passion or skill? What do you expect, mother? Do you want me to request a divorce because of this? Nobody, not even a judge, will accept a woman filing for divorce because her husband of ten years – managing director of a successful Swiss private bank, owner of luxury chalets, spender of five million francs on a wooden wall – makes love in twelve minutes and then goes to read his *Financial Times*. What *do* you want to know, mother?'

'Well,' Eugénie said.

'If I can be bothered with the charade, Mother, I have to request intercourse from my husband. Afterwards, he looks away from me and intones *ça y est*. Job done. *Veni, vidi, vici.* Do you have any idea how embarrassing that is for me?'

'Well,' her mother replied. 'It sounds like you have quite the amusing husband. You obviously take after me.'

Exhausted by her outburst, Clarice gave a hollow laugh. 'Sex is an obligation for Gabriel,' she said, 'like a chemistry exam... something he discovered in the fine print of the marriage contract after signing it... a kind of exercise that you really should make time for, even though it disinterests you entirely, like jogging, or squats... like cleaning the house. I don't know. Mother, I don't know how my husband looks at life. I don't understand the man.'

'Are you going to bear his children?'

'Mother,' Clarice said, her voice tired, 'this is an invasion of my privacy.'

'You're not in your husband's damn bank, my dear. This is my daughter's life. This is motherly small talk.'

Clarice sighed and cracked a small, sad smile. 'I don't know if twelve minutes is long enough to make a child,' she said.

'Of course it is,' Eugénie said briskly, missing the joke. 'Just try it.'

'I don't think so, Mother. It's too late for us.'

'Maybe you should try getting one of those big, soft beds, like the Americans,' Eugénie said thoughtfully, ignoring her daughter's response. 'Do you think that might make a difference?'

'Of course,' Clarice replied coolly. 'Gabriel would have to roll twice as far to get his newspaper afterwards.'

Eugénie shook her head.

'Seriously, though, Mother,' Clarice continued, 'I'm not even sure I want children myself anymore.'

'How are you going to prolong your legacy? Continue the glory of our name?'

'His name, you mean. And I don't know.'

'It's not just that. Don't you want to be a mother?'

'I don't know,' Clarice replied. 'It seems unlikely to happen in any case. Maybe I ought to make love to someone I meet on a street corner, or my horse trainer. A baby off the balance sheet, outside the accounts. A marginal baby.'

Eugénie laughed. 'That wouldn't be very Calvinistic, would it.' She paused thoughtfully. 'How old is Gabriel, anyway?'

'Forty-two,' Clarice replied listlessly.

'Well, you haven't got that much time, then.' Eugénie leaned forward, her eyes sparkling. 'Let me tell you a joke I once heard from a Polish man: This man is walking in the street, wearing jeans with the zipper gaping wide open. Just strolling down the street without a care in the world. Another man walks over, the polite sort of man who would be embarrassed to be caught with his own pants open. He taps him on the shoulder. "Sir," he says, "your zip is open. You might want to do something about that." The man shrugs and replied: "Oh, it doesn't really matter. In fact, it's better that way." The polite interlocutor is confused. "What do you mean, sir?" he asks. "Well," the man says, "when you have a dead person inside, it's good to have the window open."' Eugénie threw her head back and laughed uproariously.

'Mother!' Clarice exclaimed. 'I don't know what's got into you today. Have you been sneaking sherry in the kitchen?'

Eugénie sat back, shaking her head. 'When you're my age, you won't care so much anymore. I have done everything I wanted, suffered what I had to, done what I must.'

'I'm perfectly contented with the life I have,' Clarice said sharply.

'Of course you are, dear,' Eugénie replied. 'Of course you are.'

Chapter Six

The doorbell made a brassy sound, like a small chime being rung.

'Greetings!' Dieter appeared at the door in lederhosen, white suspenders, and a jaunty hat topped with a pheasant feather. 'I was just gardening,' he said, brushing invisible particles of dirt from his clean hands. His blonde hair flopped into his bright blue eyes.

'I hope we're not interrupting,' Gabriel said gravely with a sort of small bow, hoping desperately that a muddy handshake could be avoided.

After a moment's hesitation, his wife tentatively held her hand out to be shaken. 'I'm Clarice,' she said.

Dieter shook her hand enthusiastically. 'Welcome to Zurich,' he said. 'How was your journey?'

'Very smooth,' Gabriel replied, relieved, 'although our train was two minutes late. I find it unbelievable, this slipping of standards. Nonetheless, we found your house easily. Your directions were very coherent.'

'The old town is lovely,' Clarice added gently, 'if that is what we walked through on our way from the train station. The views of the lake from the train were wonderful, too, sparkling in the sun.'

'Oh yes,' Dieter said. He looked younger in the bright sunlight than Gabriel had remembered from London. 'It's UNESCO classified, you know. One of the most beautiful cities in the world.' He beamed. 'You will have walked right in front of my bank, too!'

'Perhaps we did, yes. I quite enjoy the Germanic style of architecture,' Gabriel said thoughtfully. 'So straightforward.'

'Did you pass by the old hotel? Such beautiful old stone cornices, overlooking the lake... But I am forgetting myself,' Dieter said. 'We can talk of architecture as long as we like, but we really should be sitting down! Come, come, into my house.'

He motioned them in through the door into a luminous entry hall. Small shoes and toys were scattered across the polished golden pine parquet, and there were vases of flowers on every visible surface. Gabriel found it all quite overwhelming: lilies, roses, orchids, blossoming white, lemon-yellow, fuchsia, crimson. In another room, someone was playing the piano.

'It's beautiful!' Clarice whispered.

Gabriel occupied himself with fastidiously unbuttoning and removing his coat.

Dieter laughed. 'The flowers are Winifred's contribution. The piano is our little Klaus. He's only eight, but he's been practising all summer. I think my wife may have finally found someone to make music with.'

'Your wife is a musician?' Gabriel asked, with distaste he thought slightly too late to hide.

'An aficionado,' Dieter answered lightly. 'Aficionada, perhaps? In any case, she loves nothing more than the opera.'

'I've never been to the opera,' Clarice confessed with a smile.

'It always seemed rather... silly to me,' Gabriel said, looking at his coat. Why did his wife seem to be making such an effort to be polite? 'All that romance, all those overweight Germans, all that loud singing when you're about to die.'

'I simply never had a chance,' Clarice added calmly. 'My family were always a little too puritanical for operas. I'm sure some of them must be wonderful.' Was that a real *smile* she was cracking?

Dieter smiled in return. 'Perhaps you might go with Winifred sometime; she loves having company on her evenings out. Which reminds me...' He paused, and walked to one of the large windows. When he opened it, the house filled with the scent of yet more flowers. 'Wini!' he called out into the garden. 'Come inside and meet our guests!'

'Dieter,' Gabriel said somewhat pointedly, 'might you have somewhere I could possibly leave my coat?'

'Right, of course.' Dieter gestured to the wooden hooks on the wall. 'Right there.'

Gabriel sniffed. '*Chérie*,' he said to Clarice, 'would you like me to take your coat?'

'No thank you,' she replied pleasantly, walking over to hang hers up. 'So, how many children do you have?'

'Three boys,' Dieter replied. 'It's a madhouse some days, I can tell you that, but what a delight! You two...' He paused delicately. 'Would you two like to use the facilities?' he finished. 'Or perhaps I can show you to your room, so you can set down your bags and come and relax? Lunch will be served in half an hour or so.'

Gabriel nodded, pleased. 'Very punctual,' he said.

Dieter gave a small bow. 'Of course,' he replied.

They walked up the staircase, towards a classical mansard ceiling. In the presence of the architecture, Gabriel almost physically relaxed. 'What beautiful wood,' he said warmly. 'How old is this house, then? Seventeenth century? Eighteenth?'

'The house is from the eighteenth century, yes,' Dieter replied.

'Amazing!' Gabriel exclaimed. 'Where did you find this wonderful wood? It's pine, yes? There don't seem to be any knots. That's a rare feature. Expensive,' he added approvingly.

'Yes,' Dieter replied. 'Swiss pine from...'

'... the highest mountains!' Gabriel finished gleefully, grinning. 'Just like in our chalet, Clarice!'

His wife formed her lips into a smile.

The bedroom was large and full of light, with vast windows overlooking the garden. Clarice opened them, brushing vine leaves and white blossoms out of the way. 'The bed is queen size, as the Americans say,' Dieter said, turning to Gabriel with a conspiratorial smile. 'So that you and your queen can rest – or not.'

Clarice did not turn around, but she suspected her host of winking.

'The sheets look like Egyptian cotton,' Gabriel said approvingly.

Down in the garden below, Winifred in her straw sunhat and summer dress was hacking away at the soil with a hoe. She was barefoot, and her shoulders were pink from the sun. A blonde-haired boy was sitting next to her, playing in the dirt. Clarice had a momentary flashback to her father, sitting unhappily in the grass. When was the last time she had seen a flower garden? She heard laughter drifting up and turned away from the window.

'Aren't my wife's flowers beautiful?' Dieter said with real warmth.

'Oh yes,' Clarice replied. 'Your garden is absolutely lovely.'

'Winifred is obsessed with roses,' Dieter said dreamily. 'All sorts of lilies, too, and orchids. Wini loves orchids. She has been playing music to them, you see: apparently it influences the speed of their growth, makes them stronger. I hear it can even change their colour!' He shrugged happily. 'In any case, even I can see the black orchids are doing beautifully. There is night blooming jasmine, too, which you'll no doubt smell tonight.'

'We can leave the window open this evening,' Clarice said with a hint of a smile.

Gabriel frowned. 'There might be draughts,' he replied.

Dieter shook his head in amusement. 'Lunch in fifteen minutes,' he reminded them. 'I'll see you downstairs.'

The lunch spread looked divine. With generous heaps of smoked herring and *viande des Grisons* lined up carefully on a china platter, even delicate curls of smoked salmon presented with capers. Small sausages were arranged next to hard-boiled eggs, and tidily cut crudités, and there was a large glass bowl of salad that looked like it had come freshly from the garden. There were lemon slices in a bowl, and what was certainly hand-whipped mayonnaise. A large basket of dark brown bread completed the rustic spread.

'I'm starving!' Clarice exclaimed, happily piling her plate with lunch meats and salad.

Gabriel poked at some herring, his expression dubious.

'We thought we should serve you French-speakers something local,' Dieter said, with a generous smile. Their host had changed, Clarice noted, into a smartly tailored suit.

'I never tire of this lunch,' Winifred said airily, slipping into her seat and brushing a wet blonde curl from her forehead. Clarice stared at her for a moment, wondering how this woman could still seem beautiful after sweating at gardening all morning. She seemed somehow unreal in her hearty, healthy beauty: a figure from Weimar Republic propaganda, perhaps. 'Something about digging and weeding gives you this wonderful, insatiable sort of hunger.'

Gabriel sniffed.

'Where are the children?' Dieter sighed with a pretence of exasperation. 'Klaus! Sigurd! Heiner!'

Several cries of '*Ja, Vati!*' resounded through the house, and footsteps were heard pounding down the stairs. A moment later, three blonde children appeared side by side, two of them flushed from sunlight and with dirt on their clothes, one of them pale and tidy.

'You must be the pianist,' Clarice said warmly to the tallest, quietest boy. 'I heard your wonderful music earlier.'

The pale boy blushed. 'Oh, I am only practising. I am not very good yet. I did not know anyone was listening.'

'Don't be silly, Klaus,' one of his little brothers chipped in. 'You love it when people listen!' The third brother giggled.

Dieter shook his head. 'Now, now, boys. Have you all washed your hands? Good. Then come sit down and meet our guests.'

'Well, I saw you in the garden, too,' Clarice said conspiratorially to the middle brother. 'Are you Heiner?'

'I am Sigurd,' he replied proudly.

'*I* am Heiner,' the smallest one said plaintively.

'Oh, well you will be the little artist whose drawing of a dog I saw on the fridge!' Clarice said with a smile.

Sigurd burst out laughing. 'That's a horse!'

'It's not a horse!' Heiner pouted.

'Children, children,' Dieter said. 'Come eat your lunch.'

'I don't really like this kind of bread,' Klaus said suddenly. '*Mutti*, do you have anything else?'

Winifred made a clicking sound of disapproval. '*Liebling*, darling, rye bread is excellent for your health. If you are not going to get any vitamins from coming out into the sun, you really must eat a few slices. Think what will happen to your piano-playing if your bones disintegrate!'

The boys giggled, and Klaus helped himself to the bread with a long-suffering sigh.

'Boys, do you know the story of pumpernickel?' Dieter asked

jovially. They shook their heads, occupied with spooning generous helpings of mayonnaise and herring onto their plates. 'What? Have I never told you about Napoleon's horse? Well, the army general always fed his horse rye bread to keep him healthy. He invaded the whole of Russia on that horse, you know. And do you know what the horse was called? Pumpernickel! Now, the Germans admired Napoleon even though he took over part of their country, so they named the bread after his horse.'

'There's no way that is true,' Klaus said primly.

'I will draw a picture of a horse later!' Heiner said. 'For my brother Sigurd.'

Clarice laughed out loud.

Gabriel looked over at her, startled. 'In Geneva, we do not like Napoleon,' he said. 'He occupied our city, taking over one of the most beautiful houses in the Old Town. He divided the Republic of Geneva, which is still to this day a republic. Did you know this?' he asked Dieter.

'Boys, did you know that?' Dieter turned the question to his sons.

They shook their heads, bored, busying themselves with the matter of constructing elaborate, open-faced sandwiches.

'The history of the city of Geneva is fascinating,' Gabriel said pompously.

'So, what do you do, Clarice?' Winifred asked with a smile. Gabriel blinked, unable to respond to this interruption.

Startled, Clarice smiled back. 'Oh, I have an art gallery in the Old Town.'

'How fascinating!' Winifred exclaimed. 'What kind of art? Contemporary? Experimental? Installations?'

Clarice shook her head, embarrassed. 'Mostly old Swiss masters,' she said. 'A few Impressionists. Views of castles on the lake, that sort of thing.'

'How wonderful!' Winifred replied, unperturbed. 'I enjoy the occasional classic. I will have to drop in on you when I am next in Geneva. I do not think I am acquainted with any galleries in the old town. Are you familiar with the art scene in Zurich?'

Clarice shook her head again. 'I have not had many opportunities to travel,' she said carefully.

Winifred clapped her hands together. 'Oh, you must come with me this afternoon, then! The men are going to have their big banking day out, and I was going to drop by my friend's opening. Do come with me! We'll look at the art, sip a glass of chilled white. It'll be a girl's day out. Do say yes!'

Clarice smiled slowly. 'Yes, I think I will,' she said. 'And you, you are a musician?' she asked.

Winifred smiled in delight. 'Yes,' she said, 'and no. I love nothing more than music, but I have never been able to make a career out of it. Raising three boys rather takes it out of you,' she added with a wink.

'Opera is Winifred's real passion, but nowadays mostly as a spectator,' Dieter added. 'She has a season ticket for the whole year in Zurich – and that's only because I convinced her it was too expensive to buy them for every single Swiss city. She still travels around.'

'I don't want to miss any, you see!' Winifred exclaimed happily. 'I just love opera so. I was a student of music, you understand.'

'Any venue, any city, any composer, as long as it's opera. She'll go to experience Puccini in a museum, Wagner in a small church, Tchaikovsky in Paris. You name it. One time,' Dieter said, looking over at his wife warmly, 'Wini begged me to take her all the way to Milan, just for one night at la Scala!'

'You didn't,' Gabriel said, without thinking.

'Oh yes we did,' Dieter said, a twinkle in his eye. 'We took the train. I didn't mind one bit.'

'Do you remember the *spaghetti al vongole*?' Winifred asked dreamily.

'Oh my,' Dieter said. 'How could I forget? And the wine!'

The boys looked at each other and rolled their eyes.

Dieter and Gabriel walked down the sunny streets of old Zurich, the lake sparkling in the distance. Dieter was looking out towards the water, which lent his profile a certain nobility. 'I like to think of us as trustworthy mountain guides,' he was saying thoughtfully. 'That is the role I would like our bankers to project. People come to us with their projects, they need to trust us with their money, their dreams, their ideas. We can help.'

'That sounds to me rather an idealised view of banking,' Gabriel said hesitantly. 'You and your lederhosen.'

Dieter shrugged. 'Perhaps you're right. My wife, however, still believes in the potential to do good through investments, so I try to listen to her advice.'

'Her advice? On banking matters?' Gabriel spluttered.

Dieter looked over, frowning in surprise. 'Of course,' he replied. 'Winifred has always been at my shoulder. She was the one who encouraged me to get involved in humanitarian enterprises whenever possible. CBS aims to help humanity through industry.'

'And how does that work, exactly?' Gabriel asked drily.

'We work with the principal industrial conglomerates: big pharmaceutical companies, food and water companies, even electronics. Financing them gives us a certain amount of say in their board meetings. If we work with the shareholders, we can have quite a lot of influence over their policies.'

Gabriel shook his head. 'I do not get involved in this way,' he said. 'We are not trustworthy mountaineers, at Von Mipatobeau. We are Swiss bankers.'

Dieter laughed aloud. 'Come then, let me show you where our work takes place.'

'So this is your bank?' Gabriel's eyebrows were raised.

Dieter nodded proudly. 'Welcome to the Commercial Bank of Switzerland,' he said, gesturing around the empty stone lobby.

An old man was standing alone behind a plain desk, in a slightly wrinkled shirt. He looked up with a smile. 'Welcome, Dieter,' he said. 'And who is your friend? Would you like to be taken to level three?'

Gabriel gawped. 'They use your name? Your first name?' he hissed.

'Of course!' Dieter exclaimed. 'I've known my dear old concierge here for nigh on ten years. How could he not use my name? This is Gabriel de Puritigny,' he added to the concierge.

Gabriel shook his head in horror and let himself be led to the elevator. 'You have only one person at the reception? We have beautiful women to welcome our clients,' he said with a somewhat condescending smile.

'Most people here are officers of the bank,' Dieter said conversationally. 'They sit in their offices. We don't see too much of them, outside of meetings. I've been lucky,' he added. 'Somehow, I got the best desk in the building.'

Gabriel smiled. 'I too have an excellent desk,' he said.

'Yet I am only one of the four managing directors.'

'Yes. You're in charge of the commercial banking?'

'Precisely,' Dieter replied.

'Level three,' said the concierge. 'Have a good day, Dieter and Gabriel.'

Gabriel shuddered visibly.

———◆———

'What a lovely view of the lake,' Gabriel said carefully. The office was vast but cold, the desk a simple piece of white marble scattered with paperwork. It was ultramodern and messy. Where were the Napoleon-III chairs? Where was the gilding and mahogany? And the paper! Weren't they worried about confidentiality at all? He could so easily catch a name on a piece of paper lying around like that! He craned his neck discreetly, trying to see one.

'Yes, I'm a lucky man,' Dieter replied. 'It's nearly thirty square metres. Most of the officers only have eight to ten square metres.'

'My desk is mahogany,' Gabriel said.

Dieter laughed. 'You know, I had to fight to get a marble desk,' he said. 'Don't you like this elliptical shape? I had it cut this way myself. Seven people can sit around it. Besides, it keeps my face cool in summer when I collapse in despair.'

Gabriel stared. 'I like mahogany myself,' he said.

'I'm joking,' Dieter said.

There was a pause. 'Do you have portfolio managers?' Gabriel asked, keeping his tone light.

'Portfolio management is less than thirty per cent of our business,' Dieter replied. 'We have it, but it's not our speciality. Opening letters of credit for trade, syndicated loans, bond emissions are our priorities. At the moment, I'm working on some very important barter of metals against refined oil products. The most important business for us right now is that of revolving credits with major food and pharmaceutical companies. In fact I am on the board of two of the pharmaceutical companies that dominate the Swiss–German sector: one is private, one is public. We also work on stock offerings, including capital increases as well as IPOs: we make a lot of money out of the Zurich stock exchange, I can tell you that. Thank the Lord for Swiss francs, eh?'

'Indeed,' Gabriel replied, looking out the window. 'So,' he said as if talking to himself, 'this is the biggest bank in Switzerland.'

'Yes,' Dieter said simply. 'Or at least we have the biggest balance sheets. We have branches in Paris, New York and Singapore, you know. We're trying to expand in Switzerland as well, but it's a little difficult with the competition from the French, German and Italians. As well as the Americans and Scandinavians.' He grinned and shrugged. 'There's a lot of competition in commercial banking.'

'I'd imagine so,' Gabriel replied vaguely. 'I suppose it is very different in the world of private banking.'

'Yes, I'm sure it is. I can't really imagine catering to private individuals.'

'Individuals, families and small corporations, really,' Gabriel said dismissively. 'We dabble in the business of apartments, houses and portfolio management, but mostly, really, our clients are high net worth individuals; princes from the Arabian Gulf, shipping magnates, that sort of thing; people who are trying to preserve money for their projects, their future, their inheritance. A lot of that kind of business operates out of Geneva. It has always been that way,' he added somewhat smugly.

Dieter laughed gently. 'Don't worry, we have no intention of competing with you guys for private portfolio management. Zurich is the centre for large banks and major investments funds. Of course, there are a few German fortunes to take into account as well, like the ones that come from heavy machinery, cars or chemicals.'

'I see,' Gabriel said grumpily. 'Perhaps you could show me the rest of your bank?'

'Of course!' Dieter replied happily. 'Come with me. After the tour, we should have coffee in the old town.'

'I don't drink coffee,' said Gabriel.

Dieter shrugged. 'Suit yourself.'

The offices were plain and neon-lit, Gabriel noted with distaste, but this was not the worst shock. The paperwork was in disarray, which he could see because the office was open plan. There were no walls. If he listened carefully, he could pick up the gist of the phone conversations.

'What about *privacy*?' Gabriel hissed. 'How do these people not have privacy?'

'What do you mean?' Dieter asked in surprise. 'It's a standard office layout. Surely it can't appear that strange? Come, walk with me!'

'Ten people are crammed into this room!' Gabriel tried to explain. 'They're all... talking! On the phone! Syndicating loans, talking to clients, whatever it is commercial bankers do all day. I can't believe it.'

Dieter shrugged. 'There is no need for that sort of privacy in commercial banking. The key is in the name. Nobody's trying to hide their money.'

'Isn't there some kind of disadvantage to this?' Gabriel asked, still staring. 'How can this be?'

'To many of our companies, it doesn't matter,' Dieter explained. 'Their assets and liquidity are published anyway, in their balance sheets, every three months. Anybody who cares to, can read it. The companies don't give a damn about secrecy: they only care about making money. And I can tell you one thing: we make more money in commercial banking than in investment banking.'

'We make all our money in portfolio management,' Gabriel replied. 'We don't even participate as investors ourselves, for fear of losing the money.'

'You obviously are ultraconservative,' Dieter said gravely. Gabriel beamed. 'Until one day you are attacked for banking secrecy,' he added in an offhand manner.

Gabriel scoffed. 'This will never happen,' he said confidently. 'If you break the laws of banking secrecy, you go to jail for five years. This is Switzerland. These things are set in stone.'

'I'm so glad we don't have to worry about this with my clients!' Dieter sighed. 'Commercial institutions are so... uncomplicated. Which isn't to say there aren't other sorts of risks involved. But risks pay off. I can't imagine that's a philosophy you'd understand, as a private banker.'

'I don't know,' Gabriel said thoughtfully. 'It depends what you mean by risk.'

'Well, for instance, our trading department is currently crazy about foreign exchange trading. One trader in our office, all he did was buy and sell Deutschmarks – I mean, options in Deutschmarks and French francs, against the dollar. Just by doing that, he's made millions and millions.'

'That's gambling,' Gabriel replied.

'Sometimes, banking is gambling,' Dieter said evenly. 'It doesn't mean CBS is a casino. The trader just bought the biggest hotel in Zurich.'

'Well, we make money at Von Mipatobeau too, but without taking risks,' Gabriel said proudly.

'As long as you have clients,' Dieter replied, teasing. 'Come, don't your clients ever complain that they only make two to four per cent with you? If they were investing properly, they could be taking home eight per cent. In share dividends they'd be making six per cent. In real estate developments, they could easily make twenty to thirty per cent. That's what commercial banking is about.'

'Making our clients money is not our primary concern,' Gabriel replied with a hint of a smile.

'You mean making your own fortune is?'

'No,' Gabriel said, his face serious. 'Keeping their money safe is.'

'Making a fortune is only incidental?' Dieter smiled and shook his head. 'I make half a million a year. What about you? The lowest-paid private banker in my acquaintance easily makes a million.'

'I can't tell you that,' Gabriel replied.

'Go on,' Dieter pressed him. 'You can tell me. We're friends! I promise no-one can hear us here.'

Gabriel paused. 'You're embarrassing me,' he said.

'Just whisper the figure,' Dieter said, teasing again.

Gabriel pursed his lips. 'Five million,' he muttered.

Dieter let out a low whistle. 'Well, this afternoon's coffee's on you!'

'Sparkling water,' Gabriel replied, dourly.

Chapter Seven

Wild swirls of colour... simple black lines... evocations of desert sand, ochre sunlight, veiled figures; the canvasses were huge: Clarice could not contain her delight, confusion and awe. 'I've never seen anything like it,' she said. She let the colours wash over her in waves, barely daring to blink.

Impulsively, Winifred squeezed Clarice's hand. 'Welcome to the world of modern art,' she said brightly. 'Or perhaps I should say modern art by women from the Arabian Gulf.'

Clarice tugged her hand back in surprise, but she smiled nonetheless. 'When you said you were bringing me to an exhibit in a seventeenth-century château, this is most emphatically not what I expected.'

'Are you one of those people who have always thought modern art is awful?' Winifred asked with interest. 'How fascinating!'

'Oh, my opinion was nothing like that informed,' Clarice said wistfully. 'My family was only interested in art with historical value. The more ancient, the more Swiss, the better.'

'The more expensive, of course,' Winifred concluded. 'Historical value is not only... historical.'

Clarice nodded. 'You must come see my gallery one day,' she said, wandering under the hanging paintings. 'It is so different from this scene, and yet in some ways alike. The smell, for instance; that sharp, strange smell of long-dry paint.'

'Goodness, are the fumes going to your head?' Winifred asked with a grin. 'Come, let me get you a glass of red to revive you. I can't bring the good little Swiss wife back to the banker, transformed into a poet!'

'Oh, no thank you,' Clarice said, embarrassed. 'I am not used to drinking in museums.' As she politely waved away the offer, she noticed that everyone in the gallery seemed to be drinking. In fact, casting a discreet eye over the chatting groups of eccentrically-dressed visitors, she also observed that almost no-one seemed to be looking at the art. Were they all so used to this scene that it bore no interest at all?

'Come, now,' Winifred pressed her. 'Perhaps just a juice?' She looked over in sudden interest at Clarice's figure, her eyes widening. 'You're not...?' She let the question hang in the air, with a soft smile.

Clarice swallowed. 'I'm not drinking,' she said a little harshly.

Winifred suddenly blushed. 'I'm so sorry,' she said.

'There is nothing to be sorry for,' Clarice said through tight lips. Seeing the guilt in Winifred's eyes, however, she relented. 'Maybe just a small glass of champagne,' she said, softening her tone.

'Yes, yes.' Her blonde friend turned away, ready to bustle towards the bar.

Following an unfamiliar impulse, Clarice laid a hand lightly on Winifred's shoulder. 'I didn't mean to snap at you,' she said. 'The subject is somewhat sensitive at the moment.'

'Of course, my dear friend,' Winifred said, turning back. Was that a tear glistening in her eye? Clarice was oddly moved. She had only met this woman this afternoon! 'We can talk about it on the drive home, if you like,' Winifred added.

Mutely, Clarice nodded, then she followed her new friend across the room towards the table of drinks.

'Isn't it a lovely drive, though, along the lake?' Winifred sighed, turning back towards her with two flutes of champagne. 'I never tire of it. Forty minutes from the city centre and you feel like you're in another country. The Black Forest, perhaps.'

'You do truly live in a wonderful area,' Clarice said wistfully. 'Your garden is marvellous, your house is so warm, and this art... Well, I've never seen anything quite like it.'

Winifred stared at her in surprise. 'But Geneva has a vivacious modern art scene! Have you truly never come across it?'

Clarice shook her head slowly. 'I suppose it's not exactly the world I deal in.'

'Of course. But you should take a private, personal interest! I can see in your eyes that the bright colours appeal to you. Don't you love that curve of golden sand? And what about the little girls riding on camelback?'

'It is all very strange to me,' Clarice confessed, tilting her head to the side. She stared for a long time at a painting of a diver leaping through an azure sky with a net clasped in his skinny arms. All around him, glowing silver spheres seemed to float through the air.

'What is strange?' a soft voice came from behind her. 'You think this art is strange?'

Clarice started in embarrassment and turned around. A beautiful dark-eyed woman in a crimson silk headscarf was standing at her shoulder, an eyebrow raised. Large gold pendants hung from her ears, and her eyebrows were drawn on in thick pencil. She looked like a painting herself.

'It's just that I've never travelled,' Clarice volunteered after a moment.

'The desert is not a hostile environment for modern women, you know,' the woman continued, peering up at Clarice. 'Nowadays, we can glory in the harsh desert sun just the same as our fathers and husbands.'

'Right,' Clarice said. She felt staid and gangly in her suit jacket, towering over this glamorous bohemian. 'I was actually looking at that diver.'

The women glanced up. 'What, the pearl diver? Oh, I wouldn't try to travel in Bahrain - terrible tourist industry, those men forgetting to breathe. The art scene is largely incomprehensible, too.'

Winifred laughed gently. 'Khadija,' she said, 'you'll scare my poor friend off. This is Clarice. She runs a gallery of historic art in the Old Town of Geneva.'

Khadija peered up at her, hawk-eyed. 'Charmed,' she said, bowing very slightly.

Intimidated, Clarice gave an awkward bow in return.

'Khadija is a princess,' Winifred said, poking her friend in the ribs with an elbow. 'She's a great art collector.'

'Oh, it's a hobby, really. And don't call me a princess – it makes people look for my tiara.'

'But you are a princess,' Winifred said gently. 'She really is.'

'Your scarf is lovely,' Clarice volunteered suddenly, awkwardly.

'Hermès,' Khadija replied, waving a plump hand. Her nails were ruby-red.

'The last time I saw Khadija, she had just spent fifty million dollars at an auction in London. Her last purchase was of a limited edition Andy Warhol.'

'It's only a copy of a lithograph,' Khadija said.

'Andy Warhol!' Clarice exclaimed, casting her mind about desperately for any knowledge of this artist. 'The American,' she finally added, lamely.

'My husband is fond of him,' Khadija replied, rolling her eyes. 'I try to indulge his tastes occasionally. Of course, I really shouldn't complain – he's one of the major financial backers of this exhibition.'

'Oh, so is mine!' Winifred said happily.

Clarice shook her head in wonder. 'My husband is a banker,' she said, 'but I don't think he's ever invested a penny in art.'

'He should try it sometime,' Khadija said, readjusting her scarf. 'I can give him some tips. Bankers and auctioneers are the only people really putting money into this scene. You can't get two coins from the government nowadays.'

'So you were involved in choosing the art for this exhibit?' Clarice asked tentatively.

'Oh yes. This is partly my brainchild,' Khadija said proudly. 'Women in the Gulf don't have many occasions to show off their art in their home countries. I'm part-Egyptian, on my mother's side, so I have a personal interest in women's lives there.'

'They're all very interesting. I think I may like the pearl fishers best,' Winifred said.

'Oh yes, the Bahraini painter,' Khadija replied. 'You mentioned that earlier. Yes, she paints these wonderful nomadic scenes. All the costumes are so detailed. My favourite artist here is actually a refugee from the civil war in Lebanon,' she continued. 'See that huge scene at an oasis? That's her. She's this wonderfully stern old woman. So political. So wise. I'd love it if you could meet some day!'

'You know the artists personally?' Clarice was flabbergasted.

'Oh yes,' Khadija replied in surprise. 'I meet everyone we exhibit.'

'Goodness.' Suddenly, Clarice giggled. 'Imagine having a drink with Ferdinand Hodler, or commenting on his hair!'

Khadija laughed.

'I'm sure he'd have been a terrible bore,' Winifred replied conspiratorially.

Clarice clapped a hand over her mouth.

'Are you talking about my husband?' A sharp voice added itself to the conversation. Turning around, Clarice found herself face-to-face with a tall, delicately boned woman smoking a cigarette.

'This is Azma,' Khadija said with a small smile. 'She is from Jordan.'

'Palestine,' Azma corrected coolly, exhaling.

Khadija shook her head. 'I know, I know,' she said patiently. 'You are originally from Palestine, but you currently live in Jordan. Your husband has made tens of millions on boats. Construction, oil trading, shipping, you name it.'

'Not just boats anymore. He's getting into the new business of gas in Qatar and Abu Dhabi,' Azma said.

'Your husband also funds this exhibit?' Clarice asked.

Azma stared at her. 'Oh no. *I* was involved in picking the artists.'

Clarice blushed furiously, sensing she had made a gaffe.

'The wonderful watermelon sellers in the corner?' Winifred intervened, pointing. 'That was her choice. A Palestinian artist also, I believe.'

'The women playing with birds outside the mosque were mine also,' Azma said. 'Would you like to buy either of those? They're very reasonably priced.'

It was Clarice's turn to stare. 'I...'

'Well, are you a woman with money?' Azma asked, somewhat impatiently. She tapped ash from her cigarette onto the floor.

Clarice drew herself up. 'I was brought up not to speak of these things,' she said.

'Azma!' Khadija said sharply. 'Must you always be so aggressive? You just met this nice Genevoise woman, who, incidentally, is new to our modern art world. Do you really want to discourage her with crassness?'

'Oh, you old Swiss types,' Azma sighed dramatically. 'You are so awfully conservative. You only eat white fish or vanilla ice cream. You only enjoy the cleanest of snowy mountains.'

'Yes, and their favourite extreme sport is walking around the lake,' Winifred said. 'We've heard your jokes before. It doesn't mean they can't be interesting people.'

'There are always interesting people in the art world,' Azma said, 'and there is always interesting money. Oil money, trading money, London banking money. German industrialists, deposed princes, Russian oligarchs, dictators with stolen fortunes. Swiss money has a flair of its own, particularly in Zurich.' She grinned.

'I thought Geneva was the centre of the banking world?' Clarice asked hesitantly.

'Oh no,' Azma said dismissively. 'You only have a few Arab princes and oil traders. The really big money is here.'

'I see,' said Clarice.

'Now, now,' Khadija said. 'Surely some of those visiting oil princes are financing this exhibit.'

'Perhaps,' Azma said drily. 'Anyway, I need another drink.'

Winifred shook her head. 'So do I,' she said. 'Clarice?'

Clarice nodded, still reeling from the encounter. Khadija narrowed her eyes, looking once more like some sort of bird of prey. Both sipped their drinks in silence for a moment. Clarice let her eyes wander up towards one of Azma's acquisitions, which seemed to be mostly populated with abstract bird silhouettes: birds of thousands of colours flying up into the sky, with silhouettes of minarets in the background. It had such energy, such strange beauty!

'I find that one rather garish,' Khadija commented.

Clarice nodded hastily, then paused. 'I don't know,' she said.

Khadija sniffed. There was another pause.

'I hope you don't mind my asking,' Clarice asked Khadija politely, struggling for a topic, 'but I find your French and English very impressive. How have you learned these languages so well?'

'Grim determination is the key,' Khadija said, with a smile.

'It's also the answer to your question. Along with, of course, an extremely exclusive and expensive education at Le Rosey school in Gstaad. I'm one of the few Arab women in the world who can ski to a competitive standard!' She laughed heartily.

'Oh, I did not realise you were Swiss!' Clarice exclaimed.

Khadija laughed. 'No offence meant,' she said, 'but I'm not sure that's a desirable epithet. Of course, I suppose it gives me an advantage over Azma. Her French is awful, and her unremarkable English just comes from a series of Berlitz classes. She hasn't been over here very long. You can probably tell from her lack of etiquette, rather than anything else. New money, you know.'

'Well, you can still be cutting in broken English,' Winifred said, returning with the drinks and shaking her head.

'You mustn't let her get to you, either of you,' Khadija laughed gently. 'She's only nasty when she feels insecure.'

'It's my fault,' Clarice said. 'I don't know how to interact in this sort of environment.'

'Don't be down on yourself,' Winifred said.

'It's simpler than that,' Khadija cut in. 'The questions we are interested in are the same, whether or not they are presented brusquely: so, what do you think about the art?'

There was a silence as Clarice looked around her once more. Yellow sand, warm feminine faces, exotic patterns. Lines and panes of colour. Mosques, birds, beaches and horses. 'I feel like there is a very accessible narrative dimension to these paintings,' Clarice said hesitantly.

'Yes, exactly!' Khadija said loudly, making her blush. 'You're onto something there. Of course, not all modern art is like this.'

'No, it certainly isn't,' Winifred added excitedly. 'Nowadays it's all people taking plastic pots of vomit and sticking them to canvases, or fresh fruit that has been crushed into a piece of plastic and then framed in black.'

'And people seem to get so into that sort of thing!' Khadija said, shaking her head. 'We're interested in something warmer, more instinctive, more feminine.'

'I see,' Clarice replied, nodding over and over.

'It doesn't have to be pretentious,' Winifred said.

'I don't think it sounds pretentious,' Clarice said excitedly. 'These are very exciting ideas. Maybe this is the future of art! Switzerland has been trapped in the past, and this is a way to move forward! It's time to move away from Rembrandt and Hodler, time to draw something more than still lives of apples and snowy funerals and, and miserable peasant children. Maybe there can be a more feminine idea of narrative.'

Khadija and Winifred exchanged glances. 'A convert,' Azma said drily. Clarice blushed furiously and tried to take a drink from her empty glass.

'Come, let's go get a drink and have a look at the paintings on the other side of the room.' Khadija gave another small bow and swanned off. With relief, Clarice took Winifred's proffered arm and walked towards what appeared to be an upside-down ocean view.

———◆———

'I don't know if I'll ever get used to this,' Clarice said, taking a deep drink of her new glass of champagne. 'It's just so... modern. Ultramodern! Some of those paintings must be three metres wide. And those big, high plastic walls they're hung up on: so unusual!'

Winifred shrugged. 'Once you've seen a few exhibits, you've seen them all. Don't get me wrong, I love the art, but you'll soon come to understand the codes, the rules, the style.'

Clarice nodded. 'I suppose that's the same with historical art. When you start out in an auction house, or working on a catalogue, you'd never be able to tell a fake from a multi-million-dollar acquisition. Now, I could do it with my hands tied behind my back. I'd like to learn about modern art, though. It must be like language: I just need a few Berlitz classes of my own!'

Winifred laughed. 'There are only three rules: big walls, bright colours, small talk. To be serious, though, there's only one way to learn about art,' she said: 'go out into the world! Come out of your shell, little Swiss wife,' she teased gently.

Clarice shook her head, as the champagne bubbles went to her head. 'You don't understand,' she said. 'I'm a hermit crab. My shell is my life. If I change, if I come out, I'll be naked. I'll get... eaten by sharks.'

The two women giggled like schoolgirls and walked on. Shortly, Clarice came upon her favourite painting yet: a scene of two women sitting in a doorway, hacking a watermelon into pieces with a long blade like a scimitar.

'It's so beautiful and so violent at once,' Clarice said aloud in wonder.

Winifred paused and looked up. 'Yes, there is clearly a story hidden there. Those watermelon women have interesting lives, I can tell you that.'

'I just love the colour of the raw flesh,' Clarice continued, getting fired up. 'That bright, bright pink, and those swathes of orange in the sky! It's so daring.'

Winifred shook her head with a small smile.

'So what is the history of the building, anyway?' Clarice asked quickly, looking up once more at the massive beams in embarrassment.

'Oh, ancient,' Winifred said, waving a hand vaguely. 'I believe it was shuttled back and forth between the old Hapsburgs and Napoleon's entourage.'

'My husband would love this parquet,' Clarice said, in an unexpectedly caustic tone. 'So shiny! So old! It gives the room... resonance,' she concluded with mock solemnity.

Surprised, Winifred laughed out loud.

'This area is most famous for the convents in the hills,' Khadija said softly, appearing again at Winifred's shoulder. 'There is something sacred about this place.'

'And so it represents our own sisterhood,' Winifred said with a warm smile, 'in art.'

'Yes, I'd like to learn about modern art,' Clarice said decisively.

'You must be so sick of dealing with stuffy old Geneva families,' Khadija said with sympathy.

'You shouldn't attack them,' she said, defensively. 'Some of the families date back to 1500! But listen to me... There is too much Genevois in my blood. I'm defending despicable people.' She downed the rest of her champagne flute. Khadija laughed.

'That's the spirit,' she said. 'Come out of your old stones. Escape your husband!'

'Yes, I think that would help,' Winifred said thoughtfully.

Clarice looked up, aggrieved. 'Winifred!' she said. 'Not everybody's life is like *The Sound of Music* with added banking.'

Khadija laughed. 'Ah, so you've been to their house?'

'Yes,' Clarice said, her lip trembling. 'It is wonderful. My life is good too, though.'

'Look, you need to inject a little excitement into your life. Buy some chilli peppers or something.' A sly smile trembled at the corner of Khadija's mouth.

Winifred glared at Khadija. 'You're as bad as Azma,' she said. 'Clarice will never want to come near modern art again.'

'There's no point,' Clarice said quietly. 'I don't even own any interesting scarves.'

Khadija laughed, throwing her head back. 'My dear,' she said, 'that much is easily remedied.' She unwound her own crimson wrap from her shoulders, and threw it dramatically around Clarice's. Clarice looked down at the bright colour, feeling dazed. It reminded her of the flesh of the watermelon in the painting she had seen.

'I can't possibly accept this,' she said.

'You must,' said Khadija. 'Refusal is out of the question. Besides, it is good for me, culturally, not to wear any scarf at all, at least when I am amongst women.' She smiled beatifically and tossed her mane of black hair. 'Welcome to the modern art world, Clarice,' she said. 'I hope we see you again soon.'

'Well, I don't know about that,' Clarice said hesitantly. 'You see, I live in Geneva.'

'Ooh,' Khadija said suddenly, 'Winifred, are you coming to the vernissage in Carouge?'

'Oh, I had forgotten about that! It's at the end of the month, right? Clarice, you absolutely must come!'

'I am particularly interested in African sculpture,' Khadija explained. 'Bronze and wood, including ebony. There are some absolutely wonderful artists working in these media nowadays, partly inspired by ancient traditions and partly radically modern.'

'Yes,' Clarice said at once, 'I will come. Although you will have to help me with the introductions. I'm not very good at talking to people for the first time.'

'Of course,' Winifred said warmly, 'though you underestimate your capacities.'

'Oh yes,' Khadija said. 'This is the art world. People are snobby by default, even to their best friends. Forget Azma. Remember me.' She fished around in a bag hanging by her side, and drew out her card. 'Here.'

'Thank you!' Clarice said. 'I'm afraid I don't have a card with me. I was meant to be here for pleasure, not business.'

'Ah, but in the art world, the two are inextricably linked,' Khadija said. 'Particularly for women.'

'I don't know about that,' Winifred said, frowning. 'Sometimes you say the most mysterious things.'

'We have our own rules,' Khadija said, smiling. 'You'll see.'

Chapter Eight

The air smelled like high forest, and golden light filtered through the large windows. An oak hawk spread its carved wings against the wall. Squirrels, foxes and mice seemed to be everywhere, their wooden bodies frozen in some sort of strange, artificial sylvan scene. Looking around, Gabriel thought he recognised pine martens, a miniature chamois and even a small wolf in dark, exotic wood. Small marmots made of pine were scattered across the floor. Gabriel hastily jumped back, trying not to crush them underfoot. What on earth was his father up to? Was that a falcon, diving from the top shelf? He walked on carefully and then shuddered, suddenly coming face to face with a life-size carving of a bear that sat at the back of the workshop. Edmond de Puritigny's face, his hair white, his skin deeply wrinkled, appeared from behind this bear. 'Ah, *mon fils*, my son!' he exclaimed, dropping the chisel he had been clutching in his hand. He stood up, dusting wood shavings off his apron. 'Welcome!'

'*Bonjour, père*,' Gabriel said stiffly. 'I see you have not tired of this... pastime.'

'Isn't he wonderful?' Edmond replied, gesturing at the bear. 'I have been working on him for months, ever since I finished the ibex.'

'The ibex. I see.'

'The ibex took four months. A marmot takes only three to four days, you know. But I am no longer interested in quantity, only quality. My dream is to create a perfect Bernese bear, you see, out of a single piece of Swiss wood. I think the oak tree this came from is almost three hundred years old. I want to make it as lifelike as possible, except for one thing. You know those wonderful honey-coloured eyes they have in the wild? Well, this one will be truly Swiss: it will have blue eyes, just like you. You will be able to hang your coats on its paws!'

'How wonderful,' Gabriel replied coldly. *I most certainly will do no such thing*, he thought. 'How much does this thing weigh?'

'A good two hundred kilos, I'd wager,' Edmond replied cheerfully. 'No, maybe more like four hundred. Close to half a tonne. It's going to take me months and months.'

'It's terrifying,' Gabriel said.

'Now, now,' Edmond replied, stroking the animal's wooden head. 'It's a cuddly beast. I'm planning to make the sides a little bit fat. I'm using only old traditional carving tools, you see, nothing electrical. Chisels, gouges, knives and saws, and a little bit of sanding around the edges.' He held up a hand to show his son the calluses on his thumb. 'See how hard I've been working?' he asked proudly.

'Don't you think this is all a little... below your class?' Gabriel said carefully.

'You're ashamed of me?' Edmond asked in amusement, dropping his hands. 'Your mother thinks it's wonderful.'

'Does she now,' Gabriel replied vaguely. 'Well.'

A twinkle came into Edmond's eyes. 'In fact,' he said, 'my plan was for you to inherit the bear as soon as it was finished.'

'What?' Gabriel edged back slightly from the overwhelming animal, stepping on a small oak mouse in the process. 'What am I supposed to do with it?'

'Well, if I were you...' Edmond continued slyly, 'back in the day, I'd probably have put it in the front of the bank, to welcome the clients. But in your case, with all your modern electronics, I just don't know if it would be quite the right touch. Besides, your multiple top-model receptionists, they'd probably be scared to death of this bear. Yes, even though it doesn't have an aggressive look, it will be very realistic,' he continued thoughtfully. 'It all depends on your psychology. Some people look at bears as symbols of aggression, but that is surely only bringing out some aspect of their own personality. Others, since the time of the American president Roosevelt, still think of all bears as Teddy, even a huge grizzly that could tear you apart with one slap of his paw.'

'Children would be terrified,' Gabriel said quickly.

'What children?' Edmond asked innocently. 'Are you telling me we're to expect grandchildren after all?'

Gabriel glared.

'Well, it's your bank, I understand,' Edmond said with a smile. 'The lovely polychrome receptionists must have their way. Why don't you keep the bear in your house?'

Gabriel stared at his father in disbelief.

'The bear... in my house. My house in Saint Antoine? Father, you must be joking. I'd... We'd have to throw a black blanket over it if anyone came over for dinner.'

'It's my favourite sculpture,' Edmond said firmly. 'It may take up to another year for me to finish it. By then, I may be dead. I'll use it as a clotheshorse in the meantime. Do I mean a clothes bear? Anyway, if you inherit it – and I think you should – you should know that I will take it as the ultimate posthumous insult if you sell it.'

'Right,' Gabriel said, swallowing. 'Tell me something, father. Are you going to put some varnish on this bear of yours?'

'Why would you ask something like that?' Edmond asked suspiciously.

'I think,' Gabriel continued cautiously, 'that if you put some kind of modern varnish like polyurethane on it, I'll be able to put it outside in the garden.'

'Son, I think that's a little bit insulting to my art.'

'Bears live outside,' Gabriel pointed out.

'If you put a bear in your garden, you'll scare off all the rabbits, the squirrels, the buzzards and birds of prey. The owls won't be too happy either.'

'What do I care about owls?' Gabriel asked in consternation. 'Father, I really don't know what you're talking about.'

'Well, when you inherit my last masterpiece, you can do what you like with it. For now, I will just put a little natural beeswax on it, in order to deepen the colour, make it more natural, closer to the true colour of a bear's coat.'

'Fine, fine,' Gabriel replied. 'Enough about the bear. Come inside for a drink before dinner.'

'A drink? How unlike you,' Edmond said, untying his apron.

'You know what I mean, father,' Gabriel replied impatiently.

Whilst Gabriel had been looking for his father amongst the woodcarvings, Avenira and Clarice were in the kitchen. Rows of golden and bright red jam in glass jars shone on the impeccable shelves. The two women were chopping potatoes, tomatoes and courgettes. Fresh garden scents filled the air.

'Every time I watch you, I find myself wishing I'd learned to cook,' Clarice said wistfully. 'Urgh! It all just seems like such a dreadful bother.'

'You're not watching, my dear: you are cooking!' Avenira said kindly.

Clarice dubiously prodded a piece of garlic with her knife. 'I wouldn't know what to do, if you weren't telling me.'

'Swiss cuisine is straightforward,' Avenira said, 'even in Ticino, where I was raised.'

'Yes, I think your taste for seasonal vegetables adds something to the endless cheese-with-extra-cheese tendency that dominates the Genevan culture...'

'You've no doubt heard Edmond's speech about what it means to be Swiss before, so I won't bore you with a repetition. But mountain life has some good lessons, including frugality. I don't mean your black-draped, mournful-faced city Calvinism – if you'll pardon the slight – but something simpler, happier.'

'Tell me again how we are going to make this stew, then; this happy, simple dish?' Clarice wiped her hands on her apron, frowning in concentration.

'It could not be simpler,' Avenira said with satisfaction, setting a pot to heat on the flame. 'First, go to your garden. Pick the ripest fresh vegetables you can find... Of course, a good local market will do in a pinch,' she added hastily.

Clarice laughed. 'Good, I'm falling at the first hurdle.'

'Nonsense,' Avenira said firmly. 'If you can learn to make this stew, you don't really need to cook anything else. You and your children will be – I mean, you will be healthy, strong and rosy-cheeked. Cut the vegetables into cubes, just as we are doing here. Add some onion, some finely chopped garlic into a little olive oil – that's the Italian touch from my heritage! Yes, just like that, into the hot pot. Wait until you can smell the garlic, then add the vegetables. You want them to fry slightly, you see. Now wait for everything to soften, and then add your stock – or water, if you're being particularly frugal. Add in fresh herbs, if you feel like it. That's all there is to it. Then you just watch it simmer, and stir occasionally.'

Clarice sighed. 'You make it sound so easy, but I tend to get bored after ten minutes... and then something burns, or the phone rings, or I get distracted, and I give up and order something from Migros.'

Avenira laughed. 'Oh, my dear, you must keep trying. Promise me this!'

'Promise you what?' Gabriel asked suspiciously, appearing in the doorway.

'Are you talking about children again?' Edmond said gaily.

'Clarice is helping me cook,' Avenira said, rolling her eyes. 'How's the bear coming, darling?'

Gabriel frowned. 'I see you've made jam again, Mother,' he said, kissing her on both cheeks.

Avenira beamed. 'Six kinds this year,' she said. 'The orchard and berry bushes have been kind to us this summer. I made strawberry last month, and then two kinds of cherry, and apricot, and most recently plum and mirabelle.'

'I look forward to breakfast, then.' He breathed in. 'Right now, though, I'm far more interested in what you're preparing for dinner.' He walked over to the stove and took the spoon out of Clarice's hands.

'Ah, your wonderful stone soup,' Edmond said. 'I will never tire of it.'

'Avenira was teaching me,' Clarice said sternly, taking the spoon back from Gabriel and stirring quickly.

'Careful, you'll crush the vegetables,' Gabriel said imperiously. Clarice glared at her husband.

'Nonsense,' Avenira said airily. 'This is soup. Everything is meant to cook down together.' She narrowed her green eyes at her son then, placing her hands on his shoulders, moved him away from the stove.

Clarice tried to hide her smile. 'Shall I fetch the bread, Avenira?' she asked.

'Come now, everyone, let's sit down to dinner,' Edmond said, ushering his son from the kitchen.

———•◆•———

Dinner was simple and delicious: the soup warm and flavourful, the homemade bread, crusty, the local cheeses sharp and tangy. They drank tap water from a pitcher. Afterwards, the men were reclining in comfortable leather armchairs by the fireplace, Gabriel sipping at his small decaf. 'I wanted to talk to you about your bank, Father,' he said. 'Our bank.'

Edmond gave a small smile. 'You always want to talk about the bank, you know.'

Gabriel ignored this, having already begun a rehearsed speech. 'All my life,' he intoned, 'you raised me to avoid risks, to limit myself to managing other people's money, taking people's deposits... to picture myself as a dragon guarding money.'

'This strategy has served you well so far, no?' Edmond asked, his face unreadable.

Gabriel nodded. 'I've been moderately, consistently successful. Yet...I can't help but wonder about the alternatives. The dragon sitting on the pile of gold coins, does he ever get to spend them? I spent the weekend with a commercial banker, you see. He's an honourable man, Dieter, a Swiss man by every part of your definition. He makes honest money. And he makes it by taking risks. I keep wondering about this other side of banking. What I might be missing out on.'

'What do you mean?' Edmond asked in amusement. 'You want to start lending money, giving it away?'

'I want to do more with our money, father, with the money that's in the bank. You know how much money people entrust to us. It's just sitting there, father. It could be...'

'I know everything it could be, my son,' Edmond cut in. 'Are you forgetting that I ran Von Mipatobeau bank my entire life? We are not interested in loans. We especially don't do Lombard loans. We don't want money going out, only money coming in! We *manage* money, Gabriel. That is what small private Swiss banks do, and we do it better than anyone in the world.'

'Yes, but managing money – couldn't it be something else entirely? Listen: I was in London a few months ago. It made me think. It made me wonder: everything we've read about England since my childhood, that it was destroyed by German bombs, that the churches were smashed –I thought there would be nothing left. But that wasn't true. It has lovely bits of architecture, and many old traditions, just like Switzerland. Certainly, it has some idiosyncrasies: drunkenness; a strange interest in foreign cuisine; terrible weather, of course. But I learned other things about the English at this banking seminar. I went to a talk that made clear the sheer variety of international products available in the world of banking today: joint ventures, mortgage lending, private placements, syndicated loans... all these relatively safe ways of making big money. Dieter is an honest man, Father.'

Edmond scoffed. 'Safe? You don't know what you're talking about. That cheap English wine must have gone to your head – or is it your new commercial friend? Have you learned nothing in all those years running our bank?' He sighed and softened his tone. 'Gabriel, my son. What is Switzerland famous for?'

'Mountains,' Gabriel said, his jaw set firmly. 'Excellent cheese.'

'This is not the time to talk back to me.'

'Privacy,' Gabriel added reluctantly.

'Privacy. Secrecy is the oldest Swiss tradition. Why do you think anyone brings their money here? Do you think clients will keep coming to us to manage their money if they hear it's no longer resting safely in a golden, padlocked vault?'

'There are no such vaults,' Gabriel said sniffily. 'There is no dragon.'

'It doesn't matter. The money is as safe as if it were in such a vault. It's not being invested. It's not being moved. It isn't going anywhere. That is the appeal of Swiss banking.'

'But imagine if they came back to that theoretical vault,' Gabriel argued, 'and found that its contents had doubled. Wouldn't they be thrilled? Wouldn't they bring more clients flocking?'

'It won't always double,' Edmond replied. 'Sometimes, their vault will be empty. And that only needs to happen once for them to leave the country with every single penny.'

'People are no longer so afraid of risk,' Gabriel said hesitantly. Hearing his uncharacteristic words hang in the air, he sighed. 'I am beginning to sound like the devil's advocate. I don't mean to say I am sure this is the way the bank should, or even could, go. I simply wanted to run these ideas past you, Father. You know how much I respect your opinion. I didn't expect you to react so strongly.'

Edmond nodded slowly. 'My son, we've been here for five hundred years,' he said. 'Our banking has always operated in the same way: high value, high morals. We take people's money, keep it safe, manage it honestly. We don't take undisclosed commissions or rob anyone with hidden charges. There is a filthy underbelly to the kind of banking you are so intrigued by, Gabriel. In a way, it is my fault for keeping you so protected from these foreign ideas. I hoped that by rejecting them without discussion, I would keep you and Von Mipatobeau safe. Perhaps I should have proceeded differently.'

'I am forty-two years old,' Gabriel said sharply. 'This is hardly a coming of age conversation. I am not seduced by the sudden discovery of commercial banking, Father. I am simply... trying to think what the best course for the bank will be, in the world of today; whether or not that is how it has operated for the last five hundred years.'

Edmond paused, staring into his coffee cup. 'Just be careful, my son,' he finally said. 'That is all I can tell you. Don't take any unnecessary risks. If there is one principle I learned from my parents and grandparents, it is that if you're not near your money, you might lose it. You can't just manage money, keeping a hopeful eye on it from afar. You have to be there with it.'

'We can't be provincial all our lives!' Gabriel burst out. 'We need to... break out of our shells. Besides,' he added, straightening his tie, 'most of the money in our bank is already international. What difference does it really make whether it stays in Switzerland?'

'History will answer that question,' Edmond said somewhat pompously. Once again, he sighed. 'Our life began in the Swiss mountains, after we came to France in the days of the Huguenots. We were farmers, simple people, like your mother's family from Ticino. Imagine that life, Gabriel. They got up every morning – just as my darling Avenira remembers doing as a child – they woke up with the sun, gathered the eggs from their hens, milked the family cows, picked the fresh vegetables from the garden for their evening soup. Perhaps they might find some fruit on the trees, for pleasure, or some leafy spice like parsley, tarragon or bay leaves. Like your mother, they would start the stew pot, leave it boiling in the fireplace and walk out to work. We are a nation of mountain workers, Gabriel. A simple, successful people. Our de Puritigny ancestors were grain brokers: then they moved onto money. But I am talking about days far back before the money lending. I am talking about real history.'

Gabriel raised his eyebrows but did not comment. His coffee cup was empty.

'Much like the pioneering days in America,' Edmond continued, 'we had to develop our own society, our own special rules, on our own. We worked hard, and we were honest. There were certain rules, rules concerning transaction with our fellow humans. That is where the Swiss reputation comes from, Gabriel, the one that makes Von Mipatobeau shine out like a beacon in the murky waters of international banking. We are Swiss, we are Protestant, and we are bankers. People came to us and they trusted us because of this tradition. Do you really think I should like to be out drinking on a yacht in the south of France, burning to a crisp and scattering banknotes into the sea? Do you think I should be sitting in some sort of overpriced English hotel, surrounded by women half my age, trying to prove something? This is not the Swiss way. We are here to work, work, work. Even our hobbies are healthy, like skiing cross-country and hiking early in the morning. This is how we keep thin and sporty, tall and muscular. As we grow older, we'll develop a few wrinkles, but stay attractive. We'll look lightly toasted, from the fresh mountain air and the sun. Meanwhile, we are here to focus, and be productive. We eat our stew, we pray, we read; some of us work on simple hobbies like woodcarving. We go to bed early. This is Switzerland.'

'I am well aware of all this, father,' Gabriel said stiffly. 'For one thing, I happen to live here. For another, I've heard this speech of yours a thousand times. It's getting rather boring. You know how hard I work. You know how deeply I respect these Swiss values. Sometimes, in fact, I wonder whether I don't embody their seriousness more than you. Carving a wooden bear, indeed!' He stood up and set down his coffee cup.

'You are offended,' Edmond said. 'I am sorry.'

———◆———

'Oh dear,' Avenira said, peering in through the window. 'The men seem to be arguing. I wonder what has happened?'

Clarice sighed, looking out over the darkening hillside. She twisted her cup of herbal tisane in her hands. In the distance, she could just make out the dull shine of the lake. 'Let's leave them be,' she said. 'I've had enough of Gabriel's tantrums already today.'

Avenira laughed. 'Marriage isn't a picnic every day,' she said. 'Life is more complicated than that.'

'Yes, it certainly is.' Clarice continued to stare out into the mountain night. 'Sometimes I think it would do him good to come back here; live with you for a while, connect with his roots; be in the mountains. He misses them, you know. He misses his early morning walks, alone with the eagles and the edelweiss or whatever on earth it is he seeks out there. Urgh.'

'Do you know, he still fits into the same pair of trousers he used to hike in when he was eighteen? Sometimes, when he's here alone, he wears them. I find them at the bottom of the laundry basket.'

'I don't understand the appeal of this rural solitude,' Clarice said, shaking her head. 'Not that I don't see the beauty in it. It's the miserable loneliness of it that gets to me. I've always been a city girl – sociable: I've always needed people around me. Gabriel's not the same.'

Avenira nodded thoughtfully. 'Do you know, my dear, Edmond sometimes says something odd about me. He says I could've been a *citadine*, but I chose to stay a farmer.' She reached over and touched Clarice's cheek gently. 'I may not have your cheekbones, or your figure, but sometimes I think I could have had a good life in the city.'

Clarice blushed. 'Avenira, I'm sure you have a wonderful life.'

'Oh, I know that!' she exclaimed. 'Heavens, I know that. We work hard, and we are happy. Did you know there is more sun in Switzerland than in the South of France? It's because we are so high above the clouds. We are... illuminated.' She gazed out towards the distant waters. 'I am a traditionalist like my husband,' she said. 'I believe in a healthy, honest, simple life. I think the Swiss, more than other people, are deeply connected to the nature around them. They understand their settings.'

'The Swiss can be blind in their conservatism,' Clarice said with unexpected venom. 'I too have been foolish,' she tried to explain. 'You see...' She faltered for a moment. 'I don't know how much this will mean to you, Avenira, but I have just discovered modern art for the first time in my life. I'm forty-two, and until now I had no idea there was this fascinating, bright world out there, pushing philosophical boundaries. I don't just mean big red squares, or... urinals, or any of that meaningless crap. I mean art, real art. Beautiful art.' She looked back down at the railing, embarrassed.

'My art form is the mountains,' Avenira said gently. 'Art, for me, is going out into the green fields and watching the cows, counting them as they wander the pastures. Do you know, I miss milking terribly. That was a truly satisfying task. And the smell of warm milk, streaming fresh into a bucket!' Clarice repressed a grimace. 'I wish I could go back to that, truly. A simple life.' Avenira paused, suddenly thoughtful. 'Can you read the sounds around you, Clarice? I am curious. I do not often spend time with... city girls, as you say.'

Clarice laughed lightly. 'I'm not sure how representative I am,' she said. 'The art world is my life, really. I spend most of my time sitting in darkened rooms. I'm not even sure what sounds you mean. I cannot recognise the songs of different birds, if that is what you're asking. I can tell the garbage truck from the *boulanger*.'

Avenira gave a mysterious sigh and finished her cup of tea. 'Well, perhaps my recent discoveries will interest you more, then. Have you read much about global warming?'

'I read the papers,' Clarice replied, 'but beyond that, I don't know much... It doesn't sound real to me. Isn't it all just scaremongering? Scientists trying to intimidate the government?'

'Oh, but it is real. Very real.' Avenira sighed. 'There are photographs of lakes shrinking into nothingness, leaving dry earth behind. Icebergs disappearing into saltwater, forever. The world is changing irrevocably, and it's all our fault.'

'But surely there has been climate change before, naturally?' Clarice ventured. 'Think of the ice ages, or... I don't know, dinosaurs.' She waved her empty teacup vaguely in the air.

Avenira gave a tolerant smile. 'Never have things changed so badly, so quickly. We have covered the planet with poison, all in the name of progress, globalisation, international travel. God knows my own husband contributed to it enough, with his endless business flights – flying to the States for breakfast, coming home by nightfall! – but at least we have tried to live a good life here, in the mountains: planting trees, tending to the earth around us. Switzerland's stance is admirable, you know, compared to the rest of the civilised world, or at least it seems that way to me. The country has made a real effort to cut down on their nuclear development, to work on funding other strategies for the production of electricity, using the country's natural resources.'

'I see,' said Clarice, unsure how to respond. 'I didn't know you were interested in science.'

'Natural sciences,' Avenira corrected her. 'But really it is much simpler than that, more instinctive. There are forces at work all around us: healing forces, gentle forces that might help to compensate for the damage we have wrought.'

Clarice looked at Avenira out of the corner of her eye. *Oh dear,* she thought. Avenira's green eyes were sparkling with excitement.

'Nature is both powerful and coherent. We are... insignificant and all-powerful at once, if we can simply learn to decode her messages. Marmots can tell the speed of the wind, they know when earthquakes are coming. They will warn small mountain birds of the arrival of hawks and eagles coming to prey on them. I have studied their calls for years. You could say I am something of a specialist in animal communication. Birds as well, of course. Soon, I believe we will be able to understand all their signs. They will be able to warn us about coming storms, the changing climate, even just strangers approaching our property. Think how useful this will be to the conservative Swiss!'

Clarice suddenly noticed she had been shaking her head gently, and stopped. Avenira was too wrapped up in her eccentric speech to notice, though. Clarice realised with horror that she had spread her arms up towards the Moon. 'Air, fire, water and earth are the forces of the world. We can understand them! We can be one with the mountains around us! We only have to listen.'

'I think we should go check on the men,' Clarice said hastily, patting her mother-in-law awkwardly on the shoulder. 'All of this has given me much to think about.'

Avenira laughed. 'I am sorry,' she said. 'Perhaps this was a bit much all at once. I have been... preoccupied. Living up here in the mountains alone, you have time to mull things over.'

'Not at all,' Clarice said vaguely. 'I am only worried about Gabriel's inevitable ill-humour, if he has been fighting with his father. I need no mountain bird to warn me of that!'

The two men were sitting side by side on the couch, hunched over in the flickering shadows, poring over pieces of paper. Pausing in the doorframe, Clarice was overwhelmed by the striking resemblance between them: the sharp nose, the shoulders, the large, deft hands.

'These movements, I designed them, you see,' Edmond was saying. 'There are so many different ways to make the hands of a watch tick forward. In this watch, look here, I designed a tiny piston, a tiny gas container, that will provide the pressure the movement needs to continue almost forever, accurately. See? It's all done through pressure, through the energy of gas.'

Gabriel was nodding enthusiastically. 'These are the new designs for small suppliers, correct?'

'Yes, I'll be sending them on to La Chaux-de-Fonds. They were very happy with my last creations. See, if you look at this illustration – I can show you the watch itself later, it's out in my workshop –'

'Next to the bear?' Gabriel asked with a wry smile.

Edmond shook his head. 'See how I have enamelled the surface several times? I do this in my lab, which is a small room out behind the garage. I was one of the first people to develop a paper-thin back for a watch, you know.'

'So this one, with the enamelling, does it work with a gas canister too?'

'No, no. This is much more straightforward; the kind of movement you'll find in most watches since the 1950s. A sort of mini gyroscope, you know.'

As Avenira and Clarice entered into the warm, fire lit lounge, Edmond looked up and smiled. Clarice's heart ached as she saw the way he looked at his green-eyed wife. 'Oh, there you are!' he said warmly. 'Our women have returned.'

Gabriel smiled thinly. 'Father was enlightening me as to his other hobby.'

'Yes, well, I thought I'd better show him something he could appreciate, if the bear really leaves him so cold.'

'I don't understand how that bear could leave anybody cold,' Avenira said. 'I think it's marvellous! So realistic, so huge. A force of nature.'

Gabriel raised his eyebrows. 'It's certainly huge,' he said, 'I'll give you that.'

'Avenira was singing the praises of your simple life,' Clarice said, sitting down in an armchair and setting her teacup down on the table. 'She makes it all sound *very* meaningful.'

'My life certainly suits me,' Edmond said, stretching contentedly. 'When I'm not carving wood, or designing watches, I'll be out cross-country skiing or hiking. When I'm at home, I'll help your mother chop potatoes for that wonderful soup. Why would I ever need anything more than the life I have in this beautiful country?'

'Don't you get bored, Father?' Gabriel asked suddenly. 'Not of Switzerland, but of this... Don't you ever think of coming back to the bank and just...'

'No,' Edmond said quickly. 'That is not the Swiss way. In our bank, we retire at sixty, and we do not go back to banking. We sell off all our shares. There is no way back. If you're out of work, you're out of ownership.'

'Such a Swiss concept,' Avenira sighed.

'Yes, it is,' Edmond said, patting her hand.

'You could still be making millions, but when you retire, you have to hand everything over to the new generation.'

'Luckily for me,' Gabriel said with a sharp smile.

'But if there's no son or relative, you still have to give them up,' Edmond said, shrugging. 'There will always be ownership management in private banking. This involves a considerable amount of liability to the owners. When there are problems, people will sue the individual people and not the bank. There is no limited liability in our bank, you see. It's part of the spirit of honesty.'

'I know, Father. Yet another reason why our clients trust us, and why nothing must change.'

'You know, Son, we are responsible. That is all there is to it. We are responsible for our management, and we are responsible if something goes wrong. In other banks, like Dieter's, where there is limited liability in the form of SA...*société anonyme*, the management cannot be attacked and neither can the bank be attacked. It's a safeguard. But it's not trustworthy. Now, when it comes to a Swiss private bank like ours, if something goes wrong, they can come for our reputation, our honour, the very shirts off our backs; certainly our net worth. Litigation notices could even come to our houses, before they come to our bank, because *we* are responsible. We put ourselves on the line with every single client, and clients know this. They respect this. This is the way it has always been.'

'You're an inspiration, father,' Gabriel said, looking at the floor.

Edmond gave a sly smile. 'In Switzerland,' he intoned, 'you have to be safe, neutral, silent, confidential. That is how to be a private banker.'

'Yes, Father,' said Gabriel, missing the tone.

'I don't understand this sudden interest in rebellion,' Edmond said. 'Don't you already make, what, five million? You have always been the most conservative of us all. I don't understand...'

'*Quelle mouche l'a piqué*,' Clarice finished with a smile. 'What kind of fly has bitten him? The fly is his lovely new friend Dieter.'

'Come now,' Gabriel said, 'you liked him too. You certainly seemed to have fun disappearing off for an entire day with his wife!'

'Can't I have friends, now?' Clarice snapped. 'Not everyone prefers the company of eagles.'

'Children, children,' said Avenira. 'Would anyone like any more tea?'

'Now your mother,' Edmond said suddenly, 'is a perfect example of a modern Swiss woman. Totally traditional in terms of her values, but she applies them in contemporary ways. For instance, she will never miss the *combats de reines*, the fights of the Hérens cows, that take place every year in the mountains near Verbier. Yet she has also recently taken a fierce interest in global warming.'

'Yes, she was telling me about this,' Clarice said quickly, keen to stop another tirade on the subject.

Edmond laughed. 'Traditional values can change, is what I'm saying. *Bio* or organic produce is another concept that is both completely local and natural, and yet fairly recent. Many of the old–

school farmers around here use pesticides on everything. Our way is older, truly.'

'You sound like hippies,' Gabriel sniffed.

'Clarice, my dear,' Avenira said with a smile, 'our son seems to get as cranky when he's tired at the fine age of forty-two as he used to as a child. I suggest it might be bedtime for everyone.'

'Well, it's nearly ten thirty!' Gabriel exclaimed grumpily. 'Of course I'm ready for bed.' He stood up and yawned extravagantly.

Edmond shook his head. 'It's that clean mountain air,' he said. 'It tires you out. It keeps you healthy.'

'Besides, the fire is burning low,' Avenira added softly.

'Good night,' said Clarice, kissing her mother-in-law on the cheek.

'*Bonne nuit*,' said Gabriel, walking from the room.

Chapter Nine

Clarice paused in the dappled shade of the plane trees. She could hear the sounds of voices, faint laughter and glasses clinking floating over the low stone wall. Would Winifred have arrived yet? She was unfamiliar with this part of Geneva. Clarice adjusted the lapels of her suit a little roughly. What was there to be nervous about? This was not her first modern art exhibition, after all. She set her shoulders, and marched towards the celadon green grille.

Inside the courtyard of the Musée de Carouge, she was overwhelmed by the greenery. Oily rhododendron leaves and exotic conifers waved in the wind. Bougainvillea blossoms drifted down along the windowsills, giving everything a vaguely Spanish air.

'She came, she came!' an excited voice was repeating in French, followed by a tinkling laugh.

'Darling!' This familiar voice made Clarice whirl around. There was Winifred, glowing in a simple white linen dress. Before she knew what was happening, Clarice was wrapped tight in her arms. She smelled of fresh herbs. 'I am so glad to see you here!'

'Yes, er, me too,' Clarice murmured into her shoulder, pulling back as politely as she could.

'This is Chloë, and this is Fleurie. Oh, and you'll remember Khadija; she's just visiting the tray of snacks over there.' A glance revealed that Khadija's pert, Chanel-clad rump was indeed bent over a selection of canapés.

Chloë giggled, extending a slender hand. A short, skinny woman with dyed platinum-blonde hair, she was wearing huge sunglasses and a very short black dress. 'Lovely to meet you, Clarice,' she said. Her voice was soft and slightly hoarse.

Clarice managed a smile, forcing her eyes back up from Chloë's bare thighs. '*Enchantée*,' she said.

'And I'm Fleurie,' the other woman said gently, sweeping her wave of golden hair back from her shoulders. She was wearing a plain grey t-shirt, jeans and rather battered sandals, but nonetheless managed a radiant sort of beauty.

'Fleurie is the real art enthusiast here,' Chloë said with a grin, putting a slender arm around her friend's waist. 'Perhaps she can show you around a little...'

'Yes, I would love to,' Fleurie said with a nod. 'Very much. I know these artists well.' Could she detect a slight Germanic accent there?

Clarice looked round the garden in bewilderment, taking in her settings a little more. Hidden beneath a grove of palm trees, next to the tables of flutes of *blanc de blanc* fizzy wine and snacks, several men were bent over in concentration, kneeling in the grass around strange shapes. 'Are those... sculptors?' she asked hesitantly. 'Are they working?' How come no-one at these modern art gatherings ever seemed to be looking at the art?

Chloë let out a tinkling laugh. 'Of course!' she said. 'It is part of the *vernissage*. These are the resident artists of the Musée de Carouge. They work with wood and metal, mostly, though you'll find them venturing into clay, or sandstone, or marble, or whatever comes into their hands.'

'They're hoping to sell,' Fleurie commented drily. 'If any of these pieces interest you, you should go inquire about acquisition.'

'No thank you,' Clarice said carefully, squinting at the hunks of rough-hewn wood and weird metal spirals. 'I don't think it's quite... to my taste.'

Chloë giggled. 'She may be a newcomer to the scene, but she knows what she likes! I approve,' she said.

Clarice had to refrain from rolling her eyes. 'I'm quite interested in modern art, actually,' she replied a little defensively.

A smile crept slowly across Winifred's face, quickly mirrored by Fleurie. 'Let me go get Khadija,' Fleurie suggested gently. 'We could go have a look inside the museum before everyone else starts swarming around; before they finish off their champagne. But oh!' she clapped a hand to her mouth. 'Clarice, you haven't even had a drink! Would you like one? We're in no hurry!'

Amused, Clarice shook her head. 'I don't really drink,' she said. Winifred cocked an eyebrow. 'Well, only on special occasions.'

As the women walked off, Chloë scrambled over to Clarice's side and forced her arm through hers. 'Quick,' she whispered mischievously. 'Let's gossip about the others before they get back! Have you met Khadija?'

'Yes,' Clarice said a little unwillingly. 'I found her quite impressive.'

Chloë sprayed her interlocutor with laughter. 'Impressive! It must be all the canapés she eats!' She threw her head back and laughed some more.

Clarice sighed, discreetly wiping spittle from her lapels. 'I meant she seemed to know the art very well. She struck me as serious, and quite well-acquainted with the business.'

'Khadija,' Chloë said gleefully, 'is a one-woman mission to change the form of the Chanel suit into a balloon.'

'What about Fleurie, then?' Clarice said quickly. 'Tell me a little about her. We have not met before.'

'Hmm.' Chloë tapped a bright red fingernail against her lip thoughtfully. 'Oh, hello, Winifred!' she said vaguely, waving at the approaching women. 'Quickly, what can I tell you about Fleurie? Nothing very scandalous springs to mind. I'd need more time. She's part French, part Swiss-German. The slight accent comes from her mother's side.'

'She was born in Alsace,' Winifred contributed, 'but was raised in Switzerland. She went to school in Contamines, then on to university in Lausanne.'

'Boring,' Chloë waved away these comments with a smile. 'Let's tell her interesting things about Fleurie! For instance, she is an incurable optimist. She's a total intellectual, obsessed with modern art. You'll notice when she gets a little carried away about a subject, she starts to sing her words. Oh, oh, and she hates Globus. She only buys her clothes second-hand, or in the July sales. Of course, you'll probably remember her for her looks. Her hair isn't even dyed!' Chloë pouted enviously, fingering her own platinum locks.

'Hello, Clarice,' Khadija said warmly, as she and Fleurie reappeared beside Clarice. Kissing her on both cheeks, she added,

'Don't let our Chloë talk your ear off.'

'It's good to see you again,' Clarice said.

'You kept your secrets well last time,' Khadija replied. 'You're a sly one. You didn't think to mention your serious art background!'

Clarice was a little confused. 'My art background? I have... Oh, my gallery, you mean?'

Khadija's smile widened. 'Oh, your little gallery,' she mimicked, 'your little gallery in Saint Antoine...'

Fleurie frowned with interest. 'The gallery in Saint Antoine? Isn't that where they have all those marvellous Hodlers?'

Clarice smiled, for real this time. 'Yes, that is my gallery.'

Fleurie arched an eyebrow. 'How wonderful!' she exclaimed. 'We must come and see you some day.'

'Didn't I tell you?' Khadija asked, wiping her lips daintily. 'Clarice is the owner of one of the most expensive and snobby galleries in Grand Rue. She has millions of francs worth of the old masters. It's the most classic Swiss gallery you could imagine: nothing but realist still lives, peasants in graveyards, and endless boating scenes on the lake.'

'I'm sure it's wonderful. I'd love to come see, some day,' Winifred cut in, smiling.

'Yes, of course,' Clarice replied quickly, relieved. 'Anytime you like.'

'Not all of us are snobs, you know,' Fleurie said with a smile. 'I enjoy my old masters, as well as more modern works.'

'When we first met her,' Khadija continued, 'Azma and I were so busy gossiping away about our own artists and projects that we hardly even thought to enquire about her own credentials. But now we know she is one of our own!' Khadija beamed.

'Well,' Clarice waved a hand vaguely in the air. 'I am still relatively new to the world of modern art. But I am learning,' she added quickly, narrowing her eyes unconsciously at Chloë.

'Come now, so are we all. Will you come with me to look at the art?' Fleurie nodded towards the entrance.

'With pleasure,' Clarice replied.

———————◆◆◆———————

Fleurie and Clarice walked a little ahead of Winifred, Chloë and Khadija. The exotic atmosphere of the garden was quite relaxing, and a pleasant change from the dark interior of the Grand Rue gallery. Palms made a dry, rustling sound as they drifted in the wind.

'Oh! Thona!' Chloë suddenly exclaimed in delight, running off in her stilettos across the grass towards a towering blonde. 'Hello!'

Fleurie gave a tolerant smile. 'Ah, Chloë,' she sighed to Clarice. 'I know she can be a bit much if you haven't met before.'

Clarice pursed her lips. 'She immediately launched into gossipy portraits of everyone in the group but herself. I believe a response in kind would be the best revenge. Tell me a little about Chloë and her history.'

Fleurie laughed quietly. 'Chloë is not afraid of gossip, even if it's about herself. She is a sort of... walking reference. She will always offer commentary on everything. Her own history is quite fascinating, though. Her father was a crook, you see. A crooked banker who ran away from Paris; a man who consistently invested in the wrong things. She's got a keen eye for business, though, maybe partly as a reaction to her father's terrible instincts. She's a powerful woman, in public and in private. Unfortunately, she also has terrible taste in men.'

'It's a great story,' Khadija commented, joining the conversation. 'She's totally off the wall, is Chloë, a bizarre import from France. Her father brought her over with him from Paris and set her up in some sort of spa. A spa, in a city where there are spas every hundred yards! Anyway, after three months, she bankrupted the place and stormed off. I mean, what could she have done so quickly to make it all fail so dramatically?' She lowered her voice. 'Our favourite theory is that she turned the place into a sort of brothel.'

Startled, Clarice made a sort of coughing noise. She looked at Fleurie.

'Seriously,' Fleurie said. 'You'll understand a little better, the more time you spend with her. She's quite a character.'

'The way she describes the spa,' Khadija said, her eyes sparkling, 'it sounds quite spectacular. Rather a shame it failed, even if it *was* a brothel... beautiful porcelain from Italy, granite and marble worth thousands and thousands; great jets of water shooting up into fountains; gorgeous hammams and steam rooms and Scandinavian pine saunas. I'd have loved to go, though I bet she tried to sleep with every one of her clients.'

Fleurie shook her head. 'That's unkind, Khadija.'

'Are you kidding? Chloë would love the idea! It's probably her fantasy!'

An urge to giggle began to well up in Clarice. She hadn't been involved in conversations like this since her teen years. Scathing and gossipy as it was, there was a kind of thrill to it.

'Chloë cares about two things,' Fleurie said with a small smile. 'Modern art, and men. Loving men doesn't make her a whore.'

Khadija shrugged. 'What's wrong with being a whore? You're always telling me what an eye for business she has. She loves to market her looks, doesn't she? Does she ever date paupers? I mean, look at her *décolletés*, look at the length of her dresses! Even the smoking is an affectation; she works so hard on that husky voice of hers. She never wears anything below the knee. She seems to be trying to be... patronising and sexy and smiley all at once.'

The oddest thing about this insulting speech of Khadija's, Clarice reflected, was how much affection seemed to be attached to this portrayal. Chloë seemed to confuse and amuse the women more than she annoyed them.

'And her jokes!' Khadija was continuing, throwing her hands up in the air. 'Those filthy French jokes of hers! They just go too far. They always seem to involve some sort of man being taken for a ride, or a dirty priest, or some man who doesn't know how to make love, or an unfortunate encounter with a gigolo.' Khadija shook her head. 'I mean, it's very entertaining. But you have to admit that she's a somewhat slippery character. Her taste in art, for one thing, is outrageous to the point of provocation. She really can come across as childish in that domain, wouldn't you agree, Fleurie?'

Fleurie pursed her lips. 'Well, she does tend to like things involving cut-up animals, or paint thrown from a bucket across a wall, or furniture stolen out of public toilets... But I don't know, she has an eye for the really radical stuff; a business eye, I mean. She tends to be able to tell a charlatan from a truly experimental artist. You know there's a market for that sort of thing, even if it's not your market.'

'I don't know,' Khadija admitted, 'but then I despise all that stuff myself. It has no meaning or intrinsic value, no beauty. Its only aim is to break the rules, and there have been no rules around worth breaking since the 1920's. It's just... infantile.'

'That's the art you're talking about, not Chloë,' Fleurie cautioned. 'Mind you stay respectful of our mutual friend. Even if she is, in your words, a whore.'

'I love her,' Khadija said carefully, 'and our lives would be much more boring without her. But sometimes she can be pretty provocative. She even occasionally comes across as racist. She has a sort of immature, uninformed xenophobia – that makes her more Swiss than the Swiss! I mean, she seems to have no problems befriending Chinese or Thai millionaires... as long as they take her shopping on Avenue Montaigne, or buy her handfuls of jewellery. Did you know she never sleeps with a man unless he buys her Chanel or Cartier? A suit or a piece of jewellery. Otherwise: no sex.'

'But... it sounds like she loves sex,' Clarice couldn't help intervening.

Khadija grinned. 'She loves money, too.'

'If you want to see her in the worst light,' Fleurie concluded gently, 'you could see Chloë as a spoiled little nymphomaniac. But there's more to her than that. She brings... colour into our lives. A sort of mad poetry. Besides, just wait till you see her doing business.'

'Business?' Khadija scoffed.

'She's learned a lot since her spa days,' Fleurie cautioned. 'You know that as well as I.'

'She still doesn't hold her own financially,' Khadija said with a shrug. '*I* know that better than anyone.'

'She will,' Fleurie said confidently.

Clarice frowned in confusion.

'We'll explain everything eventually,' Winifred said kindly. 'Just let the tide of gossip wash over you. It's a good way to get to know everyone in our little group.'

Clarice nodded. 'Shall we go look at some paintings, then?'

The museum's interior was muted and quiet, rather like stepping into someone's drawing room. The old stone was painted white, and the atmosphere was hushed. 'What a clever idea, coming in here right at the start!' Khadija whispered gleefully. 'Skipping all the chatting and drinking. I would never think to go look at the art before my third visit to the snacks corner!'

Fleurie nodded, but did not respond. Instead, she took Clarice's arm and guided her into the first room of the museum. Winifred and Khadija followed a little ways behind. 'This is a new artist, a young man who only just appeared on the scene.' Clarice cocked her head to the side, considering the large, bright aquarelle in front of her. The scene was abstract, but it evoked running water. Perhaps it was just stepping in from the summery, exotic atmosphere of the garden, but the effect on Clarice's psyche was quite pleasant. 'He started out as a Classicist, you see: perhaps you'll notice a certain quiet realism, or at least a narrative instinct? Then he fell in love with Pissarro and all those of his ilk, and started producing nothing but imitation pointillism. Now, he's creating geometrical patterns, all done in aquarelle. See this one, to the left, how much more abstract it is?'

Clarice nodded. 'Yes, this looks nothing like traditional pointillism,' she commented. 'It's wilder and more scientific all at once.'

Fleurie smiled, pleased. 'These are selling for upwards of a thousand francs a painting. I think he's ready to become a big name on the art scene.'

They walked on.

'Hmph,' Khadija said, pulling up her reading glasses. 'This geometrical stuff is really all the rage, isn't it.'

'At least in Carouge,' Clarice replied.

Khadija gave a surprised grin.

'I think it's quite interesting,' Fleurie said. 'But then I studied science for a long time. I used to want to be an architect, you know, to pursue further studies at the University of Lausanne, but the appeal of history of art was too much. They're two sides of the same subject, you know? Looking back and admiring what has been done, or looking forward and starting from nothing.'

'With all due respect,' Khadija commented, 'you strike me as more of a historian than an artist. I'm sure you would have been a wonderful architect, but I'm glad you went off into the arts.'

'Besides, your studies must give you a great deal of perspective,' Clarice added, a hint of admiration creeping into her voice.

Fleurie gave a brusque nod. 'But we are not here to talk about me,' she said softly. 'Look at this painting, here! These patterns are deeply modern, almost mathematical. I don't think they mean anything in themselves, but the colours seem highly symbolic.'

'I remember reading something in Germany, years ago,' Clarice said, surprising herself. 'Was it the Bauhaus that had a manifesto concerning the meaning of colours?'

'Yes, yes,' Fleurie replied, a little dismissively. 'Colours have always been imbued with deep significance. Of course, I have always been of the opinion that if an artwork does not offer up its meaning easily to the viewer, the meaning is hardly even there. I am not interested in decoding, or elitism.'

Winifred gave a soft laugh. 'See, you are an architect. Only interested in functional, accessible art. I rather like all that mysticism surrounding colours; even just the basic, instinctive separation between warm and cold colours. Surely even you'll admit a wall of deep blue and a wall of bright yellow have different effects on your mood? Have you never spent time in a flowering garden, in summer?'

'Most of the time, I'll admit, there is a basic emotional impact,'

Fleurie replied impatiently, 'though there are exceptions. Schoolchildren are taught these binaries. I am not sure how relevant they are to modern art.'

Clarice took a deep breath. 'I disagree,' she said, 'with all due respect. There are many different ideas about colours, and complementarity, and circularity, but surely you cannot deny the basic principle that our eyes react differently to different colours? You said you were a scientist, after all. The idea is physiological in origin: that, for instance, if you stare for a long time at something forest green – the garden outside the window, for instance – your mind will create a patch of fuchsia pink when you look back at the white wall. These oppositions and compensations are natural. Surely all artists play with them, consciously or not.' She swallowed and stopped.

Fleurie and Winifred were looking at her curiously. Khadija was looking backwards and forwards from the garden window towards the wall, widening her eyes in a rather comical fashion.

'Ah, but paint and light work in opposing ways,' Fleurie said with a soft smile. 'If you mix all kinds of light together, you get white. If you mix all paint, in theory, you get deepest black. It is impossible to reproduce what we truly see in the world in art.'

'But isn't art a quest to do so, in some way?' Clarice continued, doggedly. 'To capture light through something material.'

'I feel a little dizzy, but you're right,' Khadija cut in. 'The wall is pink now.' She paused, blinking. 'I think I need more champagne.'

'Capturing light through something material...' Fleurie repeated softly, then she shook her head. 'Yes, Clarice, you're certainly an interesting addition to our group,' she said with real warmth. 'You've given me some things to think about.'

'Most of us see this sort of art every day,' Winifred added. 'We're jaded. We hardly notice how radical some of it is – except maybe Chloë, who consciously seems to seek out the weirdest and ugliest pieces.'

'I didn't mean to get so carried away,' Clarice said, a little flustered. 'I just... have not had an occasion to talk about art theory for many,

many years. You say you are jaded: you should meet some of the old ladies in furs who come shopping for Hodlers!'

'Come, my dear, let us look at some other paintings.'

They walked on in silence for a time, along the bright white walls. Suddenly, a girlish voice drifted into their intellectual reverie. 'Yes, Thona, but he was such a dreadful *bore*. Turned out he'd already wasted his whole inheritance!'

'Hi, Chloë,' Fleurie said with a little wave. Was there a trace of mockery in the gesture? Clarice wasn't sure.

'I've brought champagne,' Chloë said, kissing her blonde friend goodbye and teetering towards them on her high heels. Somehow, she seemed to be balancing four flutes of *blanc de blanc* in the crook of her arm.

'Here, let me help you,' Winifred said, loosening the glasses from her hold.

Chloë beamed, and Clarice found herself unable to refuse the glass. 'Well, just one,' she said. She sipped at the warm, slightly flat liquid resignedly.

'Urgh,' Chloë said. 'All of these are so unimaginative.'

Clarice stepped forward. 'What do you think of this one?' she asked, gesturing. 'These geometrical patterns, drawn in oak-brown and shining mother of pearl. Don't they look like some sort of Ottoman painting? Doesn't that strike you as original?'

Chloë shrugged, then moved to take a closer look. 'Pointillism is so last-century,' she said. 'It's for bourgeoises with parasols and little dogs by their sides.'

Fleurie stopped, squinted, and then smiled. 'I'm not sure about that, Chloë,' she said. 'See, this frame of reference is accessible and radical all at once. I have to admit these colours have emotional and narrative impact. The failed architect approves. Yes, this is definitely an Orientalist work. Do you know what I like best about this artist, though? He's created most of the body of his work using only felt tip markers and pens!'

Clarice looked closer. 'Oh!' she said, delighted. 'Yes, he has!'

'How delightful,' Chloë said, walking on.

Khadija joined the two women with their faces almost pressed to the painting. 'I find this portrayal of the East, through lines and the mixture of colours, very interesting; very modern. As you know, most Orientalist painters are firmly stuck in realism – I am very interested in finding artists who go about the subject in other ways. Not like some kind of Norman Rockwell wandering the desert, nor the new Delacroix lost in a bazaar.'

Fleurie laughed. 'Well, you're obviously not alone in your approval, my dear. I happen to know this particular artist is selling for more than five thousand francs a painting. He's going places. Let's make a note to keep an eye out for his name.'

'Norman Rockwell, Norman Rockwell,' Chloë murmured, slowing down. 'Isn't he that American guy? Why does that name ring a bell? Oh, because I slept with a guy called Norman yesterday! At least I think that was his name.'

Khadija sighed and Fleurie shook her head. 'Oh, Chloë, this is hardly the time to regale us with tales of your love life! Can't you be serious for two minutes?'

'We were talking about high art, not low lives,' Khadija added, grinning.

Chloë tossed her platinum hair. 'Ah, but his is hardly the low life! Nor is mine. He's some sort of count, actually, but he was pretty boring, to be honest. I really wished I was waking up next to someone else – so I went to find one. You remember Robert?' Noting Clarice's wide eyes, she suddenly laughed. 'Oh, you'll get used to me. This is how I live.'

'Couldn't you tone it down for your first meeting?' Fleurie chided her gently.

'You love my stories!' Chloë sang out. 'You repressed little bitches can't get enough. If I had my way, I'd be with a different man every two hours.'

Clarice had to hand it to her: she certainly wasn't ashamed of her way of life!

'You'll get used to her,' Winifred said gently.

'I think the objective of life is sex. And also modern art,' Chloë was saying. 'Have you heard of this guy, Fred, who's sort of subverting children's subjects? Painting new, strange versions of Disney characters.'

'Surely you don't mean those pornographic caricatures?' Clarice asked in shock.

Chloë shrugged. 'I think Fred is wonderful. He's taken the essence of humanity, lust, Disney, and childhood cartoons, and mixed it all up in a sort of exploration of young adult sensuality.'

'Sensuality,' huffed Fleurie. 'Don't you have any other objectives in life?'

'Oh yes,' Chloë teased. 'Let's see: men, and men, and men. That's a variety of objectives, don't you think?'

Clarice shook her head. 'Is she like this every day?' she quietly asked Khadija.

'Only when she gets laid,' Khadija whispered back.

Once more, Clarice had to repress the urge to burst out laughing.

'I forgot about one of my essential objectives,' Chloë babbled on, 'preserving my youth. I mean, I'm twenty-eight now. I'm basically over the hill. By the time I'm thirty-two, I've decided I should really increase the size of my chest by four inches. Ten centimetres or so, you know. Then I'll get a nose job, to make my nose nice and snubby. Like those Scandinavian actresses in black and white. You see these eyes? I'll make them almond shaped. And I'm tired of them being brown. To go with my blonde hair, they should really be bright baby blue! You know I have to dye my hair every three days to get rid of the roots. My hair is naturally nearly black, you see. But I love this sort of ash blonde, don't you?'

There was a pause as Chloë finally stopped to draw breath. 'That's all going to be costly,' Khadija said, curiously rather than caustically. 'What else are you planning to get done?'

Chloë pouted. 'I'm thinking of increasing the height of my hips, but that's quite expensive. I'll wait another three years for that. Oh, and after that, a Brazilian butt,' she added cheerfully. 'For dancing.'

'What?' gasped Clarice; she couldn't help it.

'Oh, that's just what Fabrice calls it. Is that racially insensitive?

Fabrice just loves women.' Chloë had her head over her shoulder, trying to see her own backside.

'Who is Fabrice?' asked Clarice, her mind reeling. She noticed Fleurie was frowning.

'My cosmetic surgeon,' she said casually, straightening her shirt. 'Well, really, he's Khadija's.'

Clarice looked at Khadija. 'Khadija?' she asked in disbelief.

Khadija shrugged. 'He does my lipo,' she said in an offhand manner.

Clarice did not know what to say. Luckily, Chloë was rarely at a loss for words. 'Liposuction, I mean! Fabrice is based in Paris. He's just marvellous. Probably gay, but what an eye for the female form! You go to his office at six am, I've been told, and come out that very same evening fifteen kilos lighter. In one go! It sounds so great! I mean, it worked wonders for Khadija,' she said, straight-faced. 'She used to have to go through doors sideways!'

'Chloë!' Winifred burst out. 'You can't say things like that!'

Fleurie was beginning to shake her head.

'Well, it's true,' Khadija said, shrugging. 'Soon, thanks to Fabrice, I'll be able to fit into size 42. That's been my dream for years. Who cares if it's artificial? It means I can keep eating all the snacks I want.'

'You'll meet lots of men, too,' Chloë said approvingly.

Clarice frowned, confused. Wasn't Khadija married?

'I don't really care about men,' Khadija said airily. 'I just want to be able to enjoy life. So what if it costs me ten thousand dollars to love my body?'

'Fine,' Chloë replied, waving a hand in the air. 'You can be my wing woman.'

'Girls!' Fleurie nearly shouted. 'That's quite enough of this unhealthy chat about your bodies. Whatever will Clarice think? Bonding over hating yourselves, I mean really. And when we're surrounded by all this marvellous modern art. Don't you have anything better to preoccupy yourselves with? That Fabrice of yours is nothing but a pervert and a greasy-haired crook; and Parisian, on top of that! This practice is absolutely horrible, and a total waste of all your money. I can't believe you would do such a thing when there is such beauty in the world.' Glowering, she stomped off. Her mind reeling, Clarice looked back to the paintings, but did not follow.

Chloë shrugged. 'The thing is, Fleurie can play the intellectual all she likes: she doesn't need to worry about any of this. She's so skinny, she would look great in a bin bag.'

'I don't understand,' Clarice said in bewilderment. 'I mean, you're... you don't need... You've always found plenty of success with gentlemen, and you know how to dress well. What is the appeal of all that surgery?'

'Wouldn't you like to be just a little bit more beautiful? Don't you have a few quirks, or bits of flab, that you could do without, even if it's just on the beach, or in bed with your husband? Or do you take lovers?'

'I most certainly do not take lovers,' Clarice said sternly.

'What a shame! Well, it doesn't matter. You should really think about it,' said Chloë. 'The surgery, I mean, rather than the lovers; though of course in my most scientific opinion you should try a combination of both. Who doesn't want to love themselves? It brings a little bit of flame into your sex life, too.' She winked outrageously.

'I can't stand the idea of anybody touching me with a scalpel,' Clarice said hesitantly, 'though of course it is appealing, the idea of instant gratification. Transformation. The body as art, modern and changeable...' She shook her head slowly, staring at the geometrical patterns on the wall. 'I don't know, it's all very new to me. It seems more radical than modern art, really. When I was young, my mother didn't even think women should dye their hair!'

Chloë laughed heartily. 'Well, well, well, ladies, I don't know what you all think, but I like this Clarice of yours. I believe we can skip the traditional hazing and ritual. Shall we let Madame de Puritigny into the gang?'

Fleurie had appeared at their shoulders. She rolled her eyes. 'Chloë,' she said patiently, 'there is no gang.'

'Yes there is!' Khadija exclaimed. 'What are you talking about? I mean, we may not wear matching leather jackets, but we meet monthly in one of the major Swiss cities, depending on where most of us are, to talk about art.'

'To talk about art,' Clarice repeated mindlessly.

'We meet,' Fleurie said crisply, 'to discuss art funding: sponsoring, if you will. What Khadija is asking you, disguised as a girlish proposal of gang friendship, is if you would like to become involved in financing the modern art world, with us.'

Winifred gave a slow smile. 'This is all a little sudden, ladies. I know we don't usually make our potential candidates swim in icy lakes, or stick their heads in toilets or anything, but don't you think the proposal is a little sudden? Clarice's head must be reeling.'

'No, I think I understand,' Clarice said hesitantly. 'You already knew I had a successful gallery. You've initiated me into your gossip, and I haven't run screaming. And I've apparently demonstrated enough interest, if not enough knowledge, in modern art for you to think I might be interested in exploring further... and you think I might have money to contribute. Well, you may just be right.' She gave a satisfied smile. 'My husband will disapprove terribly, of course, but I don't really care.'

'That's the spirit!' Chloë crowed.

'The museum of Carouge is one of our strongholds,' Fleurie explained. 'We have an excellent relationship with them.'

'God knows why,' Khadija sniffed. 'I mean, it's barely even *in* Geneva. No-one's ever heard of the museum. The first time she made us all come down here, we had to take the tram. The tram! When you can get a taxi right outside the gates! Can you imagine?'

'How plebeian,' Clarice said drily.

'The taxes are lower, I suppose, to work and live,' Khadija added thoughtfully.

'The Musée de Carouge has always encouraged modern art,' Fleurie continued, ignoring both of their comments. 'Some of it high quality, some of it more dubious. Even the sculpture outside: it's not all driftwood. I know you enjoyed the geometrical pointillism, and I suspect you might like some of the more traditional sculpture. In fact, I think we should go back out into the sun and have another look.'

'And another snack,' Khadija added with satisfaction.

'We'll discuss the specifics of your theoretical contribution to our efforts, Clarice, another time,' Fleurie continued. 'Maybe over breakfast, this weekend?'

'Yes, I'd like that very much,' Clarice said, smiling. 'Very much indeed.'

———◆———

'I told you the garden was nice,' Khadija was saying, ten minutes later, munching on a piece of cheese. 'I really don't know about these sculptures, though.' She squinted in the setting sun. 'I'm glad the artists are gone, so we can take a closer look.'

'Me too,' said Winifred with genuine warmth, kneeling down in the grass with no regard for her white linen dress.

'You can tell she's a gardener, can't you?' giggled Chloë. 'A true earth mother!'

Winifred shrugged, cracking a smile. 'I've always liked woodcarving, too. It doesn't mean I worship the moon.'

'Don't you think this one is quite phallic?' Chloë asked, bending down to look closely at a twist of metal.

'You think everything is phallic,' Khadija said affectionately.

'It looks almost like Rodin to me,' Fleurie added.

'What about this lion?' Clarice asked Fleurie. 'Doesn't this remind you of Pierre-Jules Mêne's bronzes? The ones inspired by the Zoo de Vincennes.'

'I see what you mean,' Fleurie said, nodding thoughtfully. 'That one's very classic, very nineteenth-century in style. It has a sort of narrative thrust to it, too, that I suspected would appeal to you.'

'Thrust!' Chloë repeated happily.

'I like it,' Winifred declared. 'I would have it in my house, if I didn't know for a fact that my boys would hit each other over the head with it.'

Khadija let out a deep laugh. 'It sounds exhausting,' she said.

'This is why I always make sure my men use protection,' added Chloë.

Winifred shook her head, smiling. 'I love my boys,' she said. 'Exhausting though they may be.' Not for the first time, Clarice felt a strange pang.

'Anyway, I think all this cast bronze is totally bourgeois,' Chloë continued. For once, Clarice was quite happy to listen to her tide of chat. 'It's outdated and out of fashion. They should melt these lions down and make them into jewellery... for me.' She gave a little laugh, pleased with her attack.

'I quite like them,' Clarice said mildly. 'They'd go down very well in my gallery, I reckon. You're forgetting that there are still plenty of conservative bourgeois around today, especially in Geneva.'

'Oh, that's true!' Chloë exclaimed happily. 'I sleep with them all the time!'

'Well, don't you think some of your gentleman callers might have been the sort to keep a bronze lion at home? Perhaps under a dark and brooding portrait of Napoleon, or a tartan throw?' She smiled, suddenly mischievous. Chloë caught her eye, surprised, and grinned in return.

Fleurie raised an eyebrow. 'Do you usually deal in sculpture?' she asked.

'No,' Clarice admitted, 'but it might be something to consider. Do you happen to know how I can get hold of this artist?' She frowned, her mind racing.

Fleurie gave a wide smile. 'I don't,' she said, 'but I can find out!'

Chapter Ten

Gabriel pulled the door of their house in Saint Antoine closed behind him and sighed with relief, unbuttoning his navy suit jacket. Five thirty, at last! He was tired, he was hungry, and he was glad to be out of the sun, away from people, and done with banking. He loosened his tie. 'No more talking,' he muttered happily in the direction of the antique umbrella stand, slipping off his fine tooled leather shoes. They fell on the immaculate parquet with a delicate clunk. He picked them up, dusted them off lightly and set them carefully on the shoe rack.

'Darling,' Clarice cooed, startling her husband. She appeared in the crook of the doorway, a silk robe pulled around her. What kind of time of day was this to take a shower?

'Do you know where my *pantoufles* are, *chérie*?' he asked, scanning the floor. 'I'm sure I left them here this morning.'

'No,' she murmured, 'but I can look.' She paused for what seemed like a long time, then disappeared back into the darkness.

Gabriel shook his head. He sniffed the air cautiously, wondering whether dinner was ready. He couldn't detect anything – no reheated roast, no bubbling cheese. Only a dusty smell, reminiscent of old manuscripts, and the faint undertone of wood polish. He sighed. Clarice hadn't told him they would be eating late, he thought grumpily, or he would have had Caroline bring him a butter biscuit with his afternoon coffee. Where had Clarice gone, anyway?

'*Voilà!*' she said, in strangely sultry tones, handing him a pair of velvet slippers. Gabriel blinked for a moment, then pulled them on. A cloud of soft, sweet perfume seemed to emanate from his wife.

'So!' he said, with forced cheerfulness. 'What's for dinner tonight?'

'Chicken,' Clarice replied. Was that a sigh? 'I picked up some spicy chicken from Migros.'

'What do you mean, spicy?' Gabriel asked with some trepidation. Memories of dark London streets flashed through his mind.

'You know,' Clarice said impatiently, 'with plenty of salt and pepper. What do you think spicy means?'

'Oh, good,' Gabriel replied. 'I'm quite hungry. What time do you think we'll be eating, darling?'

Clarice gave an uncharacteristic and strangely mysterious shrug.

'Seven or so?' Gabriel prompted.

This time, Clarice definitely sighed. 'How was the office then?' she asked drily, retreating from the doorway in a billow of silk. Had he seen that dressing gown before? It was rather extravagant material... very expensive-looking. Had he forgotten her birthday? No, that wasn't for months.

'Work was fine,' he said, trailing after his wife towards the dining room. 'Tremendously tiring. I had to work with a series of clients who barely spoke French, or German, or English. People from Japan and the Middle East, you know. This never used to happen in Geneva; certainly not in the private banks. It's a new wave happening all over Switzerland, you know, this "globalisation" business. I guess we're late compared to the rest of the Western world, but it's still a surprise. I mean, they're bringing us millions, so it seems a little out of place to complain but...'

'You're complaining,' Clarice called back over her shoulder. 'Come sit on the sofa, my dear,' she said, her voice soft. She switched on the light, but it only cast a faint golden glow across the bookshelves and rug.

Gabriel collapsed into the leather couch. The darkness of their lounge and the faint smell of beeswax were soothing to him. 'God knows how they make their money,' he said. 'Probably selling oil, or dates, or carpets and whatnot. I don't know. We're making money, so I suppose that's all that matters.' He squeezed his toes in their velvet sheaths contentedly.

'Why now?' Clarice asked. 'I mean, how do you think these new clients have heard about you?'

Gabriel hesitated. 'I think Dieter may have put Von Mipatobeau on their radar. He mentioned some potential clients the last time we spoke on the phone.'

'Oh, you two still speak?' she asked, as if suddenly cheered by the news. 'I'm so glad you and Dieter are becoming friends!'

'I don't know about friendship,' Gabriel said carefully. 'We are simply business acquaintances. What need have I for a friend in Zurich?'

'Oh,' said Clarice, her face falling. 'It's just that I've been getting along so well with Winifred.'

'Anyway, Dieter was telling me about a number of... acquaintances of his, or contacts, if you will. I didn't understand the full picture, to be perfectly honest, though I'm quite sure it's all legal; highly lucrative, of course. I believe it had to do with hidden commissions on trade or heavy equipment sales.'

'Arms dealing?'

'Yes,' he said shortly. 'Industrialisation, if you will. Anyway, there's new money, and some of it is coming to us. I don't know how we're going to manage, really,' he concluded gloomily. 'All these Moomeens and Abdullahs and Mouhahareebs and whatnot. No more Charlies and Pierres.'

'Well, are they interesting characters?' Clarice asked, leaning on his arm. 'You know, I've met several people from the Middle East recently. Winifred's art circle is quite international. There's this one woman, Khadija, who is most entertaining. She was there at coffee this morning. I mean, I know you don't like modern art but...'

'Is that so surprising?' Gabriel gave a hard smile. 'I'm a classical man, in music, art and architecture. I only like quality. Simple, good quality objects. Maybe I'll splash out on some Empire furniture, if I'm feeling bold.'

She shrugged, unamused. 'Well, you should come out of your shell. Somebody like Khadija, or her husband, might leave money with you. There are interesting investments to be made. They make a lot of money in the art world.'

'You don't say,' Gabriel replied. 'Well, I guess I'll have to get used to strange names like Khadija, then.'

'I don't think it's strange,' Clarice said defensively. 'I mean, she used to make very expensive jewellery and sell it under her name. It sold very well. The exotic has a real appeal. I think you would like her,' she concluded stubbornly.

'Yes, dear,' he said, patting her hand. 'I'm sure.' What had got into his wife today? She had been slightly strange since that *vernissage* at the weekend. Was it in... *Carouge*? What on earth was in Carouge anyway?

'Did you even remember I was having coffee with the girls this morning?' she asked.

'The girls?' Gabriel repeated with distaste. Why did middle-aged women insist on sounding like six-year-olds when referring to people they had coffee with?

'Yes,' she said, strangely defensively. 'The club.' She giggled, suddenly, as if proud.

Gabriel stared. 'Darling, have you been... drinking?' he asked hesitantly.

She gave a short laugh. 'No,' she said. 'I did have a coffee this morning with the girls, but that's the only foreign chemical in my system today.'

'I apologise,' Gabriel said formally. 'You just don't seem like yourself.'

'The thing is,' Clarice said suddenly, as if speaking to herself, 'I thought I would be so ill-at-ease in that sort of glitzy, modern environment. I thought everyone would be terribly uneducated, and strange and... foreign. But I actually found a lot of the art very interesting. There was this woodcarver, your father would have liked him.'

Gabriel made a sort of huffing noise of dismissal. His father! Modern art! Clarice continued, unperturbed. 'Anyway, it occurred to me all of a sudden, mid-afternoon, that I wasn't bored. I was having a good time. I was giving all this art my full consideration, and having fascinating conversations. These women were... inspiring.' She blushed, as if hearing her own words suddenly. 'Anyway,' she soldiered on, 'it's not just for fun. It's a serious financial venture. I've decided to start investing in modern art.'

'What?' Gabriel couldn't help himself.

Clarice gave a steely smile. 'Each of the girls puts in eight thousand francs. Together, we sponsor new exhibits of modern art. On the side, I'm looking out for new artists who might want to exhibit in my gallery. I think this sort of thing might just sell, Gabriel.'

'You... What? Slow down a minute.'

Clarice smiled. Was she enjoying this? 'I...' she said, as if speaking to a child, 'am investing: In... modern... art... That is all there is to it.'

'Since when do you care about modern art, Madame Ferdinand Hodler? The most contemporary painting in your gallery must be from the 1800s.'

Clarice shrugged. 'People can change, you know. I've been learning a lot, lately. I've been doing some reading. Winifred lent me a bunch of books, you see. It reminded me of my art history classes from university. Some of the ideas are fascinating.'

'But isn't it all ridiculous and meaningless?' Gabriel asked, at a loss. 'Isn't it all paintings in varying shades of blue, and geometrical patterns that are supposed to represent philosophical concepts, and bunches of forks hung from ceilings? It's all pretentious nonsense! How can you think you like this sort of thing?'

'Some of it is very interesting, and meaningful, too. We had a long debate about the meaning of colour at the *vernissage*, actually. It gave me lots to think about.'

Gabriel shook his head. 'The meaning of colour... really. You might as well talk about the meaning of... chicken salad!'

Clarice sighed. 'Don't be childish, Gabriel. Can't you just support me in my venture?'

'Not if neither of us knows anything about it. I'm a banker, remember. You'll need a more coherent proposal if you want my approval.'

'Very funny. Do I need to remind you that it's my own money?'

'Need I remind you, darling,' Gabriel replied sarcastically, 'that as a married couple, our financial interests are joined till death do us part?'

Clarice sighed. 'Listen, darling, enough of this. I'm sorry for bringing money into it.' She stood up slowly, moving her silk robe flamboyantly about her. 'I think we should do something exciting tonight,' she said hesitantly.

'Like what?' Gabriel asked cautiously. Would it make dinner late? His stomach was beginning to grumble, and he was quite looking forward to sitting down with his paper afterwards.

Suddenly, without warning, Clarice grabbed her husband by the necktie. 'I think we should make love,' she said, pulling upwards cautiously. He could see a blush spreading across her cheeks, and could tell she was trembling slightly. Why this charade?

'*Chérie*,' he said gently, 'you're going to ruin my tie.'

'Yes,' she replied melodramatically, 'I'm going to ruin you, too! Let's do something... unusual!'

'Spicy chicken is unusual,' Gabriel said desperately, struggling against her choke hold. 'Darling, this really doesn't feel very good. This tie was expensive.'

'I want to make love to you!' Clarice cried. She pressed her face into his neck, whilst continuing to tighten her hold on the tie. Maybe she was drunk, after all. Did coffee have aphrodisiac properties? If only they could just eat their chicken.

'It's nearly six thirty,' Gabriel gasped, disentangling himself firmly. He pushed Clarice away by the shoulders as if she were a troublesome child, and brushed himself off, catching his breath. 'It is dinner time.'

'It doesn't have to be,' she said, slumping back into the couch, defeated. 'We don't have to be boring about everything. I met Chloë again this morning, you know...'

'... one of the girls, I presume.'

'Yes. Anyway, she will be one of my partners in modern art. She suggested initiating lovemaking in the daytime, to mix up our regular schedule. She told me I should be daring.' Clarice's lipstick had become smudged.

'So who else is in this group?' Gabriel asked, casting about for a neutral topic. 'Winifred was there, and this Chloë, and this Cat... Khad...'

'Khadija, yes. Khadija is half-Egyptian, very glamorous. Her husband is a very rich banker and they fund a lot of art together.'

She took a deep breath and exhaled sharply. 'She lives in Zurich, but travels up with Winifred once a month to have coffee with the other girls and talk about their next funding ventures. Our funding ventures.'

Gabriel did not comment. 'Who else, then?'

'Fleurie, who is tall and blonde and very intellectual. She's the serious one. She hates Globus. Then there's Chloë. She's a sort of Parisian revolutionary, with a hoarse voice from smoking. She's very sexy, she always wears short skirts. She doesn't have quite as much money as the others, but Khadija helps out with her portion. She only has to pay four thousand, instead of the eight thousand everyone else contributes.'

'Only four thousand!' Gabriel's tone was unreadable.

'Yes,' Clarice said stubbornly. 'And she has sex multiple times a day.'

'What kind of a stupid idea is that? You're bound to end up with... chafing, if not some sort of disease.'

'It's not stupid,' Clarice said firmly. 'It's French.'

'She sounds stupid,' Gabriel shot back, beginning to feel childish. Were the curtains pulled? What if the neighbours saw them in this ridiculous scene?

'Do you want to know how stupid Chloë is? She makes love to her boyfriends every two hours.'

'What? That's impossible. Nobody can do that. What sorts of boyfriends are these?'

'They're Swiss, too,' Clarice said cuttingly.

'Does she have several at once, then? She doesn't sound like a very nice girl. How did you two meet, anyway?'

'No! She's not like that. She settled here recently. Her father is terribly rich. He set her up in a business, spending millions and millions on it.'

'What kind of business?' Gabriel asked, grasping at straws in hopes of drawing the conversation away from sexual intercourse.

'A spa,' Clarice said grumpily.

'Do you mean a health farm?' he asked, his bad mood worsening by the second.

'A... It's a pool. An Oriental sort of... I mean, you can have manicures, steam baths. Exfoliation, gommage, depilation... Saunas.'

'They tried to talk us into having one of those at the chalet,' Gabriel said thoughtfully. 'I didn't like the idea of all that steam and nudity, but hot cedar wood sounded quite nice and relaxing.'

'Ugh, let's not talk about the chalet,' Clarice groaned. 'I want you now.'

'Clarice,' Gabriel said as patiently as he could, 'it's dinnertime. We can... do it before bed, if you really want. Just let's sit down and eat our chicken like normal, responsible Swiss adults.'

'It's like you need the goddamn *Financial Times* to be turned on,' Clarice shot back.

'Don't be ridiculous. Look, just the other morning I made an exception, so as to live up to your outrageous sexual expectations. I can't make new rules, new derogations, every time your hormones get the better of you. We have other things to do with our time, Clarice! I've had a long day at the office, I'm hungry and I'm tired. I am not in the mood for... rumpy-pumpy.'

'I spent all afternoon in a bath of fresh cream!' Clarice shouted back, sounding like she was on the verge of tears.

'Why on earth would you do that?' Gabriel asked gently. 'It sounds highly unhygienic.'

'Chloë said it would make my skin smooth,' she replied in a small voice. 'And Marilyn Monroe used to do it.'

'Oh dear,' he said, at a loss for words.

'You don't think I'm attractive,' Clarice said, dabbing at her eyes with a corner of her silk robe. 'Maybe the girls are right about plastic surgery. Is it my ears? Should they be smaller? Is it my waist? I could reduce it from 28 inches to 24 if I get... suction? I mean lipo, liposuction?'

'What?' said Gabriel.

'Cosmetic surgery,' she sniffled.

'You intend to paint your face?'

'No,' she said. 'It's surgery. See, I have this wrinkle on my forehead I would like to eliminate. Maybe you'll find me attractive then. Is it because I'm old?'

'What wrinkle? I can't even see it.' Gabriel tried to keep his voice soft, but he was quite close to snapping at his wife again.

'Chloë said there was a wrinkle,' she said. 'There she was, all skinny in her tiny skirt and drinking this ridiculous sugared coffee all topped with whipped double Italian cream, the kind they make cakes with, and she tells me that perhaps I could do something about that wrinkle, a little tuck. She was smoking those thin Virginia cigarettes of hers. Do you think I could use a little tuck?' She moved her face close to his, her eyes wide open. Gabriel gently took her by the shoulders and pushed her back.

'Darling, I think we should eat dinner,' he said.

'I can't. It will make me fat and then I will need more suction.'

'What the hell is suction?'

'Liposuction... they remove the fat from you with little... hoovers. At least that's what Khadija said. She lost two dress sizes. Now she always wears Chanel.'

'Darling, you already always wear Chanel, and you're already so thin. Anyway, the process sounds disgusting. What on earth do they do with the fat?'

Clarice shrugged. 'Throw it away, or sell it to science,' she said. 'But it's not only that. They have more discreet interventions, like making your eyes almond-shaped.'

'How horrific,' Gabriel said. 'And then it lasts forever?'

'Oh no,' she said. 'You have to go back. Like changing the tyres on your car. Nothing lasts forever.'

'You're putting me off my dinner,' he said, 'and that is difficult because I am starving.' He took her hand and squeezed gently. 'Is it time for dinner yet? Come now, just a little bit of chicken.'

'I don't want to,' she pouted. 'I had two *pain au raisins* this morning in the café in Carouge. It will make me fat. Chloë says surgery can improve your lovemaking, too, as an older woman.'

Gabriel shuddered perceptibly. '*Ma chérie*, I don't want you to talk about this surgery business any more. You are an intelligent adult woman. It is totally normal for you to have a few wrinkles. I... like you the way you are. You are forty-two, and you are my wife. I do not want some quack doctor dissecting you.'

'He's not a quack doctor.'

'Who isn't?'

'Fabrice.'

'Who is Fabrice?'

'Never mind.' Clarice slumped suddenly onto his shoulder, and kissed him softly on the neck. Gabriel sighed. 'It's just an hour's surgery,' she murmured.

'Who are these people you are spending all this time with? And why on earth in Carouge? They don't seem like a very good influence.'

'Carouge has lower taxes; you ought to move your bank over there,' she murmured, her voice muffled by his shoulder. 'It's a perfectly decent location to encourage modern art. I don't know why you're so threatened by change.'

Gabriel shook his head and wrapped his arm around Clarice's shoulder. 'You are a Calvinist, my dear. Remember your family, your values. I don't like the changes I see in you.'

Clarice shook off her husband's arm. 'Well, they are my choices. Now, instead of making me cry, I suggest you come upstairs with me and... cheer me up.'

'Can you not just put the damned chicken in the oven?' Gabriel snapped. 'I've had a stressful day at work.'

'No!' Clarice said, standing up unsteadily and throwing off her robe. 'No more talk of Calvinism, or Carouge.' She was wearing only black stockings, that fastened above the knee. 'Now, it is time to make love! You have to love me. It is your duty as a husband.'

'I'm so tired,' Gabriel said quietly. 'I've just been handling billions of dollars and explaining it all in hand signs because these Arabs can't speak English. Now I come home and my wife is crying about wanting... suction, and refusing to make me dinner, and this is supposed to make me want to make love?'

'Yes!' cried Clarice, spinning around in her stockings. It made Gabriel quite dizzy. 'It will reduce your boredom and stress! It will make you feel good! See how I have no more hair, anywhere on my body? I had it all removed!'

'Can you just close the curtains?' he said uneasily. 'What if the neighbours see?'

'I don't care! Besides, no-one can see through that window! Only you can see me, my dear husband. See how soft my skin is, how milky-white after that cream bath I took? Come caress me. It will ease your billion-dollar troubles.' She walked to the sofa, and took her husband's hands in hers. Her palms were clammy, and still trembled slightly. 'Come upstairs,' she said. 'For once, I want you without dinner, without pressure. I don't want to be wearing my pyjamas, and I don't want you thinking of the *Financial Times*, or timing it in your head – yes, I know you do that. I've heard you muttering under your breath. Come upstairs.'

'This is ridiculous, Clarice,' Gabriel said as calmly as he could. 'What do you want, some kind of anarchy?'

'I want variety in my life! It's always the same with you, Gabriel. The same hour, the same damn paper. It's impossible. The world is changing, Gabriel. Banking is changing. Some rich people have Arabic names, now. Some clients don't speak French. They still have the millions you need. You are going to have to get used to it. Art has evolved, too. It's not just dead fruit anymore, or children standing at their parents' bedsides. Impressionism happened. Art Deco happened. The whole of modernism happened. Art can be wild and geometric, now. Art can be urinals, or animal parts in plastic, now. But you haven't changed, Gabriel, and it's killing me.' She grabbed his hands once more and pulled him up from the couch.

'Clarice, I have no idea what you're talking about.'

'Come upstairs. I promise I'll stop talking if you just come upstairs with me. Please.'

Heaving a deep sigh, Gabriel stood up slowly and followed his wife's milk-white legs up the stairs. When he arrived in the bedroom, he found Clarice draped oddly across the bed. She appeared to be in a state of some exertion.

'Come help me move this mattress!' she panted. Gabriel suddenly understood that she was attempting to pull the entire mattress off the antique oak bed frame and onto the floor.

'Clarice, have you lost your mind?' he rebuked her.

'Help me!' she cried, with such mad insistence that he had no choice but to join her. Gabriel went to the other side of the bed, and threw his shoulder up against the heavy mattress. Slowly, it shifted over the side of the bed, then finally fell to the floor in a series of heavy thuds. Clarice wiped her brow. 'Now!' she said unsteadily. 'We make love!'

She tossed her dark, sweaty hair back over her shoulders, and leaned down to undo her stockings. Gabriel edged back uneasily. 'Do not look away from me,' she said, her breathing still unsteady from the exertion. 'I want you to make me feel beautiful. See how I'm reflected in the mirror? Look at me, Gabriel. I want you to undress me in the daylight, and I want you to make love to me.'

'Are you doing a strip-tease?' Gabriel asked in horror. 'What is this, some kind of joke? This is not a whore-house!'

'This is not a whore-house and I'm not stripping,' Clarice said soothingly, after a moment's hesitation. 'There is no music. I just want you to watch me undress. I want you to see all of me. My top. My bottom,' she clarified.

'I don't know what you're talking about,' Gabriel sighed. 'Can we please close the curtains? The neighbours can definitely see in this window.'

'So what?' Clarice said coquettishly. 'Let them look, if they want.'

Gabriel looked horrified. 'That's it,' he said, crossing the room with difficulty, since most of the floor was taken up by the mattress. He pulled the curtains shut in one brusque movement, plunging the room into darkness, and kicked off his velvet slippers. 'Fine, Clarice. Fine,' he said, angrily removing his shirt, ignoring Clarice's whimpers of protest. 'If you want us to have intercourse right now, we will have intercourse right now.' He walked back to the mattress; then, reconsidering, went back to the windows, reached through the curtains and slammed the shutters closed. 'There! Now it is dark enough for us to pretend it is an appropriate time for this sort of nonsense. Come on, then. Lie down. I will do what you want for approximately one quarter of an hour, and then you will go down to the kitchen and make me chicken.' He lowered himself stiffly into a sitting position on the mattress and removed his black socks carefully.

'Touch me,' Clarice said hesitantly. 'Roll with me on this wonderful mattress.'

'There are limits,' Gabriel muttered, closing his eyes. 'I will most certainly *not* roll.'

Chapter Eleven
Geneva, 1995

The orchestra began to tune up, the sound of their chords mingling with the mutters from the audience. The Grand Théâtre was full of glowing faces in evening dress, sipping from champagne flutes, and excitedly handing opera glasses back and forth. A circular pastel fresco of angels gazed down benevolently on the audience.

Clarice leaned over the gilded rim of their box to get a better view of the other spectators. Yes, there was the president of one of the major commercial banks, his tall, blonde daughter looking immaculate in forest green silk. Or *was* that his daughter? It certainly wasn't his wife. There were Winifred and Dieter, soberly dressed, holding hands. To one side, she saw the mayor of Carouge, apparently on his own. There were Khadija and her husband, two rotund forms in Chanel, snacking. She recognised the owners of a few modern art gallery owners from the Old Town, and made a mental note to speak to them during the interval. First, however, she was going to enjoy *La Wally*, a rarely staged opera by Catalini, a contemporary of Puccini – or so Winifred had told her. Clarice couldn't say that she was as obsessed with opera as her friend was, but over the last few years she had certainly attended a number of performances, and enjoyed herself enormously. One thing she hadn't known about opera was how dressed up people still were. She took a certain baroque pleasure in people-watching, and showing off her own expensive clothes. She was still beautiful, though she had to dye her hair now to cover up the strands of grey. Smiling, Clarice loosened her midnight blue velvet opera cape, revealing a floor-length glittering gold dress with broad shoulders. Gabriel sighed.

'Shall we get champagne at the interval?' Clarice whispered excitedly.

'Very well,' Gabriel replied, patting her hand. He had not aged as well as his wife, and in the faint lighting of the opera hall, his eyes appeared sunken into his face.

At last, the dark red curtain was pulled back, and a cardboard mountain scene appeared, topped with painted white snow. The strings swelled into the chords of the overture, and the chorus appeared onstage. Tyrolean villagers strolled back and forth in the shadow of the Alps, and silhouettes of vultures circled above. The opera had begun.

In the interval, the couple wandered down the stairs towards the main entry hall. Outside, Place de Neuve was illuminated with golden lights, and the night had turned a deep blue. Clarice sighed happily. Gabriel rolled his eyes.

'Clarice!' a familiar voice called out, and Winifred appeared, wearing a simple grey dress.

'Gabriel!' Dieter was by her side, having forsaken the lederhosen for a plain linen suit. He was smiling.

'Smile,' Clarice hissed at her husband.

'So, what do you think?' Dieter asked, as proudly as if he had written the opera himself.

'I love it,' Winifred exclaimed. 'I can't believe it's not performed more often! But then, Geneva does insist on changing its opera programme incredibly regularly. I suppose it's because the majority of seats are reserved by people with season tickets; they're there every week without fail, which means the programme has to change every week, too.'

'I think it's wonderful,' Clarice said, 'this sort of melodramatic, romantic fairy tale. It's ridiculous, but it's a lot of fun.'

'Yes, absolutely!' Winifred replied. 'The brave hunter, the sad song, the virginal mountain beauty, the repressive patriarch... It's so traditional and so radical all at once! Have you read the libretto? Do you know what happens in the end?'

Clarice shook her head. 'I like the surprise,' she said. 'I can't wait to find out.'

'The whole thing is ludicrous,' Gabriel said shortly, adjusting his tie in a brusque movement. 'I mean, why is there a dead bear onstage? I certainly hope it's not real.'

Dieter laughed. 'My dear friend, private banker and unshakeable realist. Well, I hope you enjoy the second half. There is going to be an avalanche, but don't worry, it's not real!' The couple wandered off, Winifred happily leaning on her husband's shoulder.

'Darling, shall we get some champagne?' Clarice risked a small peck on her husband's cheek. 'I'd like a little *tartine*, too, with *rillettes*.'

Gabriel sighed. 'Ten years ago, you'd never tasted duck rillettes. Now we must constantly pay ridiculous prices for your greasy treats. If you're not careful, you'll end up fat like your friend Khadija.'

Clarice stared at her husband as if failing to recognise him. 'Get me the Deutz champagne,' she said coldly. 'I will find the *rillettes* myself.'

'Deutz? Whatever are you thinking, Clarice? You know Taittinger is a client of mine. Look, I already agreed to this indulgence. Can't you be content with this?'

'What's the difference? Deutz tastes nicer, you know it does. I think the bubbles are finer, and the flavour is more biscuity.'

'Since when are you a connoisseur of fine alcohol? You'll end up an alcoholic, then, as well as fat. As for the difference, well, Taittinger already costs one hundred and twenty francs a bottle. Deutz is over two hundred.'

'But you can afford that,' Clarice said, hearing her own voice turn to a sulk. 'And I like it.' One of the gallery owners walked by, but she did not feel like engaging in conversation.

'Well, you're certainly acquiring new tastes here, my dear Clarice. What's next, a trip to the Tour d'Argent in Paris?'

'Oh, that would be lovely!' Clarice replied with a fake smile. 'I've already been to all the three-star restaurants in Geneva, and I'm rather bored of them. I'd like to go to the Bristol, to the Ritz in Paris. I hear there are two new Michelin-starred restaurants in London. Ooh, let's go to London!' Her tone softening, she grabbed her husband's hand imploringly. 'I want to enjoy this life, Gabriel. Don't you want to? We are not peasants. We have no children.' Suddenly inspired, she spun round in her golden dress. 'My children will be champagne and the biggest suite in the Dorchester...'

'You're out of your mind. That costs more than ten thousand francs a night. We are not oil magnates, Clarice. We are not princes, and we are not living in some fairy-tale opera, even if you insist on wearing clothes made of glitter. We are not oligarchs, sultans or tribal chiefs. We are Swiss. We are Calvinists. Most of all, we are reasonable people.'

'You're making seven million Swiss francs a year, *chéri*,' Clarice replied, stopping cold in her lilting dance. 'Don't pretend we're Calvinistic paupers. Come now, where are the *rillettes*?'

'This is not the golden age you seem to think it is, Clarice,' Gabriel snapped. 'Some of our French clients are suffering from troubles in real estate.'

'Don't be ridiculous. I may not be a banker, but I know how well your bank did in the 1987 crisis. I know how well you are still doing. Bank Von Mipatobeau triumphed, and held steady when everyone else got carried away and failed. Your bank is rich.'

'Not rich enough for that.'

'Then maybe it should be. If you don't think you can afford champagne when you earn seven million francs, maybe you need a few million more. You're the banker. Go on, then. If you want more money, go earn it. Go and talk to Calvin.'

'Clarice, you've become greedy,' he said, lowering his voice. People were staring. 'These girls of yours have been a terrible influence.'

'They've been the best thing in my life for years. Haven't you followed the growth of my gallery? I know you keep an eye on it, waiting for my new investments to collapse, though you wouldn't set foot in there. Well, have you noticed I've been quietly making a fortune? The girls have an eye for modern art. They know what they're doing. Following their leads, I've made a few solid choices myself. This modern stuff sells like hotcakes.'

Gabriel made a dismissive sound. 'Yes, but it's hardly worth anything. A thousand, at most, surely. There can't be that much interest in a conservative old town like Geneva! All these animal carvings and bed sheets covered in glue.'

'Well, you'd be surprised. The last painting I sold, I made three thousand.'

'That's nothing,' he scoffed. 'You used to make, what, a hundred thousand per sale on the nineteenth-century art?'

'Yes,' said Clarice, 'but those sales were almost an anomaly. I used to make a hundred thousand on a Hodler or Anker maybe twice, three times a year if I was lucky. The modern stuff sells every week; sometimes several times a week. People love it. Even some of my old clients have let themselves be tempted by the new artists! No, I swear it's true. You should come in one day and see. Every once in a while, I still sell one of the old masters. I make a good margin, and I'm on the right track to make a great deal more.'

'Well, you're clearly not making quite enough, since you're still dependent on me as your husband. If you're so desperate for people to buy you champagne, why don't you just ask one of your... girls?'

Clarice sighed. 'I don't understand why you have such disdain for my business partners. Don't you ever want to live more like them, even just a little? Why can't you just enjoy a little freedom? Use this money that you've accumulated through such hard work. Look, you'd easily be able to pay for a private jet to take me to London. You wouldn't even have to come along, but if you did we could have such fun!' Gabriel's gaze remained steely, and Clarice faltered. 'What about Cannes, or Monaco, or the Canary Islands?' she continued, keeping her voice brightly positive. 'We could visit art galleries together. I'd love to travel with Khadija to the Gulf...'

'Why don't you ask your *business partner* Khadija to lend you her private plane, then?' Gabriel's tone was scathing.

'Khadija just rents her private plane,' Clarice said calmly. 'I want to be able to rent one too. But if you don't want to travel, why don't we just have a big party at home; with champagne and caviar, and some people from the art world? You could invite some of your banking contacts. Everyone would mingle and I could wear a new dress and it would be so much fun! I know you'd love it.'

'There is no way. This is the limit, Clarice.' From the shift in the tone of his voice, and the crimson shade of his cheeks, Clarice knew she was dangerously close to being shouted at in the lobby of the Grand Théâtre. She cast apologetic glances around at the other opera-goers. 'Let me tell you something, Clarice,' Gabriel said, standing very close to her. 'Do you remember our marriage vows?'

'Yes,' she said quietly.

'Do you remember how they talk about obedience? Well, I want to exercise that trump card now. Obey me in this one thing: be a reasonable person. These excesses are unhealthy, and a terrible waste of money. You are a middle-aged Swiss woman, for God's sake. Act like one. Why spend three hundred francs a person on a meal when you can eat well for forty – or for twenty, at home with your spicy chicken? Do not let yourself be corrupted in this way. Take commercial planes, for they are perfectly comfortable. Even some of these new discount airlines are quite reasonable. There is no need for first class. There is no need for private planes. There is no need for extravagance in fulfilling a person's basic needs. For instance, this dress of yours... I didn't want to say anything, but it's a joke. Why do you need to show off in this way?'

'I thought it was beautiful,' Clarice said quietly. 'It reminded me of a Saint Laurent gown that appeared on the catwalks a few months ago. And you've already said something... twice.'

'But why this interest in high fashion?' Gabriel asked in despair. 'It's such a waste of time and money!'

'It's art,' Clarice replied. 'Besides, I'm pretty, I'm thin, and I still look good in these clothes. That won't last. Let me appreciate the good things in life, Gabriel. Come on,' she pleaded, 'get me a glass of Deutz champagne before the third act starts!'

'I buy you Chanel suits every three years,' he shot back. 'How is that insufficient? You are under no circumstances to start buying suits by Jean-Louis Scherrer or any of these crazy new guys like Gaultier and Valentino and Armani. It's all glitz.'

'Well, buy me more interesting Chanel suits, then. I'm tired of all this grey and blue. And I want it to be better tailored, to show off my body. So other people can appreciate me, since my husband doesn't.'

'As for the champagne,' Gabriel added imperiously, 'it's too late anyway. It's your own fault for starting this ridiculous argument.'

At this moment, the bell rang, signalling the end of the intermission. Clarice glared at her husband. 'I fully expect you to buy me two bottles this weekend,' she said, 'to make up for this embarrassment.'

'Embarrassment?' Gabriel hissed, grabbing her arm and marching her towards the stairs. '*Embarrassment?* I'm the one who's embarrassed! Look at us, arguing in the theatre lobby like a couple of fools! You should be buying *me* champagne! In fact, if you have all this money lying around from your modern art investments, why don't you?'

Clarice shook him off, her cheeks burning. But Gabriel was not finished. 'You know exactly why, *chérie*. It's because you're not financially independent yet. You need me, and my money. Let me just ask you one question: who bought these opera tickets?'

———◆◆◆———

They walked the rest of the way to their seats in silence, Clarice glowering, Gabriel with a grim smile. The curtain rose on the third act, revealing a stage draped in black. In the distance, the cardboard alpine peaks still glowed sharp and white. Somewhere, a church bell was tolling. Someone began to sing, Clarice couldn't really remember who. Was this the part when the girl was transformed into an edelweiss plant? What a ridiculous concept. Clarice stared at her knees, straightening her gold dress; she loved that dress. She darted a glance over at Gabriel, who was staring stony-faced at the characters onstage. 'As if you care what happens in this onstage romance!' she hissed at him, suddenly overcome with rage. 'You cold... banker!'

'Be quiet, Clarice,' Gabriel whispered back, 'or I will take you home.'

Clarice was silent for the rest of the opera, though she hardly noted the ending of the story. When an avalanche of dry ice fog flooded the stage, she almost wished it was real, so it could sweep them away. At one point, she was pretty sure Gabriel was snoring lightly. As soon as people began clapping, she stood up stiffly and wrapped her cape tightly around her. The couple walked out before the audience had even finished applauding, descending the deserted velvet stairs and crossing the empty lobby. When Gabriel held the door open for her, Clarice angrily marched through and off towards Place de Neuve. A misty drizzle was falling, glowing in the lamplight. She shivered in the cold.

'Where are you going, Clarice?' Gabriel asked ,as quietly as he could, for she was already quite a way ahead of him.

'I am walking home,' she said.

'Don't you want a taxi, in those heels?' he asked, bemused. 'When was the last time you took a fifteen minute walk?'

'No!' she shouted back. 'I do not want a taxi! I don't care about my shoes! I should like some air. Do by all means pay for a taxi for yourself, if that is what you want. After all, it's your money. You do what you want with it. And if I don't like the walk, I'll take off my shoes and walk barefoot.'

'Clarice!' Gabriel said a little more loudly. 'You were the one who ordered a taxi here in the first place. You said your feet hurt. You said it was going to rain. If we are going to have a crisis about this, can we not wait until we're home?'

Clarice spun around and walked back quickly towards her husband. 'Oh no, Gabriel,' she said, rapping him smartly on the lapel with her handbag. 'Not a chance. This crisis is happening now. After all, don't you think I'm at fault? The crisis is coming head-on. This is my new way of exaggerating, right? My capricious taste in champagne and highfalutin suites, versus your taste for living in a... matchbox in the old town, drinking flat water, and wearing the same colour ties? No, Gabriel, this crisis is inevitable. I cannot accept your way of life anymore. I am in my fifties: if I am to rebel and enjoy my life, I must fight for it now... right here in the street, if I must. Even if my hair will go terribly frizzy in this rain.'

'This is unacceptable,' Gabriel said, giving a little stamp with his right foot. 'If this is what going to the opera does to you, I'm never letting you go again. You damn melodramatic...' He coughed, swallowed, and paused to do up the buttons on his suit.

'Look, Clarice,' he eventually said, infuriatingly calmly, 'you simply must be more reasonable than this. You are going a dangerous, speculative route, just like French real estate. You know prices in central Paris used to be twenty-five thousand Swiss francs a metre? Now it's down to seven thousand. Everything has crashed. Fortunes can be lost, Clarice. You can't just spend all my money on champagne. There's no way. You may as well be holding a match to my fortune, our lifestyle, our home. If you spend all the money on alcohol and bright red Scherrer suits and travel in private jets, it'll eventually all be gone. You will come crashing down, and you will burn.' He lowered his voice again. 'Let me remind you of something, my dear. I have the key. The key is called money. This gives me a certain amount of authority in this relationship. Leverage, if you will. Who is the Swiss banker in this marriage? That's right. I've got the law on my side. So let me tell you this: you are teetering on the edge here. And if you fall, do you really think your crazy modern art friends will catch you? No. Your Calvinistic Swiss banker of a husband will save you. Deep down, you know this.'

'Do you know what the Calvinists did to the cathedral in the Old Town?' Clarice asked calmly. 'They ruined it. The hacked out the most beautiful decorations. They broke the stone statues, the stained glass, and they took those wonderful, carved, gilded cornices. They pillaged it. And then do you know what you did, you Calvinists, you stingy bankers? You kept those decorations hidden in the basement of the museum. Locked up with the mould and the dust. Now, why would you do a thing like that? Let beauty go to waste? Either for fear that the cathedral would return to its former beauty, or because you were eventually planning to sell them. Well, who's miserable and calculating now?' She hit Gabriel with her handbag again, not very hard. 'Is that what you want, Gabe? To keep me hidden away, mouldering like those fabulous friezes and carvings?

Do you want a pretty, cold stone wife who won't care, locked up in Saint Antoine? I have nothing else, Gabriel. No babies, no life, no family, no husband to make love to. Do you know when the last time you undressed me was? Three months ago. I am gathering dust. You have become impossible to reach. What does it take to excite you, Gabriel? A new Saint Laurent suit? Some ice in your flat water? Maybe a splash of rum in your coffee? Even just a bit of cream and sugar. Does anything excite you other than making money, Gabriel? Is the *Financial Times* your pornography?'

'Are you quite done?' Gabriel asked quietly. 'If so, let's please get a cab home. Look at your long dress, you can't even walk.'

'I'm just getting started,' Clarice replied. 'Let me ask you something else, if you're so embarrassed by the notion of sex. How do you make your money? No, don't try to answer. Let me tell you: you make money out of the misery of others. If it wasn't for other people's money, you would not be making a penny. People that put their so-called trust in you! What decisions do you make, Gabriel? None at all. You just take other people's money, sit on it, and add two per cent. You make your margin without taking any risks at all.'

'Clarice, you attacks are so ill-informed as to be far from hurtful. To answer your question, and your bitter, rancorous comments: no, I am not sexually aroused by the *Financial Times*. No, I do not want cream or sugar in my coffee. And no, I do not make money out of the misery of others.' Gabriel's face had grown quite red again, his glasses were awry, and his usually immaculate hair was falling in his eyes. 'If you knew anything about banking, you would be ashamed of yourself. Von Mipatobeau is actually planning to take more risks and make more money, though I can promise you, you won't see a penny of it. Yes, we are entering a new era of banking, but we are still Swiss bankers. Maybe you're right, Clarice. Maybe we Swiss bankers are cold. We are bloodless, we are greedy, even totally inhuman. You're right. But who puts bread on our table? Which of us is making seven million francs a year? What you don't understand, Clarice, is that we have to be careful. These changes come slowly.'

'Well, if you're predicting changes, perhaps I can I look forward to you becoming a human being, when you make this new fortune.'

'We can't let ourselves be corrupted by our high margins,' Gabriel said patiently, 'or defined by our incomes. I don't want you to be corrupted, my dear, because you are my wife and we live together, and because I love you.'

'That is your weakest argument yet,' Clarice replied coldly. 'As if you can love someone without kissing them, hugging them, taking them to bed. I am a statue in a cupboard, although you are the one lying in bed hard and cold as stone.'

She walked swiftly away, up the steep and narrow street leading back to the Old Town. Gabriel was left standing in the rain.

Chapter Twelve

It was windy on the shores of Lake Lugano, and the turquoise waters rippled lightly in the sun. Gabriel adjusted his Italian hat, for fear of the wind dishevelling his impeccable salt-and-pepper hair. It was late September: the trees were decked in bright summer green leaves, mixed with the first gold and crimson of autumn. A few had even started to fall, drifting across the path along the corniche. Gabriel nudged one aside with his toe, thoughtfully.

A golden-haired woman with tanned skin appeared, a tiny dog walking ahead of her on a leash. '*Ciao,*' she whispered, with an outrageous wink. Was that a tattoo between her...? Gabriel shook his head and walked on. He always took pleasure in morning walks, even in the city, but it saddened him to be away from the chalet this time of year. Clarice might even get to go there before him, this autumn, a thought which was rather galling, since she so blatantly despised the countryside. However, she seemed to have come up with some sort of harebrained scheme to take her girlfriends up there for a 'girls' weekend,' and how could he discourage her? Gabriel kicked a chestnut into the jade waters. At least it would mean some peace and quiet in Saint Antoine.

'*Mio Dio, stai attento!*' a woman suddenly shrieked. 'Be careful, *signore!*'

He looked around for the source of the voice, but before he could locate the Italian woman, a small, barking sausage-like object had appeared at Gabriel's feet, and begun gnawing at the bottom of his trousers.

'You will hit my baby with your kicking!' the voice continued imperiously.

'I beg your pardon?' Gabriel asked, whirling around and coming face to face with his interlocutor, a beautiful woman in her late thirties. As their eyes met, her expression softened somewhat, and she drew a manicured hand to her mouth, prettily. 'Oh!' she said. 'I am sorry.'

'If your animal could please stop consuming my Balenciaga suit, that would be most agreeable,' Gabriel said curtly, wiggling his foot with as much dignity as he could muster in the circumstances.

The woman giggled. 'He is playful, *signore*,' she said. 'Like me.'

'Right,' said Gabriel. 'Charming, I'm sure, but I'm afraid I have a conference to attend.'

'He's a dachshund, you know,' she continued, laying her dainty hand on his sleeve. 'They're very sweet... very affectionate. Again, he takes after me.'

'I really must be off,' he said, shaking his foot a little more. The dog seemed to take this as further encouragement, though the woman narrowed her eyes. At last, giving a small kick, Gabriel managed to disconnect the dog. 'I bid you good day,' he said quickly, hurrying away.

'My baby!' he heard her exclaim behind him.

Gabriel only slowed his footsteps when it occurred to him that it might look as if he were running away from the sausage-like thing. He adjusted his hat. The conference was not a lie: he was, once more, tasked with the duty of representing Von Mipatobeau at an international meeting. This time, the question was whether the bank would begin to expand abroad. Gabriel had his reservations about the concept as a whole, but branching out across Switzerland didn't seem like a bad place to start. He let his gaze travel the length of the lake, taking in the misty mountains in the distance. Oh, to be high in the Alps, hiking towards the peaks!

'*Buon giorno*,' a low voice purred, and he looked back from the waters to meet the sultry gaze of another beautiful Italian. The woman was in her fifties, this time, dressed in a smart Valentino suit. She looked like she could have once been an actress: her hair was dark, and swept up above her big black eyes, which were heavily emphasised with eyeliner. In her pocket, a very small and scruffy dog wearing a pink harness was lapping at her neck. Gabriel did not respond, eyeing the chihuahua with distrust, and the woman smiled and moved on. Lost in his own thoughts, he looked back out over the waters. Plenty of money came into Lugano from Italy. There were bound to be hundreds of potential clients to be found here.

But then again, this was not their territory, not their culture. Yes, it was Switzerland, but it was a different Switzerland. Perhaps Von Mipatobeau should just stick to Geneva? It was his decision, after all. There was plenty of time. No pressure. His colleagues had delegated him and Thomas to make the call: not that poor foolish Thomas was any good at making decisions under pressure! Why on earth had he decided to take Thomas with him? As a shield against the Germans, of course, but still. Caroline would most likely be running the office alone in his absence. A momentary pang struck him at the thought of his loyal secretary, with her grey hair and her perfect cardigans. When would he be back behind his dear old oak desk? He did not enjoy holidays.

As he walked on for another few minutes, his path crossed another Italian beauty: this time, a young woman in a lovely flowery dress, carrying a small dog in her Chanel handbag. This time, the woman did not have time to speak, for the dog shouted out its greetings first. Gabriel's face clearly discouraged the beautiful young woman from any further attempts at interaction. He did not smile, but he gave a small bow, in respect. As he walked away, he heard the beauty mutter a few words in Italian – chastising her animal, perhaps. *Good*, he thought. Nasty little things they were.

It started to drizzle slightly. *Thank God I've brought this hat!* Gabriel checked his watch, sighed and turned around. It was time to go hunting.

'*Ach*, I just don't see why we have to be here at all,' Thomas was whining, fiddling with a loose thread on his embroidered waistcoat.

'Do be quiet,' Gabriel said sharply. 'I had to bring you because you could be useful. With the Germans, I mean.'

'But everyone here is Italian!'

It certainly felt Italian, Gabriel was inclined to agree. The hotel lobby was a laughably baroque affair, all cream marble, velvet drapes and gilded paint. A rush of languages greeted the two men:

Italian, English, French, Japanese and German mingled together indistinguishably, with only one language more present than the others. Gabriel shook his head, watching a group of tanned men with slicked-back hair gesticulate animatedly at each other. Was one of them miming... stirring?

'There do seem to be a lot of Italians in this tower of Babel,' he said. 'Then again, that was to be expected.'

'What are we doing here?' Thomas asked again, tugging at one of his blonde curls.

'We are here for Bank Von Mipatobeau,' Gabriel replied crisply. 'We are exactly in the right place. Everyone is here to make money, or more money; either by making new international contacts, by expanding, or by looking into portfolio management. As you know, Thomas, our bank is interested in the former two; and we can offer help with the latter.'

'But we are not Italian!' Thomas cried out in despair. 'I don't even speak Italian, or... Swiss Romansh!'

'You are not a peasant, Thomas. We are in Switzerland, and everyone loves a Swiss banker,' Gabriel said sternly. 'No matter what language they speak.'

'Snacks!' Thomas exclaimed, perking up considerably. He made a panicky movement towards the other side of the hall, so suddenly that his feet slipped slightly on the waxed parquet. 'And beer!'

'Stay right here with me,' Gabriel hissed, grabbing his sleeve. 'Come now, help me find people who aren't Italian.'

Thomas sighed. Gabriel ignored him, glancing around the room, seeking lederhosen. A cluster to the left hand side attracted his attention. He pulled at Thomas's sleeve. 'Come now.'

'They have beer!' Thomas whispered back, cheerily.

Gabriel scanned their ranks, wondering if Dieter might be found here. After all, CBS had a considerable international presence. But no; though there was one fedora topped with a pheasant feather, Dieter's grin was nowhere to be found.

'*Mein Gott*, there are so many Italians here,' a tall blonde man with a hook nose was saying, looking around the room as if in dread.

One of the German colleagues took a deep drink from his glass of beer. 'That is why we are here, gentlemen,' he said imperiously.

The first man nodded fiercely. 'Of course.'

'*Jawohl!*' Thomas said, mirroring his interlocutor with a series of violent nods.

There was a pause. 'Hello,' the tall man said suspiciously. 'Who are you?'

'*Schönee Weste*,' said the beer drinker. 'Nice waistcoat.'

'We are Genevois,' Gabriel said smoothly, holding out his hand. 'I'm sorry my colleague has no manners.'

The beer drinker wrinkled his nose. 'I thought you were German. What would you francophones be doing in this Italian place?'

Gabriel laughed. 'Exactly the same as you *Deutsche*, I'd imagine. Why does anyone come to Lugano?' he asked, leaning close to the first speaker, who jumped slightly.

'The women?' Thomas squeaked unconvincingly. The beer drinker gave a raucous laugh.

The blonde man narrowed his eyes. 'What do you mean?'

Gabriel cut in. 'Imagine,' he said, 'how many fortunes have travelled through this city packed into suitcases and briefcases and stuffed into jacket linings; how much money has been smuggled through by boat, road and walking for days over the mountains... maybe even on skis. This town has been built on international fortunes. We are all here to try to claim a piece of that international cake.'

'*Ja*, you're not wrong,' the tall man replied. 'But if you think we are interested in a partnership with Geneva, you are not as Swiss as you claim. The Italian money goes to Lugano, the German money goes to Zurich, just like the French money goes to Geneva. It has always been this way.'

'Yes, but we want to be international. Why are you here, then?'

'Contacts. And beer,' the second man replied gruffly.

'What kind of beer?' Thomas asked with interest. Gabriel sighed.

'You wouldn't be interested in a little portfolio management? Our bank is a small, family operation. Very intimate, very safe.'

'*Herr...* What is your name?'

'Gabriel de Puritigny.'

'*Herr* de Puritan... Puritigny, you surely do not think you can sell Swiss banking to Swiss bankers?'

'Surely the point of this conference is mingling?' Gabriel asked, bemused. 'Aren't you interested in international expansion? Zurich is already a bastion of Germanic culture and business.'

'Oh yes,' the man replied. 'You are right about that. We are interested in dealing with the other Germans.'

'Not other Swiss?' Gabriel pleaded.

'I am German!' Thomas piped up.

'I can see that,' the man replied patiently. 'My name is Engelbert. Do join us for a beer, gentlemen, but don't for a minute think we will be interested in dealing with your little Genevois bank. You'll have to go find some Parisians for that.'

Gabriel nodded curtly and walked off. After a moment, discovering his colleague was not with him, he marched back and grabbed his sleeve. Thomas yelped, spilling beer over himself. 'This conference is going to be stressful enough without me looking after you, like a particularly unruly teenage son,' Gabriel muttered in his ear. 'Now, come help me get some goddamn business contacts. Not beer-drinking buddies.'

'It's very nice beer, Gabe,' Thomas said apologetically.

'Don't you ever call me that.' He dropped his arm hastily, and brushed himself off.

'Excusa-me,' an Italian-accented voice piped up from his side. 'You are standing on my dog.'

'What?' Gabriel looked down and saw that, indeed, a very small dog was cowering between the Italian's navy-suited legs. Its claws were probably scratching the parquet. 'I beg your pardon,' he said with a smile. 'Gabriel de Puritigny.'

The Italian frowned. 'What?' he said.

Thomas gasped at the sight of the animal, and shoved Gabriel into the group of Italians. 'Poor puppy!' he exclaimed, dropping to the ground.

The Italian, finding Gabriel's face quite close to his, grabbed his hand and shook it enthusiastically. 'Er, hello,' he said. Extricating himself from the accidental embrace, he waved a hand at his small group of friends. 'We are from just across the border,' he added.

Thomas was lavishing love on the very small dog, squatting on the ground. '*Liebling, liebling,*' he could be heard muttering.

'I am from Geneva,' Gabriel said carefully, brushing himself off. 'But we do a lot of business with the Italians.'

The man laughed. 'You can't fool me with that one! Is this your first conference in Lugano?'

'It is,' Gabriel said slowly.

'Have you noticed that there isn't a single other Genevois present here? I'm willing to bet a bottle of champagne you won't be back next year.'

'We're looking to expand abroad,' Gabriel said a little desperately. 'We have a lot to offer...'

'We have all the Swiss bankers we need, right here in Lugano. And the weather is much nicer!'

Thomas's face was currently buried in the dog's stomach. The dog was wiggling its legs in joy.

Gabriel straightened his shoulders. 'The weather is lovely in Geneva,' he said. 'It has some of the lowest rainfall in Europe.'

The Italian laughed gaily. 'Very well,' he said. 'Perhaps I will come visit one day.' He turned back to his friends. 'Adriano, you had some kind of radical suggestion...'

'Perhaps we can join in your financial conversation, at least?' Gabriel suggested, a hint of desperation in his voice. 'Mightn't we learn something?'

The man gave him a steely look. 'Adriano?'

A rather plump man in a pearl-grey suit nodded. 'Oregano,' he said.

Gabriel looked down at Thomas on the floor. Thomas looked up in confusion.

'Oregano?' The first man shook his head. 'I'm not sure, I find the taste rather bitter myself.'

Thomas suddenly stood bolt upright, letting the dog drop to the ground with a yelp. 'Are they talking in code?' he hissed at Gabriel, pulling him away from the group.

Gabriel sighed and pushed his colleague away. 'I don't think so. I think they are talking about food. You smell like dog fur.' He cleared his throat and turned back towards the group. 'Gentlemen, I wonder if you could explain something to me.' The Italian men looked up in exasperation. 'I promise it has nothing to do with banking, or cooking. As I was walking by the lake,' he continued, 'I saw many beautiful Italian women with tiny dogs. One even winked at me!'

The men nodded with hesitant approval, intrigued.

'The dog winked at you?' asked Thomas, confused.

'Now, why should that be? I asked myself,' Gabriel continued, ignoring his colleague. 'So many of them, walking in the late morning all alone.'

'Why indeed would an Italian woman wink at a Swiss man?' The Italian roared with laughter.

Gabriel raised his eyebrows. 'Indeed. I thought about this for a long time as I walked along your beautiful lake. So I came up with some answers. I decided some of these were probably the wives of millionaires, with nothing better to do than sleep late and go for constitutionals. Others will be heiresses having moved here to better survey their inherited fortunes, or widows whose elderly husbands perished in slightly suspicious circumstances. All dabbing their eyes with handkerchiefs, so sad about their dead fathers or husbands!' Thomas coughed lightly. Gabriel's tone had, indeed, become rather caustic. 'Young women are some of our best clients, you see. Rich men who have worked day and night tend to die early; it's a statistical fact. Oh, and I came up with one more category of woman: ladies of the night, who made their money early and have come here to spend it. That would explain the winking, at least.' He stopped and straightened his tie. 'I bid you good day, gentlemen.'

Gabriel spun round, took Thomas's arm and walked off.

'Gabriel,' Thomas said hesitantly, 'did you just insult a number of

IN BED WITH A SWISS BANKER

Italian women in front of a group of Italian men?'

'Nothing of the sort,' Gabriel said gaily. 'I was just sharing some of my thoughts from this morning. God, those little dogs were hideous. Can you see the cuff of my trousers?'

Thomas immediately dropped to his knees.

'Get up, get up, you fool!' Gabriel hissed, pulling his colleague up by the shoulders. 'How many beers have you had? Are you drunk?'

'I simply wanted to verify the state of your trousers!' Thomas explained, a pained expression on his face. 'You *asked* me to look!'

Gabriel shook his head. 'Sometimes I just don't know why I hired you,' he said.

'Is it because I am handsome and German?' Thomas volunteered.

Gabriel sighed. 'What time is the first study group?' he asked.

'Two o'clock, after the buffet. I think the first one is about expansion and international banking. Then at four o'clock there's one about commercial banking – we can skip that. The third is about new products. I don't know what that's about.'

Gabriel was quite impressed by his companion's memory, until he realised that Thomas was reading off a series of notes, scribbled in ink on his arm.

'Oh, you wouldn't want to miss that last one,' an American voice suddenly boomed. A shadow fell over Gabriel and Thomas, which they quickly realised was from the brim of a large hat. A cloud of cologne came with it. 'There'll be real cutting-edge discussions going on there. Brave new world kind of stuff.'

'Hello!' Thomas said cheerily, wiping the ink off his arm with his shirt cuff. 'Your hat is very large. Are you afraid of sunburn?'

'What, here in Europe? Not a chance. Have you ever been to Texas, kid?'

'I've never been sunburned in a hotel,' Thomas said, squinting. 'Is Texas in Mexico?'

'I don't believe we've met,' Gabriel intervened.

The man laughed uproariously. 'Bob,' he said holding out his hand to Thomas, then to Gabriel. 'You're Swiss?'

'Yes,' Gabriel said in relief, shaking the man's hand. 'Please excuse my colleague.'

'Oh, we all have strange colleagues,' Bob said with a wink. 'Come meet mine!' He nodded in the direction of a small group of people at the other side of the room, and began to walk towards them.

Gabriel and Thomas exchanged a glance. 'Americans!' Thomas hissed, as if they had stumbled across a rare breed of insect.

'Indeed,' Gabriel said smoothly, adjusting his already straight tie. 'Well, we're having no luck with Europeans. Why not try further abroad?'

'Because they're evil,' Thomas said calmly. 'We can't do business with Americans!'

'Oh yes we can,' replied Gabriel steadily. 'Go get yourself a beer, Thomas, or a glass of milk.'

'But you are so suspicious of the Americans!'

'Well, times are changing, Thomas. Meet me when you've calmed down. And brush the dog fur off your face, please.' He walked over.

Pre-packaged mortgage lending bonds. Derivatives. Term options. Hedge funds. The unfamiliar terms floated past Gabriel, cloaked in thick American accents. A tall woman in a white suit was slouching against the wall, chewing on a toothpick, deep in conversation with two men in cowboy boots. In the corner, another man in an expensive tailored suit leaned gracefully against a pillar, not saying a word.

'Excuse me,' Gabriel said delicately, tapping one of the cowboy-booted men on the shoulder. 'I'm a Swiss banker, from Geneva. Now, I'm quite sure that I speak decent English, but for all I understood of your discussion, you could well be speaking Japanese. Could you explain to me what you are talking about?'

The man laughed. 'It's a long story,' he said. He looked over at Bob, as if seeking an explanation for this strange character.

'Gabe is a private Swiss banker,' Bob said, putting a firm hand on Gabriel's shoulder. 'We're here to talk business.'

'Well,' the man said, 'I'll be darned. A real Swiss man in Switzerland! Welcome to the new world.' He gave a harsh laugh. 'Name's Jack.'

'These guys are the cowboys of Wall Street,' Bob explained. Gabriel noticed that the mysterious dark-haired man had disappeared from his pillar.

'I'm talking to the right men, then,' Gabriel said, leaning forward. 'Tell me about these new products.'

'Fine, fine.' Bob nodded. 'They're packaged by American investment banks, mostly. They have plenty of important speakers here: Goldman Sachs, Morgan Stanley, Lehman Brothers, Bear Stearns... They're looking for new international interest. Plenty of French banks here, from Paris and Lyon, and then of course the Germans. We were warned it would be hard to break into these circles, but we didn't realise it would really be this bad.'

Gabriel gave an oily smile. 'Europeans can be insular,' he said.

Jack grinned. 'Well, if you had told me the *Swiss* would be the most approachable of the lot, you could have knocked me over with a feather!'

'We were hoping to connect with the Japanese, originally,' Bob added, 'but they're just so damn... quiet.'

'Anyway, it's a good reason to take time off work,' Jack said. 'A little vacation by the shores of the lake. Have you noticed how beautiful the women are here?'

'Times are changing,' Gabriel said, nodding seriously. 'We are the only bank from Geneva that has chosen to attend, and it is our first time here. But I like what I've seen so far. Our bank, Bank Von Mipatobeau, is ready for new horizons. We're looking to expand abroad.' He lowered his voice. 'To be perfectly straight with you, we share your reservations about the other Europeans here. The Germans are only interested in the beer table, and the Italians are...'

'... only talking about food.' A feminine voice suddenly joined the conversation. 'We listened to a long debate amongst the Italians earlier. As I understood it, it seemed to hinge on whether one could use sour cream as a pizza topping. Things became rather heated.'

The tall woman had volunteered this. At the end of her story, she gave a broad, white-toothed smile. She was wearing a pink tie.

'This is Billy Jean,' said Bob. 'Our very own Amazon. A cowgirl among cowboys, if you will.'

'You are from Texas also?' Gabriel asked, wincing at the strength of her handshake.

'Oh no,' she laughed. 'I'm from the Midwest. I've worked in New York, Chicago and LA. I've been living in Chicago for the last year, working with Dick.' Here she inclined her head in the direction of a man who had returned to stand at the edge of the group.

'Dick Nikko,' Bob said, following Gabriel's glance. 'One of the most powerful brokers working in the USA today.'

'Did I hear my name?' Suddenly, smoothly, Dick Nikko was in the centre of the group. 'Sorry, gentlemen, I went for a smoke,' he said, stroking a clean-shaven chin. Gabriel couldn't help but admire his hair, which was smoothed into a carefully coiffed whirl. 'And who are you?' *What kind of gel did he use, this Monsieur Nikko?*

'Gabriel de Puritigny,' Gabriel said breathlessly.

'We were talking about the Italians,' Billy Jean said with a sly smile.

Dick laughed, his blue eyes sparking. 'Come now, don't insult the Europeans in front of their own. You're not some kind of royal?'

'Certainly not. Besides, I don't mind,' Gabriel said hastily. 'In fact, earlier I insulted their women.'

'Right,' said Bob, frowning a little. 'Well, you know what they're like: always speaking at cross purposes. You're trying to talk business, they're sharing tomato-growing tips.'

'As if money doesn't matter at all,' Dick said coolly. 'Very peculiar. It's a different culture to the US.'

'And to Switzerland, I can assure you,' Gabriel added. 'I've dealt with Italians before; always beating around the bush, always making vague promises they have no intention of keeping. Food and women are the only things they really care about,' he concluded with distaste.

'These are not my priorities either,' Dick said with a warm smile.

'Yes, waving their hands all over the place,' Bob said vaguely. 'You don't understand a word. These guys speak a different language: they speak... pasta, travel, girls. Throw in a few spices surrounding notions of economic growth or inflation.'

Dick sighed. 'Really, to be honest with you Gabriel, we've met nobody but reformed smugglers at this conference. I hoped to make contacts, but I sure as hell don't want my business card used to write down some lady's number later, or somebody's recipe for tomato sauce.'

Bob and Billy Jean laughed loudly. 'They did recommend an excellent pizzeria,' Jack conceded reluctantly. 'I'll give 'em points for that.'

'Jack,' said Bob, 'they probably grew up twenty miles from here. They get no credit for knowing their way round what is essentially their own home town.'

'The Germans are worse,' Billy Jean added with a sneer. 'I'd take an Italian man any day.'

Gabriel frowned into the middle distance. Where *had* Thomas gone? Peering around the room, he finally caught sight of the back of his waistcoat, its owner apparently deep in animated conversation with the group of German men. They seemed to be punching the air a lot. Gabriel sighed.

Dick waved a hand in the air. 'Enough about the damn Italians,' he said. 'Gabriel, why don't you tell us a little bit more about yourself.'

Gabriel paused and turned his mind seriously to the circle of people gathering around him. 'Very well,' he said. 'I am one of the senior managing partners of a small and quite successful Swiss private bank. Lately, we have been considering the question of international expansion. To be perfectly honest, I've had reservations for a long time about whether our private bank should become involved in international banking; whether we are really interested in picking up new products. I came here this week partly as an observer, to see what this broader world looked like. And I'll be straight with you: I'm intrigued. So tell me a little about what you do first, and I'll tell you more in return.'

Dick Nikko nodded. 'Very well, Monsieur the Swiss banker. I'm a broker. I work in Chicago. I'm involved in a lot of domains, making people a lot of money.' He gave a sharkish grin. 'Of course, most of my clients had a lot of money in the first place. Specifically, what do I do? I sell stocks and bonds. I deal with pre-packaged commodity products.'

Gabriel shook his head. 'I need more information,' he admitted.

Dick nodded slowly. 'That's fine,' he said. 'I can help you with that. You've got to learn about these new products, this new world. I can tell you're interested.' He leaned closer. 'That's why you came to this conference. Come watch us work. We're here to attract new money to our banks and brokerage firms, based on creative packaged products. This afternoon, we're going to make clear what those are.'

'I don't have a very clear idea of what these creative products could even be,' Gabriel said hesitantly. 'Our bank mostly deals in portfolio management.'

'Looking after other people's money?' Dick nodded. 'Well, let me teach you how to make those people a lot more money. Look, just imagine the car industry for a moment. If you wanted to buy a new car, you'd know to go to Cadillac, Oldsmobile, or maybe something from Chrysler's European line? You go to them for their reputation and quality, and then you buy their newest product: right now that'd be the Chrysler Cirrus, right? Well, it's the same in banking. There are new products, you just need a little knowledge to know where to find quality... where to put your money.'

'Right,' said Gabriel. 'Maybe I'll understand a little better after this afternoon's seminar.'

'Forget the seminar,' Dick said. 'Why don't you come by our offices in Chicago?'

'Chicago?' Gabriel asked, aghast. 'Chicago in America?'

'Is there any other Chicago worth the trip?'

'No, I mean I don't know... I'm sure it's... I've never been overseas,' Gabriel concluded lamely, before coughing. Where *had* Thomas gone? He felt himself curiously in need some kind of moral support, even of the unruly teenage kind. 'I mean, I have many responsibilities running our private Swiss bank in Geneva,' he added.

'Gabriel, do you know what a strangle is? What about a call? Or a put? Do you know what a documentary is, or a risk reversal, or a deposit plus? Have you heard of mortgage-backed securities? Did you know you could buy a whole tanker of oil – 300,000 tonnes of it – just on a piece of paper, without ever seeing the oil?' Dick gave a sharp laugh. 'Well, I can teach you. I can teach you how those strange words are going to make both of us a lot of money. Let me give you a little sample of my vocabulary: a call is the sale of an option, calling on you as a client, to sell your product, which could be a stock, a metal, a commodity, at a higher value. For that option, you'll get a premium in advance. Of course, if the product price goes up above your call, you are selling your product at a lower price than the market. So you will lose on your call. You will have to define the time limit to exercise the call. A put is the opposite: the possibility, during a defined period of time, to put to you the option of the client to sell his product at a certain price in the future. For that, you also get a premium, paid in advance. Either way, if you buy it as an option, you cash in a premium in advance.'

Gabriel nodded desperately. 'I see. I think. I don't know.'

'How can I explain this... You're offering your girlfriend a kiss in the future. You have an option in one month, when you go out with your girlfriend, to give her a kiss. And then you will pay a premium now of an advanced caviar dinner. Or she is wooing you, and she has the option to put to you the obligation to buy a diamond necklace in one month, in return for a kiss right now. You can't go wrong,' Dick continued. 'You make a lot of money.'

'You're paying for kisses?' Gabriel asked, puzzled.

Dick laughed. 'You're paying less than the kisses are worth,' he said.

'Except if the market goes against you either way,' Bob added hesitantly.

'Nonsense,' Dick said crisply. He swept a stray lock of hair out of his eyes. 'There's very little danger of that,' he added smoothly, 'since we know the market so well.'

'Very well,' replied Gabriel. 'Let me think about it.' *Think about what?* 'Though I have to admit I'm not even quite sure what's being offered to me here.'

'Look, Gabriel. We're both powerful men. There's a lot we could do together, if we could join forces in any way.'

'Mr Nikko, I –'

'Dick, please.'

'Dick, of course. Dick, I appreciate this offer, but I have to request more details. What exactly are you offering?'

Dick threw back his head and laughed. 'You Swiss men are as precise as they say. Tell me, do you time your love-making with a Swatch chronometer? Don't answer that question. I'll admire you if you do. Tell you what, Swiss man. You'll have to come to Chicago to fully understand what it is we do there, and what we could do together. But let me paint a little picture for you in the meantime: you make, what, two to three per cent on your transactions in Geneva, right?' Gabriel nodded. 'Well, I know a lot of very rich men. Hell, I make a lot of very rich men even richer! What if I sent a few of those dollars we make your way? You make that two to three per cent on them in your bank, and you retrocede to me, say, one and a half. As a little thank you. What do you think? I'll send you the first ten million dollars next week.'

It took a great deal of self-control for Gabriel's jaw not to drop open at that moment. 'Ten million?' he gulped. 'Just like that? But you've only just met me!'

'Oh, it's not mine. It's from one of our corporate clients.'

'I see,' said Gabriel, confused.

Dick smiled and unbuttoned his jacket. 'There's more,' he said. 'You could invest with us, too. Bonds, stocks, options, new products, derivatives: we know the market. We know what rich men should be doing with their money. You say you make two to three per cent? Well, our deals make two per cent just for being set up. Then we go on to make more like twenty per cent on the products, on churning, on managing the products. I'll explain all that to you in more detail when you come to Chicago. A hint: it has nothing to do with butter. We're not Italian, after all.' He winked. 'Then, we retrocede half of that back to you. You're a rich man, Gabriel de Puritigny, and your bank is rich. If you were interested in investing with us, I could retrocede up to fifty per cent of our profits to you. Now, doesn't that sound quite a lot better than your usual two to three per cent?'

Gabriel nodded mutely, surreptitiously loosening his tie. 'So you mean, for example, if I sent you one hundred million of our bank's money or a client's money, you would make us twenty per cent, twenty million... I mean, with that sort of return, we can charge our client a good commission back here!' Gabriel swallowed. 'I need time to think about this.' Maybe he would have a glass of milk with Thomas, as soon as this was over. How many hours till he was safely back home in Geneva?

'Let me buy you a flight to Chicago,' Dick said, setting a hand on his shoulder. 'On the house. No strings. I'm willing to take the gamble that you'll come round to our proposition if you just see our offices. Just come have a look. We'll show you our fancy computers; take you for lunch. Hell, we'll take you to dinner too!'

'I'll... I'll think about it,' Gabriel said, meeting Dick's shining blue eyes.

Dick leaned close, so close that Gabriel had to take a step back. 'Step into the American banking life, Gabe. You'll never want to go back.'

Chapter Thirteen

'Saas Fee!' sighed Chloë. 'It just sounds so... exciting!'

The white mountainside, dotted with pine trees, rushed by the train windows.

Clarice smiled indulgently. 'It will certainly be a different experience for me,' she said, 'spending time in the chalet without my husband. I find it hard to imagine the place representing anything other than total boredom.

'I cannot wait to go hiking!' Winifred exclaimed, staring wistfully out the window as a frozen lakeshore whizzed past. 'It's been so long, it's a wonder my legs haven't given up on me and stopped working entirely.'

'Well, I'm sure Dieter does his best to keep them in shape,' Chloë replied with a salacious wink.

'I don't much care for hiking,' Clarice said coolly.

'Oh, but you must try!' said Winifred, blushing. 'I mean, I've never been to Saas Fee either, but I'm sure the area is very beautiful. When we go exploring beyond the Zurich area, Dieter, the children and I usually go to Les Trois Vallées in France, and sometimes we travel as far as Austria. Somehow, Saas Fee has never been on our radar. I'm so glad we have a reason to go!'

'I'm not sure about this hiking business either, Clarice,' Khadija said gloomily. 'It sounds rather sweaty to me.'

'Look, even President Roosevelt, one of the rounder American presidents, loved walking in the mountains,' said Chloë.

'Gabriel once told me that the seventy-five-year-old president of IBM made it up the Matterhorn,' Clarice commented.

'I don't care,' said Khadija. 'I'm not Teddy Roosevelt, and I'm not the president of IBM. I happen to be very fond of flat ground.'

'Well, don't worry,' Chloë teased, 'this isn't a sporting holiday. There will be plenty of other activities. Drinking, gossiping, staying up late...'

Fleurie sighed. 'Girls, girls, girls. We mustn't forget the principal reason for this excursion.'

Khadija giggled, reaching into her handbag for a *pain au chocolat*. 'Yes, yes, the Avant-Garde Feminist Club of Geneva have Important Feminist Thinking to do.' She took a large bite of the pastry. 'I, for one, am extremely excited about our intellectual discussions.' Crumbs fell from her bright pink lips.

Winifred shook her head indulgently. 'I'm sure we can reconcile our various interests. After all, we have been friends for years and years!'

Khadija sighed. 'Yes, I suppose we have. I still think of Clarice as a newbie, somehow.'

'You'd miss my money if I quit,' Clarice said with a wry grin.

'We would not miss your husband,' Chloë added. 'Ugh, what a bore. Why don't you dump him for a ski instructor or something? You could use a little excitement.'

'Chloë!' Winifred cut in. 'That's completely inappropriate.'

'Well,' Chloë conceded, 'she wouldn't have to dump him...'

'Oh, it's all right,' said Clarice. 'I'm used to our Chloë by now. While you're right that I could use some excitement, I'm unsure some idiotic young man could provide me with what I need. I'd much rather shack up in the chalet with all of you.'

The women smiled happily. '*Pain au chocolat*, anyone?' Khadija asked.

'Where is Gabriel, anyway?' Fleurie asked. 'Didn't he mind you disappearing off to the chalet without him?'

Clarice shook her head. 'He's off in Lugano at some dreadful banking conference. He's probably forgotten where I am.'

'So many Italians there.' Chloë patted her hand. 'What about a dance teacher?' she asked. 'I know this South American guy...'

'I really do think you'll like it at the chalet,' Winifred cut in, loudly and earnestly. 'All of you. It doesn't just have to be hiking: it's late enough in the year for a little skiing.'

'That's an excellent idea,' said Fleurie, perking up a little. 'In between meetings, of course,' she added hastily. 'Winifred will be able to help organise it, since she's the only one who speaks German...'

'Skiing?' Khadija appeared outraged. '*Skiing*? No-one said anything about skiing. I haven't been skiing in years and years.'

'I thought you were some sort of ski champion in your youth,' Chloë said smugly. 'Weren't you one of the only Arab women in the world who could ski to a competitive standard?'

'There wasn't much competition,' Khadija replied, obviously offended. She took another large bite of pastry, as if to comfort herself. 'Most Arabic women have never even seen snow,' she muttered.

'Come now, I'm sure it'll come right back to you!' Winifred said encouragingly. 'We'll take it easy, I promise.'

'I don't have any gear with me,' Khadija said sulkily. 'No jacket. No poles. No *skis*.'

'We'll buy some!' said Winifred. 'The Club can fund it all!'

'What if I fall and break a leg?'

'I'm not very good either,' Fleurie added.

'Nonsense,' said Chloë. 'Fleurie is one of those people who pretend they aren't very good at sports. Then, when you agree to go along on a weekend with them, you spend the whole time running along behind.'

'Don't be silly,' said Fleurie. 'Besides, by the sound of it, we'll be left in the dust by Khadija. Maybe we can get an instructor, together.'

Khadija threw a small lump of *pain of chocolat* at her. 'Just you wait,' she said. 'I may not remember how to ski, but I certainly know how to push someone into a ravine.'

'Please, let's go skiing!' Chloë suddenly pleaded.

The others looked at her in surprise. 'I thought you mostly wanted to drink and gossip?' Clarice asked mildly.

'Ah, but I had forgotten about ski instructors. This one time, when I was just sixteen...'

Khadija threw the rest of her pastry at her.

Barefoot, the women flopped happily into the couches and leather armchairs.

'It's very white in here,' said Chloë.

'Oh, Clarice,' Winifred said happily, 'it's so beautiful! And you can see the Matterhorn from the window!'

'So pointy!' Chloë said.

'I hope you're not planning on going up there,' Khadija said suspiciously. 'I would be scared to death. That creepy little train up here was bad enough.'

'It's the most beautiful mountain in the world,' Winifred replied, her tone one of mild reproach.

'Ooh, there's a balcony for smoking!' said Chloë, throwing open another door.

Khadija shivered. 'Close that door! You European women are ridiculous, letting a draught through in the middle of winter. Indoors means inside doors, as far as I am aware. Closed doors.'

'You should come here when Gabriel is here,' Clarice replied. 'The lizard likes to keep the place hot enough to bake cheese. However, there will be no smoking in this house, I'm afraid. Chloë, you can develop cancer outside if you like. You might run into some of the farmers that live around here.'

Chloë practically flung herself towards the front door, fixing her hair.

'So, the start of winter, the start of the ski season,' Fleurie said philosophically, gazing out the window. 'The start of many wonderful things for our avant-garde feminist club, of course.'

'I don't understand why you insist on calling it that,' Khadija said, not unkindly. 'Surely we're just rich ladies who like art?'

'Modern art,' Fleurie corrected her. 'The implications are quite different. Besides, our meetings have always had an intellectual bent.'

'For you,' Khadija replied, teasing.

'Fleurie's not alone. Some of us do the reading, you know,' Clarice replied. 'Did you remember to bring your catalogues along?'

'Of course not,' said Khadija. 'I knew the rest of you would bring them. I needed more room for shoes!'

'There's snow outside,' Fleurie said, shaking her head. 'Are you really planning to go out there in your Louboutins?'

Khadija looked at the window, watching the thick flakes drift down, and was forced to bite her tongue.

'Do you know,' Clarice said thoughtfully, 'I really have learned so much since I met you all. Since I turned away from the Old Masters, and tried to look at the more difficult questions art tackles. It is all very well, when you are young, to love darkness and glorify miserable peasant scenes. But perhaps there is more to be contemplated.'

'What do you think we should eat for dinner tonight?' asked Khadija, turning away from the snow. 'Perhaps we can get some sort of takeaway.'

'If you had met me five years before, you would never have thought I could be an iconoclast,' Clarice continued, unperturbed.

'Curry or some lamb kebabs, maybe?' Khadija continued.

'My dear, when we met you seven or eight years ago,' Fleurie replied gently, 'we doubted you had a single modern bone in your body.'

Clarice laughed. 'Why did you choose me for your club, then?' she teased.

'Winifred convinced us,' Fleurie replied quite seriously. 'Of course, we quickly realised we had made an excellent decision. It was good for us, too, to have some new blood, new ideas; to be challenged by a traditionalist.'

Winifred turned back from the window, laughing. 'Wasn't it a good idea? Now here we are, in Clarice's chalet! See how beautiful the snow is? Real, pure powder, that is. I can't wait to get out on the slopes.'

Khadija sighed. 'I don't even know if they have curry or kebab houses in these sorts of villages,' she said. 'Clarice?'

'I was thinking of making dinner, actually,' Winifred said gently. 'I love nothing more than cooking for people.'

'Oh, be my guest!' Clarice said drily. 'Apparently the kitchen here is state-of-the-art. I've never used it. There won't be much in the cupboards, though.'

Winifred laughed. 'I forgot about your Migros addiction,' she said. 'Just for a weekend, let me liberate you from the tyranny of shrink-wrapped dishes!'

'Is that carpet hand-woven?' Khadija asked in admiration, wriggling her toes. 'Is that why we're barefoot? I mean, I quite like it, but it's not very Swiss.'

Clarice rolled her eyes. 'Oh yes,' she said. 'Gabriel would tell you all about it. My husband somehow manages to be boring even in the depths of his eccentricity. He'd also wax lyrical about the parquet: pure pinewood from the high mountains, without a knot in sight. Very expensive. The office is made of pears.' She laughed gently, for a long time.

'Pear *wood*, I assume?' said Winifred gently.

The other women exchanged glances. 'Clarice,' Fleurie began hesitantly, 'is everything alright? In your marriage, I mean.'

Clarice shrugged. 'When is anything alright in anyone's marriage?' she asked with a thin smile. 'We get on, you know.'

'This is the twentieth century,' Khadija said firmly. 'Women divorce. Things have come to a pretty pass if a girl from a conservative Muslim family is advising you to leave your husband. Even though now in Islam a woman can divorce her husband, based on cruelty, lack of justice and infidelity.'

'It's not that simple,' Clarice sighed. 'We are partners, as well as... well, whatever else we are supposed to be.'

'You need his money,' Khadija said shrewdly.

'Yes. But it's more than that. Gabriel wouldn't agree to it... divorce, I mean. He's far too much of a Calvinist. Respectable Swiss bankers don't get divorces, even nowadays. His parents... Well, I suppose his father would understand, he's a nice enough man, and his mother...'

'Is that the Ticino witch?' Winifred asked curiously.

Clarice laughed. 'Yes, that's her. Who knows her opinion on anything. She would probably ask a muskrat for advice.'

At this moment, Chloë flung open the front door dramatically, untwisting her long knitted scarf. 'No men,' she sighed, 'though I swear I saw a donkey in the distance.'

'We're trying to convince Clarice to leave her husband,' Khadija said coolly. 'It isn't going well.'

'Ooh,' said Chloë, sitting down on the couch, 'do go on.'

'He's just too damn respectable,' Clarice tried to explain, faltering. 'Maybe I am too.'

'So now you're stuck in this miserable, Calvinistic marriage,' Chloë commented. 'Hell, I bet John Calvin himself was more fun!'

Khadija shushed her.

Clarice sighed. 'I never thought I was marrying for love,' she said. 'It's not like I didn't know what Gabriel was like. It was a practical, pragmatic decision. I was young – we both were – and it seemed like a good idea to enter into this sort of partnership. It seemed responsible, and not just in the financial sense. And even now that I truly understand what I was committing to, back then, it seems wrong to jump ship.'

'But you hate his guts,' said Chloë.

'I hate a lot of people's guts,' Clarice replied calmly, a twinkle in her eye. 'It doesn't mean I can't live with them.'

'Hey!' said Chloë.

'If Gabriel's anything like his chalet,' Fleurie said slowly, looking around, 'I'm not sure I want to meet him. Everything is so clean and white, so impeccably tidy.'

'Look at that chandelier,' Chloë said idly. 'It's just a slim piece of wood. So boring.'

'At least it's not a pair of antlers or something covered in gold leaf,' Clarice said, shrugging. 'Gabriel doesn't like things to be tacky.'

'I mean, have you ever seen American chalets?' Chloë said, standing up and beginning to pace around the room. 'They have these incredible wooden carvings everywhere, and indoor swimming pools. Crystal chandeliers. Marble, crystal, six or seven bathrooms...'

'That doesn't sound very Calvinistic,' quipped Fleurie. 'It sounds like a five-star hotel.'

'Exactly!' said Chloë. 'And what about getting some Murano glass in? This place could really do with a few bright colours. You're not far from Venice; I'm sure they could deliver over the mountains...'

'I have to agree that it's boring,' Clarice sighed. 'To be honest, I couldn't really be bothered to get involved in the décor. Gabriel had his boys' club with the architect; he made all the interior decoration decisions. I stayed out of it.'

'It could use a modern touch,' Fleurie said hesitantly, 'if you don't mind me saying. Since your tastes have become more contemporary, maybe you might like chromed chandeliers? Something in pewter or zinc?'

'That's radical,' Clarice said, sounding rather excited. 'I must admit, the idea of redecoration is rather tempting...'

'I don't know,' said Khadija. 'I mean, everyone I know seems to live in palaces made of twenty-four carat gold. I appreciate a little simplicity. Still, maybe a painting or two on the walls would be nice.'

'What about a touch of Art Deco?' Fleurie continued, getting excited. 'That might be conservative enough for your Gabriel. Something lovely, and geometric, and modern.'

Clarice laughed. 'I wonder how I'll go about bargaining for this. 'Gabriel, tonight I will agree that we won't have sex, on one condition: buy me an Art Deco wall!' That sounds like a great tool for negotiation.'

Winifred laughed out loud. 'Withhold the need for sex, for decoration,' she said. 'I like it.'

'That's a terrible idea,' said Chloë.

'It's not like your husband can't afford it,' Khadija added. 'Just ask him.'

'Anyway, why is Winifred shaking her head? She looks like a camel,' Chloë added.

'Do you have some advice to dole out from your ridiculously successful marriage?' Khadija asked caustically.

'Oh no,' Winifred said, blushing. 'Forgive me, I... was distracted.'

'Well, go on,' Khadija said grudgingly. 'You can't tease us like that. What were you thinking about?'

'It's awfully cheesy. I was just thinking how glad I am to be a part of this group,' Winifred admitted. 'Watching you laugh, and tease, and squabble, and support each other... I don't think I ever had a group of girlfriends like this, even when I was at school. You're like my sisters.'

Chloë laughed aloud in sheer delight, then clapped her hands together. 'Let's forget about decoration!' she said happily.

'Are you drunk?' Khadija asked Winifred suspiciously. 'Did you find a bottle of *genepi* hidden in the toilet? Because I want some, if so.'

'*Genepi* is definitely *haraam*,' Fleurie interjected.

Khadija made a harumphing noise. 'God cannot see so far up as these mountains,' she said. 'He does not like climbing either.'

'I love you too, Winifred,' Chloë burst out, dabbing her eyes on her silk sleeve. 'We really are a gang. We can do anything together!'

'Well,' Clarice said drily, 'I'm glad the disintegration of my marriage has fortified our friendship.' But she was smiling.

'You know,' Winifred said slowly, 'I'm not sure my marriage is as perfect as you all seem to think. Sometimes I would love to be single like Chloë or Fleurie. Sometimes I wish the children didn't have to come along to everything.'

'Nonsense,' Khadija said warmly. 'You love them all to pieces, and we all envy you so much, we wish you would fall off a mountain.'

Winifred gave a wobbly smile. 'I'll go buy some potatoes,' she said.

'Let me walk with you,' Clarice said crisply. 'It's only a short way into the village, but there are a few tricky turns on the route...'

The path from the chalet to the village was rocky, and scattered with snow. The sky was turning deeper blue, darkening into evening.

Winifred laid a hand on Clarice's arm. 'I'd apologise on behalf of everyone, but you know the girls well enough to understand they mean no harm...'

'Oh, I know. How is Dieter, really?' Clarice asked, wrapping her scarf around her neck tightly.

Winifred smiled, brushing snowflakes from her hair. 'He's well. We're well. He's recently had a big promotion.'

'Ever the big shot, eh,' said Clarice.

'It's ridiculous, really,' Winifred said affectionately. 'He's hard to live up to. The man speaks four languages, and now he's learning Spanish. He wants the kids to be the same: sometimes, he home-schools them at the weekend. He wants them to go to Harvard, Princeton, maybe Oxford or Cambridge. Of course, that's still a few years away for the youngest ones, but Klaus will be beginning his applications this summer.'

'Gracious!' Clarice exclaimed. 'Is it really that long since we came to your house? Seven... eight years?' She shook her head in disbelief. 'They'll be men soon.'

'It's strange, isn't it,' said Winifred. 'You can't wait for the endless mewling and pooping to stop, and all of a sudden you look up and they're applying to Stanford.'

'I can't even imagine,' Clarice replied. 'I can't imagine giving that much away. I mean, it sounds like Dieter is very much invested in their lives, too. You both worked so hard for those kids, you love them so much. I don't know if Gabriel would have... In fact, I'm sure he wouldn't. I don't know if I would have been able, either.'

'Not everybody has to have children,' Winifred said gently. 'Think of all you've accomplished on your own!'

'Gabriel and I haven't made love in six months,' Clarice said shortly. 'I don't really want to talk about it, but the girls... Maybe they have a point.'

'They don't know how complicated marriage is,' Winifred said, 'except maybe Khadija. It isn't all about sex, you know.'

Clarice laughed suddenly. 'You can talk!' she said. 'How many times a week do you...?' Seeing Winifred's hurt expression, she stopped. 'You know I'm joking,' she said. 'God forbid I should start to sound like Chloë! I'm just happy that you're happy, you know.'

They walked on in the snow, the lights of the village appearing ahead. Clarice stuffed her hands deep into her pockets. 'It's just difficult to be confronted with the contrast, sometimes,' she burst out. 'Dieter just seems like such a kind, optimistic character. A sociable man, who loves travelling, who's great at marketing, appreciated in his bank, makes a lot of money without a second thought... and loves his wife and children.'

'Not all men are the same,' Winifred said softly. 'You can't compare from the outside. Dieter has his flaws. But do you know what I think his ultimate value is? Not the sex, not kindness, not money, but simply honesty. We decided very early on in our courtship that we would be totally honest with each other, and we've lived up to that promise as best as we can, throughout our marriage.'

Clarice nodded. 'I can understand that in theory,' she said. 'I don't think Gabriel is a liar, but he's not someone who would share his inner thoughts or fears.'

'Well, maybe you can work on that. It doesn't have to be about sex. Maybe it's about communication.'

'I miss them both,' Clarice said with a bitter laugh.

They walked on for a while in silence. 'That looks like the supermarket,' Winifred said, pointing.

The women hunched over the oak table in the lamplight, filling their plates with boiled potatoes, pickled onions and slices of dried meat. 'I love raclette!' Chloë said through a mouthful of cheese.

'I'll never understand how you can eat the way you eat and stay the size you are,' Khadija said ruefully.

'Sex must be good exercise,' said Clarice.

Chloë grinned. 'In that case, Winifred would have the body of an athlete, stick-thin, washboard abs...'

Winifred shook her head. 'Chloë, you really are quite silly sometimes. Come now, ladies, we didn't come up this mountain just to talk about sex, and argue about whether we were going skiing. Has everybody had a look over the catalogues?'

Khadija and Chloë rolled their eyes.

'Come on,' said Fleurie. 'You mustn't forget the whole point of this club.'

'German women never want to talk about sex,' Chloë whispered. 'But what's wrong with Fleurie?'

Clarice raised a hand. 'Fleurie and Winifred are right,' she said. 'Art is our main objective. Winifred and Khadija both travelled all the way from Zurich, to work with us on our funding of contemporary art. So, while we eat this wonderful meal that Winifred has prepared for us, let us at least have a cursory discussion about upcoming exhibitions, strategy and even, perhaps, profit.'

Chloë sighed.

'My husband had some interesting tips,' Khadija said begrudgingly. 'Some art dealers walked into the bank last week, interested in holding an exhibition in the bank lobby. I'm trying to talk them into coming to see our galleries as well. The scene is getting more and more international, you know. I've met artists from Russia, Ukraine, the Middle East, even South America. That's without mentioning the French, the Dutch, the Scandinavians and the Germans.'

Fleurie nodded. '1995 feels like a good year for modern art. I have my eye on a few works I'd like to try to acquire for the museum in Carouge.'

Khadija grinned. 'Oh, and I also visited a museum in Bern that would be interested in lending out some of their artwork, in exchange for new contacts in the francophone art world.'

'Excellent!' said Clarice. 'Perhaps you can put them in touch with my gallery...'

'I also have connections on the board of several museums in Zurich,' Winifred put in. 'Remind me. I've been to that museum in Berne. I think we could put together some fabulous shows.'

'I know two wonderful sculptors in Berne,' Chloë said thoughtfully. 'And no, I didn't sleep with them.'

'By the way, Clarice,' Winifred added, 'do you still sell Anker and Hodler? One of Dieter's old German friends showed an interest in purchasing a view of the lake next time he visited Geneva... I think his mother was from there, or something.'

'Absolutely,' said Clarice. 'Send them my way. At the moment, the gallery is, as the French say, *mi-figue, mi-raisin*. Half classical, half contemporary. It's working well enough, though.'

'You should open another gallery,' Khadija said, pouring melted cheese into her spoon. 'Just for modern art.'

Clarice raised her eyebrows. 'That would be expensive,' she said. She was quiet for a while.

'It's an interesting idea, though,' Fleurie said thoughtfully. 'Perhaps the club could contribute some funding.'

There was a pause as Clarice continued to digest this proposition.

'I suppose if it went well, I could make a lot more money,' Clarice said slowly. 'I do have a lot of contacts...'

'I might know someone who can offer you a space too,' Fleurie added. 'Let me put you in touch. After all, the club isn't just about exhibitions. We're interested in the market, too. I'm sure you can already think of a few local artists whose work you'd be willing to sell.'

'Oh yes,' Clarice said, looking up excitedly. 'Yes! I could be actively promoting modern art, not just helping it find its place in museums. People may laugh at Geneva for being old and boring, but it's incredibly international.'

'I've been thinking about international expansion,' Khadija said, setting down her fork. 'I think I need to take what I've learned back with me to the Middle East. I mean, my husband and I know some really rich people, as well as a number of incredibly talented artists.'

'I remember that expo in Zurich,' Clarice said, nodding encouragingly. 'I would imagine those painters can look forward to having as much recognition in their home countries as they've had here, thanks to you.'

Khadija nodded. 'The trouble is, most art collectors are stuck in the nineteenth century. You'll be familiar with this, Clarice, from the Old Town. Now imagine the phenomenon at the scale of the entire Arabian Gulf. It's all Orientalism, everywhere. Far too historical, far too academic. They're only buying Gérôme and Ernst and Deutsch and Rousseau. Only a few paint the old boats and the pearl-fishing of Bahrain and Dubai. I think we can shake things up a bit. Now, I know the right people to get this movement started. I know princes, ministers, businessmen who've made fortunes thanks to my husband. Oil traders. Industrialists. I even have a Lebanese cousin who married a sheikh. Everybody seems to be Mr Five Per Cent, in the Middle East. There's a tremendous amount of interest in modern art in Europe itself, but there is money in the Middle East. Well, they can start investing that oil money in me.'

Fleurie nodded excitedly. 'I reckon you can talk them into changing their outlook on life and art, just like you did, Clarice. Get away from classical forms and Orientalism into modern and contemporary.'

'Hear, hear,' said Winifred. 'See? I knew we had plenty of art business to talk about, once we got off the topic of sex.'

'Oh, you're not off the hook,' Chloë said with a grin, 'but I know when to keep quiet. It can wait till after dinner. Besides, I like Clarice's idea.'

'Not mine?' Khadija asked, offended.

Chloë waved a hand in the air. 'It's too hot over there, in the desert,' she said. 'I'll never go to your exhibitions. Clarice, on the other hand, lives very close to the best *pain au chocolat* in Geneva.'

'Clarice needs to come out of her shell, too,' Khadija said, shaking her head. 'It's not just the Middle East that's expanding — opening up. It's time for new projects, for both of us. It's time to be modern, and international. We need to bring modern art to the desert, and we need to bring the desert to Geneva.'

'I'll welcome it into my new gallery,' Clarice said with a grin, 'along with all the most radical Swiss artists I can think of!'

'Well,' Fleurie said with a smile, holding up her glass, 'I think this deserves a toast. To Clarice's new gallery!'

'Let's remember,' Winifred added gently, 'that we are not simply here as business partners. We are, after all, the avant-garde. I don't want the club to lose its intellectual, critical, analytical side. It's not just a commercial venture.'

'Yes, of course,' said Fleurie. 'After dinner, we can retire with the print-outs and sit and talk for a while. As Winifred says, we must remember that the club has more than one aim: we collect, we exhibit, we sell, we discuss art. Plus it's a friendship, too.'

'Here here,' said Chloë, through a mouthful of potato.

'By the way, before we move on to more lofty discussions,' Fleurie continued, 'we need to discuss a few practical issues, namely budget and membership.'

'Membership?' Chloë's eyes were wide. 'You want to let more people join?'

Khadija shrugged. 'Why not? More women, more money.'

'I don't know,' Winifred said hesitantly. 'I quite like the spirit of sisterhood we've developed.'

'Perhaps we shouldn't actively look for new members,' Clarice suggested, 'but simply keep an eye open, in case the right woman happens to come along?'

Fleurie nodded. 'That's a good idea, Clarice,' she said.

'I mean, what would the criteria even be?' Chloë asked, giggling. 'Rich, bored, Genevois intellectual over thirty with a complicated sex life and a snarky sense of humour?'

'I don't think sex comes into it,' Khadija said stiffly.

'No, I don't know how much of that I qualify for, either,' Winifred added.

'Ah, but Winifred,' Chloë said, 'you are our great external observer! Without you, we would have no perspective on our pathetic singledom.'

'Well,' said Fleurie.

'Now, now,' Clarice raised a hand. 'Fleurie had another important question up for discussion: the budget.'

'As your treasurer,' Winifred said, 'I can safely say that we're doing very well this year. I don't think there is any immediate necessity for new members, though, of course, any donations are much appreciated. Khadija, we really do appreciate all the outreach work you're doing in the Middle East.'

'Why don't you bring one of those princes back here?' Chloë asked innocently.

'Not your type,' said Khadija. 'Too fat — too old.' She laughed loudly.

'The budget, ladies,' Fleurie said patiently.

'Well, I had tonnes of money, but I spent it all,' Chloë said.

'Yes, we know that,' Khadija replied. 'Remind me to ask you about your new inevitable business failure. What was it, a spa project?'

'Not a spa,' Chloë said, rolling her eyes. 'Spa *cosmetics*.'

'As long as I stay married to Gabriel I'm alright for cash,' said Clarice. 'So you'd better stop pushing me to get a divorce.'

'So we'll keep the contributions the same, this year?' Fleurie prompted.

'That seems wise,' Winifred replied.

'Until one of Khadija's princes endows us with a million-dollar donation, yes, I think we should stick to that,' Clarice concluded.

'So, now that we've dealt with budget matters,' Winifred began, 'what's all this about cosmetics, Chloë?'

'Why don't I bring out dessert?' Clarice said, standing up.

'Well!' Chloë said happily. 'Since my rather reckless use of my father's funds –' here she looked pointedly at Khadija – 'I have become much more mature. Yet I am still beautiful!' She flicked her hair back over her shoulder. 'So I thought to myself: who better to create a line of beauty products?'

Winifred nodded earnestly. Fleurie rolled her eyes, half-affectionately.

'What kind of products?' Khadija asked.

'All sorts, and all natural and organic. Perfume, kohl, the softest powders for your skin. All with an international bent: rich henna hair dye from India, lotion made of tree sap from Yemen, French hazelnut cream for your fingernails. All women want to look the same, you see: high cheekbones, almond eyes, fine eyebrows, beautiful hair. I want to offer women cosmetics for the face and body. Cosmetics for the modern woman. A full-body experience.'

'Chloë,' said Khadija slowly, 'leaving aside for one moment the idea that women from all over the world should want to look the same, it really does sound like you should be running a spa. Then you could offer your clients these products.'

'Well, I *was* thinking of calling the line "spa cosmetics",' Chloë said innocently.

Khadija narrowed her eyes. 'Oh, my little friend,' she said, laughing suddenly. 'I see what you're saying, now. Were you thinking of asking me for funding?'

'Well,' Chloë said, looking up at the ceiling, 'you see, I don't think I can afford to open a spa.'

Khadija let out a roar of laughter. 'Oh, you ridiculous creature!' she said. 'Fine, fine. I'll give you four million to open a center. Just don't turn it into a brothel this time, OK?'

Clarice reappeared in the doorway with a tray of chocolates. Fleurie made a cooing noise of approval.

'Some friends of mine thought I should offer plastic surgery, as well,' Chloë said tentatively. 'For instance, you can get these fillers, made with sugar from rooster combs. It matches the sugar in your body, you see, totally natural.'

'Must we always be talking about plastic surgery?' Winifred sighed. 'It makes me feel old.'

'Yes, I agree,' Fleurie said, tucking a strand of grey hair behind her ear. 'Why don't we retire to the salon?'

'Let's get back to our art discussions,' Clarice suggested, passing the chocolate tray around. 'After all, that is what the club is all about.'

Chapter Fourteen

'God, Lugano was dreadful,' Gabriel sighed, loosening his tie and reaching for his cup of tisane. 'I'm so glad to be back to your spicy chicken salads.'

'Migros,' Clarice replied, smiling stiffly and lounging back into the leather sofa. She didn't look up from the modern art catalogue she was flicking through. 'Did Migros not have a presence in Lugano?'

'Oh, almost certainly, but I had no need to look for them.' He frowned suspiciously at his wife. 'Why?'

'I don't know,' she replied, turning the pages quickly in exasperation. The cover of the magazine featured what looked to Gabriel like something one would be upset a cat had left on the carpet. 'I was just making conversation.'

'Oh,' he said, appeased. 'Well, as I was saying, it was all dreadful. The conference hall was garish, the food was terrible, and oh, the Italians! The damn Italians everywhere.'

'I take it you didn't make any Italian banking contacts?' Clarice asked drily, her eyes still firmly on the catalogue. Was that a nail gun on the back? She seemed to be wearing some sort of glittery woollen hat. Gabriel imagined the de Puritigny family portraits looking down on it in disapproval.

'No. Nor French, nor German – although Thomas did his best to affiliate with the latter. Not even English. Not even Swiss!'

'Well, knock me over with a feather,' Clarice said sarcastically. 'I mean, given your resistance to all things non-Genevois, it's a wonder you and Thomas had to ship all the way out there to come to that conclusion.'

'Ah, but you haven't let me finish my story,' Gabriel continued in his most aggrieved tone. *Did she never listen?*

'Don't you want to hear about the marvellous time I had with my girlfriends at the chalet?' Clarice asked with what sounded a great deal like malice.

'Oh, tell me all about it! I take it I'll get the story of your haberdashery's genesis.' Gabriel's effort at sarcasm seemed to fail, for Clarice set down her art catalogue, at a page featuring a very large picture of a dead fish.

'Well!' she said. 'For once, the chalet managed not to be boring. We did nothing but drink hot chocolate and talk about modern art. The snow was marvellous, fresh powder, and we went skiing twice. And the food! The girls are just crazy about pastries, you know. We had German cakes, and the sorts of *viennoiseries* you simply cannot find in the French part of Switzerland, and of course we just walked around like a bunch of girlfriends, stomping about the town in our ski boots. Winifred cooked for us all: she made raclette, and sausages, and one night some kind of extravagant cheese gratin! I swear I'll eat nothing but salad for a month after this. All of it so... rustic, too! I don't know how Winifred does it, how she hasn't acquired a taste for luxury like the rest of us. Though of course, it turned out Khadija had sourced a bottle of Moët for us for the last night.'

'What about the hats?' Gabriel asked drily.

'Oh, aren't they just darling?' Clarice touched hers gently. 'They only cost eighty-five francs each! We decided the club needed some sort of unifying feature, just like those girls have in America, you know, sororities. A memento of the trip.'

'Speaking of America...' Gabriel began.

'Oh, and they had the loveliest wine there, too, from Sion!' Clarice went on as if she hadn't heard him. 'I mean, I don't drink very much, but just a little pinot gris from the mountains, well, I couldn't resist. We were just having so much fun!'

'What I was saying earlier, about Old Europe...' Gabriel ploughed on, determined to make his point even if it was only for his own good. 'The old failed tower of Babel. People stick to their own, speaking one language, not venturing beyond their borders.'

'Well, isn't that exactly what you like?' Clarice asked hesitantly.

She had a point. 'It's as it should be, I suppose. I'm just not sure that's the direction banking is headed. Switzerland can be quite provincial, you know.'

Clarice raised an eyebrow but did not comment.

'Anyway, what I was saying, is I ended up looking beyond Old Europe. I thought Von Mipatobeau might just need to be a little more ambitious. So I did a little... blue sky thinking,' he said with distaste, 'and I approached some Americans.'

'Ooh, how fascinating' said Clarice, picking up her catalogue again.

'Fine,' said Gabriel, hurt. 'What do you want to talk about?'

'I don't really care,' she replied, flicking through the pages. 'I just don't really care for banking chat, this late in the evening.'

'I'm so tired of hearing about your "girls",' Gabriel said, fatigue creeping into his voice. He rubbed his eyes. 'Why don't we just go upstairs, call it a night?'

'They're not just girls,' snapped Clarice. 'We have intellectual debates. And one of them is starting a cosmetics centre.'

'Wonderful,' Gabriel said coldly.

'I'm serious,' said Clarice. 'Look, you never let me talk for more than thirty seconds. Could you tell me the name of a single artist in this catalogue? I mentioned at least five over dinner this evening. Just name the ones I'll be featuring in my next exhibition. Better: just name one.'

Gabriel sighed. 'You know I have no personal interest in this art, Clarice,' he said. 'It doesn't mean I don't support you in your ventures. Look, your friends can talk to you about all this stuff. Isn't that enough?'

'No,' Clarice said stubbornly.

'You've just spent a week with those women,' Gabriel said. 'Wasn't *that* enough?'

'My life can't revolve around yours, Gabriel. It can't all be men, men, men, bankers, bankers, bankers. My friends are not going to be like your polychrome receptionists, your ancient secretary, the gum-chewing statues in the reception. These are real girls: feminists, happy, peppy, funny, sexual, sensual, intellectual.'

'Clarice, I don't care how many times you say the word "intellectual", I simply refuse to believe that is what your friends are. Especially that Chloë one.'

'Intellectuals aren't all old white men in black turtlenecks,' she shot back. 'Intellectuals can be women who talk, and hug, and drink wine, and, and...and they don't sleep on their backs like some kind of statue!'

'*Ad hominem* attack,' said Gabriel. 'Is that really the best you can do?'

'Sometimes,' said Clarice, rather melodramatically, 'I turn over in the night and I can't tell if you're dead or alive.'

'Maybe you should have stayed in a chalet longer, if you liked it so much,' Gabriel retorted, no longer caring if he sounded petty.

'Maybe I should have,' said Clarice, throwing down the catalogue and storming upstairs.

———◆◆———

Ten minutes later, Gabriel tentatively followed. The conference had exhausted him, and he was looking forward to his bed, even if Clarice would be in it. He creaked the bedroom door open slowly.

'The thing is,' Clarice said, flouncing around the room, opening and closing cupboards for no apparent reason, 'you just don't listen to me.'

Gabriel sighed. Perhaps he should have stayed on the couch. 'Clarice, I am very happy to engage with you, if only you would bring up subjects I could actually contribute something to. You know very well I have no interest in modern art.'

'I was trying to tell you something,' Clarice said, slamming the armoire door shut and throwing a beaded white dress down on a chair. 'Something...'

'You're not pregnant, are you?' said Gabriel, immediately regretting the joke. How old would they have to be, before the subject stopped being sensitive?

'I'll have you know,' Clarice said breathlessly, 'that just recently, an Italian woman conceived at the age of sixty-five. Not even in vitro!'

'Clarice,' Gabriel said as affectionately as he could, 'we are not

Italians.'

'Well, maybe if you'd tried to talk to them, you'd have managed to make some useful business contacts. We could really use the money, you know. This expansion of Von Mipatobeau, it would be useful to our family, particularly if we decided to make some substantial investments, in the near future.'

What on earth was she talking about? She was off on one of her rages, now. There was no use trying to reason with her.

'I bet you spent the whole conference off in a corner with Thomas, laughing like schoolboys at people speaking foreign languages. Switzerland is meant to be the most cosmopolitan country in the world!'

'Actually, Clarice,' Gabriel said patiently, 'I did make some business contacts. That's what I was trying to tell you, before you interrupted.'

Clarice paused, as if considering. 'Are you saying you wouldn't be willing to have a baby, if I wanted one?'

'Ah, but what would happen to the club?' Gabriel asked. 'Does your busy schedule really have time for babies? Babies cannot drink local wine, you know. In my experience, they do not enjoy *pain au chocolat* either, nor cosmetics.'

'You don't have any experience,' Clarice spat, kneeling down to sort through her shoe rack.

'I met an American broker,' said Gabriel, deciding to mirror Clarice's approach to conversation. 'His name is Dick Nikko - a very smooth character. He invited me to Chicago.'

Clarice gave a snort of laughter. 'As if you'd go to Chicago.' But the rattling of high heeled shoes quietened a little bit.

'It was an interesting offer. He's looking for international collaboration.'

He wouldn't really be going to America, but it would be amusing watching Clarice try to stop him. After all, though the couple shared very little these days, it seemed to Gabriel that they shared their distrust of all things international.

'Thomas disagrees, of course, but then that's because the Germans chewed his ear off talking about the unreliability of Americans.'

'I wouldn't listen to Thomas if I were you,' Clarice said, sitting back on her heels.

'Anyway, when I came home I found that this Dick Nikko character had mailed me these rather nice gold cufflinks. Along with a plane ticket.' He paused, waiting for Clarice to laugh.

'When?' she said.

'What?'

'The ticket. When is it for?'

'What does that matter? I mean, it's obviously...' Feeling her stare on him, he replied: 'Next month.'

'You should obviously go,' Clarice said, standing up.

'What?' said Gabriel, staring at his wife uncertainly. 'But we don't know anything about America.'

She shrugged. 'We need the money,' she said.

Gabriel continued to stare, as if hoping the answer to his wife's bizarre behaviour could be read on her face. 'You're not really pregnant, are you?' he asked hesitantly, this time honestly.

Clarice burst out laughing. 'No,' she said. 'I am most certainly not pregnant. Correct me if I'm wrong, but one usually has to have intercourse, to get pregnant.'

'I'm very confused,' said Gabriel. 'I mean, I...' A blind, confused rage was rising up in him. 'I don't even know why I spoke to those Americans,' he said. 'I was bored. They were funny. Thomas was off drinking beer. I mean, I'm not even sure Von Mipatobeau really needs to expand at all. Haven't we always been successful in Switzerland, with our mostly Swiss clientele? Why should we need to enter into these dubious dealings abroad? I mean, I'm a Swiss banker! Swiss!'

'Tell me,' Clarice said, putting her hands on her hips, 'what Switzerland means to you, and I will try to understand what it really has to do with banking.'

'Very well,' said Gabriel, drawing himself up to his full height. 'Well, for a start, cheese.'

Clarice held up one finger, as if keeping tally.

'Cheese, and beautiful mountains, and banking secrecy. *Le secret bancaire!*'

'Go on.'

'Watches,' Gabriel said firmly. 'Woodcarving. Swiss army knives.'

'Your vision of Switzerland is completely antiquated. You're like your father, chopping wood, chopping bears, chopping potatoes. It sounds rather violent, if you ask me, this idyll of yours,' she concluded grimly.

'Look, I don't know why I am allowing myself to be drawn into your ridiculous games. The bottom line is, I am not going to America.'

'The bottom line is,' Clarice said, not looking at him, 'I'm opening a new gallery, so we need the money.'

'What?'

Clarice gave an infuriating little shrug. 'I would have told you earlier, if you would just listen.'

'What?' Gabriel said again. 'When? How? Why?'

'As soon as I can get some of the funds to set up,' she said. 'Fleurie has a space in mind, very close to Saint Antoine, actually, and I've been in contact with many of my favourite artists.

'When?' Gabriel sputtered.

'This afternoon,' said Clarice. 'Khadija will be recruiting radical new artists from the Middle East, to form the basis for my first exhibition. There will be a grand opening, which is very important.'

'Why?' Gabriel said petulantly.

'To establish our reputation,' she said calmly, 'and find clients.'

'I won't stand for it,' Gabriel replied. 'This is ridiculous. I've stood aside while you dabbled in this modern art business long enough. How on earth do you come up with these harebrained schemes?'

'No, Gabriel,' Clarice said calmly. 'The application is already in. There's nothing you can do about it. There's going to be a contemporary art gallery right next to our house.'

'It simply isn't... seemly. You're betraying everything the Old Town stands for, everything Switzerland stands for! Besides, you don't have the money.'

'I am as Swiss as you are, Gabriel!' Clarice bellowed, suddenly losing her cool. 'Most of my friends are Swiss. And there is nothing un-Swiss about modern art, Gabriel. What do you want me to do to prove it, host a, a... fondue party?'

'Yes!' Gabriel shouted back. 'Why not host a damn fondue party? I'm sick and tired of your championing all Middle Eastern and... French values. We're Swiss, Clarice. The de Puritigny family has always been, above all things, Swiss.'

'Fine!' Clarice replied. 'I'll host your goddamn fondue party. I'll use it as a fundraiser for my new gallery!' With this parting shot, she stamped to the bathroom and slammed the door shut.

Gabriel sat down on the bed and waited. Eventually, Clarice emerged, brushing her dark hair fiercely.

'Look at all these grey hairs,' she barked. 'Isn't it time you stopped talking to me like I'm some sort of irresponsible teenager?' She sat down next to him, set down the brush, and wrapped her dressing gown more tightly around herself, as if creating a protective cocoon.

Gabriel sighed. 'I'm sorry I reacted so badly about the gallery. I simply didn't see the notion coming. It's none of my business, of course, as long as you don't ask me to invest my money.' Clarice was silent, sniffing and picking up the hairbrush again. She continued to run the brush through her hair with what seemed to Gabriel quite unnecessary violence. 'Clarice,' he said quietly, 'I really wasn't planning on going to America. I only mentioned it... well, I thought we could laugh about it together. You know I've never travelled overseas.'

'I was just surprised,' Clarice said. 'I mean, you went all the way to Lugano in the hopes of making new business contacts. This should be wonderful news for Von Mipatobeau. You should be excited!'

'That's the thing,' he replied. 'I'm not excited. I'm worried. Now, I'm a rational man. I don't go in for any of this instinct business. Then again, the idea doesn't hold up particularly well to rational examination, either. I met the man for, what, twenty minutes, and he sends me a free plane ticket? There's something fishy going on here. There's got to be.'

'Maybe they just really wanted to deal with Swiss bankers.'

'That's what I'm worried about. What does that tell you they're looking for?'

Clarice shrugged. 'Well, tell me more about this Dick character, then. I mean, what are you afraid of?'

'Secrecy,' Gabriel said patiently. 'I suspect they're quite keen on our dear old *secret bancaire*. I will not become involved in money-laundering.'

'Dick,' said Clarice, attempting to steer the conversation. 'Paint me a portrait. Remember, I wasn't at the conference.'

'Well, he's very tall and handsome. Chiselled jaw, impeccable suit, polished shoes. A real charmer. I can't say I quite understood everything he was offering, in banking terms. He kept using words like "call" and "reversal" and was it "corkscrew"?'

Clarice raised an eyebrow. 'Maybe you could stand to learn what he's talking about. After all, brokers know how to handle money.'

'Yes, I'm quite sure Nikko has handled a lot of money. That isn't enough to reassure me.'

Clarice leaned close. 'You could make a fortune,' she said, unable to keep the excitement from her voice. 'Europe doesn't know about this... corkscrewing. Maybe in those American offices, you can learn things about the international market that you can use to your advantage.'

'I suppose I could just go on a sort of reconnaissance mission,' Gabriel admitted unwillingly. 'It's just very far to go.'

'Why are you so against the idea of doing business with this guy? I mean, you hardly know him. I know you're wary of fancy exaggerators, but not all of them are bad people. I mean, Khadija's princes aren't all horrible men just because they have a lot of money.'

'Dick Nikko is not going to personally be buying you champagne,' Gabriel observed.

'Come on,' said Clarice, 'let's be reasonable about this. What is your resistance to outside values really about?'

'Clarice, I will not be pop-psychoanalysed...' He sighed. 'Sorry. I don't mean to be quite so on edge. I'm just worried. Do you know what being a Calvinist truly means? It's about simplification. What I mean is: I like being a boring Swiss banker. I have been extremely successful at it.'

'Well, times are changing,' said Clarice. 'May I remind you that you just came back from the border of Italy? I know Chicago is quite a few more stones' throws away than that, but the idea is the same. Von Mipatobeau is hungry for expansion, for business. You, my dear husband, are ready for it.'

'I'm not so sure,' Gabriel said. 'I'm worried about my work, my life, the future of the bank. Worried about my marriage, if I'm quite honest. You've become a bit of a... well... a gold-digger, Clarice. I'm uncomfortable with it.'

'I don't think you can be a gold-digger within a twenty-year-old marriage,' Clarice said drily. 'Besides, if you're tired of my demands for money, there are two easy solutions: one, get your bank to make some investments in America; two, help me open my gallery and watch as I ascend to financial independence.'

'Or come crashing down,' said Gabriel, unable to help himself.

'I won't come crashing down,' Clarice said firmly. 'You'll see. All of this... this is what we wanted. Both of us are ready for these changes. Both of us are ready to come out of our shells, and open up to the world.'

'The world is not just an oyster waiting to be pried open so you can grab its pearls, Clarice,' Gabriel said. 'I don't want you to get too carried away about this gallery project.'

'I know what I'm doing,' Clarice said stubbornly. 'I know the market. I've studied it. I've been successful. Gabriel,' she said suddenly, grabbing his hand, 'we've always been partners. We've always worked side by side. You helped me set up my first gallery –'

'Your only gallery,' Gabriel interjected.

'My first gallery, that I love very much. It's had a moderate success, and kept me busy. Now I'm ready for more. Won't you trust me? I'm not asking for much. Just a little help with the initial deposits.'

'I'll think about it,' he said.

'I need your help,' she said unwillingly. 'I don't want to be hanging on Khadija's purse-strings like Chloë.'

Should have thought about that before you decided to open a gallery, then. 'How about this, for a start,' Gabriel said, feeling magnanimous. 'I'll front the cash for your fundraising fondue. You can hold whatever kind of party you want, with as many rich businessmen as you want. I'd imagine that if you truly know what you're doing, you'll be able to do the rest of your fundraising right there.'

Clarice was quiet. 'Very well,' she said. 'I will have this fondue party. And one more thing.'

'What?'

'You're going to Chicago.'

Gabriel stood up from the bed. 'I'm going downstairs,' he said.

In his slippers, Gabriel padded down into the lounge, where Clarice's catalogue sat abandoned. Idly, he picked it up, and began flicking through. Modern art was just so awful, all of it! Vast geometrical designs, dead animals in plastic, entire rooms painted weird shades of grey. On one page, he came across what appeared to be a fallen palm tree, filling up the whole entry hall of a museum in Copenhagen. There was something he had not seen earlier, though: throughout the catalogue, Clarice had folded down corners, stuck post-it notes and scribbled in pencil. She'd obviously been doing her homework. Gabriel sighed. What did he know? Maybe she did know the scene. He was just quite sure it was a scene he hated. He wondered if he could justify running off to the chalet, just for a few days? But no, he had to be back at the bank in the morning. The holiday to Lugano was over. It was time to get back to work.

He sighed and scuffed his slippers gently across his beloved waxed parquet. He needed advice on this Chicago thing. But whom could he ask? Thomas was useless. Caroline was cautious. He had very few friends, let alone friends who knew about banking. Except... He glanced towards the phone. Of course! Why hadn't he thought of it before? There was always Dieter. It might be useful to get advice from a commercial banker. Perhaps he could slyly find out if these reversals and strangles were already common knowledge in all of Europe. Gabriel went to pick his agenda from his briefcase, and dialled Dieter's number.

'Hello?'

'Yes, hello.'

There was a pause.

'Who is this?'

'Er, Gabriel. Gabriel de Puri–'

'Gabriel, my friend! What an unexpected pleasure!'

'Sorry, it isn't late, is it?' Suddenly panicked, Gabriel glanced at the clock. He hadn't thought to check. But no, it was only ten. Late for Swiss bankers, but probably not too late for a family man like Dieter.

'Oh no,' said Dieter. 'It's just that I haven't heard from you in... three, four years?'

'Right,' said Gabriel. 'Well.'

Dieter laughed. 'Tell me what's on your mind. Are you planning a trip to Zurich? You're welcome to come stay with us any time.'

'No,' Gabriel blustered. 'I mean, that's a very kind offer.'

'How are you doing, then?' Dieter asked.

'I went to a banking conference in Lugano,' Gabriel said. 'It was awful.'

'Oh, but didn't you love the city? The lakeshore? The food?'

'I don't know,' said Gabriel. 'I was there for the banking. Actually, that was what I wanted to talk to you about. It was my first international banking conference.'

'Well, welcome to the modern world! It doesn't sound like your style, though. What were you up to?'

'Our bank is thinking of expanding internationally,' he said hesitantly. 'It's just that I don't know a great deal about it.'

'Did you have any luck in Lugano? The Italians tend to keep to themselves...'

'Not with the Italians, nor the French, nor the Germans.'

'Right. So the trip was a failure,' Dieter said jovially. 'Is that what you wanted to talk about?'

'No. I mean, I met some Americans. American brokers.'

Dieter let out a long, low whistle. 'Big money,' he said. 'But be careful. Those guys are class-A swindlers most of the time. They know exactly what they're doing, and how to charm a traditional banker into doing their bidding.'

'Oh,' said Gabriel, crestfallen. 'He seemed very nice. He offered to show me his offices, and fly me out for free.'

'He didn't say anything about derivatives, did he? I really wouldn't recommend getting involved in that scene,' Dieter said. 'It's fast returns, but dangerous money. I wouldn't do it, unless I had a very firm handle on the market.'

'Oh no,' said Gabriel. 'I mean, he mentioned it, but I'm not sure that's what he wants me for.'

'Well, just be careful you know what he does want you for, if you know what I mean. This doesn't sound like your scene, Gabriel.'

Gabriel sighed. 'I was hoping you'd encourage me to go,' he admitted. 'My wife... Clarice thinks we could really use the contacts, the money. Especially the money.'

'Well, far be it from me to dissuade you from something you want to do. I mean, what do you think?'

'I think it's time for Von Mipatobeau to expand abroad, and this is the first serious offer we've had. Besides, it all sounded kind of interesting. I mean, weren't you always telling me I should break out of my shell? Isn't this a great opportunity?'

'Only if you can find out what kind of opportunity it is,' Dieter said carefully.

'He's very charming, this broker, this Dick Nikko,' Gabriel tried to explain. 'He sounded like he really had things to offer...'

There was a commotion in the background. 'Klaus, one minute,' said Dieter. 'Look, I'm going to have to go – Klaus is handing in his application to Harvard tomorrow – but keep me posted, OK? I don't want you doing anything reckless.'

'I am not a reckless man, Dieter,' Gabriel said in frustration.

'I know, Gabriel. I also happen to know you're unused to dealing with men who aren't other sweet, boring Swiss bankers.'

'I am not sweet,' said Gabriel, insulted.

Dieter laughed gently. 'Look, do what you want – yes, Klaus, hold on – sorry Gabriel. If you're curious, why don't you go to Chicago? It doesn't mean you have to sign anything. Hear this Dick guy out, if you want to, but don't do more than listen. Come back to me, if you like, once you know a little bit more. You have my number.'

'I will,' said Gabriel. 'Thank you.'

'My pleasure,' said Dieter. 'Call me again soon. And have fun in Chicago.'

Gabriel sat back down on the couch. Dieter's resistance had had the opposite effect to Clarice's insistence: he *wanted* to go now, just to prove he could. What did Dieter know about what was his scene, or not? Only he knew his capabilities. He would go to Chicago. The de Puritigny portraits stared down at him from their black backgrounds and gold frames, disapproving in the darkness. Gabriel picked the art catalogue up again deliberately. He wasn't a patriarch in velvet, he wasn't wearing a ruff and pearls. He was a modern de Puritigny. It was up to him what that meant. Besides, why couldn't Swiss bankers go to Chicago?

Chapter Fifteen

'I'm so glad you're going to Chicago,' said Clarice, pouring herself a large coffee. Dusty sun filtered in through the window.

Gabriel smiled stiffly. 'Yes, well,' he said, scraping excess butter from his slice of toasted rye bread. 'It's a bit late to change my mind, isn't it.' Something was different about breakfast that morning, and it wasn't just the upcoming flight.

'You've been saying that for two weeks now,' Clarice replied pettily. 'You know what we agreed. This is a good thing in every possible way.'

Gabriel sighed, and Clarice suddenly, unexpectedly took his hand in hers. Her fingers were cool and slightly buttery. 'I'm sorry,' she said. 'I just... Well, I sort of wish I could have come too.'

'I know, *chérie*,' he said, disengaging himself gently and returning to the business of his toast. The atmosphere in the room was different, that was it. It was somehow darker, though the shutters were all open.

'If it turns out to be wonderful over there – if you make business contacts, or find some great beach – well, we simply must go back together as soon as possible.'

'It's midwinter, you know. I'm not exactly going for the scenery.'

Gabriel stirred his decaf with a silver spoon. All at once, he realised what was awry. '*Chérie*,' he said suddenly, frowning, 'what happened to the breakfast table? Has it gone for repairs?'

'Oh!' she replied. 'Don't you like it?'

There was a pause. Gabriel looked at the table dubiously. 'You don't mean...'

'I bought it! As a going-away present! It's made out of –'

'Olive wood, I presume,' he said shortly.

'I found it at the Plainpalais market,' Clarice continued, unperturbed. 'It's quite rare to make tables out of olive wood, apparently, because the trees are so short. A table for six is a rarity, or so the antiquarian told me.'

'*Antiquarian*,' Gabriel scoffed. 'Some dusty old grandfather, surely.'

'Isn't it beautiful, though?' Clarice pressed him.

'Hm,' he said. 'This is your idea of modernity?'

'Fleurie talked me into it,' she said happily. 'We went to the market together after our Carouge coffees - after we finished planning the fundraiser. She says I'm becoming more Mediterranean in my outlook, you see. She says it shows in my evolving taste in art, as well. I'd like to change some of the decoration in here to match that, if you don't object.'

Gabriel stared at his wife. 'Clarice, this is the worst possible time to have this discussion, but for the record, you do *not* have my permission to do *any* redecorating. This house has looked the same for hundreds of years. You do not move to Saint Antoine and then... modernise. Maybe things are different down south.'

'What, in Carouge?' Clarice said gaily. 'You know, olive trees grow right here in Geneva. Anyway, I think it's beautiful. Perhaps my timing is just a little bit off. We can discuss further redecorating when you return.'

Gabriel was stubbornly silent, biting into his cool, dry toast. 'Maybe in the kitchen,' he finally said, begrudgingly.

'Fine,' she said. 'Now, eat your one-egg omelette. Did you want any onions on the side?'

'No, Clarice,' he said patiently, 'I do not want onions for breakfast. Have you gone crazy this morning? Why are you trying to change everything on my last morning in Geneva?'

'It's hardly your last morning,' she said drily. 'You're coming back on Saturday.'

'Yes, well...' he said, but couldn't come up with a rejoinder.

'Khadija says onions are good for you,' she added.

'Could you please bring me some more toasted pumpernickel?' Gabriel burst out.

Clarice sighed and stood up. 'Look, *chéri*, I just wanted to have one last nice breakfast for you. I wasn't trying to offend you, or ruin it with onions. I thought the onions were a nice touch.'

'Yes, well, this isn't the Middle East,' he said.

'You'll be in America soon. Who knows what they eat for breakfast there?' Clarice walked to the kitchen and returned shortly with a basket of fresh toast. She did not seem to have stopped talking. 'Perhaps you'll meet some people interested in investing in art. I know I'll be busy, seeing my girlfriends in the gallery, planning the fundraiser, but I'll be sad you're gone. I guess I'll be the power behind the throne, eh? Well, our lifestyle has become quite expensive, and of course with the new gallery... I used to buy my Hodlers for fifty thousand, you know, and somehow, as if overnight, I can't find them for anything under two hundred thousand! It's just too much. I just don't know what direction the market is taking. I have to be careful.'

'So you do still have a touch of the old Swiss frugality under your new gold-digging ways,' Gabriel said, amused by this rambling speech.

'I'm going to need to invest a lot of capital in the near future,' she said briskly. 'I already have an eye on a few intriguing new collections, an inventory of a dozen new paintings for the new gallery.'

'Yes, and there's the matter of twelve pairs of new shoes, and a few Hermès hats...'

'Hush, now,' she said, missing the irony. 'A woman always needs more money. After all, everything I earn, I invest into paintings for the gallery.'

'All... contemporary?' Gabriel asked with distaste.

'Well, there's some modern art mixed in as well.'

'What's the difference?' he snapped.

'Of course the terms are debatable,' Clarice replied smoothly, 'but modern art is usually considered to precede what we call contemporary. Modernism, I'm sure you know, was a movement at the turn of the last century. Anyway, the Russians are becoming more interested in Picasso and Klimt, so I might pick up a few of those, if I can afford it.' She cast him an innocent glance. 'I intend to attract extremely rich people,' she said with confidence. 'The idea came from Chloë and her new Russian sugar daddies, actually. She needed cash for her spa cosmetics. Anyway, turns out there's plenty of new money in Russia, Ukraine, Kazakhstan. They just don't know what to do with it, apart from picking up villas and real estate in London or Paris.'

'I don't mind Klimt,' Gabriel said mildly. 'I mean, for a bank lobby or something. All that gold.'

Clarice made a noise that sounded suspiciously like a giggle. 'Klimts sell for a hundred thousand these days, you know,' she said.

'And how much did this olive table cost?' he asked coldly.

Clarice hesitated. 'Fifteen thousand,' she admitted. 'Of my own money!' she added defensively.

Gabriel said nothing.

'Well, the bottom line is that we need more money, whether or not we're redecorating. Just wait until I introduce you to a few of those Arab princes at the fondue party on Saturday! We'll both end up filthy rich and happy and successful. Just be a bit more aggressive, you know? It'll be good practice, spending some time in America. Doesn't every banker and executive make hundred-million-dollar bonuses over there?'

'I exceedingly doubt it,' said Gabriel. 'Could you hand me some of that toast? It will be stone cold if you talk much longer.'

'When is your flight, anyway?' she asked, setting a slice down on his plate.

'Two hours from now,' he said.

'Are you flying direct?'

'To New York,' he said, 'with Continental.'

'Don't you usually fly Swissair, *monsieur le Suisse*?'

'I prefer Swiss,' he said, 'but they had no direct flights to New York. I'd have had to drive all the way to Zurich.'

'I see,' said Clarice. Why did she always seem to have an amused glint in her eye? Was everything he said funny? 'I'll miss you,' she said suddenly.

'I'll call you when I get there,' he said stiffly.

Standing in the airport, Gabriel adjusted his tie uneasily. He had everything he needed: ticket, nearly-empty briefcase, Hermès suitcase packed with blue suits, pink shirts, underwear, two different ties. He'd also brought a large packet of muesli, in case American food was inedible. Why was he so jittery? There was still an hour until his flight's departure, which left him plenty of time to check in, buy a newspaper, drink some sparkling water. Dick would be meeting him at O'Hare airport upon his arrival in Chicago. Everything at Von Mipatobeau was in order. There was nothing to worry about. The nerves would pass, Gabriel told himself firmly, walking towards the desk. *Let's get this over with.*

Once the rigmarole of check-in and security was finished, there was nothing left to do but wait. Gabriel sat, sipping from his lukewarm bottle of Perrier, too much on edge to buy anything to read. He watched the planes touching down, wondering if any of them were coming back from the US. At last, it was time for him to walk out across the tarmac towards the huge aeroplane with *Continental* emblazoned on the side. Gabriel took a deep breath and climbed the stairs.

Inside, he was relieved to find that the plane quite resembled those he had travelled on in the past. It was larger, though, and smelled quite peculiar. There didn't seem to be many other travellers on board. No babies, he noted with relief.

'Welcome, *monsieur*,' a beautiful black air hostess murmured, showing him his seat. 'Would you like a newspaper? *Herald Tribune, Le Monde, Financial Times*?'

He nodded, gratefully accepting a copy of the latter. Gabriel walked slowly to his numbered seat, and sat down. The hard part was over: all he had to do was wait. He buckled his seatbelt and unfolded the newspaper.

'Yo! You a real Swiss dude?'

Gabriel looked over warily, unsure whether the words had been directed at him. He met the eyes of a young man wearing a neon jacket, smiling enthusiastically and nodding, and surmised that they had.

'I am in fact Swiss,' he said carefully. 'How can I help you?'

The young man burst out laughing, wrinkling his very tan skin. 'I'm Gary!' he said, nudging his companion, 'and this is Colin! We just got back from skiing. What's your name?' His companion looked up from his book, and smiled.

'I take it you're American,' Gabriel said stiffly. At the boy's questioning expression, he relented. 'My name is Gabriel,' he said, setting down his newspaper.

'Gabe! Gabe the ape!' The boy hooted with laughter, elbowing his friend in the ribs. Colin did not look back up from his book.

'I don't know you. You must be mistaken.'

'You seem real fancy, with your suit and all,' the boy said appreciatively. 'How come you're not in first?'

'First class? Oh, I asked to be moved here, actually.' The boy stared. 'It just seemed a bit silly, you know. I'm a Calvinist, a Huguenot. You have to have some... frugality in your life.'

The boy shrugged. 'Well, I guess all sections of the plane get there at the same time, don't they!'

Gabriel laughed, surprised. 'That's true, young man. I suppose we'll arrive in America at exactly the same time as those in first class.' He shook his head, and unfolded his newspaper again.

The stewardess arrived at their level. 'I'll let you in on a secret,' she said. 'You're served by the same air hostess, anywhere you sit on this here plane. Those over there just get an extra piece of chocolate. Besides, look how much space there is on this flight: if you wanted to sleep later, you could easily stretch out across these four seats.'

'You mean lie down?' Gabriel asked, a little surprised.

'Oh yes,' she said, and walked off.

Gary burst out laughing. 'Wow,' he said. 'What a piece of ass!'

'I beg your pardon?'

'I mean, well, she's a... lady,' he finished lamely. 'A very attractive lady.'

'I suppose she is,' Gabriel said, uncomfortably.

'Hey, you think there's going to be turbulence? I hear it's really snowy back home. I mean, it sure was snowy on the pistes, man oh man. You remember, Colin?'

'It was great,' Colin said quietly, not looking up from his book.

'Courchevel was just amazing, man, that powder! So fresh.'

'Do you have your own ski gear?' Gabriel asked, intrigued against his will.

'Oh yeah,' said Gary, gesturing upwards. 'It's all in here, packed up safe and warm.'

'Goodness,' said Gabriel. 'That must be inconvenient to carry. I always leave my ski gear at my chalet.'

'Man, you have a chalet? That's so awesome! Where is it?'

'Saas Fee,' Gabriel said unwillingly.

The boy shrugged. 'Never been there. Good skiing?'

'I'm more of a cross-country man myself,' he said, unsure how he had managed to engage in conversation with these youths. Were they trying to *befriend* him?

'Wow,' the boy said. 'Epic.'

'How old are you?' Gabriel asked curiously.

'Eighteen,' Gary said cheerfully.

'And how did you end up in Switzerland?'

'I told you, man, we came here to do some serious skiing. We spent a week in the Trois Vallées, stayed in Courchevel and Meribel, and then went on to spend a week in Verbier. Three valleys, four valleys! France and Switzerland! What a trip it was.'

'You have... funds for this?'

'Oh yeah, my parents paid for the trip – a little winter break. We're freshmen in college. We'll be back in school come January.'

'I see,' said Gabriel.

'I bet you want to know whether we preferred skiing in France or Switzerland, don't you?'

'Not particularly,' Gabriel muttered, but too quietly for the boy to notice.

'Well, the food in Verbier was amazing; I had the best fondue I've ever had in my whole life! But your country is just so damn expensive,' he said. 'So I'd probably say I preferred Courchevel. I mean, there were all these cute English girls in the bars. I loved the après-ski there; everybody out to party.'

'To party?' Gabriel asked curiously. 'You mean drinking? People drink when they are skiing?'

Gary laughed. 'Afterwards, mostly,' he said.

'Every day?' Gabriel said in disbelief.

'Sure, man. I mean, what's the purpose of skiing if you don't get drunk afterwards?'

Colin suddenly raised his head from his book. 'Leave the nice old man alone, buddy,' he told his friend quietly.

Gabriel was taken aback. *Old man*? 'Well, those resorts are full of tourists anyway,' he said, growing defensive against his will. 'They're the ones that are to blame for this decadence. Skiing is about purity. I mean, didn't you enjoy the views? You should go back in summer. There are the most breathtaking hikes in the Verbier area. You can walk across the tops of mountains.'

'Cool,' Gary said. 'I'm more of a high-speed guy but sure, the mountains were pretty beautiful out there.' He sighed contentedly.

'And I'd avoid Zermatt if I were you,' Gabriel said suddenly. 'It's full of Japanese businessmen.'

'OK,' Gary said hesitantly.

'I really think you should spend more time in Switzerland before coming up with these opinions,' he said.

'Hey man,' the boy said, raising his palms in an apologetic gesture, 'I loved the cheese.'

Gabriel sighed, and roughly opened his *Financial Times* to its full width.

'So what's in this pink paper of yours?' Gary asked cheerfully. 'You seem pretty keen on it.'

Gabriel sighed, letting the paper fall into his lap. 'It's an excellent newspaper,' he said patiently, 'offering insight into global politics and finance.'

'Sounds heavy,' said Gary.

'As you can see, it is a fairly slim newspaper,' Gabriel replied hesitantly. Gary giggled. 'So, what are you studying?'

'Well, Colin here is the real intellectual. I'm studying pre-med, and he's into literature. We're roommates, you see, at Cornell, in upstate New York. We're both great skiers, though.'

'You ski in America?'

'Oh yeah, but there's something fun about flying overseas for sports. I mean, sure, sometimes we ski near Lake George, or drive over to Vermont, but I guess France – well, Switzerland is more fun.' He flashed a conciliatory grin. 'And you, what do you do? Are you a businessman?'

'In Switzerland, we don't talk about these things.'

'Oh, you're one of those,' Gary said, nodding wisely. 'I see. I've heard that Swiss people are very secretive. This must mean you're a banker.'

'Well,' Gabriel said uneasily, 'yes, I am.'

Gary smiled triumphantly. 'Why?' he asked.

'Why am I a banker?'

'No, why are you so secretive?'

Gabriel shrugged. 'It's a Swiss thing,' he said. 'Books have been written about the subject, if you really want to learn more.'

'Seriously, why? Why are you so secretive? How does it serve your business?'

Gabriel sighed. 'The clients want the secrecy, not us.'

'What, because you're hiding money for some people?' Gary asked excitedly.

'No, we don't hide anybody's money. We're just very discreet. It's a rare talent,' he added pointedly, 'but a common quality among the Swiss. Nobody knows anyone else's salary, nobody talks about their savings.'

'You must be kidding!' exclaimed Gary. 'I mean, in the States, you can ask anybody about the salaries. People love to brag! Even the newspapers publish bonuses. If somebody makes fity million dollars in bonuses, they want the world to know.'

'Not in Switzerland,' said Gabriel.

'Well, America is big, so I guess it's normal that we would have bigger bonuses.'

Gabriel decided not to rise to the taunt, and was glad to observe the air hostess coming back their way. 'Excuse me,' he said quietly.

'Hey,' said Gary.

'Yes, sir?' she replied to Gabriel.

'I'm a bit tired,' he said, raising his voice for the benefit of his obnoxious companion. 'Could I perhaps order a tisane?'

'Of course. Camomile? Peppermint?'

'Camomile would be nice,' he said. 'But make it quite weak.'

'Would you like me to bring you an extra blanket? Maybe a few small cushions so you can make yourself a bed?'

'Hey!' said Gary. 'Can I get that, too?'

The stewardess ignored him. 'You look like a nice, respectable man,' she said softly to Gabriel. 'That doesn't happen too often in tourist class. Maybe I can pamper you a little bit.'

'Er, alright,' Gabriel said uncertainly.

She leaned closer. 'Would you like me to squeeze you some nice fresh orange juice from my own oranges? They're so juicy and sweet.'

'No, thank you. I don't want your oranges.'

'You're wasting your time over there. Why don't you lie down with me, honey?' said Gary. 'Plenty of free seats on this plane.'

Gabriel stared. The stewardess stood back up and straightened her outfit.

'I don't know what you're implying,' she said huffily, 'and I don't like it. This is not how you talk to an airline hostess.'

'I know they choose air hostesses based on how beautiful they are,' Gary continued, unperturbed. 'Man, you're so beautiful!'

'I'll have you know I have a degree in international relations,' she answered crisply.

'You want to relate to me?' Gary tried again.

The air hostess glared. 'This is completely inappropriate,' she said. 'Do be quiet, child.'

Gary laughed, pleased. 'Alright,' he said. 'I know when I'm beat. But would you mind bringing me a rye and ice? A little bit of the good stuff will calm my blood.' He winked outrageously.

'Very well,' the stewardess replied, mollified.

'Bring me a triple measure. Oh, and bring my friend Colin a gin and tonic.'

'That sounds expensive,' Gabriel commented.

'Oh, it's all free!' the stewardess replied, surprised. 'Would you like something a little stronger yourself?'

'No thank you,' said Gabriel, perplexed.

'Do you mind if I smoke?' asked Gary.

Gabriel sighed.

'Sure,' said the air hostess. 'Just go three seats back: that's the start of the smoking section. *Monsieur*, I'll be right back with your camomile.'

'And my rye.'

Gabriel unfolded his *Financial Times* again.

Gabriel sat in O'Hare airport, drowsily staring out into the grey snow. 'America!' he thought to himself. Here he was at last, and all he wanted was to sleep. Gary and Colin had continued to order rye whiskey throughout the night – or was it day? – so that when Gabriel jolted awake for landing, with the *Financial Times* draped across his face, he did not feel particularly rested. His first impressions of America were something of a blur: the first voices he heard were shouting their heads off about 'frankfurters.' My God, he thought. Had he accidentally flown to Germany? Yes, there were posters advertising hamburgers, as well. Were there even direct flights to Hamburg from here? At last, he figured out the mystery: airports must name their food after major travel centres. It all looked disgusting, in any case, covered with some sort of bright yellow sauce. Giving up on first impressions of America, Gabriel read the *Financial Times* over and over again, all the way from New York to Chicago, and was still half-reading it as he waited to be collected.

'Gabe!' There he was, Dick Nikko, striding across the airport lounge with a smooth smile and a pearl-grey suit. 'How was your trip?'

'Hello!' said Gabriel. 'It was fine, although everybody kept trying to shine my shoes. Do they look dirty to you?'

Dick laughed and clapped him on the back.

'I swear at least three boys came up to me. I was sure I had stepped in something awful.'

'Come on, my driver is waiting.' Dick clapped him on the back again, making him cough. 'Welcome to the windy city,' Dick continued, stepping out into the snowstorm.

'Why is it windy?' shouted Gabriel.

'Cause of the lakes, of course. Mind your step, now: even the toughest Chicago veteran can slip out here. I've lost count of the times I've almost broken my ass.'

'Is it always like this?' Gabriel asked, squinting into the gale. The wind was making his ears hurt.

'Not in July,' said Dick. They were approaching an enormous car, the door of which suddenly opened, as the driver stepped out and picked up Gabriel's bag.

Gabriel swallowed. 'This is your car?' he asked in disbelief.

Dick laughed, opening the door. 'Come on in,' he said.

'It's like a bus,' Gabriel said, bending to fit in and awkwardly sitting down on the imitation leather.

'It's a stretch Cadillac,' Dick replied proudly. 'It has a TV, a bar, and seating for eight people. See that glass barrier there? That's so the driver can't hear a thing. Some days it seems like I live and work in here. Now, would you like a J&B, a Chivas Regal?'

'I don't really drink,' Gabriel said hesitantly. 'Not in the afternoon.'

'Ah, of course,' said Dick magnanimously. 'The jetlag. You must feel like you've just woken up – or is it bedtime?'

'I don't know,' said Gabriel, resisting the urge to rub his eyes. 'To be honest, though, I'm not used to drinking strong alcohol even when I'm not jet-lagged. I only usually have wine three times a year.'

'How very European,' said Dick. 'Well, here in America, this is how we like to welcome our guests. You see, we suffered so bad here in Chicago during the prohibition, that when we got out, everybody started drinking. Even those who didn't drink before! Even children!' He winked.

'No, thank you,' Gabriel said as politely as he could.

'Is it some sort of Swiss thing?' Dick pressed him.

'It's a question of education,' said Gabriel. 'I am simply not used to it.'

'Well, I won't force you,' said Dick, pulling open a drawer and taking out a bottle of brandy, 'but you should remember you're here on vacation.'

'I'm here for business, aren't I?' replied Gabriel, trying to keep his tone light.

'Oh, sure,' said Dick, 'but this is a great time to visit Chicago. You're in for a real treat, with the snow.' Gabriel tried not to look too dubious. 'The snow, the Christmas lights, the musicians in the street, Santa Claus...'

'Saint Nicolas?' Gabriel asked, suddenly awake.

'Probably,' said Dick, dropping ice cubes into his glass. 'If that's what you call him over there in Europe. Here, you'll find one every hundred yards.'

'Right,' said Gabriel. 'So, where are you taking me?'

'Unless you have strong objections to the plan, we'll be heading straight to your hotel, as I've got some business to finish up before the evening. You can relax there, call your wife, all that jazz.'

'Wonderful!' said Gabriel.

'You'll love the hotel, I'm sure,' he added. 'I got you a suite overlooking the promenade along the Lake. It's a famous old Art Deco hotel, very beautiful. Of course, it's all prepaid.'

'Prepaid? What kind of...' Gabriel said hesitantly, before realising what Dick meant. 'Oh!' he said, embarrassed. 'I can't...'

'Of course you can.' Dick swept away his objections before he could voice them, then downed his tumbler of brandy. 'It's on the house. There's nothing you can do about it.'

'You're too kind,' said Gabriel.

'I'll let you get some rest. If you need anything: company, room service, the concierge, there will be someone to look after your needs. Tomorrow, I'll come meet you in the hotel and we'll eat some breakfast together before heading over to my office. Sound good, yeah?'

'Yes, that sounds good,' said Gabriel, looking out the limo window at trees whipping back and forth in the wind.

Chapter Sixteen

The hotel breakfast room was bustling with men in suits, women in suits, couples with small children. The air was rich with a heady smell of sugar and grease.

'So how'd you sleep?' said Dick, his hair perfectly gelled, his white shirt perfectly ironed.

Gabriel nodded, unfolding his napkin and carefully laying it in his lap. He was acutely aware of the creases his shirt had sustained in his suitcase. 'I slept well, for about four hours. Then my body decided it was time to wake up. It's... a very unfamiliar sensation. I have always been a regular man.'

Dick laughed. 'That's what happens when you fly for nine hours. Totally unnatural, and yet the body adjusts. You'll see. You're a modern man, now.' He picked up his knife and began to tap out a jaunty rhythm on the side of his plate with it. 'So, where shall we start?'

'Well, do you think I might be able to come see your office?'

'No, I mean with the breakfast!'

'Oh! Well, at home, I usually have some rye bread and a cup of decaffeinated coffee.'

Dick looked at him strangely, then burst out laughing. 'Oh, my friend, you are in for such a treat!'

'I don't think I know what half the foods in here are,' Gabriel confessed. 'Is that *steak*?'

'Oh yes,' said Dick. 'You can get steak, grits, kidneys, smoked fish, as well as donuts, waffles, five kinds of muffins, twenty kinds of cereal. You can get any kind of omelette you want. You can get a stack of pancakes covered in syrup. And above all, you must have some crispy bacon.'

'Isn't that bad for you?' he asked tentatively.

Dick laughed. 'This is America,' he said. 'Land of the free. Come on, you have to try a bite of everything.'

'Everything??'

'Just a small bite. Here, I'll go compose a plate for you.' After a good ten minutes, Dick returned with two plates: one heaped with smoked meat, fried eggs and pastries; one with more than twenty sample-sized portions. 'True to my word,' he said. 'You only have to taste.'

'If I'm going to eat all this,' Gabriel said, horrified and amused in equal measures, 'does this mean you only eat one meal a day, in America?'

'Just wait till you see lunch,' said Dick, crumpling a handful of bacon rashers over his plateful. 'I know this great place for surf and turf.'

'Surf and... what?' asked Gabriel, his mind reeling.

'Steak. With lobster. You need the energy, you see, just to be able to get through the day. It gives you this wonderful spurt of power to do all the investments in the morning, make decisions, get in contact with the important clients. Then we take a long break for lunch. Now, are you going to get started on your breakfast or just stare at it all day?'

Gabriel tentatively loaded up his fork. 'This is very strange to me,' he said, 'but I wish to appear accommodating. This is my first time in the country, after all.'

'Anyway, surely it's dinnertime in your head?'

'I don't know,' Gabriel said, dabbing his mouth with a napkin. 'I'm trying not to think about it.'

'Don't you like the food?' Dick asked. 'I mean, you don't have to eat just to be polite, but this is the way we entertain our clients. The best way to a man's heart is through his stomach. The same goes for his brain, or his bank account.' He winked. 'Don't you do the same thing in Switzerland?'

'Hardly,' said Gabriel. 'I mean, we might invite a client out to dinner when we've signed an important contract, or if we're celebrating a portfolio's exceptional performance.'

'Well, here in America, everything is important. Your visit is exceptional.'

'I guess sometimes we meet clients who love to eat, and who try to insist on meeting in restaurants: mostly the Arabs and the Chinese.

I never agree, of course, but I suppose it is not just an American instinct. Still, I've never seen anything like this. This is a real feast.'

'See, you're starting to enjoy it!'

'Steak! For breakfast!' Gabriel said, shaking his head.

'You'll get used to it,' Dick said cheerfully. 'You can have it fried in bacon grease, if you like.'

Gabriel laughed; he couldn't help himself. 'I try to stay thin,' he said.

'Well, just eat small bites, then. But eat them fast: I have the limo waiting.'

'Why don't you go on ahead?' Gabriel suggested. 'I need to brush my teeth any way.'

———— ◆ ————

Sitting on the edge of his enormous white bed, Gabriel picked up the hotel phone. 'Clarice, *chérie*. I'm sorry I didn't call yesterday – it was just so late. Yes, yes, I know. Well, America's quite something! It's an experience. There were six elevators to choose from to come back up from the restaurant. I just ate steak! Yes, it is morning here. I don't know how I feel about it, except to say that I'm quite full. The trip was fine, though I nearly broke my bones sliding on the ice on the way to the hotel. Dick brought me here in a limousine, can you believe it? Yes, it had a bar. I know! It's probably minus fifteen degrees here. My ears hurt. No, you know I never wear hats. Hats are ostentatious. Yes, I also think limos are ostentatious. It's white! No? No, you didn't tell me about that. Well, if you could only see the snow here! No. Right. Anyway, darling, you'll have to tell me about the fundraiser preparations another time, as I have the driver waiting downstairs. I feel like an adventurer, like – Yes, I'm sure it's the limo again. No, I don't think I can take a photograph. Yes. Well, I have to go: I told Dick I was going up to brush my teeth. Goodbye, Clarice.' Gabriel sighed.

He entered the large, shining elevator and nodded at his companions.

'Hi,' one of the women said.

Gabriel started, and looked back up quickly to see if he had failed to recognise an acquaintance. But no, he was in America. He knew no-one here.

'So where you from?' she continued, unperturbed. 'Europe?'

'I... How did you... Switzerland,' he concluded lamely. 'I'm from Switzerland.'

'Cool,' she replied.

'Ooh, moneybags!' another woman exclaimed.

'My son went skiing there once,' another stranger chipped in. 'Broke his leg, the idiot.'

Gabriel shook his head in utter amazement.

'So where do you guys store your money?' the second woman asked. 'I mean, all that gold.' She grinned.

'Well, if you really want to know, we store our gold in New York,' Gabriel said, rather out of the blue.

'Are you married?' the first woman chimed in.

He blushed furiously, feeling completely out of control of the situation, and got out at the next floor. He walked down three flights of stairs, and found Dick waiting by the door, a strange smile on his face.

'I don't understand the people in your country,' Gabriel said as calmly as he could. 'Are they never quiet? Have they no sense of decency, or privacy?'

'Welcome to cowboy America,' said Dick. 'Better get used to it.'

Together, they walked to the limousine.

Dick Nikko's office was nothing if not impressive. 'I see you have chosen a Versailles-style parquet,' Gabriel said approvingly.

'Yeah. Do you like the crystal staircase?' asked Dick. 'It leads up to my private mezzanine. See, my desk is crystal too!'

Gabriel looked up, observing the luminous and modern interior of the office. 'It's luxurious,' he said hesitantly. He wasn't sure if Dick was joking. The desk was certainly something: a huge hunk of sparkling glass. Everything was brightly and indirectly lit, seeming to glow. On the walls, copies of Salvador Dali and Picasso paintings were hung side by side with images of cowboys and bulls in the desert.

'You like Western art, huh?' asked Dick, following Gabriel's gaze.

'My wife's the one who knows about art,' Gabriel replied. 'I'm not much of a... modernist.'

'Ha!' Dick laughed. 'You're funny, Gabe. Do you want to know how many head of cattle are in this painting?'

'The... beefs? I forget the English.'

'Yeah, the beefs. We only call them that when we're eating them, though.'

'How many cattle are in the painting, then?' Gabriel asked. Was that a nervous blush spreading across his cheeks?

'This one time, I was sat in here, bored out of my mind, waiting for a client. The market was doing badly, the ticker over there was going down –' He gestured vaguely at the black box hung near the ceiling, with its red print blinking letters and numbers. 'I started to close my eyes out of sheer, miserable boredom. I was afraid, you know, and I'm not somebody who's afraid easily. Afraid we might go under, with all these losses. It was like ten per cent in one day, man! So I got up out of my chair, walked over to this here painting, and started counting those cows and bulls; in this seven-foot-high painting. And do you know how many there are? There are over a thousand.' He sighed. 'The guy's a great artist, I think.'

'This Western art, it comes from California?' Gabriel was ill-accustomed to feeling out of his depth, culturally.

'Further south than that,' Dick said amiably. 'No cowboys in California. Well, not that kind.' He gave a roguish laugh. 'Say, do you want a cup of joe?'

'Joe?' asked Gabriel, bewildered.

'Coffee. *Café*!' Dick said, with a ridiculous French accent.

Gabriel laughed. 'Oh,' he said. 'I see. No, thank you. Perhaps a glass of sparkling water?'

Dick looked at him curiously. 'We don't have that sort of thing over here,' he said. 'The only sparkling thing in my office is crystal!'

'Sorry,' said Gabriel. 'So,' he continued lamely. 'You like Picasso? How do you reconcile this taste for the radically modern with your interest in this old-fashioned Western art?'

'Well, it's all decorative,' Dick replied expansively. 'I like the colours, the contrast. I don't know much about art, but this looks nice next to my crystal and glass. Guess how much I paid for these prints?'

'I don't know,' Gabriel said.

'Ten dollars!' Dick crowed. 'But the frame cost five thousand.' He grinned.

Gabriel nodded, dazed.

'You should see my house! Maybe I'll take you there for dinner on your next trip. All these beautiful mirrors everywhere, and gilded frames, and we have a glass table right in our dining room.' He lowered his voice. 'I don't know if you'll appreciate this, Gabe, but I also have a crystal bed.'

Gabriel blinked. 'We Swiss don't usually talk about bedrooms,' he said. 'Not in a work environment, certainly.'

Dick laughed. 'You're a private guy. I respect that. Well, why don't we get down to business, then? I have a lot of products I want to tell you about.' He sat down behind his crystal desk, and twirled back and forth a little in his expensive-looking leather chair. 'So, let me show you our charts.' Theatrically, he spun around and pointed at the wall. 'Last year, our performance was fifteen per cent on bond trading and portfolio management of stocks and commodities. Isn't this chart sexy?'

Sexy? Gabriel nodded, not sure if his incomprehension was cultural or linguistic. 'I also deal with a few special products, like our hedge fund. We're making eight per cent on those. Those are very low-risk. By the way, how much money do you make on your portfolios?'

'We don't usually...' Gabriel sighed. When in Rome, he thought to himself. 'At Von Mipatobeau, we never make over four per cent. Our clients don't expect much more, you see. Profit is not their principal motive; they only wish to preserve their capital.'

'Ah, but couldn't you see how you could deal in a secondary market here in the States; making eight and twelve and fifteen per cent?'

Gabriel shook his head. 'I don't understand how it can be so high.'

Dick shrugged, turning back from the wall chart. 'It depends on your level of understanding of the product,' he said. 'Let me tell you about some of our most recent offerings. We've started packaging mortgages, for one. I'll explain what that means, don't you worry. What we do is this: we take the mortgages of middle-class families based in Chicago, Dallas or LA. Then we sell them on in bond form: to foundations, to savings and loans, even to little old ladies with savings. Then we make two per cent in profit, and of course the actual bonds can go on to yield around ten to twelve per cent. It's a win-win arrangement. That's the kind of thing you've got to get your people into. I can show you our brochure, if you like.' He pulled out a drawer from a mysterious space beneath his crystal desk, and set a glossy, brightly-coloured pamphlet on the table. 'Look at that beautiful real estate! On the last page, we've listed statistics from the last three years. If I remember the figures correctly, we made twelve, fifteen and eleven per cent each year respectively. Of course, there are some sexy charts, too.' He glanced up at Gabriel, and ploughed on. 'Of course, if real estate just isn't your thing, well, we could be looking into hedge funds. I have two brochures here dealing with mutual funds in Australia and the Far East. We have high yield bonds from lower grade companies. Would that be the sort of thing you were interested in?'

Gabriel hesitated, not taking the brochure. 'It's very tempting,' he said slowly. 'Isn't there any risk in this kind of dealing?'

'Risk?' Dick laughed. 'You must be kidding. There's no risk at all. This is child's play. Very intelligent option trading, and forward hedging.'

'Geneva doesn't deal in any of those sorts of investments,' Gabriel said. 'We never take those sorts of risks, nor make our clients take them.'

'It's straightforward. It's safe. You just have to know what you're doing.'

'I don't know that I understand enough, to know what I'm doing,' Gabriel said, adding hastily: 'assuming I was even interested in getting involved.'

'Ah, but that's where I come in, my little Swiss friend. I've got the technical knowledge. I can play the game for you. I'll take two per cent here, churn the bonds and make five per cent there, pick up a few bonds upon emission and sell them back two months later for a ten per cent profit. There's always profit, Gabe. Every day, we're making profit. How do you think I can afford this crystal bed, or surf and turf lunches? How would my wife pay for her plastic surgery?' He grinned. 'I have a twenty-thousand-square-foot villa. I have an apartment right here in Chicago Heights, surrounded by several acres of planned gardens, including a golf course.'

'Twenty thousand square feet?' Gabriel asked. 'That's insane! A small apartment in Geneva or Zurich would be... sixty square meters.'

'Do you play golf?' Dick asked.

'Not really,' said Gabriel. 'I always thought it was a lazy man's sport.'

'Ah, but when a rich man is lazy, that's a respectable thing,' Dick said, sighing happily. 'I happen to play every weekend, sometimes with clients. So, Gabriel de Puritigny, if you don't play golf, what do you do with your free time? Do you enjoy Switzerland?'

'I like my life, yes,' said Gabriel. 'I am very happy. I like... walking.'

'Walking. So you don't like to play golf, or drink, or eat anything but toast or muesli or some sort of egg twice a year. And you like walking.' Dick shook his head in amusement.

'The mountains in Switzerland are truly beautiful,' Gabriel said defensively. 'I also enjoy skiing, particularly cross-country. I like... fondue. I like wild strawberry picking in September, when the leaves are turning gold.'

'Wild strawberries?' Dick repeated, bemused. 'Whatever next?'

'They grow wild in our forests,' Gabriel replied, misunderstanding his interlocutor's tone.

'Well, I've sure never heard of that.'

'You must have something like that here,' Gabriel persisted. 'I have heard you have farmers' markets...'

'Everything freezes in Chicago,' Dick replied. 'We go to the supermarket. Speaking of food, though, are you hungry? Our restaurant reservation is in about half an hour.'

Gabriel laughed, before realising he was serious.

'Surf and turf, remember?'

'So why is it called by that ridiculous name, anyway?' Gabriel asked, adjusting his white napkin in his lap. Snow swirled outside the restaurant windows. 'Were the lobsters surfing when they were gathered? And what even is turf? Do I want to eat it?'

'These luxury foods come from the sea and the land. We Americans never do anything by halves, you see. We don't like to choose. We see good things, we stack them on top of each other and eat them both!'

'It just sounds confusing to me,' Gabriel said. 'It sounds like a waste. I'd rather enjoy my good things one at a time.'

Dick roared with laughter. 'Well, why don't you have lobster as a first course, and then steak?'

The waiter appeared at Dick's shoulder. 'We do a very good lobster bisque, sir,' he said. 'Or a lobster club sandwich.'

'Get me a whole lobster from Maine,' Dick said, 'followed by your best steak. What can you offer me for my main course?'

'Well, I can recommend a New York strip, or a Chicago rib-eye aged for eighteen days.'

'Aged?' Gabriel asked curiously.

'It's hung and dried in cold storage, sir,' the waiter replied. 'It makes the flavour richer, more concentrated.'

'How strange. I'll have the... strip, please,' said Gabriel. That sounded quite small.

'How would you like your steak cooked?'

'Well done,' said Gabriel.

'Rare,' said Dick.

'Very well, and what would you like to drink today?'

'I'll take a bourbon and soda,' said Dick. 'That should whet my appetite!'

'I would like a Perrier,' said Gabriel demurely.

'I'm sorry, sir,' the waiter said, 'we don't serve European drinks here. However, I can offer you New York bottled water, which is supposed to be delicious. We add the carbonation here, in our own kitchen.'

'Well, I suppose I'm eating like a local,' said Gabriel. 'It'll go well with my New York steak.'

'And with your main course, some wine perhaps?'

'Something Californian,' Dick barked. 'Maybe Napa Valley?'

Gabriel instinctively stiffened, then sighed. He was tired of fighting every single food and drink offered him. 'Very well,' he said. 'I'll have a small glass.'

'See, you are on holiday!' Dick crowed.

'We have a wonderful Napa merlot,' the waiter said.

'Perfect. We'll take the bottle. And get me that bourbon, sharpish.'

The waiter nodded and disappeared.

'You know, there are Swiss in Napa Valley,' Dick said, winking. 'They even make a sort of pinot noir.'

'How do you know that?' Gabriel asked in surprise.

'I drank some recently.'

'I didn't know there were many Swiss in America.'

'What, you thought they all died of culture shock upon arrival?'

Gabriel surprised himself by laughing. 'I just didn't know a great deal about Swiss emigration. I know a lot about those who immigrated to Switzerland in the seventeenth century, but after that... Actually, now that I think about it, Russia was a popular destination in the eighteenth and nineteenth centuries. A colleague told me that once.'

'Well, I bet America was too. Everybody loves America. Say,' said Dick, his idea brightening as an idea dawned on him, 'does this mean you've never heard of...' He paused, then shook his head.

'What?' said Gabriel.

'Never mind,' said Dick. 'I've had an idea, but it's too half-baked to share. So, have you had a chance to look over those brochures?'

The waiter arrived and set down Dick's bourbon, and Gabriel's sparkling water.

'What, since you gave them to me this morning? I mean, I leafed through in the limo... I'm planning to have a thorough perusal with my partners when I get back to Geneva. I want to study them carefully.'

'Well, you do that then. Soon as you get home, you tell them about our forty-floor building and my crystal desk.' He winked. 'I mean, look, Gabe. We're some of the biggest brokers in the world. We deal in bonds, stocks, syndicated loans, private equity investments, packaged products, hedge funds. We even have funds in some of the upcoming countries like Australia, Japan, and we are starting to work on China. We're maximisers, we're cutting edge, we go for the high returns. There's no way you don't want to work with us.'

Gabriel hesitated. 'I have to think about it,' he said, pouring himself a glass of water. 'This is a serious decision.'

'You've got plenty of time!' Dick said happily, gulping from his glass of bourbon. 'When do you need to be back in old Swissland? Just extend your ticket!'

'I can't,' said Gabriel. 'I need to be back for my wife's party. I mean, her fundraiser. She's raising funds for her new gallery.'

'When's the party?'

'On Saturday.'

'What? You're only staying one more night?'

'Two more days,' Gabriel said. 'I'm not leaving til Friday evening.'

'Well, it's Wednesday now! We'd better make the most of this time!'

The lobster dishes arrived, at this point, and conversation was interrupted for a time by discreet noises of appreciation.

'To tell you the truth,' Gabriel said, wiping his mouth clean of lobster bisque, 'I have my doubts about my wife's art ventures. She's fallen in with this awful crowd of modern women. Gold-diggers, artists, feminists – the worst sort of influence.'

'She make a lot of money?' Dick asked.

Gabriel bristled. 'She does fairly well, yes, though...' he sighed. 'I still have to provide a considerable amount of support. She's convinced opening a second gallery is going to make her rich, but she needs a lot of funding just to get the project off the ground.'

Dick's eyes were shining. 'How about I make a small contribution?' he said. 'I'm always happy to be considered a patron of the arts.'

'I don't know,' Gabriel said. 'I wasn't...'

'Oh, I know you weren't angling. That's why I'm willing to offer.'

'I'm not comfortable mixing business and personal matters. I can't accept that.'

'Doesn't sound personal to me! Sounds like mixing business and business.' He grinned. The waiter collected their plates, and swiftly returned with a bottle of wine.

Gabriel sniffed at his glass of wine dubiously. 'It smells... sweet,' he said. He took a cautious sip and raised an eyebrow. 'It's nice,' he said. He had another quick sip.

Dick smiled and poured himself a large glass. 'Ah, and here are our steaks!'

Gabriel's was stunned. 'I thought it would be the smallest steak,' he said, as two enormous steaks appeared in front of them, steaming, accompanied by salad and one large unpeeled potato covered in cream. 'What is this?' Gabriel asked suspiciously. 'You Americans eat such strange things. This looks like it came straight from a field.'

'Jacket potato!' Dick explained. 'Mash the sour cream and butter in. It's delicious. But that's not the important part. The meat is the important part.'

'Yes, I can see that,' replied Gabriel. 'It covers almost the whole plate.'

'Well, you can't come to Chicago without eating a thick steak,' said Dick. 'I eat steak every day. Nothing smaller than a pound and a half.'

'That's almost 700 grams! So why is it called the New York strip?' Gabriel asked, attempting to saw at a corner of his.

'Oh, because the biggest consumers of this particular cut of beef are in New York. The meat comes from Chicago, though, of course.'

'This is ten times the size of a steak in Geneva,' Gabriel said in despair. 'I don't know if I can eat this! I was raised to finish my plate, leave it empty. It's a question of education.'

'You're not in church now, Gabriel,' said Dick. 'Drink up. It'll help with the digestion.' He laughed, watching Gabriel struggle to cut into the thick cut of steak. 'Just eat what you can. You can always take a doggie bag.'

Gabriel looked up. 'What is a doggie bag?' he asked.

Dick laughed again. 'It's so you can take it home to your dog.'

'What dog?'

'There is no dog – really, you're taking the leftovers home for your own dinner.'

'How strange. No, I don't think I will do that. I'm staying in a hotel, anyway.'

'Well, I can always take yours with me!'

'You want my leftover steak?' Gabriel asked curiously. 'Look, if we're going to divide it for your dog, why don't we do it right now?' He began to saw down the centre of the piece of meat.

'This is what happens when you order meat well done,' Dick said. 'You end up with some very expensive leather.'

Gabriel eyed his companion's bloody steak with distaste. 'I've never liked meat the French way,' he said.

When the first bite of meat slipped into his mouth, he sighed.

'So, you like it?' Dick asked, chomping away.

'It's good,' Gabriel said, already cutting another bite. 'It's... really good.' Inspired, he began cutting into his unpeeled potato.

Half an hour later, the men sat back, sipping at their glasses of wine: Gabriel's first, Dick's fourth. 'I'm so full,' said Gabriel happily.

'Luckily, they didn't bring us a breadbasket! You'll have to carry me back to Switzerland in an ambulance...'

'I wonder what I'll be eating for dinner,' Dick teased.

Gabriel shook his head. 'I'm never eating again.'

'Why don't you take the afternoon off?' Dick asked. 'See the city. Read through my brochures.'

'I need to go and hike in the mountains for four, five hours. Failing that, I think I'd like to go for a walk down by the lake.'

'Oh, I wouldn't do that,' Dick said. 'Certainly not alone. It's dangerous down there on the promenade. You might get attacked. This city has a lot of money, you see, which breeds a lot of criminals. You're too well-dressed, too aristocratic-looking, too... thin. It's suspicious.'

'I just need a little fresh air,' Gabriel said. 'I intend to walk on that promenade, whether it's risky or not. I'd also like to walk around the city this afternoon, go to the museum, see some of these Art Deco buildings I've heard so much about.'

'Well, don't take your briefcase, or somebody is bound to snatch it.' He laughed heartily. 'Look, why don't you let me lend you a couple of bodyguards? I'd feel safer if they were walking next to you.'

'No thank you,' said Gabriel.

'I just don't want you to get stabbed,' Dick said with a smile. 'What if the bodyguards walk behind you, so you can't see them?'

Gabriel sighed. 'Fine,' he said. 'I will walk, and then I will go to bed early. Tomorrow, we'll get back to business.'

'Waiter!' Dick said, emptying his wine glass. 'Can I get two big slices of pecan pie?'

Chapter Seventeen

This time, Gabriel was prepared for the breakfast bar. He sauntered down at seven a.m., picking a corner table not too close to the hordes of pinstriped businesspeople. It was almost a delight to watch these strange men and women guzzle their outrageous breakfasts: stacks of seven thick pancakes drizzled with melted butter and syrup, omelettes piled high with bacon, waffles with blueberries, pastries on the side.

He wandered around, filling a bowl with muesli, plain yoghurt and a sprinkle of raisins. He sat down, then stood up again, dissatisfied. He decided he might as well pick up some bread and sausage on the side, since it was all free. After a moment's reflection, he added a single piece of crispy bacon. He stood for a moment, looking at a piece of steak. He couldn't, could he?

'Sir?' Gabriel turned to see a young boy, wearing white and a small chef's hat, standing at his shoulder. 'I was just wondering if you would like an egg or two with that. I noticed you haven't tried our special egg bar yet.'

'An egg bar?' Gabriel asked. 'A bar for eggs?' He looked back and forth between the plate in his hand and the bowl of muesli at his table.

'We have ten different ways you can make eggs here: soft-boiled, hard-boiled, poached, sunny side up.'

'Sunny side up?'

'That means the yellow part is like the sun, facing upward.'

'Fried. I see.'

'There's also sauce for eggs Benedict, and a variety of omelette toppings: sausage, smoked bacon, mushroom, spinach, potatoes, four kinds of cheese.' He paused. 'We can fry the eggs in olive oil, or butter, or bake them in bacon grease.'

Gabriel shook his head. 'This isn't breakfast. This is a feast!'

'It certainly is,' the boy said happily. 'See how thin I am now? In another five years I won't be able to fit through the door. I'll have to walk through it sideways.'

Gabriel sighed. 'Could you just tell me where the coffee is, please?'

'Certainly, sir. We have twelve different kinds of coffee, vanilla syrup, milk foam, soy milk...'

———◆◆———

Forty-five minutes later, Gabriel sat in the back of the limousine and slammed the door. 'I just had five different coffees!' he exclaimed. 'When I left, I saw somebody cutting a ham. A ham! What is this, Christmas? Some kind of smorgasbord?'

'Good to see you too, Mr Gabriel,' said the driver with a smile.

Gabriel paused. 'Is Dick... Mr Nikko not with us?'

'Mr Boss Man is in his office. We'll be heading there right away.'

'Oh, right,' said Gabriel.

'My name is Sanjeet,' the driver added with a smile.

'Do you like American breakfasts?' Gabriel asked. 'If I'm honest with you, Sanjeet, I think I've been seduced a little bit by them. It's ridiculous, but it's an exciting way to start the day.'

'It certainly is, sir.'

'I mean, America seems so tacky in so many ways: crystal beds and gold frames for ten-dollar prints and terrible food in airports, like frankfurters and donuts... But the breakfasts, the breakfasts are good.'

'How many coffees did you say you had, sir?' Sanjeet asked with a faint smile.

'I don't know,' said Gabriel, 'but I feel great.'

They drove on for a time.

'They have this syrup that comes out of trees!' Gabriel said. 'What is that? You can pour it on that salty, smoky, crispy bacon. Oh, it's Dick. Why is he standing outside?'

Dick opened the door to the limousine with a smile. 'Good morning,' he said. 'I have a surprise for you.' He climbed in next to Gabriel in the back of the car. 'Drive on, Sanjeet.'

'Where are we going?' asked Gabriel, utterly confused.

'I'm taking you on a little trip. It's a surprise.'

'Aren't we meant to be doing business? You were worried we had so little time!'

Dick smiled. 'I've changed my mind. I did some blue sky thinking.'

Gabriel peered out the window into the swirling grey snow.

'Keep those eyes on the road,' said Dick, 'and you might just end up guessing where we're going. I know you'll like this place.' He gave a mysterious smile. 'Sanjeet, take the lake road, not the highway.'

'Yes, sir,' Sanjeet said, staring into the snow.

'Did that sign say Geneva?' Gabriel asked suddenly, craning his neck to see back through the snow. They had been driving for over an hour. 'Geneva, USA?' His tone was disbelieving.

Dick cracked a smile. 'Why, I do believe you've guessed where we're going,' he said. 'Welcome to Geneva, Wisconsin.'

Gabriel frowned, not understanding.

'All of your pleasures seemed to be in Geneva, no?' Dick explained. 'But I couldn't afford to fly us both back to Switzerland, to continue doing business. Wisconsin can offer you the next best thing. So, do you feel at home? Look out the window, there: that's Lake Como. I know you can't see them, but there are the most wonderful rocky beaches, and pleasure boats.'

Gabriel squinted. 'That's the wrong lake! Besides, it's frozen over!' he said. 'That would never happen.'

'That's the height of Swiss rebellion for you,' Dick said. 'Coming over here and changing the name of the lake. Anything else that feels really different?'

'Well, your snow is grey,' he said reluctantly. 'Ours is always pure white.'

'Come on! Are you calling America dirty?' Dick shook his head and laughed. 'You've obviously had a charmed life. I'll have to come visit you sometime. You can show me your Switzerland.'

'Of course!' Gabriel said graciously. 'You can come stay in my chalet in Saas Fee!'

'Meanwhile, try to enjoy this place,' Dick said. 'Sanjeet, you can park over here.'

The snowfall had doubled since they had left Chicago, and flakes were now falling thickly. Dick squinted up into the grey sky and sighed. 'Why don't we go find a bite to eat? Maybe the weather'll clear, so I can show you around later. There are pretty little houses that look like chalets, and some great gift shops where you could pick up something for your wife. First, let me take you to Chez Angelo.'

Gabriel nodded. 'I wish I had my cross-country skis with me!' he said, only half-joking. This snowstorm somehow had a different quality to it than Swiss snow: wetter, more aggressive. Yet it was still snow, and Gabriel had always loved snow.

'The diner's just over here,' Dick said, motioning him forward.

Inside the bar was cosy and warm, its walls made of wood, its rickety tables made of metal. Behind the bar, a dark-haired, moustachioed man, whom Gabriel assumed to be Angelo, was drying out a glass mug with a ragged towel. He smiled, revealing a glint of gold amongst his white teeth. 'Welcome to Geneva,' he said. 'Come in out of the cold!'

'I've brought you a real Genevan,' Dick said, with exaggerated bonhomie.

'Genevois,' Gabriel muttered without meaning to. Dick frowned, but the barman's face split into a wide smile.

'*Bienvenue!*' Angelo said. Though his English had sounded perfectly American, his French was heavily accented with Italian.

Gabriel felt himself grin in return. 'You are Swiss?' he asked.

'*Oui,*' he replied. 'Please, my friends, have a seat. What would you like to drink?'

'I'll have a rye and a Schlitz chaser,' Dick said, hoisting himself up onto a barstool. It was quarter to eleven.

'What is Schlitz?' Gabriel asked.

'Two, for my friend here,' Dick said, before turning back to Gabriel. 'You can see for yourself.'

Angelo set down two short, thick glasses on the countertop and sloshed them full of amber liquid from a whiskey bottle. 'It's a cold day,' he said, opening a small fridge and taking out two beers.

'Desperate times call for desperate measures.'

'Are we desperate?' asked Gabriel, confused. Angelo and Dick laughed.

'Go on,' said Dick. 'Taste it.'

Gabriel sighed and took a small sip of the beer. It was sweet, light and crisp. 'This is not a winter drink,' he said, taking a longer drink from the bottle.

'So, my friend,' Angelo said, 'what brings you to this place? Surely you didn't travel all the way from the motherland, just to sample my beer?'

Dick clapped Gabriel on the back. 'He's a Swiss banker, as classic as they come. I invited him over here to do some business. Brought him to Geneva to seal the deal.' He winked.

'For many generations, the Swiss have been drawn here,' Angelo said, setting down the towel that had been slung over his arm and sitting down behind the bar. 'They came here looking for mountains and lakes, like the ones they left behind. They found their pleasure here, just as I'm sure you will. The same cold, the same farming communities, the same churches. What wasn't already familiar to them, they built themselves.'

'When did this happen?' Gabriel asked, apologetically. 'I'm afraid I don't know a great deal about this.'

'Well, the Swiss mercenaries were travelling all over the globe through the Middle Ages, right up to the eighteen-hundreds. Then of course, there was the question of religious persecution. Have you heard of the Amish, the Mennonites?' Gabriel shook his head. 'Big, frugal, devout Protestant sects,' Angelo explained. 'Well, they all came from Switzerland, when it was a bad time to be anything but Catholic.'

'My family came to Switzerland to escape religious persecution in France!' Gabriel exclaimed happily.

'Ah, the Huguenots,' Angelo said, nodding. 'Yes, religion was a major factor in all this. Do you know what the other one is? It may surprise you, as a successful and, I presume, rich Swiss banker.'

Gabriel tried to keep his face neutral. 'I don't know,' he said, taking another drink from his beer.

'Poverty,' Angelo said, shrugging. 'Switzerland used to be a terribly poor country, with minimal resources aside from agriculture. There was severe famine in the nineteenth century, you see. Hunger, poverty, wars: that led to big waves of emigration. In fact, the local councils were putting poor people on boats, stuffing a few hundred francs in their pocket, on condition that they never return. Those that made it to America founded towns like this one, clinging on to their Swiss traditions for dear life. Those that stayed, those that toughed it out, built modern Switzerland. That's why I've always admired the Swiss. It takes a certain type of temperament to build that strong an economy, from close to nothing.'

'What about your family?' Gabriel asked, genuinely curious.

'My great-grandfather came from the Ticino,' Angelo said, giving a gold-toothed grin. 'But everybody assumes I'm Italian, especially if I go into Chicago.'

'I had no idea there was so much Swiss emigration through the ages!' Gabriel said, shaking his head. 'How strange, that we think of ourselves as reserved, stay-at-home types.'

'You don't represent your entire people,' Dick said, joking. 'I mean, not every Swiss man is boring.'

'The history is fascinating,' Angelo said earnestly, ignoring Dick. 'I read in a book that up until World War II, there were more people moving out of Switzerland than in.'

Gabriel scoffed. 'Tell that to the authorities now! You're as likely to hear German or Japanese or Italian...' He coughed, suddenly realising his faux pas. 'Not that the mixing of cultures is a bad thing,' he concluded lamely.

'You're damn right,' Angelo said excitedly, apparently missing the slur. 'I mean, Hershey chocolate? That was founded by a descendent of the Swiss Mennonites.'

'Oh yeah,' Dick chimed in. 'Chevrolet, too! That was started by a guy from Carouge who came over.'

'And it wasn't just America they colonised,' Dick continued. 'Australia and Russia were popular destinations throughout the eighteenth and nineteenth centuries.'

'You are oddly erudite for a man running a snack bar,' Gabriel observed, finishing his beer.

Angelo laughed. 'I read a lot,' he said. 'Besides, we care about history round here. Switzerland still feels very close to a lot of people in this area. It's an American thing: we're a country of immigrants. Italians, Dutch, Cornish, Lebanese, Chinese, you name it! There's one big difference between this Geneva and the one you come from: a lot more Mexicans and Iraqis. A lot more black people. It's more diverse. That's a good thing. You'll notice people won't say: "My family's American." They'll say, "My family's Polish on my mother's side, Irish on my dad's. I'm a quarter Swedish myself." Things like that. It's not a melting pot; it's a mixing bowl. People don't forget their heritage. We care.'

'Besides,' Dick said, 'people like ghettoes. They like safety, sticking to their own, continuing to cook their own food, speak their own language. I bet every Swiss immigrant in this town spent fifty years speaking only French with a Swiss accent, before English took over.'

'Oh, more than that,' Angelo replied. 'French was the principal language of this township all the way up to 1910. Hell, I bet there are still families speaking French and that weird Swiss German in the safety of their homes, if you look far enough!' He laughed suddenly. 'Come to think of it, there was this girl working in the tourist office, I thought for years she was Quebecois. Turns out she was a recent Swiss immigrant! This city has always been Swiss, and it always will be Swiss. It's a shame you can't see it in better weather. Lake Como's a delight to sail on.'

'Yes, yes, it is!' Gabriel smiled, delighted. 'I have sailed on Lake Como, once. The other one!'

'Hey, Gabe,' Dick said, slamming his empty glass on the counter pointedly, 'when are you going to sample the good stuff? That beer is child's play.'

'It's so good to be in a place where the Swiss spirit is appreciated,' Gabriel said, buoyed by sudden patriotic spirit. 'I appreciate it so much that I will sample your American drink, even though I do not normally drink more than three times a year.'

'It's almost '96,' Dick said with a grin. 'These ones don't count.'

Gabriel closed his eyes and took a large sip of the rye. He grimaced.

'Strong, eh?' said Angelo. 'It gets easier if you have a few.'

'Say, Angelo,' Dick said, leaning forward. 'What do you have to eat? A little fondue, maybe?'

'Oh no,' Gabriel said quickly, 'not fondue. I will have to eat fondue as soon as I return home.'

'What, is that some kind of Swiss tradition?' Dick asked, perplexed. 'Like, you have to have it as soon as you get out of the airport?'

'No, no,' Gabriel said, 'I mean my wife's fundraiser. It is... fondue themed.'

'Why?'

'It... That's just the way it is.'

'Could you be any more Swiss?' Dick asked, laughing.

'It's good fondue weather,' Angelo said. 'There are a couple of traditional Swiss restaurants down the road that do that sort of thing. But I've got plenty of other options. I've got frankfurters, sauerkraut, grilled cheese sandwiches... Here, let me get you the menu.'

'*Choucroute*!' Gabriel said happily. 'Yes, I think that is what I will have. With sausages.'

Dick shook his head. 'Turns out it's easy to make a Swiss man happy,' he said. 'Just give him Swiss food.'

'You don't understand,' Gabriel said excitedly. 'I never eat choucroute at home. It's too Germanic. But here in America, everything seems possible, everything seems mixed up!' He took another sip of rye whiskey and did not grimace. Emboldened, he added: 'I also would like to try some of that strange bright yellow mustard, please.'

Dick laughed, pleased. 'Be careful: that stuff makes you sneeze every time,' he said. 'I'll have a frankfurter and a basket of fries.'

'You know, I don't think this rye stuff even exists in Europe,'

Gabriel said, sniffing his diminishing glassful thoughtfully.

'Let's have two more!' Dick said gleefully.

'No,' said Gabriel.

'I insist,' said Dick.

'It's on the house,' Angelo added. 'To make up for this horrible weather.'

'It would be rude to refuse,' Dick said, his smile fixed.

Gabriel shrugged, smiled, and finished his first tumbler. 'If you are providing free drinks,' he said with uncharacteristic flamboyance, 'you should not have to wash extra glasses.' Angelo laughed, showing his gold teeth.

Dick peered at Gabriel curiously. 'Do you know,' he said, 'I think America is good for you.'

'I'll leave you two to it,' Angelo said, setting down two large measures of whiskey. 'I'll just go give the boys in the kitchen a hand, so you don't have to wait too long for your food.'

'Thank you, Angelo,' Dick said warmly. 'Now,' he said, turning to Gabriel with a new expression, 'I think we should get down to business. Am I right in understanding you have to leave tomorrow night, for some kind of fondue party?'

'Yes,' Gabriel said glumly, having briefly forgotten.

'You're a good man,' Dick said, 'but are you sure? I mean, why don't we take a road trip over to California? Beautiful girls in Malibu. And you could hang out with Billy Jean again.'

'The cow...woman?'

'She knows some real beauties.'

Gabriel looked horrified, but recovered his composure quickly. 'I have to be home for this party,' he said. 'My wife is fundraising, remember?'

'You're not one of those henpecked husbands, are you?' he asked with forced joviality.

'What?' said Gabriel.

'That's when the wife makes all the decisions, nagging and pecking at you like a hen bothering a cock. Peck, peck, peck.'

'Oh,' Gabriel sighed. 'In that case, yes, I am hen-pecked, turkey-pecked, whatever you call it. My wife makes a lot of decisions in this family.'

'Then you obviously need a lot of money for that sort of lifestyle. We should talk turkey now.'

'I thought you said hen?'

'It's another American expression,' Dick said impatiently. 'Money. Business. Getting to the point.'

'Oh,' said Gabriel meekly. He took a sip from his glass of rye.

'Did you look over the brochures I gave you? Once you finished hiking over Chicago, I mean, and narrowly escaping being mugged.'

Gabriel laughed. 'Yes, I have read through the brochures. But I told you already, I can't answer you until I've looked through all this carefully with my partners back in Geneva.'

'What about the high yield bonds? That may be an acceptable risk level for you. You could sign right now.' Gabriel sighed, but Dick didn't seem to notice. 'They're better than stocks at any rate. Some people call them junk bonds, but they're neither junk nor disastrously risky. Some others call them "old lady bonds" – because we sell them to old ladies – but I like to call them high yields, because they tend to yield two and a half per cent more than your standard Triple A bonds. We can definitely sell you those: we have a whole department handling these things. Twenty girls. Pretty ones.' He winked. Gabriel frowned.

'We have two new products, as well,' Dick went on, undeterred. 'You remember what I told you about pre-packaged mortgages? Win-win? Well, the individual mortgages are worth between twenty thousand and two hundred thousand dollars. We package millions of these together, and we sell them in a bond form. You could buy any number of bonds you wish, but we prefer to have a minimum purchase of a million dollars. All of these are backed by house mortgages in different cities, even different states. Those are some beautiful bonds to be emitting, let me tell you. A couple of New York rating agencies have decided to classify them as A and Double A bonds, which means above-average quality. Many of the top investment banks of New York are packaging these mortgage-backed securities, just like we do here in Chicago. Like I said, they yield one and a half to two per cent above the triple A bonds of, say, Chase or US government bonds.'

'How?' Gabriel asked directly.

'Because they're emitted at this high margin,' Dick replied, unfazed. 'We have a bond trading group made up of four girls, and they made five to seven per cent last year by pure buy-and-sell of those bonds.'

'Yes, well, that all sounds very impressive, but I'm still hesitant,' said Gabriel.

'Well, we also have shares of hotel funds we could offer you?' Dick said, his voice still cheery. 'There are so many new hotels springing up in the USA, Mexico, Canada. We can give you participation in these funds. You'll make a substantial per centage as well on the capital gains, you see. The revenue is not just room rentals: the hotels themselves are bought and sold by the fund for capital gains Last year, we made twenty-five per cent on this alone. It's in the brochures, if you just read them.'

'They're in the car,' Gabriel said mildly, sipping his drink.

Dick laughed and threw up his hands in mock despair. 'OK, OK, compadre. I get it. You need to talk to your partners. Well, that's just fine. Take your time thinking about it. Say, do you want another rye?'

Gabriel shook his head groggily. 'I don't think that would be a good idea,' he said. 'I had five coffees this morning. I don't think my body is used to this... assault of chemicals.' He loosened his tie.

'Let me just make one more proposal for you and your partners to think about back in Europe, OK? I mean, it all depends on your resources; what you're willing to invest. But if you like what we're doing, we can make up a rep office here. Put the name of your bank right on it.' He laughed. 'Right in the corner of my office, there could be a plaque. You could put it on your Swiss brochures: "Representative Office in Chicago"! We could even do the same thing in New York. We'll have an employee responding to your phone calls. This will generate deposits and portfolio management for you back in Switzerland, by showing you're international! Or you can use this rep office just to get information about your account with us, or you could even manage some of your own investments here! All it will cost you is a plaque at the door. We will manage everything for you. Just think about it: you could buy land, or bonds, or your own...'

'I am not here to make private equity or land investments,' Gabriel said coldly. The room was growing slightly fuzzy around the edges.

'Fine, fine,' Dick said hastily. 'But just think about it,' he coaxed.

'Do you know the story of the bear with the red wine?' Gabriel said suddenly, setting his glass down unsteadily.

Dick looked at him uncertainly. 'No. Why?'

'It's an old folk tale I heard when I was little,' Gabriel replied. 'The story is this: a bear once came across a barrel of wine and, thinking it was honey, began to guzzle it. Realising his mistake, he reeled back and spit on the ground. But, upon reflection, the bear suddenly realised he had quite enjoyed the taste of the wine; the wine he had accidentally tasted. He went back and finished the barrel. From that day forwards, the bear was a drunk.'

'Bears don't drink wine,' said Dick, drinking deep from his glass of rye whiskey. 'I've seen bears in Northern Michigan.'

'I feel that way about America,' Gabriel continued, ignoring him. 'The crispy bacon, the ridiculous drinks, the outrageous culture. I didn't mean to taste it, and now I'm worried.'

'Two bourbons won't make you a drunk. I can tell you that for free.' Dick sighed. 'Look, man, I'm just saying we should work together, OK? I'm not trying to tell you how to run your life. A joint venture with us, you see what I'm saying? Invest a little with us. You'll join in the profits we make, just like we join in the profits you make. That's what a joint venture is!'

At this moment, Angelo reappeared, carrying a tray heaped with food. 'Hungry?' he asked.

'Oh yes!' Gabriel said, much more enthusiastically.

Dick sighed.

Gabriel dozed, on the car ride back to Chicago, barely aware of the snow settling into banks outside the car. The sky had cleared to a pale shade of blue, and the lake's icy surface glimmered.

'Yes,' Dick was muttering sullenly into his phone, occasionally glancing over at Gabriel. 'Not right now. No, he hasn't.'

Gabriel had fallen on the food gratefully, back at Angelo's, and Dick had given up on the business conversations. As the snow slowed slightly, they had toured the city of Geneva, Wisconsin, walking unsteadily by the lake as Sanjeet drove slowly behind them. 'Oh, it's just like when I was a child!' Gabriel had exclaimed, grabbing Dick's arm enthusiastically. 'I so loved the frozen lakes of Switzerland. My father and I used to ice skate across them! Oh, Lac Léman, how I miss your shores! Dick, as soon as I get back to the hotel, make sure I call my mother. No, no, I should call Clarice and tell her how much I love her.'

'You're a good man.' Dick had rolled his eyes, and signalled to Sanjeet to slow down, so they could climb in. 'Time to go back to Chicago,' he said with a very bright smile.

Gabriel woke from an uneasy slumber to find Dick roughly shaking him by the shoulder, still smiling. 'Gabe, my friend, this is where I get off,' he said jovially. Gabriel blinked. The snowstorm had started up again. 'Sanjeet will be taking you back to your hotel. You'll be picking up a few friends on the way.' Gabriel nodded, confused. Friends? Dick clapped him on the back and slammed the limousine door.

'What time is it, Sanjeet?' Gabriel asked groggily.

'About seven, sir,' the driver replied, his eyes on the road. At the next stoplight, he turned around and grinned broadly. 'The night's still young.'

'Indeed,' Gabriel replied, looking out at the snow. They drove on in silence for a time.

'Ah, here we are,' came the reply.

'Here we are what?' asked Gabriel, startled from his worried, fondue thoughts.

'Company,' Sanjeet said, his voice lowered. He rolled down his window. 'Ladies! Come in from the cold, my dears!'

In confusion, Gabriel watched as two scantily-clad young women teetered across the snow in stilettos, before climbing into the back seat with him.

'Hello,' Gabriel said. 'I'm Gabriel.'

'Hi Gabe,' the younger one purred, leaning forward to shake snow out of her hair. Gabriel looked pointedly away from her décolleté, which was practically resting on his knees.

'It's so cold out there,' the brunette added, snuggling close to Gabriel as though they were old friends. Gabriel held very still, and smiled stiffly.

'And you are... friends of Dick's? Nieces?' he asked, still bewildered.

The blonde giggled, whilst the brunette rolled her eyes, flicking her hair back over her shoulders. 'Sanj,' she said, 'where are we going for dinner?'

'That is up to Mr Gabriel to decide,' Sanjeet replied.

'I don't know about dinner,' Gabriel said, somewhat confused. 'I didn't realise... I'm quite tired, and I ate a large meal recently.'

'That's quite alright,' the brunette said, suddenly businesslike. She smiled slowly. 'We can go right to the hotel.'

'You're staying at my hotel?' Gabriel asked.

'We sure are,' the blonde said, putting her hand on his knee.

Gabriel began to sweat. 'So, are you friends of Dick?' he asked.

The brunette laughed suddenly, a harsh sound. 'Yeah, we're friends of Dick,' she said. 'Big friends. We're like this.' She held up two fingers.

The blonde looked confused. 'Who's Dick?' she asked.

'The Boss Man,' the brunette replied, idly beginning to file her nails.

'I thought he might be your uncle, or even your grandfather,' Gabriel tried to explain.

'No,' the blonde said. 'We've never met him. He's just the one who –' But the brunette suddenly shushed her. A silence descended on the limousine. Gabriel noticed Sanjeet's eyes flicking back in the rearview mirror, unreadable.

'So, er, do you go to high school?' he asked.

The brunette rolled her eyes again. 'No, Gabe,' she said in a patronising way. 'We do not go to school.'

Gabriel bristled slightly. 'Surely girls your age...' The brunette was still glaring at him, and he suddenly worried he might be offending these strange relatives of Dick's. 'I mean, perhaps you already have your maturity?'

The blonde giggled. 'Oh, we're pretty mature already,' she said.

'No,' Gabriel said patiently, 'a maturity is like a baccalaureate.'

'What's that?' the blonde asked.

'I don't know what you call it in America. When you go to school, when you sit a test to finish your studies?'

'Oh! Yeah –' the blonde started, smiling, but the brunette cut her off.

'We quit school in ninth grade,' she said coolly. 'To start work.' She looked at Gabriel pointedly.

'Oh,' Gabriel said, as amiably as he could. 'You are training so that you can go to college?'

The blonde burst into a cascade of giggles. The brunette glared at her. 'Maybe,' she said shortly. 'I don't know yet.'

After a moment, Gabriel asked hesitantly: 'I'm sorry, girls, but why are you here?'

The girls exchanged a look. The brunette smiled slowly, slyly. 'We'd like to be in your company,' she said, lowering her voice.

'Our company?' Gabriel repeated. 'You want to open accounts in Switzerland? Are you rich kids? Do you have deposits?'

'I have a deposit of kisses,' the blonde said sweetly, pecking him on the cheek.

Gabriel reeled back. 'I'm sorry,' he said, worried he had offended them. 'I'm just not accustomed to your American ways. Your jokes...'

'That's OK,' the blonde said. 'You can buy me a drink to make up for it.'

'I, er, have to go to bed early. I don't really drink,' he said, aware of the rye whiskey on his breath. 'I'm quite tired.'

'Why don't we accompany you to your room?' the brunette said quietly, laying a hand on his thigh.

'I don't have much space in my room,' Gabriel said, beginning to lose patience, 'or much time for discussions. I've had a long day.'

'Girls,' Sanjeet said suddenly, seriously, 'straighten out and stop bothering Mr Gabriel. He's obviously not in the mood. Mr Gabriel, I am so sorry.'

A light bulb lit up in Gabriel's head. Ah, so they were Sanjeet's relatives! He must have misunderstood Dick.

'No worries, no worries,' he said gallantly. 'I really must get back.'

The brunette sighed. 'Shame,' she said.

An uncomfortable silence fell.

'Mr Gabriel?' Sanjeet called back. 'Would you like me to ask the girls to leave?'

Gabriel started, horrified. 'No, no!' he said. 'They are very welcome to stay in the car with me. Aren't they staying in my hotel?'

The girls shrugged at each other.

'I have to fly back to Switzerland tomorrow,' Gabriel said, beginning to sweat again. 'My wife is organising a fundraiser for the opening of her new modern art gallery. Of course, the whole thing is poppycock,' he continued, gaining confidence in his stream of babble, encouraged by the girls' bright smiles. 'She's been talked into it by these dreadful friends of hers. It's a terrible idea, if you ask me, this explosive cocktail of art people, wealthy wives, rich dictators, it's going to blow right up in her fondue pot. She somehow managed to convince me to ask some of my clients, hoping they'll contribute, you see. Awful idea, if you ask me, mixing our business in this way. I'm sure this modern art will be near incomprehensible to the sort of conservative guys who are clients in our private bank. You're sure neither of you are interested in opening accounts with us?' he asked again, smiling as gallantly as he could. 'If my wife can mix business and socialising, then so can I.'

'Your wife,' the brunette said knowingly.

'And she wants to redecorate the house,' Gabriel added gloomily, staring out into the darkening snow.

Chapter Eighteen

The scent of garlic and white wine filled the house in Saint Antoine. Clarice looked around, torn between organisational panic and pride. The fondue fundraiser was off to a riotous start, and it filled her with a sort of excited schizophrenia. It was as if Old Clarice and New Clarice were fighting it out inside her: middle-aged, conservative Swiss Clarice, versus young, fun, modern-art Clarice. She smoothed down her billowing fuchsia silk skirt, so that the rhinestones sparkled in the dim light.

Old Clarice looked around at the crowds, wondering whether she should double-check the locks on the bedroom door, and remove the last two crystal vases from the shelves, just in case. New Clarice, however, could barely stop herself from clapping her hands together in delight. She hovered by the entrance to the carnotzet, sipping her champagne quickly. She had never met most of these people in person, and she scanned the crowds milling around the salon anxiously. Who would she recognise? Billy Bob, the Texan investor? Khadija's cousin-in-law, the sheikh? The beautiful young Chinese heiress, Juni Bao?

'*Ciao*,' a smooth young man suddenly said, appearing at her elbow. 'I'm Vincenzo.'

'Welcome,' Clarice replied, flustered. She had no memory of inviting this Italian. Perhaps he was one of Gabriel's clients?

'So this is your Swiss room; how you call it, carnu...?'

'Carnotzet,' she said, smiling. 'Yes, I had it decorated myself, just in time for the party.'

'My goodness!' he exclaimed, impressed. 'It looks very modern. May I... go inside, for some cheese?'

'Of course,' said Clarice. 'Help yourself, while it's fresh and hot. But I see your hand is empty! Have you had something to drink?'

'My sister Bettina and I just arrived,' he said, flashing a charming grin. 'She is already... making contacts. Perhaps you can point me in the direction of the drinks table?'

'Right here, in the centre of the salon. We have champagne, and

Swiss wine from the Tessin region, the Ticino I mean. I can offer you vodka, gin, scotch, and schnapps. There are a few more drinks, I can't remember them all.'

'Perhaps you have Campari?' Vincenzo asked, his expression hopeful.

'I'm sure the caterers will be able to find something for you,' she replied quickly.

'Well,' Vincenzo said gallantly, 'how about I sample some of this cheese first?'

'Yes, yes,' Clarice said vaguely, having spotted Chloë and Fleurie hurrying across the room.

'Clarice, darling, this is marvellous! I love your dress – that sexy leather belt, and the slit up the thigh! So daring,' Chloë said excitedly, kissing her on both cheeks. Catching sight of Vincenzo, her manner softened. She adjusted her décolleté.

'You're getting lipstick all over the hostess,' Fleurie said, shaking her head and rustling in her purse for a handkerchief. 'Here,' she added, wiping the pink smear from Clarice's cheek and assessing her at the same time. 'You look stressed,' she said.

'I am,' Clarice admitted in a rush. 'So many people! So many yet to arrive!'

'Let me get you another drink,' Chloë trilled. 'Perhaps this charming fellow might accompany me to the drinks table?'

Vincenzo smiled and took her arm. 'With pleasure, *mademoiselle*.'

Fleurie rolled her eyes. 'Well, that's Chloë taken care of for a little while,' she said. 'Is Khadija here yet? Are her princes? What about Winifred?'

'I haven't seen either of them,' Clarice said, 'or the princes. Oh, Fleurie, I'm so glad you're here. Did you bring the publicity brochures?'

Fleurie tapped her large handbag. 'All in here,' she said. 'I'll go spread them around the fondue and drinks tables.'

Clarice kissed her on the cheek. 'Thank you so much,' she said.

Fleurie smiled warmly. 'Here's to your new gallery,' she replied, before disappearing off into the crowd.

'Hello,' a soft voice said in English. 'I am Juni Bao?' There was a gentle lilt to her voice, almost apologetic.

Clarice took in the young Chinese millionaire, her floral dress and smart blazer, her gentle smile. 'Welcome!' she said.

'I care a great deal about modern art, and I am very pleased to have been invited,' Juni said. 'This cheese room was decorated by Swiss painters?'

'Here, let me show you,' Clarice said, happily guiding her into the carnotzet. 'I brought in local artists, from Lausanne and Basel, les Breuleux and Nods. Our architect, Serge, he designed our chalet near Saas Fee. I called him to help with this decoration project. These wonderful rural painters, they operate in the old Swiss way, you see. He put me in contact.' Clarice laughed, buoyed on a tide of artistic excitement. 'But you see how I asked them to give it all a modern touch?'

Juni nodded earnestly. 'These are almost cubist, these animals,' she said carefully.

'What do you think?'

'I think it's very interesting. These eagles, mountain lions, and some kind of deer, they are recognisable, yet modern.'

Clarice nodded. 'I had to have the whole room re-panelled,' she explained. 'A cabinet maker came in, along with the three artists that agreed to give this modern thing a try. It wasn't easy, convincing them! Do you know how much it cost? Two hundred thousand Swiss francs!'

She stopped suddenly, worried that sounded like bragging, but Juni Bao didn't even raise an eyebrow at the figure. She simply nodded earnestly, looking around at the Swiss mountain scenes, the angular faces of marmots, the geometric designs of pine needles and edelweiss.

'It is very Art Deco,' Juni said at last, smiling. 'Even the lion has a square head.'

'It took weeks, but I'm thrilled with the results,' Clarice concluded. 'See, in the corner? That is my husband Gabriel.'

Juni gave a delighted giggle. 'He posed for this, with the cows?'

'Oh no!' Clarice exclaimed. 'Gabriel doesn't even know about this room. He's away on a business trip to Chicago. It's a surprise for his return, you see.'

Juni hesitated. 'He will like it?'

'I don't know,' Clarice said, before shaking her head and laughing. 'It doesn't matter in the end: this is my party! Besides, we can always redecorate if he doesn't like it.'

'I am sure he will like the sky,' Juni said calmly, 'with these beautiful clouds!'

'Oh, thank you!' Clarice replied. 'That's a little touch from outside Switzerland. I found this artist who worked in Las Vegas casinos, he specialises in these sorts of scenes.'

'You got a cowboy in to paint these cows?' a loud American voice chimed in.

Juni and Clarice turned around in surprise. 'You must be Billy Bob,' the hostess said hesitantly.

'Sure am.' The Texan held out a large hand to be shaken delicately by each woman in turn. He had kept his large-brimmed hat on. 'So, can either of you ladies tell me what the hell this cheese stuff is?'

Juni laughed delicately, blushing.

'It is a Swiss fondue,' Clarice said slowly. 'You have never visited our country before?'

'Nope,' replied Billy Bob, 'I'm just visiting Geneva for my oil trading, and to see some bankers.' He wrinkled his nose at the fondue. 'They used to hand these ugly sets out at weddings back home twenty years ago,' he said. 'Never tried the stuff myself. Is it just melted cheese?'

'Yes,' Clarice explained, 'half gruyère cheese and half vacherin, with a little garlic and white wine.'

'And it's hot?'

'We keep a small flame under the pot,' she explained patiently.

A diminutive Italian woman joined the group, who, judging by the striking resemblance she bore to Vincenzo, Clarice assumed to be his sister, Bettina. She looked sceptically into the pots of cheese. 'Hmph,' she said, dabbing at her burgundy lipstick with a napkin.

'In America,' Billy Bob said loudly, hoping to draw in the beautiful Italian, 'we'd have at least three different kinds of dips, and a platter of grilled meats as well. Maybe some fries. I mean, you told me there was dinner involved. Did you spend your whole budget painting goats and sheep on the walls?'

'Why don't you try it?' Clarice said, as kindly as she could. 'There will also be dessert, later.'

Bettina ignored both of them, and watched for a time in horrified fascination as guests stuck their cubes of bread on long forks and dipped them in the mixture. 'It'll be full of spit!' she said, suddenly. 'They just put that kebab skewer thing in their mouth, and then back in the mix, and then they go stick it in other things! It's disgusting.'

Clarice frowned. 'You don't put the fork in your mouth,' she said coldly. 'We Swiss have manners.'

'And what are all these side dishes?' Billy Bob continued, encouraged by his audience. 'Pickles and...dried meat? Pshaw! You guys need to discover the barbecue.'

Juni laughed suddenly, a tinkling sound accompanied by blushing. 'You're funny,' she said to the large Texan.

Billy Bob stared at her in consternation, hooking his thumbs through his wide belt. The buckle was decorated with a bronze eagle. 'Sorry, lady,' he said hesitantly. 'I'm not a racist, but you guys tried to kill us all in World War II.'

Juni giggled again. 'I'm not Japanese,' she said. 'I'm Chinese.'

Billy Bob frowned. 'Oh, right,' he said. 'Well, I bet you guys have much weirder food than these Switzers, right?'

Clarice sighed. 'Fondue is a traditional Swiss dish,' she said calmly. 'If you are going to stay in Switzerland, you should get used to our Swiss ways.'

'Let me tell you something, little lady,' Billy Bob said, towering over her. 'I don't like my first impressions of this tiny country, one bit. The first thing I don't like about this goddamn place is that this room is too small, and too smoky, even if you ignore the weird paintings. I'm not used to that. I like high ceilings and large spaces. Hell, my dining room back in Houston can seat a hundred and forty people! The ceiling is twenty feet high!'

'You're exaggerating,' Clarice said coolly.

'You ever been to America?'

'No, but my husband is just flying back from there now.'

'You ask him about the ceilings,' he said, pointing his finger at her as if he wanted to jab her in the sternum. 'Just ask him.'

'There's no way you can seat even a hundred people comfortably,' Clarice said, on uncertain ground. 'I mean, surely not?'

'My kitchen is bigger than your house,' Billy Bob said affectionately, 'and better decorated.'

'I redecorated this room for this fundraiser,' Clarice said, her voice trembling slightly. 'I hired many local artists and a cabinet-maker, all of whom did a wonderful job, over several weeks.'

'I am trying to learn a little more English,' Juni piped up. 'I have never been to America either.' She beamed.

Billy Bob ignored her and smiled unexpectedly at Clarice. 'Don't look so worried, little lady. It's a swell party; just not the party for me. How about I send you a million dollars for your gallery and go eat a steak across the road at the Hilton?' With that, he turned around, and cheerfully marched off.

Clarice, whose throat had been growing tight, felt a strange mix of emotions in her chest. A million dollars! Had he truly meant that? Why would he make such a generous donation after insulting her fundraiser so thoroughly?

'What an ass,' said Bettina.

'He is handsome,' Juni said thoughtfully.

Clarice sighed. 'Look,' she said sharply, 'I really don't have time to give you English lessons right now. Why don't you go follow Billy Bob over to the Hilton and learn a few cuss-words from him?'

Juni frowned, confused. 'But I must learn English at your fundraiser,' she said. 'China is becoming more and more important in the world. We sell you cheap manufactured goods We are exporting everything.' She paused for a moment, before adding calmly: 'You know I am a millionaire, yes?'

Clarice swallowed. 'Oh yes,' she said, summoning as much cheer as she could. 'So, what kind of modern art are you interested in?'

Juni smiled. 'Perhaps your gallery has room for some modern Chinese artists? I know the scene back home quite well. Too many of our artists spend their time and energy trying to imitate Japan and Europe, you see. Our new creators need encouragement.'

Clarice nodded faintly, looking around the room for Winifred.

'My father has a lot of money,' Juni continued, undiscouraged. 'I'll send you five thousand dollars.'

'Five thousand?' Clarice said sharply. Wasn't this woman supposed to be a millionaire? 'I can't even eat lunch with that.'

Juni shrank back, taken aback. 'How much do you want?'

'One hundred thousand,' Clarice replied.

'You could feed a hundred Chinese people for two years with that kind of money!' Juni said, obviously offended.

'Fine,' Clarice said coolly. 'Fifty thousand, and you can put me in touch with some Chinese artists.'

'Done,' said Juni. 'Oh, and I will be in Switzerland for the next two months.'

Clarice tried not to sigh.

'I don't know about Chinese art,' Bettina sniffed, reappearing suddenly from the carnotzet. 'I myself will not contribute to your funding unless you bring in some Italian modern art.'

'What are you drinking?' Juni asked curiously.

'Campari and soda,' Bettina replied, raising her glass unsteadily. 'Number four, I think? This drinks table is far too international for me. I noticed some kind of coffee liqueur, and that Mexican stuff that smells like paint stripper...'

'I don't know anything about Italian modern art,' Clarice said. 'Isn't it all Renaissance and Romantic?'

'Nonsense,' said Bettina. 'There are some wonderful artists, starting right after the Art Nouveau movement. Not too modern, of course, ugh! Sculptors, painters, anything you like. You can find the most fantastic mosaics, too.' She drained her glass.

'I need another drink,' Clarice said suddenly. Her new acquaintances trailed after her.

'Anyway, I came to check out your gallery,' Bettina continued, 'but I don't think I can afford it. I mean, our whole country is verging on bankruptcy!'

A woman laughed loudly at this conclusion, tossing her curly black hair. 'You Italians think you have it bad? You should check out Greece! Do you think we can afford tossing hundreds of thousands of dollars around? It's sickening. You could heal our country's economy with that kind of money.'

Bettina huffed and stalked off.

'I don't know what you're talking about, Lavinia,' Clarice said to the Greek woman, pouring herself a large glass of lemon vodka. 'I mean, I'm mostly collecting through sales, and private fortunes. My husband and his bank Von Mipatobeau have brought us many good contacts. Then there are the Swiss fortunes, accumulated trusts and foundations, very much interested in modern art. Switzerland can afford to support its art scene.'

'This kind of fundraising, it's downright...' Lavinia lowered her voice and hissed: 'American. How can you just toss around the name of your husband's bank? I mean, I thought we were talking about a few hundred francs here and there, but this is just ostentatious. Unseemly. Un...Swiss.'

Clarice concentrated on adding several ice cubes to her drink without spilling a drop on the antique oak. 'Well, Lavinia, I'll have you know the strategy is progressing well so far. I've actually already been offered one million dollars by one of the guests.'

Juni gasped. 'You mean he was serious, the Texan?'

Lavinia sniffed. 'Americans,' she said. 'See? You people just assume everybody is so rich. I don't understand all the fuss about Switzerland. Aren't you all supposed to be Calvinists, modest, hiding your wealth, not ever mentioning salaries or figures? You've become downright loudmouthed. What about confidentiality? Your famous *secret bancaire*? And that outrageous dress you're wearing! So pink! So garish! Are those rhinestones? Is that a leather belt?'

'Lavinia,' Clarice said patiently, 'being Swiss doesn't have to mean being drab, or boring, or insular. It also doesn't mean being as poor as the Greeks. Why don't you just enjoy the free cheese and drinks, and leave my lovely dress in peace?'

'Maybe Billy Bob is in love with you!' Juni said excitedly. 'Maybe he'll...'

'And how can you throw a party this expensive and not have ouzo?' Lavinia continued.

'Shush, all of you,' Clarice said, taking a large gulp of vodka. 'Lavinia, I apologise for the oversight. If you really only drink Greek drinks, despite having a Swiss husband, then you should ask one of the caterers to run over to the Lion d'Or hotel. Juni, I must leave you here and go find my friends.' She walked off quickly, her pink skirts swishing behind her.

'Clarice!' a voice called out, and she felt her arm being grabbed. 'You must help me out!' It was Chloë, leaning against Vincenzo's muscular chest. 'We are having a disagreement about modern art.' Bettina was standing next to them, her face deeply disapproving.

'You simply cannot expect me to believe that you truly enjoy this sort of thing,' she said, her lips pursed. 'It's just a kind of rebellion, pretending to love modern art. There's no intrinsic value to it. Nothing good has been made since the 1950s.'

Vincenzo laughed good-naturedly. 'But, my dear sister, you cannot dismiss nearly fifty years of art history like that!'

'Exactly!' Chloë chimed in. 'I mean, I saw the most extraordinary show involving Italian artists recently, in Paris. It was all live, the artists painting in the street outside, tearing up their clothes...'

Bettina frowned. 'I happen to know the occasion you are referring to. It was a sham, a total scandal. At the Petit Palais, no? I shudder to think any Italians might have been involved. The most awful things happened there: people lining up garden tools and garbage cans and calling it art. Picking animal excrement off the street and exhibiting it in plastic boxes. Was that the same show where bits of war memorabilia were displayed, too? It's deeply disrespectful.'

'No, it's not!' Chloë said, her eyes glittering. 'I thought they were so exciting, the shiny hand grenades. Not dangerous, but so weighted with history.'

Vincenzo laughed again.

Bettina bristled. 'What do you know of history, child? You think you can put... pieces of the Berlin Wall on show, or barbed wire from the death camps? Bend that into a heart shape and call that modern art?' She looked ready to spit on the ground.

'Bettina,' Clarice said as softly as she could, 'we have no intention of exhibiting that sort of art in our gallery. Why don't you have a look at one of our brochures?'

'No way! I don't want to see traumatic images. Do you know about the artists who put dead people in perspex, like an awful tomb?'

Clarice looked horrified. 'Bettina! You're being ridiculous! There are wonderful movements in modern art.'

Chloë laughed gently. 'You're forgetting this is Clarice de Puritigny's gallery, not mine. I'd have made it much more avant-garde.'

'The focus is modern and international, but it still needs to appeal to the Swiss,' Clarice added, slightly shaken. 'I have contacted artists like Rivali from Italy, Pierrot from France, Hally from America.'

'Forgive my sister,' Vincenzo said gently. 'Bettina, perhaps we should go home soon?'

Chloë pouted. 'Stay! Just have one more drink! I'm not upset. Let's talk about something that isn't art.'

Bettina tossed her hair. 'Well, I've had enough of this party,' she said. 'I'll be leaving fifty francs in your collection, and *basta*. Good night, everyone.'

'Clarice!' Before she had time to recognise the voice, Clarice found herself enveloped in Winifred's welcoming arms. 'Your house smells so wonderful.'

Dieter smiled and hugged her quickly. 'But where is Gabriel?' he asked.

Clarice shook her head angrily. 'I have no idea,' she said. 'He should have been here hours ago. His flight was delayed, but I didn't think it would take this long! Anyway, I have other things to think about.'

Dieter looked worried. 'Do you know how it went, in America?'

Clarice smiled thinly. 'I think it went very well. How did you know about the trip?'

Dieter hesitated. 'He called me a while back, worried about it. I think... Well, I don't want to worry you, but I don't like these American broker types. It's all right for us commercial bankers to get involved in these sorts of schemes, but it's downright risky for someone like Gabriel.'

Clarice glared. 'So we're not allowed to make international money, but you can?'

Winifred set her hand on Dieter's back. 'Darling, maybe this isn't the time and place.'

'Of course,' Dieter said graciously. 'I'm thrilled to hear the trip went well. I'll ask him about it when he gets back. It's just... these Americans can be very seductive. I just hope my friend is being careful. Darling,' he went on, turning to Winifred, 'would you like me to bring you some cheese?'

Clarice sighed as Dieter moved away. 'Sorry, Winifred, I didn't mean to snap at him. I know Gabriel has a friend in Dieter, even if he wouldn't acknowledge it. It's just difficult, knowing how much we could use the money for the gallery opening... knowing the Americans are willing to hand it over so easily.'

Winifred smiled. 'You're afraid Gabriel will turn it down because he's too Swiss?'

Clarice laughed. 'Something like that,' she sighed. 'I think Gabriel has a complicated relationship with Dieter in his head. He envies the size of his bank, his financial success. You know my husband can be a bit of a cold fish... He acts so aloof, he finds it difficult to imagine someone would want to be a friend and help him out. There's something of Gabriel in me too.'

Winifred impulsively took her hand and squeezed it. 'Darling Clarice, I know for a fact that Dieter would never, ever try to stop you making money out of a competitive or nasty spirit. I know there's some animosity in the banking world between the commercial and the private, Swiss-German spirit versus Suisse Romande, but our friendships don't have to mirror that. There is no love-hate here. If Dieter is worried, it is for your bank's sake. For his friend's sake.'

Clarice shook her head. 'Maybe Gabriel should have coffee with Dieter, or even just speak on the phone. I don't know. I find it so hard not to be excited at the prospect of millions rolling in, just when we need them, you know?'

'Would you like a drink?' Winifred asked gently.

'Yes, please. I haven't even had time to find Khadija and her princes yet,' Clarice added, shaking her head. 'Every time I set out to find some of my friends, I run into some enemies.'

'Come then, let's go make some new friends.'

'Speaking of friends and enemies, let me tell you about—'

'Clarice! Winifred!' A familiar voice suddenly reached them, and they found Khadija standing by the side of two seated men dressed in beautiful, solemn robes.

Khadija smiled, clearly slightly frazzled. 'This is Prince Ghani,' she said, 'and Sheikh Bukhari. The sheikh is married to my cousin, you may remember.' Khadija walked over and gave Clarice a quick hug. 'I borrowed the chairs from your bedroom,' she whispered. 'I hope you don't mind.'

'Not at all.' Clarice smiled at Khadija, glad Gabriel was not present to witness this, and bowed slightly towards the men. 'You are most welcome,' she said. 'Can I get you something to drink?'

'Some tea, or juice?' Khadija quickly added.

The sheikh gave a glittering smile. 'Do you have pomegranate juice?' he asked.

Clarice swallowed. 'I'm sorry,' she said. 'We have sparkling apple juice? It's very Swiss.'

The sheikh smiled indulgently. 'That will be fine,' he said.

'Tea for me,' the prince said with a wink. 'I need to stay awake to enjoy the beauties at this party!'

Khadija shot him a reproachful glance. 'Now, now,' she said. 'Behave yourself.'

The prince laughed. 'You set up the sheikh, didn't you?'

'I don't have that many cousins,' she shot back.

'What about your beautiful friends?' he asked, leaning forward, amused. Clarice blushed. 'Perhaps one of them could help me with my plan to acquire a Swiss villa, somewhere on the lakeshore.'

'Where are you from?' Clarice asked.

'Divonne,' the prince replied, and then laughed at her shocked expression. 'Yes, I am almost as Swiss as you are! Yet I do not have a passport, so I cannot purchase land.'

'Not as Swiss as me, eh!' Khadija added.

'That's because you've failed to find me a Swiss woman, so far,' he said with another wink.

Khadija rolled her eyes and bustled off towards the drinks table.

'Tell me, Madame,' the prince continued, 'do you gamble?'

'No,' Clarice said hastily. 'I mean, unless you are referring to my style of fundraising?'

The prince threw his head back and laughed. 'No, no,' he said. 'I mean blackjack, roulette, that sort of thing. This party, to my mind, is rather lacking in entertainment.'

'Well, we have fondue?' Clarice said uncertainly. 'I... The Swiss prefer quiet activities.'

'Modern art never struck me as a particularly quiet activity,' the prince said. 'Isn't it a mad and exciting world, busy with transforming and offending?'

'There are a hundred kinds of modern art,' Clarice replied. 'We specialise in the least offensive of these. I am, after all, still Swiss.' There was a twinkle in her eye. 'Perhaps you could come to our gallery opening, if we rake together the funds in time.'

The prince laughed again. 'Ah, already you are pitching! I like your style. I like a woman who doesn't waste time.'

Clarice blushed furiously, and was relieved to see Khadija reappear. 'I am grateful for any contributions,' she said slowly, 'but there is absolutely no obligation.'

'Nonsense,' Khadija cut in. 'If you're going to drink all the juice in the house, and sit in the finest chairs, you can damn well throw in a few thousand.'

'Of course, my dear,' the sheikh said, nodding his head nobly. 'We understand.'

'Well, I'm very glad you're here,' Clarice said in a rush. 'Very happy. Very thankful.'

The prince stood up slowly and put a hand on Clarice's shoulder. 'I find you Swiss women very entertaining, very sweet,' he said, imitating her blushing manner. 'Perhaps I could invite you somewhere?'

Khadija rapped him smartly on the arm. 'Madame is married, may I remind you!' she said.

'Then where is her husband?' the prince said archly. 'Anyway, what would the harm be in leaving to do a little gambling?'

Clarice sighed. 'I am the hostess,' she said firmly. 'If you wish to gamble, you can gamble on the future success of my modern art gallery.'

'By the way, Clarice,' Khadija added, pulling her further away from prince Ghani, 'was that Juni Bao heading out the door?'

'She was here earlier,' Clarice replied, confused.

'Oh,' said Khadija. 'Well, she said she was going to the Hilton. Something about a beautiful man?'

———◆◆◆———

Clarice leaned on the balcony, looking down at the crowds. The party was getting quite rowdy, now that it was close to midnight. Lavinia, in a fit of rage, had pushed over an entire pot of melted cheese in the carnotzet, and had to be escorted out by the caterers. Vincenzo had left the party after kissing Chloë passionately for most of an hour, half hidden by the curtains in the salon. At one point, she had seen Winifred and Dieter sneak off in the direction of the kitchen. Clarice shook her head and downed her glass of vodka. Some earnest young man appeared to be trying to kiss the prince's hand, as the sheikh laughed. Was his friend curtseying? Khadija seemed to be very amused by this. Ah, but the party of Japanese bankers had arrived! She hadn't noticed. Was one of them wearing one of her decorative cowbells?

All at once, she saw a shadowy figure appear in the doorway. Gabriel! She ran towards the top of the stairs, but when she made out her husband's expression, she stopped cold. Gabriel's brows were knitted, his face drawn. He looked utterly exhausted. He ignored the guests, and made his way towards the carnotzet in a daze, as if he were alone in his house. Clarice swallowed and adjusted her dress, her heart in her throat as she began to descend the stairs.

'Clarice,' the prince said, appearing out of the crowd and catching her arm. 'We are leaving for the casino. Come with me?'

She shook her head mutely and removed her arm from his grasp. She found Gabriel standing at the entrance to the carnotzet, staring grimly into the room.

'What is the meaning of this?' he asked, his voice hollow. 'My very own home, full of drunks? There is cheese on the floor. What is this on the walls? Someone scratched the dining table.'

'It's my fundraiser!' Clarice said as gaily as she could. 'I had it redecorated!'

'I told you not to redecorate,' Gabriel said, his temper clearly rising. 'I was only gone for a few days.'

'I've been doing this in secret for weeks,' she explained. 'I called up local artists, on Serge's recommendation. I, I thought you would like it.'

Gabriel stared at her, as if failing to recognise her. 'This is our only guest room, Clarice,' he said.

'These are guests!' she said, still trying to smile. 'Guests at my fundraiser!'

'How many people did you invite? I thought this would be an intimate fondue dinner.'

'Forty,' she said, crestfallen. 'Fifty. I thought you loved carnotzets. It's just like a modern version of the one at the chalet!'

'Clarice, this is the most misjudged, the most selfish... the least Swiss...'

'I bet Dieter has fondue parties every week!' Clarice said.

'This is unbelievable,' Gabriel said, staring around at the carnage.

Guests began to drift away from them.

Clarice's tone hardened into accusation. 'And where were you, anyway? You're terribly late. You were supposed to help me host.'

'I told you my flight was cancelled.'

'You told me you would catch the next one.'

'I did,' Gabriel said shortly. 'My plane was the last one for the night. I had to spend the night in the airport, leaving in the morning. There's a six-hour time difference, Clarice. I'm utterly exhausted.'

'You knew about this party,' Clarice said, defensive.

'I did not know about *this* party. I did not expect to see so many people here. I thought you were raising funds amongst a dozen of your friends, plus a few clients from the bank that I found for you. I did not think I was inviting them to an orgy!'

'Clarice!' a feminine voice said suddenly, and Chloë deposited a drunken kiss on her cheek. 'I just wanted to say thank you for the party.'

'You're leaving?' Clarice said, turning away gratefully from her husband. 'Are you meeting Vincenzo?'

Chloë blushed. 'Oh no,' she said. 'Prince Ghani has offered to take me gambling. What fun! He said I could call him the Prince of Araby!'

'What fun,' Clarice repeated drily. 'See you on Sunday for coffee.'

Chloë waved gaily and disappeared.

'I want all these people to leave,' Gabriel said suddenly.

'I understand you're upset,' Clarice said evenly. 'Why don't you go upstairs and freshen up? Why are you so dishevelled, anyway?'

'I slept in an airport, Clarice!' Gabriel suddenly roared, startling a cluster of Greeks.

'Don't shout in front of our guests,' Clarice said, flushing crimson.

'I refuse to freshen up! I need to go to sleep!'

'Come to the bedroom,' Clarice hissed, grabbing him by the arm and smiling apologetically at the guests. They marched up the stairs, and into the bedroom. Gabriel slammed the door and threw off his jacket.

'I've raised two and a half million dollars, Gabriel,' Clarice said, her heart racing. 'It's enough to open a new gallery. The evening was a success. I did what I had to do.'

'Good for you,' Gabriel said sarcastically. 'And this included redecorating the house, spilling cheese all over my perfect parquet, dressing like some kind of fuchsia whore? What kind of respectable hostess shows her knees?'

'I love this dress,' Clarice spat back. 'It's very fashionable.'

'It makes you look like a fool.'

'I've been planning this for weeks,' Clarice said, 'for both of us. If you're thinking about turning down this American money, we needed some way to make millions. Besides, I thought you would like the carnotzet!'

'What did you spend on it, ten thousand?'

Clarice stared at him. 'You must be kidding,' she said. 'The table alone cost twenty five thousand francs! I thought you would like it; it's an eighteenth-century fondue table I bought from an antiques shop.'

'How much did it all cost, you madwoman?'

Clarice waved a hand in the air vaguely. 'Oh, over two hundred and forty five thousand francs. After all, you said you would pay for everything.'

'I'm not paying for that,' Gabriel said calmly. 'Not a cent. You cover that with the money you've fundraised.'

'I need the money for the gallery!' Clarice protested, her temper rising. 'What's the point in making seven or eight million, Gabriel, and flying out to Chicago, and... It's part of your duty as a husband! You're failing me as a husband, and you're embarrassing me, shouting at me in front of all the guests like that. After it's gone so well!'

'Letting you paint animals on the walls is hardly part of my duty as husband,' Gabriel replied. 'And ruining the house is not part of your role as wife.'

'It's not just animals,' Clarice said. 'You are there too.'

'Me?' Gabriel repeated, staring at her.

'Yes, you,' Clarice said uncertainly. 'You're a good Swiss man, herding the cows in the mountain.'

'A cowherd? After we've been bankers for three hundred years?'

'Well,' Clarice repeated stubbornly, 'before that you were probably herding cows in the mountains.'

Gabriel suddenly started laughing so hard he had to sit down on the bed. 'Oh, Clarice,' he said. 'I don't know what to say.' He laughed and laughed until tears streamed down his face. Then he put his face in his hands. 'This is my family home, Clarice,' he said. 'I can't understand how you could do such a thing. Inviting foreigners; all these people who can't possibly be interested in art... and I hate that Chloë girl! She has loose morals. Last time I saw her, I swear she winked at me!'

'She winks at everybody,' Clarice said quietly.

'I don't want her in my house.'

'Don't worry about Chloë,' she said.

'I'm more worried about my house, the money, about you, about our future... What has become of Saint Antoine? What will my clients at Von Mipatobeau think of this fiasco? You have become a scandalous woman, Clarice. You're not the woman I married. You used to believe in tradition, in family, in Swiss values.'

'These are new Swiss values,' Clarice replied, 'and we are different people. I have my own life, now.'

'People are seducing each other in my house, Clarice!' Gabriel shouted. 'That is inadmissible!'

'Well, it makes up for the lack of seduction in our bedroom,' Clarice said, her face sour.

'I haven't slept in twenty-four hours, Clarice,' Gabriel said. 'I'm not going to talk about this further.'

'Well, I'm going downstairs to finish hosting my fundraiser,' Clarice said. 'It will probably last until three in the morning. And take a shower before you get into our bed. You smell disgusting.'

'Have fun with your immoral, phoney, overly made-up friends and Middle Eastern gigolos!' Gabriel shouted.

'I'll be cleaning up 'til five, so don't expect me until then,' Clarice added, standing in the doorway. 'That's when the staff come to collect the fondue sets.'

'I'll be getting up then, to go to work!' Gabriel said in disbelief.

'Fine, I'll sleep on the couch,' Clarice said crisply. 'I'll get more comfort from hugging a pillow, than from your stony corpse lying next to me.'

'Fine.'

She paused. 'We're making de Puritigny history, you know.'

'What, with your scandalous party?'

'No. By not going to bed together. Even though we no longer make love, we always sleep together in this bed. Even after our fights. Even when we are ill.' Clarice opened the door. 'Good night, Gabriel,' she said frostily. 'I have to go take care of my guests.'

Chapter Nineteen

The pine trees rose sharply into the bright blue sky, dotted amidst the jagged mountaintops. Every year, springtime seemed to hit Gabriel with a kind of mild surprise. It wasn't that he forgot that time passed, or that the seasons changed, but every year the sudden warmth and light seemed to sneak up on him. This year was no different. Perhaps it was simply in escaping the city that he became aware of the transformations around him. Gazing out of the car window at the bright, rolling greenery of the Alps rising steeply on either side, he was amazed at how quickly the snow had melted and disappeared. He would have to go looking for the first edelweiss buds, perhaps the next morning, on his walk. Oh, it would be so wonderful to fall asleep in his beloved chalet! He couldn't wait for nightfall.

'Cat got your tongue?'

Serge, who was driving, raised an eyebrow as if mildly amused.

Gabriel shook his head. 'Sorry,' he said, smiling apologetically. 'Were you talking? I have a lot on my mind.'

'Fine, fine, I understand your subtle message. Enough decoration talk for one day, then. I'm confident I'll convince you that you need another expansion. I'm absolutely sure of it. After all, what kind of man doesn't want his chalet to be worth thirty million?'

'I'm not that kind of millionaire,' Gabriel said ruefully. 'At least, not yet. And I didn't come up here to talk business with you.'

'So you just wanted my company?' Serge sounded genuinely surprised. 'Fine, I'll take that. Very well then. I must have been misled by the mere fact that we spent all of our lunchtime discussing the chalet interior.' He gave a cheeky grin.

'Now, now,' said Gabriel, uncomfortable.

'I'm only joking. I know you're my most faithful client. How is business at the bank, anyway?'

Gabriel sighed. 'Things have been stagnant for some time. We can't seem to agree on whether it's a good idea to get involved in international banking or not.'

'What do you think about it?'

'Honestly, I'm torn. On the one hand, you should know I'm a deeply traditional man. If you'd asked me a year ago, I would have told you that Swiss banking was a matter for the Swiss. But ever since my trip to Chicago, I can't help but wonder...'

'Your partners don't want to get involved?'

Gabriel shook his head. 'They're not sure. Far be it from me to be the radical element! For now, we'll just wait and see.'

'Very well,' Serge said thoughtfully. 'Well, why don't you tell me what else is going on in your life? How is your delightful wife, for instance?'

Gabriel sighed.

Serge laughed. 'Was that the wrong question? Are you two in trouble?'

'No, no,' Gabriel replied hastily. 'Well, nothing as straightforward as that sounds.' He paused, looking out at the mountains. 'Although sometimes it seems as if... a sort of cold front has descended.'

There was a silence. 'I see,' Serge said slowly.

'Things have been strange the last few months,' Gabriel continued uncomfortably, unable to stop himself. 'Even stranger than usual, I mean. But perhaps I need to give you some context. Have I told you about my dear Clarice's involvement with the modern art scene?'

'Oh no,' Serge said. 'A midlife crisis?'

'Something of that nature, I suspect. She's met these awful women, and they've filled her head with all sorts of... notions. They drink these ridiculous coffees and spend all their time in Carouge and pretend to enjoy the most ludicrous contemporary art. All they seem to want to do is break the rules, willy nilly! I went away to Chicago for a weekend, and when I came back, she had painted... Oh, Serge, it was so awful! This sort of carnotzet.'

'Let me stop you right there,' Serge said, 'before one of us feels insulted. Clarice actually called me to ask for my advice. I put her in touch with the artists.'

'Oh, sorry, I know that,' Gabriel said, 'but did you *see* what they did? Or rather, what she asked them to do? It's modern art of the worst kind, birds with triangular heads, and these unrecognisable flower designs, and that's not even the worst part.'

'Ah,' said Serge. 'I wonder how the traditional Swiss artists felt about that.'

'The worst part,' Gabriel went on, 'is that I myself am painted in the centre, herding cows like a common peasant. In a modern style! I cannot tell you how insulting I found this charade, this farce...'

'And the party? How did it go?'

Gabriel glared out the window. 'It was a catastrophe,' he said curtly. 'Cheese spilling everywhere, drunks of all possible nationalities, and some businessman wandering around with a cowbell around his neck... and that's on top of the ruined guest room!'

Serge was shaking his head. 'At the risk of speaking out of turn, it rather sounds like you and Clarice need to work on your communication. I honestly believe she thought she was preparing a pleasant surprise.'

'Honestly, Serge, I can't even tell any more. A part of me thinks she's turned into this dishonest, manipulative, self-serving... *cow*, and then simultaneously I find it so hard to reconcile with what I know of the woman I married. If you could only imagine! Twenty years ago, I would never have questioned the notion that Clarice thought it would please me, even if that turned out to be untrue. Now, I'm not so sure. She was Swisser than the Swiss when I first met her, you know. Sweet, quiet, serious, earnest...'

'... a perfect wife. Devoted to you.'

'Yes! Well, there was always some degree of independence, but this is something else.'

'In what way?'

'Everything is just... different. In a way, I think I took this break to get away from it all. Usually, Clarice would have come with me on these weekend trips, even if she ended up spending the whole damn weekend with her nose in her art catalogues. I just needed a break. From everything.'

'Sometimes these things are necessary, psychologically,' Serge replied. 'It sounds like you should focus on the joys of the Swiss countryside, the *combat de Hérens*, all that! Maybe you'll find it cathartic.'

'Yes, yes,' Gabriel replied. 'Thank you for driving me there, by the way.'

'Oh, it's no problem. It really is on the way back to my house. I had a lovely time with you today, you know. We should meet up again for lunch sometime, even if you are postponing the chalet expansion.'

'My salad was good,' Gabriel said distractedly.

Serge laughed. 'Stop thinking about your wife!' he said. 'You're here to enjoy yourself. Don't worry, I'll leave you on your own soon. You can wallow in your marital misery as much as you like, or cast it off and enjoy the scenery. Whatever you want. Just promise me you won't wander off and miss the actual fight? I must have seen it forty times in my life, and every single time it is just the most wonderful thing. I've been coming here since I was a child. It's so wild, so exciting!'

'I thought you said it was a typical Swiss event,' Gabriel said drily.

'You'll see,' Serge replied cheerfully. 'Unless I share your wife's curse, I really think you'll enjoy this. I think I know a true Swiss man when I see one.'

Gabriel shook his head.

In truth, Gabriel had only called up Serge in hopes of hitching a free ride from Geneva to Saas Fee. However, the architect had turned out to already be in the region, and there was no discouraging his enthusiasm for face-to-face conversation. Gabriel had driven up that Saturday morning, left his things at the chalet, and rather unwillingly met for lunch in the village. He had almost forgotten about the *combat de reines* when planning his weekend escapade, and might even have rescheduled, discouraged by the crowds, had he not been so desperate to get away from Clarice. However, the scene was neither a busy nor a particularly unpleasant one, and the knowledge that he could walk back to his chalet afterwards brought with it a flooding relief.

The smell of melting cheese and the soft music of the alphorn eventually began to draw Gabriel out of his bad mood. The mountain peaks towering above the valley reminded him of the sheer insignificance of his life, his bank, his marital troubles. He was at home, here in the depths of the Swiss countryside. He was alone, even amongst these crowds of peasants. He could relax in an utterly familiar setting. Maybe he would even have a beer! He frowned, unpleasantly reminded of his American holiday. No, he told himself sternly, drinking in the afternoon would not do. A little raclette, however, might be acceptable.

From a flaking poster tacked to a barn door, he worked out that the combat itself wasn't for an hour or so. Perhaps he would have a snack, wait for the cow fight, then head back to the silent bliss of his chalet. The next morning, he would get up at dawn and walk in the mountains. Gabriel sighed, stood up from the fence he had been sitting on, and brushed a few specks of dust from his immaculate suit trousers. Yes, raclette, he thought to himself. That was what he wanted.

The cheese was melting over an open wood fire, waiting to be scraped and dripped over potatoes or rye bread by a muscular, red-cheeked woman. 'Come on, don't be shy!' she shouted in his direction, waving her cheese spatula in the air. 'Come sample Madame Fitalou's raclette, the best raclette in all of Saas Fee!'

Looking hastily behind him, Gabriel found that he had indeed been the designated recipient of this tirade. Slightly embarrassed, he joined the queue.

A gentle giggle came from in front of him, and a young woman with warm eyes turned around. 'Don't worry,' she whispered, smiling back over her shoulder. 'Madame Fitalou's like that with everyone. Isn't she just so wonderfully Swiss?'

'Madame Fitalou?' Gabriel repeated in confusion.

'Maggie Fitalou, the cheese lady!' the young woman explained. She had long, dark hair that fell down her back in a thick curtain.

'Right,' said Gabriel.

'Maggie's not a very Swiss name, is it, but maybe she changed it to appeal to tourists like me.'

'Did she now?' Gabriel replied, bewildered.

'Do you even think there's enough cheese to go around? I just love this Swiss cheese so much, I would be devastated if there wasn't! Are you Swiss?' She smiled again, revealing a soft dimple.

Gabriel surprised himself by musing that she was quite attractive. 'Yes, I am,' he said. 'Genevois born and bred. I'm a banker, actually.'

'Oh, how fascinating!' the woman said, prettily. 'A real Swiss banker, spotted in the wild!'

Gabriel smiled indulgently, then quickly stopped. What was he doing? He'd come to the chalet to be alone, not make conversation with total strangers. Even pretty ones.

'My name is Anita, by the way,' she said, holding out a tan, slender hand.

'I'm Gabriel,' he replied, shaking it. Her hand was warm, her grip surprisingly firm. She shook hands, Gabriel found himself remarking, like a man closing a business deal. He smiled almost involuntarily.

'Would you like a glass of red wine?'

'I'm sorry?' Gabriel said.

Anita giggled. 'Wine. You know, made of grapes?' she teased. Yet there was something in her tone that made Gabriel feel like he was a part of the joke.

'I don't usually drink in the daytime,' he replied honestly.

'Oh, I'm sorry!' she said, sounding mortified.

'But today, why not?' he said, observing with growing horror that his tone sounded quite jovial. 'After all, it is a sort of holiday.'

'Come closer!' Madame Fitalou shouted, scraping at the giant wheel of raclette. Her curly hair was standing out from her head in a mess, as if it too had been fried over an open fire.

'I'm not quite sure where the wine is, though,' Gabriel whispered, unwilling to anger Madame Fitalou by wandering from his designated spot in the queue.

'Perhaps we can find a glass once we've picked up our portions of cheese,' Anita suggested with a soft giggle.

The queue shifted forward a pace, and Gabriel stepped closer to this strange creature, intrigued. 'Alright,' he said, nodding slowly.

'Don't you simply *adore* raclette?' Anita continued.

'I do enjoy it, yes,' he said. 'I mean, there's no messing about with saliva, like fondue.'

Anita laughed loudly, as if he had just told a salacious joke.

Pleased against his will, Gabriel smiled. 'I mean, I'm a Swiss man, so I'm honour-bound to enjoy all the dishes of the country, but fondue? It's a little much, even for me. I mean, just this winter, my wife –' He faltered suddenly. Anita, for some reason, looked crestfallen, then seemed to force herself to smile.

'Your wife?' she said encouragingly.

Gabriel paused for a moment, unsure of how to continue. 'She had an awful fondue party,' he concluded lamely.

'Oh,' said Anita.

'And she wants to redecorate our house.'

'What a pity!' Anita said. 'I'm sure your house is lovely. You live in Geneva, then?'

'Yes,' he said, glad they were into safer conversational territory. 'I inherited the house from my parents. They have decided to live out their retirement in a chalet, you see.'

'I would so love to have a chalet!' Anita exclaimed. 'I have always dreamed of it. Cosy wooden interiors, and crisp mountain air...'

Gabriel felt his heart lift in the presence of this delightful creature. 'Oh, me too!' he said. 'Ever since I was a child...'

'But there are no chalets in Peru,' she said, 'although we have wonderful mountains. Not quite as marvellous as the Alps, though! I have never seen scenery so utterly entrancing.' She sighed.

'You are from Peru, then?' Gabriel asked, fascinated and charmed.

'Yes, I have been here only three years,' she said. 'It was always my dream to come to Switzerland. Now I am here!'

'So you are,' Gabriel said. 'Peru!'

'You there!' Madame Fitalou barked at the couple, startling them once more.

'Is it our turn?' Anita said with a smile.

'You are the lucky ones, today,' Madame Fitalou said, her red face bursting into an uneven grin. Her teeth were the same colour as the wheel of cheese she was guarding. 'Do you know what the *religieuse* is?'

'A nun?' Gabriel said coolly.

Anita giggled and slapped him on the arm. 'It is the last piece of cheese!' she said, in a tone of hushed reverence. 'Just like a fondue.'

Madame Fitalou nodded approvingly, as if Anita were a schoolchild. 'Correct,' she said. 'I am about to scrape the very last piece of the cheese onto your plates, and I want to make sure you appreciate the experience. You see, the soft, buttery part of the cheese has disappeared. All that is left is this crispy halo of perfection, a delicious crust to be slathered over your potatoes. The last bite has extra taste. The last piece of cheese is perfect.'

Gabriel raised an eyebrow.

'I'm sure you're wondering why it's called a *religieuse*,' Madame Fitalou continued, frowning at the piece of cheese held tightly in its metal base. Her cheeks were streaked with soot. 'Well, the nuns who live in the high mountains near here, they famously never throw anything away. They live pure, pious lives, you see. Even burnt cheese must be treated with respect. When you are a young Catholic, you are told to clean your plate, and always finish every bite. Yes, that is how the nuns do it, and they were rewarded for their diligence. It is a sacred act, eating this perfect, crispy bit of cheese. A meditative moment.'

Gabriel stared at Madame Fitalou. 'Thank you,' he said slowly. Anita giggled.

'There's not enough to go around,' Madame Fitalou snapped, scraping the cheese carefully from its rind, 'so you'd better appreciate it.'

'Yes, ma'am,' Gabriel said.

'*Voilà*,' Madame Fitalou said, handing across two small plates of potato and cheese with reverence. 'Enjoy.' She looked over towards the pile of fresh wheels of raclette with satisfaction.

'Could we get two glasses of red wine, as well?'

'Just over there,' Madame Fitalou replied, waving a red hand towards a tent. 'Make sure you don't miss the combat, though!'

Anita and Gabriel walked off, inhaling the scent of their fresh delicacy. 'Sit here,' Anita said, laying a hand on Gabriel's shoulder. 'I'll bring us some wine.'

Dazed, Gabriel sat down with the two plates. What a strange day this was turning out to be! He watched Anita as discreetly as he could, as she leaned up against the bar. There was something deeply seductive about her figure, both soft and tough. She had rounded, womanly hips, paired with strong shoulders. Her face was gentle and feminine, her brows as defined as if they had been drawn on in kohl. Her hair, falling down her back, reminded him of a fine, pure-bred horse. Suddenly, Anita caught his gaze and smiled, dazzlingly. Gabriel shook his head, looked away and adjusted his tie.

'What were you thinking?' Anita asked as she sat down across from him, setting down the glasses of wine. 'You looked lost in reverie...' Her expression was inviting, not teasing. How unused he had become to being spoken to so gently!

'I was thinking you looked like one of those Gauguin paintings,' Gabriel said suddenly. 'So...' Warm. Feminine. Colourful. None of these adjectives seemed appropriate. Gabriel battled to keep an image of Anita nude on an island, surrounded by exotic blossoms, from taking over his mind. In the face of his awkwardness, Anita beamed.

'I think what you mean to say,' she grinned, 'is that I don't look like a Swiss woman.'

'What I mean to say is that you are quite beautiful,' Gabriel replied, without meaning to. There was a silence.

A quick blush suffused Anita's face. 'I don't know much about art,' she said suddenly. 'Will you tell me, who is this Gauguin?'

'A French painter,' Gabriel said, beginning to cut his first potato. 'He travelled all around the world, lived on remote islands... His art was post-impressionist, if that is the right word; full of colour, like Matisse or Picasso.'

Anita was nodding fervently, whilst eating her cheese with relish.

Gabriel took a gulp of wine. 'Did you enjoy Madame Fitalou's cheesy storytelling?' he asked. 'I doubt there's a word of truth in it.'

Anita looked offended. 'Why would you say that?' Her eyes opened wide. 'Wait, do you know another story about the *religieuse*?'

'Oh no,' Gabriel said hastily. 'I am simply not... used to such enthusiasm.'

Anita looked at him, her eyes soft. She took a large bite of potato. 'I will have to find some paintings of Swiss men,' she said, 'so I can compliment you in return.'

Gabriel nearly choked on his *religieuse*.

'Anyway, I like Maggie,' Anita continued confidently.

'You have been here before, then?' Gabriel asked, trying to recover his composure. *This woman thought he was... attractive?*

Anita nodded enthusiastically. 'One time. Maggie was my guide. She explained to me the cow fights, and helped with my French. You know, "it is not a burnt nun, you eat it with a potato."' She giggled.

'Your French is fine!' Gabriel said, slightly unconvincingly. *Were there even any attractive paintings of Swiss men?* he wondered.

Anita gave a brilliant smile. 'I can always use more help,' she said, batting her eyelashes.

'Well, I know there is an excellent school near Verbier,' he said distractedly. Was it in his mind or did she look slightly saddened by this response? She had such lovely long lashes. 'Or in Geneva,' he added quickly, understanding.

'I'm actually learning English in Lausanne at the moment,' she said. 'I am living in Nyon, you see, looking over the lake. Oh, how I love Lac Léman!' she added dreamily.

'You're working there?' he asked.

She nodded. 'I am a waitress at the golf club between Coppet and Nyon.'

'Oh!' Gabriel said in surprise. 'Yes, some of my friends go there. Bankers. I have been there for lunch a few times. To think we might have crossed paths!'

Anita shook her head shyly. 'I would have remembered,' she said. 'Isn't that dining room overlooking the lake just marvellous?'

Gabriel said hastily.

'Yes,' she said. 'I love to swim in the lake so much. Sometimes, after work, I run down to the shore and simply strip out of my clothes.'

Gabriel coughed, then finished his glass of red wine in one gulp. 'So,' he said, 'I think we should go see this combat, no?'

Anita gave a shy smile. 'I have a confession,' she said. 'I did not actually watch last year. I was so worried it would be violent! I nearly fainted at a bullfight once in Mexico, you see.'

'Oh, this won't be anything like that. Swiss bulls are too proud to gore each other, you see.' He smiled. 'One usually gives up, admitting his submission, and simply turns away in shame.'

'Oh!' Anita said. 'That sounds alright.'

'Come, let us walk over,' he said, feeling oddly protective. 'I promise you, we can leave if you are not enjoying yourself.'

'You can look after me,' Anita said softly.

Gabriel walked on quickly. 'The Hérens cattle are an ancient Swiss race, famous all over the world for their fierce temper, their nobility and strength. The winner of this combat will be recognised as the strongest cow. As queen, she will lead the herd all summer.'

'Why are the cows down here in the valley, though? Aren't they mountain cows?'

'The cows travel,' Gabriel explained. 'In the autumn, they descend from the fertile *alpage* prairies, so as to be away from the snows. They come into town, covered in flowers and ribbons.'

Anita clapped her hands in delight. 'How wonderful!'

'Now, after this fight, the cows will be led back up into the mountains. This is know as the "*inalpe*" or "*réalpe*," every spring, when the cows return to the higher pastures. Oh, and one more fact: if the herd is dissatisfied with their queen, they have been known to elect a new leader, a few months afterwards.'

'How exciting!' said Anita. 'Oh look, there they are now!'

The fight appeared to be beginning. Quickly, Gabriel led Anita to a space in the crowd. Huddled between the bodies, the pair were crushed together. 'God, they're huge!' Gabriel whispered. 'I saw this once when I was a child, but I had forgotten how impressive it was!' Anita grabbed his hand and squeezed. They watched as the cows lumbered towards each other, muscular necks locked in heavy harnesses of bronze and leather, the bells swinging wildly. *My wife hates cows*, Gabriel suddenly wanted to say. *My wife drives me crazy.* He swallowed. 'See how they have large numbers written on their side in white chalk!' he said, in his most professorial tone.

Anita nodded happily. 'Switzerland is wonderful!' she said.

'Also, the meat of these cows is very expensive.'

Anita smiled. 'You're so funny! How do you know so much about cows?' she asked. The animals in front of them locked horns. One of them let out a low bellow.

'My mother,' he replied, drawing close so that they could hear each other over the cheering of the crowds. 'She taught me all about the mountains, about animals, about birds.'

'Teach me!' Anita said, delighted. 'I want to learn all about Switzerland!'

Gabriel laughed. 'Well,' he said, his face quite close to her hair, 'there are many rare birds in the mountains here. Switzerland has over sixty species. I think somebody should be writing a book about these. It's too bad that Audubon never got back here.'

'What?' Anita said, turning around. 'Who?'

Gabriel shook his head. 'I'll tell you after the combat.'

'No!' she exclaimed, moving impulsively back away from the barrier. 'Come, let's watch from further away.' She grabbed his hand more tightly and pulled him towards a patch of wildflowers. 'See? We can sit here, and still just about see who is the winner.' She spun around and sank down into the blossoms.

Gabriel smiled, shaking his head. 'Alright,' he said, sitting down gingerly.

'Now, this bird person. Who is he?'

'An American naturalist,' Gabriel replied. 'He painted birds in the most glorious detail. It's a shame he had to kill most of them to get close, but they are so perfectly preserved for eternity! The first edition is actually one of the most expensive books in the world.

The prints of the birds are life-sized, and hand-coloured. It was so big they called it the Elephant Folio.'

'How wonderful!'

'And we have better-looking birds than in the USA. I know because I travelled there, just a few months ago!'

'I've never actually been to North America,' Anita said thoughtfully.

'Really? Well, this was my first time. A business trip, for a deal that never really went anywhere.' For some reason, this thought made him rather wistful.

'It's complicated for me,' she said vaguely, waving a hand. 'But tell me about your time there!'

'Chicago was... intense and strange. A vast and cold city, unlike anything I'd ever seen in Switzerland, or Europe. Even the snow felt different! The food... the food was just crazy. There was a lot of bacon.'

'I much prefer Swiss cheese, I'm sure,' Anita said firmly.

'Yes, so do I.' Gabriel nodded thoughtfully, something like nostalgia having seized him. There was a long silence, in which he became aware that a cold wind had started to blow in from the hills. 'I think the combats are ending,' he said. He stood up, trying not to care that there was mud on his trousers.

'Would you like to get another glass of wine?' Anita asked, her eyes inviting.

Gabriel hesitated. He swallowed. She was standing quite close to him. 'No,' he said suddenly, stumbling back a little. He tried to soften his voice. 'I have to get back,' he said. 'Home.'

'I see,' Anita said, her face falling. 'Well, I have to get the tourist bus back, anyway,' she said, as if summoning a show of bravery. 'Will you walk me to the bus stop?'

'Of course,' Gabriel said gallantly. 'I mean, I really would have liked to stay longer, but I just have to get back to Geneva...' Why was he lying? Why was he babbling?

'I understand,' Anita said. 'The tour bus is just over there.'

They walked in silence past the fields. All at once, a part of

Gabriel wanted this woman gone, out of his life, so that he could be peacefully alone again. All he wanted was to go back to his chalet, and sleep, and plan the route for his hike. Something in his stomach felt tight in Anita's presence, and he wanted it to loosen. Perhaps he shouldn't have had that glass of wine.

'Here's my bus,' Anita said. She pulled her handbag open and began to rustle around in it. 'If you should ever want to call me...' She held out a card, her smile inviting.

'You're very pretty and nice,' he blurted out, 'but I –'

'All I'd like is a friend,' she said quietly. 'Maybe a tour guide.'

He nodded. 'Right,' he said, taking her card. 'Well. Have a safe trip back.'

'It was nice to meet you,' she said, holding out her hand.

Surprised, he took it, and she shook it firmly. He smiled, amused, and watched her as she climbed into the bus. She did not look back.

After the bus drove away, Gabriel began the long walk uphill towards the chalet. A chilly spring night was descending on the Alps, and the first stars were beginning to appear in the blue air. He wondered, as he slowly walked up into the mountains, if anyone had ever called him funny before.

⬦

The chalet seemed empty, with its perfect white walls and glowing waxed parquet. Gabriel sank slowly into the couch, wiggling his toes absent-mindedly in the hand-woven carpet. Was it Clarice's presence he missed? No, it must simply be that he had spent too much of the day chattering. Wasn't it good to be alone? He sprang up from the couch, shaking his head, and went to the kitchen. He filled the stainless-steel kettle and set it over the flame. A cup of weak chamomile, that was what he needed. Something to calm the nerves. Something to help him sleep. It must have been the cow fight, that was it. Quite stressful, quite violent. Or perhaps the cheese was disagreeing with his stomach. For some reason, alone in the kitchen, Gabriel began to grin. Life was exciting. Life was full of promise. Dick! He would call Dick.

Switching off the burner, Gabriel dashed back into the living room and began pulling things out of his yet-unpacked suitcase. At last, he held up his black notebook and began to flick through. There he was: Dick Nikko, Chicago. After a quick calculation of the time difference, Gabriel walked over to the phone and dialled.

'Hello?' he said, suddenly nervous.

'Gabe!' the voice at the end of the line crackled. 'Great to hear from you, my friend. It's been, what, months! I tried your office a few times but some very firm secretary told me you were out.'

Gabriel laughed. 'That must have been Caroline. I'm so sorry for the delay; I needed some time to think seriously about this venture.' Truthfully, Gabriel knew very well that he had quite firmly decided upon his arrival at the fondue party that he would steer clear of all this international business for the time being, no matter how tempting it was. He hadn't even mentioned the brochures to his partners. Yet all at once he was sure: it was time for some excitement.

'Great, great,' Dick was saying. 'So how was your trip home? Did you enjoy those little angels I sent you?'

Gabriel frowned in confusion, then remembered. 'Oh, your nieces? Yes, yes, they were very nice. Americans are very friendly, from what I've gathered.'

For some reason, Dick howled with laughter. 'Well, maybe you can introduce me to some Swiss women, sometime.'

'Yes, well,' Gabriel stammered, confused. 'Anyway, I was calling you to talk about business. I have decided that it is not a bad thing for a man to take measured risks, venture into new territory. For this reason, I have decided to commit fifteen million dollars to your high-yield bonds, and also fifteen million dollars to mortgage-backed securities.'

'Whoa!' Dick crowed. 'That's the best news I've heard all day. What's life without a little risk, after all? Welcome on board, my dear man.'

'I would like to see how these investments progress before I go any further,' Gabriel continued.

'Of course, of course. I'll keep you posted. You tell that secretary of yours to stop hanging up on me, alright? Or I'll show up at your... ski resort unannounced.'

Gabriel smiled. 'I'll call you in a few weeks,' he said. 'Maybe we can talk about a visit when we have my newfound fortune to celebrate.'

'Sure thing,' Dick said. 'I look forward to it. You take care, alright?'

'I will,' said Gabriel. He hung up, exhilarated. 'I will.'

Chapter Twenty

The crowd roared as the Swiss player sent the ball spinning to the far corner of the court. 'Fifteen-love!' Fleurie shouted, jumping up and down. 'Fifteen!'

Clarice sighed. 'Do you know where Juni Bao has got to?' she asked.

Chloë giggled. 'She went off searching for refreshments,' she answered. 'I think she was delayed by the bankers.'

Clarice swivelled around in her seat in consternation. Sure enough, the young Chinese businesswoman appeared to be deep in conversation with two of Gabriel's young colleagues. Was that Egon, perhaps, or Guillaume? 'This is what comes of insisting on watching the game from this banking box,' she said grumpily. 'I mean, if I'd known this was what would happen, I would have stayed at home.'

'Come on,' Chloë said, laying a hand on her arm affectionately. 'You know Gabe's friends only agreed to let us have this box because they knew we had our new millionaire friend with us. Anyway, aren't you glad she's funding your gallery so substantially?'

'Yes,' Clarice admittedly unwillingly. 'She's been a great help to us. I just wish she could do it from further away. Maybe with less smiling.'

Chloë snorted with laughter. 'I love bitchy Clarice,' she said. 'Are your hormones playing up?'

Clarice sighed. 'Sorry,' she said. 'It's just... I didn't sleep well last night.'

Chloë's eyes brightened. 'Ooh!' she said. 'Tell me more!'

Clarice shook her head. 'No, not like that,' she said. 'I mean...' She sank back in her seat and leaned closer. 'Well, if you really must know, I woke up in the middle of the night just desperate for it, you know?'

'For sex?' Chloë whispered back, pretending to be scandalised. 'And then what happened?'

'It must have been three in the morning, and I just couldn't get back to sleep. I tossed and turned, I was just so bored! So I tried to wake up my dearly beloved, sleeping there like a marble statue, and he was just so horrible and rude to me! I mean, I know a sort of cold front has descended ever since he got back from the States, but...'

'You mean since the fondue party,' Chloë said. 'My, what a fun time I had!'

'Well, I'm still paying for it now, and it's been almost nine months. Our fight is old enough to be a newborn baby! I mean, he cheered up a bit in the spring, after going away to the chalet alone, but then he quickly sank back into his usual desperate gloom.' She sighed again deeply. 'It's not like things aren't going well for Gabriel. His bank has been making absolutely tonnes of money ever since he started investing in Chicago. This Dick guy has made him absolutely phenomenal amounts of cash. Why we aren't moving to America right now, I can't possibly tell you! Boston, or Chicago, or maybe Hyannis beach in Nantucket...'

'So what happened, then, in bed?'

Clarice shook her head. 'Nothing, of course. As usual. The man is more boring than a boring potato. Do you know what he said to me? He said: "If you're so stressed, you should read a book or go downstairs and watch the news." What kind of romance is that?'

Chloë shook her head. 'I still don't understand why you don't just take a lover. Some nice young sprightly artist, perhaps? Don't they ever try it on, when you take them out to lunch?'

'Oh, of course they do, but mostly in hopes of their work being exhibited. No, I'm simply not that kind of woman. Gabriel is my fate. Besides, let's be practical here: there's a chance he'll be raking in the millions. This would be a terrible time to opt out.' Clarice gave a thin smile.

Chloë laughed happily. 'Yes!' shouted Fleurie, her fist punching into the air. 'Yes, yes, Switzerland!'

'What happened?' Clarice asked, leaning back lazily.

Fleurie gave a mock frown. 'You could at least pretend to pay attention, you know,' she said. 'I mean, he's a ranked player. Number two in the whole wide world! And here we are watching him in his home country, and neither of you cares at all.'

'I care,' said Chloë. 'I quite like watching his legs. And I like Italians.'

Fleurie frowned. 'Don't you dare root for the Italians,' she said. 'I will never forgive you.'

Clarice laughed. 'Fleurie, you're beginning to sound like something of a chauvinist! I would never have believed it.'

Fleurie shrugged. 'What can I say? There's something about sports that brings out quiet strains of nationalism in anyone.'

'It's an animal reaction,' Chloë said, nodding. 'All those red flags. You probably can't help it. For instance, I couldn't care less about tennis, but at the end of the match, I will make sure our Swiss man will sign my hat.'

'That's just because of his legs,' Fleurie said. 'You're probably hoping to wake up next to him tomorrow.'

'Well, doesn't that make me an excellent supporter?' she retorted.

Clarice shook her head. 'I just don't understand it. I swear with every year that passes my understanding of my people is shifting beyond recovery. I mean, aren't we a quiet, conservative nation? What is all this shouting? Those women over there are climbing on their chairs! It's ridiculous. Entertaining, but not very dignified. You'd expect this sort of thing from the Italians, but our side of the stands is just as badly behaved.'

'Well, the chants are a lot of fun,' Fleurie said defensively. 'It's all about the atmosphere. We're allowed to come out of our shells here!'

'Ooh, did you see that little girl with a tennis ball the size of her head? I think she was hoping to get it signed...' Chloë added. 'Cute, but not competition.'

'What if he doesn't sign your hat?' Clarice asked mischievously.

'I'll pull his hair,' Chloë replied firmly.

'Girls, shouldn't we go rescue Juni?' Fleurie asked, looking back at the entry to the box. 'Gabriel's partners can be downright predatory.'

'Well, she was headed to the VIP restaurant,' Clarice replied. 'I'm sure she'll make it there eventually. Not that I know why a millionaire would be so excited about free drinks.'

Fleurie shook her head. 'You're the one who took her under her wing, you know,' she said sternly.

'Yeah,' Chloë said, 'but you were the one who wanted the best seats in the house at the Davis Cup. You could at least look after her a little, instead of throwing her into the pen with those savage bankers.'

'Fine,' Fleurie said. 'Maybe at the end of this set.' She frowned. 'I don't mean to sound ungrateful,' she added, 'but how *did* we end up in this box, anyway?'

'Oh, I've been before!' Chloë said.

'Of course you have.' Fleurie shook her head indulgently. 'No, don't even tell me. Probably that Nestlé guy, right? Anyway, Clarice, why did Gabriel...'

'It was Rolex,' Chloë pouted. 'Honestly, it's like you don't even listen to me.'

'I'm not sure, to be perfectly frank,' Clarice said. 'I mean, Gabriel is still being vile to me at home, but he seems to have suddenly decided that it would be nice for all of us to be able to come here. To be honest, I suspect he feels guilty about the fondue party – for not contributing to my fundraiser. So I guess he went to talk to his partners, and asked if he could have the VIP box. He must have told them that Juni was one of us, and they must have hoped they could grab her as a Von Mipatobeau client.'

Fleurie laughed. 'I can just imagine it,' she said. 'Yes, my wife, she has excellent relations with the Arabs and Chinese!'

'Well, it's true,' Clarice said shortly. 'We do have excellent contacts. We know a lot of rich people.'

'Is Gabriel coming, then?' Fleurie asked.

'I don't think so,' Clarice replied. 'He's always been bored by sports. But there are a few seats left for the partners, so who knows? He might just show up later.'

'Why is Juni still here anyway?' Chloë asked curiously. 'In Switzerland, I mean.'

'You know the old adage: if you're far from your money, you'll lose it? Well, she seems to hold that to heart,' Clarice replied.

Chloë laughed suddenly. 'Oh my god,' she said. 'Have you guys heard about the Russian princess story?'

'What Russian princess?' Fleurie asked, curious against her will.

'So,' Chloë said excitedly, 'this beautiful young woman married an ageing Texan oligarch. When he died, she inherited his fortune. Two hundred and fifty million dollars, if I recall correctly. She moved to Switzerland.'

'Nothing exceptional about any of that,' Clarice said archly.

'Ah, but wait!' Chloë said. 'What happened next is. Her lawyer, her banker, her accountant and the family nanny teamed up to steal every single penny of it. She was left destitute.'

Fleurie gasped.

'How?' Clarice asked.

'Under cover of managing her money, they set up elaborate accounts of the ways she was spending it. All faked, of course. For instance, they bought luxury clothes from a cheap secondhand store set up in a container, and then wrote lists as though she had bought them direct from the designers. They made her look extravagant, crazy even! Later, when the case went to court, they found that the clothes were in all sorts of sizes. One pair of shoes was four sizes too small.'

Clarice laughed against her will. 'How crazy!' she said.

Chloë giggled excitedly. 'I know!' she said. 'I only recently heard this story. There's more: the lawyer's brother was a jeweller, and they had some sort of crazy setup with him as well. Some also think that her doctor was drugging her, so that she wouldn't realise what was going on.'

'That can't be true,' Fleurie said.

Chloë shrugged. 'I haven't told you the juiciest detail yet, though. The princess's banker turned out to be really into sadomasochism. He used to have women come right into his office at the Swiss bank and whip his bottom!'

'Chloë!' Clarice said disapprovingly, then hesitated. 'Really?'

'Oh yes,' Chloë said.

'And how do you know this?' Fleurie asked.

'I have my sources.' She tapped her nose. 'Apparently the bank knew about this... perversion, but they didn't do anything about it because he made them too much money!'

'Why are you even telling this ridiculous story?' Fleurie asked.

'Weren't you listening? It's proof that you can lose all your money even if you're sitting right on it!' Chloë said triumphantly.

Fleurie shook her head. 'How sad,' she said. 'Let's go find Juni.'

'The princess must have trusted all those people,' Clarice said in wonder, slowly standing up.

'Even the pervert banker!' Chloë said. 'I mean, I feel like there's another moral to this story, about the underbelly of the oh-so-pure Swiss banking world. Fraud, theft, sadomasochism...'

'Careful,' said Fleurie. 'You're talking to the first lady of Bank Von Mipatobeau.'

Clarice laughed. 'Oh, I'm quite sure there's none of that going on around Gabriel. I don't think the man would be excited, if a naked hooker walked right into his office. He'd probably ask her to bring him tea. Weak chamomile, at that.'

'Clarice!' Juni disengaged herself from the eager duo of bankers and ran over to the group, smiling widely.

'Hello, Juni,' Fleurie said with a warm smile. 'Care to come watch the match with us?'

'I do not understand tennis,' she said brightly. 'Maybe you can explain to me?'

Fleurie took her arm. 'Of course,' she said. 'This match will have five sets,' she said patiently.

'What is sets?' Juni asked.

Chloë sighed. 'Just watch the legs,' she said.

Juni frowned in confusion. 'I am sorry,' she said. 'My French is still not very good. My English, also.'

'That's OK,' Fleurie said, guiding her towards the seat next to hers. 'Sit next to me, and I will tell you what is happening.'

'I want to understand,' Juni said. 'I would like to become as European as possible in my time here.' She paused. 'I am not only in

Switzerland to hide my money, you know.'

Chloë and Clarice glanced at each other guiltily.

'Don't listen to those boyish bankers,' Chloë said. 'They were probably just trying to flirt with you.'

Juni laughed. 'Don't be silly,' she said. 'I know when a man is wanting my money. The thing is, I'm quite interested in keeping some of my fortune with Von Mipatobeau. I would not have kept... talk to them if I did not want to.'

Clarice raised an eyebrow. 'Well!' she said, slightly embarrassed.

Suddenly, there was a commotion on the court. The Italian player had thrown down his racket in a rage, breaking the handle. He could be heard shouting obscenities in his native tongue, and appeared to be stomping his feet like a child throwing a tantrum.

Chloë's eyes brightened. 'I like a passionate man,' she said.

'He's disputing the line judge's call,' Fleurie explained. 'I'm inclined to agree with him, in this case. That was definitely in!'

Clarice shook her head disapprovingly. 'Such babies, the Italians,' she said.

'You're just still angry because of that stupid woman at your fondue party,' Chloë retorted, piqued.

'You're mistaken,' Clarice said. 'I've never liked the Italians.'

Fleurie gave an aggrieved sigh. 'The man serves at over two hundred kilometres an hour,' she said. 'This is no child!'

'Wow!' Juni breathed.

'See?' said Chloë.

'And since this is the quarter-final, I would very much appreciate it if you two could keep your stupid commentary to a minimum. Look, Juni is trying to understand. We might make it to the semi! We might win the cup!'

'Yeah, right,' Chloë said sceptically.

'You're only supposed to talk between points, you know,' Fleurie added in a huff. As if to prove her point, a loud shushing noise came from the side of the court. She bit her lip.

'Do you want to go get a drink?' Clarice suddenly whispered to Chloë.

Chloë grinned. 'We'll be right back,' she told the other two, who were staring at the court; Fleurie with rapt attention, Juni with tentative enthusiasm.

'Please bring me one champagne,' Juni said, without taking her eyes from the player.

Clarice shook her head in amusement, and took Chloë's arm. They walked to the back of the box. 'Every day she surprises me,' she said. 'Oh, hello, Pierre!'

The man bowed. 'Gabriel is not here today?' he inquired.

Clarice shrugged. 'He might come along later, I don't know. Perhaps you could direct us to the drinks tent?'

'Right this way, *mesdames*.'

'He's cute,' Chloë whispered.

'You think everyone is "cute," Chloë,' Clarice replied, affectionately.

Chloë sighed. 'Do you want to know something strange? I've been bored lately, just like you.'

Clarice raised her eyebrows in mock horror. 'Surely you don't mean to say you've been lonely in your bedroom?'

'Oh no,' Chloë said hastily. 'I am not lonely, just bored. It is not the same thing, for me. My life is... somehow bereft of passion.' Clarice snorted with laughter, and Chloë joined in ruefully as they entered the VIP drinks tent. 'I mean, I know I can seduce almost any man I want. It's just that I am beginning to want something more. Do you know what I mean?'

'I suppose so, though you'll have to excuse my cynicism. It's been a long time since passion was on the cards for me.' She asked for three glasses of champagne.

'I heard another story from the young paralegal who told me about the Russian princess. Another story about Swiss bankers. One of them married a rich Swiss woman, and then immediately got bored of her. No, no, don't object yet. I know you want to tell me there's nothing exceptional there. Just wait till you hear what happened next.' She took a generous sip of her champagne. 'He hired a Kosovar to kill her,' she continued conversationally.

Clarice choked on her drink. 'What?'

Chloë gave a satisfied smile. 'He negotiated, like the banker he was, a price for the killing: four or five hundred thousand. The Kosovar, this killer, accepted, and made his way to the couple's house. The wife was supposed to be there alone. The Kosovar's preferred method of killing was to strangle, so he snuck into the house and stole one of the wife's long scarves. When he arrived in her bedroom, she was standing with her back to him. He whips the scarf over her head, and just as he is about to go through with it, she turns around and looks him in the eyes, pleading. They fall in love instantly.'

'What?' Clarice said again. 'I mean…what?'

'Isn't it romantic?' Chloë said dreamily. 'So the Kosovar goes back to the banker and says: I can't do it, I love your wife.'

'And they run away together?' Clarice asked in disbelief.

'I don't know,' Chloë said. 'The paralegal didn't tell me. Maybe he didn't know. I like to think they did.'

'Ha,' Clarice snorted. 'The banker probably had the Kosovar guy thrown in jail.'

'Maybe, but there's still such passion in the story. I want that sort of love!'

'You want to fall in love with a murderous Kosovar?'

'Maybe,' Chloë said thoughtfully. 'If that's what it takes.'

Clarice shook her head. 'My dear,' she said, 'I understand your desire to escape from boredom, even if it is a different sort of boredom to my own. Just promise me you won't go hunting for it in the wrong sorts of places.'

'What about tennis courts?' Chloë replied.

Clarice laughed gently. 'Come on, we should get back to the others,' she said.

***

As they arrived back at their seats, one side of the stadium suddenly rose up in a wave, crying with one voice. Flags were waved enthusiastically back and forth.

'Italians,' Clarice muttered, shaking her head as she slipped into her chair. She handed Juni her champagne.

'We would do the same if we won a point,' Fleurie said stubbornly.

'They are so flamboyant,' Clarice tried to explain. 'The Swiss aim to be... staid.'

'No-one,' Fleurie said, 'can be staid at a tennis match. I mean, this hall can seat more than thirty thousand people.'

Chloë giggled suddenly. 'Have you ever seen Khadija at a sports event?' she asked. The other two shook their heads. 'She's become more Swiss than the Swiss,' Chloë explained. 'She has this gigantic Swiss flag, big enough to wear as a dress, and she spends the whole time waving it over her head. Doesn't understand a thing that's going on, of course.'

'And Winifred?' Clarice asked.

'I don't think she cares about sports much,' Chloë replied, 'but I'm sure she'd be very supportive, if Dieter brought her along to a match.'

'Don't be snarky,' Fleurie cautioned her. 'You know you're just jealous.'

'Oh, I know!' Chloë said cheerfully. 'I glory in my jealousy. I only pretend to be sarcastic about it.'

'I heard from my father,' Juni said suddenly, 'that the Swiss hire their supporters for these games.'

The other women looked at her in surprise. 'Surely not!' Fleurie said, looking worried.

Chloë laughed. 'It's not impossible. I bet most of them aren't even Swiss. That would explain the enthusiasm.'

At this point, Fleurie suddenly leapt out of her seat, her cheeks flushed.

Chloë cocked her head to the side. 'Well, for most of them, anyway.'

Fleurie sighed, exasperated. 'Switzerland has never won the Davis Cup,' she said as patiently as she could. 'There's a real chance, here, of us ending up in the semi-final.'

'You said that already,' Chloë said airily. 'We just don't care.'
'I care!' said Juni Bao.
Clarice giggled.

Chapter Twenty-One

The marble, the leather, the mahogany: nothing ever seemed to change at Bank Von Mipatobeau. Gabriel walked up to his office without a second glance at the receptionists. Things were busy, these days. What was it to him if the redhead's shirt was a little generously unbuttoned? He had little time for pleasantries, let alone chastisement. Let them get on with their work, and he would do the same.

With a sigh, he sank back into the leather chair behind his mahogany desk. *Mr Schön*, he thought with a sigh, casting an eye over his schedule. *Always Mr Schön.*

'*Bonjour, Monsieur de Puritigny.*'

Caroline appeared at the door, her back slightly bowed, carrying a tray of tea.

'Coffee for me today, Caroline,' Gabriel said, removing his glasses from his pocket.

'Oh dear,' Caroline said softly, shaking her head. 'I'm sorry, monsieur. For some reason, I cannot keep track of these... changes. One cannot easily teach an old dog new tricks.' Caroline touched an impeccable fingertip to her lacquered white bun, smiling wryly. It occurred to Gabriel with a start that his secretary *was* growing old.

'Dear Caroline,' Gabriel said with warmth, 'you know my trip to the USA was nearly a year ago, now?'

'Surely not!' she said with a start. 'Goodness gracious. I am an old creature, then!'

'You'll never be old, Caroline,' Gabriel said affectionately, adjusting his glasses. 'Don't you go thinking I'll ever allow you to retire.'

'Foiled again!' A booming voice came from the doorway, immediately recognisable. 'Always miserable in my amours,' Mr Schön added sadly. 'At least the extramarital ones.'

'*Bonjour, monsieur.*' With an uncharacteristic blush, Caroline disappeared.

Mr Schön watched her go with interest. 'Aha,' he said coyly.

'Flirting with the secretary, are we? Not really my type, if I'm honest, but different strokes for different folks...'

'Mr Schön,' Gabriel said sternly. 'Hello.'

Mr Schön was wearing a bright blue suit, with a crisp cream shirt underneath. His tie was pale blue and oddly sparkly, as if coated in plastic. What peculiar sartorial decisions that man made!

'I was going to tell you about my happy and successful second marriage,' Mr Schön said with signs of melancholy. 'Aren't you interested at all?'

'Not really,' Gabriel replied.

Mr Schön shook his head, laughing. It made his tie catch the light. 'Sometimes I wonder why I keep coming to see you,' he said, 'if you don't care about my life at all.'

'Why *are* you here today, if you don't mind me asking?' Gabriel asked.

Mr Schön laughed, absentmindedly stroking his strange blue tie. 'My, my. The Swiss banker, growing forgetful? Doesn't it break some sort of secrecy agreement if I tell you what I'm here for?'

Gabriel sighed. 'No, Mr Schön, it would not,' he said. 'I know you're here to check in on your funds. What I couldn't remember, Mr Schön, is whether you had agreed to what we discussed last time: the overseas investments.'

Mr Schön made a grumbling noise, and at that moment Caroline reappeared in the doorway. 'Two ristrettos,' she said.

'Thank you,' Mr Schön said.

'That's an interesting... item you're wearing, Mr Schön,' Caroline said carefully.

'Oh, you like my Lanvin?' he asked, brushing a hand down the expensive sleeves of his jacket.

'I am more intrigued by your tie,' Caroline said, squinting at it.

'I must confess I am as well,' Gabriel said.

Mr Schön smiled brightly, clearly delighted, and reached into his pocket. Little lights began twinkling up and down the tie. 'Ice crystals!' he explained. 'It is a special pattern for this year's winter collection. I thought about edelweiss, but they're not quite seasonal, are they.'

Caroline and Gabriel stared for a moment.

'Well,' Caroline finally said, 'I'll let you get on with the work, then.'

'Where were we? Ah yes. I was reiterating my suggestion of an investment with our overseas partners,' Gabriel said smoothly.

Mr Schön narrowed his eyes. 'Yes, I recall. And who might they be, again?'

'Dick Nikko, Chicago broker,' Gabriel replied. 'Many of our clients have been dealing with them through us.'

'Yes, you mentioned this before,' Mr Schön said drily. 'I must admit, I was surprised. You always struck me as a conservative bank; essentially Swiss. I didn't expect you to get caught up in all these newfangled Americanisms.'

'Well,' Gabriel said. 'I mean, the money's simply been rolling in. None of our values have changed, of course. Our clients are very happy.'

'How long has this all been going on, then?'

'Almost a year,' Gabriel said cheerfully. 'They've helped us make a fortune!'

Mr Schön shook his head. 'Far be it from me to comment on your business practices,' he said, 'but you have to be careful with these international characters. I've seen straight through so many of them - weasels, the lot of them. Obsessed with gold. They don't care about *you* making a fortune. They only care about their own success. They're watching their own backs.'

'Be as that may,' Gabriel said, 'it's difficult to argue with the size of the bonus I've received this year.'

Mr Schön laughed. 'A part of me likes this new Gabriel,' he said, 'but you'll forgive me if I elect to wait another few months before getting involved in this new scheme of yours. I trust you, I've always been content with the service I receive at Von Mipatobeau, but I'm not used to the idea of this new change.'

'Now, now,' Gabriel said. 'You were always begging me for an extra per cent or two! I'm offering it to you now. Isn't that what you always wanted?'

'Not any more,' Mr Schön said. 'I've learned things in the last ten years. Caution, for one. I understand you should be grateful for what you have. The bird in hand is worth more than the two in the bush, don't you think?'

'I respectfully disagree,' Gabriel said, sipping his ristretto. 'I never had to let go of the first bird, you see. Our Swiss bank is still alive and well: we simply have an American subsidiary, now. We have more money. We have lost nothing.'

'Ah, but a Swiss bank with one foot in America; is that really a Swiss bank?'

'Don't get philosophical on me,' Gabriel said warmly. 'You know how I care for my country.'

Mr Schön shrugged. 'I know these Swiss mountains can begin to seem stifling to some. You're not having a midlife crisis are you? No affairs with a nubile little... No, no, that's not your style.' He sighed. 'Switzerland alone is enough. Her glaciers, her birds, her hundred-year-old trams. And the sailing. You know how I love sailing! But I digress. What I mean to say is that I am happy without straying from these borders, either in terms of my person or in terms of my investments.'

The door burst open, and Thomas floundered in. 'Gabriel!' he said. 'We must go now!' His eyes were wild, his head of curls in a mess.

'Slow down, Thomas,' Gabriel said, standing up slowly. 'What has happened? Are you alright?'

'Have you seen the papers?'

'No,' Gabriel said carefully. 'Caroline usually brings them to me if anything concerning us comes up. What is it?'

'I have read this morning,' Thomas said breathless, 'that the French banks are receiving extremely high returns on their portfolio management.'

There was a pause. Mr Schön gave a muffled snort of laughter. 'Yes?' Gabriel said, uncertain.

'Have you heard of Gérard Maigréville?' Thomas asked.

'Thomas, are you drunk?' Gabriel asked.

'Have you, though?' Thomas asked, a manic gleam in his eye.

'I can't say I have,' Gabriel replied. 'Why?'

'He's a French banker,' Thomas said. 'He's been doing such a marvellous job... He studied at the *École polytechnique* and at the ENA, you see. There is an event. He is here, in Geneva! We absolutely must see him.'

'See who? Why?' Gabriel was completely baffled. For some reason, he kept staring at the blinking lights of Mr Schön's tie, as if they might inject some sense into this situation. They were so bright and so blue!

'I think I see what your emotional German is getting at,' Mr Schön said suddenly. 'I believe I saw a poster advertising the event Thomas is referring to. This Maigréville type is engaged in much the same sort of international trading Von Mipatobeau has been wading into, and making a fortune as well.'

'Yes, yes!' Thomas said excitedly. 'He is like the most Swiss of Swiss bankers, except that he is French, and now he is working with the Americans!'

'What?' said Gabriel, growing exasperated.

Mr Schön laughed. 'I wouldn't trust the man with a penny of mine,' he said. 'He's a private fund manager, an *agent de change,* as they say.

'But what is this event?' Gabriel asked again.

'Oh, a seminar, of course,' Thomas said, handing over a flyer. 'At the Hôtel Président. He's giving a speech in half an hour. We have to go now!'

'But I'm in the middle of a meeting,' Gabriel said.

Mr Schön shook his head smiling. 'Go, go,' he said. 'Our meeting was over in any case.'

'Very well,' Gabriel said, holding up his hands in defeat. 'I'll get Caroline to postpone my other engagements. Thomas, if you could get my coat... Mr Schön, as ever, it's been a pleasure.'

Mr Schön gave a little bow. 'I'll see you next month,' he said, switching off his blinking tie.

Gabriel and Thomas stepped out briskly into the grey street. A sprinkle of early snow was falling. 'You really must meet him,' the curly-haired German was babbling. 'No, even just seeing him, that would be enough. I am sure we will be inspired.'

'I'm grateful, Thomas, really I am,' Gabriel replied, resisting the urge to pat his associate on the head in a calming manner. 'It sounds like this man shares some of our bank's recent ideas about progress and internationalism.' He was surprised, actually, at how much Thomas seemed to have taken on board of his own evolution of values, since his involvement with the Americans.

'It's not that I like the Americans,' Thomas said, prompting a sigh from Gabriel, 'but this man is fascinating. I mean, he markets himself as the ultimate Franco-American banker. Well, I thought, Monsieur de Puritigny is aiming to be the ultimate Swiss-American banker. *Ja, ja*! Once I thought about it, it was so obvious.'

'I see,' said Gabriel.

'I think we should befriend him. Maybe poach him.'

'Why?' Gabriel asked, amused.

'He has some key advantages over us, you see. Mr Schön seemed to agree that he was a competitor.'

'But he's *French*.'

'He spent three months on a management-training course at Harvard.'

'Well, maybe, but I'll bet he doesn't have anyone as successful as Dick Nikko on his side.'

Thomas shrugged. 'We don't know that. Let's go hear his speech, at least.'

They had arrived in front of the Hôtel Président, the lake's icy blue waves reflected in the glass front. 'Alright,' said Gabriel. They stepped through the revolving doors.

Inside, the place was buzzing. Staff with silver trays were meandering up and down the carpeted beige interior, stepping in and out of pools of light.

'Champagne!' said Thomas, bowing to the waiter. Tentatively, the waiter bowed back.

Gabriel sighed. 'Thomas, can you pick me up one of the brochures?' he said. As his partner scuttled off down the corridor, Gabriel looked around, noting that he recognised a few of the attendees filing into the conference room.

At that moment, a small bell rang. '*Mesdames, messieurs,*' a voice was heard, 'Monsieur Maigréville is about to begin his seminar.'

'Let's go,' said Thomas, reappearing breathlessly and handing him a piece of card.

———◆———

Gérard Maigréville peered out into the audience with small, beady eyes.

'He looks very French,' Thomas whispered admiringly. Indeed, Maigréville had a sharp nose and sported well-groomed hair.

'How old do you think he is?' Gabriel whispered back.

'Fifty?' Thomas hazarded.

'I was born to farmer parents in La Rochelle,' Maigréville intoned, silencing them both. 'It was only because of my studies that I was able to rise above my birth, and venture out into the world to conquer it. First Paris, then Harvard. Now, America is mine. It can be yours too, my banking friends.'

'Pah,' Gabriel murmured. 'The man spent three months in some university, and now he thinks he owns the whole country!'

'Quiet,' a neighbour hissed back.

'I rose through the bureaucratic ranks of the principal Parisian banks. Soon, I realised I would have to look elsewhere if I truly wanted to make my fortune. Where would I go? America, of course. But I'm not here to talk about my autobiography.' A smattering of laughter spread across the room. Gabriel made a disgruntled sound. 'The real question was: what did I bring back? I'm here to share the results of my life's quest, and to talk to you about my new Franco-American management approach.'

Gabriel sat up in his seat.

'Now, have any of you heard of Mierkov?' A murmur of assent went round the room. Thomas looked to Gabriel with a panicked expression. Gabriel shrugged. 'A broker, a financier, and a fine businessman, Mierkov hasn't had a single loss for ten years. His average yield in the last five years, in fact, was twelve and a half per cent.'

'That's still better than us!' Thomas whispered.

Gabriel shushed him, listening carefully.

'Mierkov came from nothing: his grandparents were immigrants. He only had a sharp business sense, and a disregard for the limitations of those who had preceded him.' Maigréville ran a hand through his hair, smiling thinly. 'Do you know where Mierkov keeps his money? Right here in Switzerland.'

Approving laughter went around the room.

'Now, I want to talk to you about this business model, and about America, and about investing in these very important high-return funds; the same ones Mierkov made his fortune in, and, incidentally, I did too. I'm not talking about risk-taking: I'm talking about guarantees. Do any of you know what mortgage-backed securities are?'

Thomas and Gabriel exchanged significant glances.

———— ◆ ————

At the end of the speech, the audience filed back out into the plush corridors, whereupon waiters materialised with their silver trays. Thomas grabbed two pieces of smoked salmon on crisp bread, and sat himself down in a white leather couch. 'Now, we wait,' he said.

'Well, Thomas,' Gabriel said, helping himself to a champagne flute, 'I have to admit that was quite interesting.'

'Wasn't it?' Thomas said innocently.

'I'm sure we can catch the man for a moment after his speech...'

'Oh!' Thomas suddenly set down his plate on the back of his chair. 'There! There he is.'

Gabriel stood up quickly, but Thomas beat him to it.

'A wonderful, wonderful talk,' the German said, shaking Maigréville's hand enthusiastically. 'As Swiss bankers, we feel converted.'

Shaking his head, Gabriel joined in. 'We have come from Bank Von Mipatobeau,' he explained, 'a private Swiss bank.'

'Ah!' Maigréville said, smiling and shaking Gabriel's hand firmly. 'This is good news. The more conservative Swiss bankers usually stay away from my talks. I'm always pleased when I manage to convince the Swiss to invest with the Parisian French, you know? A real turning of the tables. We've been bringing our money to you for hundreds of years. Now it's your turn!'

'We're not conservative,' Gabriel said quickly. 'And we're not...'

'Well, we have nothing to hide,' Maigréville continued bombastically. 'Everything's out in the open, laid out quite clearly in our brochures, which we've had translated into English as well. We're not like the Swiss, you know: everything so discreet it's practically invisible, a country where you don't know your neighbour's name, where everything is shrouded in secrecy...'

'No, no, no,' Gabriel said hastily. 'Not all Swiss are like that. In fact, we have also become increasingly interested in America.'

'So you're not one of those intent on making a boring four per cent every year, then?' Maigréville asked.

'Not in the least,' Gabriel said. 'Would we be here if we were?'

'Well!' Maigréville said. 'I mean, you're all originally French anyway, aren't you? If it weren't for the edict of Nantes and the Huguenots and the runaway converted Catholics, there wouldn't be a Switzerland at all. Paris was the beginning of it all.'

'So you mostly trade in Paris?' Gabriel asked, vaguely insulted.

'We're based in Paris,' Maigréville said, 'indeed. We have a whole trading floor set up on Avenue Hoche, with seven traders. We deal in hedge funds, forward trading, futures and options. The lines between banking and brokerage are growing slimmer. I sell you a put, I buy you a call; I trade, I trade, I trade. I see a hundred million every day, you know. I make a few pennies here and there, elsewhere, but at the end of the month, I always have millions in profits. You've got to join me. I have several billion dollars under my management now. Why don't you just place a few million francs with us? France is where it's at.'

'Monsieur,' Gabriel said firmly, 'I have no intention of investing in France. However, I would like to ask you about America.'

Maigréville shook his head. 'See, I told you; you Swiss are all the same. Your clients won't stick around with this four per cent nonsense! They'll all leave to the US, or come to Frenchmen like me! You cannot stay in your Swiss mountains, managing hundreds of billions of dollars by yourselves, making almost no profit. It's all coming the French way. Now, we are waking up, like Napoleon's giant.'

'Wasn't that China?' Gabriel asked, confused. 'Anyway, I...'

'Very well,' Maigréville said, throwing up his hands in mock surrender. 'You can't blame me for trying to solicit funds at the end of such a rousing speech...' He gave an unconvincing grin. Thomas laughed loudly.

Gabriel sighed. 'Look, we won't keep you long, monsieur. Really, I was just interested in your perspective on American investments. You see, our bank has been working with a Chicago brokerage firm for some time...'

'Who?' Maigréville asked suddenly, narrowing his eyes.

'A man by the name of Dick Nikko,' Gabriel replied.

'We recently invested thirty million with him,' Thomas added.

Maigréville raised his eyebrows, then began to laugh. 'You must be joking,' he said. 'We've been working with Dick for about a year now. The junk bonds, yes? The old ladies? The savings and loans? Oh, yes, it's all so exciting!' He lowered his voice. 'Did you know that Dick and his people sometimes make up to fifty million in bonuses, even more? This one guy on Wall Street made five hundred million in bonuses, just for one year. These high-yield bonds are absolutely unbelievable! How much have you been making, then?'

'Around twelve per cent,' Gabriel said cautiously.

'How wonderful!' Maigréville said, surprising Gabriel by

suddenly clapping him on the back. 'Look, I really must mingle, but we should meet up again. I think we should discuss business a little more sometime...'

'When are you next in Switzerland?' Gabriel asked.

'Wait!' Thomas said excitedly. 'Remember, Gabriel? Dick is coming here in just a few weeks, to stay at the chalet with us.'

Gabriel frowned. Had Thomas been invited on this trip? 'So he is. I'd completely forgotten. Monsieur Maigréville, would you be interested in joining our little business get-together? I have a chalet up near Saas Fee.'

'Well, I'm a very busy man, but I do love to ski,' Maigréville said.

'It'll be early December...' Gabriel said.

'Hmm, I suppose that does give me a little time to make some space in my schedule...' said Maigréville thoughtfully. 'Yes, why not? I look forward to it!'

Chapter Twenty-Two

'Was that a white donkey?' Gérard asked, staring out into the snow curiously.

'Surely not,' Dick replied, squinting. 'Are there wild donkeys in Switzerland?'

Gabriel was silent, staring at the waxed parquet that glowed in the sunlight. Steam rose from four coffee cups, and eight sets of toes wriggled in the immaculate white carpet. Well, six sets of toes wriggled. Gabriel held his toes perfectly still as he spread butter generously on a piece of toasted rye bread. Distractedly, he looked up towards the pine trees waving gently in the blinding morning sun. It was strange, having so much company in what he liked to think of as his perfect solitary retreat. Men who were nearly strangers, too! It was all right, having a few local farmers and architects over for a glass of wine, but this was different. He knew the whole trip had been his idea, but couldn't help feeling as if his personal space had been invaded. When was the last time he had come to Saas Fee without setting out on a brisk, lonely morning walk?

'I love this chalet so much,' Thomas said, eating a large piece of sausage. He was wearing what appeared to be children's woollen pyjamas, that stopped halfway up his shin and just under his elbow.

'You've come here often?' Gérard asked. The Frenchman, for some reason, was wearing a suit.

'Oh no,' Gabriel said hastily. 'Thomas is just here to make us coffee.'

Thomas laughed loudly, if uncertainly.

'Well, it is indeed a wonderful chalet,' Gérard said, nodding in approval. 'Not as large as some I have seen, but the decoration is quite interesting. Besides, I slept so well. Everything is so... quiet!'

'It's not central Paris, that's for sure,' Gabriel replied.

'It could do with a little more crystal, in my opinion,' Dick said, 'but I like the brightness. It's very different to the American chalets I have seen, certainly.'

'My wife would be inclined to agree with you,' Gabriel said

wryly. 'She wanted marble and chandeliers.'

'Ah, women...' Gérard said vaguely, before draining his coffee cup.

'You're married?' Dick asked.

'*Mon Dieu*, no,' Gérard said, running a hand through his coiffed hair and staring off into the distance.

'None of them would have you?' Thomas asked with a ridiculous wink. Gabriel choked on his coffee.

Gérard gave a melancholy smile. 'That's not far from the truth.'

'Come now,' Dick said jovially, adjusting the lapels of his silk dressing gown. 'How could a man like you let himself be tied down? No, you're leaving your options open, and I respect that. If you ever come visit me in Chicago, I'll find you some excellent options.' He winked.

Gabriel tried to repress an expression of disgust. 'So,' he said as cheerfully as he could, 'shall we go skiing today? The sun is bright, and a new coating of powder fell in the night. The conditions are perfect.'

'Yes, and the schoolchildren are still locked up at their desks,' Gérard said brightly. 'What a wonderful time to ski!'

'Let us go!' Thomas said excitedly, standing up and running off towards the carnotzet, where he had inexplicably elected to make his bed. 'I want to ski everywhere, as fast as I can!'

Dick shook his head. 'The little German has a point,' he said. 'Let's get out there on the mountain! I can't wait.'

Gabriel nodded slowly, sweeping crumbs into his hand. 'It is time, then,' he said. 'Let us get changed. We'll meet back here in, what, five minutes?' Seeing Dick's expression, he relented. 'Ten, then.'

<hr />

Gabriel looked in the mirror, adjusting the high waist of his expensive black ski trousers. Yes, the snow looked beautiful and pure. He couldn't wait to be out there, close to the bright blue sky. Gérard and Thomas, swaddled in layers of wool, had sat back down at the table in silence.

'So, how do I look?' Dick appeared in the doorway to the kitchen, grinning like a schoolboy. Turning back from the window, Gabriel blinked slowly. Gérard was silent. Thomas made a strange noise, like a mouse being trodden on, which he turned into a sort of hum of approval. 'Don't you like my ski outfit, guys?'

'Well, we certainly won't lose you in a ravine,' Gérard said.

Dick Nikko was wearing red Bermuda shorts decorated with a pattern of white flowers, with long white baseball socks pulled up to his knees. Above this, he had piled several golf sweaters over each other, and multiple brightly coloured collars from polo shirts were poking up from around his neck. Over everything, he had flung a thin cotton scarf that looked best designed for wearing by the side of a swimming pool. He was also sporting a straw cowboy hat, black leather gloves and turquoise earmuffs.

'The earmuffs are my daughter's,' he said. 'She thought I might be cold out here.'

'Oh yes,' Thomas said, 'you certainly will be.'

'Yes, an excellent outfit,' Gérard said, his expression unreadable. He clapped Dick on the back as he sat down.

'Dick,' Thomas said casually, 'do you think you might like to go for a short walk with me?'

If Dick was surprised by the suggestion, he did not show it. 'Why not?' he asked.

'You can see if you are comfortable out in the snow. Also, I know a shop,' Thomas continued smoothly, 'where you might find something to warm your knees.'

Gabriel nodded at his partner, surprised at his tact, if annoyed by the inevitable delay to their excursion.

'And we should just sit here and wait for you?' Gérard asked, a little impatiently.

'Yes,' Thomas said. 'I will make you some more coffee.'

'No, no,' Gabriel said quickly, 'let me. You two go on ahead. We'll head out when you get back.'

Gabriel stared after the pair as they made their way down the road from the chalet.

'Well, you did promise to introduce us to the real Switzerland,' Gérard commented. 'I suppose it is more of a culture shock to Dick than to any of us.'

'It's not like they don't have skiing in America,' Gabriel said in despair. 'I mean, when I visited Chicago, it was absolutely freezing!'

Gérard shrugged. 'Maybe he underestimated European winters. Americans always think they do things best. The biggest breakfasts, the coldest snowstorms!'

Gabriel cocked his head. 'Yes, perhaps that is it. Tell me, Gérard, have you spent much time in America recently?'

'Quite a bit,' Gérard said, 'although, to be perfectly honest, I seem to spend most of my time in offices and conference rooms. It's not quite the all-American experience when you're eating two of your three meals a day in hotels!'

Gabriel laughed sympathetically.

'I still think I understand something of the spirit of the country, though,' Gérard went on. 'It's a spirit that has long since lost popularity in France. Competition, hard work, inspiration to do better: these are values I am trying to bring back in fashion.'

'And you think you are succeeding?'

Gérard frowned, wrinkling his sharp nose. 'Some days, I am sure that I am. Others... Well, time will tell. I am certainly a hundred per cent confident in my financial successes; that I can say without hesitation.'

Gabriel lowered his voice, though the other two would be in the village by now. 'You trust Dick?' he asked.

Gérard paused a moment before replying. 'I trust his results,' he said finally.

'But you have... worried? People have warned you otherwise?'

Gérard frowned. 'Why are you asking me this? Didn't you say you'd been working with him successfully for months now?'

'Yes, nearly a year,' Gabriel said. 'It's just that... Sometimes I wonder if we should have ventured into all this a little more carefully. I have this friend, a commercial banker in Zurich, who told me I needed to be cautious. He suggested the venture might be reckless. You must understand how Swiss private bankers are taught to think. This interest in global methods, in the international markets, it goes completely against the grain of everything Von Mipatobeau has done so far.'

'Ah, but isn't that always the danger of the avant-garde?' Gérard said. 'Fear of the unknown must not keep us from success. We must not be afraid of breaking new ground. I have seen no signs of any of this failing,' he said. 'People like Mierkov, they are simply raking in fortunes without having to raise a finger. This is the time to capitalise.'

Gabriel nodded. 'Alright,' he said. 'I suppose you have studied the American business practices for a long time.'

'I understand that you would want reassurance,' Gérard said. 'Simply look to your statements.' He laughed suddenly, a harsh sound.

Gabriel did his best to smile. 'Oh look,' he said, peering out the window. 'The others are coming back.' He looked at his watch and sighed. The sun was high in the sky: in fact, it was nearly lunchtime. If he had been alone, Gabriel would have been on the slopes three or four hours earlier, alone with a few trim, Germanic sportspeople. Now, the runs would be clogged with chains of fluorescent six-year-olds and their fat parents. Gabriel cast an eye over his mountain companions in despair.

Dick, now mercifully freed from his Bermudas, but still sporting the earmuffs, walked confidently alongside Thomas in ski trousers and a heavy jacket. The summer scarf also appeared to have survived the transformation.

'You have to give it to Thomas,' Gérard muttered to Gabriel. 'I don't know how he managed it so smoothly. I'd have been afraid of offending the American!'

'I never thought of the man as particularly smooth,' Gabriel said with distaste, 'but I'm glad we've skirted the threat of pneumonia...'

Gérard laughed. 'I suppose health care is quite expensive in this country, isn't it?.'

Gabriel shrugged. 'Yes, well, we're not socialists here,' he said.

'Do I really sound like a socialist to you?' Gérard replied with humour. 'You'd be hard-pressed to find a set of more ruthless capitalists, I reckon, than this group of four.'

'Three,' Gabriel said, trying not to smile. 'Thomas is about as ruthless as a piece of bread.'

The men headed outside, the snow creaking under their boots. Gabriel breathed deep, feeling the ice-cold air fill his lungs. Here, he was alive!

'Ah, there are the *pistes*!' Gérard said, pointing.

Gabriel felt his heart lift at the sight of the long lines of booths moving up the slopes towards the sky. Oh, to leave all these bankers behind and fly down the mountain in blissful solitude!

Dick let out a whoop. 'Aw man! They have black runs!' he said excitedly.

Gabriel shook his head. 'Be careful,' he said, catching up with the other two men. 'An American black *piste* is about the same as a European red one.'

'No way!' Dick said cheerfully.

'It's true,' Gabriel said patiently.

'Well, I'll review it from the bottom.'

'Come on!' said Thomas. 'Let's go get our passes.'

Gabriel followed the trio, shaking his head.

The air in the restaurant smelled like grease and melted cheese. All around the banking quartet, red-faced skiers were gleefully stripping out of their heavy jackets, and clomping in their awkward boots towards the self-service. Every time the door opened, it let in a blast of cold air.

'I've got to admit you were right about the runs,' Dick said ruefully, easing slowly into a chair.

Gérard laughed. 'Yes, your backside took something of a beating there...'

'Ha,' Dick retorted. 'I wasn't the one who crashed into a snow bank by trying to go off-piste. You thought you were so fancy!'

'It was very graceful at the beginning,' Thomas said gallantly. 'Now, can I get anyone a glass of *glühwein*?'

'Thomas,' Gabriel said, 'these gentlemen won't know what you're talking about.'

'I understood the "wine" part,' said Dick. 'Why don't you bring us four glasses?'

Thomas gave a sort of bow and scuttled off. Dick laughed in a remarkably affectionate manner.

'So, what do you think of the skiing here?' Gabriel asked.

Dick shrugged. 'It's very beautiful,' he said, 'and the mountains are impressive.'

'Have you ever been skiing in France?' Gérard asked eagerly. 'It's much less expensive, and much less regulated. You can ski freely, wherever you want...'

'Yes,' Gabriel said, a hint of gallows humour creeping into his voice. 'You can ski right into a ravine, if you like, and the French government will pay for your recovery.'

Gérard laughed, a forced sound.

'Wine!' Thomas said, reappearing with four cups. A fine, spiced steam drifted into the air.

'So, Gabriel, what is the true Switzerland, anyway?' Gérard asked. 'Is it just these pointy mountains? The Swiss Alps seem pretty similar to the French Alps. I mean, after all, they are the same mountains.'

'There's the cheese,' Thomas said thoughtfully, 'and wine.'

Gabriel's glasses fogged up with steam as soon as he picked up his cup. He sighed.

'Well, we have those in the French Alps too,' Gérard said, with forced cheer. He took a large swig of his mulled wine, wincing at the heat of the liquid.

'With all due respect,' Gabriel said, peering through the wine-steam, 'the mountains are simply higher here, and more impressive. There is just something magical in the air. This is, after all, the countryside that inspired Johanna Spyri to write *Heidi*...'

'What about the Trois Vallées?' Gérard snapped.

'There is also excellent skiing in Austria,' Thomas said, 'though I personally prefer to go down mountains by luge.'

The men stared at him. Dick laughed. 'I bet you also have to *fahrt* your skis there, right?' he said, a childish grin on his face. 'I just couldn't stop laughing when I heard that word. Doesn't anybody speak English here?'

Gabriel rolled his eyes.

'Don't you make that face,' Thomas said, wagging his finger at his partner. 'You can't go ten minutes without waxing your skis.'

Dick and Gérard laughed quietly.

'Now, now,' Dick said, 'why don't we get some food? Surely we can all agree that we like cheese, French and Swiss alike.'

'Good idea,' Gabriel said a little sheepishly. 'I will pay for everyone, of course.'

The men rose awkwardly, and stumped across the room towards the cafeteria. Soon, they were sitting back down with trays of steaming hot food.

'What did you get?' Gérard asked, eyeing Gabriel's tray with suspicion.

'*Tartiflette*,' he said, breathing in the sharp smell with satisfaction.

'It smells quite... strong,' Gérard said. He had opted for a plateful of stew, potatoes and salad. He had also picked up a pitcher of red wine. How much did these French men really need to drink?

'I'm quite sure they make this dish in France,' Gabriel said. 'It's probably not quite as flavourful there.'

'Gentlemen, gentlemen,' Dick said, leaning back from his tray of steaming *steak frites*. 'I mean, we're all investing together. We can leave aside our national differences for a few days, can't we? Let's pour some wine.'

'Oh yes!' Thomas said, nodding furiously. He, too, had opted for a generous portion of *tartiflette*, and had added a sausage as well.

Dick filled four glasses with the red wine. Meanwhile, Gabriel eyed the American's plate, wondering how much that steak had cost. Couldn't he have opted for something simple, even in a ski station?

'After all,' Dick continued, cutting into the thick slab of meat and revealing its juicy pink interior, 'we work together now. We are all involved in these mortgage-backed securities, are we not?'

'Junk bonds?' Thomas asked innocently. Gabriel shot him a warning glance, but Thomas simply scooped up a thick morsel of potato, bacon and cheese, using a piece of sausage.

'Yes, there are some who call them by that name,' Gérard said, poking at his salad. 'What do we care for such allegations, though?'

'Anyway,' Dick drawled, 'anybody who says we're dealing in junk hasn't come in for a meeting with one of us. I can tell you they would change their tune as soon as their first million came rolling in.'

Thomas smiled, as if pleased to be taken down a notch. 'Excellent,' he said. He took a gulp of mulled wine, then a sip of his red wine.

'Say, on that note,' Dick asked, frowning curiously at Gabriel, 'whatever happened to that Chinese millionaire chick? You ever get her to sign on?' He wiped steak juice from his chin.

'Oh yes!' Gabriel replied. 'My wife...' He paused. 'Juni Bao is interested in modern art, and somehow got it into her head to befriend my wife.'

'Well, this wife of yours appears to have been serving Von Mipatobeau's best interests, no?' asked Gérard.

'Yes, I suppose so,' Gabriel said vaguely, 'and yes, Dick, in answer to your question, Bao recently transferred a substantial lump sum to your care. We can talk over the figures in private, if you like.'

Dick laughed. 'That's not the done thing in a chalet, is it? Well, that's fine. We Americans do have a sense of etiquette, you know, in this day and age. We can learn the customs of other countries.' He gave an ironic smile and swigged generously from his glass of hot wine.

'Of course,' Gabriel said stiffly.

'Your wife is interested in art?' Gérard asked politely. The appearance of food and wine seemed to have cheered him up.

'Modern art,' Gabriel replied, as if answering in the negative. 'She used to have a very conservative gallery on Grand Rue, but now all her energies are invested in these contemporary monstrosities. Even her old gallery is full of bright yellow plastic and pointy metal sculptures and what not. Among those glorious Hodlers,' he added wistfully.

'The world changes,' Gérard said unexpectedly, swilling his wine around in his glass. 'I myself have been somewhat converted to some of the values of modern art. The abstract and the melancholy, the empty plane of colour...'

Dick began to laugh loudly. 'Good grief,' he said, 'are you drunk? Or is this just what French guys are like all the time?'

Thomas joined in the friendly laughter.

'I mean,' Dick continued, encouraged, 'I thought being in Switzerland would tone down your emotions a little.'

Gérard smiled weakly, as if in appeasement. 'I must admit this Swiss stew is quite tasty,' he said reluctantly.

Gabriel smiled, extremely pleased.

Dick began to laugh. 'Ah, the Swiss stew! I have heard about this before. You guys eat this every day, right? Maybe fish once a week, and chicken for Christmas. That's why you live for a hundred years!'

Gabriel gave a tight smile.

'As I understand it,' Dick said, leaning towards Gérard, 'the Swiss stew was born of their great frugality and boring national psyche. It's a mountain dish, made to stew all day while you're out cutting wood or whatever, in six feet of snow. You cook it in one pot, throw whatever fresh produce you have into it, add salt and pepper and a lot of water. Maybe, if you're feeling particularly inspired, you might throw in something exciting like a tomato, or something weird like a courgette. You do this even if your income is five million dollars a year.'

Gérard laughed and laughed.

'You sound like you know a lot for an American,' Gabriel sniffed. 'I can certainly tell you my family does not eat stew every day.' His mother made a spectacular stew, but he would not share this information with them.

'I've spent a fair amount of time in Geneva, Wisconsin,' he said with a smile. 'They have excellent rye whiskey there.'

Gabriel looked up, wondering if there was a threat in his voice, but Dick appeared to be smiling placidly. He took a large bite of steak.

'Gabriel's mother makes an excellent stew,' Thomas piped up.

Gabriel sighed.

'So, Dick, are you loving Switzerland?' Thomas asked suddenly, his voice eager. 'Had you visited many times before?'

'I can't say I had, really,' Dick replied with a smile. 'Only a few trips to Lugano, and one to Zurich. Mostly for business, and you can't guess much about a country from the inside of a hotel room... Though I'm sure our friend Gabriel told you all about his adventures with the American Swiss?'

'Ah yes,' Thomas said, nodding wisely. 'As I understand, you got quite drunk together.'

Gabriel shot him a strange look. Had he told Thomas about that day?

'It sounded fun!' Thomas added, floundering.

Dick laughed, a little harshly. 'Don't look so ashamed,' he said. 'I was telling your partner about our escapade. Nothing compromising.'

Thomas looked mortified. 'I'm sorry, Gabriel,' he said. 'It was a good story.'

Gabriel shook his head. 'Don't apologise,' he said. 'I was merely concerned. I thought perhaps you had been gossiping with Clarice.'

Everyone laughed merrily at this weak attempt at a joke, and Gabriel looked down at his vanishing *tartiflette*.

'Tell me, Gabriel,' Gérard said with a smile, 'do you time your lovemaking with a Swiss chronometer?'

Gabriel sighed. 'Gentlemen,' he said, pushing back his empty plate, 'what do you say we head back to the slopes?'

'So, what are we having for dinner?' Dick asked, putting back on his earmuffs.

'I don't think they do surf and turf around here,' Gabriel joked, his patience with everyone beginning to wear dangerously thin. Was there some way he could get away from the group?

'Where shall we ski first?' Gérard asked.

'How about on the pistes?'

'I have an idea,' Gabriel said suddenly. 'Why don't we split up, ski wherever we would like, and meet up at the bottom of the village in two hours?'

'Oh,' said Thomas, a little sadly.

'That sounds excellent,' Gérard said cryptically. Gabriel suspected he would spend his time gingerly gliding down blue and green slopes, after the morning's humiliation.

'I could come with you, Gérard,' Dick said quickly. He too must have been suffering from his earlier enthusiasm. What was his level like, anyway? Gabriel wondered. He'd hardly paid attention earlier, trying his best to enjoy the snow despite the company. *They probably just want to go sit in a sauna, anyway*, he thought with disdain.

'We'll meet at the bar at four, then,' Gabriel said, striding firmly off in the opposite direction. Now, to find a deserted black slope and fly down it alone!

'You don't want company, then?' Thomas asked tentatively.

'No, thank you,' Gabriel said. 'You go and enjoy yourself.' *Go find the luge piste*, he thought. He walked away quickly, and he did not look back.

———◆———

'I can't believe you fell over again,' Dick cackled, holding a large mug of mulled wine in his gloved hands.

Gérard shrugged. 'The snow is different here in Switzerland,' he said. 'Its quality is nothing like good French snow.'

Gabriel smirked into his glass of whiskey.

At this point, a large group of teenagers entered the bar, each more fluorescent than the last. The men looked at each other in despair.

'Do you know what's worse, though?' Gérard asked, lowering his voice and forgetting his patriotic skirmish in the face of a common enemy. 'Those six-year-olds who plough past you without poles. How humiliating, to be outrun by a baby!'

Gabriel laughed. 'I try to avoid them,' he said. 'This is usually a good time of year to dodge the school crowds, but you never know when a busload will turn up from abroad. French, Italian, German...' He shuddered.

'Where *is* Thomas?' Dick asked suddenly, looking around as if he might have come in without them noticing. There was a note of genuine concern in his voice.

Gabriel shook his head, amused. 'I'm sure he's tobogganing away happily somewhere, maybe with some six-year-olds.'

Gérard laughed, and for a time the men forgot about the fourth member of the group. But as time began to creep on, a niggling concern grew in Gabriel's breast. Where *had* the obnoxious German gone? He tapped his fingertips on the tabletop nervously. Had Thomas ever been late for a meeting with him?

'Do you think we should go looking for him?' he asked suddenly.

Dick frowned. 'He is nearly two hours late,' he said.

'Surely that's unusual, for a Swiss man?' Gérard said.

'Swiss German...' Gabriel said distractedly.

'Well, the German are extremely punctual also,' Gérard added.

'It just doesn't seem like him,' Dick said. 'Maybe we should call the police?'

Gabriel repressed a smile at the broker's concern for their ridiculous companion, then sighed. 'Yes, I suppose we should,' he said. 'Just in case something's gone wrong.' What would they even do? Send a pack of dogs out? Would they spot him by his curly hair?

———◆◆◆———

'They've found him!' Dick shouted, setting down the bar phone for the fifth time or so. 'He'd fallen in a ravine! They had to haul him out with a rope!'

'What?' Gabriel asked, exhausted and bewildered. They had

been sitting in the bar for nigh on six hours by then, and the night was pitch black. For a time, the three other men had tried to keep a positive front going, talking about business and joking about their countries, but after a while, as the weather outside grew increasingly icy, their spirit began to lag. Gabriel, particularly, was slowly consumed by a nagging doubt. Was this all his fault? Perhaps Thomas wasn't used to going out skiing alone. But that was preposterous! Surely he would have said... Gabriel's heart had sunk lower and lower, until the three men just sat in silence, occasionally jumping guiltily when the police rang up or clumped in through the door in their black boots. Now, at last, he let out a sigh of relief.

'Is he OK?' Gérard asked. 'Is he hurt?'

'He cracked his head on a rock,' Dick explained. 'Apparently he skied over a giant hole in the mountain, which had been hidden by ice and snow.'

'*Mon Dieu*! I told you,' Gérard said. 'Off-piste in Switzerland is dangerous.'

'How did they find him?' Gabriel asked, ignoring the Frenchman.

'The police have some kind of machine, apparently,' Dick said, sitting back down across from them. 'It makes a beeping sound when it comes near to a mobile phone.'

'Surely there's no network coverage up there?' Gabriel asked, confused.

'You don't need it,' Dick explained. 'It has to do with the battery, or something.' He grinned suddenly. 'Maybe we should invest in these machines! They sound very clever.'

'All that ice,' Gabriel said, staring into his long-empty glass. 'Poor Thomas!'

'Let's have some more beer,' Gérard said.

'A small glass,' Dick replied. 'Then we should go find our friend.'

'We'll look after him,' Gérard said. 'Let's make sure he spends the night with us at the chalet, not locked up in some dreadful rural Swiss hospital.'

Gabriel bristled, but he had to agree. If at all possible, Thomas should be with them, not alone in a lonely ward. They would drink their beer, and they would go rescue their friend.

———————◆◆◆———————

Later that night, when Thomas was tucked up safe and warm in his bed in the carnotzet, and the other two men had fallen asleep, exhausted, Gabriel sat up late, staring out at the blue glow of the snow outside. How could such a dangerous place be so simultaneously wonderful? The mountain was not to be toyed with. It was the very essence of Switzerland: pure, tough, and utterly beautiful. For the first time in months, suddenly, Gabriel remembered Anita.

Chapter Twenty-Three

Clarice sighed, setting down her empty coffee cup. 'I don't know, Monsieur Tibbali,' she said. 'I mean, the gallery opens in just a few months. There's no time for more fundraising.' Where *was* Gabriel? He should have been back from Saas Fee early that morning.

Felix Tibbali slouched back into the sofa, twirling a pencil in the air. He was wearing a tight black polo shirt under a wrinkled silk jacket, over blue jeans so light they were almost white. 'It's your choice, Madame de Puritigny,' he said, his tone ingratiating. The skin on his cheeks was taut and unblemished, as if lightly brushed with powder. 'I merely assumed you would want the very best for your new modern art gallery.'

'Very well,' Clarice said reluctantly, adjusting her skirt. 'I guess you can talk me through your designs, at least, before I show you the door. We'll return to the question of your rates later.' She smiled thinly. Perhaps Gabriel had fallen into a ravine.

Tibbali laughed quickly, a false, high sound, before elegantly unfolding a large sheet of paper. 'So, this is Rue de la Cité, where the new gallery is to be.' He gestured at the spidery drawing. 'Over here, off to the left of my sketch, is Saint Antoine, where we are sitting now.'

Clarice nodded impatiently. Perhaps Gabriel had gone on an impromptu road trip with his new business buddies. Perhaps he was having an affair. Clarice bit her lip to stop herself from smiling at the ridiculous thought.

'Here is the small building you have rented,' he continued smoothly, leaning on the words 'small' and 'rented' in a slightly unpleasant fashion, 'and here is the courtyard behind it. It is only logical to have an expansion into this courtyard.'

Clarice shook her head. 'I have already vetoed this suggestion. We simply don't have the budget, or the permits. I hired you to discuss the refurbishment of the building interior, in which I will have my *small* modern art gallery.'

Tibbali swallowed. 'Yes, of course,' he said, flipping over rather melodramatically to the next sheet of paper on the pad. 'This is the heart of my proposal,' he said, licking his pencil absentmindedly. 'This is my marvellous creation.'

Clarice peered at the drawing. 'This looks like a high-fashion boutique,' she said coolly. 'I've seen many similar places selling women's clothes in Saint-Germain-des-Prés.'

The architect's giggle turned into a sneer. 'Don't insult my creativity,' he said, jabbing the wet pencil eraser in her direction. 'This is no shabby quarter of Paris. This is the beautiful, UNESCO-classified centre of *Genève*.'

'Please,' Clarice said. 'My family has been in Geneva since the fifteenth century. Who are you, some upstart Italian, to tell me the value of my city?'

Tibbali waved his thin arms in the air helplessly. 'No, no,' he said. 'That's not what I mean. I simply think this would make such a wonderful gallery!' His expression shifted into something suspiciously resembling a pout. 'Besides, my family has been in Lugano for a hundred and fifty years. We're just as Swiss as you are.'

'Pff,' said Clarice.

Tibbali's large, expressive eyes shifted nervously from side to side. 'My apologies,' he said, his tone turning syrupy. 'I'm sure you are much more Swiss than I could ever claim to be. Please hear me out.'

'Let me just remind you that this is not my first gallery,' Clarice said sharply, twirling her empty espresso cup in her hand. 'Go on then, talk me through the rest of your precious creation.'

'The floors would be made of beautiful French reconstituted marble,' Tibbali said, 'in the colour of your choice.'

'Switzerland has at least five kinds of native marble, far more beautiful than this fake nonsense. You want to sell me some pathetic stone paste from Lyon or Alsace, when we can get the real deal for only two hundred francs a square meter?'

'I can also source marble from the Ticino,' Tibbali said weakly, 'if you like.'

'Very well,' Clarice said. 'Please continue.'

She noticed beads of sweat forming on Tibbali's brow. 'So, I wanted to decorate the walls in this very shiny brown lacquer, that makes all wood look like beautiful *loupe d'orme*. Do you know what that is? A noble sort of –'

'Yes, I know what *loupe d'orme* is,' Clarice snapped. 'My husband is rather fond of the lovely, overpriced stuff. All that money for a few more knots! You should see our cupboards upstairs.'

'Well, don't you love that sort of wonderful glowing, constellated effect? It would be so fantastic for a gallery, I think, because of the shining reflections of your paintings.

'I don't want that!' Clarice exclaimed. 'People should be looking at the paintings, not at the walls.' *Constellated*, she thought, trying not to roll her eyes.

'Well, I'm sorry,' Tibbali said rather sulkily, 'but everything I do is very shiny and reflective.'

'I'm sure it's alright in a women's fashion boutique, just not in a gallery.'

At this point in the conversation, the sound of a door closing made them both jump slightly. 'But what is that?' Tibbali asked nervously, as if he might be about to be thrown out by a pair of guards.

'Gabriel?' Clarice called out.

'*Bonjour, chérie*,' his voice came back clearly. 'Sorry I'm late! You won't believe what happened with Thomas...'

'Where were you?' she asked, unable to stop the accusation from creeping into her voice. 'I was worried.'

'I called to tell you I would be late...' Gabriel stopped at the doorway, looking confused. 'Sorry,' he said, 'I didn't realise you had company.'

'This is the man who knows about *loupe d'orme*?' Tibbali asked, looking suitably in awe.

Gabriel looked to Clarice, who shrugged. 'Er, yes, I suppose I do,' he said. 'It's one of my favourite... but who are you?'

Tibbali looked aggrieved. 'You have not told your husband about our project?'

'There is no...' She paused and smoothed her hair back with a pained expression. 'Firstly, if you think that in this day and age a woman has to keep her husband up to date on all her activities, you are seriously in the wrong. Secondly, there is no 'our.' We do not have a project together, Monsieur Tibbali, nor are we likely to, at any point in the foreseeable future. You have a proposal for *me*, one which I do not like so far.'

'What?' Gabriel rubbed his eyes. 'Clarice, can you tell me what's going on?'

Tibbali, starry-eyed, opened his mouth as if to explain, but Clarice cut him off. 'This man is trying to suggest I should pay two million Swiss francs for the renovation of my new gallery space… as well as having to shell out a hundred thousand for these designs alone.'

'Wait,' Tibbali said weakly. 'You haven't heard everything! Monsieur, you must know that I…'

Gabriel marched over to the table and flipped through the pages quickly. Tibbali cringed. 'Is that solid wood or just a veneer?' he asked, squinting at the design.

Tibbali produced a wobbly version of a confident smile. 'Like many cabinet makers these days, my supplier prefers pressed wood: this is MDF.'

'MDF!' Clarice cried out. 'This is ridiculous. Have you even designed a gallery before? How *did* Chloë get your number?'

'Mademoiselle Chloë was dating a friend of mine,' he said sulkily. 'A very attractive one, too. It was a terrible shame.'

'Ah. Well, you didn't seem like her type,' Clarice said archly, before realising the source of Tibbali's sadness was his friend, not Chloë. 'Anyway, that's beside the point. MDF is completely inappropriate for this type of setting. After four years in a temperature-controlled art gallery, it will dry up and begin to emit poisonous fumes. Do you know what MDF is made out of?'

'W–'

'Don't you dare say wood. Glue, Monsieur Tibbali. Glue. Do you know what happens to glue in a hot, dry space? Paintings have to be dry, in case you didn't know that. Your stupid MDF would not only ruin my paintings, but also make visitors ill from breathing poisonous gases.'

Clarice stopped to catch her breath, and noticed Gabriel looking at her with something like admiration. 'Listen,' she said, 'there's obviously been a misunderstanding. With all your shiny *loupe d'orme* and your chemicals and your reconstituted marble, this all sounds like something from a beach bar in St Tropez. It just isn't right.'

'You would have the most fabulous gallery on Rue de la Cité,' Tibbali said hopefully, grasping at straws. 'So many people walk down that street! What kind of paintings will you have? Andy Warhols?'

'Urgh, I hate Andy Warhol,' Gabriel said.

'Oh,' said Tibbali.

'Monsieur Tibbali, Felix,' Clarice said softly, 'I'm really sorry, but we're going to have to reject your design.'

'But madame! I've already spent three hundred hours coming up with these designs for you!'

Clarice sighed.

'Monsieur,' Gabriel said, 'I'm a banker, as you know. Why don't we simply terminate this contract? We'll pay you for your... three hundred hours of work. We'll pay you two hundred and fifty francs an hour, which will make you seventy-five thousand. I'll send you a cheque this week. Don't you agree that's the best deal for everyone?'

Tibbali's lip wobbled. He began to shiver, and his pen dropped from his hand. Then tears began to course down his face. Clarice and Gabriel simply stared for a moment.

'Monsieur Tibbali,' Clarice said hesitantly.

At this point, the tears turned into sobs, and Tibbali threw his arms around Clarice's neck, beginning to weep in earnest.

'Clarice,' Gabriel said, but Clarice glared at him.

'Monsieur Tibbali,' Clarice said, trying to extricate herself. 'Come now.'

Gabriel pulled the handkerchief from the top pocket of his coat and handed it gingerly to his wife.

'There there,' Clarice said awkwardly, trying to dry the architect's tears.

'Would you like a scotch?' Gabriel asked.

'It's not even lunchtime,' hissed Clarice.

'Maybe a fruit infusion,' Tibbali whimpered.

'Come, now,' Clarice said again briskly, grabbing him by the shoulders. 'There is no need for a fruit infusion just because we are closing a business deal. Come now.'

Gabriel hesitated. 'Clarice, it's raining cats and dogs.'

She threw him a furious glance. 'Felix,' she said coldly. As the door into the street swung open, she realised guiltily that her husband had been quite right. As Felix Tibbali, still crying, walked out into the rain, he slipped and nearly fell. Clarice and Gabriel watched for a moment as the slender man slid away down the street.

'Well,' Clarice said, 'thanks for all your help.'

'What do you mean?' Gabriel asked.

'I don't appreciate being made to look like the bad guy in front of a business contact. Since when do you offer strangers scotch? In the middle of the day?'

'Well, he's hardly a business contact anymore, is he? Besides, you weren't exactly applying the soft touch...' Clarice sighed deeply. 'What's wrong?' Gabriel asked, softening his voice.

'It's not going well,' Clarice said tensely. 'This is the second designer to come to me with nothing but harebrained schemes. We're running out of money to pay these fools to waste my time.'

Gabriel laid a hand on her shoulder, which she shook off impatiently. 'You have the building,' he said, 'and the artists. I'm sure you will work something out.'

Clarice took a deep breath and leaned against him ever so slightly. 'I'm sorry,' she said. 'I've just been so preoccupied with all this gallery business.'

'Don't worry,' he said. 'Why don't I give Dick a call? He's probably back at home by now. I'll bet he knows some interesting, avant-garde interior designers who might be able to give you a hand.'

'Really?' Clarice asked hesitantly. 'I... Well, yes, that would be nice.' There was a pause. 'Thank you,' she said, before standing back upright and taking a step back. 'So, how was the chalet?' she asked, adjusting her skirt. 'What were you saying about Thomas?'

'I'll tell you later,' he said. 'Once I've called Dick.'

'Well, I've got to run a few errands,' she said. 'I'm having a lunch meeting with the girls... I was supposed to tell them about Tibbali's plans.' She waved her hands in the air vaguely.

'Don't worry,' Gabriel said, surprisingly gallantly. 'I'll help in any way I can.'

But Gabriel did not immediately call Dick. Instead, he walked slowly upstairs to the bedroom and closed the door behind him. He sat on the bed and listened as Clarice bustled around. When he heard the front door close, and the clicking sound of his wife's high heels had vanished into the distance of the Old Town, he relaxed. A part of him wished she had made more of an effort to hear his news, after appearing so put out that he was late... Yet he was strangely relieved to be alone. Something had changed within Gabriel, late that night in Saas Fee. An urge had been growing in him, first too subtle to notice, but stronger every day. Now, it was becoming irresistible. He didn't want to tell Clarice about the incident with Thomas, that was the thing. There was someone else he wanted to call with his news. Someone he had only met once.

For the fifth time that day, Gabriel drew a wrinkled piece of paper from the inner pocket of his jacket. Ten digits were scrawled across it, and five letters, scarcely legible but unforgettable: ANITA. He stood up slowly and walked across the bedroom. He picked up the phone, took a deep breath, and set it down. Stumbling slightly he walked back to the bed. This was a terrible idea: he barely knew the woman; he had met her once. He was Swiss! This was ridiculous. Perhaps he would call Dick instead. Yet that intoxicating mixture of softness and strength, and the way her face had appeared to him deep in the mountains... He bolted across the room and, before he could change his mind, had rung the number. The dial tone made him hesitate, but before he could hang up, he heard a familiar, feminine voice.

'*Bonjour*?' Her gentle South American accent thrilled him to his core.

'Yes, er, good morning,' he said, before coughing slightly.

There was a pause. 'Who is this?'

'Oh! Er, it's Gabriel. You probably don't remember me, or recognise my voice... I'm so sorry to disturb you, I don't know what I was –'

'Gabriel! My God, how lovely! Do you know, I think about you often.'

Really? 'I mean, it's been months,' he said.

'Yes,' she said stubbornly, 'but I never forgot about you. I didn't have your number so I couldn't try to get in touch. Listen, do you want to meet up? Shall we go for a pizza or something?'

Gabriel swallowed, his heart pounding. 'I don't really eat pizza,' he said awkwardly, struggling a little. 'How are you?'

He heard a soft laugh. 'I'm alright,' she said. 'I've been living in the Pâquis district. It's noisy, but it's cheap. It has atmosphere. I share a place with a few friends, Peruvian girls. We split the rent, we cook for each other. Sometimes we share a bed for warmth.'

'Oh dear,' Gabriel said, loosening his shirt collar.

'It's a difficult life, but I don't mind it,' Anita said, her tone casual.

'I'm so sorry,' Gabriel said, shaking his head.

Anita laughed. 'You weren't calling me with a job offer, were you?'

'No, no,' Gabriel said hastily, 'I mean, I just wanted to speak to you. What are you doing now?'

'Now?' she asked coyly. 'I'm just putting my pants on.'

'Oh,' Gabriel sputtered. 'Sorry. I didn't mean to interfere with your personal life like that. Do you... Do you ever go walking by the lake?'

The amusement in Anita's voice was clear, but gentle. 'I love the lake,' she said. 'I go down there every time I get a break from work.'

'What kind of work are you doing?' Nervously, Gabriel pushed his glasses back up his sweaty nose.

'Well, I lost the waitressing position, so I'm mostly taking on odd jobs these days: cleaning, ironing, looking after kids...'

'And this makes you happy?'

Anita paused, as if considering. 'Well, it's not consistent with my education, but it pays the rent. But I don't mean to burden you with my worries!'

'No, not at all!' Gabriel said. 'I just want to talk to you.'

'What do you want to talk to me about, Gabriel?' Again, that playful note creeping into her voice.

'I don't know,' he said lamely. 'You, I suppose?' He shook his head furiously. 'Perhaps... Perhaps we could meet up in person, and talk further.'

'Oh yes!' Anita said. 'This morning's rain has almost cleared. Why don't we meet up by the lake? We could go for a walk, or something.'

'Now?' Gabriel asked, panicking mildly.

'Why not?' Anita replied.

'Alright,' Gabriel said suddenly, firmly. 'Yes. I have to make another phone call, but why don't we meet at the Botanical Gardens in an hour?'

'Are you sure you want to see me?' Anita asked, her voice softening into a purr. 'I mean, you're a big banker and I'm...'

'Yes,' Gabriel said quickly. 'I would love to see you. At the Botanical Gardens.'

'Well. That sounds delightful,' Anita replied. 'I'll see you there.'

Gabriel set the receiver down, feeling a little dizzy. What was he doing? Yet the Botanical Gardens were a safe place, he reassured himself: if an acquaintance should run into them there, it could look like an accidental meeting rather than a... rendezvous. He shook his head vaguely, before picking up the phone again.

'Gabe!' Dick's voice on the line was slightly fuzzy. 'How the hell are you? Long time no see!' He laughed raucously.

Gabriel sighed. 'Surely the real question is: how "the hell" is Thomas?'

'Oh yeah, of course!' Dick said, his jovial tone slightly guilty. 'How is the little German fellow?'

'He's OK,' Gabriel said. 'Still a little disorientated; keeps clicking his teeth and making strange noises. Sometimes I'm not sure he knows where he is. I stayed an extra day with him up there, so he could go for some extra scans, but nothing showed up. Medically speaking, he's absolutely fine.'

'Well that's great!' Dick said. 'So you're back with the old ball and chain in Geneva, then?'

'What?'

'Your wife!' Dick said, with great enthusiasm.

'Er, yes,' Gabriel said, a little too slowly.

Dick laughed again, loudly. 'Say no more, say no more,' he said. 'Had to check in on the mistress first? Well, well. I bet old Thomas was a great excuse.'

'That's not... I'm just glad Thomas is alright,' Gabriel said firmly. 'Anyway, that wasn't what I wanted to talk to you about.'

'Don't tell me you want to talk business?'

'Something like that. My wife...'

'So it is about your wife! What, you want me to take her off your hands for you?'

'Are you drunk?' Gabriel asked sternly.

'Me? Sort of. Probably.'

'Isn't it about eight o'clock in the morning where you are?'

'Yes, but I might have stayed up quite late last night.'

Gabriel shook his head. 'Right,' he said. 'Let me tell you the reason I'm calling, and then I'll let you get back to your... coffee. As you may remember, my wife is opening a new modern art gallery in a few months' time.'

'Is she?' said Dick.

Gabriel ignored him. 'She's already paid two architects to try and create a striking design for her, but they've both been a catastrophe. Now she has six months to put something together, get the permits, and have the whole thing built and ready for the opening. It has to be something extraordinarily modern, and it has to fit in the courtyard.'

'That doesn't sound very Swiss,' Dick commented.

'No,' Gabriel admitted. 'It doesn't. That's why I'm calling you.'

'I know this Filipino guy,' Dick said, without missing a beat. 'He designed this great sort of crystal ball thing for a friend of mine, an art dealer.'

'A crystal ball?' Gabriel was suspicious.

'You know the Louvre?'

'Yes, I am familiar with the Louvre,' Gabriel said patiently.

'Well, think about that glass pyramid. Now, imagine the same thing as a crystal ball. The great thing about this guy's designs, though, is that you can move them around. They're not officially permanent structures. Do you see where I'm going?'

'So you don't need a permit?' Gabriel said slowly.

'Exactly! They're luminous, and adaptable. You can buy them prefabricated, I think, from Saint Gobain in Paris, or Waterford in Ireland. I can call the guy, if you want. How much is your budget?'

'I think my wife has about two million left,' he said hesitantly.

'That'll be fine, then,' Dick said. 'I'll get him to call you.'

'He can call Clarice,' he said, before hesitating. 'No, wait. Maybe he should call me first. I don't want to get her hopes up for nothing.'

'Whatever you like, man. It's nice to see a guy being so gallant these days!'

Gabriel ignored Dick's sarcasm once more. 'Well, thanks for your help,' he said. 'I really must be going.'

'Another woman to meet?' Dick crowed with laughter.

'Goodbye, Dick,' Gabriel said, setting down the phone. Ignoring the watchful eyes of the de Puritigny portraits, he walked slowly back up the stairs to the bedroom. Clarice probably had several lovers, he told himself. Besides, taking a walk in the Botanical Garden hardly qualified as adultery.

———◆◆———

Anita was wearing a white dress under a black suede jacket, her black hair falling loosely over her shoulders. She stood on a small bridge near the entrance to the gardens, the curve of her hips pressed up against the wood. Her shoulders held back like a dancer, she was throwing small pieces of bread to the ducks below.

'Anita,' Gabriel said, and she turned towards him at once. The young woman was wearing very little makeup, but her cheeks were flushed. Around her, he was strangely aware that water still dripped from the green leaves, and the ducks splashed in the dark pond.

'Gabriel,' she exclaimed delightedly, running forward and holding out her hand.

'You recognised me!' he said in surprise, taking her hand in his. It was slender and cold, and returned his handshake firmly. 'After all these months...'

'How could I forget?' she said, solemnly. 'A tall, good-looking banker with such dreamy eyes... That beautiful chin, that fantastic nose, and those perfect ears!'

'Ears?' Gabriel echoed, dazed. His hand rose up unconsciously to touch them. They were cold. 'Quite honestly, I've never thought about my ears,' he said.

'I liked your ears when I first saw you,' she said. 'What lovely ears on this beautiful man, that was just what I thought!'

'That was probably the raclette talking.' Gabriel felt his ears flush bright red. 'Maybe I'll start looking at them in the morning,' he joked awkwardly.

'Did you know that in some South American tribes they judge your looks based on the size of your ears? The larger the soft part of your ear, the better.'

'You mean the earlobe?'

'Yes, that must be right. Is that the word for this?' Charmingly, she tugged lightly at her own earlobe.

'Yes.' Gabriel was briefly at a loss for words.

'Probably this place is much more beautiful in the summer,' Anita said. 'But I have always loved nature, at any time of year.' She took his arm and her face opened up into a smile. Those dimples! 'I wrote my dissertation about Mayan depictions of flora, actually.'

'I know very little about foreign... ancient art,' Gabriel stammered. Anita's body was warm beside his, the curves pressed against him.

'Oh, the ancient Peruvian civilisations are just so fascinating! The pyramids, of course, and I'm particularly fond of the paintings of animals. There have been some fascinating studies about the role of fauna in Mayan worship.'

'I like animals,' Gabriel said lamely.

'I've always been fascinated by dolphins, in particular,' she continued with enthusiasm. 'They are such intelligent animals, you know, and so strong! When I was a child, I always dreamed of swimming with them, as if I could become part of the pack, and swim off into the wild. Sometimes, when I look out over Lac Léman I...' She blushed.

'Go on,' said Gabriel.

'Well, sometimes, among the sweet ducks and geese, I imagine I see dolphins swimming around.' She smiled. 'It's a childish fantasy, I know. Of course, I can't even afford to buy myself a fish, let alone a dolphin.'

They laughed, walking arm-in-arm past the wet evergreen bushes, the bedraggled cacti, and up towards the greenhouse.

'So what did you study, in Peru?' Gabriel asked, utterly charmed.

'History of Art,' she replied quietly. 'Sometimes it just seems like such a waste, such a shame... I worry a lot about my future these days: what I should have done, what I want to do now.' She lowered her eyes and batted her long eyelashes sadly.

'I don't think you should worry,' Gabriel said passionately. 'I... I'd like to spend time with you, talking about your future. I'm sure you can find solutions to your problems.'

Anita beamed. 'Shall we go to the greenhouse?' she asked.

'Yes,' Gabriel said. 'Perhaps I could take you for a slightly late lunch afterwards?'

'That would be wonderful,' Anita replied. They walked along the wet gravel path, as grey clouds scudded overhead. 'So what about you? What have you been up to?'

'Work, work, and more work,' Gabriel replied wryly. 'Things

have been going well for the bank, but it's all getting a bit overwhelming. I just came back from a visit to Saas Fee, actually.'

'Oh, how lovely!' Anita replied. 'Is it very snowy there?'

'Yes, it's beautiful. I was there on a business trip, and all I could think was how much I wanted to be alone, flying down the empty slopes. The peaks are just stunning this time of year!'

'And your companions did not share your enthusiasm?' Anita asked sympathetically.

'Well, one of them fell down a ravine,' Gabriel said glumly.

'Oh dear!' Anita said. 'Is he all right?'

'Yes,' Gabriel said, gratefully. 'Yes, Thomas will be fine.'

'I've always been a little scared of skiing myself. I don't like being cold.'

'Ah, but you're not cold if you have a woollen scarf, and the right waterproof boots, and a fireplace to come home to!'

'I'm sure that's true. If only they had places like this in ski resorts!' Arriving at the greenhouse, Anita swung open the glass door, letting a blast of warm, steamy air out. 'Come in quickly!' she said. They found themselves alone inside, overwhelmed by the damp warmth, which smelled of earth and vanilla. All around them, red blossoms and vines cascaded over the iron railings.

'I haven't been here in years,' Gabriel marvelled, basking in the combined heat of the atmosphere and of Anita's presence next to him.

'It reminds me of home,' Anita said. 'I find the Swiss winters beautiful, yes, but harsh, too. They are still strange for me.'

'I wish I could show you the wonder of the winter mountains,' Gabriel said, more passionately than he had intended. 'But yes,' he added hastily, 'this greenhouse is beautiful, too.'

'So, mister Swiss banker,' she said gently. 'Do you still want to take me for lunch? I haven't eaten much since yesterday morning.'

Gabriel laughed, leading her to the door of the greenhouse. 'You poor thing,' he said. 'Perhaps you would like some fish from the lake, like your precious dolphins?'

Anita laughed. 'I don't think I've eaten fish often in Switzerland,' she said. 'It's just so expensive here! I used to love it at home, though.'

'Don't worry,' Gabriel said gallantly. 'I will buy you *filet de perche*, or perhaps you would prefer *omble chevalier*?'

'I don't know what either of those things are,' Anita replied. 'Is that... *omble* thing really a name for a fish?'

Gabriel smiled. 'Now that you mention it, it is rather a stupid name. Switzerland is full of delicious fish, though. Noble fish. Have you ever heard of *féra*?'

Anita shook her head. They began to walk towards the gate of the Botanical Gardens. 'Well,' Gabriel said, 'it used to be one of the most popular fish caught in Lac Léman, so popular that it became extinct. Apparently, it was delicious, though.'

'What a shame!' Anita exclaimed. They began to walk down along the lake, sparkling even in the grey midday light. 'Stories about extinction make me worry about life, about fate. Do you know, I used to be so ambitious?' Her breath formed a white cloud in front of her. 'I wanted to... change things. Go places. Now I've managed to go someplace, in a literal sense, but I just don't seem to be able to find a job, or truly become integrated here. The Swiss only seem to want to hire other Swiss.'

Gabriel gave a hollow laugh. 'That may be true, but it's changing,' he said. 'I used to be one of those Swiss men, you know, completely closed to the possibilities offered by globalisation. I wanted no part of an international future. Now, one of the bank's principal partners is an American brokerage firm, and we've just signed a deal with this Frenchman, Gérard Maigréville.'

Anita was quiet. 'I'm glad you're open to international possibilities,' she said slyly. She squeezed Gabriel's arm, making him laugh.

'Let's eat at La Perle du Lac,' he said suddenly, spontaneously, as they passed the restaurant. What did he care if one of his stupid Swiss acquaintances saw him there? It was a great restaurant, and this wonderful young lady deserved nothing but the best.

'Goodness,' Anita said. 'Are you sure? I mean, we could just go for pizza...'

'I don't like pizza,' Gabriel said gallantly. He waved a waiter over and requested a table for two.

Anita sat down slowly, slipping her stockinged legs under the white tablecloth with an expression of wonder. 'Goodness,' she said again. 'I don't know what to say. I don't think I've ever eaten anywhere this nice before, in my whole life.'

The waiter handed them two menus. Was that a smirk? Gabriel frowned, but no, on closer inspection, it was simply a solicitous smile.

'I think I'll be having the *omble chevalier*,' Gabriel told her. 'If you've not tried it before, you really must.'

'I trust you,' Anita said with a brilliant smile. 'Do you mind if I have French fries with it?'

'Of course not! Have anything you like!' Gabriel said, his heart melting. 'Have some vegetables, as well.'

Anita squinted at the menu. 'What is a mange tout?' she asked. 'Doesn't that mean *eat everything*?'

'Why yes, I suppose it does,' Gabriel said, charmed. 'Come to think of it, that is a pretty stupid name for a bean. As if you were supposed to eat your fingers and your plate as well!'

Anita dissolved into peals of laughter.

'Try some!' Gabriel said. 'If you like strange vegetables, you should try some *salsifis* as well. They are like little worms.'

Anita shook her head. 'You Swiss people are so strange.'

'It started with the Huguenots, you know,' Gabriel said. 'In those days, you never knew if immigrants were Catholics or Protestants. People were afraid of their neighbours. You didn't tell anyone your name, your history. You didn't make friends. I'm convinced, Anita, that this whole Swiss obsession with secrecy started back then. Confidentiality, discretion, jealousy: it all stems from the sixteenth century.'

'How fascinating!' Anita said. 'So you are from an old family?'

Gabriel nodded. 'Yes, our house in Saint Antoine was inherited.' He paused, the word 'our' hanging in the air between them. 'It has the most wonderful parquets,' he concluded weakly.

'Wonderful!' Anita said, slightly more enthusiastically than necessary. At that moment, the waiter reappeared.

After they had given their order of two *omble chevaliers* with four kinds of vegetables, he bowed slightly. 'Would you like something to drink with your meal? I can recommend a local pinot gris, or perhaps the *johannisberg*?'

'Just Coca-Cola for me,' Anita said.

'Are you sure?' Gabriel asked.

'Oh yes,' Anita said demurely. 'I have to go back to work later this afternoon.'

'Right,' Gabriel said, slightly deflated. 'Well, in that case, a Coke for me too.'

An awkward silence fell, which was swiftly dispelled by the arrival of their drinks and a small bowl of olives.

'I like the Swiss,' Anita said casually, 'and I like Switzerland. Yes, they may have their flaws, but they seem to me to be very honest people, deeply attached to their land.'

Gabriel beamed. 'Have you travelled much in the country?' he asked.

Anita shook her head. 'I haven't found the time or the money,' she said. 'I know it's a terrible shame. Maybe one day!'

Gabriel was silent for a time, lost in thought. When the fish arrived, he watched with pleasure as Anita devoured everything on her plate. The fish was tender, swimming in an herbed butter sauce, and it disappeared quickly once Anita set into it. She also devoured a basket of thick, crunchy fries sprinkled with sea salt, and two helpings of sweet mange tout.

'I don't know how anyone could not love Swiss food,' she said in delight, mopping up the creamy salad dressing from her plate with a piece of crusty bread. 'All that wonderful cheese, too!'

'Would you like a cheese plate?' Gabriel offered. 'Or perhaps dessert?'

Anita's eyes twinkled. In the end, they ordered a crème brûlée and a bowl of blueberry ice cream with toasted coconut flakes.

As she lifted a spoonful of ice cream to her lips, Gabriel took a deep breath. 'I wondered if you would like to see Switzerland with me,' he burst out.

Anita smiled, surprised. 'What do you mean?' she said.

'I mean, I mean,' he struggled to explain, 'I'd like to show you a few sights. I think you would appreciate them. Not as a... just as a sort of tour guide.'

'I'd love that,' she said. Gabriel beamed and dug into his crème brûlée. Time passed, the only sound the silvery tinkle of spoons in china bowls.

'OK,' Anita said at last, sighing. 'Switzerland has vanquished me and I am so happy to be conquered! I couldn't eat a bite more.'

'Neither could I!' Gabriel said, leaning back in his chair. 'I don't think I've eaten this much at lunchtime since I was in America!' Anita blushed. 'Oh, don't... I mean, it's a pleasure to meet a girl with a healthy appetite!'

'It isn't that,' Anita said slowly. 'It's just that, Gabriel, I don't have anywhere enough money for this. This is a very fancy restaurant.'

'I told you not to worry,' Gabriel said. 'I'll cover it. It's my pleasure. I've had a wonderful time.'

'So have I,' she said softly. She dabbed at the corners of her lips with a napkin. Her mouth was full and soft.

Gabriel glanced at his watch, and swallowed. 'Tell you what, Anita,' he said, as casually as he could. 'Will you let me order you a taxi? It's the least I can do.'

'No, no,' Anita said firmly. 'I cannot accept that. I can walk back from here. This lunch was *my* pleasure. I don't know how I can ever thank you for it.'

'Just let me call you again sometime,' he said warmly. 'I'll plan an itinerary.' Silence fell over the table. 'And look, don't say anything...' He rustled in his pocket, and, as discreetly as possible, drew out a hundred-franc note from his wallet. He pressed it into her hand and closed her fingers over it. 'I want you to start eating better,' he said gently, holding her hand.

'Oh my god!' she gasped, opening her hand. 'I've... never seen one of these before.'

'It's nothing. I'm worried about you,' Gabriel said. 'Let me call you again soon.'

'Of course,' Anita said, apparently at a loss for words.

'Will you... let me walk you back to your apartment?'

Anita shook her head, blushing suddenly. 'Thank you,' she said, 'but I can't bear the thought of spoiling this perfect lunchtime by showing you where I live. You've made me feel like a Swiss lady, Gabriel. I don't want to break the spell.'

It was Gabriel's turn to blush again. Shyly, he reached across the table and took her hand in his. 'You are a Swiss lady to me, Anita,' he said. She smiled.

Chapter Twenty-Four

Clarice stared at the crystal wall, watching it shift from a soft pink glow into deep blue. It was more of a sun colour than a moon colour, she decided, pleased. The paintings hung still from fine silver wires, as if suspended in the air. Was everything ready? The champagne flutes were lined up, expectant. The trays of caviar and smoked salmon were laid out, the ice glistening in the changing light.

'It's beautiful, *ma chérie*,' Gabriel said, kissing her cheek. 'You've done wonderful work here! Is there anything else I can do to help before the guests arrive?'

Clarice shifted her gaze to her husband's smiling face, struggling to compute. 'Are you quite alright, Gabriel?' she asked. 'You seem strangely... cheerful.' In the background, the light shifted into the huge red-and-white cross of a Swiss flag.

'I am cheerful!' he said. 'I'm so proud of my lovely, talented wife for opening this stunning new gallery.'

'Well,' Clarice said. 'Having Simosa as the architect was your idea.'

'Nonsense,' Gabriel replied. 'It was merely a suggestion. You carried the scheme out. Besides, the real beauty in this room is you. Have I seen that black dress before? The neckline is quite stunning.'

'It's... It's Chanel, actually,' she said. The crystal wall shifted to a light turquoise, before becoming perfectly clear, and Clarice found herself blushing. What on earth was up with Gabriel?

'In any case, I'm happy with the results of the scheme, as you call it,' Clarice said lightly, 'and I'm glad the weather has held up.'

The golden autumn light filtered through the leaves, sending lovely patterns of light and shade into the gallery.

'I still think you were very clever, waiting until the start of the autumn to have this *vernissage*. The Swiss summer is just full of silly little gallery openings.'

Clarice shrugged. 'Well, as you know, we discussed it at length with the girls. Geneva basically empties out at the end of June, as the middle classes all take their squealing brats out of school and ship them across some sea or other. I don't even know where they go, these people: China, Thailand, France... anywhere but Switzerland.'

'In any case, it's a drought for business,' Gabriel said thoughtfully, nodding.

'Khadija made a strong argument for opening in June, you'll recall,' Clarice said. 'She argued quite convincingly that there are a lot of visitors from the Gulf in summer. They all seem to come running away from the heat of the desert.'

'They must love the cool of the mountains,' Gabriel said, somewhat wistfully.

'It's not even that cold in the mountains in July! However, I told Khadija I hadn't seen that many Arabs buy paintings from me, and that was that. Besides, their Rolls Royces might not fit up the narrow cobblestone roads.' She gave a grim smile. 'That is, if they can even bear to leave the Hôtel Président and the Hôtel de la Paix to come to the Old Town.'

Gabriel nodded vaguely.

'In any case, we knew the Swiss wouldn't be there, so why assume the Arabs would be?'

'So you waited for the *rentrée*,' Gabriel said, 'for everyone to come back from their holidays.'

'Yes,' Clarice said briskly. Was her husband drunk? 'A time for new beginnings, when there is very little in the way of entertainment.'

'You're so terribly clever,' Gabriel said, his eyes bright. 'Sometimes I don't know if I married you because you were so smart or because you were so beautiful. Today, I think it's both. Your analysis of Swiss society is simply stunning: they all go away in the winter, and they all go away in the summer. Of course, I shouldn't be surprised at your brilliance.'

'Why don't you... check on the canapés? Make sure the caviar has plenty of fresh ice, and that the lemon wedges have arrived.' Clarice shook her head. This wasn't just an isolated event. Her husband had been acting strangely for weeks and weeks. Clarice sighed, looking around the glowing room, trying not to look at Gabriel, standing awkwardly by the banquet table. Perhaps she was a fool to worry.

After all, hadn't Gabriel been unusually pleasant? Maybe things were going well at the bank. Maybe he was entering a new phase of middle age. She ran her hands over the crushed velvet of her bodice nervously.

Clarice's troubled train of thought was interrupted by the sound of voices at the door. The guests were beginning to arrive: overcoats were removed, makeup was adjusted, and smiles were produced: the crème-de-la-crème of Genevois society was out to play. Clarice stood in the centre of the room, watching with a pleased, feline smile as the guests began to mill around.

'What an original design!' they exclaimed as they walked around, craning their necks, wafting clouds of expensive perfume.

'Oh, and such fancy canapés!'

'Perhaps one of these would look nice in our lounge, *mon chéri*?'

'This is no ordinary gallery.'

Clarice's smile grew more pronounced, as she recognised the last speaker.

'Yes, it was actually designed by a Filipino architect,' she said casually, in reply to one of the comments. 'A friend of my husband's. Brilliant, really. We carried the whole thing out in less than six months.'

Mr Schön, startled, gave an oily smile. On this occasion, he had produced a suit in a sort of lurid orange colour, worn over a shirt that could only be described as golden. His tie was bright green silk, and decorated with a pattern of feathers. The effect, Clarice thought to herself with amusement, was highly reminiscent of a pheasant, trimmed and ready to be served up as a fancy roast.

'Madame de Puritigny!' he said. 'What a pleasure! I'm sure I have not seen you in, what, ten years? You've not aged a day.'

'I don't believe we've met since that fateful dinner at the bank,' she said. 'How many bottles of Château Latour did you drink during that business deal? Two, or was it three?'

Mr Schön laughed heartily, his thumbs strumming his golden braces. 'Come now,' he said, 'you can't begrudge me a bit of youthful exuberance. Those days are long past. I no longer get to spend much time on my boat.'

'You can't have been a day younger than forty,' Clarice said, keeping her expression polite.

Mr Schön raised an eyebrow. 'The Swiss banking scene is changing, I regret to inform you. You'll find it's mostly peopled by international rogues these days.'

'As opposed to good old Swiss rogues such as yourself, I presume?'

Charmed against his will, Mr Schön laughed heartily. 'Madame de Puritigny, it is a pleasure,' he said, pretending to doff an invisible hat.

'Perhaps you would be interested in purchasing something?' Clarice asked.

Mr Schön waved a be-ringed hand in the air. 'Maybe later,' he said. 'Do you have any Château Latour?'

'I can't remember what red wine we had brought in, but you can check with the steward. Meanwhile, can I recommend you try one of the smoked salmon toasts? They come with a caper and dill sauce, and would, I suspect, look quite divine with your suit.'

My, she was having a wonderful time! Clarice strode off confidently.

'Hey!' A female voice startled Clarice mid-stride. Who had spoken? She turned around, following the source of the sound. American, she thought. A woman in a tacky, polyester suit and cowboy boots was squinting at one of the paintings. A banker, probably one of Gabriel's contacts. Could this be the speaker? She was wearing a baby blue tie, and her hair was pulled back in a ponytail. When she looked up at Clarice, she grinned, confirming suspicions that the loud voice had indeed been hers. 'You selling these?' she asked. 'This one here is just so exciting.'

'We're selling everything here,' Clarice said, walking over slowly. Her high heels clicked lightly on the polished parquet floor.

The American woman laughed loudly again. 'Good,' she said. 'I like a fellow businesswoman. You ever been to a gallery opening where it turns out they're only selling half the stuff? I don't get it. You're not a museum.'

Clarice cracked a smile. There was something likeable about this character. 'I'm Clarice de Puritigny,' she said, holding out a hand.

'Billy Jean,' the American replied, smiling broadly and shaking her hand firmly. 'This trip wasn't meant to be for pleasure, but I must say I'm tempted. I mean, Switzerland isn't exactly the place I go to relax! But when Dick suggested I might like to check out this new modern art gallery...'

'You're a friend of Dick's?' Clarice asked, relaxing a little.

'You could say we're business associates. He's a weasel, is Dick, but a charming one. Sure, I guess you could say we're friends.'

'I've never met him,' Clarice admitted. 'He was here a few months ago for a ski trip, but I couldn't bear the thought of all those businessmen together in a chalet...'

'Ha!' said Billy Jean. 'It sounds completely awful.'

'One of them ended up falling into a ravine,' Clarice said, with a small smile.

Billy Jean shook her head. 'Some men,' she said, 'just aren't really men. But we're not here to chit-chat about guys. Let's cut to the chase and talk prices...' It was not long before the two women had come to a deal. Clarice was just inwardly congratulating herself on her negotiation skills when a familiar clean, earthy scent with floral overtones gave away Winifred's presence. A linen-clad arm was slipped through hers. 'What were you doing with that woman?' Winifred asked, her nose wrinkling in distaste.

'Are you talking about our first client of the night?' Clarice asked, a twinkle in her eye. 'She just carried off that wonder in the corner. You know, the blue one.'

'Oh,' Winifred said, as if in deep disappointment. 'I rather liked that one. Well, I guess you can't stop those people from buying up Swiss art.'

'Winifred!' Clarice said, pulling her arm away from her friend's. 'I'm surprised at you. Is age turning you into some kind of snob? You should be happy the night is off to so successful a start!'

'I hope I'm not a snob,' Winifred said, apologetically. 'It's just... I don't think these types of people ought to be residents of Geneva.

There's something colonialist about the way Americans think they can turn up anywhere and live there.'

'I think she's only here for a business trip,' Clarice said gently. 'And she paid just over half a million.'

'Oh!' Winifred said again. 'Well, in that case, I take back the bad-mouthing. It's just that in the past few months, I've had to sit through so many dreadful conversations with Dieter's work contacts. They think they dominate the world, these people! I don't think they want the best for Switzerland, or for the Swiss.'

'Dieter can take care of himself,' Clarice said firmly, 'and so can we. Anyway, I quite liked the woman's straightforward approach to money, you know? Come on, let's go find some more rich people to criticise.'

'Ooh!' Winifred said suddenly. 'Look, our rivals from Carouge have turned up!'

Clarice peered at the crowd milling in through the door, a cluster of tall, Germanic-looking women. 'Yes, you're right. I recognise Thona and Kadiz, and is that Silvio?'

'Yes, and that dreadful Dale!'

'Come on, let's go get drinks before we're cornered. I suppose we should be flattered they're checking out the competition... They must realise this is a big deal. Winifred, I think I'm rather pleased with this development!'

Winifred laughed softly, and took her arm again. 'By the way, before I forget, remind me to tell you about the paintings I might have for your old gallery. They're too big for this crystal ball, you see: if I understood correctly, they're about three meters long and two and a half meters high. You'll need wall space to hang them. They were acquired by a couple in Zurich, sponsored by Dieter's bank. Beautiful monochromes. I really think you'll like them.'

'Excellent,' Clarice replied. 'I look forward to seeing them! Do you think you could send me some pictures, or put me in touch with the couple?'

'Of course. I'm sorry Dieter couldn't be here, by the way,' Winifred said. 'He's been so stressed out with work.'

Clarice's laugh came out guttural and a little bitter. 'You should see the effect stress is having on my husband,' she said.

Winifred raised her eyebrows. 'Oh dear,' she said. 'Is he being difficult? Is he finding it difficult to make time for you?'

'He's being absolutely charming,' Clarice said cuttingly. 'I don't understand it. It's as if he developed a sense of humour overnight.'

Winifred frowned. 'I'm afraid I don't understand.'

'He's being nice, Winifred,' Clarice snapped. 'Nice for no reason. It doesn't feel right. I don't like it.'

Clapping a hand to her mouth, Winifred couldn't stop a giggle from escaping. 'Oh,' she said.

Against her will, Clarice began to laugh as well. 'Oh, Winifred, I'm sorry. I just don't understand what's going on with my husband. I know you can't possibly...'

'My marriage isn't perfect,' Winifred said softly.

'No, I know that. But I suspect you two are much better at communicating than us.'

'It's key, you know,' Winifred replied. 'I don't know how we would manage without it.'

'Speak of the devil,' Clarice said suddenly. 'My dearly beloved husband!'

'Who is he with?' Winifred asked curiously.

Clarice squinted, then sighed. 'The British,' she said.

———◆◆◆———

'Baron Armagaunt!' Gabriel was saying, with exaggerated warmth. 'Lord Cecilian de Rollo de Vicambush! What an absolute pleasure to have you here.'

'Yes, well,' the more elderly lord blustered, 'wouldn't want to miss the free bubbly, would we.' There was a distinctly Scottish burr to his voice.

'Come, come,' the baron replied. 'We're not students anymore. Don't pretend we can't afford a nice drink.' His nose was threaded with bright red veins, and his white hair stuck out at odd angles.

'I thought you were here because of your personal taste for modern art,' quipped Lord Vicambush.

'Now, now,' Armagaunt said. 'I'm fond of a few rather modern names. Erm, Caillebotte, for instance, and Henry Moore. I even like some of Picasso's more sedate works.'

'Well,' Lord Vicambush replied, not to be outdone, 'I happen to be quite fond of David Roberts. A fellow Scotsman, you know. He coloured these beautiful books by hand. His lithographs of Egypt are quite exquisite!'

'He's hardly a modern artist, though,' the Baron scoffed.

'Have a look around, gentlemen,' Gabriel said. 'Perhaps you'll find something to each of your tastes. It's not all that radical, you know.'

'It sounds like business is going well for you,' the old lord said. 'I'm pleased with the change in Swiss banking we've witnessed recently.'

'Eight per cent,' Armagaunt replied, 'is still not as much as the Americans.'

'Our office in Chicago is working on that,' Gabriel replied smoothly. 'Now, can I interest you in a little Estonian caviar?'

Clarice, observing the scene, let out a burst of suppressed mirth. 'You can't keep a banker away from his clients,' she said drily.

'And you can't keep the clients away from their money,' Winifred added.

They found Chloë and Fleurie at the other end of the table of champagne flutes, pink-faced.

'Ladies!' Chloë said expansively. 'What a surprise to run into you here.'

Fleurie shook her head. 'I couldn't keep her from the fizzy wine,' she said, mock-apologetically. 'Clarice, I must say you've done a splendid job. The place looks absolutely marvellous!'

Chloë nodded enthusiastically. 'I just sold one of the wooden sculptures,' she said. 'You know, the curvy ones?'

Clarice couldn't help but smile. 'Ah, the Austrian sculptor! I wondered whether he would sell.'

'You really have an eye for quality,' Fleurie said admiringly.

'Yes, she has such marvellous taste! That particular artist seems inspired. It reminds me of a lot of excellent work being produced in lower Germany,' Winifred said.

'Ah, but what about the Russians?' Chloë purred.

'You just love Russians,' Clarice rolled her eyes. 'Which are your favourites? Was it Smirnoff or Stolichnaya?'

Chloë narrowed her eyes, but Fleurie cut in before she could argue: 'Where's Khadija?'

'I haven't seen her,' Clarice replied. 'I think she had to pick up those princes of hers from the airport. Maybe their flights were delayed.'

Chloë let out a snort of laughter. 'You mean their private jets?'

Clarice ignored her. 'In any case, I'm sure she'll be here in time for the speech.'

'Of course,' Fleurie said.

'By the way, who are those rich-looking guys Gabriel was talking to?' Chloë asked innocently.

'They're British,' Clarice said, almost mournfully.

'Old money,' Fleurie sniffed, dismissively.

'Inherited fortunes,' Winifred said, more respectfully.

'They're just tax evaders,' Fleurie argued fiercely. 'Snobs.'

'Now, now,' said Winifred.

'She's right,' Clarice said apologetically. 'I mean, they're clients of Gabriel's, but he's not once gone to visit them in Britain. Every time they come here, they want to convert their money into ingots of gold and have it hidden away in safes. Then they go skiing and have a marvellous time until somebody falls in a ravine.'

Chloë laughed. 'I don't know what's got into you these days, Clarice,' she said, 'but I like it.'

'I think Gabriel is being a little strange,' Winifred explained.

'When was Gabriel ever anything but?' Chloë inquired.

Clarice shrugged. 'Stranger than usual,' she said. 'Or perhaps simply strange in a different way.'

'Oh, look, Clarice,' Chloë said suddenly. 'It's that odd little German man!'

Clarice turned around and saw Thomas, smiling radiantly and wearing his favourite embroidered waistcoat.

'Madame Clarice!' he exclaimed, rushing towards her, his curls flying in every direction. 'It is so good to see you!' Exuberantly, he grabbed her hand and kissed it.

Clarice blushed, pleased. 'How is your head?' she asked.

Thomas shrugged. 'Oh, you know... Ever since I started work in the banking world, I have asked myself the same question.'

Clarice laughed, before remembering herself. 'This is Chloë,' she said.

'Oh, I remember,' Thomas said, blinking wildly.

'What a peculiar little man you are!' Chloë said, kissing him on both cheeks. Thomas turned the colour of a ripe beetroot.

'Have you had any champagne?' Clarice asked. 'Help yourself at the table.'

Thomas shook his head. 'I feel I am intoxicated enough,' he said, still blinking quickly, 'by the presence of your beauteous acolyte.'

Chloë giggled. Thomas made a sort of clicking noise.

'Well, my dear Chloë,' Clarice said with a small smile, 'why don't I let Thomas regale you with the story of his skiing adventures?'

'Yes!' Chloë exclaimed, tipsily leaning into Thomas, who turned an even more extreme shade of crimson. 'Tell me about the ravine!'

Shaking her head, Clarice walked off. A few more paintings had discreet 'sold' stickers on their slim silver wires, she noticed. Business was booming. She would have to order new stock in the very next day! A strident feminine voice interrupted her mental calculations of profit.

'Khadija!' she exclaimed, relieved. 'I thought you might have forgotten.'

'Forgotten? Forgotten?' Khadija asked indignantly, puffing up like an angry sparrow underneath her gigantic black fur coat. 'These...' She closed her eyes, breathed deeply, and rearranged her ruffled feathers. 'My dear friends Prince Ragheb and Prince Sattar were delayed going through customs.'

'Pleased to meet you,' Clarice said, looking up at the pair. One had a roguish look, with a trimmed beard and gold chain around his neck, while the other had cultivated a more scholarly appearance with a long wiry beard, and kept his eyes on the floor. 'Let me show you to the refreshment table. We have apple juice and several kinds of tea.'

'Isn't there champagne?' Prince Ragheb asked, in mock horror.

'Yes, of course!' Clarice assured him, surprised. 'I just wasn't sure...'

'I'm here to have a good time,' he replied with a grin. 'And to buy some paintings.'

Clarice gave him her most brilliant smile. 'Khadija, if you could usher these lovely people towards the drinks and snacks... It's almost time for your speech!'

'I'm very much looking forward to your speech, cousin Khadija,' Prince Sattar said softly. 'I am very impressed with your work.'

'Yes, yes,' Khadija said, bustling along. 'Now go get yourself some juice and find a nice corner to stand in.'

Clarice smiled as the two men walked towards the refreshments.

Khadija unbuttoned her coat. 'Where's Chloë?' she hissed. 'I thought I could palm Ragheb off on her. He's a dreadful flirt, that one. Guaranteed to buy something to impress a lady.'

'You'll never believe who Chloë's working her charms on now...' Clarice took Khadija's arm and walked towards the platform that had been set up on one side of the crystal structure.

———— ◆ ————

With her heavy eyeliner, black leather boots and bright green silk scarf, Khadija looked quite impressive. Her charcoal grey Chanel suit fitted her beautifully, Clarice thought to herself. She would have to remember to mention it to Gabriel.

Khadija tapped on the microphone with an immaculately manicured fingernail. 'Welcome, ladies and gentlemen, ladies particularly.' A few subdued laughs were heard around the room. 'Yes, you heard me correctly. Ladies, you are welcome here, as artists, investors and buyers alike. We have entered a new era of female empowerment,' Khadija said. 'Could you ever have imagined that five women alone could raise the funds for this venture, liaise with the artists, find an architect and have this whole marvellous thing built in less than a year? Most of you will remember Clarice de Puritigny's famous fondue party, and many of you will know her original gallery. Some of you might already be familiar with the work of our architect, Simosa, a jewel from the Philippines. Yet none of you, I am sure of it, could have guessed what you were going to see tonight: this changing, luminous dome, and this wonderful modern art from all over the world. I understand Monsieur Simosa is a private person, so I won't embarrass him by making him come up to the podium, but I'd appreciate it if we could at least give the man a round of applause.' The audience obliged. 'I mean, this is a monument; this is the pride of Geneva. In my opinion, it can compete with all the UN buildings and all the great hotels by the side of Lac Léman. It is a château. If I could, I would live in this crystal ball, gazing at all the art. But I guess that's Clarice's job.'

Next to the stage, Clarice spotted Simosa, a man soberly dressed in a black suit and a tan turtleneck, blushing furiously beneath a head of black curls. She smiled.

'I don't think it would be much of an exaggeration to say this is the most modern gallery in all of Switzerland today. Ladies and gentlemen,' Khadija continued, 'this is all thanks to you. Well, no, actually. It's mostly thanks to us.' She paused for laughter. 'You may already know that I am one of the major investors in this entire project,' Khadija said proudly, 'but you may not realise how closely we five women have worked together for this. Clarice, Fleurie, Winifred and Chloë are four of the smartest, most driven, most infuriatingly beautiful women I've ever met.'

Scattered laughter erupted once more, and the girls chinked their champagne flutes. 'We hope this gallery will have a high turnover of paintings, which we collect from skilled *rabatteurs* all over the world. To all the fundraisers who have come back to see the results of their investment, I hope you are pleased. We are so thankful for your help. We hope you will become our buyers, or at least our advertisers! As you can probably see, this is not a gallery like any other, and this is no ordinary *vernissage*. We have no intention of serving you two-week-old smoked salmon and a small shish kebab. We are offering you white truffles from Italy, the most expensive truffles in the world! That caviar – if there is any left – is not dyed freshwater fish roe, and in your glasses, you'll find no *crémant* or *clairette*. This is how much we value our project: our gallery, our artists, and every one of you. Welcome, dear ladies and gentlemen. Enjoy yourselves, and if you enjoy yourselves, remember to tell all your friends, especially those with a taste for expensive paintings. After all, we need the cash to pay the outrageous rent.'

Laughter and applause washed over the room, and Khadija gave a small, satisfied smile as she descended from the podium. Gabriel appeared at Clarice's shoulder, grinning ear to ear. 'Ladies, I'm so proud of you,' he said. 'Would you like me to get you a glass of champagne?'

'No, thank you,' Clarice said, a little impatiently. 'Khadija!' She found herself enveloped in a tight hug from her friend before she could embrace her. 'Such a wonderful speech, thank you.'

'Well, I really should get back to my clients,' Gabriel said. 'Great speech, Khadija.' He shuffled away.

Khadija ignored him. 'It really should have been you up there. This is your project.'

Clarice shook her head. 'You shine in the limelight,' she said. 'Public speaking never really was my speciality.'

'Well, I really did mean what I said. I'm so proud of what you've done. I remember when I first met you, you know, when you'd hardly seen any modern art in your life.'

'My life changed for the better when I met you,' Clarice said, with complete conviction. It occurred to her suddenly that a similar thought had never crossed her mind regarding Gabriel.

'What was Gabriel wheedling on for, anyway?' Khadija asked.

Clarice shrugged. 'He's been behaving strangely, these days.'

'Well, at least he gave up quickly. Never quite understood that man,' she said.

'A Swiss banker never leaves the company of his clients,' Clarice explained with a wry smile. 'He's too afraid they'll be stolen by somebody else. Gabriel will know some of his rivals are present this evening. He thinks he has to stick to those lords of his, for fear – God forbid – they should speak to anybody else.'

'Poachers?' Khadija asked. 'Well! I'm almost impressed. I get bored of the constant Swiss moralising, you know. I like a little dishonesty, a little scandal.' She rubbed her hands together.

'Well, if you want banking scandal, you really should ask Chloë,' Clarice said. 'She has some crazy story about sadomasochism in the office...' The two women strolled towards the drinks table.

'Simosa!' Khadija said suddenly. 'No, don't run away.'

The architect gave a shy smile, cowering like a child in front of a school-teacher. 'Hello,' he said, in a lilting accent.

Clarice smiled warmly and took his hand. 'Thank you for everything,' she said.

'I think,' Simosa said shyly, 'we can all agree that this opening was a success.'

'Yes, indeed,' Khadija said, reaching for the champagne. 'A great success.' She handed flutes to Clarice and Simosa. 'Let us drink to our victory, then, and to our future. To our glorious future in art dealership!'

'And to Clarice de Puritigny,' said Simosa.

Khadija smiled. 'To Clarice,' she echoed.

Chapter Twenty-Five

Cowbells rang out in the clear mountain air, and the last of the summer blossoms waved in the wind amongst the first fallen leaves of autumn.

'Oh, Switzerland is so beautiful!' Anita exclaimed, whirling around and around with her arms held up in the air. Her long blue dress spun with her.

'It is,' Gabriel said, the giddiness catching up with him. He unbuttoned his shirtsleeves and rolled them up to his elbows. 'I cannot believe this weather,' he added.

'Is October too late for a romantic Indian summer?' Anita asked, running back to him breathlessly.

'I guess not,' said Gabriel, 'though it's certainly unseasonable for Switzerland.'

Smiling, she grabbed his hands and spun him around with her. The green and ochre mountains behind them blurred, and Gabriel felt his blood singing out with sheer love of his homeland.

'Now I feel like eating some cheese,' Anita said, stopping suddenly.

'But we've only been walking an hour! It's not even lunchtime!'

'I like hiking,' she replied, a little too quickly. 'No, I really do. It's just...'

Gabriel shook his head, unable to stop himself from smiling. 'Let's head back to town, then,' he said. 'I suppose I'm feeling rather peckish myself.'

After a speedy descent, driven by hunger, the pair then made their way at a leisurely pace into the centre of Gruyère. The cobbled streets were quiet, the fountain playing its quiet music to itself. Anita ran up to it and buried her face in one of the baskets of flowers. 'Oh, a bee!' she cried out, as if utterly charmed. 'But where is the famous Gruyère cheese museum I read about? What could be more Swiss than going to the cheese museum!'

'It's that red building just there,' Gabriel said, pointing. 'Follow me.'

They entered in reverent silence, somewhat overwhelmed by the waves of scent.

Anita wrinkled her nose. 'Well, it certainly smells like cheese,' she said. 'Ugh!'

'Our most ancestral smell. Come on,' said Gabriel. 'Let's take a tour.'

Anita consulted a stack of leaflets. 'Which language would you like?' she teased. 'Arabic? Chinese? Romanian?'

Gabriel opened his mouth to comment on how Switzerland was too small a country to be overtaken by hordes of international tourists – but then bit the words back. After all, what was wrong with a little globalisation?

As they walked towards the staircase, the sound of cowbells and mooing could be heard emanating from small speakers overhead. 'What *is* that noise? Are there real cows in here?' she asked, slightly fearful.

Gabriel frowned. A moment later, the soundtrack changed to a burbling mountain stream. 'I think it's just a tape,' he said, rolling his eyes. 'It looks like this experience may be... interactive,' he added with some trepidation, eyeing the huge billboards on the walls, showing pictures of cheese.

Shortly afterwards, sure enough, their nostrils were assaulted with a variety of strange smells: hay, flowers, and something suspiciously milk-like. Noticing Gabriel's expression, Anita began to laugh.

'Come on,' she said. 'Let's go watch how they make the cheese. Then we can get out of this strange place and go eat some.'

'I'm not sure I want to anymore,' Gabriel said grimly, following Anita blindly through the museum's labyrinth. 'This is too modern for me. I'm a traditional man. I didn't expect all this. I thought we would just see some cows, and maybe some big stirring th... Ah.'

They had arrived in front of a series of huge copper vats, where mechanical hands were stirring milk. All the different stages were visible, right the way through to drying and storage. 'Oh,' said Gabriel. 'Yes, this is the sort of thing I was expecting.' They looked up in awe at the shelves and shelves of huge, round cheeses.

'It's like a bank of cheese,' he added, quite impressed.

'How much do those things weigh?' Anita asked.

'Probably ten kilos,' he said. 'I don't know, really, why this isn't worth more than gold. Sometimes…' He paused, trying to find a way to voice his sudden frustration. 'Sometimes I just yearn for a simpler life. When I think of all this cheese, of the walk we took this morning, of the flowers by the fountain, I find myself longing to get away from my life in Geneva.'

Anita made a strange face. 'I'm sure you'd miss it,' she joked awkwardly, 'once you were living in poverty.'

Gabriel wasn't really paying attention. 'I mean, some days I truly hate it, this culture of accumulation. Money, money, money… Look how simple this is!' He gestured wildly at the shelves of cheese. 'You take milk from a cow, and make it into these delicious golden wheels. In real life, isn't that worth more than gold? Something to feed a child, or a… beautiful woman,' he stammered. 'All from the teat of a cow.'

Anita burst out laughing. Then, catching sight of Gabriel's bewildered face, she rearranged her expression into something more sober. 'I understand,' she said. 'You're… this cheese is truly inspiring. So much so that I think I want to taste some.'

Gabriel brightened. 'I'm sure I saw a sign earlier pointing towards a tasting room,' he said.

Sure enough, leaving the golden wheels of gruyère behind, they found that the next room contained a series of plates laid out on several tables, the whole space kept at a lower temperature than the rest of the museum.

'They taste so different!' Anita exclaimed, shivering as she munched through a few samples. 'This one is sweet, and this one is so… farmy!'

Gabriel shuddered as he swallowed his first bite. 'That one was far too strong for my taste,' said Gabriel. 'I like my cheeses mild.'

'Like your women?' Anita teased.

Gabriel coughed.

'Come on, let's go find the café,' Anita said suddenly, grabbing his hand again. 'Those samples were too small for me.'

Having made their way back through the maze of corridors to the museum's entrance, the couple eventually located a small on-site café. Gabriel spoke briefly to one of the waitresses, who, in a thick accent that reminded Gabriel of distant mountains, indicated that they could sit outside, if they desired. Thus, Anita and Gabriel found themselves huddled at a small plastic table, perusing the cheese-themed menu. A cool wind had begun to blow, sweeping up the leaves from the ground.

'Raclette, fondue, fondue, fondue,' Gabriel said. 'You'd think we Swiss would get bored of all this, wouldn't you?'

Anita giggled, wrapping her scarf more tightly around her. 'I'll never tire of Swiss cheese. Look, they have a few more experimental suggestions towards the end. Gruyère and bacon scones, candied walnut gratin, and even a pear tart with gruyère in the crust!'

Gabriel made a face. 'I take back what I said. I'll stick with the traditional stuff, myself. No Swiss person would ever eat such things.'

'I think I'd like dessert,' she replied. 'Just reading all these dishes makes me feel like I've just eaten a whole wheel of cheese. Shall we share a portion of meringues with double cream instead?'

Gabriel smiled. 'I used to love that dish as a child,' he said. 'Now, it's a little too heavy, for anything but special occasions. Of course, this *is* a special occasion,' he added hastily. Anita smiled sweetly.

When the dessert arrived, Anita dipped her spoon into the mounds of crunchy meringue and thick cream greedily. She closed her eyes. 'I think I'm in love with this place,' she said a moment later.

'Well, I hope your love doesn't have too many holes in it,' Gabriel said cheerily. 'I mean, er, like a Swiss cheese.'

Anita did not reply, but she smiled and took another spoonful of cream. 'It doesn't,' she said. As she licked her lips, Gabriel was reminded of a cat. He shivered.

———◆◆◆———

'Where would you like to go next?' Gabriel asked, as he and Anita drove out of Gruyère. Clouds had begun to gather in the sky.

'Let's go see the bears in Berne!' Anita replied, clapping her hands together.

'Oh, I have an idea,' Gabriel said, as if he hadn't heard her. 'There's the most wonderful museum in Bienne, the Maison Anker. Have you heard of Anker?'

Anita shook her head, somewhat irritably. 'I told you, I know hardly anything about Swiss art. And I said Berne, not Bienne.'

'I know,' Gabriel assured her. 'But Biel, as the Germans call it, is on the way to Berne. It would be an easy stop, and Anker is such a wonderful artist.' He bit back the words *my wife*. He could talk about the artist without mentioning her gallery, couldn't he? 'He paints the human condition, you know? Children on bridges, and suffering, still-lives of fruit and bread, and some beautiful scenes of Lake Geneva.'

'I see,' said Anita. She smoothed down the skirt of her dress.

'These beautiful, innocent-looking orphans. He's a humanist, you see,' Gabriel said, growing agitated. 'Very Swiss.'

'Does he paint the mountains?' Anita asked, her tone unreadable.

'Oh yes,' said Gabriel, enthusiastically. 'Mountains, and lakes, and families. He's just such a wonderful artist! Not like all these modern...' Gabriel looked over at Anita, who was staring out at the road. 'Do you like modern art?' he asked hesitantly.

'Some of it,' she said vaguely. Was it just in his mind, or did she look a little sad?

'I've never understood these people who paint with only three colours,' he said quite vehemently. 'I've never been able to swallow... I mean, why are people so obsessed with things that could have been painted by a three-year-old?'

Anita was silent. 'I guess it's just a matter of taste,' Gabriel concluded lamely. 'Maybe people are lacking spice in their life. Maybe...' He swallowed. 'Maybe what they really need is something like you.'

Anita perked up at this, and turned towards him with a sweet smile. 'Can we go see the bears now?' she asked.

Gabriel sighed, not unhappily. 'Of course we can, dear Anita,' he said.

Evidently satisfied, Anita settled back in her seat and closed her eyes, a small smile playing about her lips as she dozed. Gabriel stole glances at her every so often, admiring her black hair and striking brows, as they cruised along the motorway. So absorbed in her beauty was he, in fact, that he almost missed the exit for Berne, having to swerve abruptly onto the slip road and, in so doing, rousing Anita from her slumber.

Gabriel cleared his throat as she yawned and stretched. 'I have a few friends here,' he said as they descended into the centre of town. 'Let me show you where Einstein lived! Oh, and near his house, there's the most marvellous clock tower!

Anita smiled politely. 'The bears,' she said. 'I should like to see the bears.'

'I suppose they are the key attraction of the city,' Gabriel admitted. 'Alright - let us go, then, to see the famous Swiss bears!'

'Will they be scary?' Anita asked, her expression thrilled.

'I don't know,' Gabriel replied honestly. 'Maybe. I haven't seen them since I was little. My father is very fond of bears, you know. He's into woodcarving these days, you see, in his retirement. He made this ridiculous sort of wooden statue of a bear to hang coats on and tried to give it to me!'

'How wonderfully Swiss!' Anita exclaimed.

'Did you know that Swiss bears have very fine heads?' Gabriel asked, smiling a little. 'My father taught me that. Something about the shape of the skulls. The bears in the mountains here are famously big and brown, with incredibly soft fur. Back in the old days, people used to make fur coats out of them, to go out hiking in the snow. They also made wonderful, thick rugs. You'll come across them in expensive chalets.'

'Oh, how sad!' Anita cried out. 'Though I'm sure a bearskin rug would be just wonderful... Maybe one day we could lie together in front of a fireplace on one, just you and me. On the wooden floor in your chalet, perhaps, with Mozart playing!'

'I don't...' Gabriel blushed furiously. Anita giggled.

'I'm teasing,' she said.

They drove on in silence for a time. Eventually, Gabriel pulled into a parking space and stilled the ignition. 'We can walk from here,' he said, his embarrassment subsiding. The blue sky was struggling to widen the spaces between the grey clouds, and Anita pulled her coat tight around her as they climbed out of the car.

The trees whistled in the wind, and Gabriel put his arm around Anita's shoulder. At the top of a winding path through a park, they found a sign with the city's crest, of a black bear on a red and yellow background.

'Look at it, sticking its red tongue out!' Anita exclaimed.

'They must be near here,' Gabriel mused, and sure enough, around fifty metres away, they spotted several children pressed up against a guard railing.

'They're throwing bread at them!' Anita said in delight, quickening her pace.

'So they are,' Gabriel replied, taking her hand. 'Well, let's go see these great Swiss bears!'

They looked down into the pit, where one distinctly bedraggled-looking bear was snoozing. The other was pacing back and forth, in front of a stonewall, pawing at the mossy ground. They looked, Gabriel realised, rather miserable.

'Oh,' said Anita.

The couple were suddenly startled by a commotion nearby. A man, shouting in German, was running down the path towards them.

'What's going on?' Anita asked.

'Those kids are being shouted at,' Gabriel realised. 'I guess we're not allowed to feed the bears.'

The frightened children began to run as well, and disappeared into a park nearby. Their hunks of bread lay in the pen, ignored by the sleepy animals.

'Excuse me,' Gabriel said to the policemen. 'Is there a gift shop where I could buy a pamphlet about Swiss bears? I'd like to give it as a gift to my friend here. She is from abroad, and very interested.'

The man raised an eyebrow. 'Swiss bears?' he repeated, sternly. 'Is this a joke?'

Gabriel frowned. 'What do you mean?'

'There are no more bears left in Switzerland, sir,' the policeman answered. 'There haven't been for decades, at least not wild ones. The last Swiss bear was shot at the turn of the century.'

'That's not possible,' Gabriel stammered. 'I mean, what about these ones?' He gestured at the pit.

'We imported those from China some years back,' the policeman answered, his tone softening.

'Oh God,' Gabriel said, reddening as he realised his mistake. 'I'm so sorry!'

'Well,' the policeman said, embarrassed in turn, 'I mean, I'm sure there is reading material about Swiss bears to be found somewhere. There were once bears in the mountains, it is true.'

'Were they dangerous?' Anita asked.

'Sometimes, no doubt,' the policeman replied. 'That is why they were shot.'

'Oh!' said Anita.

'I wouldn't recommend jumping down there with them,' he added.

Gabriel frowned. Was the man trying to make a joke? 'Well, thank you and good day,' he said pointedly.

The policeman nodded and walked off. Anita looked down over the railing.

'They look very sleepy,' she said dubiously. 'I bet I could jump down there and be just fine.'

'Maybe they're jet-lagged,' Gabriel said bitterly.

'Come on,' Anita said gently, 'it doesn't matter!'

'They're the laziest bears I've ever seen,' Gabriel continued, defensive and embarrassed. 'I don't know how we could have thought they were Swiss. They're like... like clients who never check their accounts.'

'Come on, Gabriel,' Anita said, tugging on his coat. 'I'm still glad we came.'

'They're probably drugged,' said Gabriel glumly.

Anita laughed and slipped her arm through his. 'I'm getting peckish again,' she said decisively. 'Shall we go find some cake?' She indicated a cosy-looking café a little way ahead of them, beamed up at Gabriel, and then steered him firmly towards the door.

The warm atmosphere that enveloped them as they entered the café cheered Gabriel up a little, even if it did fog up his glasses. The place was bathed in golden light, and the air smelled of hot coffee and sugar. At a table next to them, a young couple were gazing hungrily into each other's eyes, lost in each other.

'I'll have a *renversé*,' Gabriel said, feeling indulgent.

'What's that?' Anita asked. Her cheeks were flushed from the warmth. 'Doesn't that mean spilled? Are you going to spill your drink, or are you going to fall over?'

Gabriel laughed. 'I suppose it does mean that,' he replied. 'It's just a milky coffee. I assume... It's probably called that because the proportion of coffee and milk is the reverse of what it usually is. It's a kid's drink, really.'

'I'll have one too,' said Anita. 'It sounds nice. Back home, I often drank milky coffee. It seems over here people only ever drink espresso.'

'Yes, we are usually in a hurry with our coffee,' Gabriel replied. 'People would probably just as happily take a caffeine pill.'

Anita laughed. 'How dreadful,' she said.

A waitress in a white frilly apron appeared and took their order, before disappearing. The couple next to them had moved to the leather *banquette* against the wall, and were now caressing each other's faces.

'It's the world that we live in,' Gabriel muttered, staring at the tabletop.

'Pardon?' said Anita.

'I mean, the caffeine pill idea,' he explained lamely. 'I suspect it's the American influence. Efficiency, effectiveness, skill, and speed... That didn't use to be how things were done. Not in Europe, anyway.'

'I thought you were open to America now,' Anita teased.

Gabriel sighed. 'Yes and no,' he said. 'There are some cultural differences that remain, no matter what.'

'Business at the bank is going well, though, isn't it?' she asked, as if hoping to lift his spirits.

Gabriel nodded. 'Who'd have thought that Von Mipatobeau would be the stage for an international banking revolution? Certainly not me, a few years ago.' He smiled wryly.

'You were always very traditional, then?' Anita asked, frowning a little. 'Very Swiss? Not too many espressos?'

'Yes, that's about right,' Gabriel replied. 'I used to only drink sparkling water in my office. As for private Swiss banking, well, it was always renowned for its locked doors, its secrecy. Now, I find myself interested in the world outside our borders, though it is still unfamiliar.' The neighbouring couple, Gabriel noted, were now kissing with lascivious abandon. 'I have guides, of course, though, at least where banking is concerned.'

'You mean you work with Americans?' Anita asked.

'Yes,' Gabriel said, 'among others. One American in particular, and one Frenchman. They are... hungry men, if you know what I mean. In another time, you might have called them conquerors. I merely follow in their footsteps.' A sad expression flashed across his face. 'Have you ever heard the folktale of the bear who drank wine?' he asked. It seemed fun to use the story again.

Anita shook her head. 'Tell me!' she said.

'I suppose it's appropriate, after our little misadventure... In short, the bear drinks wine from a trough, thinking it's honey. He pauses, when he realises he was wrong, but it's too late: he knows he likes it. He can't forget the knowledge, or go back to a life of honey. He drinks a little more. It's not honey, but it's delicious. And lo and behold, slowly, the bear becomes a drunk.'

Anita giggled. 'Maybe the bears in the pit were drunk rather than drugged,' she said.

'It's a cautionary tale,' Gabriel continued as if she hadn't spoken. 'I think of it from time to time.'

'What does it mean?' Anita asked. 'Don't be a drunk?'

Gabriel laughed. 'Something like that. It's a warning that one should always pay attention, be careful. This high-stakes banking, for example – it's thrilling, but it's dangerous too. I think... I think one might easily become addicted to the lifestyle, if one isn't careful.'

'But you will be careful,' Anita said simply. 'You are Swiss, after all.'

Their coffees arrived, two glass cups brimming with milky liquid. Anita emptied a sachet of sugar into hers. Gabriel had to wipe his glasses again, from the steam.

'Where shall we go next, then?' he asked, feeling he had turned the mood a little toward melancholy.

'On our whirlwind tour of Switzerland?' Anita joked. 'I don't know. Aren't you the tour guide?'

'Well, yes, but you are my guest.'

Anita sipped her coffee slowly, considering. 'Maybe we could go on a boat,' she said.

'OK,' said Gabriel. 'I can work with that. Have you ever been to Lucerne?'

'I haven't.' There was a silence. The door of the café slammed shut with a sound of little bells as the amorous young couple vanished into the street. 'Gabriel,' Anita said at last, her voice low and soft, 'are you... Is this OK?' She looked up at him, her dark eyes full of feeling.

'I don't know what you mean,' he replied, looking down at his coffee. His heart rate accelerated slightly.

'I mean, we will travel together tomorrow again, won't we? And sometime again after that?'

'I should like that, yes.' Words seemed to be coming to his mind more slowly than usual.

'You will not be missed?' she said carefully. This time, she did not meet his eyes.

Gabriel took a drink from his cup. 'I have a meeting in Zurich early tomorrow morning,' he said. 'After that, no-one will be tracking my movements. I won't have to be back in Geneva till the evening.'

Anita smiled slowly, her cheeks crimson. 'Good,' she said.

Gabriel cleared his throat. 'What about La Chaux-de-Fonds?' he suggested. 'To end today's tour, I mean. I've always loved Art Nouveau, and there are plenty of watch factories to visit there.'

Anita shook her head. 'You are the most Swiss man I have ever encountered,' she said. 'Watch factories? Cheese factories? Who cares how watches are made?' Her tone was tender.

Gabriel frowned, stung. 'Have you ever seen inside a watch? It's fascinating! The gears of a Rolex are nothing short of a work of art.'

'I've never understood the world's fascination with expensive watches,' she said. 'Why spend a year's salary on something you could drop behind a radiator?'

Gabriel looked horrified. 'Why would you do that?'

Anita paused. 'I guess it's just that I can't imagine ever having that much money.' She shrugged. 'I can't even afford a Swatch,' she joked lamely.

'I'll buy you a Swatch,' Gabriel said grandly, unsure of his tone. 'Then you'll understand the beauty of Switzerland. Come on, just a short stop in Chaux-de-Fonds! We don't even have to go to a museum.'

'Alright, then, Swiss man,' Anita replied. 'You're the tour guide.'

'Tomorrow, we will meet in Zurich, if that's all right. I will give you money for the train fare,' he added hastily.

Anita smiled. 'Thank you,' she said.

Gabriel signalled to the waitress.

———•◆•———

From a distance, it was hard to tell the grey skies of La Chaux-de-Fonds from the boringly symmetrical streets. Lonely smokestacks rose above the city's blocky lines, piping more faint grey into the air. They drove down a long hill through the green countryside, the Germanic forests disappearing as they neared the city limits. Tall, orange poles marked the limits of the coming snowfall: metres and metres high.

'Look!' Gabriel exclaimed. 'Watchmakers!'

Indeed, the windows of a watchmaking factory were outlined in a neon green against the darkening sky, with shadowy figures moving soberly to and fro amongst the chunky machinery.

'It doesn't look like a glamorous industry from here, I must admit,' Gabriel commented.

'Let's stop and walk around!' Anita said. Gabriel nodded.

Though evening was falling, as they wandered through the watchmaking city, Anita and Gabriel discovered bursts of colour: orange and aquamarine facades, bright green and saffron leaves, red graffiti spray-painted on the walls.

'It's very quiet here,' Anita said, uneasily.

'Yes,' Gabriel conceded. 'I suppose the watchmakers tend to stay at home at the weekend, with their families.'

'So many workers live here?' Anita asked.

'Oh yes,' Gabriel replied, 'although the city has a substantial population of artists as well.' There was a silence. 'Do you know,' he said, with an expression of uneasy cheer, 'this would be a great place for you to make it, Anita. Have you ever heard of Nicholas Hayek?' Anita shook her head, nonplussed. 'Well, he's the founder of Swatch. He left Lebanon without a penny in his pocket, and made billions right here! He was famous for always wearing two of his own watches on each arm. See, Switzerland is a country of opportunity!'

'Four watches?' Anita asked, dubiously. 'What's the point of that?'

'I don't know,' Gabriel replied, a little deflated. 'I suppose you could set them to different time zones? Realistically, though, I suspect he just wanted to show off his products.'

'The watch shops are closed,' Anita said suddenly. 'You won't be able to buy the latest Patek Philippe!'

Gabriel stopped abruptly. 'I hadn't realised it would be so late,' he said. He had almost forgotten it was Saturday, and as the realisation dawned on him that there would be a chicken salad waiting for him at home... a gnawing feeling of guilt began to brew in the pit of his stomach. 'I really... I really should be heading back to Geneva.'

'I understand,' Anita said, a little too quickly. 'Don't worry. We will meet again tomorrow.' She slipped her hand into his, where it felt small and unfamiliar.

'I'll buy you a Swatch in Geneva, I promise,' Gabriel said quietly, his tone uncertain. 'You could even choose the design, there are hundreds of them.' Was this woman only a girl to be cajoled?

Anita did not reply, but squeezed his hand.

They walked on, along the long, straight streets. A few cars crawled by. The streetlights shifted slowly through their colours. Leaves fell.

Tomorrow, Gabriel thought. *And then what?*

Chapter Twenty-Six

'So?' Dieter asked jovially, stirring his coffee with abandon.

Gabriel squinted into his own cup, trying to ignore the clinking sounds and liquid spatters emanating from the other side of the table. 'Yes,' he said vaguely, without looking up.

'Gabriel,' Dieter said patiently, 'I asked you a question.'

'Oh?' Gabriel said, looking up from his coffee guiltily. The light streaming through the windows of the house in Zurich was very bright. It was too early in the morning for a friendly coffee. Both men clearly sensed this.

'You look tired,' Dieter said kindly. 'Is everything alright at home?'

'Oh yes. Quite,' Gabriel said, his eyes still on the windowpane.

'Our dear Clarice,' Dieter pressed him, 'she is well?'

'As ever,' Gabriel replied. Surely Winifred would have filled him in on the gallery's success? He had no desire to rub salt in the wound of his wife's newfound independence. Besides, talking about Clarice made him feel a little queasy.

Dieter looked at him for a long time, then began stirring his coffee again. 'I am a little perplexed,' he said, 'as to why you have come to see me.'

Gabriel started guiltily. 'I wanted to see you,' he blurted out. 'As, er, my friend.'

'Yes. I gathered that from your phone call last night. Yet you have nothing to tell me?' Dieter's tone was still extremely friendly.

The house was as full of flowers as it had been the first, and only other, time he had visited. The polished pine parquet was a little scuffed, a little darker. The signs of the presence of children had dissipated.

Gabriel gave a deep sigh. 'I'm so sorry,' he said. 'I've... not been sleeping well lately. I don't mean to be so damnably distracted.'

'I know a homeopathic doctor,' Dieter said gently. 'My wife recommended him to me. He has these little capsules, they help when I'm stressed at work.'

Gabriel shook his head. 'I'm not into that sort of thing,' he replied. Herbs and bells and Eastern music weren't going to cure him of his desire for infidelity, he thought with a discreet snort of laughter, if that was what 'homeopathic doctors' offered.

Dieter sighed.

'I didn't mean to offend,' Gabriel said. 'I just... I have an important banking meeting in half an hour, and I thought it would be nice to meet you first, but it turns out my mind is on work.' He swallowed. His mouth felt oddly dry. What need had there been, indeed, for this meeting with Dieter? Clarice would never double-check his whereabouts. She didn't give the tiniest hoot about where he was.

'I see,' Dieter said. He peered at Gabriel, as if trying to read his mind. 'Clarice called earlier,' he added conversationally. 'She asked if you were here.'

'Ah,' Gabriel said, his cheeks flushing. 'Perhaps I have forgotten something important at home and she wanted to let me know. Did she say what it was?'

'That was the strange thing,' Dieter said. 'She didn't explain why she called. She just hung up.' Dieter's glance lingered on Gabriel's face slightly longer than necessary.

'I should probably call her back,' Gabriel said, having no such intention. 'Yes, yes, I will do so after my banking meeting.'

There was a pause. Outside, in the street, a group of children ran by.

'How are things at the bank, anyway?' Dieter asked, his eyes straying to the clock above Gabriel's head.

'Fine, fine,' Gabriel said, before shaking his head. 'Sorry, Dieter. I mean, everything has been going extremely well since we started our international investments.

'Against my better judgement, you mean?' Dieter asked. He seemed to be having a little trouble maintaining his jovial façade.

'Well, no, I mean... I mean, we were aware of the risks. We explored them carefully, and decided to proceed anyway. I valued your input enormously, of course.'

Dieter shook his head. 'Right,' he said. 'Despite not having spoken to me in, what was it, years?' It seemed to Gabriel as if this was meant to be a joke, but the tone hadn't come out quite right. Dieter took a deep drink from his cup of coffee, wincing slightly.

'I mean,' Gabriel said, feeling a headache begin to gather in the back of his brain, 'I mean... I guess we are making money.'

'My coffee is cold,' Dieter said, making no move to remedy the situation.

'Have you ever been to the library in St. Gallen?' Gabriel asked, in a desperate attempt to manage an impression of friendliness.

'Many years ago,' Dieter replied, a little frostily. 'It is very beautiful. My wife loves it.'

'An...' Gabriel swallowed, having just nearly blurted out Anita's name. He coughed slightly. 'Another time,' he said, 'I should like to take my wife there.'

'I see,' Dieter said, a little more softly.

'Perhaps the four of us could go together?' Gabriel said desperately, knowing even as the words left his mouth that this would never, ever take place.

'Yes, good idea,' Dieter replied, apparently sharing Gabriel's assessment of the event's likelihood. 'Well, Gabriel, I'm sure you must get going to your bank meeting. On a Sunday morning. Would you like me to walk with you to... which bank was it?'

'Oh! I, er, we're meeting in a café,' Gabriel said, feeling sweat beginning to drip down the back of his neck. 'The... international client and I, we are... it is a private meeting,' he added somewhat wildly. 'I know the café. I can walk myself,' he concluded. 'I mean, I have my car parked just outside.'

'Very well,' Dieter said, standing up slowly.

There was a sound of footsteps, and a teenage boy appeared on the stairs, rubbing bleary eyes.

'Heiner!' Dieter said warmly. 'You may not remember Gabriel. It's been a long time since we've seen him.'

Gabriel blinked, trying to reconcile his memories of a small blonde child with this messy-haired teenager. Was that a piercing in his left eyebrow?

'Hi,' Heiner said, shrugging. 'Sorry, I must have been pretty little. *Vati*, can you drive me to the cooperative later? I need to pick up some art supplies.'

'Of course,' Dieter said. 'There's freshly baked bread for breakfast in the kitchen.'

Gabriel felt a pang of hunger, having been offered no such delights. 'The cooperative?' he asked Dieter. He tried to make the question sound like it carried a sort of complicity, but really he betrayed nothing but dismay and confusion.

Dieter gave a permissive shrug. 'An artist's association my son has become involved with. Some of the work they produce is quite interesting. Winifred thinks a few of them might be ready for consideration by Clarice.'

'Right,' Gabriel said, somewhat horrified to think of his wife dealing modern artworks drawn by young Swiss-German punks. 'I'll let her know.'

'I'm sure Winifred has already,' Dieter said, showing him to the door.

'Well, thank you for the coffee,' Gabriel said, pausing in the doorway.

'You haven't forgotten your briefcase?' Dieter asked.

'Oh, I left it... in my car,' Gabriel replied, gesturing vaguely down the street.

'Have a nice day,' Dieter said. 'Enjoy your meeting.' The door closed slowly.

Gabriel gave a sigh of relief and began to walk down the road. Once inside his car, he sat in silence for a time, clearing his mind of the awkward encounter with his old friend. Had they really ever even been friends? Would they be able to maintain the charade after that morning? It didn't matter, he told himself. It didn't matter anymore.

It was a short drive to the train station, and Anita would be waiting outside in the cold morning light. And all at once there she was, wearing a red dress, and stockings, he noticed at once, loosely wrapped in a grey wool coat and scarf. Gabriel slowed the car and waved. She looked stunning, Gabriel observed, as she began to walk towards him. Anita opened the door.

'Hello,' Gabriel said, reaching out a hand to shake hers, which was awkward at such close quarters.

Anita giggled, kneeling on the passenger seat, and kissed him on the cheek. 'Hello, friend,' she said, sitting down and buckling her seatbelt. 'Are you ready to be my tour guide again?'

'Yes,' said Gabriel. 'Shall we drive to St. Gallen first? It's only an hour away, and you absolutely must visit the ancient library there. Then you can decide which lake you would like to see.'

'Alright.' Anita settled into her seat, leaning her head against the car window and readjusting her scarf. 'Tell me about St. Gallen,' she said.

Gabriel smiled with something like pride at his protégée as he pulled out onto the highway. 'Well, let's see.' He turned the heating up in the car slightly. 'First, make sure you have your geographical bearings: we're heading right up to the north-eastern edge of Switzerland, close to the borders of Germany and Austria. We'll be close to Lake Constance as well, which is where my parents now live. Now, St Gallen was a medieval hermitage,' he continued hurriedly. 'The monks founded the abbey, which is now a UNESCO-classified site. Some of the books in the library there date back to the ninth century.'

He glanced over at Anita, whose eyes were half-closed, with a dreamy smile. 'Go on,' she said.

'I remember reading somewhere,' Gabriel continued, 'that the city was built on extremely soft, unstable ground. Thus, many of the buildings are supported by special foundations.'

'Just like Venice?' Anita murmured sleepily.

'Well, perhaps not quite as romantic.' Gabriel's stomach, without warning, gave a loud grumble. 'I'm terribly sorry,' he said, blushing. 'I had to leave the house quite early.'

'So did I.' Anita giggled. 'Perhaps our illustrious tour guide would like to stop for some croissants and coffee before our library visit?'

'Yes,' Gabriel replied, smiling, 'that might be wise.'

The couple were still brushing almond flakes and powdered sugar from their coats and faces, when they arrived in front of the abbey's impressive façade. Across the bright green lawn, two gothic towers pointed straight up at the sun, decorated with colourful clock faces. It was quite breathtaking.

'How beautiful!' Anita said.

'It is impressive, isn't it,' Gabriel added, nodding happily. 'I haven't been here in years. Come on, let's go find the library.'

It didn't take long: ten or fifteen minutes later, they were padding up to the main door with a small group of early-rising tourists. Inside the abbey, the atmosphere was hushed. They opened the oak door into the library, and were still for a moment, overcome. Marble pillars, curlicues of gilding, carved balustrades: the whole room shone the rich colour of stained, waxed oak.

Anita gasped. 'There are so many books!' she exclaimed. So there were: leather-bound, painted with gilding, crumbling almost black, the books were neatly stacked side by side, cabinets and cabinets full. 'What a lot of reading the monks must have done.'

'Just look at the parquet,' Gabriel sighed. 'So intricate! So many types of wood!' Such simple beauty, he thought to himself, the interlocking of pale golden pine with oak the colour of burnt sugar in patterns of diamonds and crosses.

Anita smiled softly, a little indulgently. 'Are we allowed to look at the books?' she asked.

'A few of them,' Gabriel replied. 'Let me see if I can find something interesting.' He walked to a glass cabinet, where open manuscripts were on display. 'Well, here's a biology book,' he said.

Anita giggled, before clapping a hand over her mouth. Charmed, Gabriel smiled. 'Look,' he said, leaning close to the illuminated case, 'how strangely they imagined the bones of the body in the Middle Ages!'

They stared for a moment at the strange illustration. 'Look at the hips!' Anita said.

'Bizarre, isn't it,' said Gabriel, a little disturbed. They walked on to another volume.

'What an interesting diagram of the hand,' Anita said, taking his in her slender fingers. 'What is the girdle of Venus?' she asked, reading from the page.

Gabriel found himself blushing, not looking at their clasped hands. 'It's the top of the palm,' he explained, squinting at the fine print of the explanation. 'It says here that the denomination has persisted in the fields of palmistry. Palm-reading, that is.'

'Perhaps it has... romantic connotations,' Anita added helpfully, squeezing gently. How was her hand so warm in this cold autumn weather? His heart was pounding.

'It's a load of nonsense, of course,' Gabriel said, a little more harshly than he had intended, his chest still heaving.

'Yes, of course,' Anita said quietly, letting go of his hand. There was a pause. 'It says here also,' she read from one of the cases, 'that blood was once thought to flow back and forth from the heart, like a tide...'

'When now we know it is a cycle,' Gabriel finished her sentence. His hand hung limply by his side. Why hadn't he taken hers again?

'Yes,' Anita said. 'They believed the impulses of the heart could be read in the hand. Don't you think... I feel like I can understand how and why they thought that.' She swallowed.

'So!' Gabriel said, a little too loudly. He straightened his posture and took a purposeful step back. 'Shall we go see the dwarves of Appenzell next?'

Anita frowned. 'What?'

'The dwarves in the nearby Alps! They're extremely Swiss, very nationalistic... I mean, they're dwarves. I don't know if you're interested in dwarves.'

Anita was quiet, her face unreadable. Was that a hint of disdain curling at the edge of her lips? Or was it just neutral disinterest? Gabriel realised with a start that he cared what this woman thought. 'What about Neuchâtel? No, of course, we were there yesterday. Or, or,' he said a little desperately, 'we could go to St Moritz! But no, that won't do. It's completely the wrong time of year to go there. You have to visit at the height of the ski season, when the snow is pristine. That's when Sotheby's have their jewellery auctions, and there are horse polo tournaments... No, in fall it would be boring.

'What about the boat?' Anita asked. She looked tired, suddenly, in the soft light of the library.

'Oh yes!' Gabriel said, relieved. 'I'd almost forgotten. Of course, if you want a boat, we'll find a boat. We can have lunch there, as well,' he added, as if coaxing a small child.

Anita was quiet, and she turned away from his slowly. 'I'm a little cold,' she said. 'Let's go back to the car.'

By the time they arrived at the shore of Lake Lucerne, the sky had cleared a little, and Anita was all smiles once more. Gabriel congratulated himself on his inspiration of turning on the radio. Not that that had any effect on the weather, of course, but women's moods were so gloriously fickle! All it took was some silly American pop song about beaches to cheer Anita up. She'd removed her coat, and her hair was lying loose down her shoulders. Without the coat, she seemed to cross and uncross her legs more than was entirely necessary, reminding Gabriel from close quarters that they were clothed in shimmering nylon.

'Time for the boat!' Gabriel said cheerily.

Anita pretended to pout. 'But there won't be any music! And it's so cold outside!'

'I promise I'll sit close and keep you warm,' Gabriel said, catching a flirtatious tone in his voice and trying not to care. 'I'll sit so close you'll be sick of me in an hour, and then we won't even be sad when we part ways this evening.'

They clambered out of the car, into the cold sunlight. Anita pulled on her coat and shook her hair free over her shoulders. 'I will be sad,' she said decisively.

Gabriel laughed.

'Will you be cross,' she added coyly, 'if I tell you I'm a little hungry again?'

Gabriel checked his watch. 'With a little luck, we can catch one of the lunchtime cruises,' he said. Without thinking, he took her hand in his and squeezed. They walked towards the shimmering shore of Lake Lucerne, and the blue-grey sky beyond. The sight of the distant mountains made Gabriel's heart soar.

A boat proved easy to find, and soon the pair found themselves venturing out onto the crystalline waters, spray blowing in their hair. The soft peaks rose sharply, as if conjured by the deep lake. Their dark green was tempered with orange and gold, this time of year.

Anita sighed happily. 'This must be so beautiful in summer,' she said.

'Don't you like the autumn leaves?' Gabriel asked, surprised.

She sighed. 'Well, maybe, but you can't swim at this time of year. Wouldn't it be nice if we could dive into the water? As for the leaves, I guess they make me melancholy. It's as if... As if they're a sort of reminder of death.'

'It's so wonderful, though, to walk amongst the colours this time of year, and the smell of falling leaves. Just look at the snow sprinkled on the Alps beyond! Isn't the coming of winter a wonderful thing, for you? I love it so.' Gabriel sighed. 'The cold, the freedom... the cheese.'

Anita laughed, but then her expression grew more sober. 'I think I understand why you feel this,' she said slowly. 'Peru also has mountains like these, and I have known men who were drawn to them in this way. Not that I understand why, but this is to say it is not only the Swiss who have this obsession.' She smiled, a little sadly. 'A friend of my mother's, he liked to climb, you know? He... fell in a snowstorm, a blizzard, is that how you say?' Gabriel nodded. 'They never found the body.'

Gabriel took her hand and squeezed it again. 'I'm so sorry,' he said. He paused. 'For what it's worth, what draws me to the mountains is not the danger. I like the peace, the calm of their beauty. It's like a sort of magnificent... neutrality.'

Anita's eyes sparkled. 'Neutrality?' she repeated, amused. 'What a Swiss idea to like!'

Gabriel shrugged. 'There is a certain pleasure in feeling insignificant,' he said.

'I beg to differ,' Anita said, moving closer.

Gabriel swallowed, his smile a little crooked. 'Shall we find some lunch?' he asked. One last time, he glanced up at the mountains.

They wandered down the boat's deck until they found an entrance to a small restaurant area, walled off by three panes of glass. Inside, the tables were laid with white linen, and soft music played. Gabriel smiled at Anita's obvious delight.

'This looks perfect,' he said. 'But are you sure we won't be too cold outside? I think there's another restaurant below deck.'

'Oh no,' Anita said. 'Let's stay here, please! This will be lovely, just the two of us.'

Indeed, most of the other tourists seemed to have decided the area looked too windy, and the pair found themselves alone. Gabriel wasn't sure why this felt like such a relief. They sat down at a corner table, next to a potted flowering vine, and, leaving her coat on, Anita grabbed the menu hungrily.

'Ooh!' she said. 'They have so much fish! Big fish, little fish, extremely expensive fish... What do you recommend?'

'This time,' Gabriel said, shivering a little, 'I might suggest you try the *fillet de perche*. We had *omble chevalier* last time, didn't we?'

'Fillet de perche it is.' Anita nodded seriously. 'With fries again, please. I trust your judgement, Mr Swiss Man,' she said.

Gabriel shook his head, almost playfully. A few dark clouds were blowing in from the East. 'Now, now,' he replied, 'am I really just Mr Swiss Man to you?'

Anita lowered her eyelashes becomingly. 'No,' she said, her voice low. 'You are much more than that.'

Gabriel felt his heart rate begin to accelerate again. 'I mean,' he said as jovially as he could, 'I don't know how much value the Swiss nationality really has, if I'm honest. We are all French originally, in any case. We just ran away for religious reasons! You're lucky you don't have that sort of thing in your history.'

Anita frowned a little. 'What, you think I'm some sort of fire-worshipper? Do you imagine me naked, singing songs to the moon, or practising human sacrifices in the Pâquis?' The disdain in her voice was as sudden as it was cutting.

'No, no,' Gabriel said hastily. How easily he seemed to upset her! 'I don't think that at all. Are you...Catholic, then? We've never talked about religion.'

Mollified, Anita nodded. 'Yes, most of us were converted by missionaries a good four hundred years ago. A terrible shame,' she added, a smile creeping back. 'Human sacrifice seems like a lot of fun.'

'Catholicism is quite foreign enough for me,' Gabriel joked. 'I'm so used to the sombre prudishness of Calvinism, even a little glimmer of sin seems as bad as human sacrifice!'

Anita laughed. 'You mean if there is gold on the altar, or stained glass in the windows, you are going to hell?'

Gabriel shrugged. 'I mean that as far as I can tell, Catholicism is a little more forgiving.'

Anita narrowed her eyes, as if gauging his tone. 'I understand now,' she said, deciding to joke. 'You like me because I'm a Catholic, just like your ancestors!'

'No, no,' Gabriel said again, struggling a little. 'I love our friendship for other reasons! Many other reasons.'

The word 'love' hung in the air between them for a moment. The flowers on the vine moved softly in the wind.

'Time to order our fish!' Gabriel said. Slightly desperately, he motioned over a waiter. Anita sighed deeply.

'You're sure you're not cold?' he asked. If he caught pneumonia out here, it would prove a little difficult to explain to his wife.

Anita shook her head but did not reply. 'I don't know how forgiving Catholicism really is,' she said, a little mournfully. 'My father certainly didn't think so.'

'Your father?' Gabriel asked. 'I don't think you've mentioned him before.'

'I didn't know him well,' Anita said. 'He died when I was little.'

'I'm sorry,' Gabriel said quickly.

Anita shrugged. 'He was very Catholic,' she said, 'and not very kind. Certainly not very forgiving. He would not be proud of me for coming over here.' She looked down at her menu, her expression dark and unreadable.

'My family is very traditional too,' Gabriel said.

Anita did not reply.

'Well, I'm glad you're here,' he added very quietly.

A ghost of a smile appeared on Anita's face.

Still, the couple were relieved when the fish arrived. Above, the clouds had gathered into a solid mass, and a cooler wind was blowing, bringing with it droplets of lake water. Anita didn't seem to mind. 'Look at them swimming in their little puddle of butter sauce,' she said, poking the fillets with a fork tine. 'And the little bundle of chips!'

'I highly recommend a squeeze of fresh lemon,' Gabriel said, pulling his coat collar shut.

A fish-filled silence followed, and Gabriel found himself sighing.

'Anita,' he said tentatively, 'I'm sorry I keep cutting you off when you say kind things to me. It is difficult... I appreciate your friendship enormously.' He took a deep breath. 'I think you're kind, innocent, and funny. You have a calming influence on me. I can't tell you how much that is worth, the fact that I feel at peace in your presence.'

Anita was very still, and said nothing for a time. A fine mist was clinging to her eyelashes and to the grey wool of her coat.

'Thank you. I will not ask more than friendship of you,' she said finally, 'not unless you want... No, I will not ask more.'

'I can't,' Gabriel began earnestly, but Anita held out a hand to stop him.

'I know,' she said softly.

'It's getting cold,' Gabriel added. 'Shall we go downstairs?'

Anita nodded. In earnest, now, a cold wind began to blow. She slipped her hand into his and held it tight.

Chapter Twenty-Seven

'You're in a good mood, Gabe!' Dick exclaimed, punching him on the back.

Gabriel smiled, looking up to meet the broker's eyes. 'Yes,' he said, 'I am.'

Dick laughed, taking a drink from his champagne flute. 'Keep your secrets, then,' he said. 'I know a man in love when I see one.'

Gabriel shook his head. 'Not everybody thinks with what's in their trousers,' he said.

'Yeah, right,' said Dick, sarcasm dripping from his voice. 'The Swiss man is a man of the mind.'

And the heart. Gabriel leaned on the railing, looking out over the lights that glowed in the evening light. He repressed the instinctive thought, sharply, and focussed on the clouds scudded softly across the blue-grey sky. 'What do you think of the view?' he asked, keeping his tone casual. 'Just here, the lake turns into a great river. Isn't our Geneva quite something to behold?'

Dick shrugged. 'You have nice fizzy wine, I'll give you that,' he said.

'It's not just natural power you're looking at. You can see most of the big Swiss banks from here, too,' Gabriel said. 'Along Rue de la Corraterie, down from the Old Town towards the ancient fortifications, then along Rue du Rhône, and towards the Bel-Air area, overlooking the lake.'

'Of course,' Dick said, 'you'll be telling me the most beautiful of them all is the one on whose balcony we're standing.'

'On the balcony of which,' corrected Gabriel, 'and yes.' Noticing Dick's slight frown, he hastily added: 'It's strange, though, this clustering together of all the biggest banks. It's as if they're drawn to water, just like they're drawn to money. They're just like a bunch of goats.'

The ruse worked: Dick gave a raucous laugh and turned away from the balcony. 'Garçon!' he said to the maître d' hovering by the doorway. 'More champagne for the goats!'

Gabriel stood for a moment longer, watching the indigo, red and gold lettering flashing on, the scattered lights reflecting in the surface of the lake. Banks, financial companies, brokerages by the hundreds, all advertised in those pure waters, along with the high fashion lines and jewellery companies. For some reason, all at once it made Gabriel rather sad. He turned back to the guests.

Gérard, wearing a bright red silk scarf over his grey suit, was engaged in some sort of heated discussion with two of Von Mipatobeau's younger partners. What were their names? Jean-Charles? No, Pierre-Yves, and the other one was Guillaume. It was a little hard to keep track of the new blood. He wasn't entirely sure why they had even been invited to this meeting. Still, Gabriel supposed it was his duty to keep in touch with the lower ranking officials. He let a smile play around the edges of his lips. Just because he was due a million-franc bonus in time for Christmas didn't mean he should lose track of the realities of banking.

Gabriel adjusted his tie and walked over to the other men.

'It just doesn't sound stable to me, Monsieur Maigréville, with all due respect,' Pierre-Yves was saying earnestly. 'It goes against everything we were taught.'

Gérard was sniggering. 'Yes, but we make the rules that future generations will be following. Don't you want to be a part of that movement?'

'Gentlemen,' Gabriel said, 'I trust your glasses are full?'

Pierre-Yves and Guillaume, startled, smiled and nodded quickly, like a pair of lapdogs with their tongues out. Gabriel gave an ingratiating smile. 'Gérard, I trust you're not upsetting my colleagues?'

'Oh no,' Gérard replied, playing with the threads of his scarf. 'I was merely giving them a little lesson in reality.'

Before Pierre-Yves could leap back into the argument, Gabriel said: 'I think this reality can always be improved by a little touch of our two good friends, Moët et Chandon.'

The men laughed lightly. Dick wandered back over. 'What merriment am I missing here?' he asked.

'It seems you have beaten us to the champagne,' Gérard said amiably, eyeing up his full flute.

The maître d', as if on cue, arrived and refilled everyone's glasses.

'Have you noticed we are on the seventh floor?' Gabriel asked. 'It's one of the best views in Geneva, this. We're lucky the weather held.'

'Is it always this warm in October?' Dick asked. 'Back home, they'll be salting the sidewalks and readying the snow ploughs!'

'Ah, but Switzerland has four seasons, you see,' Gabriel said, 'unlike Chicago.'

'Touché,' said Dick. 'My esteemed colleague has a point.'

'You can go for long walks in the mountains all the way through November, as long as the sun holds,' Gabriel said, a little dreamily. 'Then you need to get out your snowshoes.'

'Or sit down cosily in front of your TV,' Dick added.

Gérard laughed.

'We're a good six hundred kilometres south of Paris,' Gabriel said, 'and seven hundred south of London. It's no surprise, really, that it should be freezing in Chicago! Besides, I mean no disrespect. I was there in the winter, and the city had its charms.'

Dick smiled. 'Young bankers,' he said, turning to Pierre-Yves and Guillaume, 'please forgive me for forgetting your names.' The men hastened to introduce themselves. 'Remind me to give you my card at the end of the evening. Any colleague of Gabe's is a colleague of mine. You'll always be welcome in Chicago.'

'Just wait for the summer,' Gabriel added with a wink.

'*Bonsoir!*' A chorus of feminine voices interrupted them. All four men turned at once, to see the three beautiful receptionists emerging from the elevator.

'Ah, Samantha!' Gabriel said, to the eldest of the trio. His mind a little fuzzy from the champagne, he felt almost nostalgic, remembering when each of them had joined the company: Ségolène, an incredibly educated Parisian blonde, four years before, and the brunette – what was her name? Léa, that was it – she was a little unpredictable, but barely a day over eighteen. Then there was Samantha, now the head of the team, short-haired, sharply suited and professional. What a beauty she had been in the 1980s! He was lucky to work with such women.

'Which one of you mademoiselles is mine?' Dick crowed, swaggering forward.

Samantha sighed. 'Call me madame, please,' she said, not unkindly.

Of course! Some days Gabriel forgot how quickly things changed. 'I'm afraid Madame is already spoken for,' he said. 'She had the ill fortune of falling prey to the charms of one of our best clients, Mr Schön.'

Samantha smiled affectionately.

'Oh, what a terrible shame!' Dick said. 'Is there no chance of remedying this?'

'I'm afraid I was married seven years ago,' she said.

'Well. I've always had a weakness for the exoticism of redheads, but let's see what else is on offer.'

Gabriel tried to hide the wave of repulsion that washed over him at this chauvinist display. 'Why don't we all walk together?' he said. 'I'm sure the maître d' will be ready to serve dinner any minute.'

'What about our friend Gérard?' Dick continued, unperturbed. 'I mean, don't you know the French need company?' He gave an outrageous wink.

'No, no,' Gérard said mournfully. 'I have no interest even in such beauties as these. My heart has been bruised too many times.' It was difficult to tell if he spoke in earnest: he certainly seemed to.

'But,' Léa piped up, 'we were only sent up to escort you to dinner!'

Pierre-Yves winked at her, not very subtly, and the girl blushed furiously. This did not go unnoticed by Dick.

'What, they're all taken?' he said, his face an aggrieved mask. 'Ah, Switzerland, how you break my heart! I'll have to drown my sorrows in more champagne.'

'Come, now,' Gérard said, 'we're all getting hungry.'

Ségolène repressed a smile, and brought over the bottle of champagne. 'Now follow me, sir,' she said, taking Dick's arm. 'You seem like a man with a preference for blondes,' she added coyly.

'Actually,' Dick replied, 'I've a preference for sets of three receptionists. But I'll settle for a beauty such as yourself.'

Almost imperceptibly, Ségolène rolled her eyes, before leaning into him with a sweet smile. 'You Americans,' she said. 'You're always so brash.'

As they entered the dining room, two maître d' in long, ink-black tailcoats were waiting by the door. Gabriel noted their expensive white bow ties and waistcoats with pleasure. It was good to see that people still made an effort in certain circles. The five men slotted wordlessly into their seats. The receptionists had disappeared without a word. Gabriel's gaze swept down the length of the massive Napoleon III mahogany table, made to seat twenty-four people. In perfect secrecy, too: not a word uttered in this room could be heard in the corridor outside, and guests could be ushered in without passing through the bank's entrance. Von Mipatobeau had always had a wonderfully Swiss sense of discretion, Gabriel thought with satisfaction. It was good to see that modernity hadn't ruined everything.

There was a commotion at the doorway. 'Monsieur,' Léa's voice was heard, apologetically, 'I'm so sorry, I couldn't stop him.'

Gabriel whirled around in his seat, only to see Thomas grinning madly, his favourite embroidered waistcoat buttoned up wrong. His edelweiss tie was askew. 'Oh,' said Gabriel. 'Come in, Thomas. Léa, that's quite alright. Thomas *is* invited to our private bank dinner, he is simply a little... late.'

'Gabriel, I'm sorry, my head these days...' Thomas made a clicking sound, waving a hand by his head.

'That's quite alright,' Gabriel replied, wondering if this was true.

Dick grinned and stood up from his seat. 'Tommy, my friend!' he said, grabbing the German in a bear-hug. 'Welcome! How's your head?'

Gabriel shook his head ruefully. 'Of course, Thomas, you remember Dick and Gérard.'

Gérard nodded politely. 'It was a memorable trip indeed,' he said. Pierre-Yves and Guillaume looked at each other, then smiled.

'Gentlemen, the first course,' the maître d' announced quietly. 'A homemade pâté of duck foie gras, with orange peel, gingerbread and a thyme reduction. This will be accompanied by a local vintage of Montbazillac wine.'

A hungry, contented silence fell over the table.

'There I was, skiing freely over the virgin snow,' Thomas was saying, an intense look in his eye. 'I was alone, with the cold air whistling by and the sky powder blue, when I spied a patch of ice. Careful, I thought to myself, that will be slippery. What I hadn't realised was that it was thin, too, and covering a deep gash in the rock, leading right to the heart of the mountain itself.'

Pierre-Yves gasped, his pâté of duck foie gras lying forgotten on his plate.

'It just looked like an icy patch of snow, glistening in the winter light, but when I skied over, it gave way beneath me. Crack! Just like that, I was falling down into the pitch darkness, into the unknown. Then I hit my head against a rock, hard, and everything went black.'

'My god,' Guillaume said, as wide-eyed as his contemporary. There were gingerbread toast crumbs all over his shirt front. 'How did they find you?'

Thomas shrugged. 'To this day, I believe I was watched over by some benevolent Swiss spirit. A country knows when it is loved.'

Gabriel tried not to roll his eyes. 'Also, the police had a device that located his mobile phone signal.'

Thomas looked up with a faint smile. 'That, too.'

The second maître d' began to bustle around the table, removing the empty plates. Soon afterwards, a tureen of green liquid appeared in the centre of the table.

'What is this? When is the meat coming?' Dick asked, looking with suspicion at the porcelain bowl in front of him.

'Cream of broccoli soup,' Thomas said happily. 'My favourite!'

Gabriel shook his head. Personally, he quite enjoyed the simplicity of a savoury soup. A delicate texture, a touch of cream, a sprinkle of freshly ground pepper... And what was that, a touch of tarragon? Anise, even? Suddenly, from the depths of his soup-contemplation, Gabriel became aware of the hushed, heated discussion that was taking place next to him.

'I mean, I heard that one Swiss private bank gave twenty million dollars in profit share bonuses to each partner,' Gérard said, his voice low and intense. 'Some private banks are expanding their marketing to the Russians, the Japanese, the Arabs, and they're coming away from it all with millions.'

'I guess you guys are turning out just like our homegrown Wall Street crew,' Dick added, rather approvingly. 'I mean, our boys distribute tens of millions to each other like candy.'

'You're talking about brokers, though,' Gabriel replied, piqued.

'Ah yes,' Dick replied. 'You mean they don't have that degree of respectability that private banking conveys.' He winked.

Gabriel frowned in displeasure. He did not like being made fun of.

'Do you know,' Gérard said sadly, 'I make that kind of money for my clients every year, but I don't debit their accounts in that way. You can't have those sorts of commissions, not in France. You forget we're a far more conservative country than either the US or Switzerland.'

'That's a surprising claim from Monsieur the capitalist socialist here,' Gabriel said, still smarting from Dick's slight. 'Enlighten us.'

'You're forgetting about the Bank of France,' Gérard said, still mournfully. 'It watches over us like the church of old. Money is dirty, you see, it's anti-Catholic. We can't exaggerate about money the way some of us would like to.'

'Don't tell me you don't exaggerate,' Dick said, waggling a finger at him. 'I saw the way you were savouring that Montbazillac earlier.'

A glimmer of humour crept into Gérard's expression. 'Oh, don't get me wrong. I certainly have my small pleasures. I mean, we can spend as much as we like on three-thousand dollar bottles of Puligny Montrachet or Château Margaux or even Cheval Blanc, but we can't *earn* as much as we like.' He shrugged. 'It is a very French paradox. If there is any talk of two-million bonuses, everybody goes up the wall, and we get the satirical newspapers writing about us, and the government breathing down our neck. So even if I make thirty million for my shareholders, I don't see any of it.'

'How tragic,' said Dick, his tone unreadable. 'Have some more wine.'

The soup plates were removed, Gérard's untouched, Thomas's wiped sparkling clean.

An expectant silence fell, as the main course was awaited. 'May I present a fillet mignon of Simmental beef,' the maître d' said at last, as the waiters set down four beautiful plates of red meat. 'Served with salt butter, fresh pea shoots and baked rosemary potatoes.'

'Swiss beef,' Thomas said with satisfaction.

'I was near Simmental just a few weeks back,' Gabriel said, the memory of Anita hitting him in a sudden pang. 'It's a beautiful region.'

'Tell me, then,' Dick said, 'did you eat tiny European steaks?'

Gabriel frowned, confused.

'Don't you remember your experience in Chicago?'

'Oh yes,' Gabriel replied, shaking his head. 'In America, I had not understood one was meant to consume the entire... beef in one meal.'

Thomas laughed merrily, and began sawing into his piece of steak. 'How strange everything is, outside Switzerland,' he said. 'I'm not sure I'd like to live there.'

Gabriel gave a tolerant smile. The thought reminded him of his previous self, an incarnation of Gabriel de Puritigny he suspected was disappearing further and further into the past.

'I mean, what if they don't have gruyère?' Thomas continued, laughing a little at what seemed a fantastical thought. 'What if I don't understand what people are saying?'

A delicate cough interrupted him. 'The wine that we are serving alongside this course is something quite special.' The maître d' delicately poured ruby liquid from a crystal carafe into Gabriel's glass. 'This is a Romanée-Conti from 1972. A very good year.'

'Oh God, yes!' Gérard held out his glass with a reverent expression on his face. 'To call that *un bon cru* would be an understatement.'

Dick frowned curiously at Thomas. 'You really mean you wouldn't like to see America? We have really beautiful...'

'Landscapes?' Gabriel suggested.

'Women,' said Dick, a nasty grin appearing on his face.

Thomas shrugged. 'I would happily see other places in the world, but Switzerland is my home. It is where my heart is. I am used to certain ways of doing things.'

'What about your bank's successful international investments?' Dick asked, his smile growing a little sly.

Gérard was silent, concentrating on his wine with a serious expression. He held the glass up to the light and swirled the liquid slowly, like a scientist making an important discovery.

'Again,' Thomas said, 'I understand that we've had success in this way. I have enjoyed working with people from abroad. But I'm still not sure it's exactly better than what Von Mipatobeau was doing before.'

There was a tense silence. Thomas continued chewing his beef, unaware of the glances exchanged.

'I understand where he's coming from,' Guillaume suddenly piped up. 'We aren't educated enough in these new products, these new trade systems. Foreign ways are... foreign to us. We may be profiting from them in the short term, but we have no experience; no way to know if they are the best choice in the long run.'

Gérard sighed. 'Not this again,' he said. 'Weren't you listening to me on the balcony?'

Dick let out a penetrating shout of laughter. His steak was already half gone. 'You Europeans!' he said. 'You're so worried about everything. Can't you just relax and enjoy yourselves for a couple of years? Look at the money rolling in! What does it matter?'

'It matters a great deal,' Guillaume said quietly.

'We are pioneers,' Gabriel said suddenly, unexpectedly, surprising even himself. 'There is always a risk in changing the way things have been approached. One must take responsibility, in these contexts, but one must not be afraid. You young bankers are used to doing things by the textbook. When you're my age, you'll learn to make difficult decisions. I don't resent you for your doubts: it would be unreasonable not to doubt undertakings into the unknown. However, I trust the bank's current projects. I trust our international partners. They have brought us nothing but success, and we have experienced nothing but progress.'

'Some of our oldest clients left the bank,' Pierre-Yves said, a little hesitantly.

'And for every Swiss person that left, a hundred Americans and Frenchmen and Swedes and Turks came and took their place,' Dick said, loudly. 'Didn't they?'

Unwillingly, Pierre-Yves nodded.

At last, his eyes slightly glazed, Gérard set down his wine glass. 'Nothing is ever certain,' he pronounced, 'but I can tell you from the perspective of someone who became involved in this a long time before you, that it was entirely worth it. I gambled my whole career on this approach. I was shunned by many of my contemporaries. Now I make a hundred times their salary every year. Isn't that proof enough?'

'You are not afraid?' Guillaume asked, his voice full of cautious admiration.

'What does one gain from fear?' Gérard replied. 'Life is here to be enjoyed, to be lived to the full. Taste your Romanée-Conti,' he added. 'Swirl it around. Breathe deep. Take a sip. That is how life should be approached. Yes, if this fails, I will lose everything. How would my life be better if I worried about it?'

Guillaume smiled and lifted his wine glass. 'This is indeed very good wine,' he said.

Gabriel smiled, the pleased smile of a successful host. 'I'm glad you appreciate it,' he said. 'This dining room and its associated area so rarely get used.'

'I hope you don't mind us voicing these concerns here,' Pierre-Yves said. 'I know this dinner is meant to be a celebration.'

Gabriel gave a generous smile. 'Of course not,' he said. 'It's important for me to stay in touch with the concerns of the younger generations at Von Mipatobeau. Besides, your doubts aren't stopping you from celebrating our successes, are they?'

'No,' said Pierre-Yves, 'though I have moments where I wonder if I truly understand them.'

Dick gave a bright smile. 'Let me enlighten you kids,' he said. 'Do you know anything about derivatives?'

Guillaume and Pierre-Yves exchanged glances. 'Yes, of course,' said Guillaume, just as Pierre-Yves said, 'Not really.' Gérard gave a pleasant laugh, his cheeks roughly the colour of the Romanée-Conti he was sipping his third glass of.

'Derivatives,' Gabriel said, 'are financial instruments, along with equities and debt.'

'Yes, I know that,' Pierre-Yves said, blushing slightly.

'OK,' Dick said. 'So a derivative is essentially a contract; one that takes its value from the performance of an underlying asset, whether it's a stock, or a bond, or a type of currency.'

'Right,' said Guillaume.

'So let's say you're selling and buying a Put and a Call. Or you're speculating by the sale forward of a foreign exchange or a metal or a bond. Then, at the maturity date, you cash in.' Seeing the expressions of the two younger Swiss men, Dick paused. Gabriel repressed a smile. 'I mean,' Dick said, more slowly, 'You could do that with any kind of money or asset. What's key here isn't a series of technical terms. The key here is that if this operation goes well, you can pocket the profits yourself, or share with your client. If you don't want to share with a client – and I sympathise with you – well, that's fine, but if your product starts to lose value, you could put it in a client's account.'

'No, no, you can't,' Gabriel said sharply. 'We don't do that sort of thing in Switzerland.'

Dick shrugged. 'What, no dumping? OK, well then that wasn't a very good example for you honest mountain people.' Pierre-Yves narrowed his eyes. 'I mean, that's just one of the options available to you,' the American continued. 'In general, you cover your risk with various options at different maturities.'

'How do you do that?' Guillaume asked curiously. 'Isn't it dangerous?'

'Not if you follow the pricing daily,' Dick replied. 'If you keep your eyes open, there's always a way out. You could always buy back your Put or Call and limit your risk. There's no danger if you keep out of the way of a cascade of loss.'

'This is what hedge funds are for,' Gérard piped up from the background.

'OK,' Pierre-Yves said, obviously a little dazed.

Dick smiled. 'Trust me. In any case, you don't need to understand the specifics. You should just be content with the twelve per cent I'm generating for you out in Chicago. Have some more wine and just accept it.'

'Wine,' Gérard scoffed dreamily. 'This is more than just wine.'

'I'm still catching up,' Pierre-Yves said, 'and not a little worried.'

Dick gave a tolerant smile. 'We do have certain securities outstanding,' he said, 'and others on offer. In the case of many of the packaged products that we sell to our clients, once it starts to cost us, we pull back the product in the process of redemption. The client gets his money back, and this gives us a chance of protecting our revenue. The client still gets a certain amount of assured return or a stop-loss.'

Gabriel nodded vaguely, tuning out the conversation. He noticed for the first time just how many flowers had been set up in the dining room; large bouquets of orchids, roses and thick, waxy green leaves. It gave the place an exotic atmosphere that belied its business function. He was glad the room was getting some use: the bank rarely splashed out on inviting clients to dinner, and when it did, only one or two of the bank officers were ever invited. These days, Gabriel was feeling generous, though, as well as disinclined to return home to Clarice.

Guillaume was nodding in bewilderment, and Dick suddenly began to laugh. 'You Swiss men,' he said. 'You're just as white as snow. I wish we had more Swiss clients. It would be so much fun.'

Pierre-Yves laughed, then paused, then glared. 'We have always been very good at looking after people's money,' he said.

'Yes,' Dick replied, 'but you weren't that good at making them more of it.'

'Dessert!' Gabriel exclaimed, relieved, as the maître d' began discreetly to clear away the plates.

'Oh, just one more glass!' Gérard said, catching the maître d's sleeve. 'It's a dream, this wine. It's so perfect. So perfect,' he muttered.

The maître d' gave a tolerant smile. 'I will bring you another small glass,' he said.

'So what happened to those girls, anyway?' Dick asked.

Gabriel shook his head.

Conversation continued on other subjects for a time, the table splitting among smaller, friendly topics. Eventually, the plates were cleared away, and silence settled once more. It was an ingenious setup, Gabriel had to say, contemplating the room again. Swiss clients tended to be uncomfortable being seen entering the bank: they could enter from the terrace, through the back staircase, just as they had after their champagne. The room had controlled temperature and humidity, and was entirely soundproofed. Gabriel's attention wandered back to the table as the maître d' re-entered with his silver tray. Little cups of dark chocolate mousse, a warm pineapple *tarte tatin*, and tiny caramel and pistachio macaroons appeared in front of the guests.

'I guess it's Thomas' turn to be overwhelmed,' Pierre-Yves said with a smile, nodding at the German man. Indeed, Thomas's mouth had fallen open in sheer, childish delight.

Gérard sighed. 'Will there be wine with this course?'

'I think the chef mentioned a *muscat* dessert wine,' Gabriel replied. 'Something Californian.'

The maître d' appeared at his shoulder and nodded. 'Indeed, sir. This wine comes from a very late harvest. The grapes are naturally very sweet.'

'Could I have a cup of warm milk?' Thomas asked.

'Of course,' the maître d' replied, his expression neutral.

Thomas smiled beatifically.

'What the hell are these? They look like tiny hamburgers,' Dick said, prodding at the macaroons.

Gabriel laughed. 'Try one. They melt in your mouth.'

'They are nothing like tiny hamburgers. They're not even savoury!' Thomas said, offended.

Gérard wrinkled his nose. 'They're really not my personal favourite,' he said. 'Far too sweet.'

'I'm sure they are, after all that red wine.' Dick bit into one and grimaced.

The maître d' reappeared and set down Thomas's milk, along with a pot of coffee. 'This is Robert Heli coffee,' he said, 'some of the best in Italy. You'll notice a delicate acidity, with a hint of cedar.'

Dick scoffed. 'I don't want any trees in my coffee,' he said.

'Not even a very small one?' Thomas asked.

Dick grinned, as if at a cheeky younger brother. 'Well, maybe,' he said. 'Just this once.'

Gabriel shook his head, enjoying his macaroon. Wasn't cedar poisonous?

'So, about those girls...' Dick said again thoughtfully, stirring his coffee.

Gabriel sighed, but it was Thomas's turn to laugh. 'I'm afraid Mr Schön beat you to the chase,' he said. 'He has many excellent ties and hats.'

'And there's no chance she'd be tempted into an affair with a suave American businessman? I could buy some new ties?'

Thomas looked thoughtful. 'Well, Mr Schön has been spending a lot of time in the Arabian Gulf this year... Maybe Samantha is lonely, gazing out the window, her auburn hair...'

A disapproving frown crossed Gabriel's face. 'Thomas,' he said, 'I know we've become very modern and everything, but discussing clients' private lives in this manner is a little unprofessional.'

Dick crowed with laughter. 'I think you'll find,' he said, 'that you yourself let that little titbit slip in the first place.'

'Oh,' said Gabriel. 'Well...'

'Don't worry,' said Thomas. 'The impulse was a noble one. You were only trying to discourage Dick. I'll tell Mr Schön about it when we next see him.'

'You'll do no such thing,' said Gabriel, blushing.

'The Arabian Gulf,' Dick said thoughtfully. 'You know, I have to admit I have a little bit of respect for this Schön character. Even if he's stolen the potential love of my life right from under my nose, there's something savvy about heading over there to do business. I've wondered about it before.'

Gabriel shrugged. 'I must admit the idea had never occurred to me. I mean, we've always dealt with civilised... Well, I mean, places close to us geographically. Culturally.'

Dick laughed again. 'You guys are close, though, geographically! It's a hell of a lot closer than Chicago. I mean, this crazy oil euphoria, it's all over the Middle East. Do you know the price of oil has jumped up again recently? It's gone up another fifteen per cent in one go!'

Gabriel raised his eyebrows. 'That's a huge increase,' he said. 'But we don't trade oil.'

'Are you suggesting that these oil men, who are making incredible fortunes in oil, are going to keep all their money in their sock drawers?'

'Well,' said Gabriel, 'no.'

'I thought Muslim culture had some sort of strange ideas about banking,' Gérard said suddenly. 'This came up occasionally with our clients in Paris. We had to find... creative solutions so that no-one was doing anything against their religion, or their principles. I mean, personally I feel that if these people come over here to France, they should –'

'Bring all their money!' Thomas interrupted. Gérard paused, then made a sort of coughing noise.

'Yes,' he said. 'Of course. We have no trouble dealing with international clients. Any money is good money.'

Oblivious to the dynamics around him, Dick was drumming

his fingertips on the table. 'I mean, those guys must have been accumulating hundreds of millions of dollars, maybe billions. What if the price goes up? What if it's, like... fifty dollars, or more? There's no way their ideas about banking won't have evolved under the influence of those kinds of earnings.'

'It is easy to find people who speak Arabic,' Gérard said begrudgingly. 'Paris is full of Egyptians and Algerians.'

'I'd love to go to Egypt!' Thomas exclaimed, his eyes lighting up. 'Wouldn't it be fun?'

'I'm not talking about Egypt,' Dick said. 'I mean the real oil places. The Gulf. I'm thinking, you go talk business with those guys, they won't know what they're doing. There's no way they're familiar with the market, or how to invest. This is what has stopped me from following this train of thought before. But you, Gabriel, and your straightforward Swiss banking... That's got to have some appeal to them. Do you follow my drift?'

Gabriel nodded very slowly. He did not, in fact, follow Dick's 'drift' at all.

'I mean, you head over there with your Egyptian or whatever,' Dick continued excitedly, 'you eat their stuffed camel, you tell them how to make money, and then *bam*, you sell them our products. Even if that doesn't work, they'll still hand over the money to the Swiss banker. You see, there's no way they'll be willing to fly over to Chicago. Their arms would freeze right off. Cannes or Monaco, maybe, but that's complicated to organise, and expensive.'

'I think we should go there!' Thomas said again.

'Where?' said Gabriel, a little bewildered. *Eat a camel?*

'Anywhere!' said Dick. 'What are those places called, anyway? Bahrain. Qatar. Iraq?' he added, pronouncing it 'Eye-rack'. Gabriel winced. 'All those four-letter ones President George Bush didn't like, so he pummelled them with bombs.'

'We would get suntans,' Thomas said dreamily, 'and eat honey pastries.'

'This is unfamiliar territory,' Gabriel said, struggling. *Bombs? Pastries?*

'I think it's a great idea,' Guillaume said suddenly, unexpectedly. 'After all, historically we have strong ties with the Middle East. No offence to our guests, but I'm more comfortable with this than working with Americans.'

Gabriel stared at him, and Dick began to laugh again. 'I'm so confused,' Gabriel said, trying to focus, 'but I'm listening to you all. It may take some time to process this.'

'No offence,' said Dick, 'but it's not about culture. It's about cold, hard cash.'

'Hot cash,' said Thomas, tolerantly. 'It's sitting in the desert. How could it be cold?'

'You see them in Paris all the time,' Gérard added, 'these princes and sheikhs and businessmen, coming to Paris to spend their fortunes. I think it would probably be quite savvy if we can get them to put that money in our banks, instead of watching them spend it on... furs, or whatever it is.'

'Nobody wants furs in the desert,' Thomas said, frowning.

'They won't understand about hedges and derivatives and packages,' Dick said, 'but I'm sure they'd be able to comprehend the notion of putting some deposits with us. This is a job for you, Gabriel, not for me.' He sat back and drained his small glass of muscat. 'I won't lie,' he said, 'this idea didn't just come to me this evening. I've been toying with the concept for a few months. I just hadn't thought of putting it into action through you. I mean, who would think of sending mountain men into the desert!' He laughed raucously.

'Who, indeed,' said Gabriel.

'What I'm getting at is this: I actually already have a few contacts over there. Names, addresses. You could go visit them. You could be our pioneer.'

Gabriel raised an eyebrow. 'OK,' he said, 'that's a little different to turning up at an airport and just shouting at rich-looking guys.' His mind was racing. 'My wife has a friend with many contacts in that part of the world. I'm quite sure Khadija would hand over some names.'

'The returns would be out of this world,' Dick said, 'eventually. We'll coax them in with something very Swiss, two or three per cent, to start with. Then, once they're hooked, we explain they could be making twelve per cent if they invest in our products. Boom! They'll come running to us. It's worth a try, isn't it?'

'Even if it doesn't work, we'll have a great vacation,' Thomas said smoothly.

'We have to be careful,' Pierre-Yves said suddenly. The other men looked over, surprised. 'I just mean, we can't change everything about the way we do business. We're still Swiss bankers.'

'We're modern Swiss bankers,' Gabriel said. 'We can try new things. I'm willing to give this a try, as a sort of fishing trip.'

Thomas looked at him as if he'd gone mad. 'It's the desert,' he said. 'What fish?'

'Fishing for clients, I mean,' Gabriel said patiently, nodding slowly as the idea began to take shape in his mind. 'I mean, Dick is right. There could be a lot of money in this. It's unknown territory, but it could be a land of milk and honey. Metaphorically, of course,' he added hastily to Thomas.

'Mm, honey,' Thomas said dreamily.

'So when do you want to go?' Dick asked.

Gabriel straightened his shoulders. 'If Von Mipatobeau needs a pioneer, let me be that pioneer. I'll go as soon as I can.'

'I'm coming, too,' said Thomas.

'Let's go, then,' said Gabriel. He finished his glass of wine, gazing into space with an expression of determination. *A pioneer*, he thought. *A banking pioneer.*

Chapter Twenty-Eight

Beads of sweat glistened on Gabriel's brow. From the window, he watched dust blow down a hot dirt road. A filthy black goat wandered slowly by; a few ragged palms moved back and forth in the wind. In the distance, the majestic turrets of a mosque rose from the haze.

'We're not in Switzerland anymore,' Thomas whispered, wide-eyed. 'Did you see that camel, over there, by that awful white car?'

Gabriel craned his neck. 'Where?' he whispered back.

'I trust your journey was smooth?' Both men jumped a little guiltily, and looked up. The speaker was Toufan, a smooth-faced sheikh wearing a sand-coloured robe with blue trim over black leather shoes. His voice was deep and resonant, like the voice of someone accustomed to persuading people. Toufan had just returned to his office, carrying a silver tray of wet glass cups.

'Oh yes,' said Thomas, sweating profusely. From the glance he shot at the glasses of crushed ice, he looked about to lick his lips.

Gabriel shot him a look, before smiling back at Sheikh Toufan. 'Yes, of course,' he said.

Through his mind, there flashed an image of their plane landing unsteadily in the middle of a vast, swirling sandstorm. He recalled Thomas holding his hands over his mouth to keep the hot, dirty grains from flying in as they walked towards the airport, and the abrasive feeling of the wind on his cheeks, and how the waves of humid heat and jet-lag made him feel deeply nauseous.

'Very smooth,' he added. Thomas grabbed a glass full and drank it in a single gulp.

Toufan gave an unreadable smile. 'I'm glad.' He settled back into his leather armchair. 'Please, help yourself.'

Gabriel felt sweat begin to drip down the back of his neck. Their host gestured at the tray. 'They are made with fresh fruit. The ice is safe, of course.'

Gabriel gave a little bow, and chose a bright red glass. 'Thank you for sending someone from the hotel to pick us up,' he added.

'I mean,' Thomas chimed in, taking the third glass and draining it before Gabriel could intervene, 'I can't believe how many taxi drivers seemed keen to take us! It was like they were fighting over us!'

The sheikh laughed, apparently unfazed by the loss of his ice drink. 'Well done for not giving in, then,' he said. 'It is the first test of every visitor to this part of the world. Apart from the heat, of course. I trust you are not too uncomfortable?'

'Oh no,' said Gabriel, feeling as if he might faint.

'Is it always this hot?' Thomas asked, his tone falsely casual. Earlier, in the taxi, he had been fanning himself desperately with an airline magazine.

'Certainly not,' Toufan replied. 'The temperatures start to go down in a week or so. October is the last month of this heat. It only starts to heat up again like this in April.'

The two European men exchanged glances, and Gabriel's eyes narrowed. He wondered whether Dick had been aware of this when he booked their last minute flights. Thomas licked his lips and picked up a honey sweet from the tray on the glass office table.

'I have a cultural question for you,' Gabriel remembered, thinking of the hotel. 'Are we supposed to tip everyone who asks? There seemed to be so many servants at the hotel!'

'Oh no,' Toufan replied. 'Of course, you can express gratitude when someone has been helpful, but you are not obliged to throw cash in all directions, even if it feels like that is what is expected of you.' He gave a deep, slow laugh. 'Most of these scuttling men are from the Sudan, or Lebanon. Do not consider their service a great luxury.'

'Very well,' said Gabriel. 'And the meal that will be served at the hotel, it is... safe?'

Toufan laughed again, this time lightly. 'Of course,' he said. 'You are hardly the first people to come there from the Occident. However, this evening, I would like you to be *my* guests.' He waved away their protests. 'Please,' he said. 'I have already ordered the lamb.'

'Lamb!' Thomas said happily. 'I love lamb.'

'This is very generous of you,' Gabriel said.

Toufan gave a slow smile. 'I cannot simply welcome such illustrious guests in my prefabricated concrete office, can I? You must see more than the town centre. There are truly beautiful buildings in the old town, where my family home is. I should like you to see them, when we drive to my house.' He frowned suddenly, as if anxious. 'You wouldn't prefer a camel, would you? If I had known earlier about your arrival, from my assistant, I could have procured...'

'I, er, have never ridden one,' Gabriel said nervously. 'I assume they're difficult to mount?'

Toufan burst out laughing. 'No, no,' he said, 'I mean to eat! It is one of our most traditional dishes, and delicious as well!'

'Oh!' said Gabriel. 'You eat camel? I thought that was your mode of transport!'

'Isn't that like a sailor eating his ship?' Thomas added.

Toufan shrugged. 'You'll find it's delicious,' he said, 'as well as being a very comfortable way to get around, but I personally prefer lamb for dinner. The flavour of the meat is more delicate. Besides, there are only three of us. A whole lamb should suffice.'

Gabriel and Thomas exchanged glances, at a loss for words. 'I'm sorry you didn't have more warning of our arrival,' Gabriel said at last. 'We tried to contact you by fax, but that wasn't very successful. In the end, it was suggested to us that we simply send a handwritten letter and hope for the best.'

Toufan nodded. 'That was correct. In this part of the world, we are simply not used to such last minute trips! We do things slowly.'

'You must forgive us,' said Gabriel. 'Our approach to planning was not ideal. We should not have shown up without warning here, yesterday.'

'No matter, no matter,' said Toufan. 'I was simply very busy. I'm sorry you had to wait for so long.'

'Oh no,' said Thomas, his voice strained. 'It was only two or three hours.'

Gabriel elbowed him in the ribs. 'We are here now,' he said

smoothly, 'and for that we are grateful.'

Toufan nodded. 'You are here now, and after dinner, we shall do business together. Shall we drive, then?'

The three men stood up and left the office, and walked slowly down a carpeted staircase. The air was stuffy and hot. Opening the front door into the street did nothing to relieve this, even though the sky was slowly darkening towards the blue of evening. Dazed, Gabriel and Thomas wandered towards a battered white car.

'Please, sit,' Toufan said with a gracious smile.

The ride was bumpy; the interior of the car dilapidated. A metal charm jangled from the rearview mirror. Thomas had his nose glued to the window, but Gabriel found it easier to focus on the creases of his suit trousers. He tried to repress the rising wave of nausea.

'This is the oldest part of the city,' Toufan was saying. 'Soon, we will arrive at my house.' Gabriel nodded vaguely. All these streets looked the same in the dim light. 'Do not be surprised,' the sheikh added after a pause, 'when the lamb is slaughtered in the courtyard. It is a traditional way to welcome our guests. It is a matter of courtesy and honour.'

Gabriel's head snapped upright. Had he heard that correctly? 'The lamb you said you ordered... is not dead?' he said awkwardly.

Toufan laughed. 'Of course not! Its throat will be cut in the ritual manner.'

'What?' squeaked Thomas.

'One swift, sharp, cut with a knife,' Toufan replied, calmly. 'Then all the blood must be drained from the meat, so that it is considered halal. The name of God must be invoked at this moment, so that the meal may be blessed.'

There was a silence. 'I see,' said Gabriel.

***

Later, the three men were sitting on the floor, arranged cross-legged on a number of beautiful rugs. Another tray of cool, sugary drinks appeared. There were fresh flowers on the table, the perfumed scent overwhelming. From the kitchen, a rich smell of roasting meat was wafting.

'I have always been a merchant, you see,' Toufan was saying, his hands making an elegant gesture in the air.

Thomas selected a fruit drink and sipped it slowly.

Gabriel, his eyes still slightly glazed from witnessing the slaughter of the lamb, sat in silence as Toufan told them the long version of his life story. 'I sell goods from all over the world: grains, imported wool, anything you can name. It is a good trade. These things are always needed. Now, we are expanding into sugar, tanned leather, and some industrial products like cork and pressed wood. It is quite an exciting time. There are many opportunities.'

Gabriel nodded. 'You have been successful,' he said. Thomas finished his drink.

Toufan smiled widely. 'You could say so, yes. But then, so have both of you. I have heard of your bank many times before, though I know little about trade in Switzerland.'

'I am flattered,' Gabriel said, unconvinced.

The host turned to Thomas. 'I see you appreciate our fresh fruit beverages. Would you perhaps like something stronger? In our culture, we are not supposed to drink alcohol near the family, but I have some hidden away in a cupboard. If you like, I can go find some whiskey or some gin. You see, we do not have wine or beer because smuggling is a question of volume: it costs just as much to bring in wine as it does whiskey, so it makes financial sense to opt for the stronger liquors.'

'Oh, yes please!' Thomas exclaimed.

'Thomas!' Gabriel intervened. 'I'm so sorry, sheikh Toufan. My friend has little experience of what is culturally appropriate.' He glared at Thomas.

Toufan laughed. 'Oh, it's no trouble,' he said. 'Let me get you a little something.'

Thomas glared back at Gabriel. 'I can't help it if I'm thirsty,' he hissed at Gabriel. 'It's hot in this place!'

'These are people who kill lambs in their own gardens!' Gabriel whispered back. 'We don't understand what we're doing! If we offend Toufan, we probably won't end up doing business with him at all! Then what will this trip have been for?'

'He's a nice man!' Thomas hissed again. 'I like him.'

The men looked up again, as Toufan re-entered the room. 'I knew I had a little Johnny Walker black label hidden away somewhere,' he said with a wink. 'In Arabic we call it *hannah mashy* – like the grain mash they use to make whiskey! I hope you don't mind it if we drink it in these clay cups, though, so that no-one will be able to tell if they walk in.'

As if on cue, a tall black man appeared in the doorway, wearing an elaborate robe. He bowed slightly. In his hands, he was carrying a tray. On the tray was what looked like a roast lamb's head.

Gabriel swallowed.

Toufan clapped his hands. 'Dinner!' he exclaimed happily. 'This is a delicacy; a very young lamb, only two months old. Now, I don't know how familiar you are with Arabic tradition, but you will probably only want to eat pieces of the cheeks. I personally prefer the ears and the eyes, but I know this usually horrifies our guests, so feel free to avoid them. All the more for me!' He laughed his deep laugh.

Thomas and Gabriel stared at the animal's head.

'We eat with our fingers?' Gabriel asked shyly.

'Bon appétit!' said Thomas, weakly.

A little while after this, the rest of the lamb was carried in on a large copper dish, surrounded by oily-looking rice. Toufan showed his guests how to eat, rolling the rice into balls in his right hand, and pulling the meat off the bone with his fingers. The meat was rich and flavourful, Gabriel had to admit, though he was uncomfortable with his hands being so greasy. Eventually, the conversation turned to trade, collaboration, and banking products. Gabriel began to relax into his role, helped along by his secret clay cup of whiskey.

'I understand you're already a rich man, Sheikh Toufan,' he said, 'but I am confident we can make you much richer. I won't push you into anything you're not comfortable with, but I can advise you.'

'I do not want to take risks,' Toufan replied calmly.

Gabriel nodded. 'I understand. None of us do. That is why we have advisors in France and America, helping us keep track of the global market. We won't take any undue risks. We won't let you down.'

'We are your Swiss security,' Thomas added, nodding sagely. He had finished his entire plateful of lamb, and four glasses of fruit juice.

Toufan laughed suddenly. 'Your friend,' he said to Gabriel, 'looks quite sleepy.' He checked his watch. 'I suppose it is near midnight! You must be jet-lagged, and we've been talking for over three hours.'

Gabriel nodded reluctantly. 'I hope we have not been too boring,' he said.

'Let me find a bowl of fresh water so you can wash your hands,' Toufan said, standing up slowly.

Gabriel nudged Thomas. 'Do you have the gifts?' he whispered.

Thomas looked panicked for a moment. 'Gifts? You can't give chocolate in this sort of climate!'

'Not chocolate! Watches!'

Thomas looked dubious. 'I have the watches you gave me, yes. They are a gift?'

'Yes!' Gabriel replied, exasperated.

'For him? Why would you give someone watches? There are watches everywhere!'

'This isn't Switzerland, Thomas!'

Toufan re-entered, bearing an engraved silver bowl with blossoms floating in it, along with a towel. 'Please, be my guests,' he said.

The men washed their hands, and dried them, feeling tired and refreshed.

'Before we leave, we have a small gift for you,' Gabriel said, looking pointedly at Thomas.

Thomas rummaged in his pockets, drawing out two slim boxes. 'We're sorry we didn't bring any Swiss chocolates,' he said, glaring at Gabriel. 'This will have to do.'

Toufan laughed, taking hold of the wrapped boxes with a curious expression. 'Do not worry about chocolate,' he said. 'It is not a very popular food here. Everyone eats sugar-based sweets, and honey, and pistachios.'

'Oh,' said Thomas. They watched Toufan unwrap the presents. His expression, upon discovering two Rolex watches, was one of utter delight.

'You are the most wonderful Swiss men,' he said, holding one watch in each hand. 'I cannot believe this gift! This one is gold-plated!'

'It is nothing, just a small token of appreciation. Thank you for dinner,' Gabriel said. 'We should probably get back to our hotel.'

Toufan produced another one of his deep, rumbling laughs. 'Now, now,' he said. 'Just because our culture does not offer puddings or desserts does not mean you have to hurry to your hotel rooms without closing your deal. It has been a pleasure to host you in my home, but I know why you have come, and I respect that.' Gabriel and Thomas were silent. 'Since you've honoured me by dining here in my home, I would like to give you fifteen million dollars or so to invest with your bank. I look forward to hearing news of these fantastic per centages you were promising me.' He held up a hand to interrupt their thanks. 'Just tell me how you accept your deposits. Do you take gold coins?'

Gabriel nodded. 'We can take just about anything. Gold, silver, or any currency. Of course, the easiest for us to handle are dollars and Swiss francs.'

Toufan was thoughtful for a moment. 'Most of my money is currently hidden under my mattress. Can I give you a suitcase of hundred-dollar bills?'

Thomas let out an incredulous laugh, which he quickly turned into a cough.

'That's not the easiest for us,' Gabriel said as tactfully as he could.

'It would be difficult to get through customs with forty kilos of cash,' Thomas added, deadpan.

'We'll simply need to find a foreign exchange dealer,' Gabriel said smoothly, 'to change the money over. Then we can have it transferred to us from a transient account. I can help you organise that, perhaps tomorrow.'

Toufan bowed. 'Wonderful,' he said. 'Thank you. Furthermore, I will write you a card with the address of my friend Mourshawa. He is ten times richer than me, and I suspect he would benefit greatly from a partnership with you. He has made his fortune in the oil business, you see, and I think he's also interested in things like land speculation and real estate. He can tell you all about this. It is unfamiliar territory to me.'

'Oh, thank you!' said Gabriel. 'Yes, we will contact him at once.'

'Perhaps tomorrow,' Toufan replied.

'Of course,' said Gabriel, blushing.

'We'll see if we're in any state to make calls tomorrow, after eating about half a lamb!' Thomas joked.

Toufan smiled. 'You'll be fine, little German man,' he said. 'Just maybe avoid asking Mourshawa for alcohol, alright?'

Thomas nodded enthusiastically, unembarrassed.

'Next time you come for dinner with me,' Toufan added, 'I will serve you the kidneys also, fried, and part of the liver. Some people eat the lungs and stomach as well. It's all part of the entertainment.' He winked.

'Very good,' said Gabriel, as enthusiastically as he could.

'We will bring you chocolate,' Thomas added firmly.

They shook hands and headed out into the dark street to find a taxi.

———◆———

'You're very bad at sitting cross-legged,' Gabriel told Thomas. The sun was blinding, and the stretch of desert around them seemed never-ending. Waves and waves of powdery gold and white lay in all directions, with sand blowing gently across the top.

Thomas grinned. 'And you're getting a sunburn,' he said. The German had elected to wrap his head in a long cotton scarf.

'Well, at least I don't look like a ghost in a school play,' Gabriel retorted. The grit was making his eyes water. 'I'll stick to my native customs, thank you very much.'

'Yes,' Thomas said, 'I noticed you brought your briefcase. Perhaps you should have brought your skis.'

'Whose idea was this walk, anyway?' Gabriel said, grumpily. 'I'd have been quite content sitting in our hotel room, drinking very cold bottled water until it was time to go meet this Mourshawa character.'

'Oh, look!' Thomas said, ignoring him and pointing down at the sand by his feet. 'A fossil!' He fell to his knees and began to scramble around in the powder. At last, he stood up and dusted himself off. 'This must be at least two million years old,' he said reverently.

'What do you know?' Gabriel retorted. 'For all you know, this rock fell out of a tractor yesterday.'

'Yes, I'm sure there are many tractors here,' Thomas said, amused. 'Tilling, planting seeds...'

'You know what I mean!' Gabriel shouted back. 'Anyway, it's not like the thing has its date of creation written on it like a dollar bill. Since when are you an archaeologist?'

Thomas shrugged. 'It has a print of a fern on it, look.'

Gabriel squinted, unconvinced. At last, he sighed. 'Fine,' he said. 'Keep the rock, then. Maybe that will make us rich.'

'Why are you in such a bad mood?' Thomas asked, tentatively.

Gabriel was silent. 'I am not in a bad mood,' he said tersely. 'It is just very hot here.'

Thomas shrugged. 'OK,' he said. 'Come on, let's head back to the hotel.'

The truth was, Gabriel had suffered the small disappointment of trying to call Anita from the hotel bedroom: she had not answered, and a strange wave of homesickness had flooded over him. He stared at the fruit bowl for a long time after hanging up, his throat tight. The intensity of the moment saddened him and troubled him in equal measures, to the extent that he had agreed to Thomas's stupid idea of a desert walk. As for Clarice, she had barely crossed his mind. Let her get on with her gallery. She probably was glad to have him out of the house.

'Who is that small person?' Thomas said suddenly, squinting into the swirling sands.

'It would appear to be some kind of nomad,' Gabriel replied. 'A child, I'd imagine.'

'Ooh!' said Thomas, in obvious delight. 'Let's go talk to it!'

Gabriel sighed. 'Very well,' he said. 'We talk to the little nomad, then we head back to the hotel.'

'Yes, sir!' said Thomas, scuttling off into the desert.

The child was about ten years old, dressed in a dirty pink t-shirt with an unreadable slogan on it. He stared at them in enraptured amusement, before holding out a hand.

'He wants chocolate,' Thomas said. 'Why didn't we bring chocolate?'

The child continued to stare at them, quite intensely. Suddenly, Gabriel remembered something. 'I have an orange!' he exclaimed, rustling around in his briefcase.

'Is that why you brought the briefcase?' Thomas grinned.

Gabriel found the fruit, and drew it out. The child's eyes widened further. Cautiously, Gabriel put the orange into the child's hand. He turned it over in wonder.

'I don't think he's ever seen one before!' Thomas said in wonder. 'What strange breakfasts these people must have!'

The child was still clutching the orange in his small hand, bemused.

Thomas' eyes lit up. 'Wait a second,' he said. 'I stole some stuff from the breakfast buffet as well!' He reached into his pocket.

'Is that an egg?' Gabriel asked in consternation.

The child's eyes widened further.

'It's hard-boiled!' said Thomas.

'Put it away,' Gabriel said sternly. 'One strange new food a day is probably enough.'

It occurred to him suddenly that the child wouldn't know how to peel the fruit. Smiling, he kneeled down gingerly and gently took the fruit back from the child and began to remove the peel, releasing the sharp scent into the hot desert air.

'You're making me thirsty,' said Thomas.

'You're always thirsty,' Gabriel replied, concentrating on his task. When he had finished, he motioned to the child that he should eat a piece. The child grabbed the segments, and crammed one into his mouth. His expression of delight made both of the men laugh. Suddenly, the child darted towards Gabriel and kissed him on the cheek.

'Oh!' said Gabriel, nearly falling backwards into the sand.

'He's running away!' said Thomas.

'We're going to be late for our meeting,' said Gabriel, dusting himself off.

───⬤◆⬤───

Mourshawa was wearing sunglasses, a tailored dove-grey suit and several gold rings. His office was decorated with stylish pictures of desert landscapes. Blissfully, the room was air-conditioned.

'Can I offer you anything? A brandy on ice, perhaps?'

Gabriel and Thomas stared at him for a moment. The sheikh had a moustache so slim and carefully trimmed that it seemed to have been drawn on with a pencil.

'No, thank you,' Thomas said at last, a little primly. 'We understand your customs.'

Mourshawa laughed, a rough sound. 'I can see that from your headdress,' he said. 'Very original.'

Thomas blushed, pleased. 'Thank you,' he said. 'I made it myself.'

'Well, I hope you don't mind if I pour myself a little something,' the sheikh said. He pulled open his desk drawer, and produced a tumbler and a bottle of scotch. Expensive scotch, Gabriel noted, trying not to raise his eyebrows. This man was obviously accustomed to dealing with Western clients. There would be no stuffed camel today.

'As you probably know already, I made an enormous amount of money ten years ago, at the height of the new oil boom.' Mourshawa had large, smooth hands, Gabriel noticed, and fingernails that looked manicured. 'As I understand it, Swiss banks can usually offer three or four per cent. This has never particularly interested me. However, am I correct in understanding that you are offering me twelve per cent?'

'That's right,' said Gabriel, thinking that Dick would be better off in this environment than he was. 'That's our guarantee, and our starting point.' Should he be offering him drinks? Steaks? Women?

'I like it when my money makes me money,' Mourshawa continued, leaning back in his black leather chair and spinning back and forth slightly. He was not a slender man. 'This is why I have been buying buildings in London and New York for years. However, I am *particularly* keen on my money making me money without me having to lift a finger.'

'That is essentially what we can offer you,' Gabriel replied. 'You'll be making twelve per cent just from a piece of paperwork. It's as simple as real estate, except there will be no maintenance, no plumbing, no rats.'

Thomas glanced over, obviously surprised. What was so strange about making a little joke? Mourshawa laughed, in any case.

'I am not a bureaucrat,' he said, his face growing stern again. 'So I am not sure how I feel about paperwork. You Europeans are so fond of paper. Out here in the desert, it burns in the sun.'

Gabriel swallowed, making a mental note to communicate with this potential future client by telephone. 'It's not exactly paperwork,' he said hastily. 'We're talking about bonds, stocks, products that have been refined over the years until they are good financial instruments. We are not risk-takers.'

'I like risk-takers,' said Mourshawa, narrowing his eyes.

'I mean, we are risk-takers,' Gabriel said, stumbling, 'but the Swiss sort. Reasonable risk-takers.'

Mourshawa burst out into his harsh laugh again. 'Don't worry, I'm only teasing,' he said. 'I am not afraid of gambling, but I don't like to lose. If you can offer me something safe, reliable, that sounds good to me. I have enough reckless investments going already.'

Gabriel swallowed and played his final card. 'Last year, the brokerage firm we work with in Chicago made an average of fourteen per cent.' He could not resist a small satisfied smile at Mourshawa's hungry expression.

'How interesting,' Mourshawa said. His eyes flicked around the room, as if calculating.

'You have a certain reputation,' Gabriel continued bravely. 'We know the kind of money you make, and the kind of money you want to make. We'd like to offer you higher returns. We think we can give you a better deal. Starting today, if you want.'

'American-style investment with a Swiss touch?' Mourshawa sounded convinced.

Gabriel nodded. 'Yes, exactly.'

'I've always been more of a London man,' he said, caressing his tiny moustache, 'but I can see the appeal of those mountains. Look outside here,' he said. 'Everything is flat! Fifty degree heat and sand blowing everywhere.'

'Why don't you come visit us in Geneva?' Gabriel offered, without thinking. 'You seem like someone who would really enjoy skiing.'

Thomas made a funny noise.

'It does sound rather fun,' Mourshawa said thoughtfully. 'Tell you what: why don't I make a starting investment of twenty million dollars, and come visit you in a year or so to check on them?'

There was a stunned silence. 'Yes,' Gabriel said at last. 'Yes, that sounds good.'

'We know this sort of money is nothing to you,' Thomas added, sweating.

'There is no entertainment in this part of the world,' Mourshawa said, almost mournfully. 'What can you offer me in that domain?'

Gabriel took a deep breath. 'Well, we have really excellent cheese.' There was a pause. 'Also great restaurants, a beautiful lake, erm, medical facilities... Fantastic hotels.'

Mourshawa and his moustache smiled thinly. 'Girls?'

'Of course,' said Gabriel, hoping he sounded confident. 'Swiss women are very beautiful. There are also women from other countries. I mean, I don't know how to find them for you, but they are available.' He gave a forced laugh.

'I suppose Swiss men are like that, yes,' Mourshawa said in wonder. 'Better at finding money than women. How fascinating. OK, I'm sold. I can write you a cheque right now, if you like.'

'Goodness,' said Gabriel. 'Yes.'

'I don't believe in making out cheques to banks,' he added. 'You guys have a very strange name. I'll make the cheque to you, Gabriel, right here, right now. I trust you. Can you spell your last name out for me?'

'Well,' Gabriel said, his heart racing. 'I, er, I guess that would be alright. D-E- P- U- R-...' What would the partners say! 'Maybe I should take it and run away to South America,' he added.

Mourshawa laughed, a little too heartily.

'No, sir,' Thomas said worriedly. 'Don't do that. You need to sign it and endorse it.'

'Don't worry, German guy. I trust the Swiss.' Mourshawa signed the cheque with a flourish and handed it over. 'Do you want me to introduce you to some more people?' he asked casually.

'Yes,' Gabriel said breathlessly. Then, bravely, he added: 'In the meantime, could I perhaps try a small glass of that Scotch?'

<hr />

'And then Thomas handed this poor desert child an egg! Yes, that's right, an egg! He had it in his pocket. No, I don't know why. I have no idea. I know! Of course the child didn't know what to do with that either. So we both ignored Thomas, and I showed him how to eat the orange, and then he was so pleased that he, he... He gave me a kiss. I know. Later, in the taxi, Thomas ate the egg himself. I really do wonder sometimes if that fall in the ravine was good for him. Well, no.'

Gabriel leaned back against the pillows of his hotel bed, his ankles crossed, his cheeks flushed. Anita's voice had such a soothing effect on him. Well, that combined with the two glasses of scotch in Mourshawa's office, and the one he'd poured himself from the minibar. But no matter. Everything was better, now he could hear her.

'Yes, I feel like it's all going really well. I can't really believe the success we've been having. Both sheikhs signed up, and I suspect they'll pass the word around. Do you know, I made a joke in one of our meetings? Thomas looked like he might faint. I know! I think the returns are going to be something really special. That's good news for my Christmas bonus, isn't it! I'm sorry, I don't mean to boast. Well, it's not very Swiss of me. Well, alright. I mean, maybe I can buy something nice and sparkly. Would you like that?'

Gabriel caught a glimpse of his face in the hotel mirror, pink and pleased. He looked five, maybe ten years younger than he remembered. Probably the sunburn, he told himself.

'I can't wait to see you either! We'll have ristrettos, no, we'll have champagne. We'll have *omble chevalier*. Are you laughing?' There was a long pause. 'Oh, I can't really disagree with you there. I was as surprised as anyone. Then again, why not? Hilary went to the Himalayas: why couldn't a Swiss man go to the Gulf? Well, apart from the mountains of sand, and the heat, and the sweat, but you know.'

Gabriel, to his mortification, found himself giggling.

'Of course I miss Switzerland. I can't wait to be cool again. But enough about my trip! Tell me what's going on in my beloved home country.'

There was a long silence on Gabriel's end of the line, as Anita chattered away about her new waitressing job, her walks by the lake, and the weather in Geneva.

'My love, I'm going to have to go,' he said at last, reluctantly. 'I'm so tired, and I have another few clients to see tomorrow. Yes, new ones. Yes, I did really call you my love. Of course you're my love. Was that really the first time? Well, it won't be the last. Good night, my love.'

He put down the phone and lay back on his clean, starched sheets. From the shimmering turrets of a nearby mosque, the haunting sound of the call to prayers began. No doubt he would regret that conversation with Anita in the morning, but right then, he could not have been happier. He took another sip of his scotch and stared out at the lights of this unknown city.

Chapter Twenty-Nine

Clarice readjusted a painting, tugging on the fine silver wires. The glowing crystal walls of the gallery were changing from turquoise to indigo, as the sunset outside began to darken Rue de la Cité slowly. Soon, it would be time to walk home to her husband. She hesitated, staring at the swirls of colour without understanding.

'Khadija, where is that red painting?' she called back. 'You know, the abstract one, by that young Bangladeshi artist?'

'I'll have a look,' Khadija's voice came from inside the building.

'What are you daydreaming about?' Chloë asked, appearing at her side with a stack of catalogues. 'And where would you like me to leave these?'

Clarice gave a deep sigh. 'Sorry,' she said, 'I've been a little distracted today. The catalogues can go on top of my desk.'

Chloë stayed by her side, still holding the catalogues. 'How come? Is it the gallery? Aren't you pleased with your phenomenal success?'

'It's not that.' Clarice stared out through the luminous glass at the cold stone walls of the courtyard. 'Gabriel came home from the Middle East last week, and I can't help but feel... strange about it.'

'You mean you liked it better when he was gone?'

Clarice shrugged. 'I don't think it's that. One does get used to one's husband, you know.' She wanted her tone to be ironic, but it didn't quite ring true.

'Is he telling boring stories?' Chloë asked, frowning.

'Well, yes, of course,' Clarice replied, 'but that isn't the problem either. He just seems very absent, these days. There was only one stupid story about Thomas, for instance, and *no* stories of hating the local food. It just isn't like Gabriel at all.'

Chloë grinned. 'Thomas!' she said fondly. 'How is that strange little man? He has such nice waistcoats.'

'I don't know, you see,' Clarice replied, a little piqued. 'Gabriel barely bored me at all before running upstairs to make a call. He closed the bedroom door.'

Chloë raised an eyebrow. 'He couldn't be...'

Clarice shook her head quickly. 'This is Gabriel we're talking about,' she said quickly, a little sharply.

Khadija appeared, set down the large red painting and gave Chloë a little slap on the head. 'Please excuse our Chloë,' she said. 'Her desire for gossip makes her forget herself.'

'I am sorry,' Chloë said, her tone genuinely apologetic. 'Of course I wasn't suggesting... Let me put these catalogues away.' She scuttled back into the building, her high heels tap-tap-tapping on the varnished floor.

'What's going on?' asked Fleurie, peeking into the crystal ball.

'It's alright,' Clarice sighed after Chloë, a little too late. 'Er, nothing. Khadija, can you help me lift this painting up?' The women manoeuvred the heavy gold frame into place, and Clarice adjusted the wires so that it hung correctly.

'That looks lovely,' Khadija said, standing back. 'Very impressive. I'd bet it gets snapped up in two weeks.'

'I say one,' said Fleurie. 'Remember how quickly that silvery landscape of his went?'

Clarice gave a pleased smile. 'I really am happy with the gallery, you know,' she said. 'It just really irks me, that I should have to be thankful to Gabriel for any of this.'

'You're not really,' Khadija replied. 'This is all your work. You have nothing to thank that man for.'

'I don't understand you girls. Gabriel was so lovely at the *vernissage!*' Fleurie smiled. 'I don't know why you always seem so unhappy, Clarice, when he's obviously a changed man.'

'The change is what we don't trust,' Khadija added crisply.

Fleurie frowned, disconcerted for a moment. 'What are you talking about?'

Clarice sighed. She had no desire to tell Fleurie about her meeting that morning.

'Where is Winifred, anyway?' Chloë asked, reappearing. 'She's not pregnant again, is she?'

'Chloë!' Clarice rebuked her. 'Don't be cruel.'

Chloë shrugged. 'She seems to be the only one here having regular sex. Isn't that how it works?'

'I must admit, I'm curious about Winifred's whereabouts as well,' Khadija said, ignoring Chloë. 'I haven't seen hair nor hide of her for weeks.'

Clarice frowned. 'That's strange,' she said. 'It just occurred to me that we haven't seen her in Geneva since Gabriel went to have coffee with Dieter in Zurich.'

Chloë giggled. 'Maybe *they're* having an affair,' she said.

Khadija hit her on the back of the head again. 'Chloë, you're a nasty piece of work,' she said. 'Isn't it time for you to met one of your hundred men for a date?'

Chloë tossed her hair back. 'I don't have a date,' she said. 'I'm an independent woman.'

Khadija scoffed. 'Then leave us married women alone for a bit,' she said. She made a shooing motion, and Chloë, sighing and huffing, went back inside.

'Wait for me!' said Fleurie, waving quickly at Clarice and Khadija and following Chloë.

Khadija collapsed into one of the gallery chairs. 'I love those girls,' she said, 'but their youthful enthusiasm does have a draining effect on me.'

Clarice sat down slowly in the chair next to Khadija's. 'I don't think it's Chloë or Fleurie who is draining me,' she said quietly.

Khadija sighed. 'Tell me all about Gabriel,' she said. 'What is going on?'

Clarice was silent for a moment. 'Things have been strange. I went to see someone,' she said slowly. 'A counsellor.'

'Aren't you meant to go see those people as a couple?' Khadija asked gently.

Clarice shrugged. 'I know,' she said, 'but I was desperate for advice... new advice,' she added hastily. 'Professional advice.'

'No offence taken,' said Khadija. 'I don't want to hear the graphic details of Gabriel's failures in the bedroom.'

Against her will, Clarice giggled. 'It's not like we get far enough to even have failures,' she said.

'Oh,' said Khadija. 'So, this counsellor...'

'She's crazy,' Clarice said, before laughing. 'I mean, I really think she has problems of her own. She's this tan, athletic Germanic woman in her fifties, skinny as a beanpole.'

'She sounds awful already,' said Khadija, adjusting her jacket.

'Her eyes bulge right out of her head. Her name is Gazelda,' Clarice added, feeling like giggling again. 'Gazelda Flick. She was wearing a bright yellow blazer.'

'Tell me more!' said Khadija, laughing.

'The whole thing was a joke,' Clarice sighed. 'A very expensive joke, at four hundred francs per hour. She basically suggested we should have more sex. As if I didn't know that! She barely even seemed to want to hear what I had to say. She mostly wanted to stare at me with her weird bug eyes.'

'She didn't have any fresh suggestions?'

Clarice rolled her eyes. 'She said I should try doing anything Gabriel wants. She doesn't understand that means rolling myself in the *Financial Times*, then going to sleep. But that isn't the best bit. The best was her next suggestion. Gazelda Flick wants me to put a recording device under the bed the next time Gabriel and I have sex.' The women broke out into peals of laughter.

'What?' said Khadija. 'Why?'

'So she can listen to it! She's a pervert, that's what she is. I asked her if she didn't think that was a bit dishonest, and she got all defensive, suggesting it might save my marriage! Honestly.' Clarice sighed. 'If I made a recording of our lovemaking, it would be the most boring, repetitive sex tape in the world. Like counting sheep. I bet I could sell it as a sleeping pill, and make a fortune.'

'Don't be ridiculous,' said Khadija. 'It's not really my place to comment on your sexual personality, but I have no doubt who the boring one is in your marriage.'

Clarice laughed, a little sadly. 'So what do you think I should do?'

'I think you should call your mother. That's what I would do. None of this silly, expensive counsellor business. And don't call Chloë! That's even worse. After you talk to your mother, I think you should pour yourself a nice glass of wine, and try not to be discouraged. Put on a new dress, and smile. Maybe Gabriel really is just distracted at work.'

'Maybe,' Clarice said glumly. She stared at the crystal wall, which was turning violet. 'In any case, I think it's time to go home.'

'Yes, Maman,' Clarice said, rolling her eyes and holding the phone pressed tightly between her cheek and her shoulder. The grass in the courtyard of the house in Saint Antoine was wet with dew. 'No, I know what Papa...' Her tone grew vicious. 'I mean, what Adam Louis Saint-André-Tobbal thinks of my husband. It's none of your business, really. Neither of you.' She sighed, leaning her forehead slowly against the stone kitchen wall. 'No, Maman,' she said. 'I am proud of my heritage, yes. I also stand by my own decisions. Nothing is wrong with my marriage,' she added, her tone of voice escalating. 'I wish you would be more interested in the gallery's success. That's what I called you to talk about. I was hoping you would cheer me up, not insult me and make me feel miserable. And no, I still do not have the least interest in having children.'

Eugénie's voice buzzed in the silence of the kitchen. Against her will, Clarice felt her throat growing tight. 'What kind of a mother is more interested in saying nasty things about her daughter's husband than in congratulating her on her extremely successful business venture? Need I remind you that neither you nor my father made the effort of driving down for the *vernissage*? At least Gabriel was there.' There was a long silence. 'You sound like a hippie, Mother. I am not in the least interested in seizing the day, or rolling in the grass, or whatever it is you're advocating. As if *your* marriage is anything to be proud of!' She slammed down the phone, tears pricking her eyes.

'Well, that certainly cheered me up,' she said bitterly, aloud, to nobody in particular, smoothing down her skirt aggressively. Khadija's suggestion that Clarice might want to turn to her mother for advice had sounded comforting, but she should have known better. Where even was Gabriel? It was nearly dinnertime, though she hadn't had the heart to prepare anything. Maybe they could go out to eat, as a treat.

She marched from the kitchen, across the living room, up the stairs and to their bedroom suite. In the delicately lit bathroom mirror, she took a long look at herself: perfectly ironed shirt, hair swept severely back, crow's feet, slightly red eyes, stern expression. She sighed and tried a crooked smile, but she only looked old and tired. Slowly, Clarice untied her hair, trying not to mind the grey streaks. She let the dark, flowing mass of it fall over her shoulders. That was better. She unbuttoned the top of her shirt, then a little further. When had she started wearing such boring underwear? Clarice sighed, and a real hint of a smile crept across her face.

———◆◆◆———

Gabriel opened the bedroom door, loosening his tie. He was tired, and a little giddy from coffee and champagne with Anita. Clarice hadn't been in the kitchen. He wondered what was for dinner. When he saw his wife, standing by the side of the bed in a state of luxurious undress, his eyes darted wildly from side to side, as if to avoid looking at her.

'Clarice!' he exclaimed, trying to keep the surprise from his voice.

Clarice smiled what she clearly hoped was a slow, seductive smile.

'Hello, Gabriel,' she said. 'I've missed you.' She let the silk kimono slide slowly down her shoulders, revealing black lace.

Gabriel's eyes did not follow the kimono, instead choosing the armoire, the bed, and the bathroom door. 'Right,' he said, 'yes. Hello.'

'You're home late,' she said, not accusingly.

Gabriel frowned. 'I had to meet a client after work,' he said quickly. 'It was only one drink.'

She paused. 'Of course,' she said, her confidence clearly faltering. 'I...'

'What's for dinner?' Gabriel asked, trying to keep his tone

cheerful.

Clarice glared. '*I* am for dinner,' she said, a little more petulantly than she had intended. 'I mean, how can you think of...' She paused, swallowed, and made a valiant effort to adjust her tone. 'I'm just glad to see you. We can worry about food later.' She let the kimono fall a little further.

Gabriel swallowed. There was no hint of desire in him, only a great wave of fatigue. He didn't even want dinner any more. He just wanted to go to bed, and hide from his complicated world. 'You look quite lovely, sweetheart,' he said, 'but I'm really just not in the mood, right now. Everything's quite stressful at the bank.'

Clarice pursed her lips and hiked the kimono back up a bit. 'Yes, I've noticed you've been quite busy,' she said, accusingly. 'Too busy to touch me for about nine months. Where have you been, Gabriel? It can't just be Dick from Chicago or Gérard from France, not just trips to Zurich and to the desert.'

'Yes it can,' Gabriel said, childishly. 'It is.'

Clarice straightened her shoulders and pulled the kimono back up over them. 'Fine, then,' she said. 'In that case, you may as well say you're married to dollars and cents and whatever they use in those hot countries. What is going to happen next, Gabriel? Will you be always in... Japan and Australia and Thailand?' She was growing incoherent, and finding it difficult to care. 'Why don't you just buy a big hat and become a cowboy, then? You're some kind of ridiculous nomad. You didn't even tell me any boring stories about your trip. Didn't Thomas do anything stupid?'

'Well, yes!' Gabriel said. 'One time he went into the sea in his pinstriped suit!'

'Well, why didn't you tell me that?'

'Because you don't care.' Gabriel crossed his arms.

A silence fell. Impulsively, Clarice darted forward and put her hands on her husband's shoulders. Her hands were cold. 'What's wrong, my love?' she said, imploring now. 'Something is troubling you. Something has changed.'

Gabriel's stomach felt like ice. Where could he escape to? 'Nothing has changed, Clarice, it is only the natural passing of time. We are no longer newlyweds.' This came out more sharply than he had intended.

'And what do you mean by that?' Clarice asked, drawing back. 'Does our marriage have no meaning for you anymore?'

'What are you talking about, woman?' Gabriel said, having difficulty controlling the nasty flood of emotions sweeping through him. It was taking an effort not to bolt for the door.

'I'm talking about something the English call sex,' Clarice shouted, losing her temper in turn. 'It's spelled S-E-X. Do you even remember what that means? Or can you only say that word in other languages?'

'I know what sex is, Clarice, though if this is your way of trying to get it, it's a strange one.' He glared at his wife. 'I don't like what you're implying,' he added. 'Why are you insulting me like this?'

'I'm not insulting you,' she said, 'I'm trying to understand. I'm giving you one last chance to truly make love to me. You say it's natural, but I don't agree. All my married friends are still sleeping with their husbands.'

'That's what they tell you,' he snapped. 'They're probably all off having affairs, like that dreadful Chloë.'

Clarice tightened the belt of her kimono angrily. 'Don't you dare insult my friends,' she said. 'I get more love from each of them than I ever get from you.'

Gabriel gave a bitter laugh. 'So, the truth of the matter,' he said. 'You act as if I have abandoned you, but when have you been available? You're always at one of your galleries, or having some kind of stupid coffee with those women, talking about art or feminism or whatever it is you do.'

'You're dodging the point, Gabriel. Most people still have sex in their fifties. We should be doing it more, in fact, before it's too late!'

'So you're some kind of statistician now?' he scoffed. 'Go on, show me the figures that prove your point.'

'No! I'm not a statistician! I'm just a woman trying to make love to her husband. I'm just a woman trying to keep her failing marriage together.'

Something stung in Gabriel's chest when he realised that Clarice's eyes were full of tears. Then anger rose and overcame it.

'Adolescent seduction is hardly the way to fix this marriage. What kind of way is this to have a reasonable discussion? This is the first I've heard of your marital woes, anyway. We hardly talk anymore. If I'm married to my pennies, then you're married to your paintings. What is this I hear about you acquiring naked African statuettes?'

'What are you talking about?' Clarice said, angrily wiping her tears away. 'What do you care about what I'm selling?'

'As your husband, I care about your morals,' Gabriel said, loudly and unconvincingly. 'I'll bet Chloë acquired them by sleeping with some sort of African dictator. He probably flies them over in his private jet.'

Clarice's expression was chillingly disdainful. 'Actually, the woman who sculpted the statues you're referring to happens to have a long career as an aid worked for the UN behind her. Her husband is a human rights lawyer. And I bet they still have sex.'

Gabriel ground his teeth. 'These naked statues, they're distasteful. It's cultural exploitation, mixing that in with wonderful old Swiss art. It's going to depreciate your gallery.'

'I won't engage with this line of attack,' Clarice said. 'Which one of us is the successful art dealer, Gabriel? Why don't you look after your own business?'

'I think you should mind you own business too, Clarice, and let me have friends outside our household.'

There was a silence. 'Friends?' asked Clarice, her tone cutting. 'And who might these friends be?'

'Bankers,' Gabriel said tersely, internally cursing himself.

Clarice glowered at him. It was as if he could see his wife's respect for him draining away, Gabriel thought to himself. As if he was shrinking in her eyes into something pathetic and shrivelled.

Clarice squared her shoulders. 'You came home at nine three times last week. That's just not normal. What time do we normally eat?'

'Six thirty,' Gabriel admitted unwillingly.

'So what has changed? Where have you been?'

'Don't treat me like a teenager,' said Gabriel. 'I will not have a curfew in my own home. I've been very busy, alright?' A sudden illumination struck him, and it took an effort not to grin. 'Look,' he said as calmly as he could, trying to keep his tone casual, 'I was planning on going to the opera tonight, and I'm going to be late. So why don't you just let me change my tie, and I'll be off.'

There was a stunned silence. 'You're missing dinner?' Another disbelieving pause followed. 'You think opera is better than sex?'

'I'd rather go hungry to the opera than have dinner with you,' Gabriel said bluntly, no longer caring. 'You're a veritable bulldog, Clarice. Biting and biting and not letting go.'

Clarice's eyes widened. 'You are cruel. I begged you,' she said quietly. 'I lay myself down at your feet and said: take me. I would have done anything. What kind of a man would act this way? Something is not right, Gabriel. I don't understand.'

'I don't want to have sex right now,' Gabriel said, unnecessarily. 'That's all there is to it.'

'There is a great deal more to it,' Clarice said coldly. 'You insult my gallery, you insult my body, you insult my dinner, you insult our marriage. In our bed, you read the *Financial Times* and then turn over like a cold statue. Do you have any idea how much of an effort I've put into fixing this hopeless, stone-cold marriage? Well, those days are over. This is the final straw, Gabriel. Go to your opera alone, if that's what you want. I am going to put my clothes back on, and when I come back, I will go order us twin beds. I no longer want to share my bed with such a cruel man.'

Gabriel blinked, taken aback. 'Clarice, are you suggesting a separation?'

'No,' said Clarice, coldly. 'I'm suggesting we sleep in separate beds. That is not the same thing.'

'Isn't one a sign of the other?' Gabriel asked, worried.

'What's the point of us sharing a bed if we don't have sex? See, you don't have an answer. I've never given an ultimatum in my life, but this is it. There is only one thing that separates our life from that of a brother and sister, and you refuse to give it to me. Either you have sex with me, or we sleep apart. That's it. That's the end of the story.'

'I don't like what you're saying about our future,' said Gabriel, hesitantly.

'Neither do it,' replied Clarice. She walked to the bathroom and closed the door.

———— ◆ ◆ ◆ ————

Gabriel walked quickly down the cobbled passage to Place de Neuve, his breath coming in quick puffs that hung in the cold air. Separate beds! Separate beds! The strangest thing was that, mixed in with the anger and frustration, there was a certain sense of relief. If he and Clarice were essentially separated, what was so criminal about spending time with Anita? He strode purposefully through the gathering fog, towards the crowd milling around outside the Grand Théâtre, in their black silk and velvet.

Still, the conversation had shaken him, and he was glad he was going to the opera alone. Wagner had begun to appeal to him of late: something about the bombast secretly thrilled him, in a way he had not felt possible, in his first forays into classical music. Mozart and Verdi had always pleased him, with their pleasant chords and romantic plot-lines. But Wagner? When he felt angry or triumphant, Wagner thrilled Gabriel to his very core. The brass, the drums, the sheer Germanic volume! It wasn't a fascist instinct, Gabriel was sure of this, but it was certainly a rebellion against his gentle Swiss heritage. What cowherd could ever develop a taste for fierce shield-maidens and palaces in the sky? A triumphant banker, however...

Gabriel smiled, as he was waved through the gilded entrance into the front hall. It was funny, really, how quickly one became used to a new life. How many years previously had Clarice talked him into their annual subscription? A permanent seat at the opera had seemed trivial, an indulgence. Yet how many times had he ended up there alone, seeking respite from his wife's needs and accusations? Like the soldiers chosen in battle by the Valkyries, he was destined for a higher purpose. With such success as his, he could afford to bend the rules a little. Gold, swords, magic trees: there might be no Peruvian maidens here, but the message of freedom was clear.

He settled into the plush of his seat with satisfaction, gazing up at the twinkling lights above the stage. Yes, it had been a good idea, coming here. It occurred to him suddenly that there would have been an excellent joke to make, as a retort to Clarice's comments about brothers and sisters. Coming to see *The Valkyrie*, an opera involving incestuous twins! Not that she would have appreciated even highbrow humour at that point. He looked away pointedly from the empty seat next to him, then flung his coat across it. *Take that, Clarice*, he thought with grim satisfaction. This opera was far too much a celebration of life and death for her tastes, anyway. What did those modern artists know about the harsh, essential values? He had no need for abstraction.

The red velvet curtain opened, and the sound of horns blared out. Onstage, a woman was lost in a raging storm.

Gabriel sighed with satisfaction and settled back into his chair. Perhaps he would have ice cream at the break. Or did he want champagne? Maybe he could have both.

Gabriel shivered as he crept up the stairs to the marital bedroom. Clarice couldn't have found separate beds yet, could she? Soon it would be winter. Wouldn't they be cold? He would need warmer pyjamas. Maybe his mother would buy him some nice wool ones for Christmas, like the ones he had as a child in the mountains. He opened the door slowly and found Clarice still in their shared bed as usual, but turned towards the window. He noticed with relief that she was wearing pyjamas, apparently having forsaken her alarming tendency of late, towards nakedness. If their life was a Wagner opera, he thought with a grim smile, he would have put a sword in the middle of the bed, to keep them safe from physical congress.

'Did you set the alarm clock?' Clarice asked sleepily, without turning around.

'What?' Gabriel jumped a little at her voice. 'No,' he said.

'Did you turn out the lights in the bathroom?'

Gabriel squinted at her figure in the darkness. 'No,' he said. 'I haven't been to the bathroom.'

'Are you going to take a shower?'

Gabriel shook his head, and began to unbutton his shirt. 'No,' he said.

'Have you turned off the heating?'

'No.' He slipped on his silk pyjamas as quickly as he could.

'How was the opera?'

'It was alright.' Gabriel hovered at the edge of their marital bed, like a man hesitating before diving into a freezing pool.

'Were there lots of singing women? With large breasts?' Clarice asked.

'Yes,' said Gabriel, climbing gingerly into bed. He felt almost tender towards his wife, now that her aggressive advances seemed to be over. There was a silence. They kept their bodies carefully apart.

'Are you feeling sexy?' Clarice asked meekly.

Gabriel's heart sank. 'No,' he said, quickly.

'Are you sure?' Clarice asked again, snuggling up to him.

At the touch of her body against his, Gabriel sprung up suddenly. 'Oh my!' he said. 'I've forgotten to call Dick! You see, there's a seven-hour time difference with Chicago, so he'll still be in his office. I need to ask him something. I'll go do it right now.'

'Call him from the bedroom phone,' Clarice said, her tone unreadable, her face still in her pillow.

Gabriel paused, having been ready to run from the room. 'Oh, good idea!' he said with false cheer. His heart racing, he dialed Dick, hoping he had calculated the time difference correctly. 'Dick! Hi! Yeah, it's me. Listen, I forgot... Yes, actually, that's about right. I want to place ten million more in the prepackaged mortgage-backed bonds.' Gabriel noticed he was sweating slightly. 'Yes, I want you to book the principal amount of ten million without any deductions for commissions. You can do that? Great! OK, thanks, my friend. Talk to you soon!'

'Pre-packaged? Mortgage-backed?' Clarice said scathingly, her voice muffled. She still hadn't turned around. 'What do those stupid words even mean?.' She pulled the covers up around her neck. 'You don't know what you're getting yourself into with Dick. At least with me, you know what you're getting your... self... into.'

'I'm going to turn off the heating,' Gabriel said, 'and get a glass of water. Don't wait up. Goodnight, Clarice.'

He closed the bedroom door, sighed, and tiptoed down the stairs. Sneaking into the kitchen, he found the remains of a chicken salad, which he brusquely moved aside. He picked up the phone and dialled. 'Anita!' he said softly. 'How are you? Yes, I've had a wonderful evening at the opera. It was Wagner, actually. You'd have loved it. Next time I'll bring you along.' He noticed the grass in the courtyard was freezing over. Soon it would be winter. 'Oh, my dear, I've just remembered another funny thing Thomas did,' Gabriel whispered. 'I just had to tell you. One day, we were walking down by the sea...'

Chapter Thirty

Gabriel stood glumly at the window, staring out into the freezing rain. The velvet curtains were dusty, he noticed. He ran a hand through his hair. Where was his comb? It didn't matter. He sighed, took off his glasses and rubbed his eyes slowly. What had happened to his marriage? When had it stopped surprising him when Clarice slept turned away from him, or started slamming doors? It seemed as if everything had changed so quickly, but perhaps that perspective was false. Perhaps the trouble could have been avoided years before. But how? Gabriel was at a loss. All the confidence born of Wagner, banking successes and the temptation of adultery, was fading away in the grim light of morning. Clarice was at work, and soon he would have to follow. But why? Why should he even care about Von Mipatobeau? Why was he trapped in this dreadful, tiny, dirty city? Why was everything in his house so old?

A strange, sudden instinct for flight seized him. Perhaps he could visit Dick in Chicago, or return to the Arabian Gulf! But no, no, that would not be very Swiss. He was expected in his office: he had a meeting with Mr Schön; Caroline would be disappointed. He heaved a profound sigh and slowly adjusted his tie. He closed the bedroom door softly, and walked down the stairs, ignoring the baleful gazes of the de Puritigny family portraits. Their love lives had surely been disastrous, in any case. How could they judge him?

All of a sudden, stepping out into the icy street, Gabriel was overcome by a strange pang of homesickness. He wanted stew, and to sit at his mother's table, and to be comforted by his father's proud banking stories. He wanted a cup of hot chocolate, and to sleep in his childhood pyjamas in his childhood bedroom, with the mountains close by. Embarrassed, Gabriel suddenly realised that tears were stinging his cheeks. It must be that vicious winter wind, he told himself. He removed his glasses and sharply wiped his eyes on the back of his hand. His skin was dry. How ugly the city seemed that morning.

He entered through the glass doors of Bank Von Mipatobeau, and stamped up the marble staircase without a second glance for the scuttling *huissiers*. He arrived at Caroline's desk a little flustered.

'*Bonjour, Monsieur de Puritigny,*' Caroline said, after a split second's hesitation. 'Is everything alright?'

'Yes,' Gabriel snapped.

Caroline faltered, a blush spreading across her pale cheeks. She looked old, Gabriel noted sadly. He wondered whether she was married, and thought it strange that he shouldn't know. Then again, why should he? He had never shown an interest in the lives of his staff. It wasn't his business.

'Mr Schön is waiting outside your office,' she said. 'Would you like two ristrettos?'

'Yes,' Gabriel sighed. 'That would be perfect.' He resisted the urge to rub his eyes again. 'Maybe some chocolate almonds as well.'

'Of course,' Caroline said softly. After a moment's pause, she added: 'Forgive me if this is the wrong time to mention it, but someone called Anita rang here earlier. She didn't leave a message.'

Gabriel looked up. Though her stern face tried to hide it, there was a glimmer of interest, even excitement, in Caroline's eye. More than the fact that Anita had called, this loosened the knot in his stomach a little. He even managed a terse smile. 'Did she now,' he said, somewhat mysteriously.

Caroline pretended to dab at her lip liner, obviously hiding a smile. Gabriel began to smile as well, sensing the question burning at his secretary's lips, and admiring the Swiss restraint that stopped her from asking it. He relaxed a little. 'Yes,' he said finally, 'in case you were wondering, she is my lover.'

'What?' Caroline's eyebrows nearly leapt off her face, then a real smile spread across it. 'Well!' she said, and was silent for a time. 'Well!' she eventually said again. Gabriel watched her face closely as flickers of emotions dashed across it: surprise, excitement, even something like jealousy. Gabriel felt a wave of tenderness rise up.

'My dear Caroline, I'm sure you're shocked, but you and I have known each other long enough that I felt I could confide. I apologise if the gesture is inappropriate.'

'Oh no, monsieur!' Caroline exclaimed. 'Actually, I couldn't be happier for you. I don't think I've ever known one of our senior bank officials to go so long without some kind of... light entertainment, if I'm perfectly honest.' Something like a smirk appeared on her elderly face.

'Do you know something else,' Gabriel added, emboldened, 'I think I'm going to take her for tea on Rue du Rhône this afternoon. I no longer care if anyone sees us. My wife doesn't care. My partners don't care. Even my dearest, conservative secretary doesn't care.'

'It's about time you found time for a little diversion,' Caroline said briskly. 'Go on, then, take her to Rue du Rhône. You could even buy her some chocolate at Auer.'

'She's twenty-five years younger than me,' Gabriel said wistfully.

'People will probably think you're interviewing a new secretary,' Caroline said with a sly smile.

'I would never do that,' Gabriel replied, smiling in turn.

'Well, at least this explains why your moods have been as changeable as a schoolboy's of late,' Caroline said. 'I was beginning to worry the money had gone to your head.'

'Maybe it has,' Gabriel said with a grin.

'Well,' said Caroline, 'you really should be heading to your office. You wouldn't want to be late for Mr Schön, would you.' She gave a conspiratorial wink. Gabriel shook his head. Had Caroline always been this sharp, this witty? What else had he been missing by keeping such a distance between himself and his employees? Another grin rose up, unstoppable. Next thing you knew, he would be learning the names of his neighbours and making jokes with strangers in the streets!

'Look who's in love!' Mr Schön boomed, removing an inexplicable green fedora. Leaning nonchalantly against the wall, he was wearing a sort of bright jade suit jacket over mustard slacks. His bow tie, the hand-tied sort, was decorated with a pattern of bird feathers. The jacket's buttons were gold.

Gabriel shrugged, as if buoyed up. 'Everyone needs a way to keep warm in the winter,' he said, barely resisting the temptation to wink. 'Not all of us can wear jungle outfits.'

Mr Schön gave a broad smile and slapped him on the shoulder in a congratulatory manner. 'Well done,' he said. 'Who is she?'

Gabriel winced. Schön's socks, Gabriel noted with distaste, were also a lurid shade of green.

'Now, now,' he said, 'let's not get carried away. Next thing, you'll be asking for her bank account number.'

'Those are not the sorts of feminine numbers that interest me,' Mr Schön replied with a slightly unpleasant wink.

'Why don't you come into my office?' Gabriel said, unlocking the door.

Mr Schön strode through the doorway thoughtfully. 'Although, for the record,' he mused aloud, 'they get expensive quickly, women, you know. I wouldn't recommend more than two at a time. Of course, now it's been seven years, my ex-wife has found some new rich businessman to support her. A Greek, if you can believe it! From the pictures she's shown me, I believe he must be seventy years old.'

Gabriel shook his head. 'Come sit down,' he said, gesturing to the mahogany table. 'I've ordered chocolate almonds and two large ristrettos. Caroline will bring them in any second.'

Mr Schön's eyes widened. 'It's not Caroline, is it?' he asked, lowering his voice.

'No,' said Gabriel, 'but I wouldn't tell you if it was.'

Mr Schön threw his head back and crowed with laughter. 'Well, enjoy yourself,' he said. 'Maybe this lady will be the right one, eh? Not everybody has to make as many mistakes as I did...'

'You're happy with Samantha, though, aren't you?' Gabriel asked curiously.

'Oh yes,' Mr Schön replied. 'I won't say there isn't the occasional temptation, but I've managed to stay quite faithful to your beauty of a redhead.'

'Just as you've stayed faithful to Von Mipatobeau,' Gabriel observed. 'Obviously, you're not as fickle as you might think.'

Mr Schön shook his head. 'You never know,' he said. 'Still, as long as I'm satisfied, I see no need to go looking elsewhere. Besides, Geneva keeps me interested. Love is like sailing: the wind is always changing. It's difficult to get bored.' He gave another outrageous wink.

'In any case, your accounts are in excellent shape this year,' Gabriel said smoothly. 'If I'm not mistaken, by the close of December, you should be looking at a net gain of fourteen per cent.'

Mr Schön raised an eyebrow. 'Fourteen?' he exclaimed. 'Why, those truly are interesting figures. You're approaching American returns.'

'Yes, we are,' Gabriel said proudly. Mr Schön's company always left him feeling oddly confident in his sartorial choices. He smoothed down his plain white shirt and adjusted his silver cufflinks – the sole addition to his unchanging panoply.

There was a delicate knock on the door, and Caroline appeared with a silver tray. The smell of freshly brewed coffee filled the room.

Mr Schön gave her a broad wink, to which she replied with a stony stare. Gabriel blushed. 'Milk?' he offered. 'Sugar?'

Mr Schön accepted both, and began to stir his cup enthusiastically. Gabriel focused on his chocolate almonds until Caroline had left the room.

'So you've been expanding your involvement abroad, then?' Mr Schön asked curiously, still stirring.

Gabriel nodded. How could one man make so much noise with a teaspoon? 'Our last trip was to the Arabian Gulf,' he added.

Mr Schön winced. 'How strange!' he said. 'Wasn't it terribly hot?'

'Oh yes,' said Gabriel. 'Thomas spent the whole time with a wet tea towel wrapped around his head. We ate camel, and stuffed lamb, and walked in the desert!'

'I see,' Mr Schön said with interest. 'And you are sure you're not taking on any unnecessary risks?'

'Oh no,' said Gabriel. 'Only the necessary kind.' He allowed himself a sharkish grin.

'Right,' Mr Schön said, nodding slowly. He took a slow sip of his coffee. 'Please don't misunderstand me. I'm sure you bankers know what you're doing. However, you see, there are certain reasons why one places one's funds with Swiss bankers. Safety is one of them.'

'Discretion is another,' Gabriel replied. 'Haven't we been the model of both over the years?'

'I suppose so,' Mr Schön said reluctantly, 'but...'

'Listen,' Gabriel said sternly. 'We have to break away from our two to four per cent rate of return. The only way out is international equity and debt placements. How many times, over the years, have you begged me to produce higher returns? Do you expect that we would be able to do that, give in to our clients' demands and attempt to transform the veritable bedrock of private Swiss banking, without changing our approach, our policies?'

'Well, no,' said Mr Schön.

'If I had come along on your fancy yacht, ten years ago, got drunk on champagne, and agreed to make a few high-return investments with your not inconsiderable fortune, you would have been thrilled.'

'Well, yes,' said Mr Schön.

'So how is this any different?'

Mr Schön ate a chocolate almond. 'I suppose it's not,' he said. He brushed invisible crumbs from the lapels of his green jacket.

'Look, I won't push you to invest anything more with us until we know for sure the end-of-year figures,' Gabriel said calmly. 'I'm only asking you to keep trusting us, as you have always trusted us. We are still the same bank. We still have the same values. We have only opened up a little to the modern world.' He picked up his coffee cup and drank deeply.

Mr Schön nodded again, slowly, as if trying to talk himself into being satisfied.

'We'll talk about new investments in the new year, then,' Gabriel said. 'Now, if you'll excuse me, I have a phone call to make.' He knew exactly which tearoom he would ask Anita to meet him at.

Anita's eyes were bright, and her cheeks were flushed from the cold. Those beloved eyes darted about the marble tearoom nervously, taking in the floor-to-ceiling mirrors, the gilding and the fresco paintings.

'I can't believe you brought me to a place like this, my dear,' she whispered into her menu.

'This is hardly the fanciest place we've eaten together,' Gabriel joked. He loosened his collar. The air was very warm, and smelled of chocolate. Exotic plants spilled from tall stone pots. It was a little overwhelming.

'You know what I mean,' Anita said very softly, not meeting his eyes. 'So central.'

The blush that spread across Gabriel's cheeks had nothing to do with the heating. 'Don't be silly,' he said, more brusquely than he had intended. 'What do I care if I am seen in public with a friend?'

Anita winced slightly, as if stung, and instantly Gabriel regretted his bombast. It was true, he felt more exposed than he had intended. Every besuited back could be a colleague; every pair of high heels could belong to a friend of his wife's. Still, it was hardly Anita's fault. It had been his idea. 'What do we care?' he said to Anita, and to his own fears. 'We're doing nothing wrong. My wife certainly doesn't care.'

Anita kept her eyes downcast, her cheeks bright red. Gabriel wished he could take back his remarks and replace them with something kinder, but his tongue stuck in his throat. 'I think I'll have hot chocolate,' he found himself saying. 'It always reminds me of my childhood.'

'In Lake Constance?' Anita asked, very quietly. She looked down at her hands folded in her lap.

Gabriel nodded. He swallowed. 'Which reminds me,' he said, impulsively, 'that I've been meaning to take you there.'

Anita looked up, her expression cautious. 'To the lake?' she asked.

Gabriel met her eyes and held her gaze. 'To meet my parents,' he said.

'Oh!' said Anita, her face melting into a smile.

Gabriel felt his heart rate accelerate, but he didn't care. 'Yes,' he said, 'I would love to show you where I grew up. My mother makes the most wonderful stew, and at night you can see the stars so clearly, up in the mountains.'

Anita nodded, as if thrilled. There, Gabriel thought. He had fixed his faux pas.

'I will have an Irish coffee,' Anita said, 'to celebrate.'

'Have you ever been skiing?' Gabriel asked curiously.

'No,' said Anita. 'I would love to, though.'

'Well!' said Gabriel. 'Perhaps we could take a little trip to a ski resort, like St Moritz. We could stop in at my parents' on the way.'

'That would be lovely,' said Anita.

'I could even teach you to ski,' Gabriel added, getting carried away.

Anita beamed at this. 'I think I will have a *forêt noire* gâteau too,' she said, somewhat breathlessly.

Gabriel motioned over the waiter. It really was very warm in the tearoom.

'So, how is work going?' Anita asked timidly. Her cheeks were pink.

Gabriel beamed. 'It's going well, actually. I just had a meeting with one of our oldest clients. He seems pleased with the returns, though I think a part of him is instinctively worried. It's as if the Swiss aren't mentally prepared for success.'

'What is he worried about?'

Gabriel shrugged. 'Things he knows very little about, really,' he said, his tone cavalier. 'I mean, his only job is to leave his money with us. It's our job to make him more of it.'

The waiter reappeared, bearing their drinks. Anita held her cup of spiced whiskey coffee up to her nose and smiled. 'It smells divine,' she said.

Gabriel smiled into his cup of thick, dark chocolate. 'I simply love this drink,' he said, 'even if it's a little indulgent.'

'You were going to tell me something about your client,' Anita prompted him.

He sighed. 'Well, to come back briefly to the question, I suppose he's intimidated by the international markets. I was, too, in the beginning. Only, since all this money has been coming in from the Arabian Gulf, I find it hard to believe we haven't made the right decisions.'

'So your trip was profitable?'

'Oh yes!' Gabriel said happily. He lowered his voice. 'Incredibly so. We've had over thirty million come in from the sheikhs we visited, and another fifteen million in the works from various other contacts. I'm really proud of our progress.'

Anita smiled, a smudge of chocolate cream on her upper lip. Gabriel leaned forward and wiped it away with his thumb. Anita blushed furiously.

'Everything is going well,' Gabriel continued. 'Even the foreign exchange rates just keep going up and up. The Swiss franc is doing well. And so is our bank.'

'You sound like you've wanted to boast about this for a while,' Anita observed, smiling.

Gabriel laughed. 'Do I? Well, I suppose you're not wrong. It's not very Swiss, you know, getting to enjoy one's successes in life. I don't really have anyone I can talk to about my life.'

Anita swallowed. 'What about your wife?' she asked, bravely.

Gabriel was silent for a moment, then gave a nod, as if making an important decision. 'It is difficult to open up to my wife,' he said. 'We have been drifting apart for years. In her own way, I suppose she is happy for my successes, but only because it means I can funnel some of my earnings into her crazy new gallery. It's difficult to say no to her. Whatever she asks for, I give.' He paused. 'At least financially.'

Anita was still smiling, her expression complicated. Gabriel couldn't figure out what she was thinking. 'Sometimes I can't read you,' he said at last. 'I hope you don't mind me talking about Clarice.'

Anita shook her head. 'She's the elephant in the room,' she said firmly. 'I don't mind acknowledging her existence. As long as I know that you care about me.'

Gabriel reached quickly across the table and grabbed Anita's hand tightly. 'I care,' he said. 'I care very much.'

'Then that is all I need.' Anita squeezed back.

'Do you want to know something I haven't told anyone?' he asked. Anita nodded happily.

'There's talk at Von Mipatobeau of me becoming a senior partner.'

'Oh,' said Anita.

Gabriel shrugged happily. 'So my personal life may be a little complicated, but at least I'm making enough money.'

Anita laughed out loud.

'I mean,' he added hastily, 'I'm very pleased to be here with you, right now, in beautiful Geneva. I really don't understand how anyone could be unmoved by its charms,' he continued. 'I mean, the beautiful lake and the river, the clean water, the fresh air, the excellent security...' He stared up at the fresco on the tearoom ceiling, as if seeking inspiration. 'Of course, the quality of the produce can't be topped, and the schools are marvellous as well.'

'It's a very international city,' Anita chipped in, 'right in the centre of Europe. People come here from all over the world, bringing their cultures.'

'Yes!' said Gabriel. 'And yet Switzerland maintains its independence from the rest of the world, whilst dealing with everyone. I mean, the president of the USA could be jogging down by the lake and nobody would look twice. Major negotiations about world conflicts take place at the UN buildings every day, and everybody leaves them alone. It's a wonderful, beautiful, safe place, and I love it.'

'I love it too,' Anita said firmly. 'I hope I will be able to stay here.'

'I hope so too,' said Gabriel. 'Would you like another coffee?'

Anita paused. 'No thank you,' she said sweetly.

'And what about the music festivals, and the museums, and the sports facilities?' Gabriel continued, waving his hands in the air.

'Geneva is a mini New York, a mini Paris, a mini London, a... mini Zurich. The architecture is fantastic too.'

Anita nodded earnestly.

Gabriel sighed happily. 'There's so much more for us to do together, here.'

'Yes,' Anita said gravely.

'So where would you like to go skiing?' Gabriel asked.

'I don't know!' Anita replied. 'I've never been before!'

'Oh yes, of course. Well, perhaps Klosters? Or Davos? Or Saint Moritz? Unless you want to go to Italy.'

'Oh no,' said Anita. 'I'm fed up with Latin countries.'

'Even the European ones?' Gabriel asked, confused.

'Yes,' Anita said firmly. 'I love Switzerland, and I want to stay in Switzerland.' She paused. 'Besides, I don't have a visa for Italy.'

'Oh!' said Gabriel. 'I hadn't thought of that. Well, Switzerland it is, then! How utterly wonderful.'

Anita gave a slow smile, and sipped her sweet drink.

———◆◆◆———

As he walked back towards his office, his hands jammed deeply into his pockets, Gabriel blocked all thoughts of Clarice from his mind. He refused to be made miserable by his wife's failure to understand him. There was someone new in his life, someone who loved him and his country. Anita was the best friend he had. He would be good to her. What did Clarice care for, apart from sex and art? Anita understood him. Anita understood Switzerland. Why hadn't he allowed himself to be happy? Gabriel asked himself, trudging along the cobblestones, his breath a grey cloud in the air. Didn't he deserve to be happy?

Chapter Thirty-One

Snowflakes drifted lazily past the car windows. Gabriel took the opportunity to glance at Anita. She appeared to have fallen deeply asleep, as she often did when he was driving. Her cheeks were rosy, and her dark hair fell in a tangled cascade over the front of her coat. God, she was beautiful! Yes, he had reservations about introducing her to his family. Yes, perhaps the proposition had been somewhat rash, even foolish. Yet it was worth the stress just to spend a little time with his beautiful, innocent, fascinating Peruvian lover. It was only a daytime visit, anyway; time to sit together for a short time over a cosy winter meal with his parents, before heading off on their ski weekend. Gabriel sighed, as the landscape became more familiar. There was the turn towards Lake Constance: soon, they would arrive at his parents' house. His stomach grumbled quietly, for it was almost lunchtime.

'Anita, darling,' he said, 'wake up! See how pretty the lakeshore is in the winter?'

Anita rubbed her eyes and sat up. 'Oh!' she said. 'There's so much snow!'

'Yes, and there will be even more when we get to St. Moritz!'

Anita grinned sleepily. 'I'm hungry,' she said.

'We're almost there,' Gabriel replied. 'Just around this corner...'

The car pulled up the drive in front of the old, weathered wooden house.

'It's enormous!' Anita exclaimed. 'And so Swiss!'

A squirrel skittered up a pine tree, sending snow falling from the branches.

Gabriel couldn't repress a smile. 'Welcome,' he said. 'It is time for you to meet the other de Puritignys.'

Anita tumbled from her side of the car, and nervously adjusted her dress as they walked towards the front door. As if seeing the place through new eyes, Gabriel took in the beautiful wooden carvings and the statues scattered through the garden. 'My father went through a woodcarving phase,' he explained.

Anita nodded distractedly. They had arrived at the small side door. Gabriel rapped the heavy knocker against the wood. Anita swallowed audibly.

The door creaked open, and Edmond de Puritigny's wrinkled face appeared. 'Gabriel!' he said. 'How nice to see you! Why do you always insist on coming in through here?' Edmond glanced at Anita, and a faint frown passed across his features. He seemed flustered.

Anita darted a worried glance at Gabriel.

'Hello, Father,' said Gabriel, as jovially as he could. 'You know I always use this door. I've always done, since I was a child. Sorry to surprise you, though. I hope we're not too late for lunch?'

'No, no,' Edmond said distractedly, stepping back. 'Do come on in.'

The corridor was filled with the faint scent of chocolate, which grew stronger as they approached the back of the house, where Edmond had his workshop.

'It smells delicious!' Anita ventured timidly.

'Ah yes,' said Edmond, somewhat irritably. 'So it does. I have been making chocolates, you see. You caught me in the middle of a batch.'

'Chocolates?' Gabriel repeated, surprised.

'Yes,' Edmond said firmly. There was an awkward pause. 'Would you like to see?' he asked reluctantly.

'Of course!' said Gabriel.

'We'll just stop by quickly before heading to the kitchen,' Edmond said. 'Your mother would never forgive me if I distract you too long with another of my hobbies. I suppose if you insist on coming in through this door, I can't very well walk you past my chocolate room without letting you have a quick look...'

'You certainly have been keeping busy in your retirement,' Gabriel commented.

Edmond threw him a sharp glance, as if trying to tell if he was joking. 'Yes,' he said shortly. 'I do not like to laze about, like many of my contemporaries.' He flung open the workshop door and strode across the room.

Gabriel leaned over to Anita. 'My father is the very spirit of Switzerland,' he said. He laid a hand on her lower back to guide her into the room. Sunlight streamed through the windows. Anita smiled. 'How utterly wonderful,' she said.

The workshop still smelled faintly of sawdust, which gave a certain richness to the redolence of chocolate. 'Your mother wouldn't let me make my chocolates in the kitchen,' Edmond said, 'so I had to have a second stove installed in here... a sort of chocolate annexe! See my large cauldron? I try to make everything by the most traditional means possible. December is the best month for me, of course, because of Christmas.'

'You've been doing this for a long time?' Gabriel asked in real surprise.

Edmond shrugged. 'A few months,' he said.

Gabriel looked round the room slowly, taking in the racks and racks of copper and silicon moulds, and the boxes piled on the shelves. 'You really have been productive,' he said. 'Do you sell these? They seem expertly packaged.'

'Some,' Edmond said. 'It didn't seem right to make chocolates just for us. I started sharing them here and there, and word got out. The packaging is actually by a well-known Zurich chocolatier, as you'll see if you look closely at the boxes. They buy the chocolate, wrap it up in gold and ribbons, and send a few back to me in thanks.'

'My word!' said Gabriel, genuinely impressed.

'They like it because I make the chocolate daily, you see,' Edmond said, visibly relaxing. He sat down on the chair by the cauldron. 'It's a claim few large companies can make, so they like to import from smaller chocolatiers like me. It only takes an hour or so to deliver to Zurich every week. It gives them an artisanal charm, I guess. The Swiss city dwellers go crazy for it.' He smiled, for the first time since they'd arrived.

'It sounds like you've been successful!' Gabriel said, shaking his head.

'I think I'm currently making more money from chocolate than I am from farming,' Edmond confirmed. 'I've been having a lot of fun, actually. I make all sorts of unusual specialities. Chocolate-covered apricots, juicy ones from the South of Italy. In the dead of winter, I started to have the fruit shipped from Africa. Figs, too, coated in ninety per cent chocolate: nearly pure cocoa! The combination of sweet and bitter is irresistible. I also make chocolates with smoked, grilled almonds. See that bag over there? That's twenty kilos of hazelnuts from the Swiss mountains.'

'This all sounds delicious,' said Anita.

Edmond gave a curt nod. 'Everybody loves my chocolates. And I don't put salt in any of the recipes either,' he barked. 'Just caramelised brown sugar, sometimes a little honey.'

Anita wilted visibly, but she bravely tried another question. 'What about milk?' she asked timidly.

Edmond glared at her. 'Milk?' he asked. 'Disgusting. Milk rots, you know, even in chocolate, until it becomes like cheese. What a disgusting idea!'

Anita's eyes were wide, like a puppy that has been shouted at. Guilt rose up in Gabriel's breast, and anger.

'Actually, I would have thought that milk was the only thing that would set Swiss chocolate apart from its competitors,' he said, rather sharply. 'All the other ingredients are imported from elsewhere; it's only the milk that would make it truly Swiss.' Edmond opened his mouth to argue, but Gabriel pressed on smoothly: 'Anyway, are you planning to expand further?' He smiled in Anita's general direction in what he hoped was a reassuring fashion. Anita shrank back, not meeting his eyes. Later, he thought, when they were alone, he would hold her close and make her forget his father's terseness. Soon, they would be in St. Moritz together, and this family ordeal would be over.

'Oh, maybe a little,' Edmond replied. 'I have this idea to make chocolate bars filled with praline, but really big ones, maybe half a square meter. Then you can cut them by hand and sell them.'

'What about international expansion?' Gabriel asked curiously. 'It sounds like you have some really exceptional products, here. People all over the world love artisanal Swiss chocolate.'

'I'm absolutely not interested,' Edmond said sharply. 'Swiss chocolate should be right here in Switzerland. The best of the Swiss are best appreciated only by the Swiss.'

Anita coughed discreetly. 'Excuse me,' she said softly, a little sadly, 'but could you tell me where the bathroom is?'

'It's just outside here, on the left,' Gabriel said, motioning towards the door.

'I'll be right back,' Anita said quietly. She closed the door behind her.

An awkward silence fell. Edmond turned to his son and glowered.

'I don't know why everyone always thinks the logical next step is the international market. There is everything you need right here in Switzerland, right by our beloved lakes, and there always has been.'

'Well,' said Gabriel. He stopped and coughed. 'I happen to disagree.' There was another long pause.

Edmond squared his shoulders in an even more disapproving manner. 'So, is that your secretary?'

'No,' said Gabriel, trying to keep his expression stern and neutral.

'Is she an employee of your bank?'

'No.'

Was his father doing this on purpose?

'Is she your driver?'

'No,' said Gabriel. He took a deep breath. 'Actually, she's my girlfriend.'

Edmond frowned. 'What on earth do you mean, your girlfriend? What happened to your lovely wife Clarice?'

'You should know, Father, that Clarice and I have not been getting along very well. Not for a long time. We have been having... trouble. We sleep in separate beds.'

Edmond waved a hand in front of his face, as if this could stop him from hearing the unwelcome news. 'This is none of my business,' he said. 'I do not want to hear about these matters. You are married, son, and that is all there is to it.'

'No, that is not all there is to it,' Gabriel said. 'You don't understand. Clarice also has new priorities, these days. She has a lot of work to do in her galleries. Meanwhile, I need... company. Anita has provided me with a great deal of support at a complicated time. Her conversation is sweet and refreshing. She is nice.'

'Nice?' Edmond repeated, his frown having deepened and his cheeks turned pink. 'Nice? Do you think a man leaves his wife of twenty, thirty years because he meets someone nice?'

'Anita is kind, and patient, and she understands me,' Gabriel added, unable to stop himself. 'She's introduced me to all sorts of international food. I've eaten Peruvian and Cuban food, and Portuguese food. Just a few weeks ago, after I came back from my trip, we discovered Arabian food together! We ate stuffed lamb.'

'That's disgusting,' said Edmond, wrinkling his nose. 'Your mother and I would never dream of such a thing!'

'What do you mean?' said Gabriel, getting angry. 'You live on a farm! You kill chickens! How is a stuffed lamb any different?'

'Lamb is for Easter,' Edmond said, primly.

'Father, I live in the modern world,' Gabriel retorted. 'I have no desire to be as conservative as my forebears.'

'I can see that,' sniffed Edmond.

Before Gabriel could intervene, his father had launched into the rest of his speech. 'What kind of Swiss man could do such a thing? What de Puritigny has ever nourished such ignoble thoughts? What about tradition, religion, moral values? What will people say about you? You're a famous banker, Gabriel, from a respectable old family. You live in the house you inherited in the most beautiful, historic part of Geneva. How can you do such a thing? If people find out... You might lose half your clients!'

'It doesn't work like that any more, Father,' Gabriel replied, his ears burning. 'My clients are not moralistic fools. Times have changed, even in Switzerland. I'm far from the only banker with a girlfriend. Besides, why would any of our clients find out about what happens in my private life?'

'It always happens,' said Edmond, slamming his fist down on his chocolate-making table. 'You are underestimating Geneva. What about your Calvinistic friends, hmm? They all have strict morals, as far as I understand. They are good people. You are not a Catholic, son. You can't just go to church and confess the crime of having two women at the same time!'

'I don't have two women!' Gabriel cried angrily. 'I hardly even see Clarice these days. We are living separate lives! To be perfectly honest, I don't think she would even care if she found out I had a girlfriend.'

'You are going to tell her?' Edmond asked in disbelief.

'I don't know, Father,' Gabriel replied, as firmly as he could. 'It's none of your business.

'Gabriel, listen to me,' Edmond said, 'Clarice may be none of my business, but you and your life are. You're already in your forties. You have a stable life, a successful banking career. You must be making, what, five to eight million a year by now? So why are you jeopardising all this by messing around with young girls? Stay put. Enjoy your life. Why do you always need to go looking for more?'

'I'm sorry I mentioned any of this,' Gabriel said curtly. 'I should have known you wouldn't understand. I just wanted better communication within our family, but I can see I was mistaken. That is clearly not the de Puritigny way. Why don't you just pretend that Anita is my secretary, or my driver, or whatever lie makes it easier for you, to live your deluded Swiss life?'

'I will,' said Edmond. 'That is exactly what I will do.' He popped a chocolate into his mouth and chewed it angrily.

There was a silence. 'What time is lunch?' Gabriel asked coldly. 'I don't know where Anita has gone.'

'Eleven thirty,' said Edmond. 'Or at least, it should have been, if our guests weren't late.'

Gabriel sniffed. 'That's ridiculously early,' he said. 'Besides, we would be on schedule if you hadn't just spent twenty minutes showing us your silly chocolates.'

'We have always eaten early,' said Edmond. 'We rise early, we eat early, and we go to bed early. That is the Swiss way.'

'That is no longer my Swiss way,' Gabriel said shortly. 'I'm going to find Anita and Mother.' He stood up and left the room.

The bathroom door was open, and Anita clearly no longer there. So where had she gone? Gabriel sighed. He hoped she was not too upset. Surely she hadn't gone back to the car? He would go greet his mother quickly, then go and search for her. He walked on to the end of the corridor, the scent of chocolate dissipating.

When he opened the door to the kitchen, a wave of rich, savoury steam engulfed him. The beams were hung with pine branches and little twinkling lights, and red ribbons dangled from the doorway. Everything was warm and golden, and smelled utterly delicious. When the steam cleared, and Gabriel gathered his senses, he realised his mother and Anita were sitting side by side at the kitchen table, chopping vegetables.

'Mother!' Gabriel said in surprise. 'Anita!'

Avenira looked up and smiled warmly. 'What a marvellous young woman you have here, my dear,' she said. 'It is a pleasure to have you both.'

Gabriel blinked, then walked over and kissed his mother on the cheek.

'You can kiss your girlfriend if you like, too,' Avenira said with something suspiciously close to a wink.

Gabriel stared at both women, until Anita burst out laughing. 'Your mother is very sweet. I turned the wrong way, coming back from the bathroom,' she explained. 'I walked into this room, that just smelled so marvellous!'

'I was in the middle of preparing the vegetables for the stew,' Avenira added, 'and this considerate young woman offered to help.'

'She gave me a taste, and after that I couldn't resist!' Anita said. She paused. 'You're not angry, are you?'

'Angry?' Gabriel repeated. 'Certainly not! I just...' He sighed, removed his glasses and rubbed his eyes. 'I just had a slightly difficult conversation with my father.'

'You didn't try to convince him to sell his chocolates abroad, did you?' Avenira asked in concern. 'It's a lost cause.'

'Something like that,' said Gabriel, putting his glasses back on. 'In any case, we came to an agreement.' Coming to his senses at last, he turned to Anita and kissed her lightly on the cheek. 'I'm glad you two seem to be getting along.'

'Anita is a delight,' Avenira said. 'I mean, she's such a pretty young girl! Such human warmth to her! This, Gabriel, is not a woman who will abandon you to spend all her time in art galleries. Certainly not one who would mock you as you were jumping into icy waters!'

Flabbergasted, Gabriel's mouth opened and shut a few times. Anita flushed bright red.

'Besides,' Avenira added, a mischievous glint still in her eyes, 'she has a beautiful figure.'

'Mother!' Gabriel exclaimed, then he stopped. 'Thank you,' he added, more gently.

Anita looked down at her vegetables, smiling and blushing. 'What icy waters?' she asked timidly.

Avenira rolled her eyes. 'My wonderful son made the brave decision to swim in Lake Geneva at the start of this month, and his wife could think of nothing to do than to turn up with her girlfriends and mock him!'

'Wasn't it very cold?' Anita asked. 'You're so brave, Gabriel!'

Gabriel shrugged. 'A few of my partners at the bank have been doing it for years. I thought it would be fun to join them, for once.' He sighed. 'I can't pretend Clarice was particularly kind or supportive on this occasion.'

'That's an understatement!' said Avenira. 'What was it she said? "Take a look, girls! This is as much of Gabriel's body as any of us will see this year!" If I'd been there, I swear I would have slapped her.'

Anita gasped, then blushed furiously. Avenira shook her head, then laughed.

'Mother,' Gabriel said gently. 'Please.'

'I'm serious, though,' Avenira continued. 'I mean, this could be the best thing that ever happened to you. You could move away from the snobbery of that cold fish. Clarice is colder than an *omble chevalier*! I can tell just from looking at her that this girl is down to earth.' Anita's face, if possible, turned an even deeper shade of crimson. 'This could be a good future for you. Why don't you two lovebirds get married?'

'Mother!' Gabriel said again, appalled. He glanced at Anita, who was not looking up from her vegetables. 'I mean... if I separate from Clarice, there will be a scandal from Neuchâtel to the Ticino.'

'So what?' Avenira said calmly. 'She would be good for you. You'll be renewed, you'll be youthful. I haven't seen you smile this much in years. Just look at her peeling those turnips! I can tell this woman knows how to cook. You see, she comes from a background where girlfriends and wives support a man. They're the powers behind the throne. Clarice, on the other hand, has been a weight on you, pulling you down.'

'Please,' Gabriel said, his ears red, 'I really am not comfortable with this line of enquiry.'

'Fine,' said Avenira, shrugging. 'But just look how pleased your Anita is.'

Anita was, indeed, still smiling ear to ear.

'So, um, I see you've got into the Christmas spirit,' Gabriel commented, desperate to introduce a new subject.

'Of course!' his mother replied. 'It's a shame you never celebrate Christmas with us anymore.'

'You do not come here for Christmas?' Anita asked curiously, looking up. 'But it's so lovely! Besides, I'm sure the food is delicious.'

'You're right about that, young woman,' Avenira replied.

Guiltily, Gabriel shook his head. 'I would if I could,' he said, 'but Clarice always insisted on us having a quiet, family Christmas.'

'Yes, and your Geneva friends all have swanky parties with lots of glitter and champagne, I know. Still, it's a shame.' A twinkle appeared in Avenira's eye. 'Perhaps things will change in the future.'

Gabriel stared at his mother in disbelief.

'Besides,' Avenira continued, 'I already have some gifts wrapped up for you! You can take them back for your tree. You must take some homemade chocolates away with you, as well.'

'I have not spent Christmas with my family in a very long time,' Anita said suddenly, wistfully.

'You are a Catholic?' Avenira inquired.

Anita nodded. 'It is a great celebration, for us, even if the weather is warm. I miss my family very much.'

'Do you still have a lot of family in Peru, then?' Avenira asked.

'Everyone is still there,' Anita replied, 'except my father, who passed away a long time ago.'

Gabriel stared. How long had these two women known each other?

'I'm so sorry,' Avenira said, setting down her knife and taking Anita's hand.

Anita shrugged. 'I was only a child,' she said.

'Family is essential,' Avenira said firmly. 'We are so lucky to have those who are still with us.'

Anita nodded earnestly. 'I am very close to my mother,' she said. 'We often speak on the phone.'

'She also gets along well with her brother and her three sisters,' Gabriel added quickly, keen to prove his knowledge.

Anita smiled up at him. 'Yes,' she said, 'and now I have Gabriel to depend on too.'

These words conjured up a complicated set of emotions in Gabriel's heart. Of course, he was thrilled that Anita should feel so safe with him. Yet, at the same time, he was still married to Clarice.

'Do not worry,' Avenira said softly, as if reading his mind. 'I'm sure you two will do just fine.' It was then that Gabriel realised she was answering Anita.

———•◆•———

When Edmond returned from his workshop, conversation became a little more stilted. Nonetheless, the obvious bond between Avenira and Anita lightened the atmosphere considerably. The simple vegetable stew was delicious, flavoured with tarragon and freshly ground pepper. They ate thick slices of crusty, homemade bread, slathered with salt butter.

'There's a terrible storm brewing,' Avenira said, looking out the window. 'Do you see those clouds in the distance?'

Gabriel squinted out the window. 'It's not even snowing anymore, Mother,' he said. 'There were only a few flakes on the drive down.'

Avenira shook her head. 'This morning, no birds were singing,' she said. 'It's a sure sign. I really don't think you two should take the road again today. It isn't safe.'

'We have a hotel booked in St. Moritz for tonight,' Gabriel said. 'We can't stay.'

Edmond choked on his soup. 'St. Moritz?' he repeated in disbelief.

'It's only three and a half hours away,' Gabriel said, defensively.

'You have to be the Shah of Iran to afford that place,' Edmond muttered.

'How lovely!'Avenira said, quickly and loudly. 'So work is going well, Gabriel?' she added.

Gabriel glanced up at his father with some trepidation, but Edmond appeared studiously absorbed in his soup. 'It's actually going extremely well,' he replied. 'Since I came back from the Arabian Gulf, our client base has expanded massively. The French and the Americans are still arriving in droves.'

Edmond made another strange coughing sound, but said nothing.

'Edmond,' Avenira said, her tone one of warning.

'What?' Edmond spat, looking back and forth between his wife and his son. 'You expect me to sit here and listen to Gabriel listing the ways he is ruining his life, as well as our bank? My bank?'

'You are retired,' Gabriel said quietly. 'It is no longer your bank, Father.'

'I may be retired from running Bank Von Mipatobeau, but you can bet your bottom Swiss franc that I am not retired from caring what you do with it.'

'Gabriel is doing extremely well,' Avenira said. 'It would be indiscreet to mention his salary over lunch, but I can tell you that it is more than you were making in your day.'

'Inflation,' Edmond said dismissively.

'It's not inflation,' Gabriel said angrily. 'I've worked hard for the bank's expansion abroad. It's been a difficult transition, and I think I've managed it well.'

'And what happens at the end of this expansion, hm?' Edmond asked, now infuriatingly calm. 'Do you know what happens at the end of a rise like this?'

'There is no rise,' Gabriel said. 'This is not artificial. We have just found a large number of new clients. That is all there is to it.'

Edmond straightened his shoulders and spooned up some more soup. 'I just find it difficult to stand by, watching my son bring shame on our family.'

It was Avenira's turn to glare. 'Mind your tongue, Edmond,' she snapped. 'Be respectful of our guests.'

'Guests!' Edmond said. 'As if I care what Gabriel's *driver* thinks. Or was she his assistant?' His tone was no longer guarded, and had become downright malevolent.

'Fine,' Gabriel snapped back, 'call her my driver. She's driving me to happiness.'

'You're a fool,' said Edmond, 'and she's a floozy.'

'Edmond!' said Avenira. 'Apologise at once!'

'No need,' said Gabriel, standing up and throwing his napkin on the table. 'Anita, my dear, let's go. Mother, thank you for a wonderful lunch.'

'No!' Avenira said, rising in turn. 'You really mustn't go now. The storm will arrive soon!'

'We'll be fine, Mother,' said Gabriel, marching over and kissing her swiftly. 'Anita, do you have everything?'

Anita nodded, her face crimson, putting on her coat with her eyes on the table. Avenira kissed her cheek. 'You two be careful,' she murmured. She slipped a wrapped present into Anita's pocket.

'Yes,' murmured Anita. 'Thank you.'

Without glancing back, Gabriel took Anita by the arm and marched down the corridor to the door. Outside, the air was bitterly cold.

Chapter Thirty-Two

'I can't believe it!' Gabriel said, clutching the steering wheel so tightly that his knuckles turned white. 'What an utter... I mean, how can you pretend to be an upstanding Swiss gentlemen, and then say such things to one's guests?'

Anita dabbed at her eyes with a handkerchief. 'It's nothing, my dear,' she said. 'Really. Your mother was lovely.'

'Good,' said Gabriel. 'Good.' He banged his fist on the wheel. 'I just don't understand why my father has to be so unpleasant! He made his intolerance clear. He should have just kept quiet after that.'

'He obviously felt quite strongly about the issue,' Anita said quietly.

'Well, so do I,' Gabriel said, more angrily than he had intended.

There was a silence. Snow was swirling around the car in great, drifting sheets. At times, it obscured Gabriel's vision of the road entirely. Much as it galled him to admit it, his mother seemed to have been right about the weather. The sky was a brooding shade of purple-grey, turning darker and darker. Soon, it would be night.

Still, how dare his father? They were both grown men, and should be able to communicate like adults, even if they disagreed about every essential idea. It was awful, though, Gabriel couldn't help feeling. He had spent nearly his whole life looking up to his father, admiring his values and beliefs. What a terrible disillusionment for them to be fighting like this now! Edmond had always been proud of the way Gabriel had taken over the bank. And how was he taking Clarice's side? The two of them had never even been particularly friendly! It was such a shame, such a terrible shame. Was that a turn in the road? Gabriel squinted into the thickly falling snow. He wasn't sure. No, he was probably on the right track.

'Gabriel?' Anita ventured timidly. 'I'm a little cold.'

Gabriel turned up the heating. 'There, my dear,' he said soothingly. 'Just relax.'

'Are we very far from St. Moritz?'

Gabriel hesitated. In truth, he had no idea. It had been miles since the last signpost, and at times he could barely see the sides of the road. 'It should only be another hour or so,' he said as confidently as he could.

'Tell me again about the hotel,' Anita said sleepily.

Gabriel smiled. 'Very well. The Badrutt's Palace,' he said, 'is one of the best hotels in the world. It's a historical building, purchased by the Badrutt family at the end of the nineteenth century – if I remember correctly. I've only been there once, in summer, but winter is really the right time to see St. Moritz. It's when the jewellery auctions are taking place, and there is the famous horse polo in the snow...'

Anita clapped her hands together. 'That sounds so wonderful.'

'Hopefully we'll be there soon,' Gabriel said, with some trepidation. As far as he could tell, the snowfall had turned into a real blizzard. What would they do if they got lost?

'It's going to get dark soon, isn't it?' Anita said, quietly.

She had a point. They had left his parents' house around 2 pm. The drive from there to St. Moritz was three and a half hours or so, and indeed, the sky was getting darker by the minute. He could no longer see any streetlights. 'Yes, I suppose so,' Gabriel replied.

They drove on for a time in silence. Snow was whipping around the car, so fast and hard that the wind made an unpleasant howling noise. It was now completely dark. The scene reminded Gabriel unpleasantly of stories he had heard of being caught in the heart of an avalanche, tumbled over and over with no control, lost in a wave of snow.

Anita gasped. 'What was that?' she asked.

There was a sinking feeling in Gabriel's stomach. 'The car slipped a little,' he said as calmly as he could. 'Nothing to worry about. We have snow tyres.'

'But the snow is so high,' she said, sitting bolt upright, a note of panic appearing in her voice.

'I know.' The car had slowed to a crawl. 'I know.'

'Is it safe to drive?' Anita insisted.

All at once, with the crunching sound of compacting snow, the car ground to a halt.

Gabriel swallowed. 'I'm so sorry, Anita,' he said. 'I don't think I can go any further. I don't even know where we are anymore. The snow has blocked the road.'

Anita grabbed his arm. 'But what are we going to do?' she whimpered. 'Where will we go?'

'We're going to pull off to the side of the road until the blizzard slows down,' he said. 'We have plenty of petrol in the car.'

'It sounds like a tornado,' Anita cried. 'Are we going to die?'

Gabriel squeezed her hand. 'I'm going to pull over, and then I'm going to wrap you in my arms. Then we'll be warm, and safe. It's not safe on the road.' The sound of his voice seemed to soothe her, so he kept talking. 'We can climb back into the backseat, so we can lie in each other's arms. We'll keep the car motor running so we're not cold. As far as I can tell, we must be only a few miles from Klosters. As soon as the snow clears, we'll drive on there and stay the night. Then we'll head on to St. Moritz in the morning.' The car was now nestled on the side of the road, under a copse of tall pine trees. The noise of the storm raged around them.

'I'm frightened,' Anita said quietly.

'Come on,' Gabriel said, switching on the light and clambering through the space between the front seats. 'We'll be nice and cosy back here. Follow me.'

Reluctantly, Anita hauled herself into the back. Gabriel, as confidently as he could, took her in his arms and pulled her shivering form close.

'Hold me tight,' she whispered, her voice muffled by his coat collar. 'I'm so cold.'

Gabriel obliged. Snow was gathering on the car window in thick ridges, creeping higher and higher. Would it reach the roof and cover them entirely? Anita's face was turned into his neck, and he was grateful she would not witness the snow's progression. Her breathing had slowed, and her hands had slipped inside his coat, holding his waist.

'Kiss me,' Anita murmured.

Gabriel obliged. He supposed it would keep them warm. Anita pulled him close, kissing him softly. Gabriel ran his hands up and down her arms, hoping to rub some heat into her. After a while, they settled into a comfortable embrace, dozing in the warm interior. The snow was slowing, and a chunk of black sky was visible through the car window.

'Look at the stars,' he whispered.

'Ooh, I have chocolates in my pocket!' said Anita.

It was almost midnight.

Light streaming through the windows woke them. The gathered snow had subsided, and the road was clearly visible. Gabriel stretched, and kissed Anita on the forehead. 'Good morning, my dear,' he murmured.

'We're still alive!' said Anita.

'All thanks to those chocolates,' Gabriel smiled.

'Thanks to your kiss,' Anita murmured.

'Now, let's see if this door will open.' He pressed his shoulder against the door and heaved. With a crack of breaking ice, it flew open. Freezing air blew in, fresh and bright.

Anita scrambled across the seats. 'Let's get out of here!'

'Just help me clear off the car,' Gabriel said, handing her a scraper. Much of the snow had shifted from the vehicle, but the roof and the front windshield were still deeply buried. The pair worked together, slowly and carefully, without complaint.

'I promise we'll have hot chocolate as soon as we get to St. Moritz,' Gabriel said, 'to warm our hands.'

'I don't want to eat chocolate ever again,' Anita said, shaking her head. 'I think I'll need something stronger!'

Gabriel laughed. 'OK,' he said. 'Now, let's see if everything still works.' He pulled open the front door, and sat down in the driver's seat. The motor was still purring happily. He switched the ignition off, then on again, and pushed down on the accelerator. The car slowly edged onto the road, where the snow still lay thickly. The car thermometer indicated that the temperature was between 2 and 3 degrees, however, so there was little risk of ice. Gabriel speeded up a little, and the car eased down the snowy road. 'Look, Anita!' he said. 'You can see the peaks again!'

There they were, in all their glory: the Alps. They must have already passed Klosters, then. Perhaps they weren't that far from St. Moritz after all. They drove on under the bright blue skies.

'I can't believe how nice the weather is now!' Anita exclaimed. 'That crazy blizzard just blew in out of nowhere, and disappeared again.'

'Snow is unpredictable,' Gabriel said. 'I know we're in Switzerland, but not everything can be well ordered.'

Anita giggled. 'Oh look!' she said. 'There's a small lake there!'

'That's St. Moritz,' Gabriel replied happily. 'We must be nearing the city.' They looked out at the cluster of pretty little chalets and church spires, hidden away amongst the towering peaks. The car followed the winding road through a series of long tunnels, then down the mountainside towards the valley where the lake lay glistening. Everything around them was white, glistening almost blue in the bright morning air.

'If you could just open the glove compartment,' Gabriel said, 'you'll find a piece of paper with the hotel's exact address.' Anita handed the slip over, and Gabriel nodded slowly, looking back and forth from the text to the road. 'Very well,' he said. 'We're very nearly there.' They entered town and aimed for the lakefront.

'Oh, is that it?' Anita gasped. 'It looks like a castle!'

In front of them, they found a blocky stone building, towering above them. Gabriel smiled. 'Yes, that's it. Welcome to Badrutt's!' He pulled into the drive.

A cluster of well-dressed staff immediately sprang forth from the golden doorway, waiting to usher them in, carry their luggage, and satisfy their smallest demands. 'Would you like to eat or drink anything, monsieur, madame?' a tall waiter asked as soon as they arrived in the entry hall.

Anita, overwhelmed by the finery of the setting, took a moment to reply. Then she smiled. 'Yes, we would,' she said.

The waiter led them down a long, wooden corridor hung with paintings of saints. 'If you're hungry, I would recommend the breakfast buffet.'

Anita and Gabriel exchanged a glance. Finally, they entered a vast room panelled with glass, overlooking the lake. 'We can eat anything we like?' Anita asked cautiously.

The waiter smiled. 'Of course,' he said.

'It's just that we were trapped in the snowstorm overnight,' Anita confessed.

The waiter raised an eyebrow. 'Goodness me,' he said.

'We're quite alright,' Gabriel hastened to add, a little embarrassed.

'You're very lucky, you know,' the said. 'Getting stuck at a thousand meters of altitude is no laughing matter.'

'Yes,' Gabriel said shortly, 'and now we are very hungry.'

He picked up a tray and two large plates, and they began to tuck in. Buttery raisin pastries lay piled up next to flaky croissants and *pain au chocolat*. A large glass jar of bircher muesli sat next to three pitchers of freshly-squeezed juices and steaming silver jugs of tea and coffee. There were boiled eggs, and two kinds of rye bread, and a selection of Swiss cheeses and dried meats with pickles. There were also iced cinnamon stars, dried figs and dates, and fresh oranges and grapes.

'Now this,' said Gabriel, '*is* a breakfast buffet.'

Sitting beneath the ancient wooden ceiling and crystal chandeliers, the couple were quite overwhelmed. Through the window, they could see the rippling lake and the white valleys of the mountains.

'We need our strength, after all,' said Gabriel, 'if we are to explore St. Moritz. Do you still want to go skiing?'

Anita was quiet for a moment, busy with a boiled egg and some buttered toast. 'I'm not sure,' she said hesitantly. 'I do want to learn, but I feel quite exhausted. Perhaps we can simply walk around the city today?'

'Of course,' Gabriel said, smiling. 'There is usually a polo match on Sunday. We might be able to see that.'

'Oh, let's!' Anita exclaimed happily.

He nodded. 'Very well. I'll ask the waiter about the times.'

'Maybe we should order some mimosas,' Anita added thoughtfully.

Gabriel smiled. 'Anything you want,' he said.

As if on cue, the waiter reappeared. 'Madame would like to order something?' he inquired.

Anita nodded. 'Yes, please,' she said. 'One mimosa.'

'And monsieur?'

'I'll have one as well,' Gabriel said, indulgently. 'We were also wondering what time the polo takes place?'

'Around four o'clock, monsieur,' he replied. 'In the meantime, I might recommend visiting the town's Christmas market.'

Anita's eyes lit up.

———— ◆ ————

'Would you like another mulled wine?' Anita asked, her arm linked through Gabriel's, her cheeks rosy. In the twinkling lights of the market stalls, she looked young and exhilarated.

'No, thank you,' said Gabriel. 'If I have another cup, I'll end up dancing on the tables by the end of the afternoon! I'll bet my Christmas bonus on the horse polo!'

'That sounds fun,' Anita giggled. 'Go on! Ooh, and let's try those little balls of fried dough. They look delicious!'

'I saw a foie gras stand up ahead,' Gabriel suggested. 'Why don't we stop there instead?'

'How festive!' Anita said. 'I feel so glamorous!'

Gabriel sighed, gazing up at the braided pine boughs and the red velvet ribbons. 'It's wonderful,' he said, 'but I'm afraid I can't get my father's words out of my head. What happened yesterday... I wish we hadn't left quite so hastily. What if we'd had an accident last night in the snow? He would never have forgiven himself for his harsh words.'

'That's his responsibility, not ours. That means it's up to him to apologise,' Anita said stubbornly.

'Well, yes,' Gabriel admitted, 'it is. But he's my father, you know?' Anita's face clouded over, and immediately Gabriel was overcome with guilt. 'Oh my darling,' he said, 'I didn't think.'

Anita smiled. 'It's alright,' she said. 'I know we're not talking about me. Listen, if it's weighing you down like this, you can speak to him. I simply feel that you... that both of us deserve an apology from him.'

'You needn't worry,' Gabriel reassured her. 'I know my mother will talk him round. Next time we go there for lunch...'

Anita smiled sadly. 'I don't know if there should be a next time,' she said. 'I mean, in a way, he's right. There is nothing legitimate about our union, even though nothing has even happened between us.'

'That's not true,' Gabriel said, stung. 'We kissed last night. Doesn't that mean something to you?'

'Of course it does,' Anita replied, 'but I'm afraid, Gabriel. I'm afraid of losing you.' She clung to his arm, suddenly passionate. 'You are tied to another woman by law, in the eyes of the church. How can we ever truly be together while that is the case?'

Gabriel kissed her forehead softly. 'Anita, this is all very new,' he said. 'Give me some time to think this over. I'm sure we will come up with a solution.'

'Fine,' said Anita, bitterly, 'but don't make me go to lunch with your awful father again until we have a good one.'

Gabriel stared at her, then began to walk quickly through the market. They marched on in silence for a time, Anita scurrying to keep up, glancing distractedly at the wooden stalls selling glass baubles, candles and biscuits; ornaments, tiny sausages and soap.

'Christmas markets are silly,' Gabriel declared suddenly, making a nearby couple jump and glare disapprovingly. 'We are not children. It's just an excuse to make us spend money.'

'Gabriel,' Anita said softly, slipping her hand into his, 'don't be angry with me. I'm sorry I said your father was awful. I only mean what happened was hurtful to me. You see, I've never introduced a boyfriend to my parents, or been introduced to anyone's family. To fail so spectacularly...' Tears sprang to her eyes.

Gabriel, mortified, wrapped her in his arms and held her tight. 'Oh, my darling, you didn't fail!' he said. 'They failed you. Switzerland failed us. Hundreds of years of Protestantism failed us!'

Anita giggled. 'Besides, Christmas markets aren't stupid,' she said. 'Have some more mulled wine.'

'Let's have some foie gras, too,' Gabriel said decisively. 'Then we'll go find this famous horse polo.'

'And then,' Anita said, squeezing his hand, 'we can go back to the hotel.' Gabriel squeezed back.

'Oh, it was so exciting!' Anita sighed, collapsing onto the dark blue silk sheets of the canopied bed. 'I simply love horses!'

'I seem to remember you being quite fond of cows, as well, when we saw the combats de Hérens.'

Anita threw a crisp white pillow at him. 'You know I love animals,' she said. 'Even the violent ones.'

'You enjoyed the polo, then?'

'Oh yes! Although I was so cold! I wonder if there's going to be another snowstorm tonight.' She glanced coyly at Gabriel. 'Maybe we should drive out into the snow again.'

Gabriel laughed, delighted. 'What, do you mean you want to be trapped, near-death, almost smothered by the snow?'

'In your arms? Any day,' Anita replied.

Gabriel blushed, looked away, and walked to the window. The room was truly luxurious, with several couches, a mahogany desk, and a crystal chandelier. The flowered curtains opened to reveal a large bay window overlooking the sparkling lights of the city, and the dark expanse of the lake.

'What would you like to do tomorrow, my dear?' Gabriel asked.

'Let's go back to the Christmas market! I want to live this

afternoon over and over!'

Gabriel smiled. 'Well, we can certainly do that, but why not add in a little variety? Perhaps we could try to attend one of the auctions? They sell the most expensive jewellery. Diamonds and gold, that sell for princely sums.'

'How much?' Anita asked, curiously.

'I don't know, sometimes around five million? I mean, I've never been a buyer.'

Anita laughed. 'What other entertainment can you offer me, Mr Swiss Man?'

'I don't know,' Gabriel replied. 'Perhaps a ride in a horse-drawn carriage? A lunch of fondue? We really must try the spa, here. It's supposed to be fantastic, with saunas and Jacuzzis and little splashing fountains...'

'What about skiing?' Anita suggested.

'I thought you weren't sure about the idea?' Gabriel asked.

'Oh, no, I definitely want to try!' she said. 'When you describe it, it sounds just like flying. And I love the Swiss mountains so much, you know! I was just too tired and fragile today, after last night's ordeal.'

'I thought you said you loved it,' Gabriel teased.

Anita gave a playful frown. 'I prefer this suite,' she said. 'It must have been horribly expensive, though!'

Gabriel shrugged and looked away again. 'It doesn't matter,' he said, 'as long as you're enjoying yourself.'

'No, really,' Anita pressed him, 'I really don't know how I feel about such an extravagant gift. I don't know how I'll ever repay you!'

'You don't have to repay me,' Gabriel said passionately. 'I want you here with me, and I want you to be happy. That's all I need.'

'Seriously, though,' said Anita. 'How much did it cost?'

Gabriel sighed. 'Around three thousand francs,' he said.

Anita's eyes widened. 'Oh my,' she said. 'Oh my! I know successful engineers in Peru that earn that much in a year!'

'Don't worry about it,' said Gabriel. 'I'm doing this because I want to, because…because I love you.'

Silence fell again. 'You love me?' Anita said.

Gabriel swallowed and turned quickly back to the window. 'Yes,' he said at last. 'I… I realised it at my parents' house. I mean, I've known for some time that I had feelings for you, but when I got angry, when I heard you attacked like that, I just couldn't control myself. It was like… like I was a fireplace, and somebody had filled me with little branches, branches that had been drying in a shed for a long time. No, that's not quite right. I mean, how can my father talk of fidelity to Switzerland? You're more Swiss than the Swiss. What does it matter how legitimate our union is? I mean… I just mean…'

Anita's bare feet had made no sound as she padded across the carpet to him. She wrapped her arms around him and turned him to her. 'I love you too, Gabriel,' she said. 'Now,' she went on, kissing him gently, 'let's enjoy this fancy bed.'

'You know,' Gabriel said, pulling back, 'some of the larger suites cost around ten thousand a night. This is really nothing.'

Anita tugged on his hand, looking up at him coyly.

'I mean, these chandeliers probably are only cut glass,' Gabriel babbled. 'You can tell by the colour.'

Anita slowly removed his glasses and set them on the night stand.

'Although they do have that fantastic mini swimming pool,' he murmured.

Anita pulled him into bed and began to kiss him. Gabriel fought off visions of mountain roads, Clarice in her kimono, his father with his chocolates, and, inexplicably, the chalet, before closing his eyes and succumbing to her embrace. After all, it was quite pleasant, Anita was very beautiful, and it *was* a fancy bed.

———◆◆———

The bed was a magnificent four-poster, decorated like the room in a sort of eighteenth-century Germanic style, with a golden canopy hanging down above the lovers. The mattress was topped with a vast, thick eiderdown. The couple lay under the covers, holding each other close.

'Goose feathers are much better than any other kind, you know,' Gabriel said, happily. 'Wild geese are the best, and softest.'

'How wonderful,' Anita said, snuggling into his shoulder.

'There really is a lot of gilding here, don't you think? Almost too much. And silk sheets, aren't they a little tacky?'

'I like gold and silk,' said Anita. 'They make me feel like a princess. Shall we order room service?'

Gabriel kissed the top of her head. 'What would you like, my love?'

Anita sat up. 'Maybe a steak?' she said. 'And a bottle of red wine.'

'Whatever you want,' Gabriel said. 'I'll just have some toast.'

Anita stretched happily. 'I could get used to this,' she said. Gabriel was quiet. Anita picked up the phone and ordered, then nestled back into the duvet. She reached up and stroked his hair softly. 'Gabriel?' she asked tentatively. 'Did you enjoy that?'

Gabriel blushed furiously. 'I, er, yes,' he said. 'Of course. It was extremely enjoyable.' He wriggled away. 'Must you mess up my hair like that?'

Anita kissed his cheek. 'I enjoyed it,' she said. 'I like the Swiss style. I mean, I never understood why people liked skiing, but now I understand why people like those bendy legs.'

Gabriel shook his head. 'You'll find out soon enough if you like skiing,' he said. 'I'm quite looking forward to being out on the slopes. It's been a while.'

'Well, I quite like *this* new form of exercise,' she replied.

'Exercise is good,' Gabriel blurted out.

'This is less death-defying than skiing,' Anita said thoughtfully.

'Well, I hope so,' said Gabriel.

Anita laughed. 'Do you know, I don't understand how your wife and her girlfriends could laugh when you were swimming. You have a very athletic body!'

'I do a lot of walking,' Gabriel said stiffly. 'I like being in the mountains.'

'I like being in the mountains too,' Anita said, kissing him again.

'I wonder if they have the *Financial Times* here,' Gabriel mused aloud.

'Shall we do it again?' asked Anita.

'Alright,' said Gabriel, not unwillingly. 'Let's do it again.'

'*Chéri?*' There was a knock on Gabriel's bedroom door.

Gabriel sighed and lowered his copy of the *Financial Times*. 'Yes, Clarice?'

'May I come in?'

'Of course,' he replied. He removed his glasses and rubbed his eyes. The bifocals made reading in low light rather tiring, but he simply could no longer manage without them. He glanced at the clock: it was just before seven.

Clarice entered hesitantly, wearing a floor-length linen dress in a wild, exotic print. Her greying hair was pulled back in a loose bun, and she held a newspaper in her hand. 'Have you seen the news?' she asked. 'Not the pink one,' she added with a trace of irony. 'I mean, the local papers.'

'No, I can't say I have,' Gabriel replied. 'I don't tend to keep up with local gossip. Besides, I don't really have time to read more than one paper before work.'

'Well, if you have a spare minute, you might find this week's edition interesting,' she said mildly. 'Your partner Pierre-Yves is splashed all over the covers.'

Gabriel sat bolt upright. 'Pierre-Yves? Why? Has something happened?'

Clarice smiled slyly. 'You might say that,' she said. 'He's been hosting crazy sadomasochistic parties all over town, with his twenty-year-old mistress.'

Gabriel rolled his eyes. 'He's only a kid,' he said.

Clarice raised an eyebrow. 'He's forty-five,' she reminded him. 'I hardly remember you getting into any such... shenanigans at that age.'

'Well, I wasn't interested in that sort of thing then, and I'm not interested now, in my sixties,' Gabriel said flatly. 'What Pierre-Yves does in his private life does not concern us professionally. He is one of our most dedicated partners. His work with the Arabian accounts is flawless.'

Clarice lowered the newspaper, but did not leave the room.

'How are you, then?' Gabriel asked stiffly. It seemed rude to start reading the *Financial Times* again until she was gone. 'Did you enjoy your early coffee in bed?'

'It's April,' she said hesitantly.

What was wrong with drinking coffee in April? Gabriel frowned. Or... had he forgotten some important date? He was meeting Anita for dinner the next evening but no, that wasn't it. There was the conference at Von Mipatobeau, which would no doubt require some last-minute preparation over breakfast, but that wasn't it either.

'It's been thirty years, you know,' Clarice said quietly. She gave a strange little laugh. 'I wondered if you'd like to go to dinner.'

Their anniversary! 'Oh, *chérie*,' Gabriel began to apologise, but Clarice waved a hand in the air.

'Save the pleasantries for your girlfriend,' she said drily. 'I simply wanted an excuse for a nice, quiet meal.'

'Right,' said Gabriel, awkwardly, feeling rather exposed in his pyjamas. 'I see. Of course. Where would you like to go?'

Clarice shrugged. 'Surprise me,' she said. 'I haven't been anywhere new in a long time.'

'A fondue?' Gabriel suggested. 'Since it's been so unseasonably cold?'

'No, no,' Clarice said. 'You know I'm on a diet. Besides, I really can't stand that Swiss traditional stuff any more. It's all the same. Cheese, cheese, and more cheese on top. So greasy and heavy.'

'Very well,' Gabriel said, 'no fondue, then.'

'No more fondue parties, no more raclettes,' Clarice said firmly. 'No *omble chevalier*. No *pierrade*.'

'Alright, alright,' Gabriel said irritably. 'Nothing even the slightest bit Swiss.'

'Where do you usually take Anita?' Clarice asked casually. 'I don't really know her tastes. Maybe she's more fun than you are.'

'Clarice, you know I don't like...'

His wife held up her hand. 'Nonsense,' she said. 'It's a bit late to be polite now. I mean, you've been with this woman for, what, ten years? You can't pretend to be embarrassed every single time I mention her. After all, it's hardly your position to be upset, here.' She pursed her lips and enunciated the next words carefully: 'I - don't - care. Now, where are we going for dinner? Maybe something Chinese, or Italian, or even for one of your strange Arabian dishes? Do they eat things like Khadija does in Arabia, or is it more like Lebanese food?'

'Well, if you're going to be so damn cavalier about it,' Gabriel replied, incensed, 'how about a Peruvian restaurant? I know a wonderful little place.'

Clarice looked taken aback, then amused, then a little disgusted. 'And what do they eat in Peruvian restaurants?' she asked.

'You wanted something different,' Gabriel said. 'Well, they have absolutely delicious beef steaks, fantastic oxtail soup, gizzards, grits... Beautiful fresh cuts of buffalo and horse.'

Clarice gritted her teeth. 'That doesn't sound like you at all,' she said.

'We haven't eaten out together in a long time,' Gabriel said, pleased against his will at having offended her. 'My tastes have evolved.'

'I can see that. Fine,' she said. 'I'll eat your... gizzards and soup. Anything that isn't raclette.' When she was angry, it was evident that Clarice was no longer a young woman. Her cheeks were pale and drawn, and the wrinkles around her eyes deepened when she frowned.

Gabriel sighed, suddenly tired. 'Clarice, I... We don't have to talk like this. You don't have to – We can eat anywhere you like. This all makes me terribly uncomfortable. If you don't care anymore, don't you want us to divorce?'

'Oh, don't be ridiculous,' Clarice said, crossing her arms. 'Are we having this conversation again? After all this time? What difference would it make? I won't waste our time discussing this yet again. A divorce would be a scandal. For what purpose? I already let you do what you want with your time, and with that South American hussy. I've already put up with you for thirty years.'

'Yes, and you already have my money,' Gabriel added wryly. 'Alright, then. Look, we'll eat someplace else. I'll have a think about restaurants.'

'I'll go prepare breakfast,' Clarice replied, relenting. 'Have some ideas ready by the time you come downstairs. I need something non work-related to look forward to.'

Gabriel shook his head, as the door slammed behind Clarice. How did his wife manage to have so much energy? He got out of bed, stretched, and gingerly removed his pyjamas. Having showered and shaved, he dressed in blue suit trousers, a starched white shirt, and a light red silk tie. Then he pulled on the suit jacket and buttoned all three buttons. Finally, he looked at himself in the antique gilded mirror, adjusted his thick bifocals, and ran a hand through his bristly grey hair. He sighed and turned away, then quietly walked to the bedroom door, along the corridor, and down the stairs.

———— ◆ ————

Most of the parquet was now hidden under exotic patterned carpets, and the de Puritigny family portraits were surrounded by an array of small abstract paintings: a bright blue triangle next to the patriarch in velvet, a dark red painting covered in squiggles next to the infant with her dog, a sort of paper collage next to the grandmother in her cap. Gabriel sighed apologetically in their general direction, before sitting down at the new glass breakfast table.

'I made eggs,' Clarice said cheerily. She had pinned her hair up with a chopstick. 'I thought it would be a nice change, since the weather is so miserable.'

'On a Monday?' Gabriel frowned at her suspiciously. Perhaps she had a lover too. Why else would she be so cheerful? 'Is everything going well at the gallery?' he asked, airily.

'Oh, it's so wonderful!' Clarice exclaimed, her cheeks flushing. 'A very important American artist has agreed to come give a series of talks, all for free! The benefits are to be split between his favourite charity, and our galleries. It's a perfect windfall! The Swiss art scene is just going to love it!'

'Oh,' said Gabriel. 'Congratulations?'

'Of course, there's also the exhibition going on in the old gallery, focussing on young Chinese artists. Juni Bao is the main sponsor. It's been an absolute success! We've already sold three sculptures and a huge mural. Juni had the whole gallery repainted just so the paintings would be shown to their best advantage. It must be nice, being a millionaire, mustn't it?' Clarice giggled. 'Then again, you would know.'

Startled, Gabriel's ears reddened.

'Lighten up, Gabe,' Clarice said, landing an unexpected peck on his head. 'Just be happy for my successes.'

'I am, of course,' he said reluctantly. 'And how are, er, your friends?'

Clarice narrowed her eyes for a moment, then smiled. 'They're very well,' she said. 'Chloë and Khadija are in Paris, getting facelifts and discussing the new chain of Spa Cosmetics spas that are opening all over Europe. Oh, and it's Winifred and Dieter's fortieth wedding anniversary soon. Can you believe it? They're having a huge party in the Black Forest.'

'Oh good,' said Gabriel, unconvincingly.

'So what is she like, this Annie?' Clarice asked cheerily.

'Anita,' Gabriel replied, unhappily.

'I don't understand why you're so reluctant to let me have any information at all regarding your little bit of crumpet. What is she, some kind of tribal girl, intent on invading Switzerland?'

Gabriel refrained from rolling his eyes. 'She loves Switzerland,' he replied shortly, 'but no, she has no intent of invading.'

'I'm joking,' Clarice said, drily. 'I wonder if she has any art contacts over there?'

'Clarice! That isn't... appropriate.'

'Forgive me for not understanding,' Clarice said, shrugging. 'How am I supposed to know what is appropriate when you tell me nothing?'

'What do you want me to tell you?' Gabriel cried, losing his temper. 'I don't care where she comes from. All I know is that she wants to be with me, even though I'm still married. All I know is that she laughs at my jokes, listens to me when I talk, and keeps me company. She's a warm person, Clarice. What could you possibly understand of that?'

'Now you just sound bitter,' Clarice replied calmly. 'What do you mean, anyway? She's like some kind of radiator? That sounds awful.'

'Are you playing games with me?' Gabriel shouted. 'Do you have... somebody else?

'Else? *Else*? As if I have anybody in the first place! Besides, when would I have time? No, Gabriel, I'll have you know I've been perfectly faithful to you all through our thirty years of marriage. Oh, I relish how that must make you feel!'

'I'm really looking forward to our anniversary dinner now, Clarice,' Gabriel observed. 'Thirty years of dissatisfaction and cynicism over steak. Look, you're the one who didn't want to give me a divorce. Don't act like this is my fault. I'm still happy to get divorced anytime you want, Mademoiselle Saint-André-Tobbal.'

'How dare you! I'm de Puritigny till I die, and there's nothing you can do about it. Besides, you're bluffing. You'd hate the mess of a divorce as much as I would. It would be terrible publicity for both our enterprises.'

'In banking circles these things no longer matter,' Gabriel said coolly.

'What about your traditional Swiss values?' Clarice retorted.

'If we can buy bonds in Chicago, and trade in Bahrain, and everybody applauds us for our modernity, I can divorce my wife with respectability.'

'Your father won't like it,' Clarice added. 'I can tell you *he* would not be applauding.'

'No, but my mother will,' Gabriel said, cuttingly. Clarice winced.

'That Ticino witch!' she said sharply. 'As if I cared what she thinks, while she's cooking her soup at six in the morning.' She blinked quickly. 'Fine, then,' she said. 'Let's just carry on as we've been doing, living in separate rooms, sleeping in separate beds.

What does it matter?'

'You wouldn't even notice if I moved out,' Gabriel said. 'You're never home.'

'Ah yes,' Clarice said, 'I knew this was coming. I'm cheating on you with my gallery, is that it? The way you treat me for working, it's positively medieval! Honestly, you would probably be less upset if I told you I had taken a lover than if I simply mentioned I was going for coffee with my four beloved girlfriends.'

'I don't care about your ageing girlfriends,' Gabriel said. 'Forget I ever asked. Shouldn't you be using a more dignified moniker, now that most of you are in your sixties?'

'Nonsense,' Clarice said crisply. 'We don't care. We are still the Avant-Garde Club. We are extremely open-minded. In fact, why don't you just invite your radiator girlfriend to one of our *vernissages*? It might be interesting to her.'

'Not a chance,' Gabriel retorted angrily.

'Why not?' Clarice asked innocently. 'Isn't she interested in modern art? Perhaps she'd prefer a buffet.'

'She studied art history, actually,' Gabriel replied. 'I'm sure she has far better taste than your little crew.'

'What do you think is going to happen, if I meet her one day?' Clarice asked curiously. 'I mean, do you think I'm going to scratch her eyes out? After ten years? You should get over yourself and just introduce us.'

'I can't believe this,' Gabriel said weakly. 'What do you want, some kind of *ménage à trois*?'

'Ha! This isn't even a *ménage à deux*,' Clarice replied. 'Our relationship has been dead in the water for a long time. It's very Swiss, if you think about it. We have this lovely big house here in the most beautiful part of Geneva, where even the parking lots are UNESCO-classified. Everything is meticulous and clean. Inside, everyone is dying of boredom, as if living in a sort of state of repressed depression. The only way I can get out and express myself is through my gallery. Most of the Swiss don't understand me, apart from the young bourgeois and the artists. You should know, with all your Chicago dealings, and your Arab clients. The Swiss don't like the art I sell, they don't like the crystal cupola. Foreigners, though, they love everything I do!'

'This is a joke,' Gabriel said. 'You don't know what you're talking about.'

'I know one thing,' Clarice replied smoothly. 'It's been ten years since we last touched each other, and yet nothing has changed. Your lifestyle, give or take a girlfriend, has stayed the same. What are you doing with your millions?'

'It's none of your business,' Gabriel said flatly. 'All you need to know is that I'm doing well. I'm content, and I don't want to change. I don't want to rock the boat, either in my love life or in the world of portfolio management. I don't want to upset my partners and friends. I don't want to redecorate the chalet. I am still a Swiss man.'

'A Swiss man who likes Peruvian food,' Clarice replied, amused. 'Well, I think we should go there after all. Maybe you'll get some testosterone out of your steaks. Maybe we'll end up coming home and making love.'

'I highly doubt that,' Gabriel said calmly. 'We Swiss men are very famous for suppressing testosterone. It doesn't have any effects on us.'

'Very well,' said Clarice. 'Well, I must go meet the girls for coffee.'

'And I have a meeting at the bank,' Gabriel snapped, not to be outdone.

Clarice sighed.

———————◆◆———————

Gabriel walked mechanically through the spinning glass doors of Bank Von Mipatobeau, ignoring the besuited *huissiers. Another Monday*, he thought, trudging up the marble staircase, *and everything still the same.* He arrived at the third-floor reception.

'Hello, Samantha,' Gabriel smiled, nodding at his secretary.

'Good morning, monsieur,' she replied crisply. Samantha's hair was still mostly red, despite a few streaks of grey, and she was wearing a sharply-tailored navy suit. Her hair was tied back in a tight French braid, and she wasn't wearing any jewellery.

'You received a card from Caroline,' she added, 'from somewhere in the Bahamas.'

Gabriel shook his head. 'Well, I'm glad she's enjoying her retirement,' he said. 'Good for her. How is everything else in the office this morning?'

'The other partners are already waiting in the conference room,' Samantha said briskly. 'Coffee is on its way.'

'Thank you, Samantha,' Gabriel said. 'Well, I'll go in.'

'Say hello to my ex-husband when he comes in,' she said coldly, shaking her head slightly, so that her braided hair flew back over her shoulder.

Gabriel nodded. Just before he walked through the door to the conference room, he consciously donned a smile.

'Gabe!' Dick shouted, striding over towards the door and clapping him on the back with unnecessary force. 'Great to see you, man. How have the last few months been treating you?'

'We spoke on the phone just last week,' Gabriel replied, wincing.

Dick laughed. 'Yeah, but I barely would have recognised you. What's with all the new grey hairs? Is your wife to blame, or your girlfriend?'

Gabriel ignored him. '*Bonjour*, Gérard,' he said. '*Bonjour* Pierre-Yves, *bonjour* Guillaume.'

A chorus of greetings came back to him, and he joined the little group at the table. Clarice was right, he suddenly realised. These men were no longer young whippersnappers. When Guillaume had arrived, he had only his good looks and aristocratic background to advance him in clients' esteem. Now, he was on track to become a senior partner in a few years' time. As for Pierre-Yves, well, he had always been a sort of a loose cannon, for a Swiss man. Still, he was a useful addition to the office, always happy to contribute new ideas or work overtime, as long as success seemed to be promised. Idly, Gabriel wondered what these parties of his really had involved. Was the press just seizing onto anything to make a story? Or had there truly been scandalous behaviour?

Dick followed Gabriel, slipping into a chair and grabbing himself a cookie from the plate. 'So, Pierre-Yves,' he said. 'Do you have any juicy stories to share?'

Pierre-Yves blushed furiously, but Gabriel cut both men short. 'No, he doesn't,' he said. 'You two can discuss whatever you like outside of office hours, but this is an important meeting. We have a lot to get through before lunch, and I have no intention of staying late.' Silence fell in the room, and, contentedly, Gabriel formed his fingers into a steeple. 'Now. Shall we start with a discussion of our progress over the last few months, or shall we begin planning our next trips?'

Before anyone could respond, the door to the room flew open. 'Hallo!' a cheerful German voice could be heard. 'Sorry I am late. I could not decide which tie to wear.' Thomas skipped across the room, his reddish brown curls bouncing. Did he dye his hair? Gabriel wondered. He settled into his seat, making a most peculiar clicking sound as he nodded his head from side to side. 'Do you think I made the right choice?' Grinning, he held up a plain black tie.

'Very professional,' Gabriel said drily. 'Now, if we could...'

'Hi, Thomas!' Dick said happily. 'So glad you could make it!'

Gabriel sighed. 'Let's get down to business. As we all know, the bank is doing exceedingly well.'

'My last bonus was eleven million!' Dick crowed. 'Can you believe that? Can you imagine that happening in Switzerland?'

'Yes, we have bonuses like this,' Gabriel said shortly. 'Mostly from good Swiss business.'

Gérard gave a sad smile. 'Mine was much less than that,' he said, 'because we are made to pay over fifty per cent in taxes by the damned French socialists. It's unlikely we'll ever be able to make the sorts of bonuses one can make in a private bank in Switzerland!'

'Well, next year all of us will be making a lot more money,' Dick said cheerfully. 'You know, you really should think about moving to Geneva. You'll make more money and pay less taxes!'

'Oh yes!' Thomas exclaimed. 'You could move in with me! We

could spend the weekend making fresh pasta together, and drinking French wine.'

A silence fell. 'I'll come visit you guys,' Dick said with a laugh. 'I'll bring some DVDs.'

'Gentlemen,' Gabriel said, his tone aggrieved.

'Go on, go on,' Dick said. 'Let the Swiss man speak.'

Gabriel sighed again. 'Furthermore, as I was saying, the Swiss franc has doubled against the other currencies over the last four years, especially the dollar.'

'Yeah, it's now pretty much equivalent to the dollar!' Dick chimed in. 'Sorry,' he added guiltily, catching Gabriel's expression, 'but it's true.'

'Yes, it is,' Gabriel replied stonily. 'I am very pleased with this development, even if it affects our exports. As you know, I have never had any intention of changing the way our bank handles its portfolio management just because the Swiss franc has gone up. While I am extremely pleased with our overseas returns, and our agreements with various brokerages, we must remember that Von Mipatobeau is still above all a private Swiss bank.'

'You're even conservative in your choice of investments and bonds!' Dick added. 'Big pharmaceutical companies, food companies, low risks.'

'I have taken risks,' Gabriel said slightly defensively, 'with you. But I cannot say I regret them. The products are going through the roof in terms of profitability.'

'We're talking fifteen, sixteen per cent!' Dick said happily.

'Many of our partners, employees and colleagues say that this is a bubble that will burst,' Gabriel continued. 'They tell me there is no way this will last. They tell me to look at the real estate situation in London, or at the global derivatives market. Well, I have looked, and I see nothing that we need to worry about. After all, most products we invest in are reinsured by other companies that insure banking and derivative risk.'

'That's a very American money management strategy to come up with,' Gérard commented.

'It's worked for us so far,' said Gabriel. 'I am not putting this business of insurance underwriting into question.'

'We need to invest more abroad!' Guillaume suddenly blurted out.

Gabriel paused. 'Yes, Guillaume?' he said.

'Sorry,' Guillaume muttered. 'It's just... Well, I was wondering if you were going to question our investments overseas, and, well, I wanted to disagree.'

Dick began to laugh heartily. 'No way are we going to reduce our international deals!' he said. 'They're the life and soul of this millionaire's party!'

Reluctantly, Gabriel nodded. 'I have to agree with Dick, here,' he said. 'Although I do not wholly enjoy his expressions of greed. Guillaume, you have nothing to worry about. In fact, I have several ideas of regions that we should be more involved in.'

'There is no bubble,' Pierre-Yves said quietly, his face still red with embarrassment, not quite managing to raise his eyes from the table.

'Let's go back to the Gulf!' Thomas chimed in. 'We can teach more children about eggs and oranges.'

The men frowned, confused, but Gabriel nodded. 'There is still plenty of wealth to be found in the Gulf, but we need to think about new areas of expansion, too. Now, many European countries, especially within the Schengen area, are beginning to change their rules with regards to holding your assets abroad, in countries like Switzerland. If the foreign client wants to maintain Swiss secrecy, for instance, it's difficult. The Swiss banks are obliged to withhold twenty-five, thirty-five per cent taxes, on behalf of the foreign governments Obviously, this is preposterous. The politicians are fighting amongst themselves. As a consequence, Swiss secrecy is starting to evaporate.'

'It's because of the treaties,' Gérard said quietly. 'All the countries are starting to work together. It's a tragedy.'

'It's not a tragedy unless we make it one,' Gabriel said crisply. 'You see, there are plenty of countries that fall outside these treaties. Eastern Europe, for one, seems ripe for development.'

'The Gulf?' Thomas said hopefully.

'Russia, Ukraine, Kazakhstan, Romania,' Gabriel said. 'China, too. Maybe South America. There is plenty of room for expansion, if we take the time to plan carefully.'

The men nodded with interest. 'What about the rest of Africa?' Thomas piped up.

'There's not too much money there,' Gabriel said. 'Besides, it's very hot, and quite dangerous.'

Thomas shrugged. 'Can I go to China, then?' he asked.

Gabriel sighed. 'Maybe,' he said. 'Now, we have to remember that Swiss secrecy is still a strong selling point. Its value has not diminished over the years, no matter what is going on with these treaties. In fact, the aura of difficulty and constraint is to our advantage. We have something precious to offer, something that recalls the power of Old Europe.'

'Well, we don't want to go to really poor places,' Dick intervened. 'I mean, those people will just have suitcases of cash. Is that really what we want to deal with?'

'You're underestimating the attraction of capitalism in the ex-USSR,' Gérard replied. 'I'm sure there are plenty of hidden millionaires out there, who don't yet know where to come for good banking services.'

Dick grinned. 'You mean they don't know how to invest their money?'

'Exactly,' said Gabriel. 'I'll convince them their money will be safe with us.'

'These people don't want Swiss portfolio management,' Dick said. 'They want to make big money, fast. They'll be asking for at least ten per cent dividends. You can still only offer three or four.'

'The greedy ones, I'll send to you,' Gabriel said smoothly. 'Where do you think all your new clients come from? Where do you think that eleven-million-dollar bonus came from? I know how to funnel the ambitious ones into investing with you. Meanwhile, we get to look after their fortune. It's very safe.'

Dick laughed. 'I shouldn't have forgotten who I was dealing with,' he said, sounding pleased.

'It doesn't matter if they only have suitcases of cash either,' Gabriel added. 'We want that cash here in Switzerland, or in Chicago.'

Guillaume coughed. 'There are rules,' he said, 'from the banking control organisations. They prohibit a bank from accepting cash if you don't know the provenance.'

Gabriel stifled a noise of impatience. 'I know,' he said, 'but there are ways around these rules. Systems of commissions, fast track funding, ways to make a profit. We will have to learn. This year will be full of challenges. It is time to face them, and to make a fortune.'

Dick began to clap slowly. 'Here, here,' he said.

Gabriel kept his smile plastered on. How hard it was to preach conquest when all he wanted was a quiet weekend in his chalet! He saw it in all their faces, the spark he lacked: the greed, the energy, the deviousness. Only Thomas seemed free of these emotions, and simply glad to be included in the discussions. Dick, on the other hand, was still a wild card. Gabriel would need to keep a close eye on him.

'Dick, since you're in town for a few weeks, maybe you can come with me on some of these trips,' Gabriel continued.

Thomas opened his mouth sadly, and began to make a clicking sound.

Gabriel sighed. 'Yes, Thomas,' he said, 'you will come too. I am quite sure you will be with me on all my trips until you retire. Now, shall we start with Eastern Europe or Asia?'

'I vote China,' said Dick.

'I will bring my folding bicycle on the plane,' Thomas said, pleased.

Gabriel gave a sigh of exasperation. 'Thomas, last time you rode a bicycle, you fell on your head and ended up in a coma for two days.'

'I know!' Thomas said, rather proudly. 'In Germany! It was such an adventure. When I am retired, I will ride my bicycle all over the world.'

Samantha knocked on the door, and entered discreetly. 'Gentlemen, I'm afraid it's almost time for Monsieur de Puritigny's next meeting.'

Dick laughed. 'Oh, you poor thing!' he said. 'Are you afraid of running into your nasty old ex-husband? Why don't you come for a drink with me? I'll help you forget him.'

'My ex-husband is long forgotten,' Samantha said frostily, 'and I have no interest in drinking at eleven. Monsieur de Puritigny, if you will follow me...'

Gabriel bid his goodbyes to the assembled company and followed Samantha. Her heels clicked down the corridor as she walked, quite fast, back towards his office. 'The cheek,' he could hear her muttering. 'The damn cheek.'

'Samantha,' he said gently, 'you can go to the front desk now. I will meet Mr Schön myself.'

Samantha paused and blushed furiously. Gabriel noticed her hands were clenched at her sides. 'Why don't you take the elevator?' he added, resisting the temptation to pat her shoulders. Angry as she was, she seemed likely to burst into flames. Gabriel walked slowly to his office, relishing the prospect of his lunch break. Later, of course, there was the matter of his Peruvian dinner with Clarice, but he didn't need to worry about that yet.

Turning a corner, Gabriel came face to face with Mr Schön, slowly staggering down the corridor, propping himself up on a gilded cane with a clawed foot. He was wearing a pearl-grey suit jacket over bright yellow trousers, and a tie decorated with daffodils.

'How are you feeling today, Mr Schön?' Gabriel asked, as solicitously as he could, pulling back a chair for him.

Schön groaned. 'Oh, you know,' he said, 'the same as always. Terrible. And how is my beloved ex-wife this morning? Still ignoring me? I didn't see her in the hall.'

Gabriel shook his head. 'She's still angry at you, by the look of it,' he said.

'After four years!' Mr Schön laughed. 'Well, you know how it is. We men... we make mistakes. We might as well enjoy them.'

Gabriel did not reply, nor did he acknowledge Mr Schön's outrageous wink. In fact, he had to fight quite hard to stop a tide of sadness from rising up within him. It was all so pointless, this life, these lies, these days all the same... The silly Peruvian dinners. It was all such a waste of time.

'So, how are my accounts doing?' Mr Schön asked.

'Same as ever,' Gabriel replied. 'Same as ever.'

Chapter Thirty-Four

Gabriel looked out over the glorious white mountaintops and sighed happily. The Alps! Nothing could surpass their beauty. Here, at last, he was alone, gazing down on the blue shadows of the valley of Davos, the quiet town nestled in the valley, the sweeping slopes of dark pine trees –

Gabriel jumped and quickly moved to the side of the piste as a gaggle of tiny skiers, clad in neon jumpsuits, zigzagged unsteadily by. He sighed. *Who would bring their children to the conference?* he thought to himself with distaste. A wife or lover was enough of a distraction. Speaking of which... He turned back towards the pine forest, craning his neck in the direction of the ski lifts. At last, Anita appeared behind him, huffing and puffing along on her short skis. Her cheeks were bright red under a pair of enormous goggles, and strands of her dark hair were escaping from under her colourful Peruvian bonnet. She looked distinctly out of sorts.

'Alright, my love?' Gabriel called back.

Anita smiled heartily. 'Oh yes,' she said. 'Just a little tired. Is it time for lunch yet?'

'It's ten thirty,' Gabriel replied patiently. 'Would you like a hot chocolate?'

Anita caught up with him and removed her bonnet. 'Yes,' she said, wiping sweaty strands of hair from her eyes. 'I would like that very much.' She leaned towards him for a kiss, and Gabriel smiled, but her arms began windmilling and her skis slipped towards the run. Gabriel caught her arm firmly.

'I'm learning,' Anita said crossly. 'Every year, I get a little better.'

'Of course, my love,' Gabriel said sweetly, privately disagreeing. 'I'm so glad you can be here with me.'

'I don't know how you do it,' Anita said, struggling against Gabriel's strong grasp. 'You're older. Your knees should be weaker than mine.'

'Yes, but I'm Swiss,' Gabriel replied. 'I've been doing this since I was a child.'

Anita sighed. 'I liked *ski de fond* better,' she said.

'Yes, but every year we said we would try this at least once.'

'I've tried enough. Now it's time for some hot chocolate.' Anita shook Gabriel off and unsteadily began to move forward.

Gabriel shook his head, smiling. How many times had the two of them skied together? Saas Fee, Zermatt, St Moritz... And still she was absolutely hopeless. He watched her flounder into a snow drift and, as if in slow motion, fall to the side. He hurried to her side and helped her to her feet.

'I'm walking down!' Anita said, furiously attempting to stomp on the back of her skis, only managing to cross them in the thick, powdery snow, and coming close to losing her balance. 'I don't care how long it takes me, I'm removing these stupid, dangerous slippery things from my feet this instant!'

'Here, let me help,' Gabriel said, pressing down with his pole on the catches that released the skis. 'There. You're free.'

'Good,' said Anita, beginning to trudge doggedly down the hill, leaving her skis in a pile. Gabriel sighed and leant down to pick them up. Another line of six-year-olds zipped by. Thank God it was only a green run, he thought to himself.

Having made his ungainly way down the mountainside, lugging Anita's skis over his shoulder, Gabriel arrived outside the bistro-café that marked the end of the run. He unlatched his skis, unzipped his jacket and breathed out a great cloud of steam. It was good to be in the mountains, no matter what the circumstances. He removed a soft chamois cloth from his pocket and began polishing the fog from his bifocal lenses.

Anita was already sitting at a table, sipping an enormous china mug of steaming hot chocolate. 'Hello darling!' she said cheerfully, waving with a mitten. 'Would you pick me up a croissant, please?'

'Of course,' Gabriel smiled, shaking his head slightly at his lover's insatiable appetite. That was one thing that hadn't changed over the years, at least where food was concerned. He blushed at the thought, and hurried over to the counter to order a *ristretto* coffee and two croissants.

'Sorry for making you carry my skis,' Anita said, reaching for the croissant. 'I just get so frustrated up there, knowing the only way to get down to the nice hot chocolate in the valley is to slip and slide! Why would anyone do that when you can just walk?'

Gabriel laughed gently. 'Do you remember that time in the Trois Vallées when you kept taking the ski lift to the top and then right back down again?'

Anita giggled. 'Yes, like a dog running back and forth to its master.' The hot chocolate seemed to have cheered her up. 'I don't know what it is,' she said. 'I mean, I grew up around mountains! And I love the Swiss scenery!'

'Yes, and you have very strong muscles, and flexibility...'

'... but no coordination,' Anita finished.

Gabriel nodded. Now that Anita's hair was loosed over the shoulders of her cable knit sweater, it was obvious that its raven tones were peppered with silver. Her figure had filled out, too, though its curves were currently belted into a bright turquoise jumpsuit.

'I mean, skiers like you are so muscular, it's like you're deformed!' She giggled. 'It's an unnatural way to exercise your muscles. Human beings are not seals or penguins. We are monkeys. We are built for walking, not sliding.' She sighed, running a hand through her mane of hair. 'More than ten years in Switzerland and my language skills have improved, my accent has improved, I understand the currency, I know the names of all your strange cheeses and fish, but skiing? Skiing remains beyond me.'

'Do you know, sometimes you even have a bit of a Swiss accent?' Gabriel added, amused.

'Really?' Anita beamed. 'How funny! At least it's a Swiss-French accent, not a Swiss-German one. I find it so strange, that sing-song tone, the aggression to the ear!'

'It's even hard for native German speakers to understand it,' Gabriel replied. 'To me it sounds almost Scandinavian. The pronunciation is strange, the expressions are different...'

'Yes, but that's the case in Swiss French too, surely?'

'In a much lighter way, yes. I mean, it's hardly a different language, but there are a few odd turns of phrase. The numbers, for instance, occasionally surprise someone like Gérard in our meetings.'

'Well, I like the Swiss way of counting far better,' Anita said. 'It makes so much more sense to say *septante* and *nonante*!'

'I happen to think so too,' Gabriel replied.

'I wish I spoke as many languages as the Swiss,' Anita said wistfully.

Gabriel gave a wry smile. 'I hardly speak them well,' he said. He swirled his dark coffee around in his cup.

'You speak German sometimes, don't you?' she pressed.

Gabriel shrugged. 'A little, I suppose. It's a sort of obligation in Switzerland, really, since most of the country speaks it.' He glanced at his watch.

'Do you have to go?' Anita asked sadly.

'Oh, not quite yet,' he reassured her. 'I have an important conference right after lunch, and I may have to head back into the valley to prepare, but for now there's no pressure.'

Anita smiled. 'I'm glad we haven't run into any of your colleagues. It's nice to have time with you like this,' she said, 'away from our lives in Geneva.'

Our lives, Gabriel thought with no little sense of melancholy. He raised his coffee cup to his lips and took a sip.

'We should escape more often,' Anita continued. 'Other places, too.'

Gabriel raised an eyebrow. 'You don't like Davos?' he asked.

Anita shrugged. 'I mean, it's not exactly my dream destination, no. I'm not a banker, am I, and I don't like skiing.'

Gabriel blinked, deeply surprised. 'I mean, I've been coming here for nine years, every year,' he said. 'You've never expressed an objection before!'

'Oh, I know you like it,' Anita said, smiling faintly.

'Well,' Gabriel blustered, 'it's just that my clients like to meet me here, near enough to their money in Geneva but away from the stifling atmosphere of the bank.'

Anita smiled. 'They think Von Mipatobeau is boring?'

Gabriel sighed. 'A lot of the Americans do, at least. I can't think why. In any case, people like to meet face to face, and Davos is a glamorous place to do it. Besides, there's the hope that after skiing down the slopes, going to a party with their girlfriend and exchanging business cards with international high fliers, clients will be more inclined to leave a few million in our bank. After a few glasses of wine, most people will sign anything. Or perhaps the next morning over breakfast, guilty and a little bleary-eyed...'

'I just don't understand the expense!' Anita exclaimed. 'I mean, what does it cost to come here, a hundred thousand dollars... just to participate in the conference?'

'Not quite! Well, fifty thousand dollars,' Gabriel admitted unwillingly. 'But it's fun!'

Anita snorted with laughter.

'Look,' Gabriel said defensively, 'since I'm obliged to come here for work, I may as well enjoy myself. It's a wonderful place to ski, and the hotels are beautiful. What does it matter if I have to sit through a few talks about saving the world, eliminating inflation, or promoting emerging markets?'

Anita shook her head. 'So, apart from private Swiss bankers, who can afford to come here?'

'Oh, a lot of people,' Gabriel said dismissively. 'Presidents, kings and queens, corporate sponsors, visiting dignitaries... Heads of large multinational companies, various billionaires, ministers of oil and finance, that sort of person. Oh, and of course half the people here are lawyers and brokers. They come to show off, you see, as if they were campaigning for a vote.'

'Goodness!' said Anita. 'I'm even more glad now we haven't run into these people!'

'I don't think a lot of them care very much about skiing,' Gabriel said. 'They are not de Puritignys like me. People come here to socialise, network, show off, rub shoulders...'

'Be with their mistresses?' Anita smiled coyly.

Gabriel did not respond. 'The genius of it is,' he said instead, 'that this is a perfectly neutral country, so no-one in the world can be faulted for showing up here. Besides, two thousand metres high up in the mountains, you could hardly be in a more perfectly isolated place.'

'Getting away from it all?' Anita laughed.

'Yes,' Gabriel insisted. 'It's a perfect space for peaceful discussion, since it's so damn hard to get to.'

'How do people get here from the Gulf and, say, China or America?' Anita asked curiously.

'Often by private jet and helicopter, at least for the last stretch of the journey,' Gabriel said with distaste. 'Many people also use taxis for an extravagant proportion of their travel here.'

'I still think it's an odd, isolated place to choose,' Anita said stubbornly. 'I mean, what if you don't like skiing?'

'Most people...' Gabriel paused, coughed. 'Do you know something funny?' he asked instead. 'In my nine years here, I've found the food to be mostly terrible. They bring in the most expensive caterers, but even the best cooks struggle in these Germanic kitchens. If some good food materialises by accident, it was probably imported by helicopter from northern Italy or Zurich, from a great two-star Michelin chef. In that case, furthermore, you can almost guarantee that the service will be terrible. Labour, in these mountains, just isn't reliable. All trainees and students, hired for a few francs an hour. In this place with thousands and thousands of dollars pouring in! It defies logic.'

'Well, I like the food,' Anita said. 'But why Davos? Why not, say, Saas Fee?'

'I'm not sure,' Gabriel replied. 'All I know is that this place has an excellent reputation, historically. Originally, Davos developed as a recovery centre for people with tuberculosis and emphysema. That's why there are so many hotels, you see. The air is very fresh, because of the altitude.'

'The air is very fresh in Saas Fee too,' Anita said.

Gabriel sighed, a little irritably. 'Surely you wouldn't want all these lawyers and dictators turning up at the chalet, would you?'

Anita smiled indulgently. 'Speaking of Saas Fee, how is your mother?' she asked.

Gabriel smiled, pleased. 'She's well,' he said, 'as always. I'll tell her you inquired.'

'I love her so!' Anita exclaimed warmly. 'I wish we could...' she paused, letting the words hang in the air. 'Never mind,' she added, as if embarrassed.

'I know,' Gabriel said, his air of gloom returning. 'You wish we could spend more time with my family. The words every husband longs to hear!' he added.

Anita laughed a little sadly. 'Well, our circumstances are exceptional,' she said softly. 'We are not like other couples.'

'My little Peruvian,' Gabriel said tenderly.

'Stop it,' Anita said playfully. 'I'm Swiss now, remember? Oh, how I wish I could be Swiss!'

Gabriel took her hand in his and squeezed. Anita reached across the table to stroke his greying hair. 'My beloved Swiss man,' she sighed. 'How little you have changed in these ten years!'

Gabriel shook his hair. 'I've gone old and grey,' he replied. 'You must be blinded by love,' he added, laughing a little.

Anita threw her head back and began to laugh, so loudly that various skiers turned around to stare.

'Do you know,' Gabriel said quietly, amused, 'I think you're the only woman in the world who has ever found me funny. No, the only person!'

Anita laughed some more. 'I'm sure Thomas finds you funny,' she teased.

'That's hardly reassuring,' Gabriel retorted.

'I like your humour because it is very different from the sense of humour I grew up with,' Anita explained. Idly, she had begun untwisting the croissant into a flaky spiral.

'Ah, so you like me because I am not very Spanish?' Gabriel shot back.

Anita shrugged. 'Something like that. Not Peruvian, not Quechua, not Spanish... No, I love you because you are Swiss.'

'I am not even a Catholic,' Gabriel said. 'How can you live with that?'

But the joke seemed to fall flat. Anita looked up at from her croissant with sad eyes.

'I, er,' Gabriel stammered. 'I mean, Peru is one of the largest producers of silver in the world. Don't you wish you were involved with some rich Peruvian?'

Anita stared at him, her eyes wide with reproach, then very slowly began to smile, and finally broke into a giggle. 'No,' she said, now smiling coyly. 'I much prefer a Swiss man and his gold.'

It was Gabriel's turn to laugh. 'You'll turn into an old Swiss lady soon enough,' he said, 'hiding your ingots in a safe, shivering out into the street at dawn to buy your baguettes...'

'What?' said Anita.

'You know, gold ingots! The Swiss are famous for buying up small gold ingots and hiding them away, then selling them off when they're old, and living off that income. We handle this all the time at Von Mipatobeau.'

'Oh, I see,' said Anita. 'I thought we were talking about Nazi gold.' She took a large bite of her croissant.

Gabriel shook his head ruefully. 'As if the silver production industry in Peru was entirely run by good little Catholics.'

'At least we don't have to carry it around!' Anita retorted. 'Can you imagine the weight of the handbag? I'd have to be one very strong old lady to manage that...'

Gabriel snorted. 'That's because silver is worth twelve dollars an ounce, while gold is worth about twelve hundred.'

'Don't be such a banker,' Anita sniffed.

Gabriel laughed. 'You know I'm only joking, darling,' he said.

'I know, but it makes me sad. I mean, I'll never be an old Swiss lady, gold ingots or no gold ingots. I'll probably end up deported.'

'Don't talk like that!' Gabriel said sternly. 'Nothing of the sort is going to happen.'

'What about when I'm too old to work? I have nothing, Gabriel,' she said sadly, staring down into her empty hot chocolate mug. 'Nothing.'

'If you need money...' Gabriel offered tentatively.

'It's not about money,' Anita snapped back. 'Why do you have to make everything about cold hard cash? I don't know why you care about it so much. Why don't you do something good with your enormous fortune, instead of trying to increase your bonuses? Why don't you give to charity, or invest in art? Yes, why don't you give your money to your wife's gallery?'

'What?' said Gabriel. 'I don't understand...'

'I don't care about money,' Anita said passionately. 'I've never cared about money. I don't even think *you* care about money, really, except as something to look after in the bank. I mean, you never really spend any of it! What do you think money is for, Gabriel? I mean, you've never had children, and soon it'll be too late for me. I'll be an old maid at forty! In Peru, if I had married a good Catholic man, it wouldn't matter if he worked in the silver mines or as a hotel janitor: I would have ten children by now.'

'Anita!' Gabriel said, appalled. 'How can you speak like this? Are you really so unhappy?'

'Unhappy? Unhappy I'm not married to some kind of Inca, speaking Quechua to my ten squalling babies? No. Unhappy I can't be married to the man I love, a kind, sweet man who has stood by me for ten years and yet refuses to leave his damn wife? Yes, that makes me unhappy. And it always will.' Anita fell silent, and Gabriel could only stare at her, overcome with guilt.

'Come now,' he said, in what he meant as a cajoling tone, but the words stuck in his throat. 'You mean everything to me.'

'In the eyes of God,' Anita said, her voice hollow, 'we are living in sin.'

'But Anita...'

Anita cut him off. 'In many ways, yes, I am your wife. We're growing old together, bickering, sharing all our struggles. We're having less and less sex... I hope to God you aren't still sleeping with her too, or my heart would break!'

'Anita!' Gabriel reprimanded her. 'You know for a fact I haven't touched Clarice in ten years. I am faithful to you.'

'Faithful,' Anita scoffed. Violently, she swept her croissant crumbs to the ground. 'Faithful! And you tell me you never lie. Not to your clients, and not to me.'

'It's true,' Gabriel said, growing agitated. 'I have always been as open as I could be, both with Clarice and with you! My wife and I have different beds in different parts of the house. Sometimes we don't see each other for twenty-four hours at a time! It's not a marriage anymore, it's a kind of old friendship. Like, like a bond,' he said desperately. 'You get the dividend, you don't think about the investment anymore, you don't think about its risks. It becomes second nature. It becomes your life. You can't bankrupt the company without warning, even if the romance goes out. Even after thirty years.'

'You're still married to her,' Anita said, 'and you tell me you love me. How can you pretend to be honest? What kind of honest banker are you? What kind of Swiss banker?'

'There are bigger issues at stake,' Gabriel said. 'Family. Tradition. Reputation.' He clasped her hand again, passionately. 'We can't rock the boat. A divorce would ruin us,' he said. 'Can you imagine what they would say about the senior partner of the private Swiss bank who ran away with his South American girlfriend?'

'Is that what you think of me?' Anita said, her lip trembling. 'Am I just some kind of joke to you?'

'No, no,' Gabriel said hastily, 'but you must understand what it really means to be Swiss. It's better to stay the way we are, discreet, with everybody tolerating it.'

'I can't tolerate it!' Anita burst out. 'I love you with all my heart and you are telling me not to rock the boat?'

'It's not just rocking the boat,' Gabriel said desperately. 'It would capsize the boat. They would start talking about us in horse clubs and nautical clubs. Whispers would spread through the city. Every lunch, every restaurant dinner would become a paranoid nightmare.'

'Are you so ashamed of me?' Anita cried. 'I don't care about any of that! I only care about loving you, being with you, having your babies!'

'Babies again?' Gabriel shouted, losing his temper. 'Anita, you know I love you, but you are gravely mistaken if you think I would agree to have little monkeys climbing on my back. I am sixty years old!'

'Fine,' said Anita. 'I'm sorry. I'll stay with you no matter what. Just let me marry you. I want to be your wife. I want to be Madame de Puritigny, and show the world how much I love you! I want to be seen in public with you everywhere, not just in Davos and our apartment in Geneva. I want to be with you in a house: I want to go every other weekend to the chalet in Saas Fee, I want to travel to Chicago with you, I want you to come meet my mother in Peru! I want you to do all this with me! I want to be in Switzerland with you, as your wife!' She paused, and took a deep breath. 'Marry me, Gabriel. Please.'

'I can't,' Gabriel said, lowering his voice and his eyes. 'I just can't.'

'You're married to the snow,' Anita said, her tone becoming melodramatic. 'You're married to your bank and your international conferences and your nautical and equestrian clubs and your restaurants... I mean, do you ever go on a boat? No. Do you ever ride horses? No. So why are you a member?'

'I,' Gabriel hesitated. 'I go there to network,' he finally said, defensively. 'It's marketing for the bank. I have received many deposits for Von Mipatobeau in this way. It's the same reason we're here, in Davos. I have to think about my work,' he concluded a little plaintively.

Anita stood up abruptly. 'Why don't you go to your precious conference, then,' she sniffed. 'Go learn how to make another few million. Meanwhile, a woman who loves you will be waiting at the hotel.' She clumped across the wooden restaurant floor in her ski boots, then turned back at the door. 'I've been waiting ten years, Gabriel,' she added.

Gabriel looked around apologetically at the other people in the restaurant, before rising and gathering his things. Anita would have left her skis outside, and he really needed to do a little preparation before the afternoon's seminar.

———◆◆◆———

Back in the hotel room, Gabriel was rather relieved to find that Anita had gone out, presumably to sulk in the sauna or with another over-priced hot chocolate. He showered, shaved and changed into his white shirt, red silk tie and blue suit trousers. He cleaned his glasses and looked through his notes one last time, then locked the door and took the elevator down to the lobby.

'Gabriel de Puritigny!'

Gabriel froze in his tracks, sighed and plastered on a smile before turning around. Only one of his clients turned up at Davos every single year. Of course he would be attending Gabriel's seminar.

Grinning, Mr Schön walked over, his swagger turned into something of a stagger by his golden cane. He was wearing a canary-yellow blazer over a red shirt and blindingly white trousers. His tie was decorated with gold coins. 'Fancy seeing you here,' he joked.

Gabriel maintained his uneasy grin. 'Yes, I was just heading over to the conference room,' he said, hoping to convey that he was in a hurry,

'A little early for your seminar, no?' Mr Schön replied. 'Wouldn't you care for a little coffee with me?'

'I'm afraid I need to look through my notes,' Gabriel said apologetically, vaguely shaking his folder of papers in Mr Schön's direction. 'Perhaps we can catch up later.' He began to walk towards the door to the conference room, noting with a sinking heart that the door to the room was surrounded by a surging crowd. Surely these weren't all potential attendees? Why on earth would a seminar on portfolio diversification attract so many people? Perhaps there had been a mix-up in the programme.

'Our financial saviour!' an ancient British voice croaked, and a wrinkled hand came down with surprising force on Gabriel's shoulder. 'Are you going to tell us how to make our next million now, or wait until after your talk?'

'Lord Vicambush!' Gabriel exclaimed in surprise. 'I haven't seen you in years! Is Lord Armagaunt with you also?'

'I'm afraid the baron is no longer with us,' the elderly lord said, lowering his eyes. He leaned closer to Gabriel. 'The drink, you know,' he said, shaking his head.

Gabriel nodded. 'What a shame!' he said.

'Drink?' A smooth voice interjected, and Sheikh Mourshawa appeared at Lord Vicambush's shoulder.

'Mourshawa! I didn't know you would be here either!' Gabriel exclaimed, reaching out a hand nervously for the smooth sheikh to shake. Mourshawa laughed and pushed his sunglasses up into his luxurious dark curls.

'Well, you never invited me skiing, so I thought I'd come see these famous Alps for myself!' The frames of his sunglasses twinkled with small crystals, and a thick gold chain hung into the chest hair revealed by the open collar of his crisp white shirt.

'Welcome,' Gabriel said nervously. 'How lovely to see you again. This is Lord Cecilian... de Rollo de Vicambush.'

'Would you like a brandy?' Mourshawa asked the lord conspiratorially.

Lord Vicambush sniffed. 'I hardly think that would be appropriate,' he said.

The sheikh smirked, his pencil-sharp moustache curving upwards. 'You wouldn't care for just a splash of this Courvoisier VSOP I happen to have in my pocket?' Discreetly, he drew forth an ancient-looking silver flask from the silk lining of his jacket.

Lord Vicambush raised an eyebrow. 'Courvoisier, you say? VSOP?' He put an avuncular arm around Mourshawa's shoulder. 'And what did you say your name was?'

Gabriel shook his head. All these clients! They simply seemed to love Davos. Or money, he corrected himself ruefully. These people certainly loved money. He checked his watch and realised it was time to begin. Pushing through the crowd, he walked quickly down the carpeted central aisle towards the stage. Trying to slow his heartbeat, he focussed on the podium: when he arrived, he stared at the microphone for a long time, fiddling with his notes and hemming and hawing nervously. When he looked up at last, he found the auditorium to be three-quarters full already.

He squinted out at the audience, recognising several Swiss clients, a handful of Texans, and even a few Italians. There were several Middle Eastern princes, he noted, and over there on the left, a very high-ranking Russian diplomat. He would have to make sure to corner him at one of the numerous champagne receptions!

Suddenly, a bell-like sound rang out from the corner of the room, and silence fell. Gabriel cleared his throat and tapped a finger on his microphone. 'Greetings,' he said. A wave of nods went around the room. 'I must say, I had no idea so many people would be interested in portfolio diversification! Let me congratulate you on being such a shrewd crowd of investors, and note that if you have come to this conference room by accident, you may get up and leave now without any embarrassment.' A ripple of laughter went around the room, but no-one moved.

'Well,' Gabriel continued, 'I'm afraid you'll have to listen to me now. It is a real privilege to have been appointed as the moderator of this study group. In previous years here, I have talked about private banking and direct investments. Today, I wish to share with you some of the most intimate secrets of the trade. There is an old joke about Davos, that says: Davos is not about Swiss banking, it's about Swiss talking. Well, I'm here to prove that proverb wrong. I'm not here to pontificate about world poverty, or act like some sort of megalomaniac who thinks he can change the world. There will be no dubious metaphors involving earthquakes, no encyclopaedic explanations, no long and pompous sentences that could be interpreted to mean almost anything. I'm here in Davos to tell you, my dear clients and potential clients –' Here, he paused for laughter, which was duly scattered around the room – 'how to make a great deal of money.

'The game has changed, you see. International investments are the name of the game, now. The internet has connected us all, opening up new ways of communicating, investing, doing business. This is why it's exciting to me to see a crowd such as this assembled here in Switzerland, from all over the world. At the risk of sounding like another of the men spouting Davos platitudes, it gives me hope for an international future. To counteract that idealistic note, let me give some practical advice, in the domain of recruitment: search all over the world. Find people who are young, dynamic, sporting, attractive, multilingual, multicultural, and open to change. Teach them. Train them. Value them. Make sure they learn about the main stock markets, New York, London, Tokyo. Teach them a little bit about commodities: make sure they know the price of copper and gold, platinum, palladium, silver. Teach them the principal types of foreign exchange, the euro and the dollar and sterling. Teach them the ridiculous slang: the cable, the SEK and the NOK, the kangaroos and the kiwis. Hire them as trainees, for a start, so that they only cost you a few hundred dollars a month. Then, as they become more knowledgeable and more efficient, you can start to pay them according to their performance, especially according to the new money they bring in for your portfolio management. Which brings me to my primary theme.

'Most of you will be acquainted with the basic workings of private banking, so I won't bore you with that. I'm here to talk to you about diversification. Now, why would one do that? Well, diversification in a portfolio serves to protect both the banker and the client. There are many different types of diversification, of course. You can diversify your investments into different currencies, for example, or split your portfolio between bonds, stocks, equity investments, derivatives and hedge funds. That's my job, so I won't bore you with the specifics. The important thing for you bankers out there to take away from this, is to understand that a banker is safe in this scenario, because he has covered all his bases. For the investor, of course, this is very good news. Your returns will immediately surge. As an investor, it's a far better strategy than picking up fifteen per cent in some backstreet office, off some smart aleck portfolio manager in New York city, dealing junk bonds, or launching all your cash into some sort of dotcom IPO. This is far, far safer. Of course, if you are an inveterate risk-taker, there are also plenty of opportunities to use this portfolio as a springboard. The important thing is that there is always a discussion, and there is always a choice. It's about returns, it's about margins, My benefit is your benefit.

'It's the private banking philosophy: diversify, diversify, diversify. Bankers, listen to me: this means we don't need to think very hard, and it means we can't be blamed for anything. Clients, don't worry: it also means that your money is looked after extremely safely, whilst generating a huge and diverse amount of income. Now, doesn't this sound like good news for everyone involved? It's a very Swiss strategy, so Davos seemed like the right place to share it. Switzerland is an honest country. Its bankers are not robbers. We know how to look after our clients, and we know how to look after your money.'

A hand shot up in the audience, startling Gabriel. 'Yes?' he said hesitantly.

A tall, well-dressed minister from South America stood up. 'Mister de Puritigny,' she said, 'how soon will you be back in Geneva? I'd like to transfer ten million dollars to your private bank.'

Laughter erupted sporadically all over the room. Gabriel smiled indulgently. 'Next week,' he said. 'Of course, we'll have to know the source and the use of the money, and your investment risk profile,' he cautioned.

'Monsieur!' Another voice rose up, this time from a towering man Gabriel seemed to recall was associated with some West African country. Perhaps he was a dictator of some sort?

'Yes?' Gabriel replied.

'I came in my private jet,' the man said, grinning. 'I have brought my money with me to Switzerland. My question is this: is there any danger of it freezing in this infernal weather?'

Laughter filled the auditorium again.

'No danger at all,' Gabriel replied gaily. 'Money never freezes, you see. The bills have been designed to withstand extreme temperatures. There have been many studies: a hundred-dollar bill will escape unscathed from minus forty degrees centigrade to plus forty! So really, you have much less reason to worry about storing your money up here in the mountains than under your beds at home, where the rats and mice could get at it. Bank bills are not designed to withstand being treated as a handy snack!' After the laughter died down, he added: 'Now, if there are any more questions, you can find me this afternoon at the first champagne reception. I will be happy to talk to you.'

He bowed and stepped down from the podium, to desultory applause. A tall, handsome man Gabriel vaguely associated with the Gulf immediately clapped him on the shoulder. 'Great speech, monsieur,' he said warmly. Surely this wasn't someone he had met on the desert trip? No, the answer came to him in a flash. Khadija's cousin-in-law, from the fondue party.

'Thank you, Sheikh,' Gabriel said, smiling.

'Would you mind giving me your card?' he asked. 'I only make it to Switzerland every ten years or so, but business can be conducted in many different ways in this day and age.' He gave a glittering smile.

Gabriel nodded, and retrieved a card from the inside pocket of his jacket. 'Of course,' he said.

'I am glad the Swiss are no longer underestimating the rest of the world,' the sheikh said thoughtfully. 'There is money there. Vast resources, mostly oil.'

'Yes, and palm trees and dates, too,' Gabriel said with a thin smile. 'I look forward to hearing from you. Now, if you'll excuse me...' He began to push towards the door once more.

'Hey!' A loud female voice startled him, just as he was reaching the end of the central aisle. 'Great speech!'

Gabriel looked up, smiling, to meet the eyes of Billy Jean, the American businesswoman. She was wearing a blinding white suit decorated with sequins, and her eternal cowboys boots. Her hair was now bleached a bright, Californian blonde.

'Hello,' said Gabriel. 'How is everything in the Wild West?'

'Great, great,' Billy Jean said dismissively. 'Hey, you got any good investment ideas for me right now?' She grinned, her white teeth glinting. 'I mean, what products have been giving you the best returns lately?'

Gabriel smiled, flattered. 'Well, last year we made twelve per cent in the commodities market. Structured projects, you know. Coffee and wheat and corn. Precious metals, too.'

Billy Jean nodded. 'Yes, I see. That sounds like a far more interesting market than the one for fiduciary products.'

'In Switzerland, they sometimes refer to this method as deposit plus. There are other products too, such as Pearl plus capital gains or a kick-in-goal.'

Billy Jean smiled. 'Maybe you can give me some more tips.'

Gabriel tried not to sigh, instead rustling in his jacket pockets. 'Here, why don't you take one of my cards?' he offered. 'I'll get back to you when I'm in my office in Geneva. Now, if you'll excuse me, I really must get back to my–' He paused, suddenly embarrassed.

Billy Jean's eyes narrowed. 'And how is your wife? Clara, was that her name? Such a peppy Swiss woman, full of energy! I completely loved that crazy crystal gallery of hers! Beautiful, just beautiful.'

Gabriel glared at Billy Jean. 'Clarice is very well, thank you,' he said stonily.

'Well, say hi!' Billy Jean replied airily. 'You two have fun in your hotel!' She gave a sly little wave and walked off in her heavy boots.

Gabriel sighed. Americans! He walked slowly up the carpeted stairs, exhausted, preparing his apologetic speech for Anita.

Chapter Thirty-Five

A wet and freezing March wind blew down the cobbled streets of Saint Antoine, as Gabriel marched reluctantly to work. What a strange and awful year 2008 had been so far! Everything was... hitting the fan, as Dick might have said. Gabriel didn't even crack a smile at the thought. In fact, his frown grew even deeper. Tensions in the banking world had been growing over the last few months, and the tremors felt in America had at last revealed themselves to announce a global financial earthquake.

Gabriel had waited till Friday morning to call his emergency meeting, hoping against hope that the situation would stabilise and clarify, that he could convoke the men and women of Von Mipatobeau to his Napoleon III conference room with a coherent message of reassurance, or at least with something approaching a solution. But this global crisis was swelling, not subsiding, and in his position as a senior partner of the bank, Gabriel could no longer ignore it. If he could speak to hundreds of people at Davos, he could lead his own bankers. He had called Samantha, and Samantha had called the meeting, and now Gabriel was arriving at the marble archway of Von Mipatobeau bank, his coat soaked with rain and his heart cold as ice.

He removed his coat immediately upon entering, handing it brusquely to an unsuspecting *huissier*. '*Merci*,' he said tersely, already halfway to the elevator.

'*Bonjour*,' the youngest receptionist ventured tentatively, but the golden doors had already slid shut. Gabriel drew a cloth from his inside pocket and cleaned his rain-wet varifocals, then found a comb and neatened his wet salt-and-pepper hair. Then he took a deep breath, loosened his tie, and opened the door.

'*Bonjour*,' he said to Samantha.

'*Bonjour*,' she replied. Samantha did not look like she had slept well this week, either. 'They are in the conference room,' she said, with a sympathetic look.

Gabriel forced himself to smile, nodded, and walked down the carpeted hallway. He opened the oak door.

———◆◆◆———

The mood in the conference room was grave. Gabriel slowly looked around the oval mahogany table, meeting pair after pair of worried eyes.

'Ladies and gentlemen, you've all heard the news,' he began. 'You've all read the papers.'

A murmur of anxious assent went around the room.

'This has been a dark week,' Gabriel continued, his face weary, his tone sombre, as he began his carefully considered summary of the situation. 'You've no doubt spent it glued to your laptops, calling your contacts in America, and trying to reassure your clients, or watching the news ticker fill with worse and worse news. As you all know, the world's banking system has suffered a series of terrible losses, day after day. Buyout funds are bankrupt. Businesses are in jeopardy. Corporations are toppling under the weight of unsustainable debt. No-one can fulfil their commitments to reimburse loans. Companies have been announcing profit drops of around ninety per cent. Illusions, globally, are being shattered. Everyone is begging to be saved from bankruptcy, asking for bailouts. The US Federal Reserve injected over two hundred billion dollars into the American banking system. The question we must all ask ourselves now is: will that be enough? Will Wall Street be brought to its knees? And how will this affect Switzerland?'

A hand was raised. Gabriel nodded.

'What about insurance?' Guillaume asked nervously. 'Aren't there... protections in place? A safety net?'

Gabriel shook his head sadly. 'The insurance companies like AIG are themselves asking for a hundred billion dollars to help them out of possible bankruptcy. There is no salvation there. Only insolvency, and the vague possibility of help from the federal governments.'

Guillaume swallowed, and did not reply. The younger bankers around the table exchanged panicked glances. Karl, Julie, André:

what did the future of banking look like for them? Gabriel didn't know. Thomas was mechanically turning his bow tie around and around his neck.

'So what does this mean for us?' Pierre-Yves asked, keeping his voice calm, though his hands were trembling slightly.

'It is difficult to tell this early on,' Gabriel replied, 'how this American crisis will affect Europe, or whether the private banks will suffer. One thing is for certain: our work with our broker friends in Chicago is at an end.'

'Have you heard from Dick?' Thomas asked, worried. His bowtie currently sat at a jaunty angle on the side of his neck.

Gabriel shook his head. 'I will be calling him after this meeting,' he said. 'I will be able to offer more information at that juncture.'

'What about the products?' Pierre-Yves asked, accusingly.

'Ah. The products, you see, were secured by mortgages.' Here, Gabriel was unable to keep a tremor from his voice.

'But the mortgages bubble has burst! There's no money left there! You're going to lose millions for your clients,' Pierre-Yves said in horror. 'It'll be a global scandal.'

'Some of these products have turned out to be... less than perfect, yes,' Gabriel admitted. 'But remember that the situation is more complicated than it may seem: above all, here at Von Mipatobeau, we deal in portfolio management.'

'That's not all we deal in,' Pierre-Yves shot back. 'Not anymore.'

'Listen,' Gabriel said patiently, 'nothing drops from twelve per cent to minus thirty in an instant, like that. It's not possible. There will be explanations. There must be a recovery. I'm sure everything will improve. Remember 1987? Some of you were right here with me, in this very room, when the crisis hit. Well, remember what happened? Not only did Bank Von Mipatobeau survive, but we prospered. We had, and we still have, staying power. We stick with our investments, and we stick with our clients. We are a Swiss private bank, and we will recover. Don't fight each other about this, like dogs in an alleyway. Don't let your hair turn white from lack of sleep. Don't jump out of a skyscraper window, like those poor, frazzled men on Wall Street. Let's not panic, let's stay calm. Go back to your offices and make yourself a cup of tea. Leave me to talk to Dick.'

'You convinced nearly all of our clients to invest abroad with him!' Pierre-Yves said, accusingly.

'As if we didn't all follow him!' Guillaume piped up. 'We were all excited, swept up in this spirit of conquest and greed. Now, we must pay the price. We will take a terrible hit on our bonuses and returns this year.'

There was a choking sound from Thomas, as his bow tie burlesque came to an end. He pawed at his neck, until the offending piece of silk came untied, and lay on the table in front of him.

'Steady on, now,' Gabriel said, beginning to sweat. 'Nothing is settled. Nothing is certain. Let me speak to Dick - to Monsieur Nikko. Let me find out what is really happening in America. Maybe it's not as bad as it looks from here.'

Silence met this declaration.

'It is bad,' Charles said suddenly. The younger banker's ears turned red as the people in the room turned to face him, but he persevered. 'The international portfolios are going to hell. The over-the-counter market too. NASDAQ is going down. The commodities market is down. Fanny Mae and Freddy Mac are down.'

'Why should we care?' Gabriel said, as patiently as he could. 'Remember, we are a private Swiss bank dealing mostly in portfolio management.' He could feel his shirt sticking to his back with sweat.

'Why didn't we invest more safely?' Karl chimed in. 'Why didn't we encourage our clients to turn to Nestlé, or Shell oil? At least they would have received their three per cent every year.'

'We got talked into this international garbage,' Pierre-Yves spat out. 'We were told nothing. Now we have nothing but these terrible products from the American investment banks. They were the ones who sold us these bad deals. Dick sold us the worst deals.'

'Couldn't we have stuck to Switzerland?' Karl added, sadly. 'We didn't need any of these American brokers and high flyers. Everything was fine, before.'

'Yes,' Guillaume said, somewhat sarcastically. 'We were happy and content in our quiet little mountains. Why did we go out looking for more? I'll tell you why: because we all wanted more money. Our clients wanted more money.'

'There was pressure on us from all directions, gentlemen,' Gabriel cut in. 'I beg you not to start turning on each other in this fraught time. Please, wait until the situation becomes clearer.'

'Just because you went to Davos a few times,' Pierre-Yves sneered, 'you think you're in charge of us all?'

'Pierre-Yves!' Guillaume cried. 'Think of what you're saying! We must stay together. We are not dogs. We are Swiss men.'

Gabriel raised a hand. 'Karl and Guillaume are right,' he said. 'We are Swiss. We are good, honest, mountain people. Responsible people. Calm people. And as Swiss men and women, we must stick together in difficult times, in order to survive. No matter what. If we begin to argue with each other, we will lose even more.'

'Why has this happened?' Thomas said, his tone mournful.

Gabriel hung his head. 'I don't know, Thomas,' he said. 'The causes probably won't be obvious for months. The complexity of the financial market and its products, undisclosed conflicts of interest, a failure to regulate, an obsession with high risks...'

'I mean my tie,' Thomas said sadly. 'I think it is ruined.'

Gabriel sighed. 'Gentlemen,' he said, 'unless there are any more questions, I'm going to close this meeting and postpone any practical decisions until I have spoken to the Americans.' He looked around at his partners' expressions, their long, white, miserable faces. 'Remember, it's nearly the weekend,' he added half-heartedly.

Grumbling, the bankers rose from the table and walked from the room, leaving Gabriel alone with the dishevelled Thomas.

'Are you alright, Monsieur Gabriel?' Thomas asked tentatively, his bow tie now looped around his wrist.

Gabriel nodded. 'Thank you, Thomas,' he said. 'You can go back to work.'

Thomas gave a sort of bow and retreated after the others, closing the door softly behind him. Gabriel sighed deeply, resisting the urge to plunge his face into his hands and weep in desperation. Dick, he thought. He must call Dick. No matter that it would be dawn over there. He needed to speak to him.

There was a quiet knock on the door. 'Monsieur de Puritigny?' Samantha's face appeared, looking worried. 'A call for you in your office.'

'Oh!' Gabriel said, leaping up from his seat. 'I'll just be a moment. Is it Dick?'

'No,' said Samantha. 'It's Gérard.'

Gabriel walked slowly to his office, closed the door, sat down and took off his glasses. Then he picked up the phone.

———◆◆◆———

'I don't know what to do either,' Gabriel said, cradling the phone to his ear. The sound of Gérard's trembling voice, his habitual melancholy augmented to desperation, made him feel like crying. 'I know, I know. I don't know why we trusted the Americans. We just... Do you think? No, they're not all cheating. There will be bailouts. There will be help.' Nervously, Gabriel twisted the buttons of his suit jacket. 'No, I don't think it's all a question of Ponzi schemes. It's more complicated than that, less black and white. These are major institutions we're talking about, a global crisis. We cannot blame ourselves. You can't blame yourself, Gérard. We all knew there were risks involved.' Gérard's tinny voice continued, gabbling desperately. The jacket button's threads became looser.

'Surely all your portfolios aren't lost,' Gabriel said, as confidently as he could. Then he was silent again, in the face of Gérard's terrified tirade. 'Yes, you'll have to face the big French families. Yes, the dentists and the lawyers, the politicians and the patriarchs. You'll have to take responsibility. You can do it, Gérard. You'll be fine. No, I have to agree. We'll probably lose our bonuses. No, Gérard, we're not *capot*. We're not finished. Stay strong.' Another long silence, punctuated by Gérard's distant voice. The button Gabriel had been worrying suddenly snapped from its thread, coming off in his hand. He was no better than Thomas, he scolded himself, before forcing himself to listen to Gérard, who was inquiring how things were in Switzerland.

'I don't know. I don't know how Von Mipatobeau will come out of this,' he said, finally. 'Eighty per cent of our portfolios are still Swiss, so hopefully we won't be too affected. But as for our investments with Dick, the junk bonds and derivatives... Yes, I suspect we will lose money. Yes, I'm about to call him. He deserves to be woken up in the middle of the night, frankly. It's good to hear you laugh, Gérard. Take some time off. Get some sleep. Maybe get out of Paris this weekend. This will all get better. You too. Goodbye, Gérard.'

Gabriel slowly hung up the phone. Gérard's frightened voice had affected him more than he would have liked. If things were that bad in France, perhaps Switzerland wasn't as impervious to the crisis as he had hoped. He took a deep breath, then exhaled slowly. It was time to call Dick and find out once and for all how bad things really were. He picked up the phone again.

'Who is this?' Dick's voice crackled.

'It's Gabriel,' he replied hesitantly. 'Gabriel de Puritigny.'

Dick gave a harsh laugh, like a bark. 'What a surprise,' he said.

'I'm sorry to bother you,' Gabriel began, but Dick interrupted.

'Do you know how many phone calls I've received today?' he asked. 'Do you know what time it is over here?'

'Yes, I'm so sorry...'

'You hope I'll be able to save you,' Dick growled. 'Is that right?' He began to laugh again. 'You want Daddy to come hold your little Swiss hand and tell you everything is going to be OK?' His voice slurred a little, and it suddenly occurred to Gabriel that Dick sounded quite drunk.

'Have you been up all night?' Gabriel asked.

Dick's laughter, this time, sounded quite hysterical. 'What do you think?' he asked. 'I've been up all week! I slept two hours on Wednesday afternoon, I think. That's the only break I allowed myself. I must have fielded hundreds, maybe a thousand phone calls from idiots like you.'

'I'm worried,' Gabriel said.

'Everyone is worried,' Dick said coolly. 'Some of my clients are going to lose everything. At least you've diversified, haven't you? Why are you calling me? Shouldn't you be having meetings with your partners, to discuss what to do with your Swiss stocks and bonds and fiduciary deposits? Aren't the European banks going to bail you out?'

'I don't know,' Gabriel said hesitantly. 'I haven't heard anything about that. I think the banks over here are too big to fail, just like yours...'

'Yes, money will solve the problem,' Dick said, with something suspiciously like a giggle. 'Let's print lots and lots of shiny new banknotes!'

Gabriel sighed. 'I don't think the banks here are doing well, either. There are... problems in the UK, in Ireland, in Greece.'

'Oh no!' said Dick, sarcastically.

'We're talking about the possibility of catastrophic bankruptcies,' Gabriel said, as sternly as he could. 'I thought you might be able to offer advice. What are you going to do? I mean, what am I going to tell my clients, our clients?'

'What is it you want to hear from me, Gabe?' Dick sneered. 'That the products will be fine, that the mortgage-backed securities will be fine, that everything will be fine, in some mysterious way that perhaps I'll be able to produce, from my beautiful crystal office?'

Gabriel did not reply, expecting more hysterical laughter, but Dick was silent.

'Well, fine, then,' Dick said at last. 'You want a sugared pill, I'll give it to you right now: you've been making twelve, fourteen per cent through me for years. Didn't you put some money aside, for times like these? When you were cashing your old ladies' cheques, and putting their gold nuggets in your underground safes, didn't you plan ahead? Or did you think good ole Dick would look after you?'

'No, I didn't...' Gabriel struggled to interject, but it was no use.

'Wasn't it fun?' Dick continued, implacably. 'Didn't you enjoy it? It lasted for a good few years, you know. Well, you should have enjoyed yourself more, slept with prettier girls, drunk more expensive wine, because those glory days are over now. Bye-bye!'

'This is ridiculous,' said Gabriel, struggling to contain his temper. His hand was viciously twisting another of his jacket buttons. 'I didn't call for this.'

'You've been screwed, Gabriel,' Dick replied. 'I've been screwed. The world's been screwed. Get used to it! It's time for the Swiss to get a little taste of what globalisation truly means. Get rich quick, yes, that's what you thought so far. Take a few more risks, taste the thrill of it. But you weren't prepared, were you? You're not used to being screwed, Gabriel, no matter how many nice little Swiss girlfriends you pick up. This is going to be tough on you, but in Chicago we get screwed every day. We're the prostitutes of banking. We're used to all this. You're nothing but a stupid virgin,' Dick spat down the line, his tirade unstoppable.

'I feel sorry for you, Gabe, but I also think you've been an asshole. That's right. Do you know why? Because you didn't enjoy all the fun that comes with risk-taking. What's the point of high risk without high enjoyment? You tried to stay a mountaineer while you were gambling, when really you should have just become a gambler. You stuck to your cheese, when there was caviar and champagne available.'

'I was only trying to do the best thing for my clients,' Gabriel struggled to defend himself. 'I was trying to find a balance.'

'Yes, and what a great balance that was,' Dick retorted. 'No fun, high risks, and now a terrible downfall, without having enjoyed yourself in the least. That's what happens when you play the whore without admitting to being a whore.'

'Dick!' Gabriel cried, appalled.

'At least we brokers admit what we are,' Dick said calmly. 'We don't screw our clients over, under a guise of claiming to look after their best interests. We don't pretend to be responsible, nice, mountain–'

'Enough,' said Gabriel. 'I've heard enough of this. Clearly, you are abandoning us in this troubled time.'

'The world is abandoning us,' Dick muttered. 'The markets are abandoning us. Don't come crying to me. I take no responsibility for your failures, Gabriel. Now, if you'll excuse me, I have another hundred people waiting to blame me for a global financial collapse. Goodbye, Gabe.'

The dial tone rang for a long time in Gabriel's ear. At last, he swallowed and, with shaking hands, hung up the phone. He took off his suit jacket and sat perfectly still for a very, very long time.

———•◆•———

When his breathing had calmed, and his hands had stopped shaking, Gabriel picked up the phone one last time and dialled a number he knew by heart.

'Anita, my love,' he said breathlessly.

'My darling Gabriel!' she replied cheerfully. 'How are you?' There was the muffled sound of a glass clinking.

Gabriel felt the knot in his stomach relax. 'How wonderful to hear your voice,' he said. 'I've had the most awful day.'

'Oh, tell me all about it!' Anita exclaimed.

'No, you first,' Gabriel said, forcing a smile – for whose benefit, he wasn't sure. 'Tell me about your day.'

A chair scraped across the floor. Perhaps she had sat down. Was she in her kitchen? Yes, no doubt, preparing supper and sipping a glass of wine. Gabriel's stomach tightened jealously at the thought of such insouciance.

'Well,' Anita began, 'this morning I went to the market in Plainpalais, to buy a young chicken to roast, and some vegetables. You know, they sell the most wonderful freshly-pressed juices there! I bought some strawberries, too. It was raining, but I didn't mind. I had my beautiful green umbrella! Still, it was a little cold, so I went for a coffee, and ran into a friend from my days waiting tables by the lakeside. Well, you know how it is, catching up with someone like that, so I didn't get home with my chicken till early afternoon. Then I had to get changed quickly and go to my tutoring session – you know, the young Spanish boy – and before I knew it, it was time to start preparing supper.' She paused, satisfaction filling even the silence.

Gabriel felt slightly ill after listening to this banality. He began to wish he had called his father, or Clarice: someone less enthusiastic, with a better grip on the hardships of reality. He needed someone to shout at him, to loosen the knot in his stomach and lessen his guilt.

'Anyway, how are you, my dearest beloved?' Anita chirped. 'You said you'd had a bad day.'

'The bank is in trouble,' Gabriel said, without preamble, feeling his stomach sink and his heart rate accelerate again. 'We're losing money, I'm losing money... Dick, the broker in Chicago, he abandoned us. The world's economy is crashing. I don't know what we're going to do.' He steadied his breathing, trying to slow the chaos of his thoughts, but they came to him in an emotional rush. 'Everyone is so worried, Anita, and they're turning to me for comfort. I don't know what comfort I can give them, these hard-working people. I don't know what I can tell my clients, either. It's a mess, Anita, a terrible mess.' He hung his head, defeated.

'It's OK, honey,' Anita replied softly. 'There's always good news with bad news. You can't have it all, you know: no-one can. These things happen.'

Gabriel tried to feel reassured by this reply, and failed. 'What do you mean?' he asked, somewhat petulantly.

'Well, isn't there some bright side you can find in all this? Perhaps you'll have shorter hours at work, and you'll be able to visit me more often.'

'I'm going to lose a great deal of money, darling,' Gabriel said shortly. 'That's hardly good news for anyone. My bonus...'

'Let me go to church,' Anita said soothingly. 'I'll pray to the Virgin Mary. Perhaps God will be able to recover your bonus. Or perhaps there will be another path for you, hope that springs from these dark days!'

Gabriel bristled. 'Who are you to advise me in this way? I'm in danger of failing the bank completely, and you think this could be good news, in any way? Our family has run this bank since the 1600s. We've never, ever lost money. Who are you to tell me how to recover my losses?' He took off his glasses and pressed his fists into his tired eyes. He should have just gone home.

'Darling,' Anita said calmly, 'I am not trying to offer you banking advice. I am suggesting that you look away from this stressful situation, and turn to higher powers for comfort.'

'I am not a Catholic,' Gabriel spat out, more violently than he had intended. 'You know this. The Virgin Mary is not going to bring me any comfort.'

There was a pause. Then Anita, in a softer voice, spoke again: 'Why don't you come see me, then? Come on over and I'll make you happy. We can eat this chicken. It's roasting now: it smells delicious.'

'I'm not hungry,' Gabriel said shortly.

'Then we won't eat,' Anita said, lasciviously. 'I'll clear your mind of these worries. Just give me two hours.'

Gabriel sighed. 'That's not a solution,' he said sharply. 'Sex will not make me forget my misery: the bank, our clients, the global economy, Dick abandoning me, Thomas and his bow tie...' He sunk his face into his arm, barely holding the phone to his ear. 'Anita, I just need to be alone. I'm sorry I disturbed you.'

'Please,' Anita said softly, 'don't be upset. Just come see me.'

'I can't,' said Gabriel. 'Goodbye, Anita.' He hung up, his mind in turmoil.

There was no help to be found there: his confused love for Anita could offer no help in this troubled time. He was not capable of great emotions, he told himself, after hiding them for fifty years. Love did not triumph over all, nor would it bring him peace. What had he been thinking, that he would weep down the phone to Anita and then feel better? It was a preposterous idea, and deeply un-Swiss. No, Anita was not the solution. He would go home, and sit alone with his thoughts, too Swiss to cry.

Chapter Thirty-Six

It was raining again. Gabriel walked swiftly down the road towards the bank, cursing the water that splashed onto his glasses, obscuring his vision of the roiling, blue-grey Rhône. He was exhausted, overworked, and coming down with a vicious cold. Perhaps a coffee and a fresh warm *pain au chocolat* would help. He happened to glance up at one of the kiosks by the side of the road, and froze at the headline.

LEHMAN BROTHERS CATASTROPHE. The words were splashed across the front page of the Swiss newspaper.

'Lehman!' he gasped under his breath, rustling in his pocket for a few spare Swiss francs, the *pain au chocolat* forgotten. 'Lehman!' he repeated again. This was bad. This was very, very bad. He opened the newspaper, ignoring the falling rain, then shut it again swiftly. He looked around nervously, hoping nobody he knew was in the street. He mustn't be seen in such a state of worry. He would read at his leisure in his office, with a ristretto to ward off the September chill. Quickly, he began to march towards the bank, but a hand suddenly caught him by the shoulder. He spun around, his heart in his mouth, only to see Thomas.

'Thomas!' he blurted out, half exasperated, half reassured. 'What are you doing here?'

'Hello, Monsieur Gabriel!' Thomas said cheerfully. 'I'm walking to work, of course.' He frowned, looking worried. 'You haven't hit your head or something, have you?'

'No, no,' Gabriel replied. 'It's just, well, have you seen the news?' He held up the newspaper.

'How do you feel about watermelon for breakfast?' Thomas asked, conversationally.

Gabriel blinked, still holding the newspaper aloft. 'What?' he asked, lowering it slowly. 'Why would I want that?'

'Because it tastes good with cheese,' Thomas replied, smiling. 'It really does!'

'The world is falling apart, Thomas,' Gabriel intoned, trying not to lose his temper, 'America is falling apart, the biggest leaders of the capitalist system are in disarray, Wall Street is collapsing, and you want to eat cold watermelon and *cheese* at 9.30 in the morning?'

'But it is so good and sweet!' Thomas replied. 'Anyway, I already knew about Lehman.' He smiled again, infuriatingly.

'What?' asked Gabriel. 'How?' He opened the newspaper again, slightly suspiciously, as if Thomas might be mentioned within.

'I heard the rumour from my sources in Berne,' the German said smoothly, 'that one of the oldest and most famous banks was going down.'

'But Lehman Brothers, my God!' said Gabriel, his eyes travelling the length of the pages desperately. 'That's a sprawling, billion-dollar bank! And no-one would buy it. No-one would save it. It says here it can't pay its shareholders, or any dividends, or anything. This will be yet another massive shock to the whole market.' Panic, a now deeply familiar sensation, began once more to rise in his throat. He sneezed, violently.

'*Gesundheit*,' said Thomas.

Gabriel glared at his partner balefully, as he rustled for his handkerchief. 'Thank you,' he muttered.

'Stocks are going down and down,' Thomas observed. 'The government is printing money, desperately trying to save companies that were judged too big to fail.'

'I know, Thomas,' Gabriel said, the newspaper in his hands shaking. 'This week, I had to tell my clients that the very safe domestic bonds they owned had lost thirty per cent, as if overnight. They don't understand: going from twelve per cent returns on perfectly preserved capital to zero returns and capital losing thirty per cent! These are people who lent their money to us for safekeeping. Old ladies, aristocrats, great Swiss families... All lost. It's unimaginable. There is no salvation. The bank will be ruined.'

'How?' Thomas asked, brightly. He began to wiggle his eyebrows in a most peculiar manner.

Gabriel found he was ready to cover the whole terrible collapse of the banking system, caused by greed and stupidity 'There is already

IN BED WITH A SWISS BANKER

widespread panic in the markets,' Gabriel replied. 'No-one trusts anyone else, so no-one is willing to lend. Companies are unable to rely on banks to pay their employees, so they're freezing their spending in order to hoard cash. There's a seizure in the worldwide economy. The markets are concluding their collapse,' Gabriel said, the pitch of his voice rising. 'Banking as we know it is over. These last few months have caused terrible, irreversible damage in Wall Street. A veritable cascade of bankruptcies: failing banks borrowing from other banks, or selling them bonds that end up in default. Everybody losing all their money. Some of these banks are having to talk about negative net worth. In New York! Can you imagine?'

'It's the same in London,' Thomas replied calmly, 'though America still has experienced some of the worst failures this year. Did you hear about the Secretary of the Treasury who is planning to inject hundreds of billions of dollars of taxpayers' money into buying up toxic assets?'

His mind reeling, Gabriel shook his head. 'Regulation,' he muttered vaguely. 'Isn't there supposed to be some sort of regulation?'

Thomas shrugged. 'Modern banking wasn't prepared for a crisis of this sort. Not for these complex chains of debt. I'd even say lack of regulation was one of the causes of this whole situation, as well as terrible preparation.'

'Stop acting so clever!' Gabriel snapped. 'I'll tell you what caused this crisis: idiots like you and me sitting around, trying to make more money. Risky investments, deregulation of derivatives, excessive borrowing, and a lack of transparency that borders on the mendacious. A breakdown of accountability and ethics from people like us. This crisis is our fault, Thomas,' he said viciously. 'We are all responsible.'

'It's all going to be fine, Gabriel,' Thomas said softly.

'I don't even know what the governments can do at this point,' Gabriel added glumly. 'Print more money? Try to intervene in the distribution of their bailout funds? Everything they've done so far has been hopelessly inconsistent.' His wet newspaper flopped weakly in his hands.

'You sound quite fragile, my friend,' Thomas said gently. 'Psychologically.'

Gabriel snorted. 'Coming from you...'

Thomas bowed slightly, as if flattered, a clicking sound coming from his mouth.

Gabriel sighed, feeling defeated. 'It's true, though,' he said. 'I feel like I've been under a lot of pressure lately.' He held up the newspaper as an illustration, or perhaps as a defence. His expression suddenly became more worried. 'You don't think we're inside, do you?' he murmured, attempting to flick through the sodden pages. 'Von Mipatobeau, I mean. Do you think we'll be listed along with all the other failing European banks, all of those in the UK?' He sneezed again, violently, and Thomas stepped forward solicitously to take the newspaper from him.

Gabriel sighed and found his handkerchief again.

'*Mein Gott*,' Thomas said suddenly.

Gabriel's head snapped up, and he was tempted to grab the newspaper back at once. 'What? Is it us?' Gabriel asked, his heart racing. 'Are they writing about Bank Von Mipatobeau?'

Thomas pointed to a corner of the sopping page, where the ink running could not disguise the title of the article. ANOTHER BANKING SUICIDE.

'It's Gérard,' he said weakly, before bursting into tears. 'My little Gérard!'

Gabriel wrestled the now essentially destroyed newspaper from Thomas's shaking hands, and began to read.

'How? *How*?' Thomas began to cry. 'Why?'

'Apparently he poisoned himself with insulin and barbiturates,' Gabriel read, frowning. Thomas let out a sort of howl, and began tearing at his hair. 'I suppose it's more of an American thing, jumping out the window,' he added callously, no longer caring. 'Courageous. Showy.' Why should the Frenchmen get to end it all, choosing the easy way out, when the rest of them had to fight through the mess every day? Still, it was not a glorious way to go.

Thomas glared weakly at him, and Gabriel relented. 'It's awful,' he said. 'Poor Gérard.'

Thomas wiped his eyes and made a sniffing noise. 'I will miss him so much,' he said. 'No more Dick, no more Gérard.'

Gabriel raised his eyebrows. 'What do you mean, no more Dick?'

'He won't answer my calls,' Thomas said, his face a tragic mask. 'We were such good friends! Once, I think he picked up, but he hung up without saying a word.' Tears began to trickle down his cheeks.

'Now, now,' Gabriel said as firmly as he could. 'We are going to be just fine without all these foreign influences. We are Swiss men, and private bankers. A safer category of humanity, I couldn't imagine.'

Thomas gave a watery smile. 'We're going to look after each other,' he said.

Gabriel nodded. 'Just as we have for the first part of this terrible year. Listen, for a start, I've decided to announce that I'm giving up my bonus this year.'

'What, from eleven million to zero?' Thomas exclaimed.

'I don't mind taking the penalty,' Gabriel said stoically, 'even if I'm entitled to something like five million.'

'There are provisions!' Thomas said. 'You don't have to do that!'

'We are not an American bank,' Gabriel replied firmly. 'We do not publish our balance sheets, and because of this, our reputation is, so far, intact. This is not a gesture for the world to see. This will be a gesture so that my partners and employees understand how much Von Mipatobeau bank means to me, how much it must continue to mean for us all.'

'It is all we have left,' Thomas said darkly.

Gabriel took Thomas's arm in his. 'Come then,' he said. 'Keep your chin up. Let's walk to work together. Things can only get better.'

Eight hours later, as Gabriel walked slowly through the marble doorway into the wet street, he recalled his words that morning with some bitterness. 'Better?' he muttered under his breath, squinting into the rain, which was still falling faintly. 'Things can get a whole lot worse before they get better.' He sighed deeply. He had no desire to go home, but where else could he go? His relationship with Anita had suffered somewhat over the last five months, and he had learned not to go to their apartment when his mind was full of work worries. He still loved her, of course, but he kept that love separate from the rest of his life, more fervently than ever.

He wondered, sometimes, in his darker moments, why he and Clarice still chose to move through life as if shackled to each other. In the end, perhaps it was for the best, this strange state of affairs. It allowed him to keep a small parcel of romance in his life, but in a safe, distant, controlled sort of way. Meanwhile, Clarice still meant a great deal to him. After all, they had been married for thirty years. After all, his home was in Saint Antoine.

Gabriel pushed open the door to the house, narrowing his eyes into the darkness of the entry hall. 'Clarice?' he called out. Surely she should have prepared his supper by now. He hung his coat on the peg and walked into the lounge. Suddenly, he realised Clarice was in fact sitting there on the couch, immobile in the half-light. She was wearing a long green dress, which gave her figure the impression of being surrounded by deep shadows. She had not taken off her high heels.

'Clarice!' he exclaimed. 'You startled me.'

Clarice looked up, her expression blank, and for a moment did not respond. Then she held up the newspaper.

'Oh, you heard about Gérard?' Gabriel guessed. 'A tragedy,' he added, uncertainly. Clarice had still not spoken.

Unsettled, Gabriel sat down by her side. 'Clarice?' he ventured at last.

'It just keeps getting worse and worse,' she said hollowly, not turning to look at him. 'Do you know how excited my father was when I first mentioned I was getting married to a private Swiss banker? He was positively ecstatic with pride. Now it just seems like banking is one horrible collapse after the other, some new and awful scandal every day.' She set the newspaper down on the table unsteadily and turned the full force of her blazing eyes on her husband.

'What do you mean, my dear?' Gabriel asked uneasily.

'The sadomasochistic parties. The mistresses. No, don't say anything. The markets collapsing. The Ponzi schemes uncovered. The billion-dollar bankruptcies. The accusations of theft. The endless losses. Dentists and lawyers suddenly penniless. The clients rushing to your doors, banging on the gates, and no reply from within. All of you hiding in your Napoleon III dining rooms, sweating, clutching your gold to your chests. The men leaping from sixtieth-floor balconies or poisoning their vodka tonics. The headlines blacker every day. What are we supposed to do?' She waved a hand in the air, vaguely, listlessly, turning away from him.

'You mustn't lose hope,' Gabriel said, too tired to inject any real sentiment into the words. Where was his supper?

'The embarrassment,' Clarice repeated dully. 'The sheer, daily embarrassment of having to bear your name, the family name, the name of your failing bank.'

'Clarice,' Gabriel said as patiently as he could, 'we are doing the best we can.'

'Yes, poor little Gabriel sacrificed his bonus. Boo-hoo. No private jet trips to Davos this year! No Dolce & Gabbana for your Peruvian gold-digger.'

'Clarice, are you drunk?' Gabriel snapped, beginning to lose his patience.

'No,' said Clarice, staring straight ahead. 'I am extremely upset.'

'We are all upset, Clarice,' Gabriel replied, 'but we need to stick together in the face of this crisis. I need you on my side. I need your support, as... as my wife.'

Clarice made a sort of snorting sound. 'You need my support,' she said, her voice oddly muffled. 'Now, all of a sudden, you need your beloved Clarice's support.'

Misunderstanding her accusation, Gabriel flushed red. 'Why, has there been trouble at the gallery? Have I not been paying enough attention to your concerns? Is there... Is there anything I can do to help?'

Clarice gave a desperate laugh. 'Help!' she repeated. 'I suppose you want to offer me money from your failing bank? Perhaps you want your name to go into our brochure, as a famous and important donor. Perhaps you want to be seen walking down the streets arm-in-arm with Chloë and Khadija and me, basking in our success? No, worse, thinking you are in some way responsible for our success!'

Baffled, Gabriel drew back. 'I don't understand,' he said.

'I want a divorce,' Clarice said, enunciating slowly and clearly. There was a heavy silence.

'Now?' Gabriel said at last. 'You want a divorce now?' he added haltingly.

Clarice did not reply immediately.

'I've been asking for ten years,' Gabriel said, aggrieved. Restraining himself, he fell silent. 'Why?' he asked at once.

'I've been trying to fall in love with you for thirty years,' Clarice said quietly. 'I've been trying to get you to talk to me, to make love to me, to be with me... We could have done great things together. But you know what, Gabriel? I've done great things, all on my own. My friends have helped me more than you can imagine. They know me better than you could even begin to conceive.'

'I helped you,' Gabriel cut in. 'I helped you a lot, all along.'

'You gave me money,' Clarice replied coldly. 'That is not the same thing. Besides, you only contributed as much as you did, to assuage your guilt for beginning your affair with that little Latin strumpet.'

'You needed the money,' Gabriel said as harshly as he could. 'You still need the money.'

'Not anymore,' Clarice said coolly.

A chill went down Gabriel's spine. 'Is that why you've stayed with me all these years, refusing to grant me a divorce? And now the money's run dry, because of a global crisis in the economy, you cast me aside?'

'I don't need your money any more,' Clarice said simply, 'because you've made a mess of your life, not just in banking. You screwed up, Gabriel, in your work, in your love life, with your family. Anita... You took her to meet your parents – how dare you? Taking your girlfriend to Davos, and probably to your banking lunches... Oh, but this is so, so much worse than your affair. And you think I am the one dragging our reputation through the muck, with my modern art? With my modern girlfriends? Gabriel, you've ruined your family name. I've seen Von Mipatobeau in the papers. I've seen your name, *my* name, next to those headlines. The ones talking about catastrophe, and failure.'

'We are not Lehman Brothers,' he protested.

'You are the same,' Clarice said firmly.

'Everyone is failing,' Gabriel said quietly.

'Don't you care about your reputation any more?' Clarice sneered.

'This isn't my fault,' Gabriel said, wincing at the childishness of his defence. 'You're accusing me of... The crisis is a global one. The factors are far beyond our reach.' He paused, and took a deep breath, choosing a different tactic. 'Listen, our bank is solid. You know this. It has always been so. We are a private Swiss bank and you know what that means. We are, we are... the last bastion of the current financial world. The last safe store of liquidity in the whole world. Everything can fall apart and we will not,' he said with a conviction he was far from feeling. 'We retain the last credibility, the last honour, the last good management, and the last low-risk option to be found anywhere.'

'Do you really,' Clarice said, slyly. 'You think you're in control of the situation?' She watched in satisfaction as Gabriel began to sweat visibly. 'We're here discussing the end of a thirty-year marriage and you're talking about risk management?'

'You're telling me you're asking for a divorce because of the state of the bank. I'm only answering you on your terms. You know I've been asking you for a divorce for ten years. Begging, even. Waiting patiently. You didn't want it, and now you say you do. Well, if you're going to blame banking, you're going to have to understand what banking means to me.'

'Ah, your real mistress,' Clarice said mockingly. Colour had returned to her cheeks.

'Yes,' Gabriel said doggedly. 'Banking is more important to me than any woman.'

'So it's like a secret society?' she asked. 'A Masonic cult?'

'No,' said Gabriel.

'So you're not a close-knit group with rituals and secrets, methodologies, pretensions, costumes? What about the mahogany tables, and the *huissiers* in their jackets, and the beautiful polychrome receptionists? What about your obsession with Switzerland, and speculating on gold? You're in a world of your own, you Swiss bankers,' Clarice concluded, condescendingly. 'Don't tell me how important it is. Just remember it's the reason I'm divorcing you.'

'If I understand correctly,' said Gabriel, his voice strained, 'you're divorcing me because you're ashamed of me.'

Clarice smiled slowly.

'Everyone is failing,' Gabriel said again, very quietly. 'It isn't just Von Mipatobeau. It isn't just me.'

'*I* am not failing,' Clarice replied, with emphasis, 'and I will not be held back by your failure. I don't want your name anymore. I am my own woman. I am Clarice Saint-André-Tobbal, and as such I will go forth in the world and succeed.' There was a light shining in her eyes: Gabriel suddenly wondered if she had rehearsed this speech. A sudden doubt occurred to him.

'Why now?' he asked. 'What does the Lehman Brothers scandal, or Gérard's suicide, have to do with our marriage? Why is today worse than the other days?'

'Every day has been worse than the last,' Clarice said, the words striking Gabriel like barbs. 'Every day for the last thirty years, or at least the last ten. Why not now? Why not take risks, since the world is falling to pieces anyway?'

'What happened to "de Puritigny till I die?" Gabriel asked. 'What happened to your values, and your beliefs?'

'It's over, Gabriel,' Clarice said. 'I don't have to justify myself any further.'

'This isn't very Swiss,' Gabriel said, petulantly. 'You really think this is the way to rescue your reputation? You think this is what will finally make your idiot father be proud of you? That you're taking back his godawful name?'

Clarice winced at this. 'You and your Switzerland,' she cried angrily, turning towards the wall once more. 'As if I cared for this nation of cuckoo clocks and stupid family portraits. There is nothing here, no resources, no future, only what we make. Even the chocolate is imported! Even the materials for your precious Rolex watches! My gallery is not Swiss: it is mine.'

'Switzerland means something,' Gabriel shouted back, desperately. 'Think of the mountains!'

'The mountains?' Clarice scoffed. 'An accidental occurrence that took place millions of years ago. You're proud of that?'

'What about sincerity? What about secrecy, and service, and creativity? Honesty. Quality. Maintenance. We have standards.'

'This is the worst tourist brochure I've ever heard,' Clarice sneered. 'I'm happy to stay here, because the country is rich and attracts intelligent investors. My attachment goes no further than that.'

Outside, the rain was drumming loudly on the darkened windows. Tears sprang to Gabriel's eyes, though he blinked them angrily away. 'You're lost, Clarice,' he managed to say.

'You're the one who's lost, Gabriel. Just go back to your mistress,' Clarice said. 'Doesn't she just *love* Switzerland?'

'If this is about Anita, it's a little bit late,' Gabriel said desperately.

'It's not about Anita,' Clarice said patiently. 'I have nothing against the poor girl. Does she know she'll be cast aside like a used handkerchief as soon as she stops offering you comfort? Does she know she only exists in your mind to prop up your failing ego, like a crutch you pick up from the wall on the days you feel weak and miserable? Oh, I'm sure you think you love her. You've probably been seeing her twice as much since the bank has been in trouble. Well, guess what: the crisis may have brought you closer to one woman, but it has taken your wife away from you. It's over, Gabriel.'

We're over. Anita is nothing and you are nothing. I want to step away from this mess and never look back. Just give me a divorce.'

'You're wrong,' Gabriel said, stung, but his pride kept him from revealing any further details of the state of affairs with Anita. 'She is not a handkerchief.'

The corners of Clarice's mouth twitched, and she smoothed down her green skirt very slowly, very carefully. 'Alright. Then you should be pleased, shouldn't you?' she asked. 'Now you can scuttle off and marry your beloved, like you always wanted. Gabriel and Anita, together at last.' Her voice had a singsong lilt.

'I will,' Gabriel said, angry and hurt. He stood up from the couch and swiftly adjusted his tie. 'You just wait and see.'

Chapter Thirty-Seven

Gabriel smiled, looking out over the mountains from the slowly rotating restaurant. The Jungfrau. The Mönch. The Eiger. He had known these impressive peaks intimately since he was a child, and would have recognised them in any weather or any light. Spring was just beginning in the Swiss Alps: the mountain streams were filling with icy meltwater and the first buds were appearing on snow-encrusted branches. From Interlaken, the view was stunning. Gabriel wondered if the spring birds had begun to appear yet, flying back along ancient migration paths from sunnier climes. Soon, the first mating calls would sound in the high pine branches, and woodpeckers would begin to drill among the trees, and pairs of eagles would be spotted circling high overhead. His mother would know, he thought with affection. Perhaps he would call her later on, or perhaps he and Anita could even stop by on their drive back to Geneva...

His train of thought was interrupted by Anita's return to the restaurant, which she had left to powder her nose. How beautiful she was! Gabriel thought, his heart overwhelmed by the mountain surroundings, against which she appeared. The restaurant had rotated slightly in the interval she had been away, Gabriel noted with satisfaction.

'I'm back, my dear,' Anita said, leaning in to kiss Gabriel before sitting down and putting her napkin in her lap.

'I was just thinking about migratory birds,' he said.

Anita smiled. 'Migratory,' she repeated. 'Like me. Nobody talks about immigrants birds, do they?'

Gabriel shook his head. 'Nonsense,' he said. 'You're as Swiss as I am,' he added firmly. 'Unless you're intending to fly back to Peru when the snows come?'

She shook her head and smiled back, affectionately. 'Have you decided what you'd like to eat today?'

'Well, what would James Bond eat?' Gabriel joked. 'His name seems to be everywhere in this station.'

Anita giggled. 'He would be drinking a martini, silly,' she said.

Gabriel looked worried. 'Is that really his style?' he asked. 'I thought he was a spy. Doesn't someone engaging in intelligence activities need to be sober?'

Anita laughed. 'I'll never get over your lack of interest in popular culture,' she said warmly. 'We can watch *On Her Majesty's Secret Service* when we get back to our apartment.'

'I've never even heard of that one,' said Gabriel. 'What's it about? The Queen?'

'You mean you don't recognise this restaurant?' Anita asked, puzzled. 'Why did you decide we should come here, then?'

'I just... thought it was a nice idea, to have a view of the mountains,' Gabriel replied, embarrassed. 'I thought all the 007 paraphernalia must have been advertising for some new film.'

'Don't worry, it's not one of the best Bond films,' Anita said soothingly. 'All I can really remember is this restaurant, and that George Lazenby does a lot of fighting in the snow. It's very sexy.'

'Who's he?' Gabriel asked, confused.

'James Bond, of course,' Anita replied, 'though he's not one of the more famous ones.'

'Oh,' said Gabriel, flustered. 'Well, I think I'll just have a coffee, myself. But feel free to order whatever you like.'

Anita smiled. 'I think I should like some cake,' she said.

Gabriel was gazing out at the snow again. What a shame it was that Anita did not enjoy winter sports! He couldn't wait to be out there, with his cross-country skis or a pair of snowshoes, alone with the fresh scent of pine and the promise of birdsong...

'Darling?' Anita said.

'Yes?' Gabriel smiled quickly, interrupting his train of thought.

'Why *have* we come here?' she asked.

'To see the mountains, of course,' Gabriel stammered. 'Don't you enjoy our little trips around Switzerland? I thought it had been a while since we'd had one.'

'Well, yes,' Anita said brightly. 'I love exploring Switzerland, and the little train up here was simply darling. Besides, you're right, we haven't had enough time to go anywhere but the ski resorts. You've been so busy with work, and everything.'

'Yes, but let's not talk about that here,' Gabriel said, somewhat wearily. 'I wanted to get away from Geneva, partly to escape all of that.'

'Of course!' Anita replied. 'Not another word, I promise. I was only wondering if there had been some sort of... special occasion.'

Gabriel did not look up from his menu. 'No, no,' he said. 'None at all. I mean, I thought it might be a nice time to try out my new camera,' he stammered. 'It's been so grey in Geneva, and the light... And, well, it's been years since I've taken any good nature photography, I...'

At that moment, the waiter appeared and took their order. For a while, Anita and Gabriel sat in awkward silence, each staring out at the snow. Gabriel's heart was pounding. He could feel the small, square jewellery box in his breast pocket as clearly as if it had been made of hot iron. Ever since his fight with Clarice, he had been waiting for the right moment to speak to Anita, his feelings a confusion of love, anger and vindictiveness. Sometimes, Clarice's voice came to taunt him, hissing 'Gabriel and Anita, together at last.' He *did* want to marry Anita, he reminded himself. It wasn't just an angry gesture. He didn't have anything to prove to anyone. It was simply the right thing to do. Nothing was holding him back anymore.

'Darling, you seem distracted,' Anita said again. 'Are you thinking about your camera?' Luckily, the waiter arrived with a loaded tray before Gabriel had to think of an answer. He set down two steaming coffees, and an enormous slab of gooey black forest gâteau. What a sweet tooth Anita had, as well as a sweet heart!

Gabriel felt as if all the blood in his body had rushed to his head, and he suddenly grabbed Anita's hand, quite tightly. She looked up in surprise. 'Are you alright?' she asked warmly. 'Do you need to step outside?'

'Dearest,' Gabriel said unsteadily, then paused. 'No, I'm fine,' he said. 'I mean, I wanted to...' He fumbled awkwardly inside his jacket with his free hand, then took a deep breath as his hand closed over the box. 'Anita, *ma chérie*, you know how much I love you. You've been my salvation through such difficult times, and such boring times, my trouble with the bank, and with Clarice and...' An awful thought flashed through his head. *Was this how he had proposed to Clarice?* But it didn't matter. This was a different kind of love, a different kind of marriage. That was not the time to think about Clarice. 'What I mean, Anita, is that you have come to mean the world to me, in all this time we've spent side by side. You have done everything for me, and I want to do something for you in return. I want to say something now, for you and for me.' He glanced up, to see that Anita's expression was puzzled, pleased, and full of hope. Gabriel took a deep breath. 'Will you marry me?' He pulled the box from his jacket pocket, and after a moment's one-handed struggle, revealed the diamond ring inside.

Anita let out a squeal, and nearly leapt out of her chair; then she sat down and reached for the ring, and then her hands flew to her mouth. It was as if she didn't know what to do with herself. Her eyes sparkled with tears. 'I knew it,' she cried joyfully, flinging herself across the table to kiss him.

Gabriel, flustered and pleased, felt the eyes of the restaurant turn towards them. 'My darling,' he said, 'must you be so Peruvian about this?'

Anita laughed happily. 'Don't be so Swiss!' she said.

'Now, we can be Swiss together,' Gabriel corrected gently. He delicately lifted the ring from its box, took Anita's hand, and slipped it over her finger.

Anita's smile trembled, and she looked as though she might cry. 'Oh, darling, do you really mean it?' she asked, her enthusiasm bubbling over. 'Do you really, really mean it? About getting married and becoming Swiss. I want to be Swiss so badly! Swiss with you, I mean! I want us to be the perfect Swiss couple, as soon as possible!' As if sensing that Gabriel was a little troubled by this outburst, she added: 'I love you so much, my darling. You've been a godsend to me, and I will be yours all my life. All yours and only yours.' She paused. 'Don't you think we should get married quite soon, though? I mean, I can hardly wait!'

'Any time you want,' Gabriel said generously. 'We can even get married this summer, if you like.' Of course, summer was quite an outrageous proposition, what with all the organisation, but surely he would be able to talk her round to something more reasonable, perhaps the following summer. After all, this was not the time for boring specifics. This was a time for emotion. He took a sip of his coffee.

'What about this spring?' Anita ventured.

Gabriel nearly spat out his latte macchiato, but managed to hold himself back. 'This spring?' he repeated, his voice strained. 'I mean, it's spring now.'

'I would marry you right this second if I could,' Anita replied, her smile bright and happy. 'I would marry you in this restaurant, in our hotel bedroom, or out there in the snow. Oh, Gabriel, I want to marry you in a matter of weeks, of days, of hours!' she said exuberantly.

'Let me see what I can do,' Gabriel said cautiously. 'I mean, we don't have to decide now.'

'No, of course not,' Anita replied. 'I am only getting carried away because I am so, so happy. Oh, Gabriel! We're getting married!'

This last announcement had been rather loud, and a scattering of applause broke out through the restaurant. Gabriel, feeling his face turn pink once again, felt rather pleased. How happy Anita seemed to be marrying him!

—◆—

Anita practically ran up to the door of their hotel, pressing the large, rusty old key into the lock and rattling it around.

Gabriel repressed a smile, brushing the snow from his collar. 'You know, my darling, we'll still be newly engaged tomorrow. There's no hurry.' They had walked back down to the village at an impressive speed.

Anita opened the door and rushed in, before turning back to throw him a smile. 'I know, my darling,' she said, 'but I'm just so excited! I want to tell everyone I've ever met.' Seeing Gabriel's expression, she laughed. 'But I'll start with my mother. Let me just change into something more comfortable.'

Gabriel shook his head, smiling as Anita dashed into the dressing room of their luxurious suite. How heavy with history this building was!

'I simply love this daybed!' Anita called out. 'This room will be my boudoir!' she giggled.

Gabriel smiled. A paragon of ancient Swissness, he thought with satisfaction. What a perfect place to make the decision to marry Anita, to enter once more into that ancient and sacred institution! Gabriel sat down on the edge of the bed and peered down at the parquet. Oak, he thought to himself, eighteenth century or even earlier. He scuffed his foot thoughtfully across it. From the dressing room, he could hear Anita whistling, and he smiled wryly when he realised the tune was 'Edelweiss.' *The perfect Swiss couple*, he thought, the words somehow sitting oddly.

'What kind of dress do you think I should wear?' Anita's voice came through the doorway, slightly muffled.

'I don't know, my darling,' Gabriel replied. 'We'll only be going out to dinner, perhaps a stroll around the town. Maybe wear something warm? It was snowing quite heavily by the time we arrived here.'

A tinkle of laughter came back to him in reply. 'I mean for the wedding, silly,' Anita said. 'A big fluffy meringue, in the traditional style? Or perhaps something a little sexier?' She poked her head through the doorway, grinning. 'Don't worry, I'm only joking,' she said. 'I want to be the most traditional Swiss bride Switzerland has ever seen.'

'*Chérie*,' Gabriel said hesitantly, 'you do know we won't be able to get married right away, don't you? I mean, if we want to do this wedding properly, it will take some time to organise.' He softened his voice, seeing her crestfallen expression. 'I mean, shouldn't this be the most special day in our lives? It's just that, well, I must know a thousand people in Geneva alone,' Gabriel continued. 'Then there is catering, and flowers, and we'll need a venue, and you'll have to shop for that perfect dress...'

Anita reappeared, wearing jeans and a silk blouse, and gave a bright smile. 'It doesn't matter,' she said. 'We can decide about all that later. Just as long as you promise me that you'll marry me as soon as you can.'

'And you'll marry me back,' Gabriel said, taking her hand and kissing it.

'Oh, I will, only I think I'm getting hungry again,' Anita sighed. 'I wonder...'

'You're insatiable, my love,' said Gabriel, smiling. 'Would you like me to bring you something from the hotel bar? Or a patisserie from that bakery you liked so much yesterday?'

Anita smiled. 'A small pastry would be lovely,' she said enthusiastically. 'After all, this is a day for celebration!' She paused. 'Why don't you take your camera out for a bit of a walk, while you're at it? Why don't you go enjoy the snow a bit on your own? I know you love being out in it so, I don't want to hold you back. I'll make a few phone calls while you're out, so take your time.'

'Thank you, *chérie*,' Gabriel said gratefully, if slightly taken aback. He stood up from the bed and put his winter coat back on, then picked up his camera case from the coffee table. He kissed Anita on the cheek and creaked open the heavy hotel room door.

As he walked down the dark, carpeted hallway, he tried to calm the nagging chaos in his mind. Why did he feel somehow worried? It was wonderful, that she was so excited. What was wrong with wanting to be married at once? He should be excited, too. Wasn't he? Hadn't he made the right decision? Another unpleasant thought flashed through his mind. Had Anita been... herding him from the bedroom? It was true that she sometimes seemed embarrassed to make calls back to her home country in front of him: he assumed it was something about speaking Spanish in front of him that made her feel ill-at-ease. Yet hadn't it been quite hasty, even more so than usual?

No, that was ridiculous. All was well. He was just unused to making big life decisions. Of course his mind would be in turmoil. Perhaps she just wanted to be alone in the bedroom to gather her thoughts. Or perhaps she really did just want to tell her mother. He should be making a few phone calls himself, starting with Clarice... But no, that was petty. He wasn't marrying Anita to prove anything. They had had a long and fruitful affair. Didn't she deserve the wedding she so dearly wanted? Hadn't she been patiently biding her time for ten years until Clarice was willing to back down? Nothing was holding them back, now. They could build a life together, an honest life, open to the world. They would be happy together. Why shouldn't it be as soon as possible?

Gabriel emerged into the hotel lobby, to discover that a veritable blizzard had begun outside. He sighed. This was always a danger, in early springtime. How changeable the weather could be, this time of year. How swiftly the promise of springtime could disappear into the dark and cold of winter! There would be no lovely photographs of flower buds breaking through delicate crusts of snow, no meltwater, and certainly no birdsong. Nothing but a heavy coat of powder. Of course, this did mean that the pistes might be good for skiing the next morning... Gabriel cheered up at this thought, even as he turned around to walk back to the bedroom. Perhaps he could talk Anita into coming out with him, even just for an hour or two.

He padded back down the carpeted hall, and creaked open the door. He heard Anita's voice at once, a veritable torrent of South American Spanish. She had stayed in the dressing room, perhaps sitting on the daybed. Her tone was excited, even flustered. He only caught a few words in the babble. Was *cabron* a goat? Gabriel had always considered Spanish and Italian to be kinds of deformed French, but at this speed, it was quite difficult to follow. Was he the goat? Who was she talking about? Silence and a click announced the end of the phone call. Something in Gabriel's chest stopped him from going into the other room or announcing his presence. His heart thumping, he sat uneasily on the edge of the bed, setting down his camera. After a brief silence, he heard Anita dial another number.

This time, she spoke in a mixture of Spanish and English, so that Gabriel could understand a little more than half of what she was saying.

'Yes, he finally, finally proposed!' Anita was saying. 'Yes, it's so exciting. I know! He made me wait so long!'

Was this a school friend? Someone she knew in Geneva? Anita had always kept Gabriel so separate from her social life. It pained him, suddenly, to realise how little he knew of her life away from him. *I mean*, he thought, *will I be meeting them all at the wedding for the first time?* Suddenly, he froze. He stared at the unlatched door to the other room, feeling as if someone had punched him in the throat.

'No, I don't know how soon I can get the documents,' Anita said, wistfully. 'I mean, I'm hoping I can talk him into signing the marriage papers ahead of the ceremony. He wants to have some kind of big party, bless him! He really does love me. Yes, of course I love him too, in a way. Yes, I know it's boring. Yes, of course he's boring. How could a Swiss banker not be boring?' She laughed, a vicious, high-pitched sound.

Gabriel suddenly felt very cold, and very small, as if a James Bond villain had shrunk him down with some sort of ray gun. He kept staring at the wall, clenching at the bed sheets.

'I don't know how long it will take,' Anita was still speaking, thoughtfully. 'I'll file for citizenship as soon as I get the marriage papers. I think I should be eligible for it in another year, instead of the seven I still had to wait otherwise! I know, it's so exciting! A lovely red passport all of my own!' It sounded as if she had clapped her hands together joyfully. For a moment, Gabriel thought he might be sick. Abruptly, he stood up.

Quickly, quietly, he slipped through the door, closing it silently behind him. In the corridor, he tried to steady his breathing. What was he going to do? He stood in the hallway for so long that the timer lights went out, leaving him in total blackness. No-one came down the corridor. Gabriel was left alone with his thoughts. After a very long time had passed, when his heart rate had slowed, he reluctantly opened the bedroom door and walked back in.

'Anita,' he said at once, loudly, 'I need to speak to you.'

There was a silence, and the sound of covers rustling as Anita no doubt stood up from the daybed where she had been sitting. She appeared in the doorway, looking slightly pale. 'Darling!' she said. 'I didn't hear you come in! Have you...'

'I just came back,' Gabriel said, a little more sharply than he had intended. There was a pause.

'Did you take some nice pictures?' Anita asked brightly.

His jaw clenched, Gabriel glanced over at the camera, sitting on the bed. 'Yes,' he said. 'I mean, no. I wanted to, but...' He swallowed, trying to slow his heartbeat. He barely dared meet her eyes, not because he was afraid of seeing her betrayal in them, but because he knew that they would look the same as always: warm and loving. How false a woman could be! How quickly an illusion was destroyed! For some reason, the image of the swirling snow swallowing the first buds of spring came back to him. 'I received an urgent call,' he finally said.

'But you...' Anita looked confused. 'Weren't you?'

'In the lobby,' Gabriel said, his thoughts coming to him laboriously. 'I hadn't left the hotel, because the snowfall was so heavy, and a waiter just happened to hail me.' He swallowed again, his throat very dry.

'So no pastry for me?' Anita asked cheerily.

'I'm afraid not,' Gabriel said quietly.

Anita opened her mouth, as if to say something, then closed it again. 'Never mind,' she said.

'We have to go back to Geneva,' Gabriel said blankly.

Anita's eyes widened. 'Did something happen?' she asked hesitantly.

'I don't know,' Gabriel replied. 'They said it was an emergency.'

'On the weekend?' Anita ventured tentatively.

'Yes,' Gabriel said coldly. 'I'm afraid so.' He turned towards the bed, and mechanically straightened the covers, then walked over to the pile of clothes carefully folded on the armchair. 'Why don't you pack?' he added. 'We'll need to leave immediately.'

'We can't stay for dinner?' Anita protested. 'They had that lovely-sounding veal *escalope* on the menu. I mean, by the time we get back, it'll be far too late to do any work. Won't it?'

'It's urgent,' Gabriel repeated, still staring at his clothes. He did not apologise.

'Right,' Anita said, meekly. He heard her retreat to the dressing room. After a time, she spoke again, hesitantly. 'Do you know, I had the loveliest idea for the invitations...' Her voice trailed off, and it occurred to Gabriel that she was testing the waters.

'Let's talk about this later,' he said bitterly.

———◆———

The Musée d'Art et d'Histoire was empty, and Gabriel's footsteps echoed on the cold stone floor. He had barely slept, having left Anita at their apartment without a word and knocked, stony-faced, at Clarice's door. His ex-wife, in her defence, had let him in without asking any questions. She was already gone when he awoke, probably meeting her art friends for coffee. Another solution would have to be found, he thought to himself, bitterness welling in his breast. He stared without seeing at a medieval painting of a country scene, snow falling on the peasants and their thin animals. He did not want to be somewhere Anita could call him, or contact him in any way. He did not want to see her face, or hear her voice. Gabriel's sense of betrayal was so profound that he could not imagine venting it, not to Anita, not to anyone. Instead, it festered in his mind like a wound. He walked on to another painting, of a slender, snakelike dragon impaled on an angel's sword. The gilding was beautiful, he noted. Perfectly preserved. He swallowed, feeling his throat tighten, and walked through to another room.

Here, the paintings were of a much later style, all shadows and gold. Anker, he thought, maybe Hödler. Beautiful old Swiss paintings, with the stark realism that he had studied his whole life. He stopped in front of a portrait of a child, holding an apple in its pudgy fist. Not everything was lost, as long as there was still art like this hidden in empty museums. Even the portraits of this sad humanity. There was beauty even there. A solution suddenly occurred to Gabriel: he would drive to Lake Constance. He would stay with his parents until he had figured out what to do. Yes, that was it. He would call the bank the next morning and take a few days off.

Gabriel looked up at the child's face again, its sweet bow lips, its eyes shining with innocence. Only then did he let a tear fall.

Chapter Thirty-Eight

The morning sun was bright, and snow glinted at the side of the road. How could anyone not think Switzerland was the most beautiful, fascinating, exciting country in the world? The mountains! The chalets! The perfectly maintained roads! Gabriel raged as he gripped the steering wheel tightly. These were roads he had known since his childhood, with the long alleyways of trees and the rolling fields either side, their freshly ploughed furrows now decorated with snow. Over the crest of the hill, the deep and sparkling lake would appear, and beyond that, the distant peaks of the Alps. Soon, his parents' house would come into sight. He felt a slight trepidation at the thought, but it was quelled by the rising tide of anger in him.

How could a Swiss man not be boring? Anita's words were galling, not just because they were a jab at him, but because they were such a profound insult to his country. Switzerland, the place Anita had claimed to love so dearly! The country they had visited every mile of together, as lovers! Gabriel sighed. The way she had laughed! It was as if she didn't know him at all, as if in those ten years she had walked by his side without really seeing him. Besides, what was wrong with being a boring man? Perhaps he *was* boring. He was reliable, predictable, punctual, and honest. Why did all these women seem to mind so terribly? Well, almost always honest. Gabriel frowned. Why would the pain not lessen? Something would have to give. As the road sped by, he had the feeling that he was headed to a crossroads, a place of great change. Perhaps his parents could help him see the light.

As he began the descent into the valley, and the house came into sight, Gabriel suddenly heard strains of cheerful, lilting music. The sound was sharp, yet modulated: a man's voice, carried by the wind over a great distance. Someone was yodelling, Gabriel realised with pleasure, filling the mountain air with ancient Swiss songs. Was this the one about the lost sheep, or about the brook trout? The yodeller must be close by, he thought, perhaps even very near to the family home. As he approached the house, his mouth fell open, for it was his father he saw standing in the front yard, singing his heart out.

I came one day to the mountain path and looked up to the stars
The bluebells sang in the mountain wind and our voices carried far:
Yo-de-lay-ee-oo! Yo-de-lay-ee-oo! Yo-de-lay-ee-oo!

With his sharp nose and hulking shoulders, Edmond looked very much like Gabriel, which made the vision even more striking. Gabriel felt a wave of mirth rise up in him, and had to slow the car down for fear his father would see him laughing.

I walked all night by the mountain streams, left footprints in the snow
My darling spring flower, she is gone: where else then can I go?
Yo-de-lay-ee-oo! Yo-de-lay-ee-oo! Yo-de-lay-ee-oo!

Edmond noticed the car and the yodelling stopped abruptly. Squinting, he quickly recognised his son, and gave an embarrassed smile.

Gabriel slowly clambered out into the cold air, memories of Anita clearing from his mind. 'I see you've taken up yet another new retirement hobby, Father,' he said.

'Will you ever learn to call before driving down here?' Edmond replied, not unkindly. He was wearing his hiking boots, and a leather vest embroidered with edelweiss blossoms.

'Perhaps you can teach me to yodel loudly enough to inform you of my arrival, like the cowherds of old,' Gabriel said with a smile, closing the car door. 'I'm sorry for turning up without a warning: the idea came to me rather suddenly.'

'The key to yodelling is in switching between your chest voice and your head voice, you see,' Edmond said seriously. 'A real yodeller can do this gracefully and swiftly, and their voices echo from village to village. Sometimes I go out into the mountains and find a perfectly echoing valley, so that the music can echo off the rock faces. My favourite song is one about a bridge over a frozen stream...' Seeing Gabriel's expression, Edmond was quiet. 'It keeps me busy,' he said defensively.

Gabriel laughed. 'I'm glad,' he said. 'I can't wait for my own retirement, frankly. Maybe I, too, will turn from a banker into an old Swiss peasant.'

Edmond raised his eyebrows, surprised. 'This is a change of tune from you. Why don't you come into the house and tell me about it?' he said.

'Where's Mother?' Gabriel asked, following his father towards the front door.

'Oh, she's out on a walk,' Edmond replied. 'She found an eagle's nest up in the valley the other day, and now she checks on it daily. It's quite sweet, really. I'm sure she'll be back soon, though. Her legs aren't as strong as they used to be.'

'My knees are already starting to get tired,' Gabriel said. 'God knows what shape I'll be in, in another twenty or thirty years!'

'Just keep walking and skiing,' Edmond replied, as they entered the house. 'One in the summer, one in the winter. It's the time-honoured Swiss way to keep healthy.'

They walked down the dark corridor, turning to enter the drawing room. 'Would you like a coffee?' Edmond offered.

'Perhaps something lighter,' Gabriel replied. 'Do you have any chamomile tea? I like it quite weak.'

As his father nodded and headed for the kitchen, Gabriel sat down heavily on one of the leather armchairs. He could hear Edmond softly singing: '*I came one day to the mountain path...*' How many times had he found comfort in this dark and fire-lit lounge, curling up in his childhood pyjamas or reading an old paperback? The room seemed so small, compared to his memories of it. How sad it was, that everything had to change.

'Is it cold enough to feed the fire another log?' Edmond inquired, reappearing. He had removed the edelweiss vest. 'I've been outside all morning, so it feels warm enough in here to me, but I know I've a farmer's instincts for these things. Soon, I'll go out hiking in the morning without a coat, like the shepherd on the other side of the hill.'

'It's fine, Father,' Gabriel replied. He watched as his father set down a tray with two cups and a steaming silver pitcher of hot water. 'How is the farm life treating you these days, anyway?'

'Oh, it's marvellous,' Edmond replied. 'I don't think I will ever tire of the peace and quiet, the view of the lake, the mountain hares that wander by...'

'The weather is so beautiful here,' Gabriel commented. 'Geneva was so cloudy this morning, you'd almost think you were in England! I think a storm may be on its way.'

'It has been a calm spring, weather-wise,' Edmond replied, before falling silent. He was looking at Gabriel with a curious, piercing expression, as if expecting to read something on his face. It made his son deeply uncomfortable.

'When we last spoke on the phone,' Gabriel said a little too enthusiastically, 'Mother told me you were raising chickens?'

Edmond grimaced. 'That is one aspect of our current life I may well end up tiring of. Have you ever heard a chicken laying an egg? The noise is unbearable, rather too much like a woman giving birth! No, there are some aspects of farming that I cannot get used to, even after nearly eighty years on this earth.'

'Do you have many eggs to gather, then?'

Edmond shrugged. 'Some days, we find nearly twenty. Other days, we are not so lucky. I sell them in the village, of course.'

Gabriel smiled. 'Ever the businessman,' he said.

'It's far more fun than banking, counting eggs. Better than a bonus curve, better than the profitability of Wall Street, and more exciting than the Swiss stock market.' He laughed softly.

'Chocolate, watches, and now eggs,' Gabriel shook his head. 'Will you ever entirely retire?'

'I don't know,' Edmond said thoughtfully. 'I suppose we'll find out.'

There was a silence. 'Do you ever miss it?' Gabriel asked tentatively. 'Banking, I mean.' He did not look up at his father, but picked up the silver pitcher and began to pour water into his cup. The fresh smell of chamomile filled the air.

IN BED WITH A SWISS BANKER

'Your small talk is growing more and more Swiss with every passing year,' Edmond said, eventually. 'You'll make a farmer yet. How are your chickens? How nice the weather is! How many eggs do you gather? It's amazing how quickly your mindset changes, you know, once you find yourself far from the fast world of banking. Everything slows down, and you become much more focused. It's as if you rediscover how to be calm.' He filled his own teacup and removed the tea strainer almost immediately, setting the silver ball down next to his son's. 'In some ways, though, I do miss the excitement of banking, the feeling of power I had, leading all these men, looking after so many people's life savings. However, I have learned to appreciate a different set of values, now.'

He nodded slowly. Edmond's piercing gaze eventually forced Gabriel to look up into his father's worried eyes.

'Gabriel, what has happened?' he asked at last.

'A fiasco,' Gabriel said, his voice hollow. In the silence that followed, as he tried to piece his thoughts together, he could hear the grandfather clock ticking. 'I can't sleep. I can't think straight. I no longer know what to do. The financial world is in catastrophic shape, as I'm sure you're aware. Von Mipatobeau is floundering, and the partners don't trust me to save us. They think I've dragged us into the muck by getting involved in the international market in the first place. They think I've sacrificed Swiss values for my own profit. Sometimes, I wonder if they're right. I don't know if things will ever be the same.'

'You are not responsible for a global crisis, my son,' Edmond said quite softly.

Gabriel shrugged. 'There have been investigations,' he said darkly. 'Americans are accusing us of fiscal fraud and illegal solicitation. There are murmurs about taxes, and about retrocessions that shouldn't have happened... Apart from that, I've incurred enormous losses for the bank. Everything I believed in, everything I was excited about, everything I felt I had discovered was a failure and a lie. The mortgage-backed securities, the sub-prime fiascos, the junk bonds, everything has been a total loss. All this high-risk rubbish led us into trouble, and there is no way out. People can't even pay back their loans. They lost, we lost. I'm being blamed for everything. This internationalisation has been a disaster, for me and my partners. It's over, now.' He was a silent for a time, and Edmond did not respond. At last, he added: 'I think I'm headed for a confrontation with the partners. Something has to give. What's the line from that poem? *Things fall apart, the centre cannot hold.* Well, I have been the centre of Von Mipatobeau, and I am falling apart, Father.'

'It has been a long time since you have come to cry on my shoulder, Gabriel,' Edmond said. 'I suspect the last time this happened, you had scraped your knee whilst trying to climb too high up a rocky mountain slope. Well, I suppose this is no different. Gabriel, do you think this is the first failure in this family? Do you think this is the first time Von Mipatobeau has faced trouble? Do you truly think you can be wholly responsible for this disaster? Life is complicated, and cannot be controlled, but it must be dealt with. You cannot be passive. You must always act, no matter how bad it gets. You should have enough of your ancestors' blood in you to understand that. You cannot just give up, as if there was nothing you can do. You must find the best solution.'

'There is no solution,' Gabriel replied. 'I have tried.'

'I don't mean you should try to fix the bank,' Edmond said sternly. 'I am talking about your life.'

'What do you mean?' Gabriel said, somewhat mournfully.

'Well, have you considered early retirement?' Edmond said.

Gabriel stared at him. 'Retirement?' he said. 'But you just said I shouldn't give up?'

'I'm not talking about giving up,' his father replied calmly. 'If they're going to fire you, why don't you pull out with dignity? Keep matters in your own hands? It's not like you're going to get a bonus this year. Why don't you simply leave, and cut your losses, instead of waiting to be thrown out?' Edmond shrugged. 'I know it may sound a little harsh, but I see no excitement in your eyes when you contemplate a future in banking. Of course, I am only making a suggestion, not imposing a course of action. There are many options for you, my son. You must simply find the best one for you.'

'I did not expect this from you,' Gabriel said, feeling quite confused. 'I thought you would give me some sort of pep talk, and give me the courage to go back to our family bank and recover my pride.'

'No-one can give you that courage,' Edmond said. 'Besides, aren't you going to be ready for retirement soon anyway, in two or three years? What difference do a few years make? You could come back here, help me with my watch designs, look after the chickens, take long walks in the countryside. You were always happy in the mountains, Gabriel. Or have you forgotten?'

Gabriel stared at his father. 'I don't know,' he said. 'This is all so sudden. I'm not sure if returning to childhood is what I need right now.'

'You could start slowly,' Edmond said. 'I know rich financial consultants who go back to the countryside at the weekend to milk the cows. You could simply start spending more time at your chalet. Maybe come down here at the weekends, spend time with me and your mother. Go down to the village for fondues. Walk up in the mountains in the morning. I think it would do you good to reconnect with your country, Gabriel.'

'Sometimes I am afraid I have left old Switzerland too far behind,' Gabriel said coldly.

'Don't be so hard on yourself,' Edmond said, 'and remember how far we have come, as a people. Being Swiss is a flexible concept, but there are core values at its heart. This is a mountain without resources, and out of this barrenness Swiss men and women found a way to create perfection. High-quality watches, beautiful chocolates... They started with cuckoo clocks, and ended up with Rolexes. Now, they sell their expertise as hard-working honest people of the mountains all over the world, and they call it banking. That's what the Swiss have done for the past three hundred years. That is how they became a successful people. They go out into the world and engage with it, and they keep coming back to their origins. That is what you have done until now, and it is what you must continue to do now.'

Gabriel smiled wryly. 'Are you saying we are naturals?' he asked.

Edmond smiled in return. 'In a way, yes,' he replied. 'We are survivors. All we need is stew in the morning, and a good walk in the crisp mountain air. All we need are a few vegetables, and a few chickens.' He paused, then looked his son in the eye. 'I know you. It would do you good, you know. You ought to come over and stay here, where you were raised. Spend some time under these clear skies. Find your childhood memories.'

'There are things I have to figure out,' Gabriel replied. 'A lot of what you're saying appeals deeply to me, but I suspect I have many loose ends to tie up before I can forge a new path. I don't know if it's as simple as you seem to think.'

Edmond looked at him hard. 'So it isn't just about banking, is it. You said things were falling apart. What do you really mean?' he asked.

Gabriel swallowed. 'Clarice. Anita. Von Mipatobeau. My reputation,' he said.

'Anita?' Edmond repeated, raising an eyebrow.

'Don't you dare take pleasure in my failure,' Gabriel said, gritting his teeth. 'Don't you dare presume to tell me you told me so.'

'I mean nothing of the sort,' Edmond replied, shaking his head. 'I am sorry you are unhappy.' He paused.

'I am disappointed,' said Gabriel. 'I don't think that's quite the same thing.' He was silent for a moment, before giving a bitter laugh. 'Maybe it's God's punishment,' he suggested, 'for failing with Clarice. I thought I could abandon one woman for another, start from scratch with someone else. But these women do not fit into my life. They try to force me to fit into theirs. I have felt... used, for my money, for my passport.' His throat felt tight, and he stopped speaking. 'Anita,' he said at last, rather curtly, 'is an ambitious young woman with her own plans, and her own future to worry about.'

'I am sorry she hurt you,' Edmond replied.

'Don't tell me you knew all along,' Gabriel said quickly.

'I won't, and I didn't,' Edmond said cautiously. 'I had my...
reservations. But now that you've truly left Clarice, I see a new kind
of hope for you.'

'Hope?'

'Well, are you still tied to these women? Are you not a free man?
What is Clarice planning to do? You don't have to tell me the details.
I only want to understand to what extent you are... limited. Does
she still need your presence, or your support?'

Gabriel sighed. 'Clarice has changed,' he replied. 'I'm sure you'll
recall the Clarice I married: a nice girl from a good Swiss family,
modest and reserved. You should see her now.'

Edmond shrugged. 'I guess people can grow apart,' he said
tactfully.

'None of these women truly loved Switzerland,' Gabriel burst
out. 'They didn't love my country, so they could not understand
me. I should never have abandoned my heritage. Not in my place
of work, and not in my relationships. We are mountain people. We
should have remained in the mountains, doing business with people
that came to seek our advice. People we trust. Nobody but people
with honest, hard-earned money.'

'Everything changes,' Edmond replied. 'No-one can hold the
world still.'

'I don't want to change! Some days I feel as though I truly have
been losing my Swiss values,' Gabriel cried. 'I want to get them
back. I want to be the man I used to be, before all these people wore
me down. I don't want to change for other people's benefit. I *want* to
be boring. I want to be happy.'

'Sometimes failures can be blessings in disguise,' Edmond
suggested. 'After all, haven't you made enough money over the
last thirty years? Your career was wonderful, while it lasted. You
became one of the top bankers in Switzerland. Why not call it a
day? I know you feel disappointed now, but in a few years you'll
look back on your past glory with pride. Why keep toiling on in
disappointment?'

'Are you saying you're disappointed in me?' Gabriel asked.

'No, no,' Edmond said, his face flushing red. 'I know we've been hard on you over the years, but only because we wanted the best for you. I'm so proud of you, Gabriel, and I'll support you no matter what you choose.'

'All this time as a farmer has made you soft,' Gabriel joked, his throat tight. Then he reached over and gave his father's hand a quick squeeze, before dropping it awkwardly.

'More tea?' asked Edmond.

Gabriel smiled. 'No, thank you,' he said.

'I really do think it could do you good to come back to a farming lifestyle,' Edmond said again. 'It will bring you comfort, and stabilise your psychology. Bring you back to your roots. Your mother and I are here for you. Come be my partner in everything that you were raised to do.'

'And what is that?' Gabriel asked, affectionately. 'Farming? Cheese-making and chocolate and yodelling? I think I may need to move forward in my own direction, although I appreciate the offer.'

'Or something similar!' Edmond said. 'You need the mountains, Gabriel. You need lakes. You desire simplicity. You must take the time you need to figure out, well, what it is you need.'

'I don't know,' Gabriel said hesitantly. 'I have a lot to think about. My retirement, my savings, what I want to do with the rest of my time. Where I want to live. What kind of work I should be doing. Whether I want anyone by my side.' He took a deep breath. 'I have projects, Father. I'd like to organise my archives, the family photos, my childhood stamps.' He smiled, suddenly. 'I'd like to do some cross-country skiing, more walking, more reading. Yes, there is a great deal about this future that appeals to me, and I appreciate your advice enormously.' He paused.

Edmond nodded once, gravely.

'I may go spend some time at the chalet,' Gabriel said, 'as a sort of first step towards this change in lifestyle. I could visit you more often, to go fishing or hunting. Maybe sometime you can teach me how to yodel.' He held up a hand hastily. 'But not now.'

'No, I don't think you're quite in the mood,' his father replied with a smile. 'But I hear noise in the kitchen. I suspect your mother will have returned from her walk. Come, let's go help her with her stew!'

⬧

Later, his belly full of tarragon vegetable stew and his mind full of confused hope, Gabriel found himself in the garden with his mother. The sun was still high in the sky. He wondered how his mother's baby eagles would do, out there in the wilderness.

'You notice the coming of spring so much more in the mountains,' Gabriel said. 'How long the days are becoming. How the sun lingers just a bit longer on the peaks.'

'Yes, isn't it wonderful?' Stooped over the freshly turned earth, Avenira was digging into the ground, loosening new potatoes with her bare fingers. 'See how small they are!' she exclaimed in delight. 'They will make a perfect salad.'

'I see you have asparagus, too,' Gabriel replied, tapping a clod of earth with the tip of his city shoe.

'They will be ready soon,' Avenira said with satisfaction, before giving a delighted giggle. 'You know, every year it surprises me, the return of spring, just as I cannot quite believe it every time you are back here.' She craned her neck back, looking up towards the distant mountains.

Gabriel smiled, then reached over to pat his mother awkwardly on the back. 'Perhaps I shall be coming here more often,' he said, 'now that the spring days are so full of sun.'

Avenira nodded. 'I thought that might be the case,' she said. 'I don't wish to pry into your private life, my son, and I could tell by your expression that you had already opened your heart to your father.' She held up a hand before Gabriel could protest. 'Some things are best shared man to man. I had to learn that when you were quite young! I only want you to know that if you ever need us, we will be here for you. No matter what happens. No matter what choices you make.'

—549—

His throat tight, Gabriel found himself unable to respond.

'And I really must show you the little green strawberries,' Avenira continued, smiling to herself. 'They hold such promise!'

Chapter Thirty-Nine

Clarice appeared on the gallery stairway, wearing a floor-length orange satin dress with a fitted bodice and a chiffon skirt. Outside, a few snowflakes were falling. She had set the glowing crystal ball to a spectrum of gold, salmon and ochre tones, to perfectly complement the display inside.

'It also goes rather well with your choice of outfit,' Khadija had observed, grinning.

Clarice shrugged. 'But of course,' she said. 'I own this gallery. Why should I not match my surroundings? Besides, these Fauvist paintings from all over the world are simply wonderful. One cannot imagine looking drab standing next to them.'

Khadija nodded. 'Such strong colours,' she said. 'Such...violence.

Chloë gave a mock shiver. 'I understand why the original French movement were known as the *Fauves* – "the wild beasts",' she said.

'I thought the movement had relevance in the contemporary world,' Clarice said thoughtfully. 'Besides, our last few exhibits have been quite daring. Perhaps a little too daring.'

'Yes, those Egyptian metal sculptures were quite strange,' Khadija replied. 'Oh, and that guy who dissects all those fish!'

'Quite,' said Clarice, smiling. 'I thought we should have a return to painting, for once. After all, selling paintings was how I took my first steps in the art world. Now that I am a new woman - a divorcee - it seems right to acknowledge that.'

'So you should,' said Khadija.

Chloë grinned and put on a grave voice, wagging a finger at Clarice. 'Perhaps it is God's punishment, this divorce, for your modern ways.'

Clarice smiled slowly. 'Perhaps it is God's reward, to be freed of the yoke.'

Khadija hesitated, as if about to say something, then was quiet. 'You should be proud,' she said at last.

Clarice took a sip from her champagne flute, her expression unreadable. To think that six months had passed since the divorce!

How quickly life could change, as if in the blink of an eye, after all those years of misery and waiting... 'Is everything ready for the guests?' she asked.

Khadija nodded briskly. 'As always, my dear,' she said.

Clarice smiled indulgently. 'Yes, I suppose we have this routine down by now.' She laughed gaily.

Chloë adjusted the plunging neckline of her black dress before saying, casually: 'Anyone on the guest list we should be worried about?'

For a moment, Clarice felt a pang of worry: did she mean Anita?

'Are you really asking if there's anyone eligible?' Khadija asked, smirking.

Relief surged through Clarice. Of course not. Besides, what did she care about Anita? What did she care about Gabriel? It was all in the past.

Chloë pouted. 'No,' she said, a glint in her eye. 'I was asking nothing of the sort. I was more worried about past conquests coming to haunt me.' She paused. 'Still,' she added casually, 'there isn't anyone eligible, is there?'

Clarice smiled slyly. 'Well, I believe our dear Thomas will be here tonight...'

Chloë blushed furiously. 'Be careful, Clarice,' Khadija interjected, laughing, 'I think you'll find Thomas has a plus one on the guest list.'

Clarice raised her eyebrows. 'A girlfriend?'

'It seems unlikely,' Chloë said rather grumpily. 'That peculiar little man!' Her cheeks were still quite pink.

Khadija shrugged. 'Well, we'll see, in any case.' She checked her Rolex watch. 'Ladies, it's almost time. I think we should unlock the doors.' She trundled off, jangling the keys in her hand.

Clarice turned to Chloë. 'Where is Fleurie?' she asked.

Chloë shrugged. 'She mentioned something about having to go for a jog,' she said. 'She'll be here, just a bit later.'

'Fleurie's out jogging in the snow? She *really* hates the small talk, doesn't she,' Clarice replied, amused.

'Well, that's quite alright,' Chloë said. 'You and I can go on a charm offensive.'

'Just please, for the love of God, don't unleash it on Thomas,' Clarice said.

Chloë grinned mischievously, then her expression grew more thoughtful. 'If Thomas is going to be here, does that mean Gabriel is coming?'

A cloud passed over Clarice's features, and she sighed. 'I don't know,' she said. 'I doubt it.'

'Sorry,' Chloë said hastily, 'I was only wondering.'

'No, you have every right to,' Clarice replied. 'After all, for a long time, he was one of our principal sponsors. But he isn't any more, and we have to remember that. He is no longer my husband, and he no longer has any link to the gallery. He hasn't called in a few weeks. I don't even know where he is. Still...' For a moment, she appeared to cheer up. 'He gave up his shares in the gallery, you know, as part of the divorce settlement. I thought that was rather decent of him.'

Chloë nodded. 'A nice gesture,' she said. 'Not that he ever cared about art at all!'

Clarice laughed sadly. 'No, that's true. Of course, in exchange I gave up the chalet.'

Chloë giggled. 'Oh, that must have been so sad for you,' she said, her voice heavy with irony. 'I know how much you love hiking in the mountains.'

'I told Gabriel I would be getting my own chalet,' she said, a little defensively. 'One with marble bathtubs and crystal chandeliers. One nobody had committed adultery in.' Clarice laughed as gaily as she could. 'That boring, sinful place! I never want to see it again.'

'You won't have to,' Chloë said gently. 'We'll have a few girls' weekends up in the mountains. We'll help you find a new place, somewhere far more exciting than silly old Saas Fee, and we'll come back and help you decorate it with fur rugs and crystal and silver and all the modern art you could possibly want.' She took Clarice's hand in hers and squeezed. 'After all, that is what the Avant-Garde Feminists' Club is for.'

Clarice smiled warmly, the pain in her heart subsiding. 'Do you know, I think I'm going to like being a divorcee,' she said. 'It sounds rather grand and glamorous, don't you think?'

'Oh, absolutely,' said Chloë. 'It's much more interesting than just being single.'

'No-one would ever have the gall to call you "just single",' Clarice teased. 'Perhaps outrageously single, or wildly single, but not "just".'

Chloë laughed. 'Oh look, there's Fleurie!' she said.

'Still in her H&M,' Clarice said, shaking her head. 'Some things never change!'

Chloë shrugged. 'Not everybody can be as glamorous as us. Besides, it makes us look sexier.' She ran up to Fleurie and kissed her on both her flushed cheeks.

'How was your run?' Clarice asked.

'Oh, it was marvellous!' Fleurie replied. 'Sorry I'm so late, but I'm training for a half-marathon. I really can't miss a day at the moment.'

'Did you run down by the lake?' Chloë asked. 'I love it so, down by the botanical gardens! Of course, I always take a taxi there...'

Fleurie smiled. 'Yes, I did,' she said. 'Of course, the gardens are looking quite bare this time of year, but I caught the last rays of the sunset. I don't know why more people don't appreciate the beauty of this city, this country. On days like this, I simply love Switzerland!'

'Well, I love Switzerland too,' Clarice said, 'as long as I know there's more out there, beyond those mountainous borders. I mean, just look around this room, at the paintings on the walls! We have artists from France and Ethiopia, Papua New Guinea and Peru!'

'All inspired by a modern European art movement,' Chloë said coyly.

'Well, I don't know if they were *all* inspired by the Fauvists,' Clarice said. 'I simply picked artists that seemed to represent the movement's values in the modern world.'

'The International Legacy of Fauvism?' Fleurie said, smiling as she repeated the exhibition's title.

Clarice laughed softly. 'Why yes, in fact,' she said. 'And before I start boring you both to death by reciting the catalogue text I wrote myself, why don't we go find a little more champagne?'

'Hello! Hello!' Juni Bao appeared at their side, wearing a cream and pink flowered dress. Chloë wrinkled her nose at her choice of outfit, before producing a beaming smile. 'Welcome!' she said.

Clarice resisted the urge to laugh. 'Hello, Juni,' she said. 'I trust your journey went smoothly?'

'Oh yes,' she replied. 'I am very excited about Fauvism!' She appeared to hesitate, smoothing down the folds of her dress.

'What is it, Juni?' Clarice asked kindly.

Juni swallowed. 'Have you seen Billy Bob?' she asked wistfully.

Clarice frowned. 'The Texan? I haven't seen him in years! Not since he made that impressive donation.'

Juni sighed. 'I know,' she said sadly. 'I invite him every time, and he never replies. One day, though, I am sure he will be here.'

Chloë quickly turned her noise of mirth into a loud cough. Clarice shot her a warning glance. 'Of course,' Chloë said, the corner of her mouth trembling. 'I'm sure he'll come back here.'

'Come,' said Clarice. 'Why don't you join us for a drink?' Juni Bao beamed.

The four women walked over to the drinks table, Clarice's keen eye scouring the slowly gathering crowd. So far, she recognised Italians, Germans and Americans, princes from the Gulf, and a scattering of Swiss investors. A good collection of potential buyers, she thought to herself with satisfaction, along with a pleasing number of newcomers.

'Madame de Puritigny!' A heavily-accented German voice reached Clarice's ears, just before Thomas came into sight, his grey curls bouncing up and down in enthusiasm.

'Thomas,' Clarice said warmly, turning away from the drinks table and kissing him on both cheeks. 'You must remember that I am Clarice de Saint-André Tobbal now, though!'

Thomas turned the colour of a ripe beetroot. 'Of course! Of course!' he stammered, before beginning to make a clicking sound. 'I, er, how is Gabriel? No, no, that is not the right question.'

Clarice frowned, surprised. 'Surely I should be the one asking that question? I mean, I certainly don't know the answer, but shouldn't you?'

Thomas turned an even deeper shade of red. 'I'm sorry,' he said. 'Of course, of course you have not seen Gabriel either.'

'I'm sorry?' Clarice raised an eyebrow. 'Do you mean *you* haven't seen Gabriel lately?

'No, not at all!' exclaimed Thomas. 'You mean...' If a man could be said to turn purple, then that was what Thomas proceeded to do.

'Did something happen?' Clarice asked, growing alarmed. 'You must tell me, Thomas!'

'No! No! No!' Thomas wailed, tremendously upset. 'I simply mean that he took early retirement.' Seeing Clarice's expression, he sputtered: 'It happened quite recently! I mean, he mentioned it to a few people, and then gathered his things and made a... a quiet, dignified exit.'

'Well,' said Clarice, flabbergasted. 'He left Von Mipatobeau? For good?'

Thomas nodded. 'He seemed... tired. Tired and happy,' he volunteered.

'My goodness gracious me,' said Clarice. 'How unexpected! He didn't mention anything to me during the divorce hearings, and we've had very little contact in the months since then...'

'I believe he had a conversation with his father a while back that had a great deal of influence on him,' Thomas added, terribly embarrassed. 'He started spending almost all of his weekends with his parents, or alone at the chalet.'

'Alone?' Clarice repeated.

Thomas stared at her, his eyes bulging from his head, and proceeded to turn crimson again. 'Well, yes,' he finally said. Clarice would not have been surprised to see steam issuing from his ears. 'He, I, we, well...'

'It's all right, Thomas,' Clarice said as gently as she could, for the Swiss German had started making a rather alarming humming sound. 'I just... have been rather out of the loop.'

'I, um, I have to go,' Thomas said nervously, casting his eyes around the room. 'Now.'

'Please,' Clarice said softly, 'stay. I didn't mean to embarrass you. You couldn't possibly know I wasn't in touch with Gabriel anymore. It doesn't make me sad, you see. Our divorce was an amicable one, but we no longer have much in common. We will not be staying close friends, but that does not mean I don't care about him.'

'Thomas!' said Chloë, suddenly reappearing at Clarice's shoulder. 'There you are! How are you enjoying the *vernissage*?'

Thomas blinked several times before replying. 'Fine, fine, fine,' he repeated mechanically. 'I have just made a terrible faux pas and now I do not know what to do,' he said. 'Now Madame de Saint-André Tobbal will not let me leave.'

Chloë giggled. 'Don't worry,' she said. 'It's difficult to upset "Madame de Saint-André Tobbal".'

Clarice cast her a grateful, if somewhat exasperated, look. 'Exactly,' she said. 'That's enough about Gabriel, anyway. I'm just glad nothing terrible has happened to him without my knowledge.' She shook her head wryly. 'Why don't you tell us about you, Thomas? Is your friend here with you tonight?'

Thomas immediately beamed, his face resuming its normal pallid colour. 'Agatha?' he said. 'Oh, Agatha, she could not come with me tonight. She is singing in a bar in the Pâquis.'

Chloë raised an eyebrow, half intrigued, half amused. 'So, who is my rival, then?' she teased. 'Is she very beautiful?'

Thomas turned red again. 'None could be your rival, Chloë,' he said gravely, 'but I'm afraid Agatha is my girlfriend now.'

'And how did you meet?' Clarice asked curiously.

'Well,' Thomas said enthusiastically, 'I had gone bicycling in Brazil... I was in the country for work, and it was around carnival time, and the weather was blisteringly hot, but the music was so loud and fun!'

'Von Mipatobeau have been in Brazil?' Clarice asked, surprised.

Thomas shrugged. 'Now that we have started down the road of international investments, there is no going back,' he said rather sorrowfully. 'Still, I liked Sao Paulo. There were lots of ladies with feathers, and excellent fried snacks, and I may have indulged in a stein of beer or two. This did not lead to the most high-quality bicycling, as I'm sure you can imagine.'

'Did you fall in a ravine?' Chloë asked.

'No,' said Thomas, sounding rather offended. 'I fell in a ditch. That's when this vision appeared to me, with enormous coloured plumes on her head and sequins on her... everywhere. I thought I must have fallen into a coma again, or perhaps died and gone to a very Brazilian heaven!'

'And this was Agatha,' said Clarice.

'Yes,' Thomas beamed. 'She was so beautiful, and so... big. She pulled me to my feet, dusted off my waistcoat, and began to dance with me! I left my bicycle right there in the ditch and followed her into the crowd of the parade. We danced for hours, until I thought I was going to faint, she was so dominating and sexy and big! We spent all of Mardi Gras together, and it was perfect. I fell in love at once, just as I had fallen in the ditch.'

'She's big?' Chloë repeated, obviously trying not to laugh.

'Yes!' Thomas said happily. 'Big and very tan, with very long hair! She is probably thirty centimetres taller than me. It is wonderful!' He lowered his voice. 'She used to do mud wrestling, you know. I can't wait to see her in the mountains!'

'And she came back to Switzerland with you?' Clarice inquired.

'Oh yes,' said Thomas. 'She wants to go dancing all the time, you know, to those late night discos, when I would really be quite happy eating dinner at five o'clock and reading my book! But I love her. I think she is simply marvellous. If she wants me to dance, I will dance.'

'And what does she do?' asked Chloë, innocently. 'Is it just the singing?'

Thomas shrugged. 'She is... making her way in the world,' he said, with the air of a man repeating someone else's words. 'She doesn't need a visa, you see. I am simply so happy she is living with me! She is so exciting. Every day with her is exciting. I'm taking her skiing next weekend for the first time.'

'Do be careful,' said Clarice, genuinely rather concerned.

'Of course,' Thomas said gallantly. 'I will look after her very carefully.'

There was a short silence. 'Well,' Clarice said, 'look after yourself, Thomas, and be sure to enjoy the show. I look forward to meeting Agatha some day.'

Thomas gave a stiff bow. 'I will go look at all your paintings now,' he said.

The second he was out of earshot, Chloë dissolved into giggles. 'Oh, Thomas,' she said. 'A Brazilian!'

Fleurie reappeared. 'What Brazilian? Who? What happened?' she asked.

'Chloë's paramour has taken a new lover,' Clarice said drily. 'Thomas has a Brazilian girlfriend.'

'I like Brazilians,' Fleurie said decisively. 'They have a lot of great football players.'

Clarice shook her head in amusement. 'He must look like such a little lackey, trailing behind this Amazonian goddess in his embroidered waistcoat...'

'Brazilians are a curious breed,' Chloë said. 'Either they work really hard, or they don't work at all.'

Fleurie laughed. 'You should write a guidebook to international dating,' she observed.

Chloë laughed. 'I might, when I'm not so busy with Spa Cosmetics!'

'So business is going well?' Clarice asked.

'Oh yes,' said Chloë happily. 'With Khadija's help, the line has become quite successful. I'm actually thinking of expanding into pedicures. Have you heard of fish pedicures? There are these fish called doctor fish, that like to nibble on your skin...'

'Urgh,' said Clarice, wrinkling her nose.

'Well, it's very popular in California,' Chloë said defensively, 'and apparently it feels very nice. It's a kind of purification, you see.'

'It doesn't sound very hygienic,' Clarice observed, 'and it certainly doesn't sound very Swiss. I mean, this is the country that makes Rolexes and Patek Philippes, not some third-world country where we expose our feet on a street corner and have some fish eat the dead skin!'

'There's big money in fish pedicures,' Chloë retorted. 'We'd replace the water regularly, of course. It would be very clean.'

'Yes, and I'm sure you'll find some illegal Thai immigrants to help you.' Clarice shook her head. 'It seems like everything they do in South-East Asia has to do with fish or algae!'

Chloë giggled. 'Well, in any case, business is going well.'

Fleurie laughed. 'You did ask,' she pointed out to Clarice.

'What about you, Fleurie?' Clarice asked. 'What did we miss at the drinks table?'

Fleurie grinned. 'A potential client,' she said, nodding in the direction of a distinguished-looking old lady. 'In fact, I should get going: I told her I was going to show her some paintings that look like Gauguin. Perhaps I should try to sell her a pedicure as well.'

'Well, run along then,' said Clarice, smiling. 'We wouldn't want to miss a good opportunity!' She shook her head as Fleurie walked off.

'So, back to our previous conversation,' Chloë teased. 'Am I to understand that you still care about Gabriel and his boring ways?'

Clarice shrugged. 'I was just surprised. I mean, he's quit his job, and maybe left his girlfriend? That's big news! It feels strange not to know.'

Chloë nodded, a little guiltily.

'It's true, you know,' Clarice said thoughtfully. 'That I care. Marriage doesn't just dissolve overnight, no matter how miserable it might have been at times. Besides, if you feel even a twinge of jealousy at the mention of this enormous Brazilian, you can't really fault me for still caring about my ex-husband. Even if he is very boring.'

Chloë looked rather sad. 'I'm sorry,' she began, but Clarice cut her off: 'Don't be.'

'Oh look,' Chloë said suddenly, with a palpable sense of relief,

'Khadija is bustling over with a serious look. What have we done wrong now?'

Clarice glanced at her watch. 'Goodness!' she said. 'I think it's time for me to make a speech.'

'I'll go find a good seat,' Chloë grinned.

Clarice laughed softly. What a strange world love was! She was much more comfortable talking about art. Nodding to Khadija, she crossed the room towards the raised podium, and climbed the steps. The room was full of familiar faces, from all stages of her career: even some of her regular clients from the Anker and Hödler days appeared to have been converted to modern art by the exhibits at her second gallery. That alone was enough to be proud of, without taking into account their huge international following. She smiled and tapped the microphone lightly to get people's attention.

'Ladies and gentlemen,' she said, and paused. 'Welcome.' Clarice looked out at the audience and straightened her back. 'We do not live in easy times,' she began solemnly. 'Switzerland is changing. The financial world is changing. My own life has been irrevocably changed.' She let an uncomfortable silence settle around the room before slowly smiling. 'But I am not here to talk to you about the economy, or about the EU, or about my divorce. I am here to talk to you about modern art, and its unchanging force.' A scattering of spontaneous applause greeted the statement. Chloë, who had looked horrified for a moment, grinned widely.

'I am here to talk to you about hope,' Clarice said loudly. 'I am here to tell you about taking charge of your life, your values, your decisions. Now that the whole world economy is in crisis, now that everyone has lost their confidence in money, it's time to make a change in Switzerland. It's time to recognise the pure value of art, unchanging, even eternal. Switzerland is not just a country of cowboy bankers and cash cows. It is a country of art aficionados, the likes of which the world has never seen. It is a country of sensitive artists, and intelligent investors. At least, I hope it is.' She smiled widely, then gestured at the paintings on the walls around her.

'Art immortalises colours, shapes, ideas. Yes, trends and tastes may evolve, but art lasts. What goes around comes around. If you don't believe it, you should know that I've been making two hundred to three hundred per cent profit on the art I've bought! People use paintings and sculptures as a store of value, you see. It's far safer than putting cash in the bank, as I think we've all learned the hard way.'

Several people in the audience tittered.

'*Les Fauves*, whom I believe to have inspired most of the paintings in the gallery today, were modern artists in the original sense of the term. They cared about simple patterns and bright colours, creating strikingly original paintings. If they saw a yellow tree trunk, they would paint it gold. If they saw a blue shadow, they painted it in the boldest cerulean tones. Red leaves became vermilion. Thus, they transformed the world around them. Artists all over the world have contributed their vision to tonight's *vernissage*. They are inspired by colour, by light and by life.'

People in the room were beaming as they looked around them. Khadija was nodding fiercely.

'Art is art for its own sake,' Clarice continued, 'but art is also capital. We all have access to this wonderful, invaluable capital. Look around you, at these paintings from all over the world. See the bright colours that they bring to this dark, old Swiss building? See the wonder they bring to a cold winter's day? That is what art can do. It brings the desert and the rainforest into our sitting rooms, into our imaginations, into our lives. When we look at a painting, we travel, even if we are just sitting on the same couch as every other night, eating the same chicken salad. We open our minds to the whole world.' She gave a seductive smile. 'And that, ladies and gentlemen, is why you should buy these paintings. Thank you.' She raised her champagne flute and stepped down from the podium, blushing, to a shower of applause.

A wave of sheer happiness washed through her. What need had she, a successful woman, for a husband or a lover? She had started not one but two art galleries on her own, and had made a fortune from them. She had a close group of wonderful, intelligent friends, and a wider circle of admirers she could visit. Just look at all these people who had come to listen to her speak, who had come to buy the art she had collected! What need did she have for a frowning face waiting on the couch, beneath the circle of ugly portraits? The portraits were gone from the house in Saint-Antoine, she recalled with satisfaction. She had replaced them with a collection of bright, abstract paintings from around the world. What need did she have for a grumpy man, waiting to be served chicken salad? Clarice ate out most nights of the week these days, and had excellent caterers at her disposal for the evenings when she wished to stay home with her catalogues. She had everything she needed. Alone, she was happy.

'Oh Clarice,' Chloë gushed, 'you were simply wonderful!' She opened her slender arms, as if to gather her friend in her embrace, but Khadija had got there first, wrapping her plump arms around Clarice and holding tight.

'You are a very clever woman,' she said gruffly, before stepping back and straightening her blazer's lapels.

'Yes,' said Chloë, hovering as if wondering whether to try for a hug again. 'You've put that foolish banker husband of yours to shame, with the sheer volume of talent you've brought to Switzerland.'

'Not to mention the money,' Khadija said drily. 'I'm really proud of the Clarice we created, you know. This wonderful, bright, materialistic woman who has left behind all of her conservative pretensions. This Clarice is modern, aggressive, and she gives a great speech. She won't just wait for people to wander into her gallery and buy paintings, she'll go searching for them, out on the streets.'

'And every three months,' Chloë gushed in return, 'there is a new gallery opening for a show: sculptures and war paintings and, oh, Post-Impressionists and cowboy art and anything you can think of.'

Clarice laughed at her friend's assessment of their exhibitions.

'Whatever it is,' Khadija said, 'she'll buy them for twenty thousand and sell for at least eighty.'

'Oh, you girls are too kind! Do you really think I'll have convinced anyone to buy?' Clarice asked coyly, and Fleurie laughed in delight.

'My dear, people were already making offers to us during your speech. The Fauvists have made quite an impression! The artists must be so pleased.'

'I will have to make sure I email those who couldn't make it here, to tell them what success they're enjoying,' Clarice said thoughtfully. 'Especially that young Peruvian woman. Such style! We've already sold two of hers, including that big blue landscape from the back wall.'

'Oh, I'll contact the artists,' said Chloë. 'Don't worry yourself with the details. You're the owner, after all, and the hostess.'

'The belle of the ball,' Fleurie said cheerfully, 'and the most beautiful woman here.'

'Except for me, of course,' said Chloë with a pout.

Fleurie gave a mysterious smile and did not reply.

'I have you, my friends, to thank for all of this,' Clarice said firmly. 'I couldn't have done it without you, and I hope I never have to.'

Chloë flung herself at Clarice once more for a hug, this time beating Khadija to it. Fleurie clapped her hands together happily.

'More champagne?' said Chloë.

'Definitely,' said Khadija.

'I've been wondering something all evening,' said Fleurie. 'Where is Winifred?'

Clarice sighed. 'Oh, don't bring her into it,'

Chloë tittered, and did not leave for the drinks table.

Khadija raised her eyebrows. 'You sound a little bitter,' she said. 'Has something happened?'

'Oh no,' Clarice said hastily, 'we've just... drifted apart. Gabriel and Dieter had something of a falling out, I believe, and after that it got a bit awkward when Wini and I ran into each other. She only wanted to talk about the education of her sons, or about the banking scene in Zurich. I mean, I'm no longer married to Gabriel. I don't want to hear another word about the golden boys of banking, or their foolish wives! It's a shame, really, but I guess people change.' She paused. 'Besides, sometimes I think she might have known about Gabriel and Anita, and I simply can't bear the thought of being friends with somebody who would have kept that secret from me.'

'She was always a bit too much of a good little wife to be truly Avant-Garde,' Khadija said quickly, decisively. 'I think she had mixed feelings about feminism.'

Fleurie looked unsure. 'I had coffee with her recently,' she volunteered, 'and we talked about art a lot. Well, and about other things.'

'I'm not saying we should throw her out of the group!' Clarice said hastily. 'I simply mean... Well, I sent her an invitation to the *vernissage*, but I wasn't surprised in the least when she didn't respond.

'She and Dieter might be moving to Lugano,' Fleurie ventured.

'Goodness!' said Chloë. 'How exciting! Maybe you could go visit her there, Clarice? Drink wine by the lake and reconnect?'

Clarice laughed softly. 'You go do that, Chloë. I know how much you love the Italian border. But I think Winifred and I have gone our separate ways. There is no reason for bitterness. She is happily married, I am happily divorced.'

The girls laughed.

'And how is Gabriel?' Fleurie asked kindly.

Clarice shrugged. 'I think he's happy,' she said simply. 'If you ladies take away one lesson from all of this, let it be this: if you're not happy, if you're not getting along with your partner, don't try to make a relationship last. Don't force it. Don't be afraid to give up. I was so afraid, because of tradition and religion and reputation and family... I admit to all of this, and I admit that I was wrong.

'I mean, Switzerland has a higher rate of divorce than anywhere else in Europe, but they also have very few babies born out of wedlock. This means that everybody gets married here because they feel they have to, and then change their minds later, realising what a terrible mistake they've made. Well, not everyone: sometimes I think I might have been jealous of Winifred and Dieter.' She paused and shook her head. 'Now, looking back, I don't know why Gabriel and I stayed together as long as we did. I think it was out of fear. And fear should not govern our lives. I truly believe it has been the best decision for both of us, moving apart.'

Khadija shrugged. 'I think you're right. People stay together for so many of the wrong reasons: avoiding stigma, keeping their children happy, keeping their wealth in the same aristocratic families... Reputation and materiality, that's what it's all about. Except, of course, that's not what it's about at all.'

'Exactly,' said Clarice.

Chloë giggled.

'I'm not saying it's impossible to have a happy marriage,' Clarice added. 'If you love each other, and listen, and care for each other no matter how difficult it might be. But married life is not for everyone.'

'Hear, hear,' said Fleurie. 'We are strong, independent women. Let's go have some more champagne.'

'I'll go,' said Chloë. She sashayed away.

'I have been thinking,' Clarice said, 'how important the question of female friendship has become to me, of late. Not simply on a personal, emotional level, but in terms of our careers.' She paused. 'I wonder... How much you know about women's liberation?'

'Well,' Khadija replied, 'wives of dictators are certainly rather liberated. They have access to enough money! I suppose anyone rich enough can be independent these days: I know some French lawyers, too.'

'Yes, and I have a friend who runs a major technological organisation in the US,' Fleurie added thoughtfully.

'To be liberated is to have power, not just money,' Clarice interjected. 'This gallery, and our Avant-Garde friendship, have given me both. They gave me the strength to leave Gabriel without leaping straight into the arms of another man.' She smiled. 'Well, at least not into wedlock.'

Khadija laughed. 'You know we're better off without them,' she said. 'I hardly see my own husband anymore. It's perfect! When we do meet up, we're thrilled to spend time together, because we're not sick to death of each other.'

'Feminism is a serious issue,' Fleurie replied.

Clarice nodded. 'I feel exactly the same, Fleurie,' she said. 'I actually have been thinking about all this for some time. Maybe, to some degree, since I met you ladies. Unlike in the USA, there isn't a coherent feminist movement in Europe. I'm beginning to think perhaps we could establish one together. Hold conferences. Invite interesting, intelligent speakers, so that women all around the world can share their discoveries, the different ways to independence. Whether that's leaving your boring husband or simply becoming financially independent from him. Whether that's starting your own business...'

'Or opening a gallery,' Khadija concluded. 'I love the idea, Clarice! We could have conferences every year: in Geneva, in Cannes... Why not in Los Angeles? The... International Women's Liberation Organisation.'

'WILO,' Fleurie said suddenly. 'The Women's International Liberation Organisation.'

'It has a certain ring to it,' Clarice said thoughtfully. 'Interesting.'

'What's Willow?' asked Chloë, reappearing with a tray of champagne flutes.

She wrinkled her nose when Fleurie explained. 'It doesn't mean we have to burn our bras, does it? I'm quite partial to my bras.'

'No,' Clarice said patiently. 'It just means we're proud to be intelligent, independent women.'

'Well, we already knew that,' said Chloë. 'Can we hold international conferences?'

Khadija laughed. 'Yes,' she said, 'and we'll have parties at the Kempinski and the Hotel President, don't you worry. It will be a glamorous sort of liberation.'

'I'll be the secretary,' Chloë said decisively.

'Clarice will be the president,' Khadija retorted.

'Is Winifred invited?' asked Fleurie.

'She can go fly a kite,' said Clarice.

'I will be the treasurer, then,' said Fleurie, smiling.

'We'll let her come to our conferences,' said Chloë.

Clarice, Khadija, Chloë and Fleurie each took a champagne flute from the tray, and held it up to the light. Around them, the gallery crowds milled happily.

'To the most wonderful group of women in the world,' said Clarice.

'To our new projects!' said Chloë.

'To a new era,' said Khadija, solemnly.

They clinked their glasses together and drank deeply. Outside, the snow was still falling.

Chapter Forty

The sky was blue, the clouds were crisp and white, a coat of fresh powder had fallen in the night, and Gabriel's snowshoes crunched pleasingly through the snow. Left, right, left, right: his poles left their faint imprints in the virgin white. It was Tuesday morning, he realised, as he rounded a bend and the full view of the Alps struck him in all its savage glory. Was that a white donkey in the distance? How far his banking days seemed already! The peaks rose high, their crags dusted with white, their shadows turning blue. Above, a few wild birds rode the air currents in widening loops.

Such purity! Gabriel smiled faintly, imagining what his ex-colleagues would be doing: striding through the unchanging marble hall, greeting the sparkling receptionists, taking the elevator, navigating the dull corridors. Soon they would be pulling up their leather chairs, sitting at the mahogany table, rustling distractedly through papers and waiting for Samantha to bring coffee on a silver tray. How boring it all seemed! Gabriel sank his poles into the snow and began walking uphill. The air was so fresh and clean, its biting cold purifying. He could hear birds calling in the distance. He was alone and everything was perfect.

Isolation: every man's dream, he thought to himself. No neon children skiing by, no women requesting chocolate cake, no Germans falling into ravines. *If you were alone*, Gabriel contemplated, *you would never disappoint anyone. You would need only please yourself: and your easy to please.* He lifted his snowshoes high and brought them crunching down into the snow, heading for the peaks.

———◆———

Upon his return to the chalet, Gabriel slipped off his shoes and enjoyed, as he did every day, the feeling of the soft, hand-woven white carpets caressing his feet. He had waxed the gorgeous butterscotch-coloured parquet to a golden sheen the previous day, and the light from the fire he had lit that morning flickered across it, most pleasingly.

He walked to the corner of the lounge, and flicked on the state-of-the-art silver kettle that sat on a small table there. After all, why should he need to go all the way to the kitchen just to make himself a cup of tea? An Art Nouveau glass bowl held a selection of herbal teas. Gabriel selected chamomile, and filled a delicate silver strainer. He sighed. These were his simple joys.

When the water had boiled, he poured it into his white china cup, releasing the scent of flowers. Gabriel crossed the room slowly, contemplatively, and sat down by the glass coffee table. He set down his tea and distractedly wiped some dust from its corner. Every once in a while, it struck him how little he missed the bank. Wasn't it strange, that a person could invest so much of their time and energy into something so... unnecessary? He smiled, a little sadly. Perhaps the same could be said of his marriage.

He swirled the hot water around his teacup. Von Mipatobeau seemed like a distant dream. How glad he was to be away from it all! No-one smiling sharkishly and typing things into enormous calculators. No-one in overly colourful suits trying to sell him anything. No-one forcing him to make small talk, or drink horrible strong coffee. No more awkward business dinners in strange locations. No more wandering around conferences, wishing to be left alone!

He stood up, and walked to the fireplace. The flames were low, so he selected a fine pine log, pulled open the glass door, and added it to the blaze. He smiled softly, recalling how Clarice used to call him a lizard for his love of warmth. Now, no-one but he had any say in the temperature of his house. He could drink what he wanted, walk when he wanted, eat what he wanted, sleep when he wanted.

The phone rang, startling him from his luxurious rêverie. Gabriel sighed and stood up from the white couch, brushing invisible particles of dirt from his trousers. He walked slowly into his office, panelled in smooth, salmon-coloured pear wood, and picked up the phone.

'Hello, Thomas,' he said.

He reached over and poured himself a glass of water from a cut-glass pitcher.

'Gabriel!' Thomas exclaimed happily. 'How have you been?'

'Very well, thank you,' Gabriel replied, wondering if this would be a long call. Thomas had made something of a habit of checking up on him, ever since he'd left Geneva and moved to the chalet permanently. He often seemed solicitous, even worried, as if there was something strange about leaving the city. How wrong he was! He couldn't imagine how happy Gabriel was.

'How was your weekend?' Thomas asked. 'I went dancing! Did you go dancing?'

Gabriel shook his head. 'Oh, I spent the weekend with my parents,' he said, smiling faintly.

'Did you pick berries?' Thomas asked enthusiastically. 'Did you dig up potatoes?'

'The ground is frozen, Thomas,' Gabriel said affectionately. 'I help my father with some of his new designs for watches, and I split logs with my mother, and we spent a lot of time sitting by the fireside, just enjoying each other's company.'

'Did you drink... weak tea?' Thomas asked, almost ecstatic.

'Yes,' Gabriel replied, amused. He glanced at the window, ascertaining with relief that the sun was still high in the sky. There would be plenty of time for another walk, later.

Thomas sighed happily. 'It just sounds so idyllic, this country life,' he said. 'You've only been gone from Von Mipatobeau what, two years? Your life is completely transformed.'

'Well, so is yours,' Gabriel reminded him. 'I mean, since your baby was born, you've been working part-time, haven't you?'

'Yes,' said Thomas, 'and I love being a father! But oh, how I too long for the countryside, to bicycle the mountains of Switzerland, my baby on my shoulders...'

Gabriel winced. 'Do be careful with that child,' he said.

'Oh, the little *Liebling* has his mother's blood,' he replied, chuckling. 'I dropped him down the stairs when he was just a week old, and he bounced. He bounced! His fat little Brazilian bottom saved him.'

Gabriel shook his head. 'And how is Agatha?' he asked.

'She is very happy,' Thomas replied. 'I spend as much time with our child as I can, and Agatha loves being with him when I cannot. She always has her friends over at our house, singing to the child, telling him stories in Portuguese, bringing fresh fruit from the Plainpalais market... It's such a wonderful atmosphere to come home to. Sometimes, when I get home from the office, they are playing music and dancing! It is so joyful.'

Gabriel made a face, looking around his own immaculate, empty home. 'It sounds... lovely,' he said.

'I made my son a very small waistcoat,' he said.

'How delightful,' said Gabriel, beginning to be bored. He couldn't imagine having children. Wouldn't they be there... all the time, jabbering away, and playing games, and making noise? Imagine having a small child on a mountain walk! He shivered at the prospect.

'I worry about you sometimes, you know,' Thomas said unexpectedly. 'You're not going to go crazy with loneliness, are you? I mean, sometimes, when you describe your life, it sounds like the life of a cow. Walking, eating, sleeping, looking up at the sky. Even cows spend time with other cows!'

'You are being very silly,' Gabriel replied, a little annoyed. 'I mean, do you think cows are unhappy? Cows have the simplest life in the world. They move slowly. They are contemplative beasts. They are in perfect synchronisation with the world around them, the birds in the sky... Even the flies do not perturb them. They eat fresh Swiss grass and drink from little mountain streams. It sounds perfectly blissful to me,' he snapped.

Thomas laughed.

'Besides, I am not a cow. I happen to enjoy the mountains, and my books, and sitting by the fireplace, and going for the longest cross-country run in the whole of Switzerland...'

'... and avoiding the tourists,' said Thomas.

'Of course,' said Gabriel. 'Especially the French.'

'And you still walk on those strange tennis rackets of yours?' Thomas asked excitedly. 'The ones made of catguts and other small animals?'

Gabriel sighed. 'Actually, the modern ones don't look like that at all,' he said. 'Mine are made of plastic, with metal teeth. They're not even that big.'

'Oh,' said Thomas, disappointedly. 'I mean, I heard you could cause your own avalanche with those shoes! You should be careful.'

'I doubt I will be causing any avalanches,' said Gabriel. 'I stick to the paths, which have been carefully marked, and I always check the day's weather warnings, when I walk by the road to the ski station.'

'I've never seen an avalanche,' Thomas said rather wistfully.

He sighed. 'Listen, Thomas, I really must get going.'

'You have some important sitting around to do, yes?' Thomas replied, giggling.

Impatiently, Gabriel prepared a sharp retort, but swallowed it. What did it matter to him if city folk did not understand his wonderful new life? It was better for him, anyway, if they didn't all come swarming out to the mountains to bother him. 'You know I like being alone,' Gabriel replied, 'and I've just got to a really exciting part of my book.' He picked up his heavy glass tumbler, and sipped the ice water.

'Oh, the one about theology?'

'Yes,' said Gabriel.

'What's it about, again?'

Gabriel sighed. 'It's about the history and philosophy of living as a hermit. Biblical stories, shepherds in the Holy Land, various saints... It's fascinating.'

'Is it a very thick book?' Thomas asked, with the air of someone deeply unfamiliar with the concept.

'Actually,' Gabriel said patiently, 'I've been listening to it in audiobook form. Sometimes, I even take my book with me when I walk. Not in the mountains, of course, which must be fully experienced at every moment, but when I have to go down into town to buy bread and cheese, I often switch it on. You should try it!'

'Yes, perhaps I should,' said Thomas vaguely. 'Well, I must be off. I think the baby has woken up from his nap. Take care of yourself, Gabriel.'

'You too,' said Gabriel. He did not mention when they would speak again, for the two spoke quite often these days. It was the perfect level of friendship for Gabriel, this long-distance sort, he thought to himself. No obligation, no time-wasting, no offence caused if a phone call was ignored.

He set down the phone and stretched luxuriously. The sun was still bright: perhaps he would take another short walk. Or did he feel like napping first? He wasn't sure. No, the weather was too wonderful. After all, a snowstorm might descend at any moment and trap him indoors. He loved the drama of heavy wind and snow, since it made his warm, fire-lit home feel exceedingly cosy, but he far preferred walking outside on a clear day.

It occurred to him suddenly that Thomas might find him boring. Thomas, the most boring man in the world, who only talked about his bicycling accidents and his small child! The thought amused him enormously, then made him feel slightly defensive. He was not boring, just because he preferred a quiet and solitary existence. Could a man really be thought boring for avoiding the company of Clarice and her mad artistic feminists? He sighed. It had been a few months since he had spoken to his ex-wife, and it really was his turn to make a friendly gesture. He just found it hard to muster up the energy. Clarice had so much…. energy for her new projects, the international women's conferences… What were they called, Willow? She had her friends, and her galleries. She was a successful, independent woman. He wondered idly if she had a new man in her life, then dismissed the question as petty. He wished Clarice all the best, he really did. He just didn't particularly care to hear the details.

He sighed. Had Anita found him boring? The question, a galling one, often came back to haunt him, particularly on rainy days when he was trapped all day in the chalet, unable to roam the mountains. Then, he occasionally found himself unable to concentrate on his book, instead roaming from room to room like a caged tiger, a potent wave of anger and sadness boiling in his stomach.

Today, he reminded himself abruptly, was not one of those days. Yes, he would go for another walk. Later, he would go down into the village and buy freshly-cut *viande des grisons*, along with a loaf of bread. Perhaps he would even indulge in a glass of wine! He frowned, sternly. There was no need for such indulgence. He would make himself a cup of green tea, if he needed stimulation. Wine! It was Anita's fault that he had started drinking.

Where was Anita now, he wondered? Was she drinking? Was she married? Did she have her citizenship yet? What did he care! he scolded himself sternly. There was no lasting bond between them. She had lied, she had tricked him, and now it was all to be forgotten. They had barely spoken since the revelation in Interlaken. There had been no tearful confrontation. Gabriel had simply given his Peruvian lover the cold shoulder until she had understood. She had tried to talk about their marriage: flowers, guest lists, catering, even to reminisce about the James Bond proposal, but he shut her down with such firm coldness that she quite quickly gave up. 'Later,' he said the first time, and then, at last, 'I don't think so.' That was the height of the crisis, his limitation of risk. After a few weeks, she stopped calling. They never saw each other again.

Gabriel swallowed. Perhaps his chamomile tea had been off, for his stomach felt rather upset. He walked quickly out of his office towards the front door, pulled his coat down from the hook and threw it over his shoulders. A walk would make him feel better.

———◦◆◦———

When he returned from his second tour of the mountains, Gabriel's cheeks were flushed and his mood was much improved. He would never tire of the view of the chain of Alps that perfectly encircled Saas Fee. Surely it was the most beautiful sight in all of Switzerland! Who cared how pointy the Matterhorn was? Here, there was such tremendous variety of beauty.

The scale of it all! *You cannot fight a mountain*, Gabriel thought with satisfaction. The mountain dominates Man, and Man vanishes in his shadow. That is the way of the world: power and solitude. To think of the sheer strength of gravity that created this Earth four and a half billion years ago! To think of the mountains surging up into the sky, like the deep sea in reverse, terrifying and glorious. Three thousand meters high! To think of the creation of these valleys, filled with life and death!

And now here he was, Gabriel de Puritigny, walking among these eternal peaks. Here he belonged, for the rest of his life. In the face of this terrible grandeur, what need did he have for a wife or a girlfriend? He shuddered. He was a free and happy man. His days of trying to please people were over. He could make his own chicken salads. He could pour his own tea. He had plenty of interesting ways to occupy his time, without the bother of human company.

After hanging up his coat and scarf rather firmly, Gabriel trundled down to the carnotzet, which he had reconverted into a sort of antiques workshop. *I'm turning into my father*, he thought with a smile. Indeed, his father had helped him set up the room, so that he could adequately access all the family heirlooms amassed there. For that, indeed, was his mission: to draw up a precise catalogue of all the de Puritigny objects. Clarice, blessedly, had agreed to return much of the furniture and art from the Saint-Antoine house. In fact, the rapidity with which she executed this scheme might almost have been insulting, had Gabriel not been so relieved she hadn't thrown any of it out, or converted it into modern art.

It took a moment for his eyes to adjust to the darkness, after the blaze of the sun and snow outside the chalet. He looked around the room, picking out his favourite family heirlooms. There were his great-great-grandfather's lederhosen, worn on the mountain paths of *Suisse Romande*. He particularly loved a granite bust of an unknown ancestor, frowning off into the middle distance. Then there was a small Anker painting of a child, rescued from Clarice's clutches, or at least from the basement of her first gallery. There were several ancient manuscripts describing the house in Saint-

Antoine, with long and fascinating annexes concerning the origins of the oak parquets. How he loved the history! But he was looking for something else, an old red folder containing his grandfather's stamp collection. Was that it, up in the corner?

He opened the heavy volume in question and found it full of coins, turning the plastic pages with satisfaction. What a beautiful collection they had amassed through all the ages! The next book he pulled down from the shelves was indeed full of the treasured stamps. Liechtenstein, Thailand, Peru... What an extensive collection! There were several pages devoted only to Queen Elizabeth of England. Gabriel shook his head proudly. His plan for the end of the afternoon was to find a missing set of stamps from Monaco, in order to complete a page. His theory was that someone had removed them, perhaps to lend them to a museum, and then neglected to put them back in their rightful place.

Therefore, they must logically be in one of the chests that sat in the corner of the carnotzet, gathering dust. Surely it wouldn't take a very long time to find them. Gabriel knelt down by the side of one, and pried open its heavy top. He coughed, as ancient particles flew into the air, but when they cleared, he could see nothing but miscellaneous items of clothing. He sighed, and closed the trunk with a bang. Perhaps this would take longer than he had thought. There must have been a dozen trunks still piled unopened in the corner of the room. Without thinking, he opened the next trunk, only to feel his heart drop into his stomach.

This was not one of the ancestral trunks, he realised too late. This was the small wooden trunk into which he had stuffed all the objects that reminded him of Anita. He had done it in a fit of rage, and clearly forgotten to lock it. He swallowed. Little trace of Anita had remained in the chalet: a flowered nightie, a toothbrush and a paperback book in Spanish. He should have burned them, he thought bitterly. The sight of those three innocent objects was enough to bring memories flooding back: of waking together in the double bed and laughing together, or of Anita laughing at him, as the sunlight poured down on them. Of sharing coffee and butter cake for breakfast. Of her humour and insatiable appetite... and lies, Gabriel reminded himself, crushing his fist into his eye to dislodge the dust that had entered. This ridiculous carnotzet! How dare Anita spoil this place of refuge, heavy with history! How could he have even thought of bringing her there in the first place? Saas Fee was his place. The chalet was his.

It was now, he reminded himself, as his breathing slowed. He was a hermit, just like the ones in the book. Anita would never hurt him again. No-one would, he thought with satisfaction. What need did he have for someone that constantly begged him for sex? What need did he have for someone who nagged, or lied, or used him for his nationality? Above all, what need did he have for someone who did not appreciate Switzerland? He straightened his shoulders. He was a self-sufficient man, now, dependent on nothing and no-one, living off his substantial pension. *Damn women!* He slammed the chest shut and left the carnotzet.

It was time for some green tea, he decided, flicking the kettle on with unnecessary force. He flung himself down on the couch, before remembering he was covered in dust, and guiltily leaping back up. He marched to the front door, removed his sweater, and shook it violently into the air. The blast of cold mountain wind that entered the house had a calming effect on him, and he almost laughed. Emotions! he thought. How they caught one by surprise! Perhaps he needed a break from the chalet.

This began a pleasing trail of thought. For some time, Gabriel had been planning an excursion to Italy by snowshoe. There was a small town called Cervinia, in a valley overlooked by the glorious Matterhorn, that he had always wanted to visit. He would walk along the rocky ridge of the Gornergrat, overlooking the glaciers. Perhaps he would see ibex or eagles on the way! It would do him good, a whole weekend of walking amongst the eternal mountains. Yes, he would book himself a nice hotel. That would make him feel better. Did he want to ask a friend? *God no*, Gabriel thought. Friends? He had friends. His friends were the blue sky and his ski poles and the works of obscure Scottish philosophers. His friends were his snowshoes, and the snow beneath his feet. His friend was the Matterhorn, looking down on his insignificance.

The boiling kettle interrupted his train of thought. Green tea would be a bit much, Gabriel decided. Perhaps *tilleul* or verbena? He sat back down on the sofa with his china teacup, watching the light shift, from blue to a light shade of orange. Sunset in the mountains: was any sight more glorious than this? He sipped his weak verbena. Yes, perhaps he was boring, but that was his choice.

He felt like himself again, after nearly sixty years of catering to others' desires: his parents, his wife, his partners, his girlfriend. He no longer cared to do so, to pay attention to a woman's whims or to the vagaries of the market. His success, he decided, was going back to his old self. After all, the Swiss had come from the mountains: they were meant to go back to the mountains. *Un Suisse est un Suisse est un Suisse*, as the saying went. No matter, once a Swiss man, always and forever a Swiss man. What could make a man prouder? What more could a man need? *Nothing*, Gabriel thought with satisfaction, sipping his warm tea. *Nothing*.

———— • ◆ • ————

At bedtime, Gabriel looked out over the faint blue glow of the snowy hillside one last time, then closed the heavy curtains. He turned with satisfaction to his bed, and the books stacked neatly on his bedside table. *Comparative Religion*, one spine read. *The Complete Works of Bertrand Russell*, said another. He was looking forward to that last one considerably. But first, he needed to finish his book about hermits. It would be overly indulgent, if not downright chaotic, reading two books at a time.

The bed was a single one: in a symbolic gesture, he had disposed of the queen-sized bed that Clarice had bought twenty-five years previously. There was no need for such an enormous, soft bed. Besides, he liked the daily reminder that he was alone now: that he could be, that he had the right to be, living simply and reading philosophy. No-one but he had slept in this bed, and the knowledge pleased him. This was the Swiss life, he thought to himself, slipping back the white Egyptian cotton sheets. Purity, modesty and isolation. Was it truly every man's dream? It didn't matter, for it was his dream.

Gabriel de Puritigny climbed into bed, laying his glasses on the locker, and switched the bedside table lamp off.

ABOUT THE AUTHOR

Parker Belmont is the former chairman of a small bank in Switzerland, and held various other directorships in financial institutions across the world, most notably in Switzerland, Germany and the Middle East. This is his first novel, and was inspired by the numerous strange and outlandish characters he met in the world of Swiss banking during the course of his glittering portfolio management career.